THE FALL OF NEVERDARK

THE ECHOES SAGA: BOOK FOUR

PHILIP C. QUAINTRELL

ALSO BY PHILIP C. QUAINTRELL

THE ECHOES SAGA:

1. Rise of the Ranger

2. Empire of Dirt

3. Relic of the God

4. The Fall of Neverdark

5. Kingdom of Bones

6. Age of the King

THE TERRAN CYCLE:

1. Intrinsic

2. Tempest

3. Heretic

4. Legacy

For Emma, the one who showed me the real meaning of strength.

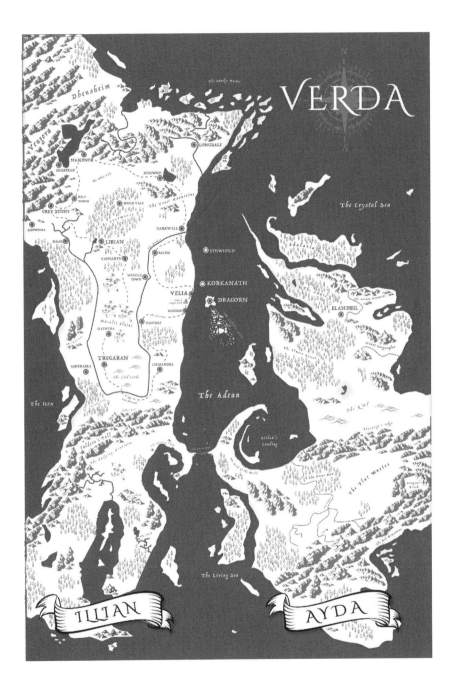

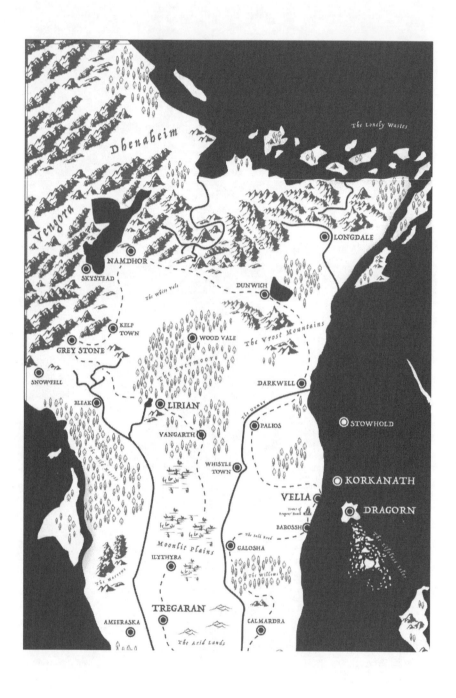

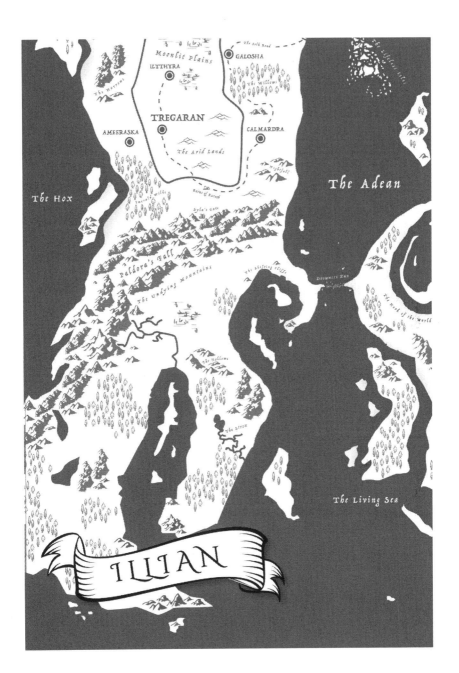

VERDA

The Lonely Wastes

LONGDALE

The Crystal Sea

STOWHOLD

Shalaria

KORKANATH

The Amara

DRAGORN

The Dervn Mountains

ELANDRIL

The Elwater Forest

Mount Gargantan

DRAMATIS PERSONAE

Adilandra Sevari
The elven queen of Elandril and mother of Reyna Galfrey.

Alijah Galfrey
Half-elf

Asher
Late human ranger and hero of the War for the Realm.

Athis
Red dragon, bonded with Inara

Doran Heavybelly
A Ranger and son of Dorain of clan Heavybelly

Galanör Reveeri
An elven ranger.

Gideon Thorn
A human Dragorn.

Hadavad
A mage and ranger

Ilargo
Green dragon, bonded with Gideon

Inara Galfrey
Half-elf Dragorn

Karakulak
King of the Orcs

Ellöria Sevari
The Lady of Ilythyra

Morvir
First Servant of The Crow

Nathaniel Galfrey
An ambassador and previous knight of the Graycoats.

Reyna Galfrey
Elven princess of Elandril and Illian Ambassador.

The Crow
Leader of The Black Hand

Tauren Salimson
High Councillor of Tregaran

Valanis
The late dark elf and self-proclaimed herald of the gods.

Vighon Draqaro
A human and friend to Alijah

PROLOGUE

10,000 Years Ago

The day began like any other for Sarkas. The bitter and unforgiving cold of the northlands disturbed his slumber with its icy embrace. Next came the shouting. His parents would inevitably fall upon their poisonous words to convey their feelings towards each other.

That was the nature of starvation, though Sarkas was old enough now to see that his parents had their addictions too. His father preferred to spend what little coin he had on drink. His mother enjoyed the out-of-body sensation granted by the Yellow Poppy.

This morning, Sarkas awoke to the same argument as yesterday and the day before that. Where would the coin come from today? How would they eat? Of course, the burden of feeding Sarkas himself always came up. Any love they had once displayed towards him had been replaced over his short life with resentment.

Unfortunately for Sarkas, today was not to be like any other.

There was to be more dark than light this day, that of the winter solstice. Every year, on such a day, The Echoes would accept offerings in the form of new servants. The order of Kaliban had swelled over the years, and the towering Citadel had grown with it. The priests needed help and they rewarded such offerings with coin.

His father's hand snapped around his wrist and dragged him from their squalor.

"You're coming with me," he growled.

Sarkas knew something wasn't right and the boy looked back at his mother with a pleading face. His tears went unnoticed as his mother closed the door without so much as a second glance.

His father marched him through the streets of Ak-tor, the capital city in the great kingdom of Atilan, first of his name. It didn't look so great from Sarkas's point of view. On the outskirts of the city, the poorest of folk dwelled in the mud and died young.

Leaving their district behind, Sarkas's father dragged him through the streets until the buildings rose so high neither of them could see The Citadel or the glistening palace. Mage Knights in scarlet cloaks patrolled the streets here, keeping order for those who could afford to pay the army's wages.

"Father, where are we going?" Sarkas begged in his little voice.

"Shut it!" he barked.

It wasn't long after that when Sarkas noticed other children, clearly from the poorer areas, being ordered through the streets by their parents. Like him, they appeared frozen to the bone and starved.

Finally, The Citadel came into view and took his breath away. The spire rose so high as to rival Atilan's palace in the west. Its stark white walls spoke of virtue and enlightenment. It was beautiful.

"You can have this one," his father said bluntly, thrusting Sarkas into the path of an Echoes priest.

"Father?"

Ignoring his son, Sarkas's father began to haggle with the priest over the price.

"A queue is forming," the priest said curtly. "Take your coin or take your boy."

Looking at his father's tremulous hand, it was clear to see that he was running out of time before the lack of drink arrested him.

"Just take him then!" Too busy counting the coins, Sarkas's father didn't even register the boy's sobbing cries.

"Prepare him with the others," the priest commanded.

Without a word, a large fiend of a man grabbed Sarkas around the back of the neck and pushed him up the grand staircase and into The Citadel. The interior was an opposing image to that of its exterior. The majestic white walls were replaced by dark and narrow corridors. The only comfort came from the heat. Even without the fiend's hand pushing him forward, the heat alone would have kept Sarkas moving.

What awaited him and the other children was not worth the warmth. Once strapped down to damp chairs, a tall priest in opulent robes gave them a speech about serving the Almighty Kaliban by serving the High Priests of The Citadel.

Sarkas noticed that the girls were taken elsewhere and saved from being strapped to one of the chairs. So too were the stronger-looking children. Where they were taken was beyond Sarkas. His attention was on the tables beside him and the others. A curved blade sat on top of an old piece of cloth which appeared to be covering other utensils.

Along with six others, Sarkas was told he had the honour of serving in the Red Tower. It was a protruding extension to the main tower and home to The Echoes council. It was said to be a place where the voice of Kaliban could be heard. Such a voice, however, was not for just any ears.

Seven men, one for each of the chosen servants, approached from behind the tall priest. Wearing long aprons, smeared with dried blood, they picked up the curved blades, disturbing the instruments under the old cloth. With brutish efficiency, the men proceeded to shave the children's hair, drawing blood in arching scrapes. Sarkas, like the others, cried out in pain as his hair dropped over his face and over his skinny shoulders.

The boy tried to blink the blood from his eyelashes as he pulled hard on the bindings around his wrists and ankles. The children screamed for their parents, but nothing would stop the fiends.

"Find comfort in Kaliban," the tall priest announced. "For your service in The Citadel, you will be rewarded tenfold when you return to His embrace."

At last, the curved blades were put down, leaving them all bloody and bald. Together, the seven fiends removed the old cloth from atop the table, revealing a row of metallic implements. Sarkas didn't like the look of any of them.

The tall priest clasped his hands inside his sleeves. "Let us begin…"

PART I

1

A PACT IN THE DARK

For hundreds of miles, The Crow had endured the rocky path his carriage had forged through The Arid Lands, navigating the ruins of Karath, and the treacherous valley of Syla's Pass.

The rhythmic sounds of the carriage wheels had worked to put The Crow into a trance, taking his mind back to memories past. When he closed his eyes, he could still see the dragons swarming above, the cities burning, and the armies of man being laid to waste.

The smell of bodies consumed by fire would never leave him, nor the sound of men, women, and children screaming for their lives. Those violent days were over now for the realm of Illian, though fractured into six kingdoms, had finally found peace.

That time would soon come to an end. It always did, after all.

This new Age was celebrated by those under the protection of the Dragorn. Both dragons and their riders had drawn a line in the sand and kept the darkness at bay.

The Crow cared little for the light or the dark, good or evil. He knew only what the world used to look like, and what it could be again. Of course, what the world needed could not be found in peacetime. To forge that which the realm required, he needed a war...

The carriage stopped abruptly, bringing an end to his musings. The Crow pulled back the curtain and opened the door to make his way across the hard desert plain in the wake of the others. His followers, devout believers all, were running to the front of their caravan, their black cloaks blowing out behind them in the rush. The Crow walked, having already seen the spectacle in his vision. Still, looking upon Paldora's Fall with his own eyes was quite the sight.

The men and women who served him stepped aside, giving him a clear view to the colossal crater at the end of the valley.

Twenty-four years ago, a star had fallen from the heavens and forever changed The Undying Mountains. Of course, no one but The Crow knew of the star's real impact, a seismic ripple effect that had spread across the southern lands and shaken loose that which was lost.

The crater itself was hard to see, shrouded by the floating boulders that continuously collided with each other above. Some were tethered by roots, destined to be knocked about and forbidden from floating free.

Paldora's Star, as it had been so named, was unique in its magical properties. Displays such as this were unusual outside of a congregation of dragons, whose proximity to one another could affect the physical world.

"Incredible..." Morvir, his first servant, was transfixed by the vista, reminding The Crow that the people of Illian hadn't witnessed all that he had. "A gift from the old gods," the smaller man said absently.

"They were never gods." The Crow's reply had the first servant cowering, fearful of his master's wrath.

Flashes of his vision returned, blinding his eyes and filling his mind with divine purpose. He saw the crater from high above, as if he were a bird. Beneath the crater was a web of earth-shattering cracks. The most catastrophic of these cracks ran to the west, deep into the heart of The Undying Mountains.

That was where they must go.

Without warning, the ground moved under their feet. The Crow looked down at the tiny pebbles vibrating on the surface. The effects were becoming stronger the farther south they travelled.

"We have lingered long enough," he said. "The journey beckons us."

Their route through the mountains took another day and night but, after coming across Paldora's Fall, the excitement among his followers was palpable. For too long they had been led astray by the fools who came before him.

"Stop!" he commanded from within his carriage.

"The Lord Crow demands that we stop." Morvir's message carried down the line, halting the entire caravan.

The sun was beginning to wane, casting long shadows across the barren ground. The Crow walked ahead of the caravan, his head low, and his eyes searching for the exact spot he had seen in his vision. The Crow parted the robes hanging over his legs and knelt, placing one hand flat against the cooling ground.

"This is the place," he said quietly to himself. "Here, the lost shall be found."

The Crow stood up and produced a slender black wand from his belt. The wizards who had followed him on the long journey came no farther, forming a line of black robes behind him.

The Crow whipped the wand around his head and brought it down, unleashing a destructive spell with enough power to break stone. The valley floor exploded again and again as he bombarded it with spell after spell. To any onlooker, it would appear he was simply laying into the ground with obtuse precision, but every strike was surgical, his wand directed by his vision. He flung his wand this way and that, removing the larger slabs of rock with ease, clearing the way.

Plumes of smoke and sand rose from the hole, making the others wait to see the sloping tunnel that lay beneath. Inside, there was nothing but an inky abyss to greet them.

Morvir crept to his master's side. "Are they really in there?" The first servant looked around at the others, their excitement mingling with fear.

The Crow looked at the others and decided it was time he fed them the lies that bolstered the resolve of all men. "Have faith. Remember, all of you, that the light of Kaliban shines within us. He will reward your strength." He felt ridiculous saying it but, as history proved, their entire order was easily manipulated.

"What are we to do, Lord Crow?" Morvir asked.

The Crow looked up at the approaching night. "Now, we wait for darkness…"

And wait they did. Long after the sun had set and its light been banished from the world were they rewarded for their efforts and patience.

The Crow heard them first, though he suspected it was because they wanted to be heard. What few myths remained of them had their kind noted as the deadliest hunters, as cunning as they were strong.

It would have been easier to communicate with them and negotiate, but this was not a breed that appreciated words. Strength and dominance was their language.

There was hesitation on their behalf, uncharacteristic of their kind. The Crow had expected this, however, since it was the first time in five thousand years that they had seen the sky or the moon.

Their eyes glowed when they caught the pale light, much in the manner of a cat or dog. It was foolish to think of them as animals, The Crow thought. Once upon a time, that way of thinking had almost cost the elves and dwarves their entire way of life.

The shuffling of his followers' retreating feet filled the night air when the first emerged from the shadows.

The orc…

The Crow stayed his ground, his wand gripped firmly in his hand. Had he not already seen how this was going to play out, he too would have taken a step back with the rest of the wizards.

The three who emerged from the tunnel were walking walls of muscle, though The Crow felt a comparison to stone would be better. Their pale flesh was pulled tight against their frames, easily seen with exposed chests that revealed a patchwork of scars, resembling cracks in a statue. Their trousers were roughly sewn with little care for their appearance, except for the random plates of armour, which told of their mastery over iron and steel.

At least they hadn't lost all of their skills under the mountain.

The closest approached him with cautious steps, torn between examining his human features and that of the stars twinkling above.

The approaching orc had a strong jaw that formed the foundation of a face made from angular features. Its straight jaw gave way to sharp cheekbones and pointed ears. Its nose and mouth were not dissimilar from any man or elf's - even its hair was dark, flowing over its slab-like chest.

A quick glance at the others informed The Crow that all three of the orcs possessed a head of horns, bony protrusions that began just above the eyes and flowed over the back of their heads. Despite being similar at a glance, their horns were unique in shape, size, and pattern, a distinction far more notable to their own kind, he assumed.

With a brow of solid bone, The Crow could only imagine what knocking heads with an orc would do to one's brain.

The orc's cautious behaviour ended the moment it thought The Crow was within reach of its sword arm. The inquisitive face stretched into one of pure aggression and the orc lunged at him with a dull serrated blade that had been hidden in the dark. The other two attacked at the same moment, their roars closer to that of a lion.

The Crow had only to lift his wand and end their assault with a whisper.

The orc to his left was folded in half and sent flying across the hard ground, its body leaving track marks in the sand. The orc to his right found it hard to move at all when its blood turned to ice, converting most of its body into a solid block.

The last orc, in front of The Crow, was lifted from its feet and suspended in the air. Its responding growl soon became a yelp when he used a spell to heat up the creature's sword. The glowing orange hilt sizzled in its grip before the orc relinquished it to the ground in favour of saving its pale skin. A quick flourish of his wand tilted the orc in the air, forcing it to lie flat and float before him.

The Crow approached the prone orc and removed an arcane translator from within his robes, a spinning top no bigger than his thumbnail. The orc writhed about in an effort to break free of the magic, forcing him to tighten his spell and prevent the creature from moving at all. With nimble fingers, he twisted the spinner, using the orc's chest muscles as a surface.

"Hear my words," The Crow said, noting the recognition and surprise on the orc's face. "You will take me to the one who owns you."

The orc bared its sharp teeth. "Release me!"

The Crow lifted his chin. "Very little is known of your kin." He leant over the creature's head. "But, I know more than most."

Beckoning Morvir with his bony finger, the first servant scurried over with a large sack. The Crow placed a hand inside and lifted out the skull of a man, perfectly intact without a single mark to ruin its features. The orc's eyes lit up.

The Crow continued, "Your people trade in bones, yes? The bones of monsters from the deep, even the bones of your own kind. That type of currency must be limited down there. Hard to come by too, I imagine, what with you all being so… *strong*. The world I have come from is not so strong, and it is full of bones like this one. Take me to your master and you can be rich."

The orc had yet to take its eyes off the polished skull. "Give me the skull," it demanded, "and I will take you."

The Crow could see the hint of a smile on the orc's face and knew of the creature's treacherous intentions. "You shall receive payment when we meet your master."

The orc didn't agree. Frozen in the air, the creature thrashed, testing the strength of the spell. The expletives leaving his mouth became unintelligible the moment the spinner became unbalanced on its chest, much to The Crow's appreciation.

Wasting no more time, he dropped the orc onto the hard ground and cast a binding spell around the creature's wrists, tying them behind its back. A thin gold leash ran from the binding to The Crow's wand, giving him complete control. It took three of the wizards to get the heavy orc back on its feet, but a twist of the wand had fire shooting through its veins, an encouragement to cooperate.

"Keep the light behind it," The Crow instructed.

Morvir stamped his staff into the ground and created a globe of soft white light, careful to keep it away from the sensitive orc. As they entered the dark tunnel, the other wizards released orbs of light to float above them and follow their route.

The orc grumbled for the first hundred yards of their journey; being a captive was far worse than being dead, apparently.

They travelled through the hidden world, buried beneath The Undying Mountains, for some time, though it was impossible to track day and night in perpetual darkness.

Just as fatigue was beginning to set in, The Crow noticed the rock change from its smooth, natural formation to hewn stone. Where there had once been nothing but a gradual decline, there were now steps and engravings marking the walls. If these telltale signs hadn't been enough, the foul odour attacking his nose certainly would.

They were finally entering the home of the orcs.

Shining eyes appeared in the darkest depths of this new world. What started as a few quickly became dozens, then hundreds. The gloom from their magic wasn't enough to pierce the orcs' dwelling, exposing only that which they passed. Whispers and grunts echoed from high above, telling The Crow that they had entered a large cavern within the mountain.

Before entering another, smaller cavern, they saw buildings chiselled from the mountain stone. As fascinating as it was to see a culture that had been buried and long forgotten, The Crow was only interested in one of them.

The king...

The prisoner spoke something in its guttural language and two double doors were opened by lumbering orcs, much bigger than the three they had encountered so far. The great beasts protected their eyes from the approaching light and retreated into the next chamber, stumbling over themselves to find comfort in the dark.

The roars that greeted The Crow and the other wizards were

offensive to their ears. It was hard to determine exactly how many orcs were inside this new chamber, but he knew that none of them posed a threat right now.

This is not how I die, he thought.

Where the orcs found comfort in the dark, he found comfort in magic. The orcs had the advantage of numbers over every race, but magic would forever be their weakness.

The Crow strode into the chamber, following the path cut out by his tethered prisoner. When the orc finally came to a stop, its demeanour somewhat diminished since its attempted assault, the leader of The Black Hand assumed he was now standing before the king.

The roars died away as suddenly as they began and the prisoner flinched. The Crow couldn't see far enough beyond the gloom to witness what had transpired, but he knew an order when he heard it. A jarring language that was harsh on the hearing filled the chamber, its volume forcing a wince even from The Crow.

He didn't have time for this. There was work to be done.

He twisted his wand again and the prisoner screamed in a single moment of agony as its arms were lifted high behind its back, pushing it down on its knees. Another twist sent lightning bolts of controlling, yet painful, magic through the orc's muscles, commanding it to bow the head and remain there, frozen in place.

The Crow came to stand over the orc, where he carefully placed the spinning top on the crown of its head, between the gap in its horns. Using his middle finger and thumb, he spun the top and gestured for Morvir to release his glow of soft light into the air. The orcs protested and the sound of weapons being drawn from scabbards bounced off the walls.

"What are you?" the leader spat.

The Crow narrowed his eyes to better see the figure sitting on the throne of bones. Having only seen three orcs in detail, he didn't consider himself an expert, but it was easy to see that the leader was old. Despite retaining his muscle and bulk, his body was as marred as the desert floor and cracked from top to bottom. There was no crown to speak of, allowing The Crow to examine the long horns that had grown and sloped over the leader's head and down his back.

What was more interesting to The Crow, however, was the tall orc standing beside the throne. It was the same orc he had seen in his vision, the one he had come so far to meet.

The tall orc possessed broad shoulders and a solid build that made an offensive sight to behold. White hair flowed over his chest and two thick horns curved over his head and flicked up at the back. Tucked under them were two extra horns, mirroring the shape of the larger ones above. For all of his features, The Crow found his expression the most telling. Where those around the throne looked on him with anger and disgust, this taller orc was *curious*.

Curiosity he could work with.

The older orc dipped his head, keeping the light from his eyes. "You're no elf."

"I am a man," The Crow replied, boldly.

The orc sneered. "You are from Neverdark…"

"An apt description," he consented. "You are the king of the orcs?"

"The tribes have no king. I am *chieftain* of the Born Horde, greatest of the nine! What are you doing in The Under Realm, man-thing? Other than filling my nose with your vile magics."

The Crow turned to glance at Morvir, who threw the sack of bones before the old chieftain. More whispers erupted from every corner of the throne room when every piece of a human skeleton scattered across the cold floor.

The Crow could see that the two armrests of the chieftain's throne were made from similar-looking skulls. Elven skulls, at least five thousand years old. In orcish society, that would make the Born Horde a very rich tribe…

"After five thousand years, you must be tired of the same old bones."

The chieftain grunted. "Years? What is *years*, man-thing?"

The Crow blinked slowly, chastising himself for the oversight. "It's been a long time since your people have set foot above The Under Realm. A new race has claimed Neverdark as their land." He put a hand to his chest. "Humans. They have allied with your mortal enemy, the elf. The orc has been lost to history, forgotten by all."

The chieftain leant forward in his throne. "And what of the dwarf?"

The Crow replied, "There is peace with the dwarves of Dhenaheim. They have grown fat and complacent in their halls of stone. The Great War is but a memory."

The chieftain considered his words while his eyes took in the variety of different bones. The Crow knew of their unusual trade system, but he had no idea what the value of each bone was.

"You have come a long way to tell us this," the old orc said. "What is to stop us from flaying you all and adding your bones to my throne?"

The Crow briefly met the eyes of the curious orc beside the chieftain. "I have knowledge of the world above. Their kingdoms. Their allegiances." He put his hand to his bald and scarred head as glimpses of his vision flashed before his eyes. "I even know of the old burrows dug beneath Neverdark by your ancestors. I could show you how to navigate the world without fear of the sun and take back what should always have been yours."

The orc chieftain laughed. "You may not be an elf, but your tongue is just as forked as theirs! Our kind has conquered The Under Realm. It is our home. We have no place under the wrath of the sky fire."

Growing tired of the exchange, The Crow announced, "I can make you *king*."

The chieftain puffed out his cracked chest. "There has been no king since The Great War, man-thing. I do not see how such a scrawny creature can make such a claim. I will, however, accept your skull as payment for bringing magic into my domain."

The Crow sighed. "I wasn't talking to you..." The statement drew a quizzical expression from the chieftain.

The curious orc, beside the chieftain, took a threatening step towards the leader of The Black Hand. It was happening just as he had envisioned. The tall orc drew his wide serrated sword, much to the chieftain's amusement.

"Bring me his skull, Karakulak."

What came next was almost too fast to make sense of. Only when the orc chieftain's head slid from his body, did The Crow note that the curious orc, Karakulak, was now facing away from the wizards, his serrated blade held out to his side with thick red blood dripping off the edges.

The Crow expected the assassination to have some effect on the surrounding orcs, be it a shuffling of feet or the reach for a weapon, but the chamber remained silent, the transition of power as absolute as the old orc's death.

"My father was weak," Karakulak said with his back to the wizards. "We have been on the brink of war with the other tribes for most of my life. But..." The orc slowly turned around to face The Crow, his pale features and sleek horns speckled with blood. "A *king* would unite the tribes under one banner. Our banner!" he shouted.

"THE BORN HORDE!" the chamber erupted in a deafening cacophony.

It was clear to see that Karakulak had allies not just within his tribe, but closer to the throne. There was every chance this exact scene would have played out in the not too distant future.

The tall orc beat a hand against his solid chest. "I am Karakulak. And *I* would be king of the orcs."

The Crow bowed his head. "*My* name is of little consequence, only my knowledge can serve the Born Horde. *We* are The Black Hand."

Karakulak lifted his chin, taking the wizards in. "Generations have come and gone since The Great War, yet still we remember the enemy. Elf. Dwarf. They drove us from Vengora, our home! I would have *them* remember *us*." The new chieftain displayed a cocky smile, a disturbing sight on an orc. "And a throne entirely of elven bone wouldn't hurt," he added, eliciting a cheer from those in the shadows.

Changing his behaviour in the snap of his jaws, Karakulak took a single stride to plant himself only a foot away from The Crow.

"My father may have been short-sighted, but he spoke a truth that cannot be ignored."

The Crow twisted his mouth, careful to conceal his smile. Everything was happening just as he had seen, right down to the very words.

"The orc has no place under the sky fire," Karakulak continued. "Besides spilling our enemies' blood, what would we want of Neverdark?"

The Crow made to speak, but he felt it better to show the would-be-king. Dropping to one knee, he placed the flat of his hand against the chamber floor. He could feel the heat radiating up, the source of The Under Realm's warmth.

Another quake rippled through the stone and rained debris from above, something the orcs appeared to have become accustomed to.

"Come Chieftain Karakulak," he beckoned. "Feel the wrath of the earth."

The orc raised an eyebrow until it became squashed against his bony forehead. Still, Karakulak relented and crouched beside The Crow, placing down a much larger hand. The heat was undeniable.

"If the orc goes to war with Neverdark, the earth will go to war with the sky fire," The Crow proclaimed. "It is written…"

"It is Gordomo's breath!" Karakulak stated proudly, slapping the floor.

"Gordomo…" The Crow repeated the name, testing it out in his mouth.

"The All-Maker, creator of orcs!" Karakulak thumped his hand into his chest.

"GORDOMO!" The orcs' reverberating praise was grating to his ears.

Knowing that the orcs, like every other race, worshipped a god that simply didn't exist only made them all the more malleable.

The Crow took a breath before responding; he wanted to deliver his tall tale just right with the perfect inflection rather than, *Once upon a time…*

"In a realm above our own, the gods conspire to change our

world. My god, Kaliban, has shown me the end of the sky fire and the beginning of a new Age. An Age of the orc," he lied.

Karakulak stood up, peering around the chamber at his tribe. "An Age of the orc?" The chamber erupted into cheers and beating chests.

"You would rule above *and* below," The Crow embellished his lies.

"Your god has shown you this?" the orc asked.

"This and much more," he replied. "Knowledge is power, *King* Karakulak. And I have knowledge that will see the nine tribes bow in your shadow or perish under it. Then the world is yours."

The new chieftain tilted his head, searching for any sign of a lie. "You would see the Born Horde rise above all others and have the orc rule over Neverdark?"

"That is Kaliban's will." *What harm was another lie?* he thought.

Karakulak spat on the floor. "I care little for the will of your god. Let Gordomo and this *Kaliban* deal with each other. *I* concern myself with the thing standing before me. Every living creature has wants…"

The Crow looked away as if considering his answer. "I have no wants. But, there is one thing I will *need* of you. After I help you to become king, that is."

Karakulak's eyes shone as they caught the light. "And what would that be? Besides your life, I mean."

Ignoring the threat, The Crow replied with calculating words, "It is said the orc was once Verda's greatest hunter, that no beast could elude you."

"If its heart beats, we can trap it," Karakulak said confidently, the bait taken. "What beast from the deep would you have us capture?"

"The beast I desire cannot be found in The Under Realm." The Crow uttered his next words with as much clarity as he could muster. "I need a *dragon*…"

2

OLD BONES

Six Years Later

Atop the slopes of Vengora there was no place a man could call home, especially for a tired old man with five hundred years under his belt. For thirty days and thirty nights, the howling wind and the weight of a heavy pick-axe had been Hadavad's only companion, but under the shadow of the whip masters, the mage had little choice in the matter.

That same shadow fell over him again, threatening to add another lash to his back. The sting from the last whipping had yet to die away. Hadavad hefted the pick-axe and swung deep into the mountain stone, doing his best to ignore the sores growing across his hands or the fatigue creeping into his bones.

"Dig, you whelps!" the whip master barked.

Hadavad paused, noticing the man beside him had stopped pounding the rock. How long had he stood there, slumped over his axe? The days were long, cruel, and bitterly cold, even in the tunnels. The mage had found keeping track of all those around him to be a task his mind simply wasn't up to.

"Wake up," the mage hissed, sure that the man was about to receive a beating along with his lashes.

A gentle nudge saw the man topple under his own weight. Hadavad sighed and gritted his teeth. That was the third man he had seen die in these wretched tunnels since he was dragged up the mountain.

"We've got another one!" the whip master called down the shaft.

A silhouette stepped into the light at the end of the tunnel, its shape slowly forming into the long black hood and robes that had plagued Hadavad's dreams for five centuries. The dark wizard, one of many who stalked the dizzying heights of Vengora, looked down on the dead man and sneered.

"Throw him off the mountain," the dark wizard ordered casually. "Another excavation site has been chosen to the east. Take ten of the strongest diggers and relocate them immediately."

The whip master bowed and went to work rounding up the youngest of the men. Though Hadavad's current body wasn't counted amongst the young, he was relatively new to the dig site and therefore still counted amongst the strong.

Of course, his true strength lay in his magic, but he would keep that to himself until the time was right. For now, he resigned himself to playing the part of a bewildered beggar, plucked from the unforgiving streets of Grey Stone and forced into slavery.

Rough hands grabbed the mage under the arms and pushed him into the line with the others. A couple of the slaves begged to be left in the tunnel, preferring what little heat it offered over the unrelenting winds outside. Furs were handed out to give them as much time exposed to the elements as possible, but the sun would still grace the sky when the first of them froze to death.

Hadavad was thrust forward and momentarily found himself face to face with the dark wizard. Cold, scrutinising eyes looked him over, boring into the mage. After a month of hard labour in the tunnels, his dark complexion and long dreadlocks had become matted with mud. Hadavad was confident that the wizard wouldn't recognise him but, just to be sure, the mage hunched over, feigning a crippled back.

"Can this one even lift an axe?" the dark wizard asked.

The whip master raised Hadavad's chin with the end of his whip handle. "He's only seen one full moon. He's still got plenty of diggin' in 'im.'"

Happy to have passed the wizard's inquisitive eye, Hadavad followed the others into the mountain's icy embrace. After five hundred years, the mage could say he knew pain, discomfort, and torment, but walking out onto the frozen plateau, high above the world, Hadavad decided he knew nothing of any until now.

The furs did nothing to protect against the wind and his hands struggled to keep a hold on his pick-axe. This was the first time since he arrived that he had been pulled out of the tunnel and made to work outside. He had heard from the other slaves that their tunnel was one of many. Whatever they were being forced to dig for, it had apparently remained elusive for some time, years even.

"We'll die out here!"

The cry came from the youngest of them, a man Hadavad guessed to be in his early twenties. The slave, once a beggar, had no strength to run and the flurry of snow would prevent him from finding his way back down the mountain. But fear was ever the keen motivator. He hobbled through the snow, breaking away from the group with a frantic whimper on the end of his frozen lips.

The dark wizard held out an arm and stopped the whip master from chasing him down. Instead, the wizard removed a slender wand from within his billowing robes and took aim.

Hadavad's first instinct was to take action and cast a shield to protect the fleeing slave, but he would learn nothing if he gave himself away now. It would have been easy to close his eyes and prevent the man's death from staining his memories, but for five hundred years he had carried with him every death that stemmed from the order of The Black Hand.

A brilliant flash erupted from the end of the dark wizard's wand and shot across the plateau, unhindered by the battering winds. The spell caught the slave in the back and tore through flesh, muscle, and bone. His body lay in the snow for only a moment before the dark wizard flicked his wand and sent the corpse flying over the side of the mountain.

"That's two in one day," the whip master commented.

The dark wizard shrugged. "Grey Stone isn't running out of beggars and criminals. Another group will be here in two days."

The casual nature with which The Black Hand took lives drove Hadavad's pick-axe that day. He dared to steal a glance over his shoulder at the black tents pitched on the ridge above them. A month in the cramped tunnels had hindered the mage from counting the necromancers' numbers, but judging by the all the tents, he guessed there to be around twenty of them.

The question was, is *he* on the mountain? The Black Hand's mysterious leader had been the bait that saw Hadavad masquerading as a poor beggar, hoping to be snatched from the streets and taken up the mountains. Why would The Crow be up here? What were they looking for that had his direct attention? The mage continued to hammer the rock, determined to survive and discover their secrets.

"They found it! They found it!" The announcement came from one of the other tunnels, just below their new excavation site.

The commotion saw the whip master and the dark wizard running to the edge, where two other wizards in black robes were making their way up to the tents. Hadavad furrowed his dark brow, desperate to lay eyes on what the wizards were carrying between them.

"At last…" the dark wizard said.

"Does this mean we can finally get off this frozen hell?" the whip master asked.

The wizard ignored the question. "Put them back in the tunnel," he commanded, making his way over to the tents above.

This was the moment Hadavad had been waiting for. Weeks of planning and a month of slavery had finally paid off.

Providing he didn't die in the next ten seconds…

He had to act quickly to ensure the dark wizard had no time to utter a spell. The whip master, a thug with no knowledge of magic, would be no bother, providing Hadavad still had strength enough to drive his pick-axe home.

He had no time to question his strength though. There was only action.

Hadavad spun on the ball of his foot and brought the wooden haft of the axe up into the man's jaw, knocking him back. A month ago the force of the mage's blow would have been enough to put him down.

Hadavad swung the pick-axe again and buried the point in the soft skin, under the whip master's jaw, until it tapped against his skull. Without missing a beat, the mage yanked the axe free and threw it end over end into the dark wizard, who had made the unfortunate decision to turn back to the commotion.

The mage staggered through the snow, exhausted already. The wizard had fallen to his knees with the pick-axe sticking out of his chest, propping him up. His expression of shock and horror could only flicker across his face before death claimed him.

Hadavad dropped to his side and rummaged through the dark wizard's robes, his numb fingers searching clumsily for the wand. It was delicate in his hands, making it far harder to wield than the thick haft of a pick-axe.

The other slaves behind him were at a loss as to what to do. Were they free or had he doomed them all?

Hadavad put a finger to his lips before saying, "That way. Run. Free any you can along the way."

The men hesitated, but it was their first taste of freedom and they weren't going to waste it.

The mage lifted the wand into the air and whispered a retrieval spell. Half of his forward planning had been the planting of his satchel on the mountainside. It took a couple of agonisingly long minutes before the leather satchel hurtled through the fog of snow and landed at his feet.

"You're a sight for sore eyes…" Hadavad lifted the flap and reached down into the satchel, its seemingly limited space easily fitting the length of his entire arm. "Where are you?"

The pocket dimension inside the satchel had grown larger over the years, making it harder to find everything. At last, his fingers seized the Viridian ruby and the mage eagerly draped its chain over his neck. For five hundred years, that ruby had accompanied him from one end of the world to the other, and he could count on one hand the number of times he had been forced to temporarily part with it.

On the ridge above, The Black Hand were abandoning their tents and running to the large pavilion in the middle of their camp. Whatever they had found buried in the mountain, it had them all excited. With their numbers and brutality in mind, Hadavad reached back into his satchel and retrieved his staff. Ash white, coated in dwarven polish, and inlaid with the hair of a griffin, the staff had been with him even longer than the Viridian ruby.

Completing his look, Hadavad relieved the dead wizard of his black robes and donned them himself. In his current state, walking among the necromancers was the only way he was going to see what they had excavated.

He was among the last of the wizards to enter the pavilion, a palace of warmth and comfort. A large fire burnt in the centre and the corners were illuminated with torches. The dark wizards jostled to reach the large table beside the fire, but Hadavad was one of the few who carried a staff and he used it to his advantage, shoving them aside.

A nasal, irritating voice cried out, "For six years we have worked the rock and stone! The Lord Crow has shown us the way and the great Kaliban has rewarded our dedication!"

The dark wizards cheered and Hadavad did his best to blend in. The man who had addressed the tent was small in stature with greasy hair and a hook for a nose. His robes were no different to the others, but if the mage had to guess, he would say this man was the first servant to The Crow. His presence was another indication that The Black Hand's leader was on the mountain top, nay, in this very tent. He shuffled around the edges until he found a place among those on the front row, where he had a clear view of the table.

The cheering and shuffling became an eerie silence when the

shadows on the other side of the fire took shape. Hadavad held his breath and gripped his staff until his knuckles paled.

For ten long years, since he killed the previous Crow in the valley of The Narrows, the mage had sought to discover something, anything, about their new leader. Who was he? What was his name? Where did he come from? Unlike his predecessors, this new Crow had kept to himself, operating behind the scenes. Whoever he was, he had the rest of The Black Hand terrified of him. Their fear was palpable, almost infectious.

The Crow walked into the light of the fire, revealing a lanky bald man, draped in black robes and a thick collar of dark feathers. Dull gold bracers adorned his slender wrists and a web of gold chains and gems hung around his neck. His face was a story of a hard life, marred by creases, bold lines, and a litany of scars. The skin around his mouth was discoloured, darker than the pale flesh that clung to his face like stone. Vivid green eyes glanced over them all before focusing on the shrouds placed on the old wooden table.

Hadavad leaned to the side, trying as he might to discern the contents hidden within the rags. The Crow held his hand over the shrouds and slowly moved along the length of the table until he reached the head. Black fingernails, as sharp as any Gobber's, dived down and grasped the rough fabric, tearing it away with dramatic effect.

"I have seen all that will come to pass," The Crow said, his voice a rasp. "The world we dare to dream of begins here. We, his Black Hand, will see the name of Kaliban risen above all others."

Hadavad heard every word but his attention was stolen by the bones laid out before The Crow. Though piled up and far from resembling a person's shape, the bones were certainly that of a human or an elf.

The skull, broken and cracked, sat facing the mage, its hollow sockets boring into him, reminding him where they were. Thirty years to this very winter, the last war of Illian had come to an end inside the caverns of this very mountain.

Valanis, an elf twisted by ancient magic, had tried to take all of Verda by force and found his end at the hands of Asher, an unlikely hero, but a hero none the less. Asher had used Valanis's magic against him and brought his reign of terror to an end at the cost of his own life.

These two were the only ones Hadavad could guess the bones originally belonged to. But why would The Black Hand want their bones or, more specifically, why would they want Valanis's bones? He could only imagine what they might do with the skeleton of a being so evil…

The Crow picked up Valanis's skull. "There will be those who try to stop us, as there have always been. Whether they worship the false gods or ride dragons, they will not find victory. With this in mind," The Crow's eyes moved from right to left and rested on the mage, "perhaps you would prefer to give up now, Hadavad? Before things become *unpleasant.*"

The mage looked up to see the leader of The Black Hand staring at him from across the fire. His gaze drew that of the others and the wizards stepped away with all haste, leaving Hadavad exposed. The mage was only too glad to shrug off the robes of a necromancer and brandish his staff.

The Crow stalked around the fire. "You look tired, old man." The bald man tilted his head, examining the mage from head to toe. "I thank you for your service. Your presence up here has been my only source of amusement."

Impossible, Hadavad thought. There was only one other who knew of his plan and he was miles away.

The Crow smiled arrogantly. "Surely, after five hundred years of fighting us, you have learnt of our greatest gift, just as we have learnt of yours?" His green eyes rested on the ruby poking out between the mage's clothes.

Hadavad puffed out his chest, doing his best to mask his fatigue. "So, you're as deluded as the rest then. All you Crows think you can see the future. Funny how none of them saw their end by my hand."

The Crow held out his hands, one of which still grasped the skull. "And yet, here we are. *I* knew you were coming before you did. But, what will really keep you up at night, Mage, is knowing that I have already seen everything you're *going to do.*"

Hadavad sneered, aware that The Crow was trying to get in his head. "What do you want with Valanis's bones?"

The Crow inspected the cracked skull and gently placed it back on the table. "You should be more concerned with yourself. I have seen your end, Hadavad, and it is not a good one."

The mage had heard enough; he hadn't fought for all these years to barter words. Killing every dark wizard in this tent would deliver a blow The Black Hand wouldn't recover from.

"The actions you are considering may seem heroic to you," The Crow baited, "but I assure you they are folly."

"Any action I take is to undo the unnatural practices of your order," Hadavad spat.

The Crow arched an eyebrow. "Are our practices any more unnatural than your long life? How many bodies have you possessed over the centuries, Mage?"

Hadavad had no options left to him but to explode with action. The mage flicked his ashen staff and cast a spell over the roaring fire, causing it to grow wildly out of control. The wizards scattered to avoid the blaze which soon licked at the fabric of the tent, setting the whole pavilion alight. His next spell caught one of the dark wizards in the chest, compressing every rib until his heart was crushed.

Quicker than the old Crow should have been capable, the wicked leader pointed his wand at Hadavad and let loose a destruction spell so powerful that it flung the mage from his feet and carried him outside. The wall of the tent ripped apart and flew out into the snow with him, wrapping him up as he tumbled. The Crow casually followed him out, apparently oblivious to the burning tent behind him.

Hadavad struggled in the wind and snow to tear the swaddling fabric from his body. The Crow wandered towards him with a dozen dark wizards at his back.

"You're going to need this." The Crow flicked his wand over the ground and sent Hadavad's staff back to the mage's side.

Hadavad knew he was being humiliated, but he wasn't going to give this new leader an inch. He snatched up his staff and released a

THE FALL OF NEVERDARK

fiery spell before reaching his full height, hoping to surprise The Crow. A backhand with his wand, however, deflected the spell, sending it into the mist. The mage growled and fired another spell, then another, and another. The Crow caught every one mid-flight, flinging them away or driving them into the ground.

"I killed your predecessors, wretch!" Hadavad shouted over the snow. "And I *will* kill you!"

A smirk crept up the side of The Crow's mouth, adding more lines to his face. "I am not my predecessors, *boy*…"

That last word caught Hadavad off guard and the necromancer took advantage, unleashing a lightning spell that would have claimed the mage's life had he not erected a shield at the last second. The magic clashed in an explosion of colour with blue lightning colliding against Hadavad's flaring red shield. Even the icy winds of Vengora couldn't keep the heat off his face at that moment.

"How long can you last, Mage?" The Crow called over the clashing spells.

Hadavad used what little energy he had left and expanded his shield, hoping to push The Crow's spell back on him. It wasn't enough. The necromancer ceased his assault and the mage fell forward into the snow, bringing him to the feet of the dark leader.

"Until the next time…" Using his wand, The Crow picked Hadavad from the ground as if he were no more than a feather.

The mage struggled within his invisible bonds but a month of hard labour had taken the fight out of him. The necromancer whipped his arm out and Hadavad flew with its motion until the impact against the mountainside brought him to an abrupt stop. He couldn't remember the fall or how he had cut so many parts of his body, but the mage looked up through the pelting snow to see The Crow and his wizards peering down at him. He was lying on the plateau below, where he had not long killed the whip master.

One of the dark wizards pointed his staff down at him, ready to bring an end to Hadavad's five long centuries of life.

"No," The Crow commanded, lowering the wizard's staff. "This is not where he dies. Gather our supplies and kill the slaves. We must return to the south immediately." The snow crunched under The Crow's feet as he approached. He bent down and handled the Viridian ruby around Hadavad's neck. "You may keep this a while longer, Mage…"

Hadavad blinked hard in an effort to stay conscious, but the cut on his head and the fatigue in his bones robbed him of further thought, plunging him into a blissful oblivion.

Hadavad… Hadavad…

The soft feminine voice called to the mage from deep in his soul, rousing him from the abyss.

Open your eyes…

Hadavad lifted his head from the snow, only to find he was lying face down in the middle of a forest. The biting chill of Vengora's mountainous heights had been replaced by the warmth of a midday sun on a summer's day. His ears were soon filled with the sound of animals going about their lives between the trees, which towered over him, so full of life.

The mage lifted himself up to his knees and parted his long dreadlocks to better see what could only be the result of a serious head injury.

There, before him, was a soft glow breaking through the trees and slowly circling him. Every colour he could imagine emanated from the glow, spreading through the leaves and the moss, increasing the vibrancy of their lush green.

You need to open your eyes, Hadavad…

The words came from within the glow as a humanoid form began to take shape inside the light. The mage was entirely captivated by the spectacle, curious as to whether he had died and found his way to the afterlife. The legs, silhouetted against the light, stalked towards him until a supple body, glowing with life, came to stand over him.

You need to open your eyes…

The light overwhelmed his every sense and banished the

summer warmth and the sound of nature. The mage gasped and swallowed a mouthful of freezing air, so cold that he feared he might choke on it. Through grunting and considerable pain, Hadavad slowly rose from the snow, discovering that he had been mostly buried beneath the powder.

How long had he been there? Why had The Black Hand left him?

Questions began to circle in his mind but the cold in his bones and the pain in the ends of his fingers prevented further thought. Then he remembered, as if it had been a lifetime ago, or another life completely. The woman in the forest, made from light. Her voice had felt familiar, like that of a mother's call.

As hard as it was, Hadavad managed to find his feet, collect his staff, and follow the narrow path back up to the plateau above. The central pavilion had been left to burn out, and the rest of the black tents had been packed down and taken. The Crow's last words echoed in his mind and he hurried to the nearest tunnel, fearing what he might find.

The mage stopped in the mouth of the tunnel. Sprawled across the cave floor was every man they had taken off the streets of Grey Stone and forced into labour. Every one of them had wounds typical of a destructive spell. Hadavad's heart sank and he slid down the wall, holding onto his staff.

Who was this new Crow? The Black Hand were powerful wizards all, but he had never fought against one as powerful as today. The mage looked up as yet more of The Crow's words came back to him. They were going south.

With a lasting look at those who had died by their dark hand, the mage set off for the mountain path. He would find them: he had to. With the bones of Valanis in their possession, there was no telling what evil The Black Hand could wreak across the world…

3

ORIGINS

By torchlight alone, Alijah Galfrey navigated the ancient caves in the hidden depths of The Wild Moores. Every step was the first any man had taken inside these dark halls for centuries, maybe longer.

This was what he lived for.

For the last four years, he had devoted himself to uncovering every trace left behind by the men of The First Kingdom. This cave was the sixth location Alijah laid claim to and he would be damned if he was going to leave any stone unturned.

With the fire from his torch, Alijah cast light over the ancient dwelling of his ancestors. Everything was coated in moss and weathered by time, but he could see the manmade objects resting on shelves carved from the stone. Above them, crude hand paintings decorated the walls, though their story was lost on him.

As fascinating as cups, tools, and finger paintings were, it wasn't what Alijah was looking for.

He pressed on, further into the cave. The air was thick and stale, an oppressive force that did its best to see him turn back. He hadn't trekked through the most untamed forest in the world to be turned back now. He had to know if this was the place.

Hadavad had spoken of the prophecy's origin for years, keen to discover the legendary cave where the priests of The Echoes had first scribed their foretellings. The old mage didn't believe that anyone could see the future, but he did believe in knowing your enemy.

The Black Hand. Alijah stopped and held his torch low, where a painted black hand decorated the smooth stone at his feet. With a delicate finger, he stroked the handprint before placing his whole hand over the top, matching every digit.

"Found you…" he whispered into the dark.

His excitement was building now and he quickly entered the next chamber, eager to set eyes on anything left behind by the priests of The Echoes. The final cave that marked the end of the network was small and intimate with a high ceiling. The centre of the round chamber was stained and dark, where, perhaps, there had once been a fire.

Then he saw it.

On the back wall, pinned to the stone, was a large piece of parchment that had succumbed to several lifetimes in a damp cave. Alijah crossed the cave and ran the torch over the surface, careful not to set it alight. His heart sank to see that so many of the glyphs had faded, their ink the victim of incessant droplets from above.

His finger and thumb gripped the edge of the parchment, gently caressing it. As he suspected, the taut scroll was, in fact, made from skin, and, if Hadavad was right, The Echoes always used human skin. His heart racing now, Alijah removed the iron pins and rolled the skin up, binding it with string. He began to search the cave for any other hidden gems: anything that might tell them more of The First Kingdom or The Black Hand.

It was his nose that made the next discovery. Alijah sniffed the air, relying on the senses he had inherited from his elven mother. The air inside the cave wasn't foul, but it wasn't exactly pleasant, making the aroma of cooked sausages impossible to ignore.

"Oh, you fool…"

He ran from the cave, only dropping his torch when the light of the world showed him the way out. The clearing beyond the cave was walled off by trees that had given in to winter's call, their branches skeletal limbs that looked ready to pluck wayward travellers off their feet. It wasn't the sinister trees of The Wild Moores that worried Alijah Galfrey so much.

"What are you doing?" he cried, upon spotting Vighon Draqaro spit roasting a line of sausages.

"Don't worry, I cooked enough for both of us," Vighon replied casually.

"I don't care how many you cooked, you bloody idiot!" Alijah kicked as much dirt as he could over the fire, smothering its flames in a bid to stop the smoke.

Vighon jumped up. "Oi! What're you doing? I've been cooking those for ages!"

Alijah ignored his friend and scanned the trees with one hand over his shoulder and his fingers nestled between the arrows in his quiver. His left hand slowly crept up his back, ready to pull loose his folded bow.

Vighon swept his furry black cloak out behind him and sat back down again. "I've already walked the perimeter three times while you've been poking around in the dark," he explained. "There's no Outlanders in these parts."

Alijah sighed. "We're in The Wild Moores. There are Outlanders everywhere…"

Vighon retrieved a tin plate from his pack and went about salvaging the sausages. "Let them come, I say. It's dull as shit sitting around here."

Alijah took one last look at the ominous forest before turning back to Vighon. "If you weren't so obsessed with swinging that sword you might use your head a little more." He removed the ancient scroll from his belt and waved it in front of his friend. "Maybe even learn something."

Vighon took a cautious bite of his steaming sausage. "There's more to fighting than just swinging a sword, Galfrey. It's an art. I'm an artist, really." He waved his sausage at the empty clearing. "And I don't know if you've noticed, but my canvas has been awfully dull of late."

Alijah tutted under his breath. "Barbarian…"

Vighon chuckled to himself. "That's never been proven."

Alijah offered his friend a roguish smile and held up the scroll. "I found it." He unravelled the skin and weighed it down with small sacks of spice left out by his hungry friend.

"That's one of those prophecy things, then?" Vighon asked, engrossed in his food.

Alijah paused before answering, "Do you listen to anything Hadavad says? You've been privy to everything I have for the last three years, and you think this is *one of those prophecy things*?"

Vighon shrugged as he salted the next sausage. "I like the old mage as much as anyone, but he talks *a lot*. First Kingdom this, ancient prophecies that, the big scary Black Hand, blah blah blah… It's simple in my eyes. You follow him and I follow you."

"Well, maybe instead of *following* me, you could take part, help me even."

Vighon stuffed the last of his sausage into his mouth and held up both hands, displaying seven digits. "Seven," he said between chewing. "Seven times."

"Not this again." Alijah closed his eyes.

"I've saved your life seven times in three years. I'd say following you pays off, especially with the way *you* gamble. How you survived working for Hadavad for a year without me is a mystery."

Alijah was happy to drop it there. Had it been anyone else, he might have argued the point of why the person who continued to save his life, and follow him across Illian, didn't simply return to their old life. But Vighon wasn't just any other person. They had known each other since they were children, when Vighon's mother had been under the employ of Alijah's parents. That aside, the life Vighon had left behind to join him was not one Alijah would have him return to. He would personally kill any who tried to drag his friend back to that hell…

"This," Alijah explained as he ran his hand over the top of the skin, "is an original prophecy, scribed by a priest of The Echoes."

Vighon rubbed the heavy stubble on his cheek. "I always get

confused when you call them that. You are talking about The Black Hand, yes?"

Alijah tried to hide his disbelief. "Yes, The Black Hand. But, when this was scribed, they were just known as The Echoes." He looked over the scroll like a hungry animal. "The oldest religion in the world, maybe even the first. They worshipped a god called—"

"Kaliban!" Vighon exclaimed. "I remember that bit. Hadavad always says it like he's got a bad taste in his mouth."

Alijah couldn't argue with that. "Hadavad's been fighting them a lot longer than we have…" Knowing how long the mage had been fighting the necromancers didn't give him much hope that they would ever win, at least not in his lifetime.

Vighon ran his finger over the narrow scar above his left eyebrow. "I still remember fighting them last year," he said. "Was it Dunwich or Longdale?"

Alijah was trying to take in every inch of the half-ruined prophecy. "Dunwich," he replied absently. "They had a temple under the lake."

Whatever Vighon said next was lost on Alijah, his voice blending into the background noise of the forest.

The glyphs had been arranged in three verses, but most of the text was gone, with no one verse left intact. At the bottom of the scroll was the painted black hand, just where Hadavad had said it would be.

"So," Vighon said a little louder, breaking his thoughts, "can you read the markings? The glyphs."

"Of course I can read it," Alijah replied. "Do you remember the ruins we found in The Narrows? Or the royal graves in The Spear? You've *seen* me reading the ancient language."

Vighon screwed his face, creasing the scar that ran down his right eye. "You see, you always remember reading this and finding that. All I remember is fighting off the bandits who felt we were trespassing or slaying the Gobbers who thought we'd make a good meal. Oh, and keeping the barbarians of The Iron Valley from ripping your limbs off…"

Alijah chewed over the smart reply on the end of his tongue, but Vighon had a point. "I'll give you that," he conceded.

It was only mid-afternoon when the sun began to wane, forcing Alijah to take the scroll inside the mouth of the cave, where Vighon could make a new fire and he could use the light to see the faded glyphs. A westward breeze blew the smoke farther into the cave rather than up into the sky, where any Outlander might spot their camp.

Alijah flicked backwards and forwards through his small leather notebook. Every page had something written down about his discoveries over the last four years. Right now, however, the most important thing was the translation key he had been maintaining. There were elves and mages across Verda who could read and speak much of the ancient language, often using them for spells and such, but unearthing The First Kingdom's forgotten fortresses and temples had also unearthed more of their language.

"Pass me my pack," Alijah said, tying his chestnut hair into a knot. "I need to write some of this down to make sense of it."

Vighon, who had been resting back with his feet up most of the afternoon, opened his dark eyes, entirely unimpressed. "I'm not your man-servant, Galfrey. Get it yourself."

Alijah lifted his head from the scroll, reminding himself that treating Vighon like a servant never ended well. He reached over and retrieved his ink and quill, eager to get the glyphs written down so that he might make light of their meaning. It was hard to understand any of it, with so much of the text ruined.

With his head down, Alijah missed the rising moon and the downpour of snow that encroached on the cave. He couldn't miss the freezing air, however.

When the cold became too much and interfered with his concentration, he sat up and wrapped his leather jacket a little tighter around his chest in a bid to fight off winter's bite, which took little notice of their fire. Vighon took pity on him and emerged from the warmth of his fur cloak to throw Alijah's long overcoat across the cave. It only came to his knees, but he was all the happier for the extra layer.

"You should really invest in some gloves," Vighon suggested, lifting his own black gloves. "Why you would choose to wear fingerless gloves in winter is beyond me."

Alijah blew into his closed hands. "Makes lifting arrows from my quiver easier."

Vighon raised an eyebrow. "And the reason you don't wear a cloak?"

Alijah smiled. "I haven't found one I like yet."

The northerner laughed. "You just think the look of a rogue is all it takes to win over a girl."

"It *helps*…"

Alijah took advantage of the precious silence that always accompanied Vighon's drooping eyelids and went back to work. The scroll had only so much to offer, but he would make sure he knew everything there was to know before he met up with Hadavad. And so the night crept on and the wind did naught but howl through the cave in its attempt to snuff out the fire.

Alijah flinched when Vighon's northern voice broke the silence. "Have there been any quakes while I've been out?"

Alijah considered the question for longer than he really should have. "No. None since we arrived."

Vighon nodded, his eyes glancing over the scroll. "I thought you said you could read the ancient language? Have you been going over that all night?"

"I can read it!" he argued, noting the irritation in his own voice. He looked up for the first time to see the pale blue of dawn's first light resting over the trees. Maybe he should have got some sleep…

"I've seen you stroke your beard like that before," Vighon continued, lighting his pipe. "You're stuck."

Alijah rubbed the back of his neck and removed the loose braids of hair that sat over his chest. "I'm not stuck. It's just hard to put together. Must you always start the day with a pipe?" he asked, holding his hand out for a puff himself.

Vighon blew a perfect circle of smoke into the cave before handing the pipe over. "You got me into the stuff. I used to prefer a good cup of Velian tea in the morning."

Alijah inhaled on the pipe, enjoying the sweet aftertaste of the weedwood. "I merely showed you a better class of smoke than that wretched stuff from Namdhor."

Vighon snatched the pipe back and let it hang from his mouth as he pulled his one-handed sword from its scabbard. The rhythmic sound of a whetstone running over the steel was another morning routine Alijah had become accustomed to over the last three years. In truth, he quite enjoyed the creature of habit his friend had become and he wouldn't have him any other way. He just wished he'd got some sleep…

"So, what have you translated so far?" Vighon asked, preventing further investigation of the scroll or indeed sleep.

Alijah pinched his nose and massaged his eyes. "Something about a *rising*… or maybe it says lifting. No that can't be right… Maybe it's talking about…"

"You're mumbling," Vighon interrupted, his hand running up and down the blade.

"I think it says something is going to be risen in the heart of a fallen star." Alijah shrugged. "I know, it sounds ridiculous. There's also mention of a dragon and something forgotten or maybe lost. The glyphs are just…" He held out his hands, too tired to think of the words.

"You've been looking at it all night and that's all you've found?"

Alijah took a breath, all too aware that Vighon knew exactly how to get under his skin. "I just need more time with it."

Vighon nodded along. "So, it's probably fair to say that you can't read the ancient language."

Alijah pointed his finger, his retort ready…

But the light crunch of fresh snow found his ears

The sound was too distant for Vighon's ears and the blundering fool continued to speak, ignorant to the volume of his own voice. Only when Alijah's hand went for his bow did the northerner stop and, credit to him, he knew not to ignore Alijah's senses.

"What do you hear?" he asked.

Alijah focused, aware now of more than one person's footsteps slowly pressing into the snow. His left hand slid up his back and unhooked the folded bow.

"Alijah!" Vighon hissed. "We don't all have the ears of an elf. What is it?"

Meeting his friend's dark eyes, he said, "We have been hunted…"

Vighon put down his whetstone and reached for his rounded shield instead. "It's about bloody time."

Alijah shot his friend a look before flicking the switch on the handle of his bow, expanding the limbs with a snap.

Before either had walked out into the snow, he had an arrow nocked as an echo of his mother's words rang in his ear. He couldn't pull on the string of any bow without his mother's guidance flooding back to him. It pained him to think of her, he missed her so much, but she was easily the best archer in all of Verda and it would be folly to ignore her council.

The falling snow and the twilight of dawn made it hard to see anything beyond the trees. But he knew they were out there. Outlanders. The wild people of the wood who refused to leave their forest and enter the civilised world, unlike their ancient cousins a thousand years ago. They weren't as big as the barbarians in The Iron Valley or as savage as the legendary Darkakin, but they were killers all.

"How many?" Vighon asked, hefting his one-handed sword and shield.

"Ssh!" Alijah turned his ear to the wall of trees and closed his eyes.

Never aim with just your eyes, his mother had said. *Feel the direction of the wind on your skin. Inhale the scent on the breeze. Listen to the world.*

Alijah released his arrow to the sound of a satisfying *thud*, quickly followed by a garbled yelp and the crunch of snow after the body hit the ground. It was a show of superior skill, something Alijah had been told was respected by Outlanders and often led to them abandoning their prey.

He had been told wrong.

A dozen faces slowly emerged from the snow, as if The Wild

Moores itself was giving birth to them. The expected rush and attack never came, however, with the Outlanders creeping ever forward. If it was a fear tactic, Alijah decided it was a very good one…

The men and women spreading out around the tree-line wielded crude axes and jagged swords. From head to toe, they were all attired in a mismatch of animal skins and furs, though they all revealed their dirty faces and tattoos. It was the black fang tattooed below their eyes that caught Alijah's attention. At this point, he was beginning to doubt the information he had been given about Outlanders, but he had heard it from his father himself that the fang tattoo was the mark of a hunter clan.

Vighon turned his head to Alijah while keeping his eyes on the Outlanders. "I'll be lucky if I see thirty winters sticking with you…"

"The only reason they found us is because you just had to have sausages for lunch," Alijah quickly replied.

Without another word, Vighon drove his sword into the ground, dropped his shield, and unclipped his fur cloak. Alijah would have closed his eyes in despair were he not fixed on six of the Outlanders who appeared to have chosen him as their prey.

"Why do you always have to do this?" he asked through gritted teeth.

Beside him, Vighon continued to go through his stretching regime, pulling on the muscles in his arms and legs. "Stretching is important before a fight and you don't always get the chance," he replied.

Alijah kept his bowstring taut and the end of his arrow resting at the anchor point behind his mouth. "You're mad, do you know that?"

With an almost playful tone to his voice, Vighon replied, "We'll see who has a sore back by the afternoon."

There should have been a question as to whether either of them would live to see the afternoon, but they had both survived worse than this. It was a cocky attitude Alijah was sure would get them killed one day. Just not this day.

Almost as one, the Outlanders took note of the cave behind the two men and shared a terrified look. A moment later, they turned and scrambled through the forest as if the dark mouth of the cave would consume them whole.

"Clearly my reputation has spread to The Wild Moores," Vighon commented.

Alijah shook his head, ignoring the remark. "They were scared of the cave. Clearly, the tribes of the Outlanders don't remember The Echoes fondly. We should leave before more arrive. Hadavad needs to see this scroll."

"I'll just fetch the horses then," Vighon said sarcastically. "Oh, that's right, you made us leave them in Lirian."

Alijah flicked his bow and collapsed the limbs. "You can't bring horses into The Wild Moores. Everybody knows that."

Vighon sheathed his sword on his hip and reattached his cloak. "Why? Because of the scary Outlanders?" He glanced at the trees. "They ran away at the sight of a *cave*."

Alijah wasn't convinced they were safe yet. "We can't stay here forever. Eventually, they'll band together and find confidence in their numbers."

"How many can there be?" Vighon asked.

Both men suddenly looked at each other for from across the clearing there was no mistaking the wild cries echoing through the trees. Judging by sound alone, the rest of the tribe was descending on the clearing and rapidly.

"Get your things!" Alijah hooked his bow to his back and dashed back into the cave to gather his pack, to which he strapped the ancient scroll.

Vighon slung his shield over his back before collecting his own pack. "It took us two weeks to reach this cave..."

Alijah looked up at the rising sun. "That's because we didn't know where to find it. We follow the dawn. We'll be at the banks of The Unmar by dusk."

"If we don't stop," Vighon said, catching his eye.

Alijah turned to the clearing, where the cries for blood were growing louder. "Do you want to stop?"

With that, they ran into the east as the first salvo of arrows impacted the ground and the trees around them. It was going to be a long day…

4

DRAGONS' REACH

With nothing but the clouds above her and the ocean beneath her, Inara Galfrey felt truly alive. As cold as the winter chill was, especially at such dizzying heights, the warmth emanating from Athis was enough to keep her comfortable, allowing them to fly together for hours.

Inara hugged the dragon's red scales and Athis briefly rose above the cloud bank, offering a view of the heavens, before diving back towards the waves of The Adean. Were her mentor not sharing the sky with them, Inara would have cheered and hollered with glee. As it was, Gideon Thorn, the leader of the Dragorn and praised hero of The War for the Realm soared below, astride Ilargo, whose green scales glistened under the midday sun.

Athis straightened his great wings, filling the soft membranes with the wind so that he might glide down and allow Inara to hear the waves. With the world outstretched before them, her sense of adventure drove her desires, daring her to fly into lands unknown with Athis and discover new realms.

Where would you have us go? Athis asked, deep in her mind.

Inara smiled, comforted by the fact that they would be forever connected. **West, I think. Beyond The Hox.**

Athis didn't seem convinced. *As long as we can go beyond The Hox. That sea is infested with monsters even dragons dare not hunt…*

Have I found a place that brave Athis the ironheart dare not fly?

The red dragon glanced back at her with one of his rich blue eyes and huffed. *You can't fly anywhere without me, wingless one…*

Inara laughed and rubbed her hand over his smooth scales. Nestled between the spikes on his back, she could see his magnificent wingspan spread out beside her. Following the spikes that ran up his neck, a head of horns gave way to the white walls of The Shining Coast, Illian's eastern edge.

Athis caught the air currents to lift them a little higher, where the white cliffs met the fields of Alborn, a blanket of green that stretched to the foreseeable horizon.

Inara looked back over her shoulder and squinted into the distance, just making out the coastal city of Velia. It had been some time since she had made this particular trip, heading south down the coast, but every time she did, Inara would look out for her parents' house.

I can see it, Athis said with a hint of smugness.

You always see it first! Inara pushed her boots into the dragon's scales and stood up to better see over his flapping wings.

There it was, not far from the edge of the cliff, a fairly modest two-storey house with stables and a few fields of sheep sprawled out before it. Of course, her parents wouldn't be inside. They never were these days. Instead, they were a few miles farther south and awaiting her very arrival. The thought of seeing them soon brought a wide smile to her angelic face.

It didn't take Athis and Ilargo long to cover those extra miles, breaking through a patch of fog to reveal the lone tower built into the cliff face.

Carved from white stone to fit in with its surroundings, Dragons' Reach rose high above the fields with a crown of silver-pointed spikes. Supporting pillars jutted out from halfway up the tower and provided reinforcement for the oval platform that extended out of the Reach, at its highest level.

Far below, Inara could see a battalion of Velian soldiers and a caravan of supplies that typically followed a king or queen around. In this instance, she knew it to be King Rayden, who had arrived with such an entourage since the tower sat within Alborn's borders, the country of Rayden's ancestors.

Inara looked for Gideon in the skies around her, feeling his presence on the periphery of her mind. Through their bond, shared with the dragons, her mentor spoke through Ilargo, to Athis, allowing her to hear his voice with perfect clarity.

You should go first, he said. *Your parents are inside…*

Inara appreciated her mentor's sentiment. It had been a few months since she had seen her parents and they would get very little time together on this trip. Also, the arrival of Gideon Thorn tended to capture the attention of any room he was in. It couldn't be helped, she knew, and Gideon often found it more of a hindrance than anything, but he was *the* Gideon Thorn, the first Dragorn in a thousand years and the first *human* Dragorn in ten thousand years.

Having been born four years after The War for the Realm, Inara had only heard the tales of his prowess in battle and the heroic way he and Ilargo had entered The Battle for Velia, at the end of the war. There weren't many who hadn't heard the stories of Gideon, Asher and her parents. Even her grandmother, Adilandra Sevari, was the queen of the elves, ruling over the city of Elandril, on the other side of The Adean. Inara felt as if she had an awful lot to live up to…

We will have our time, Athis said.

Doubtful, she replied. **There is no greater deterrent to war than the Dragorn. Our numbers grow every year. Who would be stupid enough to cause trouble with dragons for peacekeepers?**

Athis banked out to sea, adjusting his angle of approach. *We have had cause to step in many times over the last ten years together. Just last year we tracked down those slavers hiding in The Narrows.*

I'm happy with all that we've done, Athis. And I'm incredibly privileged to be living in a time of peace. It's just… I've been brought up on the stories of the war. My

mother was on top of Syla's Gate when it fell for goodness' sake! My father held off the Darkakin atop Velia's walls! They fought alongside Asher, the Asher, and were even there when Valanis was beaten. My grandmother forged the first alliance between man and elf, not to mention arriving at The Battle for Velia with an army of dragons! And then there's Gideon...

She didn't need to list her mentor's deeds. Athis had met Gideon before she was even born, before Gideon was even a Dragorn, in fact. *I just... I feel I should be doing something more. It feels like a weight on my shoulders.*

On our shoulders, Athis corrected.

Inara couldn't help but smile and pat his hard scales. *Then I'm glad yours are a lot stronger than mine.*

You always think this way before you see your parents, Athis observed.

It was impossible to argue with the observations of a being who shared your very soul. *Well, they've given me a lot to live up to.*

Athis arched his wings dramatically and brought all four of his legs up as he landed on the platform, presenting the occupants of the highest room with his chest of hardened, slate grey scales.

The dragon folded his wings in and ducked his head, allowing Inara to see the dragon-sized arch in the wall. She had only been to the tower once before since meetings such as this were uncommon, but her parents were always guaranteed to be present.

"Inara!"

Her mother, Reyna Galfrey, was the first to greet her, as always. The elven ambassador, or princess, depending on which side of The Adean she was on, embraced Inara in a tight hug that any human would find uncomfortable.

For Inara, the discomfort came from the number of eyes on her, with the chamber filled with royalty from across the realm. There was nothing any of them could do, however, to stop the Galfreys from greeting their daughter.

It felt like a lifetime before her mother stepped back, revealing a face as youthful as her own. Reyna's long blonde hair flowed over her shoulders, decorated with braids, and tucked behind her pointed ears. Her blonde hair and green eyes provided the starkest of differences to her daughter's dark hair and blue eyes, but her high cheekbones, typical of an elf, had been passed on to Inara.

"Let me get a look at you." Her father, Nathaniel Galfrey, pulled her in for an embrace of his own, before planting a kiss on her forehead.

As always, his eyes ran over her, checking for injuries, but he always glanced at her rounded ears. He had always been especially satisfied with the knowledge that he had given Inara her human ears.

"It hasn't been that long, Father." Inara embraced him again and pushed up onto her tiptoes to kiss him on the cheek.

Despite being human from birth, her father had yet to age a day since the end of The War for the Realm; a lasting gift imparted to him by the hero, Asher, in his dying moments.

At the time, it hadn't been known what the ranger had done, releasing some of the raw magic that flowed through his body into her father's. With the appearance of a thirty-year-old, it was now assumed that Asher had given Nathaniel the life of an immortal, allowing him to live with Reyna forever.

That same magic had been Asher's downfall, a power he couldn't contain, but Inara would be eternally grateful for his lasting gift.

"Athis..." Her mother ran a hand up and down the scales between the dragon's vibrant blue eyes, whose entire head and neck fitted through the arch.

"Uncle Tauren!" Inara regretted the affectionate call as soon as she spotted the array of monarchs and leaders seated around the semi-circular table, facing the arch. Still, Tauren Salimson, High Councillor of Tregaran and esteemed leader in The Arid Lands, was like family to Inara.

"It has been too long, Inara," Tauren replied in his exotic accent.

It had been some time since he had called her by one of the affectionate names he had used when she was growing up and, it seemed, she would never hear him use one again now that she bore the title of Dragorn.

"I have missed your tales," she said.

Tauren brushed a hand through his greying curls. "My stories pale by comparison to that of a Dragorn, I think. I fear you would find them boring now."

Inara squeezed his arm. "Never."

Tauren had played his own part in The War for the Realm, and as much as Inara had enjoyed hearing of it, she also enjoyed hearing of his life on the streets of Karath, fighting slavers in The Arid Lands. Back then, of course, he had been known as The White Owl.

"Inara Galfrey!" King Rayden had left his seat in the middle of the table to greet her, an unusual thing for one accustomed to others coming to him. "It is an honour, as always." The king of Velia took her hand in his own and kissed it gently.

"The honour is mine, King Rayden," she replied with the bow of her head, just as her mother had instructed her so long ago.

Rayden was young by kingly standards, with only a few years on Inara. In truth, he was closer in appearance to her father, Nathaniel.

Unlike Rengar, Rayden's father, the current king of Velia and ruler of all of Alborn was much loved by his people, though Inara suspected it had helped to have her parents and Gideon around to advise him. She also suspected that the king wanted to take her as his bride.

A union that could never be, she thought.

Beyond Rayden, the semi-circular table was lined with the ethereal images of the other monarchs who ruled over the six kingdoms of Illian.

Inara recognised Weymund of house Harg, king of Lirian and ruler of all of Felgarn, recently taken to the throne after his mother's abdication.

Beside him was Jormund of house Orvish, king of Grey Stone and ruler of The Ice Vales, a brute of a man, even when his form was that of an astral projection.

Seated at the end of the table was the oldest of the monarchs,

Yelifer of house Skalaf, the self-appointed queen of Namdhor in the north and ruler of Orith. She had fought tooth and nail against the other lords of Orith to claim the throne after the line of Tion came to an end, thirty years ago.

As always, there were no representatives from the island nation of Dragorn. It was widely known that the city was ruled by criminal guilds that presented themselves as noble houses, houses that wanted nothing to do with the troubles of the mainland.

Inara just found the over-populated island an irritation. Long ago, they had taken on the name of the order who called the island their home. Now that the real Dragorn had returned, Inara had hoped the criminal guilds would rename their city. After thirty years, it seemed that change would never come…

Standing to the side, out of the way, was Rayden's court mage, Ibn Vangodill, attired in a ridiculous pointed hat and more belt accessories than should have been necessary. The wizard, along with the other monarchs' court mages, was responsible for their ethereal presence, despite being separated by hundreds of miles in some cases. Somewhere inside their own castles and palaces, the three rulers would be sat at an empty table looking at all of their ethereal projections.

Of course, the only mage worth noting at the table was Magikar Caliko, the head wizard at Korkanath, Illian's most prestigious school for magic.

Athis audibly grunted from the balcony and shook his head as he made to back out. *Ilargo is waiting.*

Inara nodded her understanding before addressing the chamber. "Master Thorn is here," she explained, using Gideon's official title.

Athis moved out onto the platform and dropped off the edge. Inara could sense her companion's intentions, aware that he planned to lie on the ground before the Velian soldiers and put them ill at ease. For all his wisdom and honour, Athis could not be denied his mischievous side.

Play nice, she said with a smile.

I don't know what you're talking about… Athis coyly replied.

A gust of cold wind was blown through the arch, preceding

Ilargo's arrival. It seemed to Inara that the atmosphere in the room changed more than the temperature.

Dragons' Reach shuddered under the dragon's mighty weight and his wings stretched out to eclipse the pale grey of winter's midday sky. Arching his neck, Ilargo the redeemer of men poked his head into the chamber, his piercing blue eyes scanning the room's occupants.

Gideon Thorn dropped onto the platform and made for King Rayden with a rehearsed bow he too had learned from Reyna many years ago.

As close as they all were, the leader of the Dragorn could not be seen to greet anyone before a king or queen of the realm. After grasping forearms with the king of Velia, he turned to address the ethereal monarchs sat around the table, greeting them all by name.

Inara's parents took the time to say hello to Ilargo, who would be terribly offended if he was forgotten. Inara translated the dragon's greetings, telling them how he had missed them and, adding cheekily, that Gideon was still in need of Reyna's instructions.

By Inara's observation, however, her mentor was doing just fine as he went through the royal greetings. After all, Gideon's smile was as charming as it was inviting. Coupled with his status as leader of the Dragorn, he was perhaps the most loved and powerful person in all of Verda.

Inara was proud to have had him as her mentor, though she would always think of him as her teacher, no matter how long she was a fully fledged Dragorn.

In his early fifties, Gideon was actually a decade or so younger than her father but, by anyone's eyes, it was easy to see that the Dragorn was visibly older, placing him in his early forties. His short dark hair had lost some of its curls and been peppered with strands of grey, a sign of ageing that had also crept into his trimmed beard.

Of course, he would never age another day now that his bond with Ilargo had solidified. Human or not; the magic of their bond would keep him immortal and death's grasp forever at bay.

His attire, much like Inara's, was practical for flying with a short jacket of tough leather and light armour padding throughout. Their knee-high boots were brown and weathered; perfect for all terrain since a Dragorn could be called upon anywhere in Verda.

Inara could never look at her mentor without glancing over at the Vi'tari blade that rested on his hip. Mournblade was an elven scimitar with a hilt of red and gold, its pommel a hooked claw resembling that of a dragon's.

Inara gripped the hilt of her own Vi'tari scimitar, the weapon of a Dragorn. It didn't have the history of Mournblade, but its hilt of intricately decorated red wood was magnificent in her eyes, and made all the better for the crystal that adorned the end, a gift from Adilandra, her elven grandmother.

The Dragorn soon finished greeting the leaders of Illian, Tauren included, and turned to Reyna, practically lifting her off the ground in his embrace, much to the embarrassment of Inara.

"Oh, Reyna," Gideon said with a cheeky smile. "When are you going to leave this bag of old bones and come and live with me? In The Lifeless Isles, you could have your very own island!"

Nathaniel cut in with a bemused smile. "You're definitely looking older..." The two men locked arms before pulling each other in for a hug.

"We can't all look young forever, old friend," Gideon said, patting Nathaniel on the arm. "Some of us have to pull off the distinguished look," he added with a wink to Reyna.

"Alright," Inara said, placing a hand on the shoulders of both men. "The three of you just need to learn where the line is." The young Dragorn glanced at the kings and queen.

"Ah." Gideon placed a hand on Inara's own shoulder. "And so the apprentice has become the master."

"I think I overtook you several years ago," Inara replied in such a way that the seated delegation couldn't hear their banter.

Gideon raised his eyebrow. "I think I preferred it when you couldn't even spell Dragorn..."

Magikar Caliko cleared his throat. "Perhaps we should discover the reason for our attendance?"

Looking a little embarrassed, on her parents and mentor's

behalf, Inara made for her seat. Her mother walked back around the table and gave her one last squeeze of the hand before finding a seat beside Nathaniel. It was good to see them again.

Gideon leaned into Nathaniel's side and whispered, "Do you know what this is about?"

Though Inara's ears were human in appearance, they were of elven design inside, allowing her to hear everything that passed between the two men. Indeed, she was just as curious as to why they had been summoned to Dragons' Reach, for a meeting of so many was not usual.

"Nothing good," Nathaniel replied solemnly. "The recent earthquakes, perhaps."

Inara hoped her father was wrong, but Dragons' Reach had been built after The War for the Realm as a way of bringing the leaders of the world together, along with the Dragorn, to discuss the larger problems that might affect the kingdoms. It was never good.

Tauren Salimson was the only one who had yet to take his seat, instead, gesturing to one of his aides to bring something inside. Looking at him now, Inara could see how uncomfortable he was, though she knew from experience that it could not be from addressing so many; he was a High Councillor of Tregaran, after all.

"Thank you for gathering at such short notice..." The southerner gestured again for his aides.

The ornate doors opened at the end of the chamber and four natives of The Arid Lands entered the room, pulling a cart draped with a large tarp. The cart was placed in the open space, in the curve of the table between Ilargo and the others.

Nathaniel wrinkled his nose at the smell. "Well, you don't need to be an elf to smell that."

It was a nauseating smell, but Inara had come across something similar in her time as a Dragorn. It was the smell of death.

"What is that, Tauren?" Reyna asked, struggling to keep the disgust off her face.

Tauren hesitated with his hand on the corner of the tarp. "Since the war, my people have kept watch over Syla's Gate. When the last watch rotated, however, they found only death. The men had been slaughtered, some in their sleep, others in battle."

"The Darkakin?" King Rayden asked, fearing the return of those savage killers from the south.

"No, Your Grace," Tauren continued, "something *worse*. I accompanied the relieving watch myself and was attacked by the same beasts in the ruins of Karath, though we fared better. We killed all but one and tracked it to an underground cave."

"*It?*" Reyna echoed.

Tauren hesitated before pulling the tarp clean off the cart. Ilargo was the first to react, becoming distressed at the sight that greeted them. Thankfully, the dragon pulled his head from the chamber before roaring into the sky. Those still in the room could only look at the contents of the cart in horror and confusion.

"It cannot be…" Gideon whispered.

Inara looked from her mentor's contorted expression to the body laid out on the cart. She quickly rose from her seat to join the audience that was amassing around the dead body. The ethereal kings and queens were able to walk through the table and stand beside Ibn Vangodill, who was just as curious as the rest.

"I have seen every manner of monster in this world," Nathaniel said. "What in all the hells is that?"

"Something it cannot be." Gideon's gaze was fixed on the body, his hand clenched around the red and gold hilt of Mournblade.

"It looks worse than it smells," Inara commented, breathing through her mouth.

"*Gideon.*" Reyna's tone reminded the Dragorn that he wasn't alone. "You recognise this creature. What is it?"

Gideon took a deep breath. "An *orc*…"

5

RED IN THE SNOW

W hen the third arrow impacted the large pack on his back, Alijah decided it was weighing him down too much. He shrugged the pack off and dropped to his knee, quickly pulling free the leathery scroll from its binding and shoving it between the quiver and short-sword that rested on his back.

"Get up!" Vighon yelled from behind, having already abandoned his pack half a mile back.

Alijah tried to pick himself up as Vighon's rough hand cupped under his arm and yanked him to his feet.

The snow had gathered above their ankles, slowing their escape since fleeing the cave. Two more arrows sailed past them and sank into a tree before a single-bladed axe cut through the air and dug into Vighon's shield on his back, knocking the man to the ground.

Skidding to a stop, Alijah turned back to help his friend, only to see half a dozen Outlanders sprinting towards them. They were relentless in their hunt. He couldn't decide if they simply wanted to force them out of the forest or cook them over a fire.

One hand brought up his folded bow, snapping it to life with the flick of a switch, while the other hand retrieved an arrow from the quiver on his back. "Are you hurt?" he asked as the arrow flew from his bow and took down the closest Outlander.

"No," Vighon groaned. He lifted the shield off his back and pulled the axe free, using it to scrape off the four arrows that protruded it. He threw the axe back into the oncoming mob, catching one of the crazed men in the shoulder.

Alijah let loose another arrow, sighting half a dozen more advancing from the south. Judging by the howls that punctuated the air, he guessed there to be a score more of the wild folk approaching from the north, closing them in.

By the time the hunting party was on top of them, Alijah had dropped five of the fools who continued to run towards his bow.

The first of the Outlanders to make their move against Vighon was a man with bushy red hair and an axe in each hand. Vighon didn't even bother reaching for his sword as one axe after the other cut through the air an inch away from his head.

He caught the next swing with a strong hand around the haft of the axe before driving his forehead into the man's nose. A single boot to the chest had the fiery Outlander skidding back through the snow, where he would remain for some time.

Alijah knew better than to watch Vighon fight, for the man required no help and his brutal fighting style was often hypnotic to watch. More than once, Alijah had sat back and taken bets with fellow spectators on how quickly his friend would succumb to overwhelming odds. Of course, Vighon could take the punishment, always getting back up to finish the fight - often started by Alijah himself...

A stone dagger flew from the hand of a female Outlander, its sharpened point in line with Alijah's head. His inherited reflexes kicked in and he released his next arrow to intercept the dagger mid-flight, knocking it from the air.

Two of the Outlanders on his left tried to take advantage of the distraction and charge him with their crude swords raised and a battle cry on their lips. With speed they couldn't match, Alijah nocked another arrow and launched it into the chest of the closest runner, taking the man off his feet.

The second runner provided the perfect launching pad for him to kick and gain some height over the others. Before the second runner landed in the snow, Alijah was flying through the air, having fired two more arrows, each one striking true and dropping their targets. He landed with the grace of a cat to face the remaining Outlanders with a superior grin on his face.

Vighon had pulled his sword free by now and given the Outlanders something to think about. Two came at him from either side, hoping to split his attention while one of them split his skull. Vighon raised his sword and parried one blade before ducking into a roll and collecting his shield on the way back up. Now a third took their chance, attacking him from behind. Their mistake. Vighon dropped to one knee and pivoted in the snow, bringing his sword out into a sweeping arc. The Outlander caught the blade across their midriff and spun around, stumbling to the ground in a bloody mess.

Only a couple of metres away, Alijah ducked, weaved, and evaded every swing from the swords and axes that the Outlanders tried tirelessly to bury in his head. A quick gut punch had the attacker doubling over, allowing Alijah to roll over his bent back and nock an arrow. The female screamed like a banshee, waving her axe in the air, as he let loose the arrow and put her down for good.

When he rolled off the other side of the male Outlander, the man had recovered enough to bring his sword up, thrusting it towards Alijah's stomach. The rough blade would have pierced his flesh too had Vighon's sword not chopped down on it, driving the blade to the ground.

"That's eight!" he growled, before punching the Outlander with the edge of his shield. The man spat blood and collapsed in a heap at their feet.

"That doesn't count," Alijah protested. "I would have…"

"What? Got stuck like a pig?" Vighon laughed and flexed eight digits from the strap of his shield and the hilt of his sword.

Alijah looked to see that all of Vighon's attackers were lying still in piles of red snow. His observations were interrupted when an arrow whistled past his ear and found its home in the trunk of a tree. There were more coming and now they wouldn't be content with just forcing the trespassers out... now they would want vengeance.

"Time to start that running thing again," he said, firing an arrow to intercept an Outlander mid-air as he jumped down from a small ridge.

Vighon raised his shield and stopped two arrows from laying him low. "You're slowing yourself down," he said from within the shelter of his shield.

Alijah kept his bow in hand as he turned to run. "What are you talking about?"

Vighon slung his shield over his back and joined Alijah in searching for the eastern edge of the forest. "We both know you can run a lot faster than this!"

Alijah ducked his head when the next salvo of arrows landed in the snow around them. "We entered The Wild Moores together and we'll leave The Wild Moores together!"

And so they ran, often bashing into each other in a bid to navigate the bare trees and climb over the snow-covered rocks. More arrows hailed down on them, along with the occasional spear or axe, but run they did. The sun was searching for its rest and long shadows stretched over the ground when they, at last, saw the fields beyond the edge of the forest.

Any elation that might have been grasped was torn away when the mound of snow in front of them exploded with Outlanders. Whether they had been lying in wait for them or just waiting to capture their dinner for the night, Alijah couldn't guess, nor did he have the time to ponder upon it.

The closest Outlander dived forwards and wrapped his hands around Alijah's waist, dragging him to the ground. Vighon was tackled by the other two and driven into a tree. They only had a minute before the hunting party would be on them, yet they were only feet away from the edge of the forest.

The Outlander swore in his native tongue and drooled over Alijah as he pressed down with his jagged knife, pushing it closer and closer to his throat. Alijah grunted at first until he turned it into a rage-filled growl and used the anger to fuel his strength. The two rolled to the side and tumbled over the shallow rocks, giving Alijah enough time to scramble to his feet and put some distance between them.

Vighon, on the other hand, had already snapped the neck of one and was continuously ploughing the other's head into the tree, smearing his blood across the bark.

Alijah's first instinct was to reach for his bow and end the threat of his own attacker right there and then, but the Outlander was already up and charging. Alijah reached over his back and pulled free the short-sword poking over his right shoulder. The silvyr blade flashed in the dying light, the orange hue accentuating the ancient glyphs carved up the centre of the rare metal.

A part of him hated using the blade, aware that he was most certainly undeserving of it, but mostly because he had stolen it from his parents' house before running away. Still, crafted from the most precious metal in all of Verda and forged on a dwarf's anvil, the silvyr short-sword cut through anything and everything that posed a threat.

In this case; it was an Outlander who had the honour of dying by the blade of Asher.

Alijah side-stepped the charge and drove the point through the man's chest. One sharp cry escaped the Outlander before he fell to his knees, dead.

Vighon drew his single-handed sword and stole Alijah's attention as he jumped into the path of the chasing savages. The northerner's blade slashed left and right, opening guts and arteries with every strike. Alijah could only watch as his friend ran into the last of them and thrust his sword through the man's stomach until he met the hilt guard.

Through laboured breath and a curtain of hair, Vighon turned to regard Alijah. "We should really get out of here before more arrive."

Alijah sheathed the silvyr blade and resisted the urge to simply slump against a tree and fall asleep. They had been running all day and were close to collapsing from exhaustion.

"The Bovadeer bridge isn't far north of here," he replied. "We can cross The Unmar there and make for Lirian."

Vighon eyed the scroll on Alijah's back. "That piece of bloody parchment had better be valuable."

Alijah joined him in jogging to the tree line. "It's valuable to us. And it's not parchment. It's human skin…"

6

A DARK NEW WORLD

Inara looked from the body lying on the cart to her mentor. "An orc?" she repeated, her tone as incredulous as Gideon's expression.

Ilargo held his head over the cart and sniffed. His facial expressions were hard for most to interpret, but Inara could see the disgust clear as day.

"What is an orc?" King Rayden's question was echoed by his peers.

Gideon met the eyes of all three Galfreys, they being the only ones present who knew of The Great War, five thousand years past. Inara suddenly regretted not reading enough about it in the library on The Lifeless Isles. She had always been far more fascinated by flying with Athis.

In fairness, Inara thought, the Dragorn didn't believe she would ever come face to face with a real orc, dead or alive.

"Five thousand years ago, long before mankind left The Wild Moores," Gideon explained, "the dwarves of Dhenaheim called Vengora their home. So too did another race: the orc."

Inara followed his gesture and examined the creature in greater detail. Its skin was pale grey and marred with ravine-like scars. Its face had all the features of the goodly folk of the world, but its brow was a solid piece of ridged bone that led to a head of horns not dissimilar to a dragon's.

"They ultimately went to war over the territory," Gideon continued, "but the orcs outnumbered them, running the dwarves out of their home and into Dhenaheim, farther north."

"But, they didn't stop there…" Reyna added.

"No," Gideon agreed. "The orcs relished in their victory and sought more from the land. They soon attacked the elven nation and plunged all of Illian into war. It took the combined efforts of elf *and* dwarf to beat them back."

"Beat them back?" King Jormund of Grey Stone asked. "Where have they been for the last five thousand years?"

Inara caught Gideon gripping the hilt of Mournblade a little tighter. "The war finally came to an end in The Undying Mountains," he answered. "Elandril, the first of the elven Dragorn, led the charge south astride his dragon, Nylla, driving them into the mountains. Through the will and efforts of both races, the mountains were sealed and the orcs left to die."

Tauren Salimson threw the tarp back over the dead body. "I would say they didn't die."

Nathaniel cupped his jaw, his eyes still fixed on the body beneath the cover. "If they've been in The Undying Mountains all this time, how is it we haven't heard from them? They don't exactly sound friendly."

Gideon shook his head. "I don't know."

"Syla's Gate perhaps?" Weymund Harg, king of Lirian, offered, referring to the massive gates that once cut off the world below The Arid Lands, to the south. "They were brought down thirty years ago, were they not? During the war."

"Indeed, good King," Gideon nodded along. "But Lady Syla erected the original gates two thousand years ago, after driving the Darkakin out of Illian. The orcs had a few millennia in between to return north and trouble us once more and yet they didn't…" The Master Dragorn looked to Ilargo, as he often did.

THE FALL OF NEVERDARK

"If they were sealed within The Undying Mountains," Inara said, working it through, "how could they be here, now, in the northern lands?"

"They must have found a way out," Tauren replied. "It sounds like they were already adept at life underground."

Reyna shook her head. "If the elves, dwarves, and the Dragorn sealed them under those mountains then they would still be there."

"Then what?" Nathaniel asked. "We know that they did seal them in, so how is there an orc lying right there in front of us?"

Inara heard them all, but she knew to keep her eye on Gideon, who always knew more than anyone, no matter what room they were in. His subtle expressions and body language often told her what to expect or how serious a situation was. Right now, she could tell that he wasn't agreeing with anything that was being suggested, leaving her just as clueless as everyone else.

"I'm sorry for the loss of your men," Gideon said to Tauren. "I promise the Dragorn will investigate the appearance of this creature. I will look into it myself."

Tauren bowed in appreciation, but Inara could see the ethereal expressions of intrigue on the other rulers. It wasn't very often these days that Gideon Thorn himself looked into matters, though, in truth, Inara knew he just deliberately avoided matters personal to the kings and queens of the realm.

Gideon looked to Inara. "We shall leave for Syla's Gate immediately and—"

Yelifer Skalaf cleared her throat, cutting Gideon off and drawing everyone's attention to the end of the table, where her ethereal form was still seated.

The queen of the north met all of their inquisitive expressions with a steely gaze of her own. "Since we have been summoned to Dragons' Reach for no more than a history lesson and a monster hunt, I shall present a situation worthy of this council."

Gideon turned to face her. "I assure you, Queen Yelifer, the appearance of an orc is not to be taken lightly. Had it not been for the alliance, they would have consumed all of—"

"I'm sure they were wicked, Master Thorn," Yelifer interrupted again, "and I have no doubt that the Dragorn will get to the bottom of it, but Namdhor, nay the entire north, is under threat of war."

That silenced the room. Inara called upon her years as a Dragorn to control her face and hide any sign of shock, an effort not easily achieved when a monarch talks of war.

"War?" Reyna asked.

"Yes, Ambassador Galfrey, *war*." The older woman shot Inara's mother a challenging stare.

King Rayden glanced at the other rulers, his bewildered features matching their own. "Of what war do you speak, Yelifer? I am not aware of tensions between any of us."

The queen of Namdhor pursed her lips, exaggerating the lines around her mouth. "That is because you share a border with all of us, as do you all," she added. "*My* kingdom occupies the north of Illian and therefore shares a border with foreigners."

There was a pause in the room before Reyna said, "Dhenaheim? You are under threat of war with the dwarves?" she asked skeptically.

"I would say the possibility of war with Dhenaheim is of far more consequence than the appearance of some long forgotten… What were they called?"

Gideon ignored the question and pressed the queen for answers. "What could cause a war between Orith and Dhenaheim?"

"As you know, the mountains of Vengora are all that separate their kingdom from mine. It would seem we have both laid claim to the same mine."

"You're mining in Vengora?" Nathaniel asked with disbelief in his tone.

"It is my right, is it not?" Yelifer retorted. "As Master Thorn has just pointed out, the dwarves left Vengora thousands of years ago. They are part of Orith, *my* kingdom."

King Jormund's ethereal form stepped forward. "That has never been established. Vengora is neutral land."

Yelifer raised her thin eyebrows. "To reach them you would have to cross my land."

Jormund shook his bushy head. "The southern curve is in my territory!"

The queen of Namdhor was quick to reply, "I thought you just said the mountains were neutral?" That was enough to fluster the king and prevent him from furthering his protest.

Thankfully, Gideon stepped in between them. "This is not the time to debate lines on a map. Courting war with the dwarves is folly, Queen Yelifer. What mine could be of such value that you wouldn't simply withdraw and leave them to their ancient home?"

"The affairs of Namdhor are private, Master Thorn. I do not have to tell you anything, even if you do fly around on a dragon. All this council needs to be concerned with is the fact that a foreign people are threatening a kingdom of Illian. Whether the mountains of Vengora are to be claimed or not, it is certainly not within the land of Dhenaheim as carved out by the dwarves."

Inara wanted to question the queen herself, but it felt inappropriate, even as a Dragorn. She was in a room with several other rulers, two ambassadors and Gideon Thorn. There weren't many places Inara had such insecurities regarding her status, but inside Dragons' Reach wasn't many places...

"What actions have you taken? Nathaniel asked.

"The mine has been reinforced with extra guards from our end," Yelifer explained. "My scouts tell me the dwarves have done the same on their end."

"Has there been any bloodshed?" Reyna inquired.

Queen Yelifer shook her ethereal head. "Blood has been spilled, but no deaths... yet. I am officially asking this council for support."

A decidedly awkward pause befell the room as the kings, ambassadors, and High Councillor pondered the exact meaning of *support*.

In the end, it was Reyna who spoke on behalf of those gathered. "What exactly are you asking for, Queen Yelifer?"

Namdhor's ruler had a simple reply. "Soldiers, of course. I have already called upon my bannermen to rally my forces. Soon they will march on The Iron Valley."

"March on The Iron Valley? For what purpose?" Gideon asked.

"To flank my enemy and locate the northern entrance created by the dwarves," the queen replied casually. "Claiming a foothold on both sides of Vengora will secure the mine. It would also stop any dwarven army from marching south through the valley and invading Illian."

"Invading Orith," King Jormund corrected.

"Yes," Yelifer agreed. "Orith, the only land between them and the rest of you."

The king of The Ice Vales laughed, disturbing his ethereal body. "I will not supply your ranks with my soldiers, Yelifer, not over a damned *mine*! It is said that the dwarves have armour and weapons of pure silvyr. Nothing can beat that!"

Inara could see that King Weymund and Rayden were moments from agreeing with King Jormund, all responses that would see the beginning of a rift between their kingdoms.

Speak, Inara, Athis encouraged from the base of the tower. *You are Dragorn!*

"Perhaps a line of dialogue needs to be opened between Namdhor and Dhenaheim?" she finally suggested, much to her mother's approval.

"Agreed," said Gideon. "I would ask, Queen Yelifer, that you hold off from marching your forces through The Iron Valley. At least until contact has been made with the lords of Dhenaheim."

Nathaniel added, "Avoiding war with the dwarves should be our priority at all costs."

Yelifer waved the notion away. "I fear the time for words has passed. As we speak, the dwarves in that mine are being resupplied and preparing for an assault that will see Dhenaheim lay claim to Illian land. I assure you all, I will not let that happen..."

Inara was inclined to believe the queen of Namdhor. The war-witch, as she had been known, had personally spearheaded the battles in Orith, spilling blood across the northern lands for thirty years as she took over the throne, claiming the right to rule through violence alone. Now, the lords of Skystead, Dunwich, Longdale, and

Darkwell feared her wrath, preferring to bend the knee rather than revolt.

"Let us try," Reyna pleaded.

Beside her, Gideon said, "I will send two Dragorn to Dhenaheim at once."

Having already spoken up once, Inara was gaining confidence in her ability to offer advice, even if it wasn't in agreement with her mentor. "That might not be such a good idea," she said. "The dwarves haven't seen a dragon for centuries. Seeing two with Illian riders astride might be taken as an act of aggression."

Gideon's smile wasn't quite as prideful as Reyna's, but he certainly agreed with her statement. "Then a lighter touch, perhaps?" he said, looking to Inara's parents.

"You want us to go?" Nathaniel asked, barely able to keep the excitement out of his voice.

"You have long proven yourselves as ambassadors between Illian and the elves of Ayda," Gideon replied. "If you are willing and those present agree that this is the best course of action, I don't see why you can't prevent a war from breaking out." Inara caught the wink her mentor threw at her father. "Queen Yelifer, will you agree to this?"

The old queen blinked slowly as she considered her reply. "Be swift, Ambassadors. If the dwarves attack, I will not retreat." With that, Yelifer Skalaf's ethereal form lost its cohesion and dissipated into wisps of blue smoke.

"Thank the gods for that!" King Jormund bellowed. "I thought the old war-witch would never leave."

Inara once again looked to Gideon for guidance on what to do next. Her mentor had already turned from the rulers of Illian, however, and returned his attention to the dead orc. She recognised the glances he threw Ilargo's way, understanding that a conversation was taking place between them. It was clear to see that he was more disturbed by the presence of the creature than any dispute between Namdhor and Dhenaheim.

King Weymund of Lirian turned to Tauren. "It is a great loss that your men have fallen to these beasts, High Councillor. I hope that Master Thorn roots out the cause of their emergence as soon as possible and prevents further deaths in The Arid Lands."

Tauren bowed his head in appreciation. "Thank you, King Weymund."

"Yes, terrible business," King Jormund of Grey Stone chipped in. "I would also appreciate any update from the north, Ambassadors. War with the dwarves would be bad for all of us."

"Of course, Your Grace," Reyna replied in her best diplomatic tone. Inara could always hear the difference.

A moment later, the kings of Lirian and Grey Stone disappeared, returning to oversee their own countries. King Rayden offered his own condolences to Tauren and wished everyone luck in their separate errands before making to leave with his entourage and Magikar Caliko.

Inara felt as if she could breathe again when all who remained could be counted among her family. Tauren ordered his aides to remove the cart, a sight that saw Gideon's gaze linger, his thoughts too distant to guess.

Her mother took advantage of the moment and embraced Inara once more. Her father, however, kept his mind on current events.

"Should we be worried about that?" he asked Gideon, gesturing to the departing orc.

"I'm not sure yet," he replied honestly.

Inara pulled away from her mother's embrace. "What is it?"

Gideon looked to see that he was alone among friends. "I can't shake the feeling."

"What feeling?" Reyna asked.

"That the world is turning," he replied softly. "Though, for better or worse I cannot tell."

Nathaniel planted a heavy hand on the Dragorn's shoulder. "Whatever's happening here, I've no doubt that you'll get to the bottom of it. You always do."

"And you have a war to prevent, it seems," Tauren added with a lighter tone.

"I know," Nathaniel said with a smile. "I might even pack my sword…"

Both Inara and Reyna looked to respond to his inappropriate glee, but Gideon spoke first. "The road to Dhenaheim will be treacherous, no doubt. Not to mention the dwarves themselves. Perhaps a guide would be of use, someone who knows the path *and* the dwarves. An old friend even…" he added with a smile.

Nathaniel nodded. "I think I know just where to find him."

"Say hello from me," Tauren said.

"What are *we* to do?" Inara asked, catching Gideon's eye.

The Master Dragorn glanced at Ilargo before replying, "We shall leave for the ruins of Karath and investigate."

Inara could see that her mother wanted to offer cautioning words, telling her to be careful, but Nathaniel subtly nudged her elbow, a silent message that reminded the elf their daughter was a Dragorn. Inara was thankful for the intervention, especially while in the presence of Gideon.

"I'm sorry there isn't more time," Gideon added, seeing Reyna's longing look at Inara.

Reyna waved his apology away. "We all have our duty to the realm. I only hope these orcs are a lonely few, lucky to have found a way back to the surface."

Gideon made to leave, falling into a huddle of farewells among the men. Inara gravitated to her mother, sensing Reyna's need to speak to her. It was impossible to avoid another embrace and Inara squeezed her tightly, wondering when they would see each other again.

Reyna pulled back, keeping Inara held by the elbows. "Have you heard anything?" she asked, stealing a glance at Nathaniel.

Inara couldn't help but lose her smile. "Nothing," she replied quietly. "Whatever he's up to he isn't leaving tracks." She could tell by her mother's eyes that she was fearing the worst. "Alijah is still alive," Inara said firmly. "I would know otherwise." There was no explanation for that fact, but the Dragorn was sure that she would know if anything ever happened to her twin brother.

Reyna did her best to offer a smile, but Inara could see through it. Both her mother and father had suffered since Alijah walked off into the world four years ago, searching for his own path. Inara missed him every day, often wondering what adventures he might have found himself on.

In truth, she suspected he was either drunk, bedding a bar wench or hanging by his thumbs for cheating at a game of cards. Inara loved her brother dearly, but he had a habit of collecting bad habits…

7

ROGUES AND RANGERS

After more days and nights of walking than Vighon Draqaro would have preferred, he finally looked upon Lirian, the heart of Illian. Leaving the Selk Road behind, he entered the city beside Alijah, more than happy to return to civilisation.

Located in the bosom of The Evermoore, Lirian was a city of woodland folk, accustomed to a life of logging and hunting. It was a pleasant existence that Vighon had fallen asleep dreaming about during his early twenties, during his years in Namdhor. He had dreamt of many different lives while living in Namdhor…

Thankfully, a passer-by, a young man with a sack of goods slung over his shoulder, bumped into him, pulling him from the clutches of his violent memories. Vighon apologised for the collision and quick-stepped to catch up with Alijah, who was making his way down the main street.

Gleaming at the head of the city was Lirian's royal palace of pointed roofs and rounded towers, set amidst the mountain that overlooked the people. The thick clouds amassing overhead looked to dump more snow, however, threatening to blanket the city and hide the palace from view.

Vighon gripped the strap of his shield and followed his friend through the streets, their destination always the same.

A smile broke out across his face when The Pick-Axe came into view, its lanterns illuminating the wooden porch and thick smoke rising from its chimney.

Vighon patted Alijah's back. "Is there a better place in all of Illian for a man to find rest?"

Half a smile lifted Alijah's beard. "You're just thinking of Nelly…"

Vighon laughed. "How could I not? She's beautiful, loyal, and loves me more than any other man!"

"I can't argue with that," Alijah replied as he started up the short steps into the tavern.

Vighon walked in behind him, embracing the warmth and general hubbub of the rowdy tavern. That familiar scent of timber and ale filled his nose, giving him the feeling of being at home.

Alijah cleared them a way through the drinkers, many of whom were crowding around an old knight of the Graycoats, telling the last tales of his retired order before they died out.

"Well, there be a couple of rogues if ever I saw 'em!" came the call from behind the bar, where Russell Maybury, the owner of The Pick-Axe, stood washing tankards. "And in need of a drink too, I'll guess!"

Resting horizontally above the big man's head was his weapon of choice; a hefty-looking pick-axe. Vighon had tried many times to count the notches scored into the haft, a line for every beastie and monster Russell had put in the ground during his ranger days.

Being a ranger wasn't the only interesting part to Russell's past, though it had taken Vighon a little longer than Alijah to come around to the idea that a werewolf could not only run a tavern, but also refrain from killing them all.

Russell's exact age was uncertain but, from the tales he had heard, he guessed the man to be in his late eighties, at least. Of course, to look at him, it was easy to believe he was in his late forties.

Alijah slumped against the bar. "I'd rather take a bed, Rus."

Vighon didn't miss the cheeky look his friend gave to Rose, the barmaid, or the look she gave him back. Indeed, it seemed impossible for women to resist Alijah's roguish charm, though Vighon suspected his unusual looks had something to do with it.

Being half-elf, his facial features were what most would consider pretty, with strong cheekbones and a jaw to match. Vighon couldn't count on one hand how many times he had seen Alijah use his pointed ears to draw a woman in. Countering his elfish looks, and making him all the more unusual, was his beard, thick but trimmed and never seen on a full-blooded elf. And finally, ensuring that Vighon was always second in any woman's considerations, were his crystal blue eyes.

"There's always a bed at The Axe for a Galfrey!" Russell shot them a wink with one of his yellow eyes, and Alijah looked about, clearly uncomfortable with his famous surname being announced. "And a Draqaro at that!" Russell added.

Vighon nodded his appreciation when two sharp barks pierced the din of the tavern. "Nelly!" The shaggy dog bounded between the customers and into his open arms.

"She's missed you," Russell commented.

Vighon scratched Nelly's ears and waited for her to roll over so he could rub her belly. After three years of frequenting The Pick-Axe, he liked to think of Nelly as his own and ignore the fact that she belonged to Russell.

"Go grab some shut-eye, boys," Russell suggested, flicking his head in the direction of the door marked *private*. "The Axe'll still be here tonight."

Alijah glanced at Rose. "And… will the lovely Rose still be here?"

Russell dropped his tankard on the bar like a hammer, emphasising his response. "*Yes*. And she'll still be working then, so no funny business, Mr. Galfrey."

Alijah held up his hands, pleading his innocence. "No funny business," he agreed. "Which room is Hadavad in?"

Russell's face screwed up. "Hadavad? I haven't seen the old mage in over a month."

Vighon looked up from stroking Nelly to see Alijah's concern.

They were the ones who were late arriving at The Pick-Axe; Hadavad should have been waiting for them for at least four days.

"Well, if he should arrive while we're sleeping send him our way," Alijah directed.

"As you wish," Russell said. "You can take Nelly with you too, if you like."

Vighon smiled at that. "Come little one, you can keep me company."

The two made for the private door in the corner of the tavern, happy to drop into a couple of fluffy beds and forget about the last two weeks in The Wild Moores. Of all their expeditions, camping in those woods was not Vighon's idea of a good time.

Nelly, her whole body wagging, led the way across the tavern. That was when Vighon saw him. Seated in a shadowy alcove, alone, was a hooded man cloaked in blue with his feet up and a pipe in his mouth. Bar his eyes, which were fixed on Vighon, his features were entirely hidden, but there was something about the man that stood out, something he couldn't quite put his finger on.

"Are you coming?" Alijah asked from the private door.

The question brought Vighon back to the present and his fatigue continued its barrage on his senses, beckoning him to sleep. He glanced over his shoulder before walking down the steps, beyond the private door, only to find the alcove was now empty. He blinked hard, unbelieving that any man could move that quickly and remain hidden, even in a crowd such as this.

Nelly barked from the bottom of the stairs and Vighon shook his head, sure that he needed rest. After passing through the private bar beneath the tavern, both men chose their separate rooms and bade each other good sleep.

Vighon woke up to the sensation of a wet tongue licking his fingers. Seeing Nelly's happy face was a far better sight than waking up to Alijah's.

Judging by the increase in noise and feet on the boards above, he guessed night to have arrived and with it the larger crowds.

"Come on," he called to the dog. "Let's go find some food."

The private bar beneath the tavern had a couple of quiet occupants sitting together by the fire. Like all those who were granted access to the basement, they were rangers of the wilds, folk who found work hunting creatures with an abundance of fangs.

Eyeing Vighon, they stopped their conversation and watched him as he passed through. There was no uniform to a ranger, but they could always tell their own, and Vighon was not their own. He had only been granted access due to his friendship with Alijah, who was only granted access because of Hadavad, though Vighon suspected his friend's parentage had something to do with it as well.

The crackling of the fire was rudely interrupted by loud snoring that emanated from the small bar area. Sprawled out across the square table lay a dwarf - at least he assumed it was a dwarf, hidden as he was within layers of black and gold armour. The little boy in Vighon became very excited, aware that the dwarf, a rare sight in Illian, could only be Doran Heavybelly!

Another hero named in The War for the Realm, the dwarf had fought alongside the Galfreys and even Asher. Renowned for charging into battle astride his Warhog, Doran Heavybelly had been said to have actually saved Asher's life during the final battle at Velia.

He took a step in the sleeping dwarf's direction when one of the seated rangers warned him, "I wouldn't do that, lad. Waking up Heavybelly doesn't end well…"

Vighon took the warning and backed away, thanking the man for his caution.

One floor up, The Pick-Axe had come to life in a way it never did during the day. The band was twice as large and the patrons had packed out every available space to avoid the icy air outside.

Vighon navigated the dancing duo in the middle of the foyer and made his way to the bar, where Russell Maybury was already placing a pail of cold Lirian ale down in front of him.

"Appreciated," he replied, though he would much rather have

smoked his weedwood and enjoyed a piping cup of tea. "Where's Alijah?"

Russell raised an eyebrow and slid his eyes to the left, where Alijah was sat around a table with six other men, deep into some card game.

Vighon groaned and dropped his head. "What're they playing?" he asked reluctantly.

Russell handed out another tankard of ale before replying, "Last I saw, it was Galant…"

Vighon groaned again. "I hate it when he plays Galant."

"Why?" Russell asked, somewhat bemused. "I've only ever seen him win."

"It's *how* he wins that bothers me." Vighon collected his ale and found his way to Alijah's chair.

"Morning sunshine!" Alijah said with a quick glance.

"It's night time," Vighon replied dryly.

Alijah looked up from his cards and inspected the windows. "Ah, so it is. Any sign of Hadavad yet?"

Vighon didn't need to examine every patron to know the mage wasn't in The Axe. "No. Maybe we should go and wait for him?"

Alijah didn't hide his confusion. "We are waiting for him," he said, holding his hands up to the tavern.

Vighon sighed. "Maybe we should wait someplace else…"

Alijah twisted his mouth, careful to keep his retort to himself. "One moment, gents." The half-elf stood up to meet Vighon eye to eye and kept his voice low. "I'm not going to cheat—"

"And the sun's not going to rise," Vighon shot back.

"Do you like eating?" Alijah asked in hushed tones. "How about drinking? Or sleeping on a bed? These things cost coin, and I don't know if you've noticed but these little expeditions of ours don't exactly make us wealthy men."

"Coin?" Vighon quickly responded. "It wouldn't matter if you were playing for doilies, Alijah; you just enjoy gambling."

Alijah rolled his eyes like a child tired of hearing his father's lectures. "Why don't you go and smoke your pipe, have some food, and keep an eye out for Hadavad?" With that, the half-elf took his seat back and resumed the game.

Vighon turned his back on him, sure that when the fighting started, and it would, he wasn't going to be there to help the idiot. With Nelly padding around his feet, eager for attention, he returned to the bar and ordered a bowl of stew from Rose. It soon became clear, however, that he wouldn't be able to get his hand from the bowl to his mouth without being jostled.

"Come on, Nelly, let's go and find somewhere quiet to eat." With the dog in tow, Vighon pushed his way through and edged his way into the stone alcove beside the fireplace. "I'll be surprised," he said, looking down at Nelly, "if I finish the bowl before the first of them takes a swing at that daft sod."

Lifting his spoon, Vighon took a steaming mouthful of chicken and slurped on the hot broth. It would have been enough to bring a smile to his face had he not looked up and discovered a man sitting in the alcove with him. Being in such a familiar place, he managed to contain the surprise that would normally have seen him reach for his sword.

"How in all the hells did you get there?" he asked. He realised, then, that it was the same hooded man who had been watching him when they arrived at The Axe. "Who are you?"

"I'm like you, Vighon," the stranger replied cryptically. "Just another cog…"

Vighon's lips parted but the words were stolen by the ruckus that erupted on the other side of the tavern. There were shouts and complaints of cheating before someone broke a chair and a handful of coins hit the floor.

"Save your friend." The stranger gestured to Alijah with his chin, briefly exposing a smooth face from within the shadows of his hood. "Meet me down in the locker when you're done."

"Locker?" Vighon had barely said the word before the stranger left the alcove.

Nelly barked, pulling his attention back to the brawl. His head was suddenly swimming with questions, as well as the urge to leave

Alijah to a doom of his own making, but the sound of a good tussle was always impossible to ignore.

Pushing his way through the onlookers, Vighon came to a scene he had witnessed far too many times. As good as Alijah was at cheating, he always pushed it too far, always wanting more until he slipped up. Luckily for him, Vighon thought, he had the reflexes of an elf to fall back on. A sweaty man with more hair on his face than on his head threw a punch at Alijah, hoping to crack his jaw.

He missed.

His next two punches could do nothing but displace the air as Alijah shifted his shoulders, avoiding him by inches. The third punch swung over his head and caught one of the other players across the nose, whose arm flew out and knocked a tankard of ale from a patron's hand. In short, Alijah was causing his usual amount of chaos.

Vighon clenched his fist, though he wasn't sure if he was going to hit Alijah or the sweaty man.

From nowhere, the meaty hand of Russell Maybury came to rest in the middle of his chest. Vighon could feel the strength in that hand and knew he wouldn't be taking another step.

"I can't afford for you to get involved, kid," Russell explained. "I'll have the city watch in here demanding your arrest."

Vighon shrugged as if he didn't understand. "I was just gonna' throw him about a bit…"

Russell's yellow eyes bore into him. "You never just *throw them about a bit.*"

The werewolf turned to the scrap, which was quickly turning into a full-on brawl, and gripped the sweaty man by his tunic before he could throw his next punch. Russell lifted him from the ground with one hand and marched out of the front door, where he promptly ejected the man into the snow.

"Cool off!" he shouted after him. His feat of strength had been enough to calm the others down immediately and they quickly found their drinks to be the most interesting thing. Russell looked to Vighon and pointed at Alijah. "Take him downstairs," he ordered.

Vighon had no desire to argue with the man and he ushered

Alijah back to the private door. Where most would display some embarrassment, Alijah could only shrug as if he had done nothing wrong.

"This is why we can't have nice things," Vighon commented as they returned to the private bar below.

"What? I didn't do anything!" Alijah protested. Vighon shot him a look over his shoulder. "Alright, maybe I cheated a *little* bit…" The half-elf opened his overcoat to reveal a small bag of coins. "Worth it, though," he added with a cheeky grin.

Vighon shook his head in despair. "Do you know anything about a locker?" he asked, eager to avoid the gaze of both the seated rangers.

"Locker?" Alijah didn't even look up from inspecting the contents of his bag of coins. "Oh, yeah, the armoury. It's at the end of the hall, I think."

"There's an *armoury* down here? We've been coming here for *years* and you never told me there's an armoury!" Vighon placed a firm hand on Alijah's back and had them both get out from under the gaze of the two rangers.

"I haven't seen it since I was a child," Alijah replied in defence. "Was that Doran Heavybelly?" he added as an afterthought.

Vighon walked past the bedchambers until he came across a blank door around the corner. He had always assumed there were just more rooms, always hesitant to explore after coming across Russell's chamber a couple of years ago. The owner of The Axe was also the owner of a reinforced cage big enough to accommodate a couple of horses. Thankfully, he had never been visiting the tavern during a full moon…

"What are we doing here, Vighon?"

"I have no idea…" he replied under his breath.

Pushing through, the chamber beyond was a feast for the eyes. All four walls of the rectangular room were lined with swords of all sizes, axes, both single and double bladed, clubs, spears, daggers, staffs and shields. Some looked to be antiques, while others looked newly forged and polished. Padded mats filled the majority of the floor, with thick wooden mannequins situated in the corners, all lined with old scars.

Vighon could have spent hours inspecting every wall, handling the weapons and hefting the shields. He was immediately drawn to the single-handed sword on the far wall, displayed horizontally beside a tattered long coat. With all thoughts of the hooded stranger forgotten, Vighon rushed over and read the plaque under the sword.

"Jonus Glaide..." The name rang a bell but he couldn't place it.

"He was a ranger," Alijah explained. "My father knew him. He fought in The Battle for Syla's Gate and on the King's Walls at Velia."

"I think I remember his funeral," Vighon said.

"Yes, he died when we were children. We all went..."

Vighon could hear his friend's thoughts wandering down a path he would rather not have him take. He quickly moved on to examine a collection of shields, rapping his knuckles against the wood to get a feel for them. None were as good as his, however, gifted to him from Hadavad three years previously.

Behind him, a small alcove caught his eye, its contents mostly hidden behind a dusty curtain. Through the crack, he could make out a rack of dark green cloaks and a row of identical swords, all crowned with a spiked pommel.

"That's why they call it the locker," the stranger's voice broke his intrigue and startled the pair.

Standing by the far wall, though how he got there without either of them noticing was baffling, the hooded stranger shifted his blue cloak, revealing a pair of scimitars, one on each hip. Only now did Vighon realise that there was a chance he had been duped into being cornered in a room with only one door.

Vighon fell on old habits and assessed what could potentially turn into a formidable foe. His muddied boots told of a life off the beaten track, while his brown leather jerkin, layered with hardened pauldrons on his shoulders, told of a life of violence. Matching his shoulder guards, the stranger wore a pair of rerebraces around his biceps and leather vambraces around his forearms. It was following this examination that led Vighon to the man's hands, each smooth and clean; an odd companionship to his attire.

"It was *his* locker," the stranger continued. *"Asher's…"*

Hearing that, it took everything Vighon had to keep his eyes on the man and not return to the alcove. "Who are you?" he demanded.

"Look at his blades," Alijah said in the same tired tone often reserved for matters concerning his family. "He's Galanör Reveeri."

Now there was name Vighon had heard growing up in and out of the Galfrey household. During the time of The War for the Realm, Galanör's name often came up alongside Gideon Thorn's, as the pair had been together when they discovered the dragons in the south of Ayda. He had been present for The Battle for Velia and even in the halls of Kaliban, atop Vengora, when the evil Valanis had been slain. If memory served, and it didn't always in Vighon's case, the elf was also betrothed to Alijah's mother before the war broke out.

He was also said to be the greatest swordsman in all of Verda. And a ranger to boot…

Galanör lifted his hood to reveal a typical elven face of classically handsome features, marred only by a single scar that cut through his left eyebrow.

Vighon was more than used to pointed ears, having lived with Alijah and his mother, Reyna, in his earlier years, but to his understanding, elves typically styled long hair. Galanör, on the other hand, sported short spiky hair of hazelnut brown.

"Good to see you again, Alijah," Galanör said.

The half-elf nodded along. "What's it been, ten years?"

"Thirteen," Galanör corrected.

Vighon couldn't recall such a time, but he hadn't always been permitted to join the family on their trips around the kingdoms. As Ambassador Reyna's handmaiden, Vighon's mother had accompanied them everywhere but, occasionally, he had been commanded to stay behind and help out with the Galfreys' farm.

"You were just a child then," Galanör continued. "You seem to have grown up... a *little*," he added with a glance at the ceiling, referring to the recent game of Galant.

"Hang on," Vighon interrupted, looking to Alijah. "He's been... upstairs... he was the..."

"Use your words, Vighon," Alijah prompted with an amused smile.

Vighon took a breath. "He's been talking to me upstairs. He's the one who told me to meet him here."

Alijah's face scrunched up in confusion. "What's going on Galanör? From what I've heard you rarely frequent The Axe."

Galanör gripped one of his scimitars and paced the length of the wall. "It's true. I prefer my time in the wilds of the world. Still, when Hadavad calls I do not delay."

"Hadavad?" Alijah quickly repeated. "You know Hadavad?"

"Better than you, I think." Punctuating his statement, Galanör leant against the stone wall and pressed his heel into one of the slabs, activating what sounded like a series of unseen cogs.

"What the bloody hell is..." Vighon held his tongue when a section of the wall beside the elf rotated, presenting them with an entirely new wall.

"What is all this?" Alijah stepped forward, his attention captured by the wall of parchments.

Vighon paced behind his friend, keeping one eye on the elf and the other on the wall. From top to bottom, the stone was overlaid with a wooden board and a hundred sheets of parchment. A map of Verda provided the centrepiece with strings and pins connecting various points in both Illian and Ayda to the parchments. Some had drawings on, surrounded by scribbled notes, while others offered reams of information about some of the sites they had unearthed.

The top left corner appeared to be devoted to The Black Hand's more recent activity, referencing sighted movements up and down the country between Grey Stone and The Arid Lands.

"These are all the places we've been," Vighon pointed out. "Look. Dunwich, The Iron Valley, The White Vale. There's even a sketch of that old pillar we found in The Lonely Wastes..."

Galanör circled behind them. "This is just one of many, I

suspect. Knowing Hadavad, he probably has a hundred walls like this."

"I'm confused," Alijah admitted. "How *do* you know Hadavad?"

Galanör offered a knowing smile. "We're all looking for the same thing, aren't we? There are only a handful of people who know that The First Kingdom even existed and even fewer who know of its connection to The Black Hand. They pose a threat. Knowing about The First Kingdom might give us answers or clues as to how we dismantle their cult for good."

Alijah narrowed his eyes. "That didn't exactly answer my question."

"I suppose it didn't. But, if Hadavad has chosen to keep certain things from you, I can only imagine it was requested of him."

In Vighon's eyes, that answer only begged more questions, a lot more questions. "Requested of him? Who's giving the old man orders?"

Alijah thumbed at Vighon. "What he said."

Galanör held his hands up. "We all have our parts to play. But, rest assured, we are all fighting for the sake of the realm."

"Fighting for the realm?" Vighon echoed, looking to Alijah with an amused smile of his own. "What's he talking about? You must have us confused with the Dragorn. We're more like... treasure hunters!"

Galanör narrowed his brow, looking from Vighon to Alijah questioningly.

Alijah shrugged. "He's not really a listener..."

"Hang about..."

Vighon's words were cut off by the elf. "Then now is the time to pay attention." Galanör's tone had taken a firmer edge. "Hadavad was supposed to meet the three of us here. He's been late before, but never this late. Given his last errand, however, I fear he will never arrive."

Hearing it put so bluntly was shocking to Vighon, but he could see from Alijah's animated movements that it was much harder for his friend to hear.

"He can't be dead..." Alijah was wearing out the mat under his feet. "He was... he was just..."

Galanör took a step closer, focusing the half-elf. "You never really know where he is, do you? When he's not with you, that is. He sends you here or there while he travels another route."

"There's a whole kingdom that existed before any of this," Alijah replied, sweeping his hand around the room as if it were the whole world. "We have to split up to cover more ground and uncover as much as we can as fast as we can."

"True," Galanör agreed. "It's also to ensure that you never have the whole picture, should you be captured by The Black Hand. We few are the only ones who oppose them. We cannot afford to have our plans unravel."

It was clear to see that Alijah had been slapped in the face by this news. Where Vighon was used to being out of the loop, and pleasantly so, Alijah believed he was at the heart of their investigations, alongside Hadavad.

"But you know where he's been," Vighon said, catching onto the elf's arrogant nature. "Don't you?"

Galanör walked through the middle of them and pointed at the corner concerning the movements of The Black Hand. "I've spent most of my time trying to locate their leader, The Crow. Since Hadavad killed the last one ten years ago, this new Crow has pulled back on a lot of their activities, shutting down operations in all six kingdoms. This made them harder to keep track of for a while, but six years ago they came together in greater numbers than ever before." Galanör poked his finger into the map, highlighting The Arid Lands. "I followed them as far as Syla's Gate before they disappeared into The Undying Mountains."

"We've noticed an increase in their numbers of late," Alijah chipped in. "Why are they coming together more?"

"We don't know," Galanör admitted. "This new Crow would appear to have a more singular objective than those before him. It was travelling in such numbers, however, that ultimately helped to find them."

"Is that where Hadavad is?" Vighon asked. "Has he gone to find The Crow?"

Galanör twisted his mouth, clearly unsure just how much he was permitted to divulge. "After The Black Hand returned from The Undying Mountains, they started showing up in Grey Stone, in The Ice Vales. They were taking beggars and criminals and marching them up to the peaks of Vengora. They have been up those mountains for years, digging at the rock."

"Digging for what?" Vighon pressed.

Alijah shook his head with revelation in his eyes. "Not digging. Excavating…"

Galanör nodded his head. "Just as we have been doing. Hadavad has been posing as a beggar on the streets of Grey Stone. The last I heard, he had been taken up the mountain with the others. He should have come back by now, regardless of what he found or didn't find."

"Was The Crow up there?" Alijah asked with a grave tone.

"We believe so," Galanör replied.

Alijah turned away from them and Vighon could see the internal struggle within his friend. Hadavad was the one who had given Alijah another path to follow, a path that allowed him to be of service in a way he had always failed to be in the past. He didn't have the level head of an ambassador, the honour of a Graycoat or whatever it was that made one a Dragorn and able to bond with a dragon. Even if Vighon didn't know exactly what they were always doing, he knew that Alijah did, and his friend believed it to be for the greater good.

"Why weren't you up there with him?" Vighon asked the elf.

Galanör could have taken offence at the direct question, but his tone was practical in response. "Hadavad sent you into The Wild Moores to locate one of the caves belonging to The Echoes. I was to be here in case he couldn't be, so that whatever you might find could be connected to the larger picture." The ranger looked to Alijah. "*Did* you find anything?"

It took Alijah another moment to gather his thoughts and turn back to them. Vighon could see that he was hurt, not only by being left out, but also by the unknown fate of Hadavad.

Vighon didn't believe for a second that the old mage was dead. He had seen him fight with that staff of his and knew it would take some punishment to put him down for good. He hoped…

"We found the cave," Alijah explained as he removed the scroll from a deep pocket inside his overcoat. "And this. It was pinned inside the cave."

Galanör took the ancient scroll and ran his nose along it, taking in the scents as well as the texture between his delicate fingers. "It's damaged," he commented upon unravelling it.

"It's been inside that cave for a long time," Alijah observed. "I've already started the translation." He pulled out his little notebook from his inner jacket.

"I would see both in more detail." Galanör held out his hand, waiting for the notebook.

That riled Vighon up something rotten but, before he could protest on Alijah's behalf, his friend begrudgingly handed the notebook over to the ranger.

"I suggest you both eat and rest," Galanör said, his eyes still glued to the ancient scroll.

"What are *you* going to do?" Alijah asked.

Galanör finally looked up. "I will see what can be learned from this. Hopefully, Hadavad will return to us by dawn."

"And if he doesn't?" Alijah asked, stopping the elf from walking out of the door.

"Hadavad or no Hadavad," Galanör replied, "we will still have orders to follow. As long as you're willing to follow them…" With that, the ranger left the locker.

Vighon could barely wait until the elf was out of sight. "What's going on, Alijah? What orders? Whose orders have we been following all this time? I thought we were just helping the old man find some long lost treasures before those cult bastards did! And why did you give him your notebook?"

Alijah held up his hands as a sign of calm. "I don't know who's been giving Hadavad or Galanör their orders. Believe me, I would love to know. I gave him what I had because regardless of what we don't know, he's still right; we're all fighting for the sake of the realm." Alijah offered him a hard look. "They've been excavating Vengora, Vighon. Nothing good can come of that. The Black Hand are clearly up to something and it needs us to get in the middle of it."

Vighon didn't know what to do with his adrenaline. "Are we fighting a war here or something?"

"We always were, Vighon. We always were…"

8

OUT OF THE LIGHT

A s Athis punctured the clouds, Inara was given her first look at the ruins of Karath. The desert floor provided a canvas of sand that stretched on for miles to the north, but to the south, it rose up into the imposing walls of The Undying Mountains.

Syla's Pass, beyond the broken gates, cut the mountains in half, a valley that faded into the distant land. At the valley's feet lay the remains of the enormous gates that once blocked any and all from journeying south, though its main purpose had been to stop the savage Darkakin from journeying north.

Inara had never had cause to see the broken gates up close, but her mother told of the ancient glyphs carved into every inch of them, supporting the gates with magic. Seeing them now, she couldn't believe her mother had been atop them when Valanis brought them down with Paldora's Star. What a sight that would have been...

Stay focused, wingless one. I do not like the look of these ruins.

Inara drew her vision back to Karath below, another example of Valanis's power. The city had once been the gem of The Arid Lands and home to its emperor, before Tauren Salimson installed a council in Tregaran. Now, Karath's high walls topped no more than six feet, the thick stone reduced to rubble under the weight of the dark elf's magic. Every building and tower had been cracked open, their shapes forever lost. The palace in the east had been almost split in half and imploded in on itself.

Ilargo flew past them, angling towards the ruins, and Athis naturally fell in behind the green dragon. They soared above and circled the old city a couple of times before landing by the northern gate, or what remained of it.

Athis lifted his head and sniffed the air. *Smells like death.*

That's all any will find should they pick a fight with you, Inara replied with a light pat on his neck.

Be careful in there, the dragon pressed. *The sun has not yet found midday and the shadows are long.*

Indeed, the sun had yet to reach its apex, but Inara was thankful for the heat one could only find in a desert. The snows of the north had the feel that they might never leave these days.

Gideon jumped down from Ilargo's back with one hand steadying Mournblade on his hip. "We will investigate the ruins," he said, meeting Inara's eyes. "Ilargo and Athis will sweep Syla's Pass and check for anything unusual."

Inara could sense Athis's reluctance to leave her. **You worry too much.**

I worry just enough.

Inara chuckled silently to herself before joining Gideon under the broken arch of the northern gate. Athis and Ilargo turned about and walked a few steps into the desert to find enough space to take off. Their magnificent wings lifted high and beat down, kicking plumes of sand into the air and masking their quick ascent.

When she had been in her late teens, and her bond with Athis was new, Inara had hated to see him ever fly away, often feeling as if a part of herself had abandoned her. Ten years later, however, their bond was as strong as could be, allowing them to communicate with each other regardless of the physical distance between them. The half-elf was tempted to retreat into their sanctuary, a realm that only existed between the two of them, where even time couldn't bother them.

Then she caught the scent of it herself. The city *did* reek of death and it focused her intensely. At times such as this, when separated from Athis, she recalled all the more keenly that if she died... so did he.

Gideon entered first with Mournblade still on his hip. Inara followed his lead and kept her own Vi'tari blade sheathed as she passed beyond the boundary wall. They made their way up what had once been a street, though it was now indistinguishable from anything else. Debris from the buildings and the forgotten belongings of its old inhabitants littered the ground.

"They left in a hurry," she observed.

"I was on the other side of The Adean when this happened," Gideon replied solemnly. "When your mother and father told of what happened here I couldn't believe it."

Inara had heard the story a handful of times and read about it a dozen times. "They say Valanis pulled Paldora's Star from the sky."

"Yes," Gideon agreed, "but the star didn't do this. Valanis saw to Karath's end with his own hands. The people fled for their lives, led by Tauren thankfully."

"I can't believe we're really doing this," Inara commented as she inspected every corner and crevice of the ruins.

"What's that?" Gideon asked.

"Searching the ruins of Karath for *orcs*," she replied incredulously. "They've been gone for five thousand years. Why would they return now?"

"I still can't believe they survived The Great War." Gideon leaned through a hole in a wall and examined the inside.

"I've read some of the books left behind by Elandril and Valtyr," Inara said as she half climbed a wall to investigate the rooftop. "They both fought against the orc in The Great War. They both said orcs were the greatest hunters they had ever come across."

Gideon nodded along. "They also said orcs fear the light and possess no knowledge of magic." He glanced back at her with a grin pulling at his cheek. "I'd say we have a few advantages."

Inara agreed, looking at Mournblade on her master's hip. The scimitar had belonged to Elandril, the first elven Dragorn. Five thousand years ago, that blade had slain the orc king and helped to push their kind into the darkest depths of The Undying Mountains.

It seemed its job wasn't quite done...

"You don't appear too worried about bumping into them," Inara observed.

"There can't be that many of them left," Gideon replied. "The elves and dwarves slaughtered them together. I'm sure this is just a lucky few descendants who have discovered one of the ancient tunnels."

"Ancient tunnels?"

Gideon stopped by a door and slowly pushed it open. "You need to keep reading, Galfrey. During The Great War, the orcs would move about Illian via a network of tunnels to avoid the light."

"Perhaps when I'm as old as you I will have read them all," Inara quipped.

Gideon blinked slowly. "I should have seen that one coming, I suppose."

Inara stopped and turned to her left when her nose caught a stronger scent of death.

Gideon didn't miss it. "I bow to your senses. Lead the way."

The two Dragorn were forced to enter the hollowed out remains of someone's home in order to navigate around the tower that lay across the street. Entering the dark, they ducked under fallen beams and crawled through narrow spaces until finally climbing up through a hole in the ceiling. On the first floor, they had a better view of the ruins ahead since the entire wall was missing.

"That's the palace." Inara pointed her chin at the largest pile of rubble in the city.

"Let's keep heading in that direction," Gideon suggested. "It looks to have caved in. Perhaps that is where we will find our hole."

They jumped back down to street level and left the shadows behind. There wasn't a single stretch of path that could be called flat anymore, decorated as the streets were with craters and piles of stone.

Inara's head snapped to the right.

Something was knocked loose in the building and they both

heard it. Gideon kept a calm demeanour about him, emanating confidence and control. It had always proven to be bolstering for the half-elf.

You are not Gideon Thorn, Athis reminded her from miles away.

Inara rolled her eyes in the knowledge that the dragon understood exactly how she felt at that moment. Heeding his words, however, Inara followed Gideon with one hand on her hilt.

The main door was jammed in place by something that had fallen on it from the inside. The Master Dragorn tried moving it with both hands but was careful not to make too much noise in the process. He turned back to her and placed a finger to his lips before pointing to the roof.

Inara wasted no time in putting her inheritance to good use. Using the adjacent wall, she made a light step and a powerful push off the stone, using strength and agility that even Gideon Thorn didn't possess.

Her hands caught the lip of the flat roof and she deftly pulled herself up with the ease of a cat. There wasn't much of a roof to speak of since the back half of the building had collapsed into the next street. Inara waited patiently by the edge, listening for any sign of life besides the two of them.

The sound of loose pebbles falling to the ground didn't escape her ears and she pounced. The Dragorn flipped and twirled as she descended into the house with as much speed and little sound as possible. When her feet finally touched the ground, her Vi'tari blade was drawn and ready to react on her behalf.

There was nothing.

"Inara?" Gideon's call came from the other side of the door, stunning Inara for a moment.

She wanted to answer but, instead, followed her nose into the shadows. With one hand, the Dragorn swept her dark ringlets behind her ear to keep her peripheral vision clear. The darkness felt as real as a wall. She couldn't shake that feeling, the feeling all prey had when under the gaze of a predator. The half-elf turned this way and that, inspecting the shadows with what few cracks of light pierced the rooms.

A piece of wood creaked behind her. Again, there was nothing to see. A light rain of dust sprinkled down from above, filling the thin shaft of light with floating bits. For just a moment, she questioned whether it was one of the earthquakes that kept being reported.

It wasn't a quake, she knew. There was something in the room with her.

"Inara?" Gideon called again.

Inara whispered a small spell into her hand and birthed an orb of pure light to release into the room.

Not two feet away stood an orc!

The Dragorn gasped and her Vi'tari blade shot up in her defence, but the orc roared under the light and dropped its serrated blade in favour of diving for the shadows. The orb of light made its task all the harder but the orc pushed its way through a triangular crack in the wall, quickly disappearing into the adjoining building.

Get out of there! Athis warned. *We're coming back!*

The main door to the house blew in behind her in a wave of magic, shattering the awkward pillar that had blocked Gideon's way. The Master Dragorn rushed in with Mournblade in hand, his form that of the Mag'dereth, the ancient fighting style known only to the Dragorn order.

"It went that way!" Inara dropped to the crack in the wall only to find more darkness beyond.

"Come on!" Gideon was already running back outside in pursuit.

Inara knew it would be folly to climb through the hole after the creature, but she decided running along the ruined streets was not to be her path. The half-elf dashed back up the cracked walls and found her way to the roof again.

Gideon was running parallel to the block, jumping and skipping over debris as he hunted the fleeing beast. The Master Dragorn shot out his hand and fired spell after spell into the buildings below Inara's feet, every flash of light eviscerating the ruined contents.

Inara leaped from rooftop to rooftop, weaving left and right to avoid the jagged holes and serious cracks.

It didn't take her long to overtake Gideon below and catch up with the orc, who she caught glimpses of as it ran from shadow to shadow. In fact, the only reason it had yet to evade them completely was that its path was slowed by the apparent need to stick to the darkness.

One of Gideon's spells knocked out the last of one building's fragile supporting walls. Half a row of what had perhaps been shops crumpled in on itself, spreading dust and sand in every direction. Inara adjusted her trajectory and hopped, skipped, and jumped back down to the street to meet her master. Together they ran side by side, all the while listening for the laboured grunts of the orc as it pushed on into the final building at the end of the row.

The two Dragorn skidded to a stop. There was nothing but the palace on their left and an empty street between it and the final building. The orc had nowhere to go.

Inara felt the brief tingle of magic on her skin before Gideon held his hand out to the end wall and pulled away, taking the central slab with it. The wall broke to pieces, adding more debris to the street and a cloud of dust and sand into the air.

With their Vi'tari blades in hand, the two Dragorn cautiously approached the jagged hole. Inara released a new orb of light, casting the shadows away.

The house was empty. They inspected the walls from top to bottom, checking every corner and looking under the rubble for any sign of the creature. It had vanished.

"Are you sure they can't use magic?" Inara asked.

"Over here," Gideon called, drawing the half-elf to a crack in the floor. It was just large enough to fit a person, if they breathed in, and it slanted to the left, towards the palace.

"We're not going in there," Inara said.

"And we would be wise not to," Gideon replied. "Midday is approaching, our ally in this hunt. Let's investigate the palace. I don't believe this is the hole from which they crawled. Tauren said they were attacked by a pack of the brutes."

The Dragorn left the house and made for the steps that rose up into the palace. The fortress, as it was, still towered over them in its ruined state. All signs of its grandeur and luxury had either been wiped away or faded over the last thirty years. Great chandeliers littered the halls and grand mirrors lay strewn and shattered. The enormous crack that divided the palace in two provided a solid line of light from east to west, allowing them to walk through.

Inara's senses caught up with her again and she noted the foul odour coming from the passage to the south. "I think we're going to have to brave the dark."

We're almost there, Athis told her.

Inara knew what the dragon was really saying, but they didn't have time to wait for their arrival. The orc had already escaped their grasp once and they weren't about to let it escape a second time.

"Keep your wits about you," Gideon cautioned. "We don't know enough about them yet."

Inara led the way into the darkened corridors with her Vi'tari blade held out in front of her. The magic of the blade would have it react to any attack before her keen senses could even register one. The half-elf held out her free hand and readied another orb of light to take shape from her fingertips.

"Don't," Gideon said with a hand on her wrist. "We need to draw them out."

Having just seen an orc face to face, fangs and all, Inara didn't entirely agree with hunting them in the dark. But she couldn't argue with her master's wisdom, something he shared with Ilargo.

Shattered glass and pieces of broken mirrors crunched under their feet as they progressed through the old halls. Shafts of light pierced the gloom here and there, offering them some sight as well as informing them of the sun's position above. In some places they were forced to pass through holes in the walls as the doorways were blocked by fallen pillars and cracked beams.

"Is it possible this is the last one?" Inara whispered. "Perhaps Tauren and his men killed the others."

Gideon paused, looking back at her over his shoulder. "There's an orc walking the surface of Illian... at this point, I'd say anything is possible."

They continued their search of the ground floor, creeping through as many rooms as they could where debris didn't need moving. Inara caught the scent again after passing through what looked to have been an outside garden in the south of the palace. Death and rot filled her nose, leading her to a large chamber of marble beyond the garden. There were no windows or sunroofs, only a single crack in the top corner where a ray of sunlight did its best to illuminate the room.

"It's a bathhouse," Inara commented upon seeing the sunken, empty rectangle surrounded by pillars.

"Not anymore," Gideon replied, his eyes leading Inara to the massive hole in the centre of the dusty bath.

Its edges were jagged and rough, but the angle was that of a slope, allowing any upright creature to walk in and out. The single shaft of light wasn't enough, however, to give them an idea of its depth.

Gideon tilted his head to the side and held his hand out, stopping her from going any farther.

"What is it?" she asked.

"I don't think we were the ones doing the hunting…"

Inara had no time to respond before the shadows came alive. The orcs roared, their bellows resounding off the marble walls with deafening effect.

Her scimitar reacted, lifting her hand and parrying two of their blades while her left leg shot out and kicked a third orc over the edge and into the bath.

Gideon parried one of his own, raised his free hand, and released a fireball into another. The orc was launched back with enough force to crack the marble wall. The light from the fire temporarily blinded the other beasts and gave both Dragorn a quick count of their enemies.

Inara's heart skipped a beat when she realised there were too many to count.

The first of the orcs to recover from the burst of light came at the Master Dragorn with a spear. Mournblade twisted Gideon's body into an unorthodox position, allowing him to evade the pointed tip, then parry the sword of another orc before finally spinning back around to bury his scimitar into the spear-wielder's chest.

Inara could have marvelled at her master's skill for some time, but the orcs renewed their attack. They swarmed, coming at her from all sides. The Dragorn moved left and right, batting their attacks away with her scimitar between using every limb to kick, elbow, and punch her enemy.

The Vi'tari blade sliced through the air, chopping down the orcs' swords and then quickly reversing to impale another. The half-elf never stopped, weaving between attack and defence as she switched through the forms of the Mag'dereth.

With a mighty roar, one of the orcs swung his blade in the hope of cutting her in half, but the magic of the Vi'tari blade had Inara drop down and spin on one knee. The edge of the creature's sword sliced through a few strands of her dark hair as she slid beneath. There was no time for the orc to follow through with a second attack after Inara jumped back up, twisted her wrist, and brought her scimitar around to cleave the beast's head from its body.

This only served to enrage the others, who came at her with spears and swords. For most swordsmen, it would have spelled certain doom, but for a Dragorn, blessed with the magic of their dragon companions, it was nothing beyond Inara's skill. With her sword hand, she deflected one incoming blade while pushing out her open palm with the other hand. The magic that burst forth from her hand fractured the air as well as multiple ribcages, sending three of the creatures into the broken rubble in the corner of the bathhouse.

The nearest orc showed no sign of fear or regret in attacking her, despite the fact that many of his comrades had started piling up around them.

The Dragorn decided to press her own attack. Her scimitar whistled through the air, batting the orc's sword aside, before crossing the air left then right, each swipe cutting through the orc's armour and opening up its flesh.

First it dropped the sword, then it dropped to its knees, absent of any expression, and, finally, it fell face down onto the cold floor, dead. Gideon caught the corner of her eye as he dashed to the left and whipped Mournblade around with him, almost dividing his last orc in half.

Inara looked at her Vi'tari blade, thankful to have such a weapon at her disposal. Had they been wielding ordinary swords in this gloom, she had no doubt it would have been they who lay slain on the floor.

Both Dragorn stood panting, their blades dripping with blood. It was hard to say how many they had killed, piled as the bodies were.

Blood trickled down Inara's hand, its source a cut on her forearm. It was the first time she had been injured in a battle with her Vi'tari blade in hand. Then again, she had never faced so many in combat before.

Inara stood up straight with Gideon, their eyes fixed on the jagged hole in the centre of the empty pool. The light from the orb could barely pierce the abyss within, but they could see enough.

Dozens, maybe a hundred reflecting eyes looked back at them...

Low growls and feral snarls filled the bathhouse as the first of the orcs stepped out under the white glow. Some cowered, but only for the second it took them to adapt. Then they walked with confidence until their numbers filled the empty pool. Only then did Inara realise that Gideon and herself had been edging backwards. This was not a fight they could win.

Get out of there! Athis cried in her head.

The growing mob of orcs were parted by the appearance of another, taller orc with broad shoulders and a pair of thick but elegant horns atop his head, not unlike Athis's or Ilargo's. When he opened his mouth, a foul and jarring language echoed inside the chamber. His words might have been lost on the Dragorn, but Inara was sure she understood *kill them* in any tongue.

"Run!" Gideon ordered as the first wave of orcs poured over the lip of the pool towards them.

Both Dragorn turned and sprinted back the way they had come. The sound of thunderous feet behind them was almost as terrifying as the roars and growls that followed them through the darkened halls. It wasn't long before arrows darted through the air and sank into every surface around them.

"Up ahead!" Inara warned as she caught sight of two orcs barring their way, both of whom were aiming bows.

Gideon held up Mournblade and the Vi'tari scimitar reacted to the flying bolts, cutting the arrows from the air before they could cause harm.

Inara followed her master's defence with a destructive spell that swept the orcs off their feet and sent them flying down the ruined hall. Before they had even finished skidding across the floor, more orcs were rounding the corner and cutting off their escape.

With orcs in front and orcs behind, the Dragorn were forced to run deeper into the abandoned palace. Using her elven strength, Inara shoulder-barged her way through a set of closed double doors, knocking them both from their hinges.

Gideon's arm flew out and caught her before she could continue running into a hole in the floor. The sudden stop allowed the orcs to catch up and let fly a salvo of arrows, all of which were halted mid-air by the Master Dragorn.

"Watch out!" Inara dashed over the hole in the floor and put herself between Gideon and the two orcs who emerged from the shadows of another room.

Her Vi'tari blade held back the first swing and her fist lashed out, catching the orc on the bony ridge above its eyes. The creature stumbled back, but Inara learnt very quickly that punching bone was not appreciated by her knuckles.

The second orc tried to take advantage of her exposed back, only to find a magically-crafted scimitar deflecting it away. Gideon simply held up his hand to the orc's face and cast a fire spell. Inara didn't even hear the creature scream before it was slammed into the wall with most of its face melted off. Not that she had time to take note of Gideon's kill. The orc she had slugged in the face came at her again with its black blade.

"We need to go!" Gideon reminded her, making for the next hall as yet more arrows thudded into the walls.

"I'm coming!" Inara gave into the flow and let her Vi'tari blade do what it did best.

The half-elf spun on the spot as the orc thrust forward, bringing herself around its sword and able to swipe across the creature's neck. It would have been satisfying to see the orc's head fall to the floor, but over a dozen more rushed into the room, giving flight to Inara's feet.

"This way!" Gideon called in the distance.

Inara ran as fast as she could, wishing more than ever that she had inherited elven speed instead of strength. **Athis! Where are you?**

Get to the main doors, he replied. *We're almost there!*

An arrow whistled past her arm, tearing a scrap of the leather away with a piece of her skin. Gideon raised his hand to the ceiling and made a pulling down motion. Inara dropped low and skidded across the floor, narrowly avoiding the planks of wood and debris ripped from the ceiling by her master's magic. A moment later, the half-elf was on her feet again and looking back at the orcs through a thick shaft of midday sunlight.

"Keep going!" Gideon ordered. "It won't delay them for long!"

Indeed, the orcs were already searching out new passages that would see them reunited as predator and prey. The Dragorn ran through the ruined halls and dilapidated corridors with their blades held out in front of them, making certain their scimitars would catch any foe who jumped out of the shadows.

"Through there!" Gideon directed.

Inara took a breath as she slid between the crack in the jagged walls. Once on the other side, she kept watch while Gideon made his way through behind her. She could hear them coming, howling and hooting in anticipation of capturing their prey. The outside world, however, was in sight now. They were both running through the central spilt in the palace and making for the main entrance.

"Don't stop!" Gideon warned.

Orcs started appearing on the levels above them, firing arrows into the strip of light. A bulbous roof that topped one of the outer towers cast the end of the strip in shadow, but they were already running through it and into the glorious sunshine as the orcs spilled out of the darkness, filling that single line of shadow.

The Dragorn were almost doubled over in their attempt to regain their breath. Stood in the middle of the street, and entirely under the cover of the sun, they were safe from any advance. Inara kept her scimitar ready to deflect any stray arrows, but it seemed the orcs were content to simply stand in the shadows and stare at them.

The tall orc from the bathhouse strode through their ranks and made his stand on the very edge of the shadowed line. The orc tilted his head, taking in the Dragorn from head to toe. It glanced at the blue sky and squinted at the bold colour.

"What's it doing?" Inara asked.

The orc held out his hand, palm up, and let his pale flesh soak up the sun. Inara half expected to see the limb burn but it didn't; he instead closed his fist and pulled it back into the shadows.

A new shadow overcame them all and Ilargo dropped out of the sky with an ear-splitting roar that had all of the orcs retreating into the palace.

The green dragon slammed into the ground and marched on the entrance. The jet of fire that erupted from his mouth found every crack and crevice, melting anything and everything in seconds. Athis landed farther down the street and shoved his horned head through a hole in the palace wall. More fire and smoke filled the air before the interior walls could be heard collapsing.

When the dragons had finished their assault, the Dragorn approached the shaded area, waving away the intense heat emanating from within the palace walls. Charred bodies littered the ground but not nearly as many orcs as there had been.

Inara searched the remains for any sign of the taller orc. "That was not a handful of orcs who were just *lucky* enough to have found a way up to the surface."

"I agree," Gideon replied gravely. "That hole inside the bathhouse was *blown* outwards. They forced their way through."

To Inara's eyes, their pale features were very similar, along with their chiselled bodies that resembled stone more than flesh. The most notable difference she could easily spot was on their heads, where they all possessed a variety of horns. Some had a cluster of small horns, while others had only a couple of larger horns, all curved and shaped in their own unique way.

Inara crouched beside one of the dead orcs. "Have you ever seen armour such as this before?" The half-elf ran her fingers across the black metal, noting its many ridges, most of which appeared natural rather than forged. "It's like volcanic glass…"

Gideon joined her and gripped the chest piece between his fingers. "Obsidian armour. There must be a volcano in The Undying Mountains, underground too, I'd imagine. This is not easy to craft. I can't see a small band of orcs forging this. The arrows too," he said, gesturing to the bolts strewn across the sand. "Obsidian arrows is closer to dwarven skill than any other."

Inara glanced at her master and the dragons. "What's happening here? Are we seriously looking at the return of the orcs?"

Ilargo dipped his head and filled Inara's mind with his majestic voice. *Orcs do not simply return. They invade.*

"Ilargo's right," Gideon said. "Everything ever written about them suggests they *enjoy* conflict. There was also something about bones…" The Master Dragorn cupped his beard in contemplation. "I should have paid better attention when I read the books. I just never thought they could have survived The Great War, let alone swell to such numbers and find a way back to Illian."

Athis glanced back at the charred bodies. *We must learn more before meeting them in combat again.*

Gideon nodded his head and made towards Ilargo. "We should return to The Lifeless Isles and consult the library."

Inara stepped forwards. "We should finish investigating The Undying Mountains." Seeing her master's frown, the Dragorn pressed on. "Athis and I can go."

"Inara…"

"I'm not a student anymore. Athis and I can handle it. We won't even land in the valley, we'll stay high. If there are more of them out there, then there has to be some sign of activity in the mountains. We might even get an idea of how many we face."

Gideon looked from Athis to Ilargo, though she knew he wasn't communing with the red dragon as she would be able to hear him. Inara could also tell that Athis wasn't too happy about her suggestion, but he was reserving his comments while Gideon came to a decision.

"Very well. You stay high," he ordered firmly. "Should you find *anything* you are not to engage. Observe and report back. Find somewhere high to rest at night."

"We will," Inara replied with an exaggerated nod.

"I will send Edrik to assist you," Gideon added.

"You don't need to send Edrik, Master."

Gideon held up his hand. "The rising winds might not have found The Arid Lands, but the days are still growing shorter. With Edrik, you can cover more ground in less time."

Inara sighed. "As you command."

"Stay high," he reiterated. "I mean it, Inara. These aren't bandits or mindless monsters. We were lured into that palace by creatures who excel at hunting. Just don't… Just promise me you won't do anything a Galfrey would do."

Inara knew her parents had performed enough reckless, but heroic, acts to make that a compliment. "We'll observe and report back, Master."

That didn't seem to satisfy Gideon, but he still climbed onto Ilargo's back. "Be safe. Meet me at the library."

In a bid to avoid meeting Athis's eyes, Inara simply watched Ilargo take off into the sky.

Don't think your wordplay escaped me, wingless one. Master Thorn asked you to promise him one thing and you offered another, minus the promise.

It's a good thing half of my decisions are made by you, then.

Inara scrambled onto Athis's back and took one last look at the ruin of Karath. The shadows of that palace were not a place she would soon return to, nor did she ever wish to fall under the scrutinising gaze of that orc again…

9

A CROWN OF HORNS

The king of orcs released the latches on his obsidian armour and shrugged off the smoking chestplate. He glanced over the back of his right arm and inspected the burn that had blackened his pale flesh. Karakulak relished the pain, having waited for this moment for so long.

Blood had been spilled. Be it his or the enemy's, the king didn't care. The war would soon begin and he, Karakulak, chieftain of the Born Horde, Bone Lord of The Under Realm, and king of the orcs would claim all of Neverdark.

The healers interrupted his thoughts and attempted to rub a soothing balm into his burn, only to find Karakulak's hand in their face, pushing them away. Compared to others he had fared much better. The tunnels of The Under Realm now resounded with the pained growls of his tribe. The smell of burning skin stung his nostrils and he cursed all dragon-kind in Gordomo's name.

Vuruk, his war chief, called over the din, "Any who cannot walk or hold their weapon will meet Gordomo this day!"

"No!" The king slammed his hand into Vuruk's chest, halting the others from thrusting their spears into the injured. "When this war truly begins, we will not have time to treat our injured. Until then, I want as many orcs under my command as possible." Karakulak could see that his war chief disagreed, so he gripped the edge of his armour and pulled him in.

"Vuruk, you fought by my side when the Steel Caste waged war against our tribe, you led our assault against the Bone Breakers' underkeep, and by your axe the Born Horde has found victory many times against the monsters of The Under Realm.

"But this is a war unlike any we have seen. Our ancestors lost everything trying to take Neverdark. If we do not *think*, Brother, we will perish as they did. That is how we will win this war. Not with our mettle, not with The Crow's magic, and not by throwing away lives needlessly. We will win because we are *smarter* than those who dwell under the sky fire."

Vuruk bowed his head, giving Karakulak a glimpse of the orc's horns. The left one had been scorched halfway down by dragon's breath and continued down the back of his head and across his shoulder. Still, the war chief displayed no sign of discomfort; it would simply become another scar to add to the canvas of his body.

The king pushed Vuruk away and strode off, choosing the northern tunnel that would take all of them beyond The Arid Lands. Orcs of every size were running back and forth with mining tools, resources, and supplies to keep the tribes fed and watered. They had been burrowing through the ancient tunnels for six years, exploring the network forged by their ancestors.

"My king!" came the call from up ahead.

Karakulak narrowed his vision and pierced the pitch black to see Grundi, one of the few orcs he had come to trust who had not been one of the Born Horde.

The cripple, as most of their kin called him, limped down the tunnel with his signature hunch and scrawny left leg. The king knew better than to judge one of his subjects on their physical strength alone, however, and had found many ways of exploiting the orc's intellect.

Something his enemies would soon come to fear.

"Grundi, the enemy saw our horns and fled!" Karakulak clapped a hand on the short orc's shoulder and continued his stride.

"Very good, my King!" Grundi turned about as quickly as his leg would allow and trailed his lord. "We have almost established clear routes to the north, Sire. The wizards of The Black Hand have shown us a new tunnel that will lead to the most northern city in the north; the humans call it Namdhor."

"Why do I feel you are holding back, Grundi?"

The shorter orc ground his staff into the tunnel floor as he dragged his scrawny left leg. "The tunnels they have found are inaccessible, Sire."

"Most of the ancient tunnels have been inaccessible, Grundi. That is why we have been digging for so long. Do you need more supplies for your wrath powder?"

Grundi came to an abrupt stop in a small cavern where the tunnels branched. "We have plenty of wrath powder, Sire. The problem lies with those expected to move the debris…"

Karakulak finally halted his stride and turned to face the orc. "The Big Bastards…" The king paced the cavern with his fists clenched. "Those over-fed beasts should know their place by now."

"Chieftain Barghak had word sent to his tribe in the farthest tunnels," Grundi explained. "They aren't to pick up another boulder until their demands are met."

A low growl rumbled out of Karakulak's throat. "The days of the Big Bastards being *his* tribe were over years ago. They are all mine, now." The king felt as if he could rip the giant orc's head off with his bare hands, but Grundi's words sank in and gave him pause. "Barghak sent word? He isn't in the north?"

Grundi tilted his head to better see his master. "No, Sire. Chieftain Barghak resides in the spider cavern." The crippled orc gestured to the tunnel on the right.

Karakulak roared in anger, letting some of the pain from his burn into his rage. A sharp whistle had his six-legged Gark bounding up behind him, its hideous face drooling from the flaps that contained the many rows of teeth.

Without another word to Grundi, Karakulak straddled his

mount. The beast carried him through the tunnels for many miles without the need to stop, its speed and stamina unmatched by most of the creatures in The Under Realm.

Located under the heart of The Arid Lands, the spider cavern was vast and pitted with burrows and dotted with purple crystals. The crystals emitted a soft glow that baited creatures of The Under Realm into the cavern, putting them at the mercy of the spiders hiding in their burrows.

Those same spiders served the orcs now. Those that had resisted were still pinned to the cavern walls…

"Barghak!" the king bellowed, deliberately leaving out the chieftain's title. "Barghak, get your fat arse out here!"

Karakulak marched into the cavern, blinking hard to adjust his eyes in the soft glow. Giant spiders, skulking between the crystals that protruded from the ground, cowered away from his powerful frame. The orcs, who had been using the cavern as a camp for the surrounding tunnels, bowed their heads and cleared the king's path.

One of the chieftain's enormous hands wrapped around the head of a crystal as he pulled himself up with the obligatory grunts. His girth alone was often enough to dissuade most orcs from challenging him, but King Karakulak was not most orcs.

"My king calls and so I rise," Barghak said dryly, towering over Karakulak.

The king couldn't help but notice the belly that had removed all shape from the chieftain's abdomen. The Big Bastards were known not only for their great height, but also the muscle they carried. It seemed Barghak had indulged in the pleasures of his position for too long.

"New tunnels have been found in the north, yet your boys refuse to lift a single rock. Explain this to me as if your life depended on it."

Barghak stepped back in mock-surprise. "You threaten me, king? I think only of my tribe while you send them into the unknown. My boys are on the frontline of the expansion. They've been attacked by every monster that calls The Under Realm home."

"As chieftain, I would expect you to see to the survival of your tribe," Karakulak replied, nodding his horned head, "but as king, I must not only see to the survival of our race, but also to the glory of our god. By ruling over Neverdark, so too will the indomitable Gordomo!"

"You use big words, little king," Barghak spat. With both hands, the large orc adjusted his impressive necklace of bones, rattling his bracelets of smaller bones.

Karakulak pulled free the newly-forged, rectangular blade from his back. "I use a big sword too."

The cavern fell silent. Even the giant spiders sensed the tension in their masters and remained as still as the dead. Barghak looked down at the blade in his king's hand and glanced over the orcs who were present for the display. Karakulak smiled, all too aware that the chieftain of the Big Bastards was standing without allies.

Barghak took a moment to consider his next words. "These humans," he began with a lighter tone, "they claim six kingdoms..."

"So The Black Hand say," Karakulak replied, going along with the inevitable demands.

"The Big Bastards want a whole kingdom's worth of bones!"

"There are nine tribes of orc and six kingdoms of man. If I grant you one I will have to grant them all one and there aren't enough to go around, even with the elves and the dwarves. This will lead to rebellion and in-fighting that will see us returned to the old ways."

"You mean before you were king? I remember those days well."

Karakulak had heard enough. The longer he allowed Barghak to talk down to him this way, the weaker he appeared. The king could not be seen to be weak.

"You want bones, Chieftain Barghak? Then you shall have bones..." The king turned away from the overly large orc and met the eyes of his kin. "Bring me his firstborn!"

Barghak stepped forward with an expression of genuine surprise this time. There was nothing he could do, however, to stop the group of orcs running from the cavern and heading north. Karakulak spun around and pointed his flat, rectangular blade at the chieftain, an action that saw the big orc take a step back. Barghak was met by the clicking hisses of the giant spiders that closed in from behind.

"Perhaps I could get word to my boys," Barghak spluttered. "I could have them lifting rocks in no time, get us through this northern passage."

"There will be time for that," Karakulak replied, happy to stick his blade into the ground and wait.

The chieftain pleaded, bargained, and came very close to grovelling. The latter, however, would have seen Barghak stripped of his title and rule over the Big Bastards. The orcs were certainly smarter than most would give them credit for, but strength would always be valued above all else. In some way, Karakulak had hoped the chieftain would grovel and beg; at least then he could cleave the fool's head from his body and be done with it. As it was, he needed the orc to keep his Big Bastards in line.

After some time, the sound of rattling chains and heavy protests sounded from the cavern entrance. A dozen orcs surrounded the firstborn son of Barghak, pushing and pulling the orc by chains shackled around his neck and wrists. Those at the back prodded the chieftain's son with spears, angering the over-sized orc.

Karakulak took some pleasure in the look etched across Barghak's face. "You are Vandhak son of Barghak of the Big Bastards," the king stated.

Vandhak looked from his father to the king questioningly. "I am the mountain made flesh!" he declared.

"A title you deserve," Karakulak replied, taking in the sheer size of the orc. "I'm afraid Vandhak son of Barghak, that your father, the chieftain, wants bones and he wants them now." Again, the son looked to his father in confusion. "The only question is, what bone does he want?" Karakulak paced the gap between father and son, looking from one to the other, noting the rising panic in both.

"My king!" Barghak took one of his long strides towards Karakulak and found his way barred by the pincer-like legs of a spider.

"Would you like the finger bones?" the king asked. "Maybe all the finger bones? Feet too?" Barghak shook his head with every question. "No, you're right. A chieftain would be insulted to be presented with such meagre bones. A chieftain deserves a much larger prize." Karakulak looked Vandhak up and down, craning his neck as he did. "It seems the mountain made flesh has some *very* large bones…"

"I will have my tribe clearing every tunnel! They will work until they drop!"

Karakulak nodded along. "Yes, they will, because you have three sons do you not?"

Barghak narrowed his eyes, shaking his head. "I have four, my king."

Karakulak hefted his wide blade. "You *had* four…"

The king swung his sword with all his strength and hacked his way through Vandhak's knee, dropping the massive orc in a scream of pain unbefitting of the Big Bastards. The orcs pulled hard on his chains and stopped him from fighting back, while others appeared from behind the purple crystals and stopped his father from intervening.

After six hard strikes, everything below Vandhak's knee rolled away and the orc collapsed face down on the floor in a growing pool of blood. Karakulak didn't stop there. He brought his blade down on the joint where the leg met his hip. It was tough, requiring nine strikes before the orc yielded its thigh. The blood flow increased dramatically and Vandhak was dead before the king could kick the thigh towards the chieftain.

"A thigh bone, for the chieftain of the Big Bastards! It is not a kingdom of bones, but you should consider this a promise. Keep your tribe in line and you will drown in bones. Don't keep them in line and you will… well, you'll have bones either way I suppose."

Barghak dropped to his knees and roared with all his considerable might. For just a moment, the king wondered if the chieftain was going to charge him; not that he could move very fast. A second glance, however, proved that Barghak was more interested in carving out his son's enormous thigh bone, a great treasure indeed.

Karakulak grinned, revealing his fangs. He now had the most unruly tribe back under his control at the price of a single life and, at least, the chieftain of the Big Bastards had made a little profit...

10

DIVINE COINCIDENCE?

"Wake up!"

Alijah shot up with one hand instinctively reaching for the short-sword on his back. He blinked hard, coming to the realisation that he was still in bed, half a room away from his weapons and belongings. He blinked again and tried to make sense of the figure standing over him.

Galanör Reveeri.

The elf was looking down on him with judging eyes. "Do you not rise with the dawn?" he asked.

Alijah winced at the shaft of light breaching the narrow window at the top of the wall, where feet were hurrying past with the start of their day. The light, combined with Galanör's voice, was enough to remind him that he had consumed one too many ales.

"Vighon usually wakes me," he replied groggily.

"Hmph," was Galanör's only response on his way out of the room.

"With breakfast," Alijah called after him, making no effort to hide his cheeky grin.

Galanör turned back briefly with a scowl on his face. "Get dressed and meet me in the locker."

The elf disappeared down the corridor and Vighon replaced him in the doorway with a plate of food in each hand.

"What's his problem?"

Alijah waved the question away. "He wants us to meet him in the locker." He peered over the top of the plates. "Please tell me you brought bacon."

Vighon handed over the plate, making the half-elf's eyes light up. "I don't think he's slept, you know."

Alijah considered the reason why Galanör wouldn't have slept and his memories from the previous day came flooding back. The elf had spent the night translating what was left of the prophecy and might have found something important!

"We better go," he said with a rasher of bacon hanging out of his mouth. "Any sign of Hadavad up there?"

Vighon sat on the bed and finished his own breakfast while Alijah threw on his shirt and jacket.

"Nothing," Vighon said. "Rus hasn't seen or heard anything of him overnight."

Alijah's stomach lurched. He hated to think of what might have happened to the mage, surrounded by dark wizards and stuck at the top of Vengora. Still, Hadavad or not, he had a mission to carry out, just as the old mage had taught him. How long had Hadavad fought the necromancers without aid? At least he had Vighon by his side.

Inside the locker, Galanör was laying out the scroll of ancient skin on a wooden table he had placed in front of Hadavad's wall of notes and drawings. The elf was busy comparing small pieces of parchment that rested beside the prophecy to the notes pinned to the wall.

"Have you heard anything of Hadavad?" Alijah asked before anything else.

Galanör tapped his finger on one of the small parchments and sighed, his attention entirely fixed on the information spread out on the wall.

"Galanör?" Alijah prompted.

The elf finally stood up straight and turned to greet them. "If

Hadavad had entered the city I would know about it. I hate to say it, but the mage is either dead or following a new lead."

"He's not dead," Vighon stated. "That tough old bastard doesn't know how to die."

"If he was following a new lead he would have sent word," Alijah added.

Galanör appeared somewhat exasperated. "Hadavad has been fighting The Black Hand for five centuries. That's longer than I've been walking the land. You have known him for what, four years? You, three years, Vighon? *I* would say you don't know anything about the man."

That sobered Alijah's concerns. How well could he know the mage? Four years was a fraction of Hadavad's life and he had taken on more apprentices than he could count. Not that Alijah saw himself as the mage's apprentice. They were more like... partners. At least, that's what he had thought until now.

"If Hadavad was here," Galanör continued, "he would want us to keep going."

Alijah took a breath and did his best to focus on the path he had chosen to walk four years ago. The Black Hand was a danger to all, and he, Alijah Galfrey, neither knight nor Dragorn, would keep Illian safe.

"You have found something?" he asked the elf.

"Yes," Galanör replied, returning to his scrawls. "Some of your translations were accurate, some less so."

Vighon nudged Alijah's arm. "I told you, you can't translate the ancient language."

Alijah shot his friend a look before joining Galanör. The small pieces of parchment around the scroll had segments of the prophecy copied down and the translation written underneath.

"There is mention of something being found that was thought to be lost, but I can't tell if it's a thing or a person. You were right about the heart of a fallen star," Galanör said, placing his finger over the line on the scroll. "But it wasn't rise or risen." The elf picked up two pieces of parchment and put them side by side under the relevant line on the scroll. "It says, *shall be resurrected in the heart of a fallen star.*"

"Resurrected?" Alijah echoed, all too aware that The Black Hand had boasted the power of necromancy since the days of The First Kingdom, when they were known as The Echoes.

"It all sounds a bit ridiculous to me," Vighon commented. "I've never seen the dead rise and I've laid low my fair share."

Galanör shook his head. "This isn't talking about the dead coming back. This speaks of a spell that will bring back one particular individual."

"Yeah," Vighon continued skeptically, "in the heart of a fallen star? It's ridiculous!"

Galanör pointed to the notes and the map on the wall. "Not as ridiculous as you might think."

Alijah examined the wall with a keen eye, noting the movements of The Black Hand from north to south. They had been seen six years ago entering The Arid Lands and journeying through Syla's Pass, into The Undying Mountains. Since then, they had been sighted in varying numbers travelling back and forth, but there was one particular landmark that drew the half-elf's eye, south of Syla's Pass.

"The heart of a fallen star," he said aloud. "It's talking about Paldora's Fall!"

Galanör nodded his head. "I believe so."

"Wait a minute," Vighon said, raising his hand. "Paldora's Star fell from the sky thirty years ago. This was written, what, a thousand years ago?"

"Try ten thousand," Alijah replied.

"So, how could anyone know ten thousand years ago that Paldora's Star was going to fall from the heavens?"

Alijah had to remind himself that Vighon had lived a very different life since they parted ways in their teenage years. "That's why it's called a prophecy. It's a foretelling. The Echoes, that is The Black Hand, claim to see the future—"

"I know how a bloody prophecy works," Vighon interrupted. "I just... I just didn't think they were *real*."

Galanör looked from them to the scroll. "Trust me, young Vighon; I lived through The War for the Realm. Prophecies are very real and they can drive the motivations of some of the most powerful beings in Verda."

"What else have you found?" Alijah asked, not entirely convinced by the elf's convictions.

Galanör replaced the small parchments with new ones. "The next verse is mostly illegible. But, you were right, this here is the ancient glyph for a dragon."

"Now there are dragons involved?" Vighon looked to Alijah in concern.

The elf shrugged. "It's impossible to say what role this dragon will play; the scroll is too damaged."

"Perhaps a dragon is needed to perform the resurrection," Alijah mused.

Again, Galanör could only shrug. "I have seen The Black Hand raise the dead before and never once was a dragon required."

Vighon's jaw dropped open. "You've actually seen them do that?"

"Vighon," Alijah stole his friend's attention. "*We've* seen that."

Vighon furrowed his brow and shook his head. "I think I would know if I saw a dead man walking, Alijah."

"You remember the hidden temple, under the lake in Dunwich? Half of them were Reavers. I even said as much at the time."

Vighon looked away as if he were recalling the oldest of memories. "I didn't hear you say that. I was too busy trying to avoid all the swords coming for my head. And what in all the hells is a Reaver?"

"A second tier resurrection," Galanör explained. "They are capable of basic, if slightly unintelligible, speech. They retain their skills from life but they cannot think freely. They remain under the control of the one who resurrected them."

"There are tiers?" Vighon asked incredulously.

"Indeed," Galanör continued. "The most basic of The Black Hand's spells can resurrect Darklings; unthinking, mindless corpses that are good for a single task. They retain nothing of their former lives, including the simple ability to walk upright. Most scramble about like monsters."

Alijah could see Vighon's questioning gaze. "No, we haven't seen any of them," he answered.

"So there's Darklings and Reavers now." Vighon rubbed his bristly cheek as he looked upon the scroll. "My world is starting to get a little too big for my liking…"

"There is a final tier," Galanör said. "Hadavad told me of them years ago, though neither of us has ever come across one. In truth, and despite all that I have seen, I believe it to be a feat too far for The Black Hand."

"What is it?" Alijah tried not to think about the fact that Hadavad had left this out of his teachings over the years.

"They call them Astari," Galanör replied. "In the ancient language, ast means *new* and ari means *life*. An Astari is said to be a full resurrection, bringing the person back from the dead and restoring them to the life they once knew."

"Aren't they all brought back to life?" Vighon asked.

"No," Alijah answered. "Darklings and Reavers are technically still dead, they're just reanimated. They don't breathe, eat, drink or sleep. They can't even use magic."

"An Astari would appear just as you or me," Galanör elaborated. "If it is possible, I imagine it would take a considerable amount of magic to…" The elf trailed off and returned his attention to the map and the scroll.

"What is it?" Alijah couldn't see the revelation that had dawned on Galanör.

"Paldora's Fall," the elf whispered. "The Dark War, a thousand years past, was fought over a *fragment* of crystal that had broken away from Paldora's Star. That was *before* it fell. That star is a source of powerful magic and now tons of it reside in The Undying Mountains."

Alijah recalled a conversation his mother and father had with the Magikar of Korkanath, some sixteen years previously. He would always remember as their conversation took place after the Magikar had offered to take Alijah back to Korkanath with him to learn the ways of a mage. That was not something he had been keen to do and thankfully neither were his parents.

"The mages of Korkanath have tried many times to investigate Paldora's Fall," he said, recalling their conversation. "Any attempt to prise the crystal from the rock resulted in injury or death."

"So I heard," Galanör agreed. "The crystal is too volatile to be removed. But, the crater in which it lies must be a well of powerful magic. That must be The Black Hand's interest in the south." The elf walked away from the table, cupping his strong jaw. "Vengora... what did they find in those mountains?"

"To my knowledge," Alijah offered, "there has only ever been one thing of interest in Vengora..."

Galanör turned back to meet his eyes. "Kaliban," he said gravely.

Vighon stepped forward. "Valanis's fortress?"

"Oh, this you know about?" Alijah said sarcastically.

"Everyone knows about Kaliban," he reasoned. "*He* was there!" Vighon said, gesturing to the elf. "It's where Asher fought Valanis, ending The War for the Realm."

Galanör's gaze looked to pierce stone. "There's a little more to it but, yes, that is what happened. Asher died in the process and brought the whole fortress down on itself, burying him and the most evil of elves. We never found a connection between Valanis and The Black Hand, but it must be his bones they've been searching for."

"They're necromancers. It's his bones they mean to *resurrect*," Alijah corrected.

Galanör was pacing now, an unusual sight for such a collected elf. "That cannot be allowed to happen. Valanis brought Illian to the brink of destruction twice in his lifetime. He cannot be allowed a third attempt."

"We should go to Grey Stone and follow their trail to the top of Vengora," Alijah suggested. "Only then will we discover if they've found anything."

"And maybe discover what has happened to Hadavad?" Galanör added, his eyes burrowing into Alijah. "No, as much as I would like to learn of his fate, trekking up Vengora will take time, planning, and the procurement of a lot of equipment. We should go to Paldora's Fall, their final destination. I would rather be there for any such spell than reach the top of the mountains and discover we are too late."

Vighon stepped between them. "Am I the only one who thinks this is a bad idea? What are the chances that we would find that prophecy, a prophecy that's been sat in that cave for ten thousand years, and learn of its meaning just in time to prevent the resurrection of a genocidal elf?"

"You think we were *supposed* to find that scroll?" Alijah asked, seeing his friend's point.

"Maybe, though why an evil cult would want us to be present for their big party is beyond my understanding. Then again, there's always the chance that it's not a coincidence and this prophecy will come true, just not right now. The Black Hand could be digging their way through Vengora for the next thousand years before they find Valanis's bones."

"Both are very real possibilities," Galanör said. "There is, however, only one way to find out."

Vighon groaned but Alijah agreed. "To Paldora's Fall then," he said, feeling that sense of adventure rising in him again.

"Not so fast," Galanör warned. "The Moonlit Plains and the desert of The Arid Lands lies between us and Syla's Gate. From there, we will have to journey through barren valleys to Paldora's Fall. It will not be an easy road, nor a swift one."

"We have horses," Vighon said.

"And you'll need them," Galanör replied, retrieving a black orb from a pouch on his belt. "Equip yourselves with whatever you think you'll need, though I suggest something to provide shelter under a desert sun. Winter is different in the south."

"Is that a diviner?" Alijah asked, trying to better see the sphere in the elf's hand. "Who are you contacting?"

Galanör threw the diviner into the air and caught it easily. "Someone who can lessen our burden…"

11

FAR FROM HOME

The Undying Mountains were spread out before Inara Galfrey, a glorious horizon of rocky points that knew no end. To the west, where the mountains dared to reach for the heavens, their tops were capped with brilliant white snow. The half-elf was in a part of the world now that none could claim to know.

She loved it!

Or at least she would have. The orcs plagued her mind, their deadly encounter playing over and over. Inara tried to focus on the land and the valleys below, reminding herself that she was here for a reason.

It is okay to be shaken, Athis said into her mind.

I'm not shaken, she protested half-heartedly. **It's just... we've never run from anything before. We've never been...**

Hunted before, Athis finished for her.

There were so many of them, Inara continued.

There are fewer now, the dragon replied, *thanks to your blade and my fire.*

She couldn't argue with that. **There were many, but they fell as easily as any man.**

Every creature bleeds, wingless one.

Indeed they did, she thought. For ten years she had been beside Athis and for five of those years she had been granted the title of Dragorn. In that time, Inara knew she had faced dangers before, taken lives even, but that underlying confidence, that feeling of invincibility, came from having Athis as her companion.

Without him, she was vulnerable, and that made him vulnerable. She had foolishly allowed a band of the deadliest creatures ever to walk the earth to lure her into a trap. Had Gideon not been present, both she and Athis would likely be dead. The thought of Athis lying dead in the desert sent a shiver up her spine.

You forget, Athis said, *Gideon was beside you when the trap was sprung. The Master Dragorn was lured into that place just as you were. And remember, no one is born a warrior, Inara. That path is forged through time and blood. If the orcs are returning to the world, I have no doubt that you will be forced down that path.* The dragon let out a long sigh. *I would do all that I can to stall that, however, and keep you just as you are…*

Inara hugged the dragon a little tighter, enjoying the moment and the heat from his scales. She truly didn't know how to live without Athis and often found it hard to remember what life was like without him. Of course, back then she had her brother for company, and mischief more often than not.

They flew together in the dying sun, having searched the northern region the previous day. The long shadows cast by the mountains made it all the harder for Inara to see anything, especially dark holes suitable for orcs. Only when the sun was at its highest did Athis take them closer to the valley floor. Still, even in the black of night, the dragon's eyes could see everything.

We should find somewhere to rest, Athis announced as the last sliver of the sun dropped beneath the horizon. *Twilight won't last much longer and you will be blind.*

I trust you to keep searching. Just don't put us down anywhere that I might fall off the side of a cliff…

Master Thorn instructed us to be safe and so we shall. We will rest now and begin our search again at first light. Do you have enough food?

Inara knew she couldn't convince the dragon to keep searching if her safety was in the balance. The half-elf pulled on the strap tied over her shoulder and brought the narrow pack onto her chest. With only a hand inside, she could feel what was left of her dwindling supplies.

I have enough food and water for tonight, but tomorrow we will need to hunt and find clean water.

Athis let out a sharp grunt, typical of a dragon's laugh. *Preferably enough water for you to bathe in as well!*

I thought dragons were supposed to be charming!

What we are is sensitive to smell, wingless one.

They shared a laugh as Athis banked to the west, closing the gap between them and a flat plateau below. It was well above the valley floor and far from the reach of any predators that hunted under the moonlight.

After her feet touched the sandy rock, a low growl rumbled from within Athis's stomach and the dragon turned to regard her with an embarrassed look that only Inara could recognise.

It's been too long since you have eaten, she observed. *Go and hunt something for yourself.*

Athis looked from Inara to the wide world beyond the plateau and grunted with stubbornness. *I will stay with you*, he said.

We could be searching The Undying Mountains for days, Inara argued. *I need you sharp in case I miss anything.* Athis peered over the side of the cliff and sniffed the air. *I'm clearly not going anywhere. Go. Hunt.*

Unable to ignore his stomach for much longer, Athis relented. *I will be back soon.*

The dragon dropped off the edge and soared into the valley before flapping his magnificent wings and disappearing into the night.

Inara sat beside the small fire she had started and did her best to enjoy the strip of tough meat from her supplies. The water had been warm, something she hated, until the desert grew bitterly cold - then she wished the water had stayed warm.

Thinking back to her years under Gideon's tutelage, she remembered a good way to stay warm on a night such as this.

Getting to her feet, the half-elf walked a circle around the fire and used her Vi'tari blade to trace the ancient glyphs into the sand. Once complete, she whispered the spell Gideon had taught her and watched as the small fire briefly flared into the dark before settling down again.

It was much cosier inside the circle now since the glyphs prevented the heat from escaping its perimeter.

Inara rested back with her head on her supply pack. An ocean of stars looked down on her, each an inspiring orb of light that ignited the adventurous fire inside her belly. This was the kind of work she had envisioned as a sixteen-year-old girl, joining the ranks of Dragorn on The Lifeless Isles - just her and Athis in the wilds of the world, rooting out evil and exploring the land.

Inara had no clue as to how long her eyes had been closed or how much sleep she had found before her keen ears heard the lightest of steps. Remaining very still, the Dragorn shifted her eyes one way then the next, searching the dark beyond the firelight for any threat. She knew Athis was yet to return since his bulk was impossible to miss.

The half-elf took a breath and snapped up, using every muscle to flip onto her feet. In a blur of motion, her Vi'tari blade was in hand and raised into form one of the Mag'dereth. The light of the fire could only go so far, but she knew there was someone or *something* up here with her.

I'm coming back! Athis said urgently inside her mind.

A voice from behind startled her and she spun on the ball of her foot to confront the owner, paying little attention to the words. Her scimitar came to rest across the dark neck of a dishevelled-looking man, who was wise enough to hold his tongue and refrain from taking another step.

"No one calls this place home, stranger," Inara said in a hushed tone. "Who are you and why are you creeping up on me?"

The stranger gulped and his throat hit the steel of her blade. "Forgive my creeping, Miss. I have spent so long fighting those that hide in the shadows I fear I have become rather good at it myself." The stranger looked down at the scimitar held against his throat. "Or perhaps not as good as I thought…"

"You were able to climb up here without me hearing," Inara replied, happy to keep her weapon pressed to his flesh, "and with a staff no less. I'd say you were damn good at creeping. Now, feel free to answer any of my questions, *good sir*."

"My apologies, Miss. I imagine my sudden appearance must have a threatening overtone to it, but I assure you, I only made the climb because I saw your firelight. That, and I'm very hungry." The stranger glanced at himself. "This body has more muscles than the ones I am accustomed to. I'm afraid it requires more sustenance."

From his choice of words, Inara knew the stranger to be educated, though in what or by whom she couldn't say. He definitely wasn't an orc, so that worked in his favour.

It was a risk to remove her blade from his neck, but it was a calculated risk based upon her own skill. Inara stepped back, sure to keep her scimitar raised and pointed at the stranger.

"Do I know you?" he asked, his brown eyes taking in every feature on her face.

"Do not think I will offer my name before I learn of yours. And what do you mean by *this body*? You will speak sense or be gone," she added with a flourish of her blade.

The stranger held up his hands to show that he meant no harm, though Inara was far more concerned by the staff that remained standing upright all by itself.

"My name is Hadavad, and I mean you no ill will, Miss."

That name tugged on Inara's memories, distracting her for a moment. Athis, who never forgot anything, found the memory first and brought it to the surface.

"Hadavad the mage?" she asked.

The man bowed his head. "The one and only," he said with an inviting smile.

The Dragorn scrutinised every inch of the mage's appearance trying to match up what she knew of the mage who had fought beside her parents in The War for the Realm. From the tales she had heard growing up, Hadavad was a young woman!

Athis sharpened the memory in her mind and she remembered the details surrounding the mysterious mage. Those particular details had her note the chain around his neck, though she was unable to see the fabled ruby that hung from it.

"What happened to your other body? The female one, from the war?"

Hadavad looked down at his body and sighed before meeting her eyes again. "The body of Atharia Danell served me well for many years after the war. But while the world enjoyed its peacetime, I returned to the war that has continued in the background of *every* war. Atharia's body was mortally wounded during a fight in The Narrows. I won, but at a cost. My next apprentice served me for almost six years, but I caught the Red Sorrow outside of Snowfell. The disease would have claimed my life had..." The mage gestured to his current body. "Had Daro not offered his body in service of the cause."

Daro's body must have been close to fifty years with a bushy black beard and dreadlocks down to his chest. Strands of grey had begun to make themselves known, but it did nothing to diminish his capable look. Draped in robes to his knees and a heavily laden belt, it was impossible to speak of a muscular body, but the skin she could see was covered in cuts and bruises, suggesting he had recently held his own in a fight.

"Now, Miss, I have given you my name and much more, yet I know nothing of you, besides the fact that you're smart enough to camp high in The Undying Mountains and brave enough to light a fire."

"I am not a *miss*. My name is Inara and I'm a *Dragorn*," she said with pride.

Hadavad tilted his head and his dark features softened. "Ah. I see it now. You are indeed the perfect blend of your mother and father, Inara Galfrey." Voicing her family name surprised Inara, but the mage continued, "You were much smaller the last time I saw you. I was thrilled to hear of your bond with... erm, forgive me, I've forgotten the name of your dragon."

As always, Athis's timing was perfect. The red dragon, with a chest of slate, fell upon them both, shaking the rock beneath their feet. He huffed a breath and hung his head directly over the mage, a chandelier of razor-sharp teeth.

"His name is Athis the ironheart," Inara replied with the hint of a smile on her face.

Hadavad gulped as he took a step back. His dreadlocks blew out behind him under the dragon's breath and he became very still.

I have seen Hadavad through Ilargo's mind. This man does not match his memories.

He just explained that, Inara said, aware that the dragon had heard everything through her.

That doesn't mean this is the *Hadavad...* Athis replied wisely.

Inara addressed the mage again. "He doesn't trust you. He says you could be lying and, to be honest, he has a point."

Hadavad's eyes shifted nervously from dragon to Dragorn. "I have this," he said, lifting the large ruby gem from within his robes.

Athis lowered his head and sniffed the gem. *It is certainly magical in nature, but it proves nothing.*

"How do we know you didn't kill the real Hadavad and steal the gem?" Inara countered.

Hadavad raised an eyebrow, considering his response. "I could probably recite some of your father's speech the day he wed your mother, but you weren't there for that..." The mage ran his hand through his scraggly beard, keeping one eye on Athis. "Have you seen your mother's wedding dress?" he asked hopefully.

"I have," Inara answered. Her mother, Reyna, had made a point of not needing to keep and pass it on now that Inara was a Dragorn, fated never to marry. That was a thread the half-elf didn't particularly fancy pulling on right now.

"It was blue and gold," Hadavad said wistfully. "Princess Reyna wore a circlet of sapphires that shone a clearer blue than the sun on the waves. She was radiant, the envy of every woman and elf in all of Verda."

"Your recollection is accurate," Inara replied, more convinced than Athis.

"The two of you are far from home," the mage commented.

Inara could see that it was an attempt to diffuse the tension and she went along with it, for now. "Everyone is far from home in these lands. We are on Dragorn business," she added vaguely.

Hadavad glanced at the overbearing dragon before collecting his staff and cautiously moving towards the fire. "Sounds serious."

"And what brings *you* to The Undying Mountains?" Inara asked pointedly. "And what is this war you speak of? I think the Dragorn would know if there was a war going on."

Hadavad knelt by the fire and put his hands out to warm up. "Maybe they do know and you're the only one who doesn't…"

That reply saw Athis adjusting his bulk to stand over the mage again. Inara could feel the dragon emanating his emotions, pushing the feeling of being disrespected onto Hadavad. For anyone but a Dragorn, this was the only way the great wyrms of the sky could communicate with normal people. It was enough to make the mage shrink a little and hold his hands out.

"I meant no offence," he offered. "I have lived in a world of secrets for more years than I care to count. I always assume the same of everyone else. A fault of mine to be sure."

Inara subtly flexed her fingers and bade Athis to relax a little. The dragon sighed, almost blowing out the fire, and backed off.

"You don't like answering questions, do you?"

The mage seemed to miss her every word, instead, focusing on the glyphs around the fire. "That's very good," he complimented. "Do they teach magic on The Lifeless Isles or is it a skill passed through your bond? Just curious…"

Inara couldn't get the measure of the man and she hated it. The Dragorn walked around the fire and sheathed her Vi'tari blade before crossing her legs on the ground. If the threatening presence of a dragon wasn't enough to make a man talk, then what would?

"Perhaps we should play a game?" Inara suggested. "I answer a question, then you answer a question. Sound fair?"

Hadavad blew into his hands. "I don't suppose there's much else to do up here. Let's play…"

Inara considered her answer. "We learn many things on The Lifeless Isles," she began. "Magic, mediation, diplomacy, politics…" The Dragorn gripped the hilt of her blade. "How to use a sword.

We are blessed by the natural magic that flows through the dragons. It enhances our ability to use it." Inara lifted her chin and wondered for a moment how on earth she had found herself in this situation. "There, I've answered your question and then some."

"Thank you," Hadavad said with a bow. "Please, ask your question."

"What war do you speak of?" Inara asked.

The mage took a deep breath and stared into the fire. "That question comes with a long and complicated answer."

The Dragorn glanced at the eastern horizon. "Winter brings with it long nights. We have time."

Hadavad rested his staff across his lap and regarded Athis for a brief moment. "As a Dragorn, you must be privy to the secret history of the world…"

"I am," Inara replied confidently, curious as to how much of it was known by the mage.

"Then you know that humans came first. We were here before the dwarves and it was us, not the gods, who created elf kind." Again, Inara nodded along and Hadavad continued. "The people of Illian, the humans that is, still believe in the old gods; Atilan, Paldora, Naius… At the end of The War for the Realm, when we learnt the truth about the gods, we few decided to keep it from the world. There were no gods to offer them in return for taking their current deities away, so we maintained the peace."

"You are yet to answer my question, Mage," Inara pointed out.

Hadavad raised his hand. "Patience, girl. I warned you it wasn't a simple answer. Now, where was I? Oh, yes. We kept the truth of the gods from the people. Could you imagine the chaos if everyone discovered their gods were once human, and as mad as a bag of cats at that? No, we kept that to ourselves and, of course, history's secret keepers… The Dragorn."

"You're not telling me anything I don't already know."

Hadavad sighed. "As patient as your father, I see. Well, what you don't know is enough about The First Kingdom, ruled by King Atilan ten thousand years ago. That's what I've been doing, girl."

If he calls me girl one more time…

"I've been scouring the world for years trying to uncover everything there is to know about this First Kingdom of man. They were much like any other, from what I can tell." The mage held up a single finger. "With one distinct difference," he continued. "The people of The First Kingdom only worshipped the one god, Kaliban. This god was the head of a religion called The Echoes. To us, they would be considered dark wizards too stupid to understand the dangers of their work."

Inara couldn't believe she was hearing another side of the secret history that hadn't been covered on The Lifeless Isles. Not only that, but she was hearing it from a mage who was himself a part of the history books.

If he can be trusted... Athis chipped into her thoughts.

"Now," Hadavad continued, "King Atilan went to war with the dragons and reaped the rewards for taking on a superior adversary. Of course, he killed the dragon riders of the time and created elves in his mad search for immortality, but *ultimately*, he was defeated."

"I know," Inara added. "What was left of his kingdom was forced to flee the dragons and they took shelter in The Wild Moores."

"Yes, where over the next ten thousand years, they forgot almost everything about their history and became the savage Outlanders and Darkakin. But..." Hadavad looked hard into the flames. "There were those who did not forget the old ways, those who did not forsake their god."

Inara tilted her head to try and capture the mage's attention from the flames. "The Echoes?"

"Yes, only these days they go by a different name. After man emerged from The Wild Moores, towards the end of the Second Age, they began to call themselves The Black Hand. They delve into dark magic and necromancy all in the name of Kaliban."

"I've never heard of them," Inara said without meaning to.

"They operate in the shadows," Hadavad explained. "They've never been connected to any evil that beset the world, not openly at least. But, I believe they have been amassing their wealth and power for the last thousand years, waiting for the right time to..." The mage trailed off, chewing over his words.

"Time to what?" Inara pressed.

"I know not," Hadavad admitted. "I have been challenging them all my long life and never uncovered the true extent of their schemes, besides raising the dead and creating monsters."

Inara ignored that last part, chalking it up to embellishment. "Yet you go to war with them?"

"They are evil. They come from evil and if it proves true that their god is real, then he too is evil."

Inara asked in a lighter tone, "Will you go to war with a god then?"

Hadavad met her eyes and replied with bold words, "If I must."

Inara sat back, unsure what to make of the mage and his claims. On the one hand, it sounded entirely plausible while, on the other hand, it sounded as ludicrous as a weeping basilisk.

"Is that why you're in The Undying Mountains?"

Hadavad wagged his finger. "I answered your question. Now you answer mine."

Inara didn't like it, especially since this Black Hand intrigued her.

"What are the Dragorn doing in The Undying Mountains?" he asked. "You're peacekeepers and there isn't any peace to be kept south of Syla's Gate. Civilisation is that way." The mage thumbed over his shoulder, to the north.

That was a hard one and Inara instantly regretted drawing the mage into this game. "Sometimes to keep the peace we have to travel to quieter parts of the world and make sure it's quiet for a reason."

"That's not an answer," Hadavad replied, leaving no sound but the crackle of the fire.

Inara looked to Athis, weighing up the pros and cons of telling the mage why they were here.

He wouldn't know what an orc is anyway...

That doesn't matter, Athis said. *Only the council at Dragons' Reach know of the situation and this mage is not a member.*

It would be dishonourable to lie or refuse to answer now.

Then you must weigh your honour against your duty…

Seeing no way out of it, Inara straightened her back and announced, "We are searching for any sign of orcs."

Hadavad's face screwed up. "What in all the hells is an orc?"

Now it was Inara's turn to wag her finger. "I answered your question. Now you answer mine," she echoed. "You say you've been fighting The Black Hand all your life, that you've lost bodies to them."

"Sadly, yes," Hadavad agreed.

"What happened to your original body?"

"That was a long time ago," the mage replied absently. "In my first life, I was lucky enough to reach a ripe old age. After I transferred my essence into my first apprentice, I sought out an old friend in Longdale. I had him take my body and bury it somewhere dark and deep, where no one would find it, including myself."

Inara couldn't imagine living from one body to the next, man or woman, and never making any lasting connections in the world.

"What's an orc?" he asked immediately.

Inara could think of quite a few choice words that would describe the beasts, but none would accurately define them. "I'm surprised you don't know, given your knowledge about history."

Hadavad shrugged. "I do not claim to know everything. Nobody can; it's what makes life so exciting!"

Inara bit her lip. Telling Hadavad of their search for orcs was different to telling him things not known to mankind. Then again, the mage was accustomed to be being burdened with secrets…

"They're an intelligent race of beasts who emerged at the end of the First Age, after mankind had retreated into The Wild Moores. That's why humans have never heard of them before, but if you were to ask an elf or a dwarf, they would tell you of The Great War. It was their defeat over the orcs that ushered in the beginning of the Second Age."

Hadavad ran his hand through the scraggy strands of his beard. "The Second Age began five thousand years ago…" The mage looked at her across the fire. "Why would you be looking for orcs now?"

"That's two questions," Inara pointed out.

Ask him why he is here, Athis said.

"So you're at war with this Black Hand," Inara continued. "Why are you in The Undying Mountains?"

"Believe me, Inara Galfrey, I wish I wasn't. I would much rather be under the stars in The Moonlit Plains or enjoying an ale at The Pick-Axe in Lirian." The mage grew serious then, and his tone dropped to match his expression. "I was left for dead by my enemy, though, in truth, I think he meant for me to live. Why, I could not say. This new master they serve is different from the others I've fought in the past."

"So, you survived then," Inara observed.

Hadavad locked eyes with her across the flames, but he might as well have been looking through her. "I believe death would have found me had…"

"Had what?" Inara's question seemed to bring the mage out of his trance.

"I saw something, on the edge of death. You and I both know there are no gods." Hadavad's eyes lit up. "But I saw something up there… a beautiful woman."

Typical man, Inara thought. Of course, he would see a beautiful woman at the edge of death and find just enough life to keep going. "Up there?" she asked instead, hoping the mage wouldn't take it as a second question.

"I challenged them on the highest slopes of Vengora," Hadavad explained. "I should have sought out my friends afterwards, but I followed the wretches here. Whatever they have been planning is going to bear fruit soon, I'm sure of it, and I mean to get in the way of that."

"You have travelled far." Inara had spent her youth journeying up and down Illian with her parents and brother and knew well that even the lowest range of Vengora was hundreds of miles from here.

"I would follow them to the ends of Verda if it meant bringing an end to their evil."

Inara nodded along, unsure how to reply to such a bold statement.

He can stay, the dragon said in her mind, finally satisfied with the mage.

The Dragorn reached into her narrow pack and gave the mage what little she had left in the way of food. "You are welcome to share the safety of this cliff and the warmth of my fire for the night."

"Is that to be the end of our game, then?" Hadavad asked. "These orcs intrigue me. I could ask questions of a Dragorn until the sun rose, it seems."

"When the sun rises, Athis and I will resume our errand, good mage."

"I'm sure searching for long-dead creatures is of the utmost importance," Hadavad said, "but, you should come with me. With a Dragorn and a dragon by my side, we could rid the world of The Black Hand in a single night."

For all his centuries of life, Athis said, *he could never understand the threat posed by the return of the orcs.*

Inara agreed with her companion. "I'm sorry, Hadavad. We must continue with our errand, alone. I wish you luck if there is such a thing."

The mage bowed his head. "Then I thank you for your hospitality. It is the greatest honour to share such company…"

Inara took herself away from the fire after a while and sat with her back to Athis. His scales were warm and she preferred to listen to the dragon's heartbeat as she found rest. She couldn't say she trusted the mage entirely, but Athis would keep watch until she woke again.

UNWELCOME GUESTS

Vighon nuzzled his face into Nelly's head and gave her a big kiss between the eyes. She licked his face in return, wetting the bristles of what was quickly becoming a beard. He begrudgingly had her return to the warmth of The Pick-Axe. He didn't know how long it would be until he saw her again, but she couldn't follow where they were going.

Alijah exited the inn, avoiding Nelly on his way out, and pulled the new hood over his head to keep the light fall of snow at bay.

"Is that what I think it is?" Vighon asked, taking note of the dark green cloak draped over his roguish friend's shoulders.

"Galanör said we would need something to keep the sun off our faces." Alijah tightened the straps of his quiver, which was thrown over the back of the cloak with his short-sword.

"That's not just something to keep the sun off your face," Vighon argued. "That's from the locker, isn't it? That's *Asher's* cloak."

Alijah waved his observation away. "There was a whole row of them. He would never have actually worn this one. Besides, it's perfect for my needs and it's *free*."

Vighon wasn't convinced but he also wasn't in the mood to debate. They had been instructed to meet Galanör at such an hour that the sun had barely greeted the world. They retrieved their horses from the stables, having thankfully paid for their upkeep before leaving for The Wild Moores just over two weeks ago.

"Well met, old friend," Vighon said upon greeting his horse. "Have you been good while I've been away?"

"Do you have to talk to every animal?" Alijah asked, mounting his black horse.

Vighon slung his shield over his black fur cloak and climbed onto the white horse. "I've known Ned longer than... well, not longer than I've known you, but longer than we've been working for Hadavad. Or should I say, saving the world?"

Alijah shook his head. "Nothing's changed, Vighon. You've just started paying attention for the first time, that's all."

Vighon took the reins and guided Ned out of the stables and into the snow, where, side by side, the two riders made their way through the streets of Lirian. The sleeping city was coming alive now, with smoke rising from every chimney and small businesses opening, ready for the day.

On the eastern edge of the city, the interior border of The Evermoore provided a wall of towering pines that cared little for summer or winter. They chose a path between the trees and Vighon did his best to appear casual as two of the city watch observed their unusual departure from the city.

It was ill-advised to leave the city via the forest and forego the Selk Road that connected every kingdom in the realm. It seemed to Vighon that there wasn't much they did these days that couldn't be considered *ill-advised*...

The horses trotted through The Evermoore for several minutes before they came across a small clearing with a single pointed rock in the middle. Off to one side, stood Galanör and his grey horse, which was saddled with full bags.

The elf truly looked the part of a ranger when removed from civilisation. With his dual scimitars resting neatly on his hips and the armoured leathers that enveloped his body, Galanör appeared more than capable of taking anything on. His blue cloak was now overlaid with white fur that covered his shoulders and the top half of his back.

Alijah steered his horse towards the ranger. "This is a strange way to go south," he said. "The Selk Road is that way."

Galanör ignored Alijah's gesture. "We're not taking the Selk Road. The Black Hand have been up to something in The Undying Mountains for too long, and I intend to find out what. With that and Hadavad's disappearance, I fear we may already be too late."

Vighon hopped off Ned and joined Alijah. He was still coming around to the idea that the work they had been doing together for the last three years was of any importance. To his dismay, he realised that hearing the ranger talk in such grave tones was going to become a regular occurrence.

"Well, we're going to be really late if we keep heading east," Alijah replied.

Galanör walked over and ushered both of them back from the middle of the clearing. "Stand back," he said.

Vighon looked to Alijah for some kind of explanation, unsure as to why they were standing in the freezing cold in the middle of the forest. The half-elf could only shrug in response, suggesting that they just go along with it for now.

"What are we waiting for?" Vighon finally asked. "Some of us aren't immortal."

Galanör gave him a side-long glance and remained very still in front of the pointed rock. Vighon was about to press the elf when the space in front of them exploded with the black abyss of a portal.

Except for Galanör's horse, the other two whinnied and attempted to flee before they were calmed by their masters. With his free hand, Vighon instinctively reached for the hilt of his sword, but the elf's hand on his arm prevented him from drawing the steel.

Galanör walked up to the portal, which was surrounded by short bursts of lightning, and waited patiently. The elf was unfazed by the sudden appearance of the portal, a feat of magic that not everyone could pull off.

Without warning, a small leather sack came through the portal and landed in the snow at Galanör's feet. Alijah and Vighon watched it for a moment, unsure what was happening and full of questions.

Then, with just as much warning as its appearance, the portal collapsed on itself.

"What's going on?" Alijah asked. "Who opened that portal?"

"What's inside the sack?" Vighon added, though he was too slow to reach for it before Galanör scooped it up.

"I told you," the elf replied, "we're not the only ones looking into The Black Hand."

"But who tossed that pouch through the portal?" Alijah continued, never happy until he found all the answers.

"An ally," Galanör said plainly. "There aren't many we can trust; The Black Hand have infiltrated every kingdom in some regard. Not every ally can make themselves known. Now, ready yourselves."

Vighon pulled his fur cloak around his shoulders. "What should we be readying ourselves for exactly?"

Galanör untied the pouch and emptied a single crystal into the palm of his gloved hand. Both Alijah and Vighon took a step closer to better see the glowing crystal, filled with stored magic.

"It takes a great amount of meditation and focus to put magic inside a crystal," Alijah commented, his eyes on the elf. "Outside of Ayda, and your kin, there aren't many in Illian who can master such a feat."

"You are correct," Galanör answered without giving anything away. "If I had a crystal I could do this myself, but they are hard to come by. Now, *ready yourselves*," he instructed again.

"Are you going to open a portal?" Alijah asked incredulously.

"Yes, but it will take a lot out of me, especially with the distance I have in mind. I don't know exactly what will be on the other side, so be ready to repel anything. I probably won't be able to assist you…"

Vighon gripped Ned by the reins and bowed the horse's head down, hoping that the new portal wouldn't frighten him so much.

He also hoped that tending to Ned would distract him from the fact that he was expected to walk through a portal himself.

Galanör flung out his arm and threw the crystal into the other side of the clearing, where it shattered into dust mid-flight and gave birth to a new portal of pure black. The effect on the elf was almost immediate. He had just enough energy to pull himself up onto his horse and have it take him through.

"Come on, girl," Alijah said soothingly to his horse. "It's alright, come on."

Vighon watched Galanör and his friend trot beyond the wall of black and disappear across the world in a single step. Keeping his feet on the ground, for Ned would need pulling through the portal, he tugged on the reins and did his best to place one foot in front of the other until they were both through.

There was no expected sensation or pain. One moment he was in the freezing cold snows of The Evermoore and, the next, he was standing on hard, dry ground where snow had never fallen. Vighon lost control of his jaw, unable to do anything but stare up at the enormous mountain walls of the south, broken only by the valley that cut through the heart of it.

At the base of the valley, two colossal doors lay strewn in the desert, one awkwardly resting on top of the other, providing a triangular entrance into the valley beyond.

To the left and right was nothing but more desert and the endless face of The Undying Mountains. Vighon had never been this far south before, but there was no mistaking where they were, not when a pair of massive, ancient doors lay abandoned in the desert.

The portal closed behind him and he turned to see the distant walls of a ruined city on the horizon, its features just becoming clear in the rising sun. The sunrise here was very different from the ones he was used to in the north. Here, the sky was clear of the usual grey clouds and stretched out to veil the stars with a pleasant blue and streaks of pink.

"Galanör!" Alijah's alarm had Vighon turning back to the valley, where the elf was sliding from his horse.

"He's going to fall!" Vighon cried, too far to be of any help.

Alijah, blessed with elven speed, was off his horse and by Galanör's side in time to catch the ranger and ease him to the ground. The elf's horse bent down and attempted to lick his face, but Alijah pushed the animal away.

"We need to find somewhere he can rest," the half-elf said.

Vighon looked around at their barren surroundings. "We can't stay here. The doors have narrowed the entrance to the valley, making this the only way in or out. Perhaps we should ride north, to those ruins. We can find shelter from the sun and plan our next move."

"That's Karath," Alijah replied gravely. "I would not have us spend the day in those ruins. We should press on, into the valley. There might be somewhere along the walls that we can find shelter."

"As you say." Vighon bent down and pulled Galanör up onto his horse, positioning the exhausted elf over the front of his saddle. Alijah mounted his own horse and led the ranger's by its reins as the companions made their way into Syla's Pass.

They must have only journeyed half a mile before Vighon began cursing the weather. "Damn it's hot," he groaned, having already removed his black fur cloak and replaced it with a lighter cotton one.

"It's still early," Alijah pointed out.

"I was built for the north. I could sit bare arse naked in the tundras of The White Vale for an entire morning before the cold found its way into *my* bones. But this heat…"

"Yes, it's hot," Alijah agreed with a hint of irritation in his voice. The half-elf kept the hood of his new green cloak over his head, protecting him from the sun.

"I still can't believe we're even here," Vighon continued. "Have you ever stepped through a portal before?"

"No," was his friend's only answer.

Undeterred by Alijah's tone, Vighon said, "You've been to The Arid Lands before, though. I remember when you left with your parents and Inara. It was winter; I remember because it was supposed to be milder here. It wasn't bloody mild by The Shining Coast, I can tell you that. I spent the winter mucking out horse shit and, do you know what, I loved it. It was warm in the stables…"

"What are you going on about?" Alijah snapped.

Vighon shook his head in despair. "I don't even know anymore. I'm struggling to even remember why we're in this hell."

Alijah, riding in front of him, pointed over his shoulder to the bound scroll nestled between his short-sword and quiver. "To see if there's any truth in that," he answered.

Vighon adjusted Galanör's cloak, making certain the elf was in shade. "I don't know," he said. "I think we should have let the ranger see to this while we waited in The Pick-Axe for Hadavad." He couldn't see Alijah's face, but he suspected it held the same stoic expression the half-elf had inherited from his father, Nathaniel.

"Hadavad isn't coming," Alijah replied. "The Black Hand have seen to that."

Vighon could see that all hope had fled his friend and that this heat was sweating out his sense of adventure, as it was with him.

They continued their slow ride in the heat for some time. Twice they stopped as the ground was shaken beneath their horses' hooves. The quakes in these parts were certainly stronger than those they experienced in the north.

After a lazy curve in Syla's Pass, Vighon spotted a dark cave, its shaded interior beckoning from the base of the mountain. "Alijah! Over there! We would be better travelling in twilight, anyway."

"No, Vighon," Alijah warned.

Ignoring his friend, Vighon directed Ned towards the wonderful shade. There was even a cool breeze blowing out of it, soothing his face.

"Vighon!" Alijah hissed.

"What?" Vighon asked, becoming irritated himself with the half-elf. Looking back, Alijah had already unhooked his bow and nocked an arrow, but it was his eyes, piercing the shadows, that tugged at Vighon's sense of danger.

Turning slowly back to the cave, he caught the outline of what could only be a monster. Imitating the nightmares that so many shared, one pincer-like leg stepped into the light followed by another, then another. These sharpened limbs came together in the light, revealing the most hideous of beasts.

Standing on six pincer-like legs, at eight-feet, the creature's abdomen was that of a giant insect until the body formed up into a torso, not dissimilar from a man's. Two thin, but well-muscled, arms extended from the vertical torso and ended in five long fingers, each as razor sharp as any blade. The head was a grotesque amalgamation of man and spider, with two meaty fangs hiding a smaller mouth of serrated teeth.

"Sandstalker…" Vighon whispered before shouting at the top of his voice, "Sandstalker!"

He pulled hard to the right on Ned's reins, desperate to put as much distance between them and the monster as possible. A single arrow sailed past his face and intercepted the Sandstalker mid-charge, cutting off its banshee-like scream while taking some of the speed out of it.

With his heels dug into Ned, who didn't need that much encouragement to flee the beast, Vighon had the horse galloping in the opposite direction. Two more arrows were loosed from Alijah's bow before the half-elf turned his own horse and set off at a gallop.

Glancing over his shoulder, the first Sandstalker now lay dead on the ground with three arrows protruding from its chest.

But there were more, lots more…

The grotesque monsters exploded from the mouth of the cave with ravenous fury in pursuit of their prey.

Having spent most of his formative years in the capital city of Namdhor, Vighon struggled to recall all that he knew of the creatures that preyed on man. Alijah's parents had taught them many things known mostly to rangers, but those years were too far behind to draw upon. The last ten years in Namdhor had been so brutal as to replace many of his pleasant memories with hard truths, known only to the worst kind of men.

He just wished he could remember whether Sandstalkers were faster than horses.

Unburdened with the added weight of Galanör, Alijah soon

overtook Vighon with the elf's horse quickly overtaking them both. It suddenly occurred to Vighon that it didn't matter which creature was faster, you only had to be faster than the one beside you.

Right now, that meant he was to be the feast of monsters...

REUNION

The last of the blistering rain pelted Doran's armour as his chunky feet crunched in the fresh snow. It was cold enough to turn any man or elf from their task, but Doran, son of Dorain of clan Heavybelly was neither man nor elf. He was a dwarf! And dwarves could not be so easily dissuaded, especially when it came to a good fight.

As the rain died away, Doran snarled and spat into the snow, his piercing blue eyes never straying from the monster in his sights. The beastie staring back at him had terrorised the town of Wood Vale, to the north, before journeying south through The Evermoore to prey upon the good people of Lirian.

By any standards of Doran's, it was just another day in the life of a ranger, only this one was made all the more convenient by his lodgings at The Pick-Axe. He was able to hunt, slay a monster, and make the short journey back for a frothing ale. It brought a smile to his hard face.

"Aye, I've hunted yer kind before," he declared across the clearing. "Ye're a fat one, I'll give ye that! Brave one too for travellin' so far south. Ye should o' stayed in the mountains, Gobber. Still, good news for me tab at The Axe! That thin's gettin' out o' control..."

Dark green scales covered the Gobber's sloping leathery head and it stretched its neck to taste the air with its forked tongue. Hunched over on two thick, long arms, the monster dug the claws of its smaller hind legs into the snow, readying itself to pounce. Its face was closer to that of a lizard, only it possessed several more rows of razor-sharp teeth, teeth that would tear through Doran like butter.

Still, the dwarf could only smile. "I suppose the pickin's are pretty slim in Vengora this time o' year," he continued, mirroring the beast as it slowly edged around the tree line. "I'll tell ye what's goin' to happen next, shall I?" Doran brandished his fat sword in one hand and his single-bladed axe in the other. "I'm goin' to chop off yer ugly head an' take it back to Lirian. After I've collected the reward from there, I'm takin' yer ugly mug to Wood Vale, for *their* reward. Then, I'm goin' to drink 'till summer!"

The lone Gobber took a single step forward in the snow and snarled at the dwarf as if it understood his threat.

"Come on then ye dumb beast," Doran said through gritted teeth. "It's been too long since me steels tasted blood." The dwarf beat his sword across the black and gold of his plated armour.

The Gobber charged across the clearing, using the pointed fingers of bone to propel it at great speed. Doran roared and sprinted to meet it in the snow.

And meet they did.

The dwarf dropped and skidded through the powder, bringing him under the leaping Gobber. The tip of his sword sliced neatly through the monster's scaly hide, tearing through to the muscle in its hip. The Gobber screamed in agony and tumbled over its disproportionate limbs, kicking up snow and splattering hot red blood.

Doran jumped to his feet and turned to face the wounded creature. "Did I nick ye there?" He laughed. "Ye killed six people in Wood Vale an' three in Lirian. I'd say ye've got abou' eight more lashes before I put ye out o' ye misery..."

The Gobber shrieked, extending its jaw to a size that could easily encompass a man's head. It picked itself up and continued its line around the edge of the trees, this time with a limp and a bloody trail behind it. Doran remained in the centre of the clearing and pivoted to keep his eyes on the beastie.

"I don't know what drove ye so far south, but ye should o' stayed with yer pack. Ye lot are a pain in the arse when ye've got the numbers."

The Gobber hissed and charged again, determined to carve out its territory. Doran threw his axe, deliberately aiming for the ground in front of the monster. As predicted, the Gobber instinctively leaped over the axe as it ploughed into the ground, giving Doran the opening he needed.

The creature screamed in agony again as the dwarf's blade clipped its bottom jaw, cutting through to the bone. Once again, the Gobber botched its landing and rolled through the snow, bleeding from its mouth.

"Ye're down to seven now…" Doran casually collected his axe and cricked his neck.

The Gobber, enraged, kicked up the snow as it made the short dash across the clearing. It swung its long arms, left then right, swiping the air with its pointed claws. Doran stepped back with every swipe, evading every attack with more speed than a figure of his standing should be rewarded with.

Frustrated now, the Gobber lashed out with its razor-sharp teeth and tried to take a bite out of the dwarf's head. Doran ducked under the scaly maw and cut a line with his sword, opening up the monster's full belly.

"Six!" Doran yelled, spinning around to bring his axe down, across the Gobber's back. "Five!" he bellowed with glee.

The monster stumbled forward with one nightmarish hand covering the deep wound on its belly. A growl gave away its intentions and Doran lifted his sword to block the backhanded assault. Yanking his blade down, the steel sliced a red line across the monster's forearm.

"Four to go!"

The tortured beast had barely the energy to muster a rumble in its throat, but Doran had no intention of stopping now. His sword went one way, his axe the other, and the Gobber fell forward with a red X marring its back.

"Two left and I promise, ye'll die."

Thinking about the victims, one of whom was the baker's son, a boy of seven years, Doran was only too happy to extend the monster's final moments of torment.

The dwarf marched through the snow and backhanded the Gobber's shoulder with his axe, tossing the creature onto its back as it tried to rise. A quick flourish of his sword, to readjust the hilt in his hand, and Doran plunged its tip into the monster's shoulder, pinning it to the ground.

"An' that makes nine! Lucky for ye…" Doran walked around the wailing Gobber to acquire a better angle with his axe. With two hands and a mighty swing, the curved blade chopped through flesh, muscle, and bone until it dug into the ground.

Doran laughed to himself. "Ha! Back in time for some supper, me thinks!" The dwarf looked about the clearing for any sign of his Warhog. "Where's that damn pig?" A sharp whistle soon brought the stocky animal into the clearing.

Adorned with golden rings around its deadly tusks, the Warhog was saddled much in the way a horse would be, only its temperament was far more unpredictable than that of a horse. Doran strapped the Gobber's ugly head to the saddle and made for the east, back to Lirian, before the light of the world faded to black.

It was later in the evening than he would have liked but, by the time Doran found himself walking back through The Pick-Axe's wooden door, he possessed a large bag of well-deserved coins.

The tavern was quiet, the lull before the crowds came by to hear a tale or two from one of the rangers. With two hundred and forty-eight years behind him, the son of Dorain had more than a few tales of his own to tell. Maybe he could recount the battle at Syla's Gate for an extra coin or two…

A bark was the only warning he received before Nelly bounded up to him and licked all the melting snow from his armour. He gave the dog a decent scratch and dismissed her as he approached the bar, where Russell Maybury was inspecting a cracked tankard.

"This should cover me tab an' then some, Rus!" Doran threw the sack of coins onto the bar.

Russell hefted the bag of coins and measured the weight in his hand. "This'll cover half of your tab, Heavybelly."

The dwarf halted his stride to the door marked *private*. "Half?"

Russell's reply never came, his attention entirely on the front door, where Doran's Warhog stood, its body steaming. It was a mystery in itself how the hog had untied itself and made it into the tavern without a sound, but this wasn't the first time and the dwarf knew it wouldn't be the last, so he had stopped wondering.

Russell pointed his finger threateningly at the Warhog. "That pig drinks and eats more than you do, Heavybelly. Not to mention the mess it makes!"

"Bah!" Doran waved the words away. "Pig's just got a taste for that fine ale o' yers!"

The Warhog met Russell's predatory gaze with a blank stare that bordered on derision. For decades they had been at odds and more than once the barkeep had been forced to give a patron a free meal or round of drinks to compensate for the hog's mischievous nature.

"A'right, a'right!" Doran threw his hands up and ushered the Warhog back outside. "Be off with ye!"

"Aren't you even going to tie the beast up?" Russell protested.

Doran frowned, pulling his blond hair closer to his eyes. "Ye think I haven' tried that? I tie 'im up, he gets out, an' then I can't even find the damned rope!" The dwarf scratched his bushy beard. "I think he eats it…"

A cold breeze swept through the tavern as the door opened again, and Doran readied himself to tussle with the boisterous hog. The two people who stood in The Pick-Axe's entrance, however, were no hogs and they certainly weren't a pair to tussle with.

"Galfreys!" Doran yelled with a grin from ear to ear. "By Grarfath's beard, ye're a sight for these old eyes!"

Husband and wife pulled back their hoods and offered the son of Dorain broad smiles of their own.

"Doran!" they both exclaimed.

Reyna was, as ever, the most beautiful creature to walk the earth, though the dwarf would never admit such a statement. Nathaniel was as young as the day they met, thirty years ago, and still carried himself like a knight of the Graycoats.

Doran's weathered eye couldn't help but also notice the couple's gear, with Nathaniel sporting a sword again for the first time in many years, and Reyna with her bow and quiver.

"Ye don't look to be here on official business..." the dwarf commented.

Elf and man shared a look that perhaps only spouses could decipher. Before either of them could get a word out, however, Russell ambushed them both with a hug each, his thick arms easily wrapping around them, weapons and all.

"It's so good to see you both!" the barkeep exclaimed.

"And us you," Reyna replied. "I can't tell you how good it feels to be back here."

Nathaniel locked hands with Doran. "I would choose The Axe over a castle any day."

"At least ye get to choose though, eh!" Doran winked and beckoned them into the warmth.

The dwarf could tell that the comment put Nathaniel ill at ease. It seemed that, even after all these years, the old knight wasn't content with his life of comforts. Doran had known since he first clapped eyes on the man that he would have made a better ranger than an ambassador.

"Can I get you both anything?" Russell asked. "On the house!"

Doran snapped his head around. "On the..." The dwarf shook his head. "I was at Syla's Gate an' The Battle for Velia too, ye know!"

Russell ignored him and kept his attention on the Galfreys, who politely asked for anything warm.

Doran had them follow him to a quiet booth nearer to the hearth when he heard the front door open again. He kept his smile to himself upon spotting the Warhog enter the tavern for the second time. The pig appeared to be checking for threats in the shape of Russell Maybury before making his way deeper into The Axe.

"So!" Doran rubbed his hands together. "How's the old offspring? Still flyin' around I take it?"

Reyna beamed with pride. "Inara is well. She and Athis are… well, they're always busy doing something."

Doran cocked his head. "Dragorn business, eh? I've lived for nearly three centuries in a world where dragons were naught but old stories. I still can't believe they're back. I saw one ye know, 'bout a year back it was. Just flyin' over the Moonlit Plains…"

An awkward silence crept over the booth as the Galfreys struggled to ask a question of their own. Doran knew exactly what they burned to ask just as he knew the sun would rise in the morning.

Finally, Nathaniel leaned forward. "Has Alijah crossed your path?" he asked as casually as he could.

The answer was far more complicated than the poor dwarf cared to handle. Thankfully, Russell tackled the question on his behalf.

"He frequents The Axe," the barkeep answered. "He was here… *recently*."

Doran's face creased into confusion. "I've not seen the lad."

"You were drunk," Russell stated, clearing up all of the dwarf's recent memory loss with three words.

Reyna couldn't contain her questions any longer. "Is he okay?" she asked desperately.

"Where is he?" Nathaniel added.

"The boy don't want to be found," Russell replied softly. "Not yet, anyway. He's always accompanied by that boy that was always with you as a child. Suppose he's a man now… Vighon Draqaro."

"Vighon Draqaro?" Nathaniel asked skeptically. "I haven't seen him since… well, maybe a decade or more."

"He looks out for your boy," Russell assured. "Though I last saw Alijah in the company of an old friend of yours; Galanör Reveeri."

"He's with Galanör?" Nathaniel looked at his wife.

"What has he been doing?" Reyna continued.

Russell put his hands up. "Alijah has asked for privacy. I shouldn't even be telling you what I am. I just can't stand to see you fret. He's in good company and that's what matters. He's a bloody good shot and damn sure of himself; there's nothing he can't handle these days." Russell placed one of his over-sized hands on Reyna's shoulder before he left. "He will come home soon. He just needs more time…"

The news of their son brought both joy and crushing sorrow, it seemed. Nathaniel squeezed his wife's hand and they shared a look that spoke a thousand words. Doran's dwarven mind battled with guilt, an emotion his kind weren't familiar with. He had made promises to both of them and Alijah, a mistake of his own doing.

"So…" Doran dragged the word out. "What brings the pair o' ye to this neck o' The Evermoore? I haven' seen ye since…"

"Whistle Town," Reyna finished, tucking her hair behind her pointed ears. The elf blinked and any trace of a tear was consumed by her eyelids.

"That were it!" the dwarf said, slapping his hand down on the table, happy to change the subject. "Troublesome little nest o' Vorska, if I recall."

Reyna managed a smile. "The townsfolk still hail you as a hero."

Doran shrugged, hoping the heat from the fire covered his blushing cheeks. "Is that what this is abou'?" he asked. "Ye got another beastie for me to sink me axe in to?"

Nathaniel's voice cracked a little, but his eyes spoke of that resolve the old knight was known for. "Are you up for another adventure, old dwarf?"

Doran pushed himself back from the table and sat against the green leather of the booth. "I've seen that look in both o' yer eyes before. Sense tells me to stay well clear o' yer *adventures*! Is this Illian business or Ayda's?"

"Illian's," Reyna answered.

"Trouble?" he asked.

"In the north," the elf replied.

Doran chewed over it. "Well, at least it ain't south. The heat makes me armour chafe…"

"So, you'll come then?" Nathaniel pursued.

The dwarf held up his hands. "Whoa, laddy! I didn' say I was goin' anywhere. A good ranger always gets all o' the facts before takin' on a job… This is a job, aye? Some king or queen's payin' us for this."

Reyna, fully composed once more, replied, "Queen Yelifer Skalaf will accommodate our needs."

"Skalaf?" Doran echoed. "Trouble's in Namdhor, then." The dwarf thought it over for a moment. It had been some time since he had travelled to the capital of the north. "It would be nice to see some mountains for a change."

Nathaniel cocked an eyebrow. "There's a mountain right outside the tavern. King Weymund lives there…"

"Bah! That's no mountain, laddy. Just a fat hillock."

Reyna cut in, "We will be going a little *farther* north, actually."

"Farther north?" the son of Dorain asked.

Russell arrived again with two plates of steaming hot pies and a tray of tea for his new guests.

Doran looked from the tea to the barkeep. "I don't drink this swill. Where's the ale?"

At that moment, his Warhog made himself known with a great clatter and a scream from the other side of the tavern.

Doran pursed his lips and met Russell's fierce yellow eyes. "Maybe just forget the ale… for now."

Russell sighed and stormed off after the hog. "PIG!"

"So, farther north ye say. I suppose ye two are daft enough to head into Vengora in winter time. What's got Yelifer's skirt in such a bunch that she'd request the two o' ye to enter those mountains?"

Reyna put down her cup of tea. "A dispute, of sorts."

Doran ran his hand through his beard as he struggled to put together what the Galfreys weren't saying. "Disputes are for talkin'," the dwarf belched with a fist in his chest, "and for elves. No offence, me Lady," he quickly added. "Dwarves are better at disputin' with steel!"

"That's exactly why we need you, Doran," Nathaniel said, yet to tuck into his pie.

The dwarf frowned. "I'm all for goin' out into the world with ye both, but I'm not cuttin' off some lord's head because they can' agree with Yelifer, the old hag. Besides, between yer bow and yer sword, who's goin' to argue with ye?"

"Doran," Reyna began softly. "The dispute is between Namdhor and Dhenaheim."

The dwarf stopped eyeing Nathaniel's pie and focused on the princess's mouth. "Say that again…"

Reyna glanced at her husband before continuing, "We don't have all the information yet, but it seems an ancient mine has been uncovered by the Namdhorians and your fellow dwarves have taken up arms over its claim. There's an unsteady truce right now, but it won't hold for long."

Doran didn't even have to think about what he did next. "Well, it was great seein' ye both!" he said, finding the floor under his feet again. "Make sure ye take plenty of supplies with ye, it's bloody cold up there…"

The dwarf loved them both deeply, but he couldn't look them in the eye as he made his way to the door marked *private*. He marched down the steps without a second look and did everything he could not to think about his reasons for staying put.

"Doran!" Nathaniel called after him.

A pair of rangers seated around the small fire gave the son of Dorain quizzical looks, but he ignored them both and made for the locker. Perhaps hitting something would distract him.

Before the dwarf could strike a mannequin or hurl his axe at one of the targets on the wall, the Galfreys followed him in.

"Doran?" Nathaniel said his name with concern.

Reyna dropped to one knee and took the dwarf's rough hand in hers. "What's the matter?"

From anyone else, Doran would have taken the gesture and question as patronising, but Reyna Galfrey had a way of disarming everyone. She was also the most genuine person he knew. He squeezed her soft hand and turned away, looking to the tattered long coat displayed on the wall. He wished more than anything that Jonus Glaide was still here with him now.

Of all the humans he had met since journeying south into Illian's lands, Glaide had been his closest and most trusted friend. He knew all of Doran's long tale and would provide him with the council he so needed. Alas, his friend had the audacity to leave this world without him.

"Do ye know any more than ye've told me?" he asked quietly.

"No." Reyna walked around the dwarf to face him. "We thought you would—"

Doran held up his hand. "Ye don't know which clan they're loggin' heads with?"

Reyna shook her head. "Only what we've told you."

Nathaniel offered, "You're the only person in all six kingdoms who has any idea how to negotiate with the dwarves of Dhenaheim. We wouldn't ask you otherwise, old friend."

"Ye wanna' know how to negotiate with me kin? Ye don't. Me advice is simple; send a raven an' have them Namdhorians collapse the mine, collapse the whole mountain if they have to, an' forget about whatever's tickled their fancy. Dwarves throw words like *war* an' *battle* around like Velians do *picnics* an' *parties*! This'll escalate if they don't back off."

Nathaniel shook his head. "That's not going to happen. We don't know what's in that mine that has Yelifer all caught up, but she won't relinquish her claim on it. She's already talking about marching her bannermen through The Iron Valley."

Doran's eyebrows blended into his hairline. "If me kin sees them, The Iron Valley will flow with so much blood it'll melt the snows!"

"Then help us," Reyna cut in. "The realm has known peace for thirty years. Shouldn't one generation, at least, be able to live without picking up a sword?"

Doran moved aside, unable to meet the princess's emerald eyes any longer. If he hadn't known her so well, the dwarf would have been sure she was placing him under a spell with those eyes.

The curtain to Asher's private alcove was half open, revealing his green cloaks and row of swords and daggers. That man, a good man, had died so that they all might live... what good was his sacrifice if the realm fell back into bloodshed before the Age was even out?

Doran sighed. "I'll go with ye," he said softly. "To Namdhor that is. I'll barter words with the war-witch o' the north and see if we can't solve this. *But*, I ain't goin' in no mine an' I ain't talkin' to no dwarves. Namdhor. No farther."

Reyna beamed at him. "No farther."

Doran shook his bushy head. "This ain't goin' to end well..."

STATUS QUO

I nara and Athis were as far south as they had ever ventured, having followed the spine of The Undying Mountains until they could see the vast blue of The Hox in the west. It was an ocean said to be larger than that of The Adean in the east, though The Hox was entirely unexplored.

As enchanting a view as it was to see the crystal-like waves cresting under the sunlight, Inara was captivated by Paldora's Fall, just north of their position.

From their lofty vantage, the Dragorn was offered a view of the impact site in its entirety. The enormous boulders, which had once been a part of the star, as well as the ground, floated around the crater and reached for the heavens above. From here, she could see them slowly colliding into each other and floating apart, ever chained to the crater by magic.

Through her bond with Athis, Inara had seen similar effects in the original Dragons' Reach, found in the deserts in south Ayda. That place was an oasis of greenery surrounded by flat wastes, but the boulders and rocks at its heart were always floating, a result of the magical aura created by dragons congregating in large numbers.

It is not the magic of dragons that has created such a view, Athis said.

No, Inara agreed. **My mother and father were fighting at The Battle of Syla's Gate when the star fell. They said the whole world was rocked.**

The crystal from that star holds vast amounts of magic, Athis explained. *As such, it is a dangerous place to visit. I dislike unpredictable magic.*

You dislike anything that might hurt us...

Athis grunted in disagreement. *I dislike anything that might hurt you. I am Athis the ironheart! My strong chest rebuked a spear hurled by Valanis himself in The Battle for Velia.*

Alright,   alright!   Don't   start   naming   all   your achievements... again.

Athis grunted, too secure in himself to feel stung by her words but irritated enough to consider banking sharply to the right. Inara laughed, having been the victim of this kind of response before. Falling off your dragon, however, was covered vigorously during training and Inara had often enjoyed her brief flights before Athis scooped her up, mid-drop.

Come on, the Dragorn insisted. **We hugged the coast all the way south. Let's go north a little and take a closer look!** Athis continued flying in his own direction. **Athis!** she tried again. **Where's your sense of adventure?**

We have our duty to consider, wingless one. We are yet to find any evidence of orc activity. We should continue our search.

Well, maybe there's activity near Paldora's Fall...

Athis sighed. *Why didn't I choose an elf?*

Inara rolled her eyes and smiled. **We both know there is no choice, you old grump.**

The red dragon glided on the air currents and made for Paldora's Fall. As they drew closer, it became apparent just how varied the giant boulders were, from the size of a person to the size of castles.

Before they could get any closer, a shadow overcame them.

Athis instinctively banked to the left and closed in his wings, dropping them like a stone. In a blur of motion, the shadow gave way to another dragon, who plummeted past them as if thrown from the heavens in the manner of a spear.

Athis unfurled his wings and Inara felt her whole body press into his scales as the membranes filled with air.

Looking down, beside Athis's neck, Inara caught sight of a golden dragon climbing back up to their height. It wasn't long before the sound of Edrik's laughter found her ears…

"Edrik!" she chastised.

With the arrogant smile he had maintained all through their training together, the young man replied, "Just because we're the predators of the sky doesn't mean you shouldn't look up every now and then!"

Inara clamped her mouth shut before remembering to acknowledge the golden dragon between Edrik's legs. "Aldreon…"

Inara… the dragon replied.

Athis had told her years ago that the differences between Edrik and Aldreon were surprisingly few. Most dragons, if not all - a fact skewed by Aldreon - were humble but confident creatures who respected those who respected them. Aldreon was just as arrogant and boastful as Edrik, too sure were they of their superiority over everything else.

The golden dragon was the very definition of a *bad egg*.

"Master Thorn filled us in on your errand," Edrik continued as Aldreon circled them. "Have you found any trace of these *orcs*? Or are you enjoying the sights too much?" The young man gestured to Paldora's Fall in the distance.

"It seems the orcs prefer to move underground to avoid the light," Inara explained. "We have not discovered any tunnels, at least none like the one Master Thorn and I came across in the ruins of Karath!"

Sweeping his blond hair aside, Edrik shouted back, "Aldreon has spied a river just south of here! It stands to reason that even beasts as foul as orcs require water to live! We suggest searching in that area!"

It was quite the effort to keep her eyes from rolling, something the golden dragon would easily spot. "Athis and I were about to investigate the area around Paldora's Fall—"

Edrik and Aldreon were gone. The pair dived down and glided towards the river.

Inara wanted to ignore the rude little boy and continue on her own way. The Dragorn could feel the magic of Paldora's Fall rolling over her skin and calling to her.

Remember, wingless one. Just because he was granted the title of Dragorn a few months before you does not make him your superior. Your opinions matter and he should hear them.

How he was able to form a bond in the first place has forever been a mystery to me.

Their souls are alike. How you feel about Edrik isn't far from how many of my kin feel about Aldreon. Even dragons have their flaws...

Not you, though, Inara replied, nestling into the dragon's red scales.

Athis glanced back at her. *Any flaws of mine are opposed by your talents, wingless one. Now, let's see if we can beat them to the river...*

∾

The Crow stepped out of his carriage and craned his neck back to take in the ocean of blue sky above him. It had been an awfully long time since he had seen dragons gliding through the heavens but, on his journey through The Undying Mountains, he had seen one fly overhead *twice*.

He looked back inside his carriage, where a small pyramid, the size of his hand, was smoking, its metal frame charred from the exertion. A relic of ancient times, the dwarder had hidden The Black Hand's entire caravan from sight, mocking even the eyes of a dragon.

Such a long journey had taken its toll on a relic that hadn't been used for thousands of years. Still, The Crow was perhaps the only person alive who knew how to construct another.

With the dwarder depleted of magic and the skies clear of dragons, now was the opportune time to disappear under the mountains.

"Get everyone inside," he ordered Morvir, his first servant. "The chest is to stay with me at all times." He waved his wand over the small wooden chest and commanded it to float out in front of him, away from its carriers.

"My Lord Crow…" Morvir bowed his head before relaying the commands.

The Crow inspected the darkness of the cave, a source of fear for most. He was accustomed to the shadows but, in these mountains, the dark caves were home to another.

The Crow's wand produced a faint glow, a bi-product of the spell cast over the floating chest and, just as he had seen them six years ago, the eyes of the orcs reflected the light against the abyss. Morvir joined his side and added light from the end of his staff, pushing the guarding orcs back a step.

Stealing a glance at the sky one last time, The Crow stepped into the cave. The orcs of The Under Realm might be somewhat unpredictable at times, but they were allies none-the-less. The same could not be said of the Dragorn.

In its foul tongue, one of the orcs said, "King Karakulak has been waiting for you for some time, Wizard."

Learning their language had become a necessity over the last six years, since many of The Black Hand had been left in The Under Realm to assist with uncovering the ancient tunnels. Translating spinners were good when conversing with a single orc, but catching what everyone else was saying around them had proven enlightening, often saving a mage from a disgruntled or starving orc.

"Your every word delays me further," The Crow calmly replied in their guttural language.

They journeyed deeper into The Undying Mountains for what must have been many hours before they came across a dwelling of orc-make. Judging by the sigil of the broken skull stamped into the stone, they were entering a cavern that belonged to the Bone Breakers tribe. They were the first tribe to bend the knee at Karakulak's feet, thanks mostly to The Crow's knowledge of ancient passageways that gave the Born Horde a great advantage.

The space inside the cavern appeared to be massive, as if the orcs had hollowed out the mountains themselves. The Crow was sure to keep the chest floating out in front of him, more than aware of the interest displayed by the passing orcs. For a society that valued bones, they would consider the contents of this chest to be the greatest of treasures.

A foul odour that competed with rotten death assaulted his nose, leading him to the pack of creatures to his right looking down on them from a flat ridge. The monsters sneered and pawed at the ground with one of their six feet. They were somewhere between a giant wolf and a lizard, each saddled and mounted with an orc.

"Don't mind them!" the king of orcs yelled from atop the ridge, pushing his way between the beasts. "Their bark is worse than their bite!"

The Crow bowed his head. "I am sure we are safe in your presence, King Karakulak."

The mighty orc laughed. "I was talking to them!" He thumbed at the six-legged beasts, rousing laughter from the rest of the cavern. "The Garks are my greatest hunters, bred by the Grim Stalkers!"

It was a testament to his rule that the cavern, belonging to the Bone Breakers, had Karakulak of the Born Horde and orcs from the Grim Stalkers all under one roof. Six years ago, he would have been torn limb from limb for coming anywhere near their dwelling.

The king stepped off the ridge and landed easily on his feet in front of the chest. It was a drop that would have killed any man, though perhaps that was the point Karakulak intended.

Noting the king's interest in the chest, The Crow gripped his wand a little tighter. It would be a devastating blow to the cause should he be required to kill Karakulak at such a critical stage. Still, no one was to interfere with the contents inside the chest; they hadn't spent six years excavating Vengora just to have the bones spent like coins in The Under Realm.

The king led them into a smaller cave, draped in the Born Horde's banners of many fists gripping a double-sided axe. The Crow flicked his wand over his shoulder and cast a spell that shut the wooden doors behind him. He heard the satisfying sound of a whimpering Morvir before he and the rest of their caravan were locked out and left with the orcs.

"So this is it?" Karakulak asked, unimpressed with the simple chest. "This is why we have delayed attacking Neverdark?"

The Crow raised an eyebrow into the shape of a question. "Even now, after all we've done together, you doubt the results of my magic?"

Karakulak, now away from his kin, held back the typical orc response, refraining from beating his chest or boasting of their might. The king was smarter than his brothers and sisters. He knew real power when he saw it.

"My people will never accept magic, no matter how many victories we claim with it. When Neverdark is in ruins, I could build a tower to the sky fire in Gordomo's name, but if my kin were to feel I valued magic over strength, I would be... *replaced*."

The Crow examined the end of his wand. "Magic can be a weapon or a tool, much in the same way your wrath powder works. There are those in Neverdark who will wield magic against you, good king. Your people will come to appreciate magic when the first spells are cast and dragons are raining fire down on them."

The king slumped into the throne that had no doubt belonged to the chieftain of the Bone Breakers. "Thousands of years fighting amongst ourselves has dulled the minds of orcs. We have forgotten what it means to claim real victory over our enemies, our *real* enemies. I need my people to taste the blood of elves, dwarves, and your humans, Wizard. Only then will they embrace all that is required to defeat our foe and take Neverdark."

The Crow pulled his thick collar of feathers in around his neck, feeling the cool air of The Under Realm. "The orc was bred for war and so war they crave. With this," he indicated the chest, "it can truly begin."

Karakulak examined the chest. "We have produced enough wrath powder to level Neverdark, forged more weapons than we have orcs, supplied every region of The Under Realm with our kin, but now that you possess that tiny chest, the war can begin..."

The Crow calculated his words, never foolish enough to believe Karakulak was as dumb and brutish as he made out to be. The Fates had brought them together for a reason, and it wasn't because the orc could swing a blade better than most. The king was curious by nature, and curiosity often led to intelligence.

"You wouldn't have wanted to start the war before I complete this spell. Especially since you recently challenged the Dragorn and their pets, gaining their attention..." The Crow let his comment linger in the air, allowing the revelation to sink in.

"How do you know of this?" the king replied, sitting forward on his throne.

"I see all, king of orcs," he responded ominously.

The king tilted his head of horns. "You mean your little mages have been spying on us."

The Crow conducted his orchestra of lies with ease. "One day, good king, you will see my power for the advantage it is. On that day, you will stand as king of Verda, atop a mountain of bones, a king of kings!"

Karakulak tilted his head, taking in the leader of The Black Hand. "I see a change in you, Wizard. I see something your followers do not." The orc stood up slowly, deliberately. "With an audience, all I hear is, Kaliban this and the great Kaliban that..." Karakulak's dark eyes bored into him. "When there is but you and I, I only hear of *your* indomitable power, *Lord Crow*."

The Crow pursed his lips. "And I would counsel care, King Karakulak. If you continue to use such large words your own people may begin to suspect that I am influencing you, even controlling you..."

Karakulak let free a rumbling growl from deep in his throat. "You mock the orc?"

"I wouldn't dare," The Crow purred. "But I see an intelligence in your eyes, an intelligence I saw six years ago when first we met. It sets you apart from your kin and rightly so. You are fit to rule. But do not concern yourself with my faith nor the source of my power. Know only that it serves you."

That soothed Karakulak enough to take his seat again. "Why are you here, *now*?" he asked. "We were expecting you at Paldora's Fall."

"The skies are being patrolled by the Dragorn that *you* baited."

The Crow lifted his hand, silencing the king's rebuttal. "Thankfully, all is going to plan. The Dragorn can't stop what happens next, nothing can. I am here to ensure that you have held up *your* end of the bargain."

All the frustration and anger was drained from Karakulak's angled face and replaced with a sly smile. "I enjoyed hunting your beast of the sky! Judging by the nests we found, it had been in The Undying Mountains for some time. Still, it succumbed to our efforts. The orcs celebrated that day! My people hadn't hunted dragons for an Age."

"Two actually…" The Crow waved away the king's questioning gaze, too tired to get into the details of history and the passage of time that orcs knew nothing about. "I want to see it," he demanded.

Karakulak picked up his rectangular blade and sheathed it on his back. "Follow me, Wizard."

They left the private chamber and continued in the dark until they had left the Bone Breakers' cavern behind. Trailed by the caravan of mages from The Black Hand, the king led them through empty tunnels for some time. Only when they came across rows of orcs guarding the ancient stone did The Crow believe that they had reached their destination.

"Keep your lights low," Karakulak ordered the mages.

With the chest still floating out in front of him, The Crow dipped his wand to the ground, noting the fierce orcs pressing themselves into the walls and averting their eyes. It was by far their greatest weakness, alongside their less-than-average intelligence.

Two massive orcs, tattooed with the sigil of the Big Bastards - an image of an orc defaecating on a mountain - pulled hard on the heavy doors. The resounding creak of the wood echoed throughout the chamber beyond. The Crow followed the king and stepped onto a platform of rock, hewn from the mountain. Beyond the platform was a vast emptiness that dropped seemingly forever. Looking up, the darkness had no end above them either.

The two massive orcs closed the doors after Karakulak and The Crow stepped through, shutting out the mages and guards alike.

The king slowly walked to the edge of the platform, his movements somehow bold and cautious at the same time.

"Is it sleeping?" Karakulak asked aloud, eliciting a response from the previously unseen orc on the far side of the platform.

The orc made itself known in the faint gloom of The Crow's wand. There was nothing special about this keeper of beasts as he approached the edge of the platform, where the wizard now noticed the end of an impossibly thick chain. The orc removed a hammer from his belt and struck the metal of the chain, filling the void with the offensive sound.

It was soon followed by the movement of more chains, somewhere deep in the hollow. The Crow lowered his wand and the chest found its rest on the ground as he made his way to the edge. The distant sound of chains grew louder and the distinct sound of bat-like wings echoed off the rocky wall. He lifted his wand and fired an orb of white light into the dark, banishing the shadows.

"Wonderful..." he said, looking down.

Flying steadily higher to see them was a dragon of tremendous size and coated with glistening black scales. Eventually, it stopped beating its wings and gripped to the hollow's walls. It ascended fast and looked up at The Crow with brilliant purple eyes, blazing with hatred and hunger. Suddenly, the chains around its neck and legs were pulled taut and the dragon was halted mid-climb. A thunderous roar, unique in its sound, rippled over him and the king.

Karakulak placed a firm hand on The Crow's chest and forced him to take a step back before the wall of flames erupted like the fires of a volcano, eclipsing their view of the entire hollow. Both orcs could do nothing but shield their eyes, while The Crow watched the towering flames with a broad smile on his pale face. This would do, he thought.

When the flames died away, he peered over the edge and took in the sight of the dragon again. Upon further inspection, it appeared the beast had been severely beaten and tortured, his wings poked through and a handful of scales missing. A deep gash cut across his snout and over his left eye until it met a crack in his horn. They weren't old, either.

"You finally caught the dragon over a year ago," The Crow observed. "Yet he still bears injury…"

"What does it matter?" the king asked casually. "It will die in your ritual soon enough."

"You know nothing of what I intend for this dragon," The Crow quickly replied, his anger bubbling up. "You were to simply keep it until I required it. Nothing more."

"Until I give it to you, Wizard, the beast belongs to me—"

The king's next words were choked from his mouth when The Crow flexed his wrist and pointed his wand. Karakulak instinctively placed his hands around his neck, but magic was not something one could claw away at. He lifted his arm and pointed his wand downwards, commanding the orc to his knees in front of the other wretch. Karakulak's arm dashed out and stopped the orc from defending him.

The Crow took meaningful strides towards the spluttering king. "I have given you Illian on a plate," he hissed in the orc's pointed ear, ignoring the fuming orc beyond him. "From north to south and east to west, the land will belong to King Karakulak because *I* will it. You will know power unlike any has known for thousands of years. But…" He twisted his wand and watched the king's eyes begin to bulge. "If you interrupt my plans I will replace you as easily as I did your father."

The Crow turned his back on the king and returned to the chest, leaving Karakulak free of his spell and gasping for air. The orc panted and doubled over onto all fours. So sore was his throat that he couldn't even growl.

"What happens next is crucial," The Crow continued. "Without this magic," he gestured to the chest at his feet, "your army will succumb to the might of the Dragorn."

Karakulak picked himself up. "If you touch me with your magic again, Wizard, I will—"

The Crow whipped his wand up again and forced the king to the very edge of the platform. "You are far more intelligent than you let on, good king. Don't undo all that you have gained by flattening that learning curve of yours."

The wizard walked the short distance to the immobilised king. "We are in this together now. Without The Black Hand, every tribe of orc will fall to the men, dwarves, and elves of Neverdark. Without your army, the world I desire can never be. Our current arrangement sees us both claiming victory. Harm my dragon again and I shall be forced to re-evaluate our relationship..." With that, The Crow lifted the chest and made for the heavy doors. "Have it taken to Paldora's Fall," he called over his shoulder.

The king found his feet under his own control again and turned to face the only other orc on the platform.

The fate of the pathetic creature had been sealed the moment The Crow attacked the king.

Indeed, it was amusing to watch Karakulak grip the smaller orc around his chin and horns. The neck snapped with a loud crack and the king left the orc to tumble over the side.

The Crow straightened his robes and prepared for the rabble of ignorant mages on the other side of the door. He would tell them that Kaliban's will was coming to pass. Yes, he thought, that would pacify them for a while...

ALONE IN THE WORLD

Alijah Galfrey had lost count of the number of times his life had been in the clutches of death, just waiting for that malevolent entity to close its fist and take him to whatever lay beyond, but fleeing a horde of Sandstalkers on a tiring horse was perhaps the worst way he could imagine dying.

There would be no fighting back, no valiant stand, and nothing left of him to even light a pyre for. The monsters would rip him to pieces and devour every inch of his body. Still, he wouldn't leave this world with a full quiver.

The half-elf turned in his saddle and fired arrow after arrow into the Sandstalkers that reached out for Vighon, who was weighed down with Galanör's limp form.

The valley walls towered over them, funnelling the riders ever southward, offering no refuge from the monsters. Alijah sighted down his next arrow and let loose the shot that whistled through Vighon's flowing hair and into the Sandstalker's nightmarish face behind him. The creature screamed and dropped to the floor, a slave to its own momentum, before being crushed under the pincer-like legs of its kin.

Vighon drew his single-handed sword and lashed out to the

sides, giving the Sandstalkers something to think about besides how exquisite he would taste. Ahead of them both, Galanör's grey horse was the only one who would probably survive to see another day, fast as it was.

"We can't keep this up!" Vighon shouted.

Alijah could feel the fatigue of his own horse between his legs. "Keep going!" he called back.

As his last hope began to fade, his eyes caught movement on the rock face to his left. It was so subtle that Alijah assumed he had imagined it but, a moment later, the lower half of the valley wall exploded with life.

Vighon freed himself of more expletives than Alijah could register, but the half-elf had to agree with every one of them. Their chances of survival had been low, but faced now with a mob of cave trolls closing in from both sides of the valley was the nail in their coffin.

The lumbering beasts closed the gap on all four of their solid limbs, using their giant hands as feet. Their skin was coated in scales of rock that allowed the trolls to blend in with their environment. It also acted as natural armour that Alijah's arrows couldn't pierce.

The cave trolls roared and beat their chests in the brief moment before they waded through the chasing Sandstalkers, creating bloody chaos.

"Weave between them!" Alijah suggested, wondering if those were to be his last words.

Galanör's horse disappeared in the cloud of sand and thundering trolls who, thankfully, were far more interested in the horde of Sandstalkers than the riders. Alijah guided his horse this way and that, doing his best to evade the trolls and find a way through. Thanks to the curses spewing out of Vighon's mouth, he knew his friend wasn't far behind.

The cave trolls beat their mighty fists into the Sandstalkers, crushing them into the ground. The few who scuttled between the trolls never found the riders again, lost in the stampede. The roars and screams of the opposing monsters echoed throughout the valley as they rode their mounts to the other side and continued south, rounding a curve in Syla's Pass. Even with their cries growing distant, Alijah kept an arrow nocked and ready to fly.

The horses were only too happy to slow down, though Galanör's horse showed no sign of fatigue as it trotted back to greet them. Alijah could see that Vighon was ready to get down and rest, but he kept his friend going until the monsters could no longer be heard.

Transferring the elf to his own horse, Alijah and Vighon walked beside their own, leading them by the reins for the rest of the day. They could do nothing but walk through Syla's Pass and head south. Before the sun gave way to the moon, they followed a ramp that rose up into the valley wall and ascended to a plateau that gave them a view of the pass both north and south.

Only after the horses had given in to exhaustion and the pair had eaten and drunk from their supplies did Galanör stir. The elf sat up and groaned while rubbing his eyes. It took another moment for him to orientate himself and look upon Alijah and Vighon.

"Nice sleep?" Vighon asked between mouthfuls of Lirian wheat loaf.

Galanör found his feet but still required the valley wall to keep himself upright. "How far south have we travelled?" he asked.

"How far?" Vighon repeated, offended. "Never mind how far we've come! You have no idea what we've faced to even reach this far! I never thought I'd be so thankful to see a whole mob of cave trolls…"

"Cave trolls?" Galanör echoed, looking to Alijah.

The half-elf shrugged the entire exchange off. "We're about halfway through Syla's Pass," he explained. "We should reach Paldora's Fall by sundown tomorrow if we set off at dawn. Will you be fit to travel?"

"I'll be fine. Have you found any trace of The Black Hand?"

"No," Alijah replied before Vighon could say something witty. "The Sandstalkers and cave trolls were something of a distraction."

Galanör looked from the stars to his grey horse, resting close by. The elf could barely walk, but he made it to the horse's side and rested with his back to its ribs. There was a kinship there, between elf and horse - much like Vighon and every animal he came across - that Alijah had never experienced himself.

"You should get some rest," Galanör said.

Vighon stood up and pulled his cloak around him. "I suppose that's all the thanks we'll be getting..." he commented on his way past Alijah, seeking a new spot to find rest.

Once again, Alijah shrugged at Galanör's questioning expression. What else could he say? Vighon loved a fight more than any man Alijah had known, but the northman had a particular dislike for the monsters of the world. Saying that out loud, however, would offend him further.

The elf cleared his throat. "Thank you," he said meekly. "You kept me safe."

Vighon pulled his cloak a little tighter, his eyes on the valley. "It's not me you should thank. Ned's the one that took your load."

Galanör looked back at Alijah, clearly uncomfortable thanking a horse for anything. With that, their bartering of words came to an end, soon followed by Vighon's snoring. They had refrained from starting a fire, unsure what other monsters lurked in the darkness of The Undying Mountains. Under the pale glow of the moon, it wasn't long before Alijah noticed the elf's attention fixed upon him.

"You have something to say?" Alijah asked softly.

"I've never been one for saying much," Galanör replied, wrapped within his blue cloak and white furs. "But, I can't help but notice some of your gear."

Alijah glanced at the folded bow and short-sword standing against the wall beside him. His quiver, lying by his leg, was almost empty and in need of more arrows from one of the satchels hanging off his horse. Self-conscious of his things, Alijah pulled on the hood of his green cloak and had it cover a little more of his face.

"I've seen that blade before," Galanör continued. "The bow too."

"What of it?" Alijah retorted sharply.

The elf raised his hands. "I meant no offence, merely an observation. One doesn't easily forget a silvyr blade or the bow of an Arakesh for that matter."

Alijah glanced at the folded bow again. Its design was just as unique as the silvyr of his short-sword. Neither had been made for him…

"They were collecting dust above my father's hearth," Alijah said, though he wasn't sure why he felt the need to explain himself. "I thought I would put them to better use."

"They weren't given to you?" Galanör clarified.

Alijah couldn't meet the elf's eyes. "Nothing has ever been given to me."

"Your parents gave you life," Galanör countered. "They gave you love. The latter is more than I received from my parents."

Alijah rolled his eyes. "I will not be lectured about family by some ranger of the wilds. Elf or not."

Undeterred, Galanör replied, "These scimitars are better than any blades forged in Illian, made by the finest smiths in Elandril, yet neither of them has the edge, balance or strength of that short-sword. Do you know where it was forged?"

Alijah sighed, having said more about his past to Galanör in the last minute than he had to Vighon in the last three years. "I thought you weren't one for saying much."

The elf smiled. "Perhaps I just needed to find the right person to talk to…"

Bar feigning sleep, which he was seriously considering, Alijah could see no way of ignoring the ranger. "It was forged in Darkwell by a dwarf named Danagarr. It is said that the dwarf gave it to Asher by way of payment for slaying a troll in the area."

Seeing Galanör's eyes on the sheathed blade, Alijah picked it up and removed the short-sword. Under the light of the moon, the hourglass blade sparkled as if inlaid with diamonds. Ancient glyphs ran up the spine of the silvyr, adding an extra sting to any monster unlucky enough to feel its bite.

"Here." Alijah threw the short-sword into the air and the elf caught it easily enough.

"Magnificent…" Galanör observed. "It must be the only silvyr weapon in all of Illian. I wonder how he sneaked it out of the mines; the dwarves of Dhenaheim would not easily part with the metal." The elf looked up from the blade and his eyes drifted over Alijah. "Between this, the bow, and now that cloak, I would say you were about thirty years away from looking the spit of the great ranger himself."

Alijah had taken too many things in his life to feel guilt over a couple of weapons and a cloak. "Dead men have no wants or needs. But Asher had good taste, I'll give him that," he added with a disingenuous smile.

Galanör's playful manner dropped away. "Asher died so that your mother and father might live. Myself included, and your grandmother, even Gideon Thorn. I would say he had more than just good taste."

The stubbornness that Alijah hated to recognise as his mother's rose in him with ire. "I must be cursed. I left my home to make something of myself, to make a life out from under..." He bit his tongue and reconsidered his words. "Since walking into the world I've done nothing but meet people," he gestured to Vighon's sleeping form, "who have known me since childhood or people who knew my parents before I was born."

Galanör didn't respond straight away. "Maybe you were never meant to walk away from your family."

That brought an incredulous smile to Alijah's face. "You sound like a priest. We both know the gods aren't real, so let's not pretend something as ridiculous as destiny exists."

"There aren't any gods that we *know about*," Galanör corrected. "Save for Kaliban, of course, who we're all hoping is naught but fantasy. Perhaps us little folk aren't supposed to know about such beings or their plans for us."

"You know, I've decided you *are* someone who has a lot to say. And I've also decided that it's irritating." Alijah held out his hand for the silvyr blade and the elf obligingly threw it back. By the time he had sheathed it and placed it next to his bow, Galanör was hidden beneath the hood of his cloak and searching for sleep.

Alijah's choice of words gnawed at him for some time, keeping rest at bay. He had spoken harshly to an elf, known for good deeds, whose greatest curse was his eye for detail. There was only a handful of people in the whole world who could look upon his silvyr blade and bow and recognise them as Asher's. Yet somehow, just as he had said, the half-elf couldn't escape those who had a connection to his family and their history.

Forget it, he finally told himself. Forgetting his family and the life he had was the only way any of them would move on. It was his place to be alone in the world, even with Vighon by his side, an old friend who meant well but knew nothing of what toiled inside his heart. With or without him, he was doing something that mattered now, something that made a difference. Alijah repeated that over and over until sleep claimed him.

A DARK REFLECTION

G ideon Thorn's eyes snapped open. The sound of the crashing waves and the wind blowing through the torches came back to him. It was still night and the stars were almost exactly where he had left them before he began to meditate, telling him that he hadn't maintained his moment of peace for very long.

Rising to his feet, the Master Dragorn took in a breath as well as the view beyond his home. Halfway up a steep cliff, the alcove was dug deep into the rock face. For thousands of years, the hollow had housed the council's chamber as well as the Master Dragorn's personal quarters and the library. From the very edge of that alcove, Gideon was able to see The Adean below and the stars above with nothing but more rock face on the other side.

The archipelago provided the perfect place for the Dragorn and dragons to live in harmony, as it had done thousands of years ago, but even in this place, his home, Gideon couldn't rest easily. Here there was peace, but out there... out there was unrest in the north and a re-emergence of evil in the south.

The Master Dragorn sighed and glanced one last time at the restless ocean below, his attention turning back to the alcove. The torches lining the walls showed him the way, between the four pillars, and into the council chamber of hewn stone. The long table in the middle was surrounded by seven empty chairs and three murals carved out of the white cliffs.

Often he would stop and take in the history being depicted in those murals, tales of heroism displayed by previous Masters, but tonight, like so many before, he couldn't concentrate. Gideon stopped at the head of the table, beside his own chair, and contemplated which door to pass through. The one to his right would take him to his bed, the one on his left would take him to the library.

Ilargo's soothing voice sounded clear in is mind. *I would advise sleep, but we both know you're going to stay up late reading again.*

The green dragon wasn't anywhere near the cliff, but when Gideon closed his eyes he was sure he could feel the ocean spray on his face. Ilargo was likely gliding close to The Adean, hunting.

Orcs, Ilargo. No Dragorn has had to think about their wretched kind for five thousand years and now...

We should wait to hear back from Inara and Edrik, Ilargo countered. *It's possible we're dealing with a small band of orcs who are just taking advantage of the devastation wrought upon the land by the collapse of Karath.*

Did that seem like a small band to you? They filled the palace of Karath and I have no doubt there were more in the tunnels beneath.

The dragon probed his feelings. *There's something else, isn't there? Something that stops you from meditating or finding any rest for that matter.*

Gideon knew better than to keep things to himself. Ilargo was the other half of his mind that allowed him to process everything and discover a better understanding of not just the world, but also himself.

I can't shake this feeling that I have.

What is it? Ilargo asked.

The feeling that everything is about to change. The end of an Age...

The new Ages are only ushered in by times of peace or great cataclysms.

Gideon was all too aware of that fact. The Pre-Dawn had been the time of Atilan and the First Kingdom, a time that only a few knew about. The First Age began with the bonding of the first Dragorn, Elandril, and the rising civilisation of the elves.

The Second Age arose when the elves and dwarves defeated the orcs, five millennia ago, and a golden age of peace stretched across the realm.

The Third Age began when The Dark War came to an end, a thousand years ago, and mankind assumed control of the land, slaying many of the dragons and exiling the elves to Ayda.

The Master Dragorn had hoped that the defeat of Valanis would usher in the Fourth Age, but the kingdoms and their Time Keepers weren't in agreement that the current Age should come to an end just yet, despite the unprecedented peace.

The world was turning once again now; he was sure of it.

Gideon shook his head and made for the library door. Learning more about the orcs would help him to feel better equipped to deal with this new threat. Maybe then he could find some rest.

The library was a pocket dimension, a vast, three-tiered chamber, that shouldn't exist inside the cliff. Walking out onto the middle level, Gideon descended the step to the lowest tier, where the walls were lined with books and the floor was filled with glass cabinets displaying ancient relics and trophies.

The long table in the middle was already piled with various books and scrolls related to The Great War. Gideon had done his best to take in as much information from the tomes of the previous Dragorn and understand everything he could about the orcs. As complete as the records were, he felt there was always something missing and decided it was the perspective of the dwarves, who fought alongside the elves in the war.

Gideon sighed and lifted the top book, glancing at the title before throwing it down the table, towards the pile of books that offered the least insight. The last book he had read was about the ancient martial arts of the Mag'dereth, developed by Elandril during The Great War. The orcs were only mentioned in comments relating to the proficiency of the various fighting forms.

So far, the only book he had put to one side for a second read through was The Red Dawn. Written by Glanduil of house Myro, an elven Dragorn on Elandril's council, the book documented the earliest encounters with the orcs in Vengora. It was still lacking in the detail Gideon was searching for. It was the dwarves of Dhenaheim who came across the orcs first, not the elves or Dragorn.

The Master Dragorn dipped into the chair at the head of the table and examined the next leather-bound book. They were all starting to look the same to him. He needed to know the specifics of how the orcs travelled underground. Was this network still under Illian's surface? Had the ancient dwarves and elves found a way underground? Surely, the dwarves, great miners all, would have found these tunnels and sealed them.

Frustrated, Gideon pushed the next book aside and sat back in his chair. As usual, he was distracted by the relics and trophies that surrounded him, all far more interesting to look at. On the other side of the table, the display case held the horizontal blade of Alidyr Yalathanil, the long-dead general of Valanis. The short-sword had been plunged into the evil elf by Asher himself, a deed that saw Alidyr to his end. And what a violent end it was. The blade was charred and the exquisite hilt damaged beyond repair after the general exploded with powerful magic.

You're getting distracted, Ilargo warned. *You might as well seek out some rest. The books will have more clarity in the morning.*

Gideon dropped his head, feeling a failure. Perhaps the greatest evil that had ever challenged the goodly folk of Illian was once again above ground for the first time in five millennia and he, the Master Dragorn, had no explanation. He couldn't even assess the level of risk having only seen a band of them in the ruins. There were six kingdoms in Illian and he had never felt more thinly spread than he did right now.

Gideon, this isn't a war yet. You are behaving as if the entire realm is already under attack.

Gideon pinched his nose and screwed his eyes. **Something isn't right, Ilargo. I can feel it in my bones.**

I feel it too, the dragon replied softly. *But we can only react.*

What if reacting is too late?

A sense of resolve crossed the bridge between man and dragon and Ilargo's voice said clearly, *Then the Dragorn will rise up and rally the kingdoms of man, elf, and dwarf to see the threat pushed back.*

Gideon used the last of his energy to laugh to himself. **Only a predator of your renown could have such confidence.**

A confidence you should share, Dragorn. As I am the predator at the top of my food chain, so too are you at the top of yours.

I didn't feel like the top of anything running away from those orcs...

The green dragon filled his mind with a sense of understanding. *You ran because Inara would have fallen if you had stayed. Even Athis could see that.*

It was hard to argue with the logic of a dragon and impossible to argue with one who shared his very soul.

Gideon pushed back from the table and stood up to leave. As he reached the bottom step, the strangest thing caught his eye, halting him from taking another step. The Master Dragorn left the stairs and walked over to the long mirror that ran down the corner where the bookshelves met.

Standing in front of it, Gideon waited to see if he had imagined the ripple that distorted the flat mirror. Just as he was about to leave and chalk it up to exhaustion, the mirror rippled again. Gideon placed his hand on the cold surface and discovered nothing unusual about it.

He blinked once and there was a man standing behind him in the mirror. The Master Dragorn spun on the spot to face the threat, his hands already alight with the flames of his spell. There was nobody there. Gideon looked about, his hands still flaming, but there was no man but him standing in the library. Turning back to the mirror, the man was still standing there, beside the table.

"What is this?" Gideon demanded, half turning back to the empty library.

The man in the mirror smiled arrogantly, twisting his ancient features, and creasing the web of lines and scars on his bald face. Draped in black robes and crows feathers, the stranger stood very still with his hands by his side.

"This…" the stranger said, gesturing outwards with his arms, "is a form of magic that predates even your ancient order, Master Dragorn. Elegant, isn't it? Far superior to diviners—"

"Who are you?" Gideon interrupted, sure that he wasn't speaking to an ally.

"A common question. One that often bears little consequence. There is only one name that should matter to any of us. *Kaliban…*" The man pronounced the name as if it was the only word that existed. "Still, you are, after all, *the* Gideon Thorn, master of the Dragorn. You are strong among men and elves and the great Kaliban respects strength above all else. *My* order calls me The Crow."

Gideon closed his fists and the fire in his palms died away. "I take it your order is that of The Black Hand?" The Crow bowed his head. "I heard your god's name thirty years ago. He didn't impress upon me then and he doesn't now."

"Ah, but a part of you *does* believe. It has to after all that you've seen, and that part has given him life inside of you. It's burrowed deep and it feeds your fears."

Gideon could feel Ilargo's passion rising in him. "I have seen the things your order has done in the name of Kaliban. If your wicked god supports those crimes, I promise you the Dragorn will oppose him, regardless of the dimension he resides in. He wouldn't be the first god I've killed…"

The Crow clasped his hands in front of him. "You killed old men, pretenders, not gods. This is the real thing, Master Dragorn. You must have felt it… the turning of the tide, the change in the wind, the *shudder* under your feet. A new Age is coming, but not the fourth! The First Age of Peace… Something that will remain forever unattainable under the protection of the Dragorn."

Gideon kept his composure and clamped down on his snarl. "The Black Hand doesn't even number a thousand. I fail to see how you will usher in a new Age for Verda."

The Crow smiled. "Exactly. You fail to see…"

Gideon was growing tired of this little exchange. "Why are you talking to me?"

"History has repeated itself for ten thousand years. A threat rises and the Dragorn rises to meet it. Round and round the wheel turns. I wish to break this cycle. That begins tonight, Master Dragorn. Scholars will look back on this day and declare it to be the beginning of a new Age." The Crow took three steps closer in the mirror. "I'm afraid blood will be spilled this night and one of your pets will fall, never to fly again."

Gideon clenched his fist and his teeth. He wanted to lash out but there was nothing to attack but a mirror.

"More will die before you and I see each other again," he continued. "I have not seen your death, not *yet* anyway. I am sure it will be a good one…"

Gideon stepped closer to the mirror and met The Crow's eyes over his shoulder. "When I am standing over your dying body, *Crow*, you can tell me if *yours* is a good one."

The leader of The Black Hand flashed his arrogant smile again and faded from the mirror.

Ilargo…

I am coming!

Contact the council and put everyone on high alert.

What are we *going to do?* the dragon asked.

Gideon could think of only one place they needed to be.

17

EVIL NEVER SLEEPS

Alijah had never been one to use magic, but his elven heritage would forever tie him to that plane. It was that same connection that translated to the odd sensation he felt running over his skin and through his bones.

Looking to Galanör, he could see that the full-blooded elf was feeling the same powerful magic.

"What's wrong with you two?" Vighon whispered.

"Something is happening." Alijah's reply was cryptic, but it was also the only answer he had for his friend.

The three companions continued their climb up the ridge, careful not to misstep and give away their position. Peering over the lip, Alijah looked upon the majesty of Paldora's Fall, a crater to rival most cities and surrounded by floating boulders and broken rock.

"Now there's something you don't see every day," Vighon said with wide eyes.

Galanör's arm cut across them both and pointed to the valley floor. "The Black Hand…"

The two edged even closer to the lip and looked down on the cloaked mages, barring the head of Syla's Pass. Casting his eyes around the perimeter, more of the dark mages made themselves known, patrolling the outer edge of the crater.

With bright lights illuminating from the ends of their wands and staffs, the hooded men and women of The Black Hand stood out in the dark. Alijah counted more than a dozen before he stopped, coming to the conclusion that they were simply outnumbered.

"I suppose this answers our questions," the half-elf said. "They must be finished excavating in Vengora."

Vighon stretched his neck trying to see the centre of the crater between the floating boulders. "They must be digging for the crystal in there. Maybe that's what they were looking for in Vengora."

"No," Galanör replied softly. "I see no evidence of an excavation here; no tools, no manpower. The only reason necromancers would excavate anything is in search of bones."

Alijah pulled himself up into a crouch, careful not to disturb any loose rock. "Well, we aren't going to learn anything lying here. We need to get closer."

The three companions used the light of the moon to navigate the cliffs and climb down to the valley floor in the west. It appeared to be the area with the weakest patrol numbers as well as shadowed areas where the moon couldn't find them. Alijah and Galanör pushed on ahead, taking the awkward trek in their stride, agile as they were.

Vighon was less agile, but just as stealthy. His time in Namdhor had taught the young man a great many skills most would consider dishonest or downright dishonourable, but Alijah had always appreciated his ability to sneak up on others.

Galanör was less forgiving of Vighon's speed. The elf gave him many a look on their way around the crater, reminding them both that the ranger was used to working alone.

Together, they crowded behind a wide, but flat, boulder and watched the patrol of dark mages. There was a gap in which one, maybe two, could slip through undetected if they were quick enough. Coming to this conclusion together, Alijah and Galanör turned to look at Vighon.

"Oh, aye, you two might be a fast pair of shits," Vighon argued quietly, "but if just one of them idiots turns around and sees you, it'll only take a single spell to give us all away."

"We can make it," Galanör countered.

"No, he's right," Alijah agreed. "We need to see what's going on in the heart of this crater."

Galanör sighed and glanced over the boulder to assess the enemies in their way. "We could position ourselves to the north and south, wait for them to get closer or maybe lure them in. Take them both out at the same time."

Alijah nodded. "And hide the bodies," he added.

"Though..." Galanör mused. "Perhaps magic would be better to use."

"It'd be loud," Alijah warned.

Vighon sighed and shook his head. Seeing him do that, Alijah should have known that his friend was about to do something rash, but the elf was between them and it would cause a commotion to stop him now.

Proving his fears to be true, Vighon suddenly shot up and let free a small knife. The dark mage to the right took the blade in the side of his head and dropped like a stone. Before his body hit the floor, Vighon had retrieved and thrown another, larger knife from his other hand. This blade sank into the spine of the dark wizard on the left and robbed him of life before he could yell out.

Vighon straightened his dark cloak and tapped Galanör on the shoulder. "You get the body on the right, and you get the body on the left." Without waiting for a reply, he strode towards the edge of the crater. "And don't forget my knives..."

Alijah could only shrug at Galanör's questioning look of concern - after all, he couldn't deny that Vighon's unorthodox approach to life bore results. They hid the bodies in the shadows, removed the bloody daggers, and entered the crater together.

The initial declivity was steep and would force the threesome to climb down, but the floating boulders made it impossible to find a safe route. Every time Galanör attempted to make his way down, a giant boulder would silently glide past and scrape again the rock, threatening to grind him into the crater.

Observing the vast collection of rocks colliding with each other, Alijah saw another way to reach the middle of the crater. He tapped the elf on the arm and pointed up before a hop, skip, and a jump placed him neatly on the side of a boulder flying past.

He had to move quickly once he found purchase. Another jump prevented the adjacent slab of rock from flattening him as they came together. A glance below saw Galanör and Vighon copy his movements and find a boulder of their own. Using a strength that neither of them possessed, Galanör soon left them behind as he progressed farther into the crater.

Alijah dashed and jumped from one to the next, stealing a glance at Vighon whenever he could. The man wasn't as fast, but he cleared every jump as cleanly as the others. It wasn't long, however, before Alijah noticed his friend climbing too high.

"Vighon!" he hissed, hoping that the colliding boulders would muffle his voice from any mages. "You're going too high," he warned after gaining his attention. "Stay low—" Alijah clamped his mouth shut as a man in black robes walked directly under his boulder.

The Black Hand were traversing the crater via a network of veins that had been dug into the ground, saving them from any rogue boulders. He decided there must have been an entrance somewhere along the edge of the crater - somewhere heavily guarded he imagined.

The dark mage walked by, giving Alijah just enough time to leap from one slab to another without being seen or crushed. He took a breath, waited for Vighon, and continued through the maze.

The closer they got to the centre of the crater, the stronger the effects of magic were on his skin. It was somewhere between intoxicating and nauseating, but most certainly powerful.

Galanör caught his eye, resting on a high rock to his left. The rock in question was trapped in a web of vines that tethered it to the ground. It gave the elf the perfect vantage to observe the activities of the crater without having to stay on the move.

Together, Alijah and Vighon made their way over and joined Galanör on the rock. They had made it to the centre. The ground rose up here into a central dais, where, to Alijah's eye, the rock had been carved into a flat table. The burrowed veins, like the streets in a city, converged on the middle, allowing the mages to easily ascend and descend.

Looking up, the faint outline of a magical shield could be seen. It flared here and there when one of the larger boulders scraped along its surface.

On the other side of the dais, an enormous tunnel had been dug out of the crater. With only a handful of torches surrounding the carved table, it was impossible to pierce the shadows of that tunnel.

"Is there something moving in there?" Vighon asked.

Unable to answer, Alijah turned to Galanör. "What are they doing here?"

The elf ducked his head down instead of replying and the other two instinctively mirrored his movement. The sound of several feet ascending to the dais, out of the narrow tunnels, reached all their ears. Alijah dared to look over the ridge and see what was happening.

The Black Hand were filling the area around the hewn table, their dark robes hanging to the floor in the still air. Then the drumming began.

"What in all the hells is happening out there?" Vighon pulled himself up and joined him.

The drumming came from the mages stamping their staffs into the ground, perfectly in time. Through it all, Alijah was sure he could hear chains rattling in the distance. The mages to the right of the dais parted and a man, the only man without a hood, walked through the aisle.

"Who *is* that?" Vighon asked.

"I know as much as you do," Alijah said, close to his friend's ear.

Galanör was fixed on the bald man making his way to the flat table. "That's The Crow…"

Alijah tracked the man with great interest. The Crow was accompanied by a floating chest, tethered to the wizard's wand by the faintest of golden lines. As the chest came to rest on the hewn table, the stamping staffs came to an end and silence fell over the crater, filling the air with expectation.

Taking no notice of his followers, The Crow lifted the lid of the chest and carefully removed its contents... one bone at a time.

Alijah's eyes went wide as the bones slowly but surely gave shape to a person. It took The Crow some time to place every bone where it was supposed to go within the skeleton, but not a single mage protested about waiting.

Alijah could see that Vighon was about to ask another question when Galanör's hand wrapped around his mouth, silencing him. The three companions lay there and watched the skeleton of Valanis come together from skull to toe. When the bald man was finished assembling the skeleton, another mage stepped forward and removed the chest, while another handed The Crow a bowl of dark liquid. Then the drumming staffs began anew.

"Tonight," The Crow shouted, "The Black Hand do not forge a weapon, but an instrument of God!"

Alijah whipped his head around to Galanör. "We need to do something," he hissed.

"Only Kaliban has power over life and death!" The Crow continued. "We mere mortals can but breathe his life into the world! Through this resurrection, a force of nature will be unleashed upon the world once more. These are the first steps that history will note. Tonight, brothers and sisters, we secure the future our lord has imparted to us!"

The dark mages cheered and continued to stamp their staffs and feet in time. Alijah could feel the well of magic around them drawing in, as if The Crow was already focusing it.

"Galanör!" he whispered urgently.

The elf finally responded, "Not yet. A spell of this magnitude will drain The Crow. With this many of their order present, we need their most powerful to be at his weakest. We strike before he finishes."

Alijah disagreed. "If we misstep he will complete the spell and bring back the most tyrannical elf who ever lived. We must act now!"

Galanör's expression was as solid as the steel of his scimitars. "Not yet."

It dawned on Alijah at that moment that Galanör wasn't in command of him. With the exception of the brief times when Hadavad was present, Alijah answered to no-one and took no counsel but his own. He would listen to Vighon, of course, but only when it suited him.

With one hand ready to unhook his folded bow, Alijah positioned himself to leap into action. He froze, however, when the shadows beyond The Crow took shape. The half-elf felt his lips part and his expression fall flat as two purple eyes and a black head of horns rose into the light of the torches.

It had been some time since he had laid eyes on a dragon, but there was never any doubting one. Its black scales glistened like starlight. Its beauty, so exquisite, was barely marred by the scars and gashes that lined its face and neck.

Alijah was pulled into those purple eyes and the rest of the world was pushed away, leaving only the dragon and himself behind. The sound of the drumming staffs faded away and the rhythmic chanting, spewing from The Crow's wrinkled mouth, disappeared completely.

Something between a whisper and a gasp broke free from Alijah's dry lips. In a disorientating, yet hypnotic, haze, Alijah was suddenly looking back at himself through the dragon's eyes.

It was a feeling unlike any other and the half-elf had nothing to compare it to. As the out-of-body experience died down, Alijah was left feeling dizzy and disorientated to time and place. The drumming staffs beat in his ears again and Vighon was shaking his arm with concern.

"That's a..." His friend swallowed hard. "That's a bloody dragon."

The chains, wrapped around its mouth and neck, were suddenly pulled tight and the dragon was tugged back into the shadows of the tunnel. What possessed the strength to physically move a dragon was beyond Alijah's comprehension.

"That was Malliath the voiceless..." Galanör said in a tone of disbelief.

Alijah heard the words of both of his companions, but it still took him another minute to figure out how to use his voice again. "We should free him," he declared.

Both Vighon and Galanör met his words with confusion, but it was his friend who asked, "Are you mad? Did you see that thing? Besides being massive, it looked pissed!"

Galanör shook his head. "Malliath is not like the dragons of The Lifeless Isles," he warned. "He is wild, driven mad by captivity at Korkanath."

Vighon appeared more confused than ever. "The school for magic?"

"The same," Galanör explained. "The mages bound him by magic and had him serve as the island's protector for a thousand years. I last saw him thirty years ago..."

Alijah had heard this very story as a child, from Gideon Thorn. "You were the one who set him free."

Galanör nodded. "And after that, he tried to kill me on at least three occasions, so I wouldn't consider our history to work in our favour this day. I advise staying away from him."

Alijah knew, though he couldn't say why, that staying away was never going to happen. He had to free that dragon. He had to free Malliath.

"Look!" Vighon was looking down on The Crow.

Malliath's presence had distracted them from half of the resurrection ritual, which now saw the entire skeleton coated in a thick red liquid, poured from the bowl now discarded by The Crow. The bones themselves were visibly shaking on the hewn table, slowly coming together and sticking.

Valanis was rising...

Alijah had seen enough and had allowed the ritual to go on for too long. Ignoring the warning of a far wiser being, the half-elf snapped his bow to life and launched an arrow at The Crow's head. With a single shot, he could kill the head of The Black Hand, prevent the evilest of elves from returning to life and give Malliath a better chance of breaking free of his new captors.

At least he would have, had his arrow not impacted an undetectable shield around The Crow. The projectile broke against the magic, sending a ripple of energy across the sphere. It also alerted every member of The Black Hand to their presence.

The Crow looked up at them, his dark eyes connecting with Alijah. "Kill them."

After another day of searching The Undying Mountains, with Edrik Everard and Aldreon for company, Inara was ready to fly north and return home. The Lifeless Isles were a mystery to most, but to the Dragorn it was her home.

Athis was in agreement, tired of guarding his mind against the golden dragon. The last thing they needed was for Edrik and Aldreon to overhear their thoughts and opinions on the pair.

As grating as the pair were, Inara couldn't fault her master's logic. Together they had covered more ground and found several caves between them, but there had been no evidence of orcs or any bipedal creatures for that matter.

The sun had once again dropped beneath the horizon and their search had come to an end. The dragons soared through the night's sky, gliding in and around each other in perfect harmony. Below, the valleys and barren desert were shrouded in darkness.

"Over there!" Edrik suddenly called, pointing to the ground. "Aldreon has seen something!"

Without waiting for any reply, the Dragorn and his golden dragon dropped away. Inara looked around, aware that they were now flying over Syla's Pass, an area of the mountains that she had covered with Athis days earlier.

Aldreon is correct, Athis said. *The valley is littered with bodies.*

Despite Athis's quick descent, the shadows of the valley concealed any such bodies to the Dragorn. A moment later, Edrik and Aldreon disappeared beneath those same shadows, but Inara heard the golden dragon land and his wings close in. Only after submerging into the shadows did her eyes adjust and make out the shapes strewn across the valley floor.

Both Dragorn climbed down from their dragons and walked among the dead with their hands resting on the hilts of their Vi'tari blades.

"Sandstalkers," Edrik observed.

"And cave trolls," Inara added, kicking the tough leg of one of the giant beasts.

Edrik sounded bored already. "I would imagine this is a common occurrence in The Undying Mountains. It is a land of predators."

Inara focused on the ground between the bodies, her eyes doing their best in the dark to find any tracks belonging to orcs. The Dragorn birthed a small orb of white light in the palm of her hand and commanded it to follow her.

Athis walked over the bodies and bent his head down low. *There are footprints in the sand here.*

Inara ran over and waited for the light of the orb to reveal Athis's discovery. The red dragon was right, of course, having found bloody footprints walking away from the body of a Sandstalker.

"That's a wide print," Edrik commented. "I would say too wide for the average man, certainly too wide for any elf." The Dragorn crouched beside Inara and touched the edges of the footprint with his fingers. "It's deep too. You and Master Thorn are the first to see an orc in five thousand years; would you say this fits their build?"

Inara couldn't recall seeing any orc who didn't appear to be built from mountain stone. "They are a large breed," she replied. "Why were they out here?" she wondered aloud.

Edrik frowned, gesturing to the dead monsters. "I would say they were killing these beasts. Just hunting most likely."

The half-elf disagreed. "Look at their wounds. They weren't killed by weapons. Look at the position of the bodies. This wasn't a trap. The Sandstalkers and cave trolls were fighting each other. The orcs just came out afterwards and harvested what they needed."

"Harvested?" Edrik questioned. "They don't appear butchered to me, besides the obvious…"

"Look at the cave trolls," Inara pointed out. "Their hide is made of rock. How many do you see with their skin intact?"

Edrik turned on the spot, taking in the flayed trolls that surrounded them. "Master Thorn said the orcs already had armour. Obsidian he said."

Inara shook her head. "We are far from understanding how the mind of an orc works. For all we know they eat the hide…"

Aldreon's voice resounded clearly in all their minds. *Over here, there are more tracks leading away from the skirmish.*

Along with Athis, the Dragorn wove their way through the graveyard and made it to the edge, where the golden dragon was sniffing at the ground. The orb floated above and shed light on the new tracks, distinctly different from the prints of a Sandstalker, cave troll or an orc.

Horses, Athis confirmed.

Three of them, Aldreon added. *They fled the carnage and carried on south.*

"They were more than lucky to have survived this," Edrik concluded, looking back at the massacre.

"But who are they?" Inara asked, her curiosity piqued. "Orcs have lived underground for thousands of years. They don't use horses. So who would be riding south through Syla's Pass?"

"Mindless men of no concern to the Dragorn," Edrik declared. "If they aren't orcs we shouldn't busy ourselves with looking for them."

Inara had heard enough declarations spout forth from Edrik's mouth. "Well, I am," she glowered. "We have found prints most likely belonging to orcs, the only traces we have yet to find in these mountains, and now there are tracks to suggest that citizens of the realm are here too. It is the duty of the Dragorn to keep the people of Illian safe from all harm, so *I am* going to look for them."

Edrik raised his chin in an attempt to rise above the rebuking. "It is also the duty of the Dragorn to obey their master's commands. Master Thorn has charged us with finding further evidence of orc activity, not going after some fools who are too stupid to know where they aren't welcome."

No one commands a dragon, Athis insisted, *and I am going south to find these people.*

Aldreon took a threatening step closer to the red dragon. *A command from Master Thorn is a command from Ilargo.*

The four came head to head at their respective heights, locked together at an impasse. Inara had sharp words at the end of her tongue but she swallowed them when an unusual feeling rolled over the surface of her skin. She felt the hairs on her arms trying to stand on end under her leather jacket. The sensation eventually coalesced into a tingling at the base of her neck.

Edrik and both dragons had felt it too and they all turned to the south, where only an empty valley resided. Still, the feeling continued to roll over them, rippling across their bodies.

Magic! Athis exclaimed.

There was no denying it. They had all felt the effects of powerful magic before, but only on The Lifeless Isles where so many dragons were in one place. This was something else though, something that pulsed with great magic from afar.

Edrik looked at his hands, no doubt feeling everything that Inara was. "What could be using so much magic this far south of the realm? There's no one here!"

Inara dashed up Athis's front leg and left wing until she was sat astride his neck. "I don't know, but we're going to find out. Are you with us?" she asked pointedly.

Edrik glanced at Aldreon before bowing to Inara in agreement. "We are duty-bound, are we not?"

The two dragons took off into the night with Paldora's Fall in their sights.

~

"Kill them," The Crow ordered.

As one, the dark mages raised their staffs and wands and let loose a salvo of colourful spells that banished the shadows with a light brighter than the sun. It was hard to say who reacted first in Alijah's eyes, as Galanör, the seasoned warrior, was already leaping to the side and ascending the adjacent boulder. Vighon, on the other hand, yanked hard on Alijah's green cloak, sending them both tumbling backwards over the edge of the vine-wrapped boulder.

The rock was impacted by a plethora of destructive spells and violently shattered in every direction, drawing out their cries.

Alijah called upon every ounce of his elven heritage to orientate himself and flip in the air to avoid landing on his back. A quick bend of the knees absorbed the fall and he found himself in a crouch. Vighon, who was lying in a heap, jumped to his feet and barrelled into Alijah, slamming them both into one of the high walls of the crater's veins.

The half-elf would have found his friend's bear-like hug to be a huge hindrance in an escape attempt, but the shield strapped to Vighon's back saved them both. The dark mages unleashed spell after spell, filling the narrow space with dust and flashes of light.

"Run!" Vighon said through gritted teeth as two more spells pummelled into his round shield and bounced off, cracking the rock on the high walls.

Alijah had seen Vighon's shield take a beating from spells before and knew well that the glyphs Hadavad had etched into the strong wood had enough power to safeguard their retreat. Vighon, however, was unable to balance a swift escape with the resistance he needed to stay on his feet. As Alijah rounded the corner, his friend was launched off his feet and pounded into the rocky wall.

"Get up!" Alijah shouted, dragging Vighon down the next vein.

Coughing and spluttering, Vighon finally found his feet again and recovered enough to take his shield in hand. The ancient glyphs were sizzling and glowing a brilliant blue in their intricate patterns.

The half-elf nocked another arrow and let it fly past Vighon, his timing perfect. The projectile came to a sudden stop in the chest of the first mage to round the corner. His dead body quickly became an obstacle to those behind him, eager to give chase.

"This way!" Alijah beckoned, another arrow already resting in his bow.

The two ran through the maze dug into the crater's floor, following the twists and turns as best they could in the gloom. The occasional spell exploded against the rock and saw them take a different turn to avoid their hunters. The farther out they ran, the shallower the network of veins became, but the giant boulders above continued to collide and smash into the floor, raining debris down on top of them.

"We can't climb out here!" Vighon exclaimed, raising his shield to protect him from the falling stones.

Alijah looked back the way they had come. "We can't go back either..."

Proving his statement to be true, a group of dark mages rounded the sharp turn behind them and levelled their wands. Vighon raised his enchanted shield just in time to catch the first spells, though the force of them pushed him back into Alijah.

"My arm's going dead!" Vighon called back.

"Duck!" Alijah commanded, his bow aimed.

Vighon dropped only enough for Alijah to release his arrow and kill the closest of the necromancers. The shield came up again, giving Alijah enough time to reload his bow.

"They're here!" came the call from above.

Alijah held onto his taut line and looked up to see a dark mage staring down at them, his staff glowing with the beginning of a spell. There was nothing to be done to avoid the inevitable assault, nowhere to hide and nowhere to run. As on countless times before, however, luck always had its part to play in Alijah's life. A jagged boulder sailed past and swept the mage along with it, crushing him into the ground above them. The gruesome sound and dying scream were thankfully overpowered by the continued salvo of spells being hurled their way.

"I can't hold them back much longer!" Vighon warned.

The threat gone from above, Alijah aimed down the narrow vein and fired his next arrow, easily picking off another mage. It was enough to give their pursuers pause and take cover around the corner, forcing them to fire blindly in their direction.

Alijah dashed farther down the vein and found another turn. "This way!"

In the second he turned to face Vighon, a mage of The Black Hand emerged from the darkness, his wand aimed high. With no time to nock an arrow, Alijah lashed out with his bow and knocked aside the wand. The spell went off next to his ear to deafening effect.

Ignoring the ringing in his head, the half-elf clenched his fist and hammered the mage across the jaw. It hurt like hell, dissuading him from punching the man for a second time. A sharp elbow to the face drove the mage's head into the wall, putting him down for good.

Vighon came running up behind him, his shield smoking now as yet more spells bombarded the walls. They headed back into the maze of high walls and narrow veins, their sense of direction completely gone. The sound of fighting in the distance halted them both.

"Galanör?" Alijah whispered, or at least he hoped he was whispering.

Vighon sighed, slinging his shield over his back to soothe his arm. "I know *I* wouldn't want to bump into him down here…"

Alijah rubbed his ear. "Come on. We need to get back to the centre."

Vighon's hand shot out over his friend's chest. "You want to go back? Did you hit your head on the way down or what? There was a bloody angry dragon back there. Not to mention whatever's going on—"

The air was sucked out of the confined space as a bolt of lightning bounced off both sides of the vein, belabouring them with its incredible pitch. They instinctively dropped to their knees, only Vighon never made it as far as the ground. The northerner was thrown from his feet when the spell struck his shield, blasting him farther down the rocky corridor.

His hearing was shot, but Alijah's eyes caught sight of the mages through the debris. They were advancing from both ends of the vein, stepping over Vighon's still form.

Alijah coughed amid all the smoke. "Vighon!" he croaked.

Vighon didn't move.

"Vighon..." he mumbled, tears welling in his eyes.

The northman disappeared behind the massing mages, their black cloaks filling the narrow vein. Alijah did the only thing left to him in the name of survival; he went up.

"Kill him!" came the shouts from below.

Alijah leapt from one wall to the other until he gained enough height to reach the top. Rolling over the lip and onto the crater's surface saved him from the bombarding spells that exploded behind him. Again, his thoughts rushed back to Vighon just lying there, his body already forgotten by The Black Hand.

Two boulders converged on him, threatening death and robbing the opportunity to glance over the edge and see if his friend was moving. Alijah dashed out of the way but quickly found himself in the thick of a colliding rock storm.

"Find him!" The command came up from the web of veins dug into the surface around him.

Alijah dropped and rolled under another boulder, but he jumped up too soon and caught his shoulder on a smaller slab that ricocheted off another. Seeing the immediate need for two hands, Alijah collapsed his bow and tucked it away on his back, ready to climb.

Up he went, using every nook and cranny to get a hold on the floating boulders. He jumped from one to another, often clinging flat to the surface as he waited for the perfect moment to make the next leap. It was only a glimpse, but Alijah caught sight of Galanör below, his scimitars shredding the walls and mages alike.

Events had escalated somewhat. The feeling of guilt nibbled at his mind, but Alijah refused to feed it as his father's words echoed through time from a memory he could barely recall.

Acting against evil is the only thing a good man can do...

If they survived this, Alijah knew he would be repeating those words in his struggle to find sleep.

Round and round the boulders went. With each rotation, Alijah made his way back into the heart of Paldora's Fall. The last boulder he scrambled over brought him directly over the top of the dark tunnel. Malliath writhed beneath him, his chains pulled this way and that to keep him under control. Still, his handlers remained cloaked in the shadows.

Three more jumps and a partial fall saw the half-elf land safely on another boulder tethered by vines. The angle was awkward, preventing him from seeing past The Crow's black robes. The resurrection spell was yet to be completed it seemed. There was still time.

Looking around, The Crow was the only wizard present. Alijah concluded that those guarding the dragon could pose little threat since their task was mammoth by comparison to dealing with him. Just thinking about Malliath split his attention, clouding his determination. Alijah didn't doubt that the dragon was to be slain as part of this despicable ritual, and he knew then that he would never let it come to that.

The half-elf shook his head, focusing his thoughts. The Crow was protected behind a shield, but if the magic of Malliath was needed to complete Valanis's resurrection, perhaps he only had to free the dragon…

Alijah crept across the boulder and, using the vines, cautiously made his way down to the edge of the very centre of the crater. Being careful to stay behind and out of sight of The Crow, the half-elf pulled free his silvyr short-sword and slowly made his way around to the tunnel entrance.

From his vantage, Alijah could only see the hot breath of Malliath in the cold desert air. A quick glance to his side told him that The Crow was occupied and unaware of his presence. Hearing the chains rattle again, he moved with the noise and peeked around the tunnel wall.

Malliath occupied most of the available space, but Alijah couldn't miss the large creatures standing beside the dragon, each pulling hard on the thick chains. Their eyes shone in the dark, caught by the firelight from the torches around the dais. Their skin was pale, tight against a solid form of muscle that was crowned by a head of horns.

What were these beasts? He had never seen anything like them, but there were dozens of them surrounding Malliath. The dragon tugged against his restraints, forcing the pale creatures to dig their heels into the ground as they pulled harder on the chains.

This changed things. He was about to attack a large group of capable-looking beasts with a short-sword. Silvyr or not, it wouldn't be enough to see him free the dragon and make it out alive.

The magic pulsing against his skin intensified, the only warning before a powerful wave of magic washed over the half-elf, its source the dais.

Alijah felt pressed against the rock, as if the insidious energy pulsing out of the ritual was a physical force. A light had sparked from nowhere in front of The Crow, silhouetting his voluminous robes. The shaking feet of the skeleton could be seen at the end of the table, only they weren't skeletal anymore. Valanis had flesh!

Alijah took a breath. He had to act now, while The Crow was surely at his weakest. Freeing Malliath weighed heavily on him, but it was suicide to enter that tunnel. He had to kill The Crow...

With a steady grip on his hilt, Alijah pushed off from the wall and battled the waves of magic that poured out of the spell. Every step was akin to wading through a blizzard, the only sound that of The Crow's voice and billowing robes. His chanting sounded distant, as if his voice was in another world, echoing into theirs.

With one hand shielding his eyes from the light, Alijah brought the point of his short-sword to bear, ready to pierce his enemy's back.

Valanis couldn't be allowed to return. No matter what.

A cacophony of snarls and growls reached his ears from behind, but he dared not look back for any more than a glance. The creatures pinning Malliath could see him now, with a few breaking away to attack him. He couldn't worry about that now. He was so close.

In the shadow of The Crow, he approached the blinding light that shone over Valanis's body. With his blade angled upwards, he was moments from thrusting it up into The Crow's spine. Then, as suddenly as it all began, the light vanished in an even stronger wave of magic. The rock under their feet cracked outwards from the hewn table in every direction and Alijah was thrown back.

Dazed and bleeding from a fresh cut above his eye, Alijah reached out clumsily for his short-sword. His green cloak was wrapped about him and tangled around his legs. The dim glow from the surrounding torches was hard to adjust to after the magical light and it took him another moment to realise what was happening.

Only an inch from his face stood a wall of black robes. Alijah blinked hard and looked up to see the ancient face of The Crow staring down at him.

"And so it begins…" he said in his croaky voice.

Alijah looked upon The Crow's work. The spell was complete.

PART II

10,000 YEARS AGO

Sarkas hurried about his master's table, setting out the fine cutlery and the very best plates. Everything had to be perfect today. His master, High Priest Vyran, was hosting the rest of the council and The Lord Crow himself. With that in mind, everything had its place on the table, from the positioning of the candles to the layout of the various knives and forks. After six years of service, Sarkas could do it in his sleep.

He stood back from the table, satisfied with his work.

The sound of a glass shattering in the adjacent room sent shivers up Sarkas's spine. He rooted himself to the spot and clung to the back of a chair until his knuckled paled. He couldn't respond to the sound. He wasn't supposed to be able to respond to any sound.

A stream of curses were spat forth from his master's mouth. It sounded to Sarkas as if Master Vyran had cut himself. It would be he who got punished for his master's accident: not for the cause, but for the lack of attentiveness. He should be watching his master at all times.

Subconsciously, Sarkas rubbed the palm of his hand over one of his ears. It had been luck and luck alone that had saved his hearing. Strapped to that chair, with the other six children destined to be servants to the council, they had all suffered terrors that no person should be made to endure. Sarkas could still feel the slender pick entering his ear and the small hammer tapping the end. Those light taps should have caused agony and deafness, but the man had botched the angle, new to his job in The Citadel, and simply pierced the canal inside Sarkas's ear.

Hearing the agonising screams of the others, Sarkas did his best to appear in as much distress. Indeed, he was deaf for a time, since the blood filled his ears.

Now, six years later, he had the recurring dilemma of what to do when he actually heard something. The faster he reacted, the less he would be punished. But he shouldn't be responding to anything he couldn't hear...

Satisfied with the table, Sarkas decided that he would walk back into his master's chambers. The speed with which he moved showed no sense of urgency, therefore hiding the truth he felt.

"Where in all the hells have you been?" Vyran shouted.

Sarkas bowed his head and put his hands together as if he were praying. Asking Master Vyran for forgiveness was like asking the ocean to stop moving.

Dropping to his hands and knees, Sarkas began to pick up the shards of broken glass.

"You're more concerned with the glass than my hand!" Vyran waved his bloody hand in the air.

Sarkas had to ignore the words. He gritted his teeth and continued to pick up the glass as quickly as possible. Then Vyran's boot came down on his back. Sarkas was pushed down and stamped into the remains of the broken glass. Three times the boot came down before Vyran moved away.

Picking himself up, Sarkas was covered in cuts and gashes, his pale robes stained with blood. He pulled one larger piece out of his eyebrow and winced before the blood ran over his eye.

The searing pain had distracted Sarkas from his master, who strode over to the desk and retrieved his wand. Completely defenceless, Sarkas was ripped from the floor, thrown upwards and pinned to the ceiling.

Vyran looked up at him and sneered. "Useless maggot!" The master flicked his wand down and then back up, sending Sarkas plummeting to the floor before slamming him back into the ceiling.

Annoyed by the blood staining his robes, Vyran released Sarkas from his spell and let him drop to the floor, back onto the glass. "Fetch me a new robe!"

Again, Sarkas had a choice. Obey his master and reveal the truth of his hearing or lie there in the glass and await the next beating.

The young servant looked up, blood streaking his face, to the see the glowing end of his master's wand. That little stick held all the power. Even before his time in The Citadel, Sarkas had seen the power of magic, used by the Mage Knights. In magic there was strength and his master had all the strength.

Vyran flicked his wand again and Sarkas found himself stood upright in front of his master's furious face. "New-robe-now!"

Sarkas nodded and ran to the next room in search of an appropriate robe. After dressing his master, Sarkas was instructed to clean himself up and appear presentable before the council arrived. Holding back his tears, the young servant nodded his understanding and did as commanded.

A little while later, the councillors arrived and took their seats before The Lord Crow sat down. The head of their order preferred to arrive late and have the room stand to attention.

Outside of King Atilan's court, the six men of The Echoes council were the most powerful and influential in the entire kingdom. Sarkas hated every one of them.

The Lord Crow was an intimidating man, taller than the other councillors. The contrast between his black hair and pale face created an other-worldly appearance.

Along with his six brothers, all servants to the council, Sarkas lined the wall and watched their masters eat and drink as if there weren't people starving outside The Citadel.

It was at times such as this when Sarkas wondered briefly if his parents were still alive.

"This is good stuff," Master Vyran commented, peering inside his empty glass.

Sarkas reacted first and made to pour some more wine into his master's glass. He chastised himself immediately, having reacted a moment too soon in his eyes. Still, Master Vyran just seemed pleased to have his glass refilled and thought nothing of his servant's fast reactions.

The other six servants noticed. They always did and they always warned him to be more careful. They were the closest thing they all had to family and they protected each other as families should.

"It's not bad, is it?" One of the other councillors lifted his own glass for a refill. "You'll never guess who sent ten barrels of the stuff."

"He didn't?" Vyran asked rhetorically. "If old Atilan thinks that sending us some wine will replace the coin his court owes to The Echoes he's—"

"He's what?" The Lord Crow interjected. "He's still the king of an empire that spans three continents. He is still our king."

"Our king, yes," another councillor agreed, "but he is not a god."

"He certainly fancies himself as one," Vyran added before taking another sip.

The councillor sitting in front of Sarkas sighed. "Atilan has no respect for our order, Lord Crow. He needs reminding that the majority of his empire worship Kaliban."

The Lord Crow waved their concerns away. "Our great king is slave to a plethora of self-destructive tendencies. He will see to his own demise before too long, I have no doubt."

"Perhaps we could—"

The Lord Crow hammered his water cup into the table, silencing them. "I have to deal with that old wretch on a daily basis. I do not want to discuss him any more than I have to."

A tension, that Sarkas would have picked up on with or without his hearing, filled the room.

Eventually, the chamber was noisy with their merriment again as the wine took root in their minds. They ate like animals, ruining their robes and dirtying the floor as their food slipped between their clumsy fingers.

Sarkas was drawn to the wand poking out of his master's robe. Whoever held the wand, held the leash. It wasn't the first time Sarkas's fingers twitched and he envisioned the wand in his hand, pointed at the inebriated council. Not that he would know what to do with it…

As always, their conversation flowed towards the usual boasting about their power. It had been hard for Sarkas to hear at first, even *harder to control his expression, as the six men talked of their greatest trickery, passed down through the generations of their order.*

There was no Kaliban.

It was a simple truth in their eyes and a world-shattering fact for Sarkas. Years later, he stood to attention, as was commanded of him, and saw the lie for what it was.

Control.

They joked, believing no one else could hear them, that their great god had been made up centuries past to curb their civilisation's aggressive tendencies. It had grown significantly since those earlier days. Now, they were the dominant religion, commanding power, influence, and deep coffers. Even King Atilan couldn't touch them.

Learning that his god had been a fiction, a fiction created and sustained by these six monsters had almost driven Sarkas mad. It had been his brothers who kept him sane and reminded him of their need to survive.

Of course, Sarkas always asked: to what end were they surviving?

18

GREY STONE

Doran Heavybelly looked upon the kingdom of Grey Stone and conjured but a single thought.

"I friggin' hate this place…"

Nathaniel passed the dwarf astride his horse. "I thought we decided there wasn't going to be any more complaining?"

Reyna passed Doran on the other side. "We haven't even reached the north yet, master dwarf. I fear your temperament when we finally reach Namdhor."

"Oh, I'll be mighty displeased standin' in Queen Yelifer's court, don' ye doubt! But Grey Stone… there's just so many damn steps."

The kingdom before them was a sprawling mess, but it was almost entirely hidden within the base of Vengora's most southern tip. Directly ahead of them, the mountain was cut in half, providing a narrow ravine for the people of Grey Stone to set up their homes.

The ravine appeared oppressive from the outside, but inside it was only worse. Often compared to a cobweb, the city comprised of a network of ravines, its alley ways and streets, that all branched from one central courtyard.

Then there were the stairs.

Doran craned his neck to the top of the mountain, where a flat plateau housed the richer inhabitants of Grey Stone. The Lords and Ladies of The Ice Vales lived in grand castles and miniature fortresses above the din of the common folk. The upper city was connected by series of bridges that crossed the network of ravines.

Of course, to reach those dizzying heights, one had to traverse the stone steps carved into the high walls of the ravines. They zig-zagged from bottom to top and were themselves home to market stalls desperate to find any space in the cramped city.

Of all the cities Doran had visited in Illian, Grey Stone was the closest in its resemblance to the dwarven kingdoms; with the inhabitants forced to carve their homes out of the mountain stone and become accustomed to a gloomier life by torchlight. It was the smell, however, that got to the dwarf. All those humans jammed into the mountain without the appropriate sewer system or ventilation...

Doran wrinkled his nose at it.

"We could a' done as I suggested," the son of Dorain piped up. "If we had gone straight north to Wood Vale, I could o' collected the reward owed to me, an' then we could o' crossed the White Vale and been standin' at the foot o' Namdhor in no time!"

Nathaniel shook his head. "No one crosses the White Vale in winter, Doran. It's a cold death."

"Bah!" Doran waved the notion away. "Ye southerners are wimps...."

Nathaniel looked back over his shoulder. "Southerner? I grew up in Longdale, Heavybelly! That's as far north as you can go!"

Doran licked the icicles from his moustache. "Is it south of Vengora? Then ye're a southerner to me, laddy. Ye're all just summer dandies!"

Reyna's melodic laugh could be heard over the wind, which was quickly picking up some speed. As a dwarf, Doran was naturally predisposed to find elves on the irritating side, but damned if he didn't love the sound of Reyna's voice.

"So, how are we to play this one, Galfreys?" the dwarf asked, spurring his Warhog on. "Resupply, find somewhere quiet to stay the night, an' be on our way at first light?"

"Those were the days," Nathaniel muttered.

Reyna glanced at her husband before regarding the son of Dorain. "It would be improper of us to enter one of the kingdoms without forewarning the ruler of said kingdom. King Jormund is expecting us…"

Doran couldn't bring his lips back together as he stared at the grand keep at the top of the mountain. "Well… ye enjoy the good king's company, won't ye. Come get me when ye leave."

Reyna flashed her perfect smile. "Fear not, master dwarf. King Jormund has installed a pulley system. We will be raised to the keep without breaking a sweat."

The idea of breaking a sweat in this weather was preposterous, but those stairs took no prisoners. Doran, now somewhat happier, began to think of a royal reception and all the meat and ale that would come with it.

"Perhaps travellin' with the likes of ye ain't so bad after all," he commented.

The three companions rode side by side across the icy ground, making their way through the growing mist until the sounds and smells of the lower city were upon them. There was precious little light offered by the thick grey clouds that sat overhead, making the column of light from the ravine all the more inviting. Doran found it to be a confining sight, but he had to admit, and only to himself mind, that the warmth of the lower city would be much appreciated.

A group of armoured soldiers in thick fur cloaks broke away from the fire pit beside the ravine's entrance, blocking their path. The men were emblazoned with a bear's head, the sigil of house Orvish.

"What strangers arrive in the mists?" the captain asked.

Reyna removed her hood. "I am Reyna Galfrey. This is my husband, Nathaniel Galfrey. We are amba—"

"Ambassadors!" The captain bowed his head before gesturing to his men to attend their horses. "King Jormund told us to expect you. My men will see to your mounts and belongings. I will escort you to the Black Fort."

Doran dismounted the Warhog and slung his pack over his

shoulder. The soldiers happily took the reins from the Galfreys, but not one of them approached the dwarf's hog.

"He don't bite... *people*... *much*." The dwarf's honesty only acquired further scrutiny.

"My Lady," the captain began with one eye on Doran. "Has this dwarf been harassing you on the road?" His hand came to rest on the hilt of his sword.

Reyna adjusted her bow and quiver before answering the captain with perfect clarity. "This is Doran, son of Dorain of clan Heavybelly. He fought in The War for the Realm at both Velia and Syla's Gate. He's also two hundred years older than all of us and hunts monsters for a living. If he intended us harm, Captain, I am sure both my husband and I would already be dead. As it is, Doran is our friend and companion on the road. He will be treated as we are."

The captain bowed apologetically and ushered his men to take care of the Warhog. He then turned to Doran and bowed again, flustered and embarrassed.

Nathaniel's grin caught Doran's eye. "I love it when she does that," he said quietly.

"Aye," Doran agreed. "Remind me to stay on her good side..."

Free of their mounts, the companions followed the captain through the busy streets and alleys of Grey Stone's lower city. Hundreds of market stalls lined the ravine, each separated by braziers and torches. Walking past them all was an assault of sounds and smells as some cooked in powerful spices and others shouted out to sell their wares.

Most gave the captain a wide berth, the spear head of their entourage, but wide was a loose term in the narrow confines of Grey Stone's streets. Doran was all the more disorientated by the towering humans who piled in from every side, offering him only glimpses of his surroundings.

The dwarf craned his neck and tried to find the top of the ravine, but only the faintest silhouette of a bridge could be seen through the mist. It was only midday, but it could easily have been twilight. It was a miserable place, Doran decided.

After several minutes of navigating the central ravine, known to its inhabitants as *the way out*, they found themselves in the central courtyard, a junction that had seven more ravines branching off. Each one appeared just as busy and nauseating as the first. The stonework that occupied the courtyard was carved with the sigil of the bear, no doubt to remind the people of Grey Stone that they were part of a larger kingdom.

They just weren't invited to live among those who governed it.

The captain took them down another street that apparently specialised in the sale of fish if the smell was anything to go by. The lift Reyna had spoken of was fitted neatly into an alcove that ran up the length of the northern wall. Constructed from wood and surrounded with rails, the lift was ancient in design to Doran's dwarven eyes.

The call went out and the companions were slowly raised by the team on the pulley system. They ascended through the mist, leaving the sights and sounds behind, as well as the warmth.

The lift was rickety, but it finally raised them above the mist and onto the plateau that supported the upper city. Above the din was an entirely different world, a place where wealth, influence, and power provided a life of opulence and security.

Doran couldn't help but notice the increased number of soldiers up here. Having seen the chaos of the lower, and more populous, city below, the dwarf struggled to see the logic in posting so many soldiers up here.

The son of Dorain inhaled the mountain air, enjoying the icy cold as it stole his breath away.

The captain escorted them across several bridges, taking them over the ravine-like streets below, until they stood before the Black Fort, the home of King Jormund and all those of the Orvish line before him.

Most had called the slab of stone built into the mountainside an eyesore. Doran, on the other hand, felt it was closer in architecture to the homes of his own ancestors, with its straight lines and thick pillars.

Once inside, the captain handed them over to the master of

servants, a portly fellow whose name Doran cared very little for. By torchlight alone, they were taken through the dark corridors and into the mountain proper.

Doran rubbed his hands together. "This is more to me likin'! Big halls! Roarin' fires!" The dwarf wiped his finger along the wall and tasted the rock on his tongue. "Not bad stonework, either... for humans." The stout master of servants glanced over his shoulder and glowered at the son of Dorain. This was followed by a look from Reyna. "What?" The dwarf shrugged. "I said it wasn't bad..."

An extravagant hall of pillars and long tables, filled with the lords and ladies of the land, awaited them at the end of their journey. A fire pit dominated the centre of the hall, offering them only a glimpse of King Jormund beyond the licking flames. The king sat on his throne, situated at the top of a small flight of stairs.

Doran rounded the fire with his friends and took in the beastly man sat before them. His beard was as black as the bear pelt draped over his back and right shoulder. The animal's upper jaw rested neatly over his jerkin, its dark eyes twinkling from the light of the fire.

The dwarf was immediately drawn to the other bears in the great hall. The rug laid out at the base of the throne was a brown bear, as wide as three men abreast. The heads of several bears also lined the walls, though they were all dominated by the monster of a bear skull hanging over the throne.

Doran tilted his head up at Nathaniel and whispered, "He likes bears then..."

Nathaniel did a terrible job of hiding his smirk, but he did manage to nudge the dwarf, dissuading him from any further comments.

The master of servants announced, "King Jormund of house Orvish, the third of his name, ruler of Grey Stone and protector of The Ice Vales!" Jormund bowed his bushy head at the companions. "Your Grace, may I present Ambassadors Nathaniel and Reyna Galfrey." Doran sniffed loudly. "And their companion, Doran, son of Dorain of clan... Heavyjelly."

"Heavy*belly*!" Doran quickly corrected.

King Jormund stood up to his full towering height. "You are most welcome in my hall! Your journey from Dragons' Reach has been long and your errand is on behalf of us all. As such, it would be my pleasure to lessen your burden this day…"

Doran was licking his lips, praying to Grarfath and Yamnomora that the king was talking about roasted meat. The double doors to the left of the hall were swung open and an army of servants marched out with trays, plates, and trolleys of food and drink. A small band, previously unseen in the corner, began to play their ballads.

The king beamed through his thick beard. "I cannot say what reception will greet you in the halls of Namdhor, Ambassadors, but here, in the Black Fort, you will be treated as family!" The tables of lords and ladies cheered and applauded, just as they had been instructed, no doubt.

Reyna bowed her head. "We thank you for your hospitality, good king. Perhaps we could be given some time to put aside our travelling clothes before we dine." Doran scowled at the suggestion.

"Of course!" King Jormund replied after a moment's pause. He flicked his wrist and the servants reversed direction and disappeared back into the kitchens.

The dwarf sighed. "Elves…"

Still attired in his black and gold armour, Doran finally found the hard wood of a bench beneath him and a buffet of meats sprawled out before him. The dwarf smacked his lips as the smell of various meats and ales seduced his senses.

The smiles and welcomes he received were somewhat reserved when compared to the Galfreys. Most looked upon Reyna in awe, fascinated by her pointed ears and remarkable complexion. Many of the ladies admired Nathaniel's smooth chiselled jaw, a look reserved only for dwarven babies in Doran's eyes.

"I don't get it," the dwarf announced, ignoring Reyna's deliberate glance at the king, who sat at the head of their table. "Ye might as well be human in appearance," the dwarf explained. "Why does everyone get transfixed by the sight o' ye?"

Reyna replied, "The alliance between the elves of Ayda and the men of Illian has been strong for thirty years." The elf looked at King Jormund, who nodded and lifted his cup to the notion. "But," Reyna continued lightly, "even with a small population of elves settling down in The Moonlit Plains, there are very few who have actually seen an elf. My people are very private in nature."

Doran ripped a chunk out of his chicken leg. "I'm one o' two dwarves who calls Illian home, yet all I ever get is funny looks."

Nathaniel leaned down. "That's because of the smell..."

Doran whipped his head up at the man with a face of disgust. Then the dwarf sniffed under his arm and the two fell into laughter. It wasn't long before the king pulled Reyna into deep conversation, an opportunity never to be missed. The band continued with their songs and the ale flowed freely. The son of Dorain could get used to this, he thought.

"Do ye get this everywhere ye go, then?" he asked Nathaniel, saving the man from a dull conversation with one of Grey Stone's lords.

"Mostly," the old knight admitted. "They believe Reyna is the key to Ayda. All these kings and queens ever want is the knowledge of the elves. They want to know how they build their towers so high. How they make forests grow from nothing. Where their source of magic comes from." Nathaniel swallowed the last of his ale. "The list goes on."

Doran dropped the bare leg bone and reached across the table for a slab of beef. "What abou' that place in The Moonlit Plains? Ily... Ilytho... Bah! Elves and their names!"

"Ilythyra," Nathaniel said. "Most are too afraid to even approach their woodland home. A shame really. As private as they are, the elves of Ilythyra would happily welcome humans as their guests. There are only a hundred or so living there."

Doran nodded his head as he clamped down on the beef. "A hunnered elves living in Illian and dragons flyin' over the land! What a time to be alive, eh?"

A hand cut between them with a fresh jug of ale. "More ale, me Lord?"

"Oh, aye!" Doran cheered.

The dwarf watched the froth reach the top of his tankard where his eyes quickly wandered to the wrist of the man pouring the ale. From the wrist up, every inch of the servant's skin was covered in tattoos. Doran looked up at the man, who quickly lifted his collar to hide what appeared to be more tattoos, before he left their table.

The son of Dorain couldn't put his finger on why the servant's appearance had bewitched him. Servants, after all, were allowed tattoos and they were allowed to look like they had met the wrong end of a shovel more than once. Still, with a fresh ale slugging down his throat, Doran couldn't put his finger on it.

"Master dwarf!" King Jormund called from the head of the table. "The entire realm will be in debt to you after assisting the ambassadors in the north. Come, tell us something about the mighty dwarves of Dhenaheim."

Their half of the table grew quiet, eager to hear anything new that would bring entertainment to their tedious lives. Even through the haze of drink, Doran noted Reyna's displeasure at the king's direct question. Alas, the king hadn't actually asked him a question, but it would be foolish to deny his request.

"Me kin are a folk o' few talents, in truth," Doran began. "They can inhale drink like fish inhale water. They can work silvyr better than any man or elf can work steel an' iron. But, a dwarf's greatest talent…" Doran kept them waiting while he finished the last of his tankard off. "Is killin' other dwarves!"

His last statement surprised even the Galfreys. Doran ignored their looks and squeezed the ale out of his blond beard until every drop was back in his tankard.

King Jormund finally replied, "I could say the same about my own people."

Doran shook his head and created two of everything in his vision. "Yer little feuds over this and that pale compared to the wars that rage beyond Vengora. An' they are *wars*! Since me kin left

Vengora, they've done nothin' but spend the last five thousand years buryin' their axes in each other's heads."

"What are they fighting over?" the king asked.

Doran burped and wiped his moustache. "Ye name it, they kill for it. Land, mines, honour, gold. When I was only a lad, I remember two clans goin' to war over the length o' their beards!" The dwarf's gaze got away from him and he stared right through the table. "An ocean o' blood because one clan thought it was blasphemous to grow yer beard past yer knees…"

"Blasphemous?" the king echoed. "Your people have religion, then?" Jormund gestured to the pillars, where carvings of Atilan, the king of the gods, watched over their feast.

"Oh, aye!" Doran responded, his gaze focusing on those around him again. "We've got gods… real ones!" Nathaniel nudged his leg under the table. "I mean no offence o' course. Me kin worship Grarfath an' Yamnomora, the mother an' father o' the world. They made us from the mountain stone, yerselves from the mud, an' elves from the bark."

"Doran…" Reyna's cautioning voice took a moment longer than it should have to get through to the dwarf.

Nathaniel added, "I thought you said dwarves inhaled drink."

Doran blinked hard. "Aye, we can inhale it. I didn't say anythin' about handlin' it!"

The son of Dorain blinked one last time before he fell over the back of the bench and passed out on the cold stone.

19

ASTARI

Lying awkwardly on the ground, Alijah could only look in horror from The Crow to the figure trying to roll off the hewn table. He had never seen Valanis in the flesh, born, as he was, years after the tyrant's demise, but he was certain the figure struggling to sit up was not Valanis or even an elf, for that matter.

It was a man…

Disorientated and off balance, the man looked from his own hands to the world around him, taking in the floating boulders, the chained dragon, and the mysterious pale creatures harassing it. His eyes finally fell on Alijah and The Crow, adding to his confusion.

The stranger's focus quickly shifted to the silvyr short-sword resting in Alijah's hand. The recognition in the man's eyes brought with them revelation for the half-elf. The Black Hand hadn't resurrected Valanis.

They had resurrected Asher!

Alijah jumped up with a start, ready to lash out at The Crow and grab the old ranger. For all his skill and speed, however, The Crow's magic was far superior.

A black wand shot up and struck Alijah with a spell that sent a shiver through to his core. Then he couldn't move. Alijah blinked and shifted his eyes frantically, desperate to move a single limb. It was no use; The Crow had immobilised him, freezing him to the spot with magic Alijah had never seen before.

Asher swung his legs over the table, his first instinct to get in the middle of whatever was happening, but his legs had forgotten how to walk. The ranger collapsed in a heap, catching the hewn table at the last second to keep himself upright.

"What's…" Asher shook his head, blinking hard. "What's happening? Who are…"

"Hush now, child." The Crow walked back up to the dais and cupped the ranger's jaw. "You have found new life—"

Asher batted The Crow's hand away from his face. "Get… away from me." The ranger attempted to crawl away but, again, his new bones couldn't support him.

"I'm afraid," The Crow continued, "it takes some time before you acclimatise to the weight of the world. But fear not." The dark wizard turned back and glanced at Malliath. "I have just the thing to restore your strength."

Alijah groaned from within his spell. Whatever they had brought Asher back for would never be a good thing but, right now, the half-elf found himself far more concerned with Malliath's life. He couldn't let anyone hurt him!

"Bring the beast," The Crow commanded.

Alijah shifted his eyes to the right, his sight limited. The pale creatures heaved and pulled the chains as others prodded the dragon's hide with spears, ushering it towards the dais. Malliath growled, but the chains wrapped around his mouth wouldn't budge.

The Crow flicked his wand over Asher and the naked ranger was flung back onto the table. He, too, groaned and struggled to move, but appeared as frozen as Alijah, helpless to defend himself. The Crow moved around the table, giving the half-elf a better view of everything, including Malliath, who was forced to stop a few feet from the table.

The bald necromancer blew into the end of his wand and the tip glowed orange from the sizzling heat. "Mr. Galfrey," The Crow called, meeting his eyes across the prone ranger. "I apologise for the pain this is about to cause."

That statement made no sense to Alijah until The Crow pressed the end of his wand into Asher's chest. An intricate pattern glowed bright orange around Malliath's left eye and the dragon tried to roar. All at once, Asher, Malliath, and even Alijah were groaning and trying to shout in agony.

The Crow moved his burning wand around Asher's chest and, as he did, the pattern around Malliath's eye flared with roasting magic. The ritual felt as if it would never end for Alijah, though the pain wasn't in his chest or around his eye. The pain cut at him somewhere far deeper, fracturing his mind, and clawing at his insides.

The half-elf couldn't understand why he was experiencing anything at all, but he was in too much pain to take a moment and consider the circumstances.

At last, The Crow lifted his wand from Asher's smoking chest and the pain finally stopped. The ranger had passed out from the pain, but The Crow wasn't done with him. The necromancer walked around to the other side of the table and uttered a new incantation into his wand. This time, the tip came to life with a sizzling green end.

The new jolt of pain awoke the ranger in a fit of rage. Asher spat and his eyes bulged as The Crow etched a new pattern into the other side of his chest. Alijah felt no pain at first, but once Malliath began writhing within his chains, the pain expanded across his right chest muscle, burning with fire.

When The Crow had finished with this new spell, he released both Asher and Alijah from their imprisonment. The half-elf fell to the floor with weak knees. His insides felt restless and his skin far too sensitive. Most of all, his chest stung as if touched by fire, yet a quick inspection proved his flesh to be intact.

"Rise," The Crow announced over the ranger. "Rise, Asher, the first Dragon Knight of a new Age!"

Alijah looked from Asher to Malliath, struggling to comprehend the meaning of that title. It couldn't possibly mean what he thought it did. There was no magic that could force such a bond...

Asher performed exactly as commanded, only this time, he had no trouble finding the strength to stand. His face was void of any expression, the life taken from his blue eyes.

Alijah used the tip of his silvyr blade to heave himself up and back onto his feet. Asher ignored the half-elf and walked towards Malliath instead, though it was notable that the dragon had ceased its struggling.

"Don't touch him!" Alijah warned, raising his short-sword.

The pale creatures abandoned their chains upon hearing his threat and formed a line between Alijah and the ranger. Asher glanced at him but didn't pause as he approached the black dragon's head.

Alijah took in the sight of these beasts, their bodies exposed in the firelight. They all wore helmets that formed perfectly around their variation of horns but, most notably, the visors were very narrow, limiting their view. They were all well-muscled and larger than the half-elf; a threatening sight even without their jagged blades and hooked spears.

Beyond them, Asher went about removing the chains from Malliath's head and limbs. The dragon, a furious-looking creature, should have attacked them all immediately. But he didn't. Malliath appeared as content as the ranger, shrugging off the loose chains.

"You see, Mr. Galfrey," The Crow said, "nothing is what you think it is."

The revelation that Asher had been brought back to life was a struggle to comprehend, even more so when distracted by the pale beasts surrounding him.

It wasn't long before Asher came back into view, stepping out from behind Malliath's head. The old ranger had donned black leathers and chainmail as he fastened his light armour into place. A dark cloak flowed out behind him, completing the menacing look.

The torchlight exaggerated the scar across the ranger's right cheek and Alijah noticed the fabled black-fang tattoo under his left eye.

He really was back…

Without a word, Asher climbed onto Malliath's neck, where Alijah spotted a saddle strapped between the dragon's horns: an addition that no Dragorn would ever place upon their dragon companion. Malliath flexed his wings and the pale creatures between him and Alijah shuffled forwards, distracted by the dragon's enormous bulk.

The half-elf could see what was about to happen and the opportunity it would afford him.

Malliath roared once and took off into the floating boulders above. Most of the rock was pushed aside by force alone, but the dragon proved nimble and weaved between the larger slabs until he and Asher had broken free of Paldora's Fall entirely.

The sudden take off disorientated the horned creatures and Alijah took advantage. There was a rage born in him, its origin unknown to the half-elf, but use it he did. With great speed, he dashed within arm's reach and swiped his silvyr blade, cutting through the exposed neck of the nearest beast.

Dropping into a roll, he came up on the other side of a spear-wielder and thrust the tip of the blade up through the creature's armpit and into its neck. That was all the surprise he had to use before the others rounded on him with growls akin to Malliath's.

"Fight well, Mr. Galfrey," The Crow said from the dais. "Your journey is to be longer than most…"

Alijah could only glimpse the departing Crow between the beasts that came at him. They were stronger than him, but not as fast. Rather than parry their blows and jabs, he evaded and weaved between them, lashing out where he could to draw blood and wear them down. It soon became clear, however, that these monsters wouldn't tire as any man would.

One misstep saw the end of a spear whip him across the face, turning him to the large boot of another. The force of the kick lifted him from his feet and sent him rolling down from the dais, his blade clattering against the rock. Without a breath in his lungs, he was helpless to even yell when a meaty hand gripped the back of his neck.

Being lifted and brought face to face with one of these things was made all the more unpleasant by its rotten breath. Through the slit in its obsidian helmet, Alijah could see two reflective orbs staring back at him like a piece of meat. With its free hand, the creature raised its sword, ready to run him through.

Again, that rage welled up in him, a rare emotion that he had experienced only once or twice in his whole life. Alijah brought up his leg and thrust it into the creature's sword arm, preventing it from bringing the tip to bear. Using his hands, the half-elf grabbed one of its horns and tore the helmet free from its demonic face.

Exposed to the light, the creature shut its eyes as tightly as possible and yelled out in a language Alijah couldn't even begin to understand. Favouring the protection of its eyes apparently, the beast released the half-elf who wasted no time driving his silvyr blade up into the soft skin under the jaw. The weight of the falling creature forced Alijah to bend with it or risk losing the short-sword.

With three of their own dead at his feet, Alijah had hoped that the rest of the pale skins would back off, but he had only spurred them on. They beat their stone-like chests and roared in defiance of his survival. Alijah had a roar of his own just waiting to be unleashed when he noticed the increasing number of eyes reflecting light in the tunnel.

Like ghosts from the abyss, more of the creatures walked out of the shadows, clad in obsidian armour and wielding an array of weapons. An almost arrogant rage still lingered under the surface, as if he could take them all on and make them suffer his wrath. Thankfully, the gambler in him saw the odds stacked against him and sobered such violent emotions.

Alijah slowly backed up, towards the hewn table, sure to keep them all in his vision. A commotion behind him told all of his senses that he was about to come under attack, but the assault never came. Alijah dared to turn around and to his amazement, standing on the table, was an old friend.

"Hadavad!" he exclaimed.

The mage lifted his staff and slammed it down hard into the rock. The spell on the end of his lips was lost when the staff produced a light so bright it could have been the rising sun. The pale skins roared and, in some cases, even screamed in a manner unbefitting of their ferocious appearance.

Alijah shielded his own eyes from such an offensive light and, in so doing, spotted Galanör behind Hadavad. The elf was supporting Vighon under one arm, though his friend looked hardly with it.

Turning away from the light, the pale skins were fleeing the magic of Hadavad's staff, taking shelter inside the tunnel.

"We need to get out of here!" Galanör called.

Hadavad lifted his staff and the magic drew back into the end, leaving the dais in the low light of the torches. Alijah ran up to the table with a hundred questions etched across his face.

Seeing Vighon's haggard face stopped him from asking a single one of those questions.

Galanör happily handed his care over. "He hit his head, he'll be fine soon enough."

Vighon had just enough energy to stay on his feet, though Alijah's support was still needed to give him direction.

"Hadavad?" The half-elf said the mage's name hoping that all of his questions would be heard.

Hadavad jumped down from the table with a mad look about him. "Has he returned, boy?" The mage took no notice of Vighon in Alijah's care and gripped his arms. "Has he returned? Has Valanis been brought back?"

Alijah wanted to answer but the roar of a dragon broke through the floating boulders and filled them all with dread. The sound of growls and metal on metal spilled out of the tunnel a moment later, the creatures' thirst for blood renewed.

Galanör pulled free his twin scimitars. "Follow me!"

With no time to barter words, the four companions made their way down from the dais and into the narrow veins that spread throughout the crater. The bodies of Black Hand mages littered the ground, making Alijah's job of getting Vighon through the maze all the harder.

The growls of the pale-skinned creatures echoed through the rocky veins. It wasn't long before they came charging through with their weapons brandished high. Hadavad ushered the companions on while he lingered behind and loosed a destructive spell. The boom was deafening, but it gave the monsters pause and the four of them more time to escape.

"This way!" Hadavad pushed past and took them another way which quickly led them up to the lip of the crater.

Galanör made the climb first and pulled Vighon up. Hadavad commanded Alijah to go next while he kept watch down the narrow ravines.

They were all together again soon enough and crossing the rocky terrain to find their horses. It was a hard and slower climb with Vighon still nursing a sore head, but at least Hadavad was with them now, his magic an added weapon in their collective arsenal.

"Quickly now," Hadavad called. "Our enemy favours the dark and…" The mage let his words go, his attention fixed on the sky behind the others.

Alijah hefted Vighon and turned back to see what had transfixed the mage. He already knew what sight would greet him.

"Get on the horses!" Galanör yelled.

Alijah gestured for the mage to take his horse while he climbed onto Ned. The elf helped him get Vighon over the saddle, just as Vighon had done with Galanör, and together they rode hard for the north.

Malliath's flapping wings found his ears before Alijah's eyes settled on the dragon. As the boulders floating around Paldora's Fall shifted and moved, the light from the centre shone free into the night and caught Malliath's dark scales. He was coming right for them.

The dragon's roar resounded over the land, exaggerated by the rising valley walls. Malliath opened his maw and looked to snatch Alijah from his saddle. Hadavad raised his staff and emitted another orb of brilliant light. It wasn't harmful magic, but it was enough to blind the dragon and send him back into the sky. His thick, spiky tail scraped the ground behind Ned's galloping legs and kicked up a shower of sand and dirt.

"We can't outrun him!" Galanör shouted.

Malliath had flown ahead of them and was already banking to turn back around. They were now galloping towards the dragon in a valley that offered a single direction. Unfortunately, this was also the time Vighon began to regain his senses and the northerner's groggy voice soon broke into a warning cry, as if they weren't aware of the danger flying towards them.

The black dragon dropped into the valley and glided towards them, his mouth open and the smallest flicker of light visible at the back of his throat. He meant to burn them.

"Straighten up!" Alijah barked at Vighon, intending to direct Ned sharply to the left.

It was too late. Malliath was almost on top of them and his fiery breath couldn't be denied. They were all about to die.

But death would have to wait, it seemed.

From over their heads, a red dragon soared into the fray, forcing them all to duck as it glided down in front of them. This new dragon flew so low to the ground that its feet thundered across the rock and launched it back into the air, where both wyrms collided in a violent clash of claws and gnashing jaws.

Sand was kicked into the air and the riders could do nothing but gallop through the cloud and hope to avoid the swinging tails. Alijah blinked the debris from his eyes and tried to glimpse the warring dragons as they collided into the valley wall. A cascade of rock broke away and fell into the valley like a waterfall, adding more plumes of sand to mask their battle.

"Dragons!" Vighon shouted.

Alijah jostled with his friend and the shield on his back to better see the valley in front of them. The dragons, capable of covering a greater distance in a fraction of the time, clashed overhead and dropped into the valley before them. The riders pulled hard on their reins and narrowly avoided the black tail that swung around. The red dragon, however, took the force of it in the side, knocking it over in a tumble of wings and limbs.

"What do we do?" Galanör asked Hadavad.

The mage, who normally possessed all the answers, appeared just as concerned about the calamity they had found themselves in.

How could they pass through the valley with two enormous dragons taking chunks out of each other?

The red dragon jumped up on its hind legs and battered Malliath around the face with its razored claws. As Malliath's head was smacked to the side... so too was Alijah's.

The half-elf put a hand to his cheek, sure that there would be blood in the pattern of a dragon's claw upon his skin. There was no wound to speak of, but there was no mistaking the pain he had felt.

Alijah looked back at Malliath with wide eyes. They had shared the pain!

The red dragon clamped its jaws around Malliath's leg, dragging him down enough to jump up again and swipe its claws. The black dragon was larger than the red and took the streaks across its face, adding the wounds to a patchwork of others, new and old.

Alijah, on the other hand, was pulled down from his horse by a pain in his leg and thrown to the ground by another swipe across his face.

"Alijah?" Vighon asked from atop Ned. "What's wrong?"

Hadavad drew his horse over. "What's happening?"

Alijah pulled himself back up, the pain abating as suddenly as it set upon him. He ignored the questions and concerned looks and turned to the dragons. Their wings extended and tails hammered the ground, each roaring and growling as they sized the other up.

The half-elf could see that the red dragon was about to spring forwards and snap at Malliath's neck. Alijah feared for his own neck, but he couldn't fight the urge to protect the black dragon.

"STOP!" he yelled at the top of his lungs, running across the valley.

He hadn't even crossed half the distance before another dragon appeared, birthed from the stars above. Scaled in gold and equal in size to the red, this dragon slammed into Malliath's side with all four of its legs outstretched. The black dragon roared in defiance but was unable to stop itself from falling to the side.

Alijah yelled out, feeling all four of the claws jab at his ribs and hip before forcing him to the ground. The golden dragon then sank its teeth into Malliath's thigh and Alijah gripped his right leg and cried out as if snared by a beast.

"Stop…" he strained. "Please…"

"Alijah!" Vighon had left Ned behind and started across the valley to reach him.

The fighting dragons were getting out of control again and Malliath's tail curled through the air, swatting the golden dragon square across the jaw. Vighon skidded to a stop by Alijah's side and dragged the half-elf back, saving him with a moment to go before the golden dragon rolled over the very spot.

The pain faded quickly, allowing Alijah to get his feet under him and run with Vighon. Malliath and the red dragon hovered, their wings flapping, before they both crashed into the ground beside the golden wyrm. Mighty jaws gnashed in the air and claws dug into the ground as the dragons rose up on their hind legs, battling for dominance. The two smaller dragons were no match for Malliath on their own, but Alijah could see that together, they were drawing a decent amount of blood from him.

He felt every bite, claw, and strike of the tail.

"What's wrong?" Vighon asked, doing his best to keep his friend from crumpling to the ground.

"It hurts…" he replied through a clenched jaw, his hands squeezing the sand between his fingers.

"I don't understand," Vighon said, desperately trying to drag the half-elf away from the giant scrap.

"Get out of there!" Galanör's warning came from the distance.

The pain subsided just enough for Alijah to see the black tail swinging towards them. That should have been the end of them, and it would have been, if not for the invisible force that swept both Alijah and Vighon from their feet. Both hit the ground as the thick tail passed only inches overhead.

There was a woman running towards them…

A couple of seconds later, that same tail swung back, whistling through the air with enough force to shatter stone. Had Malliath's spiky tail not been on course to decapitate them, Alijah would have looked twice at the woman sprinting towards them, through the raging dragons. He resisted that urge and flattened himself to the ground beside Vighon.

The approaching woman displayed remarkable reflexes and dropped feet first, skidding under those same spikes.

Vighon was already scrambling to his feet with a firm grip on Alijah's coat. "Move!" he yelled.

Still in the thick of it, a golden tail pummelled the ground between them and the woman like a hammer on an anvil, kicking up more sand to conceal her identity. The woman jumped and twisted her body mid-flight to have her clear the tail and land back on her feet. The golden tail was already lifting back up before her feet touched the ground.

Alijah's face screwed up when the woman fell into a crouch at their feet. "Inara?" he asked incredulously.

His sister didn't offer so much as a smile but, instead, raised her hand and clenched her fist. Malliath's solid tail-end came down on them from nowhere and impacted a shield Inara had wrapped around the three of them. The shield flared a brilliant red every time the bulbous spiky end came down.

Under the bombardment, every vein in Inara's head made itself known. Still, she held. The shield took the hammering tail again and again until the red dragon leapt from the side and took Malliath into a chaotic tumble across the valley.

Inara gasped and unclenched her fist. "You need to move, *now*!"

Alijah had so many questions he couldn't think straight. "Wait. What are you—"

Hadavad and Galanör rode up beside them, blocking his view of Inara. Vighon climbed onto Ned and called for Alijah to get on behind him, as yet more of the valley's walls fell apart under the weight of the violent dragons.

Inara was gone by the time he was astride Ned and he suddenly feared for her life. How could anyone survive in the middle of such a fight?

"We need to get out of Syla's Pass!" Hadavad bellowed with his staff raised high. "Follow me!"

Galanör paused, halting them all. "There's a rider on top of Malliath... a black rider."

They all turned to see the rider, clad in dark armour and a cloak as black as the night. The ranger held tightly onto Malliath's saddle as the dragon raked at the golden dragon's neck, scraping red lines down its glittering scales. The red dragon came up behind and dropped its weight onto Malliath's tail.

Inara was astride that dragon!

That meant the dragon assaulting Malliath was Athis, her eternal companion.

"What evil has that Crow unleashed?" Hadavad asked, his dark brow creasing into despair.

Galanör looked an elf bereft of all hope and strength as he said, "He made Valanis a dragon rider..."

"No," Alijah corrected. "He made *Asher* a dragon rider."

20

FIRST BLOOD

Inara chose to fall deeper into her bond with Athis, hoping that the dragon's resolve and focus would allow her to ignore Alijah's surprising appearance.

Malliath the voiceless was certainly enough to be thinking about...

Athis clawed at Malliath's hind and coiled his tail around the black dragon's tail, hoping to pin it in place. Malliath, however, was a larger and more experienced dragon than either Athis or Aldreon. One of his claws raked at Aldreon's face, pushing him into the valley wall, while his enormous tail swiped around, uncoiling itself from Athis's grip.

Inara knew to hold on when the dragons uncoupled, for the sweeping tail forced Athis to skid around on the valley floor. The red dragon recovered quickly and turned his skid into enough momentum to dash back along the high wall and come down on Malliath.

The black dragon roared as Athis's claws sank into his back. Inara could sense everything her companion was going to do and knew exactly when to brace or shift her weight. Right now, she knew that Athis was about to clamp his jaws around the back of Malliath's neck.

A man looked up at them, giving both dragon and Dragorn pause.

Inara saw a stranger, but Athis saw Asher, the ranger and hero of The War for the Realm. The dragon's memories flooded Inara's mind and she experienced flashes of The Battle for Velia. The same man who was the focus of those memories sat beneath her now, on Malliath's neck.

Impossible!

Hold on!

The black dragon took advantage of the pause and exhaled a jet of fire upon the valley wall. The inferno ran up the rocky slab and pushed off into Athis's face. The red dragon was immune to the effects of fire, but Inara wasn't. To keep her safe, Athis was forced to flap his wings and gain some height over Malliath.

Aldreon and Edrik launched back into the melee, assaulting Malliath from the side. Looking down on the fight, Inara couldn't believe her eyes.

Asher reacted with a speed and finesse rarely seen in humans, and dashed across Malliath's back and leaped onto Aldreon's. The ranger was on Edrik before the Dragorn knew what was happening.

Get me down there! Inara yelled across her bond with Athis.

We have parted once already in this fight and you nearly died twice.

Asher gripped Edrik's collar and repeatedly hammered the man with a single fist, bloodying his face. Every hit took its toll on Aldreon, who shared the pain and knocks to the head. It was a disorientating assault that gave Malliath enough time secure a bite around the golden dragon's front leg.

Inara squirmed as Malliath shook the leg until it cracked and broke. Aldreon's roar drowned out Edrik's agonising cry.

Asher was losing his balance on the pained dragon and made a quick run and a jump onto Malliath's wing. The two demonstrated a bond that only existed between dragon and Dragorn after decades together.

The black dragon waited until Asher was back in his saddle

before continuing his slaughter of Aldreon and Edrik. Athis the ironheart, however, was far from being out of the fight. The red dragon had gained enough height to pick up some speed as he flew over Malliath's spiky back.

You can do it, Athis! Inara braced herself against him.

The red dragon dropped down low enough to snare Malliath between all four claws. Inara could feel the strain on Athis's muscles as he flapped his mighty wings and pulled up on the black dragon with all his strength. He was only able to lift the voiceless one a dozen feet off the ground, but it was enough to allow Aldreon the chance to escape.

Malliath fell from Athis's grip with a bloodied back, but the dragon failed to land, taking flight instead. Sand was kicked high into the air and the black dragon took off into the night, ascending quickly to melt between the stars.

Aldreon is hurt, Athis commented.

Inara looked down at the valley floor and found the golden dragon, limping with a barely conscious Edrik on his back.

We need to—

Inara became aware of Malliath's return as soon as Athis's heightened senses caught sight, sound, and smell of him. The black dragon came at them from the sky with enough speed to take them both from the air.

The half-elf braced, all too aware of the only option left to her companion. Athis tucked in his wings and dropped towards the valley floor, which was much closer than either of them would have liked. Malliath cut through the air a couple of feet above them, but only a second later, Athis was forced to extend his wings and glide inches above the ground.

Athis's voice sounded as clear as her own thoughts. *We need to gain height and take this fight into the sky.*

Inara agreed, recalling her training on dragon tactics. When facing a larger opponent, clashing on the ground would always give the bigger dragon the advantage of its immovable weight and deadly tail. In the air, where dragons of all sizes could dominate, the battle could become fairly pitched.

Athis's suggestion crossed the bond between dragons and saw Aldreon limping through the valley until he could take off. Edrik was only just holding on…

If Malliath attacks Aldreon in the air, Edrik will fall! Inara tried to reach out and make a connection with Edrik, but he was too weak.

Malliath is coming back! Athis warned before banking hard to the west.

Inara shifted her weight to go against the sharp angle, keeping her firmly rooted. The black dragon was a spear hurled from the heavens, missing them with a sharp gust of wind. All three dragons had left the confines of Syla's Pass now and soared through the air in circles as they searched for their angle of attack.

Inara cursed the lack of training they had received on aerial tactics. There just hadn't been cause to learn that much when all dragons lived in harmony together. Of course, no one had been thinking about Malliath, the only dragon to ever go into exile.

Height is the key, Athis reminded her. *Our underbellies are hardened and guarded by claws. The wings and neck are vulnerable spots.*

Inara called upon her lessons about dragon anatomy and visualised the drawings from the textbooks. The gap between the scales on the neck was larger to allow for more flexibility. It also allowed for teeth to sink between the natural armour. The wings were an obvious weak point on any creature that could fly.

Aware that Edrik and Aldreon were already wounded, Inara gritted her teeth and tightened her grip around Athis's spikes. ***Let's bring him down!***

Athis growled deep in his throat and banked to the north as he gained some more height. Malliath and Aldreon were flying towards each other below them. From above, it was clear to see how much larger the black dragon really was. For just a moment, Inara doubted any of them would live to see the sunrise.

Athis roared and angled his body to come down on Malliath. Inara called upon magic to provide her with enough air to keep breathing against the rushing wind.

With only feet between them, it appeared Athis was going to hit

Malliath with deadly speed and four legs of piercing claws. The black dragon, however, was not so easily ambushed. Malliath ignored Aldreon's head-on attack and twisted his incredible bulk with enviable agility, bringing his claws to bear on Athis.

Dragons, red and black, came together in a mad tangle of claws and limbs, their wings flapping furiously as they spun through the air. Aldreon glided past, missing the clash of dragons altogether.

Inara groaned in pain as Malliath's claws raked Athis's legs and ribs. The half-elf could feel blood trickling down her own legs and side, making her job of holding on all the harder. The dragons snarled and gnashed their teeth, always trying to grip the other within their maw.

Malliath used his superior wing size against them and flapped hard to take them all up, farther into the sky. The sudden change in momentum forced Athis's head aside, opening his shoulder up for Malliath's incredible bite.

Inara added her own scream to Athis's pained cry. Her left shoulder burned through to the bone and the Dragorn lost her grip. It was luck that saw her fall back through the air and avoid her companion's thrashing tail.

Inara! Athis desperately raked at Malliath in an attempt to break free of his hold and fly down to Inara.

"Athis!" she screamed through the pain that radiated from her shoulder and ribs.

Aldreon's lighter voice rang clear in her mind. *Turn around!* the golden dragon instructed.

Inara flipped around in the air and saw Aldreon gliding beneath her. The golden dragon was losing altitude too, but he was slowing his descent foot by foot until they were both falling at the same speed. Inara gripped one of his spikes and pulled herself down just in time for Aldreon to flap his wings and prevent them all from hitting the ground.

Rather than gain any more height, Aldreon opened his wings, filling them with air, and slowed to a stop. They were grounded on the flat ledge that stretched on to the eastern horizon, far above Syla's Pass.

"We need to get back up there!" Inara cried.

No, Aldreon countered. *Stay with Edrik. I will help Athis.* Aldreon tilted his wing and allowed Edrik to slide down to the ground.

Inara didn't have time to get another word in before the golden dragon took off again, leaving her with a wounded Edrik. His face was swollen and cut, but his leg appeared mangled and positioned at all the wrong angles.

The half-elf crouched down to check on him when more pain exploded up her back. Inara arched her back, lifting her head to the battle overhead. Athis had taken a pair of razor-sharp claws to the back, but the red dragon managed to awkwardly twist his head and clamp down on Malliath's lower neck.

Inara tasted the dragon's blood in her mouth before his roar found her ears.

"Inara…" Edrik managed.

Doing her best to ignore the pain, Inara picked Edrik up into her arms, cupping his head in her hand. "It's alright," she said softly. "Together they will overpower Malliath. It will be over soon."

Edrik groaned in pain as Aldreon entered the fray above. Inara could do nothing but watch as new cuts and bruises spread across his face and hands.

"We weren't… trained for this," he strained.

"I know," Inara replied, brushing his blond hair from his eyes. "But we are Dragorn," she said boldly. "We are—"

Edrik's neck snapped.

Inara gasped and sat back in shock. His lifeless eyes looked straight through her, but the Dragorn couldn't help but be drawn to the bony lump in the left of his neck.

Through tears, Inara turned her attention to the sky. Aldreon was falling fast. His wings were up in the air as his back slammed into the ground, sending quakes across the canyon.

Athis came in hard and fast after that, landing directly in front of Inara. The red dragon was exhausted, his breathing ragged and tail laid low. A moment later, Malliath landed between them and Aldreon's body.

Reptilian purple eyes fixed them within a predatory gaze. Athis dug his claws into the ground and released a low growl to rumble across the plateau.

Inara gently placed Edrik's body down before drawing her Vi'tari blade. The Dragorn joined her companion beside his head and stood her ground, her hand trembling with rage. When Malliath next attacked, Inara knew she would meet him with all her mettle and fury.

The attack never came, however, as Malliath lowered his head and Asher slid down. The ranger locked eyes with Inara and reached for his hip, pausing only when he realised there was no blade to draw. Not to be dissuaded, Asher opened his other hand and birthed a ball of blue fire.

Then he stopped.

Asher came to a halt mid-stride and turned his head to the south, as if hearing a voice on the wind. He closed his fist, ending the spell, and turned back to climb up Malliath's scales. Without any further provocation, the pair took off and flew into the night.

Inara took her first breath since the ranger had climbed down from the black dragon. Meeting him in battle would likely have spelled her doom, but meet him she would. For the first time in thirty years, since the death of Adriel, Gideon's mentor, a Dragorn and his dragon had perished. It released an anger that burned deep inside of her, an emotion she shared with Athis.

It also made her feel vulnerable.

First, it was encountering the orcs, now this. The world was not as she had come to believe it to be. The Dragorn were not invincible. And immortals could die…

I want to hunt him down.

Athis spoke wiser words. *We alone cannot defeat Malliath. The hunt will have to wait, wingless one.*

Inara sheathed her scimitar and crouched by Edrik's side. **He didn't deserve this, neither of them did.**

They died in battle, Athis replied. *A great honour for any Dragorn.*

Inara looked at Edrik's battered and bloodied body. **I think I can do without honour.**

We should put them together, Athis suggested. *They should be together in rest.*

The Dragorn wiped away her tears and lifted Edrik's body from the ground. The light of a new day was cresting the horizon as she placed him in the crook of Aldreon's neck. There was nothing to see yet, but by the next sunrise, the magic stored within Aldreon would be released back into Verda's soil. From their corpses, a small paradise would spread across the barren plateau.

It would be beautiful.

Inara stood there in silence, watching the sun bathe them in orange light. **I've never seen the death of a dragon.**

Athis lifted his head to the south, his red scales catching the first of the rays. *I fear Malliath's return may spell the end for many more of our kin.*

Inara looked up at her companion. **Was that really Asher? The Asher?**

I never met the man, but I did see him during The Battle for Velia. The rider we fought tonight is a perfect match to my memory.

The Dragorn wiped the last of her tears away and looked to the south. **How can he be back? How can he be bonded to Malliath?**

The answers will have to wait, Athis said. *Malliath is still in the area, which means the skies are no longer safe. We should return to The Lifeless Isles and speak with Master Thorn.*

Alijah!

Athis's suggestion reminded Inara that her brother was in Syla's Pass. The half-elf could have hit her own head for letting that revelation go.

Athis turned his deep blue eyes on Inara. *It was a relief to see Alijah, but we must report our findings to Master Thorn.*

Gideon's going to have just as many questions as we do, if not more. I would bet both of my arms that my brother knows something. There's no way his being in The Undying Mountains is a coincidence.

Athis didn't appear convinced and Inara could tell he was worried about the emotional implications of seeing Alijah again. It was no secret that their relationship had broken down over the last few years, before his self-exile.

Even if I didn't think he had answers, I would still need to see him, Athis. He's my brother...

I know, wingless one. But if he upsets you I cannot give you my word I won't snap at him. The red dragon sniffed the air. *They are still in the Pass.*

Inara climbed up the dragon's leg, careful to avoid the cuts and gashes that mirrored her own wounds. They were both in pain and covered in blood, but they were alive. Seeing Aldreon and Edrik, it could easily have been them who suffered under Malliath's deadly bite. With that in mind, Inara took little notice of the blood in her dark ringlets or the stiffness in her back.

Before Athis launched into the morning sky, Inara took one last look over their fallen companions. "If there is something beyond this world, I hope they find it together..."

~

The Crow walked out of the tunnel and back into the centre of Paldora's Fall. The magic rooted in the crater continued to ripple over his skin, despite the dampening effects of the resurrection spell.

Orcish blood ran between the fine cracks in the ground, weaving between his feet. He smiled. Everything had happened as it should have. The waters had been muddied, blurring the lines for the so-called heroes of Verda.

The Crow stepped over the dead orcs and approached the hewn table. It had taken more lifetimes than he could count to come this far.

"There will be peace..." he whispered.

The flapping of great wings filtered through the floating boulders and found The Crow's ears. The Dragon Knight had heard his master's call.

He waited patiently for Asher to find his way back to the dais. The man cut quite the figure, attired in dark armour and emerging from the shadows. Asher's face spoke of a lifetime of hardship but, thankfully, his soft blue eyes told of a gentle nature. Muddied waters indeed.

The Dragon Knight strode up to his master and took a knee. "I am ready to serve, Master."

The Crow's throat rumbled with glee. "What a magnificent weapon you are." He walked around the genuflecting Dragon Knight. "You have found Astari, *new life*, in the world. Yet... here you are, a slave to destiny once again, forbidden to rest."

Asher remained on one knee, his expression stoic and mouth shut. A product of two binding spells, the Dragon Knight was the most twisted form of new life, chained to the magic that shackled his mind. He was perfect.

Morvir, The Crow's first servant, strode quickly out of the orcs' tunnel. The Crow held out a hand to silence the man before he spoke, his focus still on Asher.

"Inara Galfrey is not to be killed," he instructed the Dragon Knight. "You may do anything else you like, so long as it does not result in her death." Asher remained completely still. "Does that name mean anything to you? *Galfrey...*"

Without meeting his master's eyes, Asher replied, "Nathaniel Galfrey, son of Tobin Galfrey. Formerly of the Graycoats. Abandoned his order in favour of courting Reyna of house Sevari, princess of Elandril. A proficient swordsman and expert marksman. He was a... *good man.*"

The Crow arched an eyebrow. "Rise," he commanded. The master took a confident step closer to Asher's face and scrutinised those blue eyes. "How much of you is still in there, I wonder, clawing at the walls?" The Crow tapped his wand against the hardened leather over the Dragon Knight's chest. "Claw all you like. This magic is older than both of us." The Crow stepped back, noting the absence of a sword on Asher's hip. "A Dragon Knight requires a sword. Perhaps one familiar to your grip..."

Those blue eyes twitched and met The Crow's with recognition. "Take flight then," he ordered. "You will know my commands when you hear them."

Morvir moved aside with some swiftness to avoid the Dragon

Knight. "Lord Crow, I have received—"

Morvir's words were cut off when Karakulak strode out of the tunnel and pushed the wizard aside. His dominating frame eclipsed the first servant, leaving The Crow with nothing but the orc to look at.

"My kin lie dead at your feet, Crow," the king stated. "I hope your magic was worth it."

The leader of The Black Hand met the orc's eyes, wondering if and when the king would understand his place in their arrangement. "It was worth it when my magic gained you a throne, was it not? What has transpired here, tonight, will see to your victory," he lied boldly.

"For six of your years, Wizard, you have made promises, each one as mysterious to me as you yourself…"

The Crow moved his robes with such subtlety that the appearance of his wand seemed almost natural. He was happy to see the king recoil from the sight.

Karakulak bared his fangs but kept his growl in check as he called upon his resolve. "The time for magic is at an end, Crow. My army craves battle."

"The fall of *Neverdark* may begin…" The Crow replied offhandedly, his mind struggling to stay in the present.

"What of the dragon and its rider?" the king asked pointedly, his gaze lifting to the floating boulders above.

The wizard turned his back on Karakulak, a statement in itself. "After tonight, your greatest adversary is going to be the Dragorn. Your numbers will count for naught against so many dragons and their riders. Consider it another gift."

Karakulak sneered. "You can keep your gifts, Wizard. My ancestors slaughtered hundreds of dragons in The Great War."

The Crow rolled his eyes in the shadow of the torchlight. "An exaggeration, good king." He turned on the orc with his wand clearly displayed, dissuading Karakulak from arguing the point. "Malliath and his rider, Asher, are to be considered allies. They will keep the Dragorn from decimating your army as well as distracting the more powerful individuals of the realm."

"I am to give the beast commands?" Karakulak asked incredulously.

"No," The Crow replied firmly. "The magic that binds them can only be controlled by me. Rest assured, King Karakulak, they will serve you well in battle." Having walked up the dais, Morvir came back into sight. "Are we prepared for the journey, Morvir?"

The first servant glanced nervously from the king to his master. "The Grim Stalker tribe have supplied the required number of orcs, Lord Crow."

"As *I* ordered," Karakulak added. "You may have a new pet, Crow, but the orcs obey only me."

"They obey the *strong*," the wizard corrected slyly.

His meaning hadn't been lost on the king, but Karakulak dismissed the comment. "What do you need with my Grim Stalkers, Wizard? Does your magic not suffice?"

The Crow's eyes went wide, stretching his creases and scars. "Didn't we have a conversation about using such big words?" Karakulak looked ready to rip his head off with his bare hands, but the wizard waved the comment away. "You are to attack Tregaran first, yes? As we discussed."

The orc king held The Crow's gaze a moment longer before replying, "My forces are amassing under the city as we speak."

"Excellent. The city is yours, of course, but while you are there, I would have you take one life in particular."

Karakulak tilted his head. "One life? When I am finished with Tregaran, there won't be a soul left alive."

"Yes, but I would ask that you seek out this person and see to their death before all else."

Karakulak huffed, ready to storm away. "I have a war to begin!" he cried over his shoulder.

"If you want to *win* this war, King Karakulak," The Crow's tone halted the orc's mighty strides, "I would suggest heeding my advice. I have seen how you win against the free folk," he lied. "But you must adhere to the plan…"

"Your god's plan?" Karakulak clarified with a mocking tone.

"You stand now as the king of The Under Realm," The Crow

countered, reminding the orc that *he* was the reason Karakulak held such a title. "Listen to me a little longer and you will be king of the world."

Karakulak took a deep breath and made The Crow wait for his answer. "Who is this human you would have me kill?"

The wizard smiled, happy to see that he still held the leash. The Crow walked over and tapped his thumb against the bony ridge above the king's eyes. It was an elven technique, but a useful one for transferring an image from one mind to another. Karakulak stumbled backwards and blinked hard, snatching at the air in front of his face.

"Find that man," he reiterated, "and kill him."

Karakulak reorientated himself and squared his shoulders to regain his regal composure. "Anything less than the *world*, Crow, and your head will become part of my throne." With that, the pale orc disappeared back into the tunnel.

The Crow massaged his eyes, rubbing the thin skin of his wrinkled lids. Like all kings, Karakulak was exhausting...

Morvir watched the orc disappear. "I hope I can be there to see his face when all of this—"

The Crow held a finger up to his lips, silencing his first servant. "There are ears in every shadow."

Morvir bowed his head in apology. "Everything is prepared for our journey, Lord Crow." He hesitated before speaking again. "Are we really going there, Master?"

The wizard considered his first servant's reservations, sharing many of them himself. "The blood of a dragon stains the ground, Morvir. After tonight, we will have gained more enemies than just the mage. Illian's strongest will rise up to meet the threat we pose on their way of life. We will need strong warriors of our own, warriors who do not fear the sun or bend the knee to a king."

The Crow looked over his surroundings, sad, in a way, to leave such a place. There were very few places in the world where the currents of magic flowed so freely. It felt like bathing in a warm bath, another luxury he had long forgotten.

"Come, Morvir," he bade. "The assassins of Nightfall await..."

21

ON THE OTHER SIDE

Alijah could feel his companions' eyes on him, but his own were glued to the morning sky. So much had happened in one night that he struggled to form a coherent thought.

Inara…

He hadn't seen his sister in four years and this was far from the reunion he had expected. Still, the desert skies were clear of dragons, good or bad.

"Come on, mate," Vighon encouraged Ned, his horse, to keep going a bit farther. They had ridden out of Syla's Pass with all haste and forced the horses to put as much distance as possible between them and Malliath.

"He's tired," Alijah observed, sat behind Vighon in the saddle. "Like all of us."

Astride Alijah's black horse, Hadavad dug his heels in and rode out in front to block them off. The mage fixed Alijah within his gaze and Vighon pulled on Ned's reins.

"The sky is clear and Syla's Gate is behind us now," Hadavad began. "I would learn all that you know, Alijah Galfrey."

Alijah sighed, feeling too tired to recall the night's events. He climbed down from Ned and Vighon followed him, only his friend grunted in pain and reached for his back under the shield. The hardy northerner waved his concerns away and removed his enchanted shield. Considering it had been hit by numerous spells and a rather powerful bolt of lightning, the shield appeared brand new.

"This is no time for dawdling, boy." Hadavad pushed past Vighon and came face to face with Alijah. "You said *Asher.*" The mage looked almost furious. "Did you really see him?"

Galanör climbed down from his swift steed and joined them. "He's never even seen Asher," the elf pointed out. "Alijah was born after The War for the Realm."

Hadavad reached out and gripped Alijah's arms, pulling the half-elf's attention back to him. "Was it Asher?"

Alijah pulled away and found some space. He had dirt and sand smudged over his face, his fingerless gloves were in tatters, and new aches and cuts were beginning to make themselves known. He was exhausted. When he closed his eyes, however, he could still see the skeleton on the dais coming to life.

"The Black Hand have been excavating in Vengora," Alijah finally said. "What did they find up there, Hadavad?"

The mage raised his chin. "A skeleton."

Alijah nodded. "We came to the conclusion, in your absence, that there were only two things of value in those mountains. A pair of skeletons: Valanis and Asher." The half-elf turned back to look at the distant gates strewn across the desert, guarded by the high walls of The Undying Mountains. "We assumed they were searching for Valanis's bones. We were wrong. The thing that found new life in Paldora's Fall was not an elf."

"Are you sure?" Hadavad asked with some urgency in his voice.

"Elves don't have grey hair," Alijah replied, turning back to his companions. "They don't have stubble on their face and, though I haven't met every elf, I would wager that none of them have a black-fang tattoo under their left eye…"

Hadavad bowed his head so that his dreadlocks concealed his expression. Galanör cupped his mouth and found something on the horizon to stare at. Behind them both, Vighon continued to stretch his back, almost oblivious to their conversation.

Almost…

"Isn't that a good thing?" the northerner asked. "I mean, the alternative was an all-powerful, genocidal maniac of an elf. I suppose there's still the issue of the dragon…"

Hadavad stomped his staff once into the ground, silencing Vighon. "That was not the Asher I knew. And he was never bonded with Malliath the voiceless. What happened in there, Alijah?"

The half-elf wiped his forehead, freeing the strands of hair matted to his face. "That might not be the Asher you knew, but The Crow performed an Astari ritual. Asher is no Reaver. Before The Crow cast his binding spell there was a moment…" Alijah could see Asher's first few seconds of life in his mind. "For just a moment he *was* Asher."

The mage took a step forward. "Tell me of the binding spell."

Alijah scraped his loose hair and braids back as he recalled events. "The Crow burnt an ancient symbol into Asher's chest, but I couldn't see it clearly. After that, he wasn't really Asher anymore."

Hadavad gripped his staff all the tighter and sighed. "That could be any number of binding spells…"

"There's more," Alijah said. "Whatever spell he used, it was reinforced by another."

The mage locked eyes with him. "Malliath."

Alijah nodded. "Malliath was bound and chained by those pale creatures." The thought of it still pained the half-elf. "The Crow performed another spell that bound Asher to Malliath."

Galanör shook his head. "I thought that was impossible."

Hadavad raised a single eyebrow. "The bonding of Dragorn and dragon is a mystery to most. If there is such a spell, I would assume it to be ancient and its origins that of dark magic."

"It still makes no sense," Galanör continued. "Why would The Black Hand bring Asher back in the first place? Why not Valanis?"

"Their motives and allegiance with those pale creatures remain a mystery," Hadavad replied as he leaned onto his staff. "As does the pain you experienced in Syla's Pass, Alijah." The mage's last comment turned the eyes of the other two towards the half-elf, as if they had only just remembered his fits of agony.

"What was that?" Vighon asked, the pain in his back quickly forgotten.

Alijah suddenly felt like retreating into himself, as if he had just been asked the most intimate question. Successfully lying to these particular individuals would be difficult, so he settled for the vaguest answer he could.

"As The Crow was enacting his spells, he froze me to the spot and made me watch. He said…" Alijah swallowed the truth of The Crow's apology. "He said it would hurt."

Hadavad scrunched up his face. "He said the binding spell between Asher and Malliath would hurt *you*?"

"Well, it looked as if it worked," Vighon chipped in. "Every time Malliath took a beating you knew about it."

Galanör and Hadavad shared a look, but it was the mage who spoke up. "Perhaps the spell is even more complex than I first imagined. It would seem The Crow has tied you into their bond, ensuring Malliath's and Asher's safety."

"Wait," Vighon said, holding up his hand. "Are you saying that if Malliath or Asher die, so does Alijah?"

Hadavad chewed over his answer, but Alijah didn't like the way the mage continued to share a silent conversation with the elven ranger. "I'm not sure what I'm saying. We only have pieces of the whole and it isn't enough to make a picture."

"There's a prophecy," Galanör announced ominously.

Hadavad looked from the elf to Alijah. "You found it then?" he asked eagerly. "The Echoes' cave?"

With all that had happened, Alijah had forgotten about the prophecy. "It's not intact," he warned. "The scroll we found had been in that cave for a very long time."

"But it's signed, yes?" Hadavad pressed. "With a black hand?"

Alijah pulled the ancient scroll from between his blade and quiver. The mage tentatively took it in his hands and unrolled it. His eyes lit up and took in every line and glyph with a hunger that Alijah rarely saw in Hadavad.

"This is why we came south," Galanör explained. "It speaks of—"

"A fallen star," Hadavad finished, his eyes on the second verse. The mage parted his lips to speak again, but the distinct sound of beating wings froze them all.

Alijah turned back to The Undying Mountains to discover a red dragon descending from the vast blue above.

The ground was shaken as Athis touched down with all four of his legs. The dragon flared his wings dramatically and lifted himself up on his hind legs to reveal his hardened chest of slate grey scales. As his front legs came back down, Inara gracefully landed beside Athis's head.

Alijah had exiled himself for a reason, but seeing his twin sister now made it very hard to remember why.

Inara strode towards them with the confidence befitting of a Dragorn. Her hair, a shade darker than his own, rained down in perfect ringlets, but it was her eyes that tugged at the Alijah's heart. The deep blue of her eyes was that of his own.

Attired in armoured brown leathers and gripping the hilt of her Vi'tari scimitar, Inara looked more the warrior than when they last met. Blood and dirt stained her skin and leathers, but none of it could detract from her youthful beauty, something she would maintain for eternity.

Alijah gritted his teeth and held onto the resolve he had found four years previously.

"Brother!" Inara crashed into him and wrapped her arms around him in a bear-like embrace.

It pained Alijah to simply pat her back lightly, desperate as he was to hold her close. Inara pulled away with a wounded and confused expression marring her beautiful features.

"It's good to see you," Alijah managed. "Are you hurt?"

Inara looked to be reading his mind as she took another step back. "No, I'm fine…" Her reply was absent of its melodic tone.

"Inara…" Vighon stepped forward, his movements awkward. Inara and Alijah hadn't seen each other in four years, but Vighon hadn't seen Inara in more than twice that.

It was clear to see from Vighon's expression that the torch he carried for Inara was still there, despite their decade apart.

Fool was the word that sprang to Alijah's mind.

Inara didn't appear to share the sentiment. She did, however, glance back at Alijah, the flash of her eyes asking a hundred questions at once.

Thankfully, Hadavad and Galanör made themselves known, bowing their heads at both Inara and Athis.

The mage said happily, "It is good to see you again so soon, Inara Galfrey." That statement saw an inordinate amount of confusion creep over Alijah's face.

"And your timing saved us all," Galanör added.

"So soon?" Alijah asked, ignoring the elf's comment. "The two of you have…"

"We met a few days past, in The Undying Mountains," Inara answered.

Alijah turned his confused and hurt expression on Hadavad.

The mage shrugged. "Did you want me to tell you in Paldora's Fall? Or as we fled for our lives?"

Alijah sighed and let it go, though he was entirely unhappy with the growing situation.

A sharp huff resounded from Athis's mouth. "This is Athis the ironheart," his sister said, shifting her shoulders to regard the dragon.

Alijah glanced at Athis and felt a wave of caution overcome him, drawing his gaze back to the dragon's reptilian eyes. The half-elf suddenly felt like tip-toeing around Inara and being as nice as possible.

Inara turned to face Athis and the feeling dissipated as suddenly as it came on. Having his emotions affected by a dragon was one thing, but seeing his sister hold a silent conversation that excluded him in every way was far more painful.

"It is an honour to meet you," Galanör said to the dragon.

"Wait," Alijah interjected. "There were two of you."

Inara's expression told them everything they needed to know about the fate of the other Dragorn. "Edrik and Aldreon died fighting Malliath and…" The Dragorn looked up to meet them all, her eyes searching for the truth in theirs.

"Asher," Hadavad said. "I am sorry for your loss and grateful for your intervention."

"So, it was really him…" Galanör said absently. "They actually did it."

Inara looked at Alijah but asked the mage her question. "Do you know how this came to be? How Asher has returned? His bond with Malliath?"

Hadavad twisted his mouth. "That's *three* questions, Miss Galfrey."

Whatever the mage meant by that, it annoyed Inara instantly. "I'm not playing games, Hadavad. For the first time since the new order, a Dragorn and his dragon have been killed. I want answers."

Seeing his twin become irate should have bothered Alijah but, after so long, he was, instead, forced to hide his smile. Inara had never let anything or anyone come between her and the justice that needed answering, even from a young age.

Hadavad's answer was as plain as could be. "A cult of necromancers excavated Asher's bones in Vengora. They used the magnified power of the magic inside Paldora's Fall to cast a resurrection spell."

Inara appeared to be searching for any hint of a lie on the mage's face. "The Black Hand you spoke of?"

"Aye," the mage replied. "After bringing him back, they bound him to their will as well as Malliath."

Inara shook her head. "That's impossible. A bond can never be forced."

Vighon said, "And a few days ago, I didn't think the dead could be brought back to life…"

"It's true," Alijah added, ignoring Vighon's unhelpful comment. "I saw it happen."

Inara turned away from them all and faced Athis, though his reptilian face was a mystery to Alijah. Judging by his sister's face, he deduced that they were holding another conversation.

"There's more," Hadavad stated.

Alijah's stomach lurched, concerned that the mage was about to divulge the bond that he now shared with Malliath. He hadn't wanted them to know, let alone his sister, a Dragorn.

"There were other creatures inside Paldora's Fall," Hadavad continued. "Pale and horned."

Alijah hid his sigh of relief.

"You fought them?" Inara asked.

"I killed a few," Alijah answered. "But there were too many. We had to run."

Inara looked at her brother with new eyes, as if she was reassessing all that she thought she knew about him. Inara wasn't the only one who had changed over the years.

"How many?" the Dragorn asked.

"A lot," Vighon chipped in helpfully.

Hadavad asked, "Would they be the orcs you spoke of?"

"Orcs?" Galanör blurted out. "That's what chased us in the crater?"

Inara nodded solemnly. "They have returned, and in some number it seems."

"What are orcs?" Vighon and Alijah asked simultaneously.

"A breed of monster lost to history..." Galanör said, visibly shaken.

"Just as Asher was lost to us," Hadavad mused, his eyes on the prophecy in his hand. "It seems the lost and impossible are coming together."

Inara turned back to Athis. "We need to go. Gideon must hear of this."

"Wait!" Vighon exclaimed with more emphasis than he should have. The northerner tried to plough through his awkward command. "Malliath and Asher are still out here somewhere. I think we can all agree that getting out of The Arid Lands is our best course of action right now. Perhaps a Dragorn escort would see us safely out of the desert?"

Inara hesitated but still shook her head. "This is too important. Gideon has to know what's happened here and it will take you too long to reach The Moonlit Plains from here."

"To Tregaran then?" Vighon pressed. "It's the capital of these lands; we would be safe there."

Alijah was doing his best to shoot daggers at his friend, more than aware that Vighon wasn't afraid of their journey north.

Inara silently consulted with Athis before turning back to them. "To Tregaran, but we cannot go any farther."

Alijah blinked very slowly and pinched his nose. This *adventure* had quickly turned into a nightmare four years in the making.

The twins shared one last look before they separated and made for their individual mounts. The tension between them would inevitably come to a head if he knew his sister. She let nothing go.

"I shall look after this." Hadavad lifted the prophecy before tucking it into the pouch on the side of Alijah's horse.

"That's *my* horse," he protested quietly.

Hadavad looked from the black steed to Alijah and shrugged. "Old bones, you see. Besides, you and Vighon ride so well together."

Alijah sighed, quashing the unusual rage that again threatened to consume him. The half-elf knew he shouldn't feel this way and yet his anger clawed at the bars to be unleashed.

He swallowed that fury and met Hadavad's eyes. "You and I still need to have a talk, old man. We thought you were dead."

Alijah watched the mage nod his head and trot ahead. He waited until he could only see the back of him before releasing his grip on the dagger strapped to his belt. He hadn't even realised he was gripping it.

Standing beside Ned, Vighon was watching him. His friend's intense stare posed the same question that was swirling inside Alijah's head.

What was happening to him?

22

WELCOME TO THE NORTH

D oran Heavybelly took one last look over his shoulder. Kelp Town was quickly disappearing behind the falling snow, its wooden walls fading to white. With Kelp Town and Grey Stone behind them, the three companions were well and truly in the north.

They were also without comfy warm beds and buffets that went on and on. Of course, their reception in Kelp Town paled by comparison to that of Grey Stone's. The lord of Kelp Town could never compete with the luxuries of his king, Jormund Orvish.

Still, they had been offered warm accommodation and free food and drink. The dwarf couldn't complain about that.

"Nothin' cures a nasty hangover like a northern breeze!" Doran bellowed into the icy wind.

Reyna looked down from her horse at the dwarf. "Is getting blind drunk a prerequisite for every town you visit?"

Now that Doran thought about it, he couldn't remember much of their stay in Kelp Town. "Blind, deaf, an' preferably passed out, me Lady!" he replied with a broad smile.

"I'll say," Nathaniel added. "Kelp Town was hit by one of those damn quakes last night and you slept through the whole thing."

Doran vaguely recollected some kind of disturbance, but he had chalked it up to his belching or some other kind of gas expulsion…

The three continued their journey north, rounding the southern curve of Vengora to put them on a straight shot to Namdhor. The Selk Road was almost impossible to make out in the snow, but Doran's uncanny sense of dwarven direction kept them straight.

With only two brief stops, the companions had made good tracks into the region of Orith. Only once did they pass another traveller on the road; a wagon of goods being transported to Grey Stone apparently. Doran fancied stopping and sharing some food with the driver, especially the salted pork he boasted of, but the Galfreys drove on.

When the Selk Road cut through a small wood, it offered nothing but trees for the son of Dorain to look at. After rainbows, trees were the dullest things to a dwarf's eyes.

"This travellin' malarkey is borin' as shit!" Doran announced after another few hours of silent trekking. "Nathaniel! Ye must have some interestin' tales from ye time in the Graycoats!"

Nathaniel moved his hood aside to look at the dwarf. "That was thirty years ago, Doran."

"Bah! Ye humans and yer flimsy memories… I want stories abou' hunts! Beasties! Summat excitin'! Anything to take me mind off o' me numb arse!"

Reyna offered, "Would you like to hear a tale of the elves, son of Dorain?" Even the howling wind died down to hear the elf speak.

Doran held up his hand. "Ye can save ye stories of dandies and butterflies, me Lady."

"Surely you would want to hear of Lady Syla's great feats?" Reyna continued.

Doran's ears pricked up at the name. "As in Syla's Gate?"

"Named after Lady Syla of house Arinör," Reyna explained. "It was her idea, and magic, that saw the great gates erected to keep the Darkakin out."

Doran chuckled to himself. "Well, she did a piss poor job o' that! Valanis brought 'em down in an afternoon!"

The elf rolled her eyes at him. "Before that, they had stood for three thousand years. Besides, there are far more tales of her heroism than the war against the Darkakin. Lady Syla was known throughout the realm for her skill with a bow."

"Much like you, dear," Nathaniel commented oddly.

Reyna removed her bow and held it firmly in her right hand. "Thank you, darling."

Doran raised a bushy eyebrow and looked from husband to wife.

"I have often wondered if I am as good a shot as Lady Syla," Reyna continued, this time drawing an arrow from her quiver.

"I would say so," Nathaniel replied, gripping the hilt of his sword and pulling it an inch out of its scabbard.

Now, Doran's face was a picture of confusion with a light sprinkle of irritation. "What are ye two talkin'—"

Everything happened at once and Doran's mind did its very best, while still somewhat intoxicated, to interpret the surroundings.

The trees either side of the road exploded with savage cries, a pair of axes flew through the air, Reyna let loose her arrow, and Nathaniel leaped from his horse with his sword held high.

The axes went wide, Reyna's arrow sunk deep into the chest of one of their attackers, and Nathaniel sliced open another with a perfected horizontal strike.

Doran's Warhog saw blood and went crazy. The dwarf yelled at the top of his lungs and held on as the pig sprinted towards the rushing men. The nearest of the attackers took a tusk to the leg and went down screaming. The next two faced Doran, who held a sword in one hand and an axe in the other.

An arrow whistled through the air and pierced the skulls of both men, dropping them dead. Doran turned to his right with the infuriated look of a wronged dwarf. The expletives that came to mind, however, never found their way to his mouth, as the Warhog continued its charge between the legs of Nathaniel's riderless horse. Doran was thrown backwards when his bulk met the larger bulk of the horse's midriff.

Spitting snow and shaking the powder from his armour, the dwarf rose with the fury no one should ever bring out in his kin.

"Come on then!" he roared.

Nathaniel kicked one of his attackers in Doran's direction and the son of Dorain pounced. His axe swung first, quickly followed by his sword. A betting dwarf would have wagered the man died after the first swing, but the second always felt damn good!

Reyna had abandoned her horse now and joined them in the snow. Her green eyes sighted down arrow after arrow, each one nocked quicker than a man could blink. Only one of the elf's attackers succeeded in getting close enough to actually raise their sword to her. Seeing the flat of her boot was the last thing he ever saw.

Doran swiped his axe and chopped down a man who sought to stab Nathaniel in the back. A downwards thrust of his sword ensured the man would never threaten another person. Seeing the man bleeding into the snow, there was something about him that gnawed at Doran.

A sharp pain interrupted his musings and the son of Dorain turned to see the end of a sword poking between his back plate and shoulder guard. The man on the other end tried desperately to either push or pull his sword free, twisting it this way and that. The sword wouldn't budge.

"Dwarven skin, laddy. It's almost as tough as our armour." The son of Dorain spun around, knocking the sword free of the man's grasp and his shoulder. "Ye should o' thrust harder!"

The man turned on his heel and ran north with all haste.

Nathaniel danced around the last two, dispatching them one after the other with the graceful movements of a knight. "Where's that one going?" he asked, spotting the runner.

"Nowhere fast," Doran quipped, turning his axe in one hand.

"Doran, no!" Reyna's cry was too slow for Doran's muscle memory.

The dwarf had already launched his axe into the air with a prayer to Grarfath on his lips. The axe spun through the air over some distance and height before finally coming down in the back of the runner's head. The distinct sound of his skull cracking was terribly satisfying.

"What would ye stop me for?" Doran asked.

"To get some answers," Reyna replied.

Nathaniel looked about at the bodies strewn in the snow. "I don't suppose we left any others alive, did we?"

"Answers?" Doran repeated. "They're jus' a bunch o' bandits." The dwarf kicked the nearest body with disdain. "They were jus' too stupid to know who they were dealin' with!"

Reyna was shaking her head. "These were no bandits."

Nathaniel sheathed his sword. "I agree. They're dressed too well." The old knight picked up a discarded sword and examined the steel and the hilt. "Bandits can't afford steel like this and they're not trained well enough to take it from their owners. They were forged by a professional smith, most likely from Namdhor this far north - Skystead maybe."

Doran didn't see it, but then again, he spent most of his time on the road, making him more accustomed to such ambushes. He waved the notion away and ploughed through the snow to retrieve his axe.

"I'll be takin' that, thank ye!" The son of Dorain yanked his axe out of the runner's skull, lifting the head as he did.

The corner of a tattoo on the man's neck caught Doran's eye. The dwarf huffed, thinking nothing of it, before deciding to take a closer look. If the Galfreys said that something wasn't right then it often wasn't.

Pulling back the man's shirt, Doran inspected the tattoo only to find it ran down the neck and over the torso. The dwarf rolled the body over and caught sight of another tattoo, on the man's wrist.

"Hang abou'…" Doran knew that tattoo. He roughly stripped back the sleeve and discovered it ran up his arm and connected to the mosaic on the runner's chest. "Over 'ere!" he called.

Reyna reached him first. "You have found something?"

Doran sniffed hard. "I've seen this bugger before."

"Where?" Nathaniel asked, crouching beside the body.

"Back in Grey Stone," the dwarf explained. "He was servin' drinks."

Reyna crouched on the other side, examining the tattoos on the other arm. "He was a servant of King Jormund?"

"No," Nathaniel answered firmly. "I've seen tattoos like these before, a long time ago." The old knight pointed at a particular pattern of tattoos that ran down the centre of the man's arm. "You see these straight lines, the sharp angles? That's a Namdhorian design. You see this longer one, the way it's entwined and ends with a point? That's the mark of The Ironsworn."

"The Ironsworn?" Reyna asked.

Doran spat on the ground. "Thieves, rapists, and murderers, me Lady!"

"They're a gang," Nathaniel clarified. "When I was a Graycoat, I had a few run-ins with them. I even remember them trying to establish a foothold in Longdale, when I was a child."

"That was sixty years ago," Doran said. "Times 'ave changed. The last I heard, The Ironsworn 'ave establishments in every town in the north. After that little civil war they had, the one that put that war-witch on the throne, the gang spread like wild fire. Had a run-in with them meself a few years back, in Dunwich."

Reyna ran her finger over the entwined mark. "Why would The Ironsworn attack us on the road like bandits? They clearly have a hold over the north if they have establishments in every town and city, so why go to the effort of waiting in the freezing cold to rob people?"

"Maybe robbing us wasn't the objective," Nathaniel said. "I would say we were targets if Doran saw this man in The Black Fort."

"Aye," Doran agreed. "They scouted us out and waited until we were on their turf before springin'!"

"But why?" Reyna questioned again. "Why would a gang from Namdhor go to the effort of infiltrating King Jormund's keep and then set a trap?"

"What trap?" Doran exclaimed. "Ye two knew we were bein' ambushed before they moved a muscle."

Nathaniel flashed Reyna smile. "Not much can get past an elven nose."

"Not when they smell this bad," Reyna replied.

"Still," Doran continued, "they sent what - ten men to kill us? It's bloody insultin'!"

Reyna and Nathaniel rose to their full height, looking back over the dead Ironsworn.

"Our reputations come from a war that ended thirty years ago," Reyna pointed out. "Most of these men weren't even born then."

"We're just relics now," Nathaniel concluded.

"Speak for yerself!" Doran insisted. "I've killed more beasties and bandits than ye've had hot meals."

Ignoring their comments, Reyna said, "Perhaps our presence in Namdhor is not desired, after all."

"By who?" Nathaniel gestured to the bodies. "By a gang? We were requested by Queen Skalaf. What do The Ironsworn care?"

Reyna slung her bow over her shoulder. "I wouldn't say we were *requested* exactly. I suppose we'll just have to reach Namdhor and discover the truth ourselves."

The son of Dorain stuck his fingers in his mouth and whistled, calling the Warhog. "Nothin's ever simple with ye two, is it?"

INTO THE DARK

The Crow paused by the edge of the ravine, taking a moment to marvel at the first rays of the rising sun. This was his favourite time, just before the sun crested the horizon.

One by one, the stars faded away, relenting to the awesome power of the sun. The black of night was pushed ever westward, its eternal battle with the light of day never to end.

It was beautiful.

Even now, The Crow could still remember watching the most glorious of sunrises as a child.

The Crow gripped his wand and looked over the edge of the ravine to find a canyon of darkness. It was the same canyon he had seen in his vision.

Morvir's nasal and irritating voice broke his thoughts. "Is it just as Kaliban showed you, Lord Crow?"

The wizard refrained from rolling his eyes. "Oh, yes," he lied softly. "Just as he showed me…"

"I see why they call it Nightfall," Morvir remarked, peering over the edge.

"Find the steps," The Crow commanded.

The eight mages, his greatest spell casters, began to search the lip of the ravine for the fabled steps of Nightfall. The Crow had chosen these eight specifically for their talents at resurrection and destruction spells.

"Have you ever met an Arakesh?" he asked his first servant, favouring the elvish pronunciation for assassin.

"No, Lord Crow." Morvir bowed his head, as he so often did. "But like all who fear the shadows that move, I have heard of them. It is said they fight blindfolded, that they have no need for sight."

"The Nightseye elixir..." The Crow mused.

"So the legends say," Morvir agreed. "They are forced to drink the elixir regularly as children until it changes their very blood. I have never sampled Nightseye, but I hear one's senses become incredibly heightened."

"Over here!" one of the mages called.

The Crow moved with such purpose that Morvir was forced to side-step in a bid to escape his master's stride.

It was a small jump down to the first step, hidden beyond the edge of the ravine. Carved from the rock, the steps continued to descend into the canyon, following its curving walls, little more than the width of a man's shoulders.

It was only a few minutes of traversal, however, before they came across the arched entrance to the lair of the Arakesh. It was a humble entrance devoid of carvings or inscriptions, much like the now ancient hollows of The Echoes.

Once again, The Crow was faced with the black abyss, home to predators. He gripped his wand. The first time they had entered the darkness of another's lair, The Black Hand emerged with the might of the orcs behind them. Now, he would emerge with a guard befitting of his station.

As one, the ten mages of The Black Hand entered Nightfall with their wands and staffs at the ready. They journeyed but a single foot before the first arrow sailed through the shadows and pierced the skull of a mage.

"Shields!" Morvir ordered.

The next salvo of arrows impacted against invisible shields that flared in a variety of brilliant colours as they protected their casters.

The Crow didn't bother with one, shielded as he was behind Morvir's staff. Instead, he raised his wand and summoned the Winds of Galdor, a spell that would lift even the strongest of trolls from their feet.

The blast of energy burst forth from his wand and filled the sides of the corridor as it rushed ahead. The assassins found no shelter from the spell but, instead, found the back wall more than happy to greet them. Their bones cracked and their weapons snapped before they fell back to the cold floor.

"A little light, perhaps?" The Crow suggested.

The remaining eight mages released orbs of light into the darkened corridor, revealing walls of intricate and amazing tapestries and murals carved from the stone. The end of the corridor was decorated with the dead bodies of three Arakesh.

"Come." The wizard continued, unafraid.

"What of Garrett?" Morvir asked, gesturing to their dead brother.

The Crow offered but a glance at the man's body. "We shall wake him up on our way out…"

The contingent of dark mages made their way through the narrow, maze-like corridors. There were no signs of anyone else living inside the assassins' temple: not a footstep to be heard or a sword drawn from its scabbard. The Crow was sure to keep an ear out for the distinct sound of a bow string being pulled taut.

"Why have we not been challenged?" one of the mages asked.

"If the legends are true," Morvir replied, "then they should already know we're here."

The leader of The Black Hand stopped at a crossroads of corridors. "I would say we've piqued their interest." The Crow sniffed the air. To his right was the intoxicating aroma of cooked food, straight ahead that of sweat, and to his left the stench of death. "This way," he bade, turning left.

After a couple of turns, each one taking them deeper into the labyrinth, a faint light showed them the way. The Crow extinguished half of the orbs glowing around them and walked towards the new light.

The corridor opened up into a large square, surrounded by a U-shape of balconies. The braziers in the corners were lit, shedding light on the hundred or so Arakesh standing on the balconies, looking down on them. To the right, the stone floor descended by ten steps into an adjacent room.

Moving into the square, The Crow could see the circular pit in the other room. In his visions, he had seen the assassins entering that pit to face the nightmares of The Under Realm as a final test. It was where the stench of death was coming from...

"This is highly irregular," came a female voice from the head of the room.

The braziers offered what light they could, but the woman, seated in the throne at the head of the room, remained shrouded in darkness as if the shadows clung to her for warmth.

"If you wish to utilise the services of the Arakesh, you will have to acquire a contract through the proper channels." The woman on the throne leaned forward, exposing her features to the light.

The Crow guessed her to be somewhere between forty and fifty, her attributes entirely ordinary for a woman of her age. Of course, it was her eyes that captured The Crow's attention.

Or lack thereof.

The Mother of Nightfall stood up from her throne with her hands clasped in front of her. Unlike the assassins around them, she wore long dark robes with red piping to match the red blindfolds of the Arakesh. Her lidless eye sockets bored into The Crow.

"I require thirteen of your best assassins," the wizard announced.

"Thirteen?" the Mother repeated in disbelief. "I assure you, whatever the task is, only one Arakesh is needed."

"I require thirteen all the same," he reiterated. "Your best."

"You believe that you can enter our domain, kill three of our order, and demand thirteen of my greatest assassins?" The Mother gave a sharp laugh. "Magic or no magic, you will never see the sky again."

The Crow nodded along having lost track of the number of

threats he had received in his long life. "If you could at least present the thirteen I have requested, it would be appreciated."

"You fanatical cults..." the Mother said with disdain. "So arrogant. *Our* reputation comes from centuries of proving our worth."

The leader of The Black Hand mused over her terminology, considering his followers. "A cult today... a religion tomorrow." He glanced at the small shrine off to the side. The inscription indicated that it was a shrine to Ibilis, the god of shadows. "Even the infamous Arakesh will worship Kaliban when we are finished." The ignorant mages lapped up his words.

So easily manipulated...

The Mother stood perfectly still, a pale statue devoted to stoicism. "Tell me how you found Nightfall and thirteen of the world's greatest killers will make your death a swift one."

The Crow was impressed. Standing around them, on the same level, were thirteen assassins with their twin short-swords in hand. How they had come to be standing there was beyond him.

"If you survive this, I will show you." It was as bold a statement as it was threatening.

"Very well," The Mother sneered. "Make sure they have enough body parts left to torture them," she instructed.

Morvir stamped his staff into the stone floor, eliciting a loud crack and a flash of light. The blindfolded assassins were undeterred by the mage's actions and came at them from thirteen different angles of attack. Their twin blades rebounded off a flaring yellow bubble that had engulfed The Black Hand.

Raising his voice, The crow said to no one in particular, "These thirteen are to remain *intact!*"

Without eyes, it was difficult to assess The Mother's expressions but, if The Crow had to guess, he would say she displayed amusement followed by confusion. That confusion quickly turned into outrage when the first wave of dead Grim Stalkers emerged from the pit.

Before emerging from The Under Realm, The Crow had seen to the deaths of his Grim Stalker escort personally. His spells had ripped through their flesh, tearing their obsidian armour asunder. Now, they rose from the pit as true monsters, Darklings all.

The undead orcs roared and growled as they filled the adjacent room. The Arakesh in the balconies above them reacted immediately, jumping down to intercept the invaders. Safe inside their shielding orb, The Crow and the others watched the two sides collide in battle.

The Mother shot out from her throne with a wide scimitar in hand. The blade whipped across orc throats and cut through their dark armour as if it wasn't even there. The wizard noticed that the other assassins gave her a wide berth rather than close ranks and protect her, as soldiers would their king or queen.

Sadly for the Mother, the Darklings refused to stay down. As long as their head remained attached to their bodies, the monsters would come.

One Arakesh was unfortunate enough get his blade lodged in the helmet of a Darkling orc. The assassin was quickly swarmed and found himself flattened against the shielding orb. Blood exploded from his mouth and splattered across the shield before the Darklings finished the job with their claws and teeth.

The Darkling Grim Stalkers proved their worth, scaling the walls and ceiling to take any advantage they could over the superior killers. While in greater numbers than the assassins of Nightfall, the orcs were not as efficient in the art of killing, since a great deal of maiming often came first. Watching the Arakesh now, The Crow could see that they were trained to end life as quickly as possible.

It didn't take them long to realise the key to laying the Darklings low. The mounting orc bodies were testament to that fact...

Still, more monsters poured out of the pit and filled Nightfall's central chamber. One Grim Stalker dropped from the ceiling and drove an Arakesh to the ground, where the orc proceeded to headbutt the man until his bony brow split the assassin's skull open. The Mother's ravenous scimitar lashed out and removed the Darkling's head in a single swipe.

The Arakesh utilised their agility and danced around the Grim Stalkers. They weren't fighting any ordinary foe, however. Darklings behaved more akin to animals than anything else. Animals that felt no pain.

For all their skill, the assassins of Nightfall couldn't hold back the tide. The Crow cared very little for the numbers lost on either side. As far as he was concerned, this was evil killing evil. There would be no place for either in his new world, no matter how strong they were.

Limping now, the Mother was using her scimitar as more of a crutch than a weapon. Like others of her order, she was retreating into the darkened hallways of Nightfall. There would be no hiding from the Darklings in there, he thought. The Arakesh required elixirs to see so well in the dark, but those that challenged them now had been hunting in the dark for millennia.

The Crow stepped forward, breaking the shield that surrounded them. With a levelled wand, he fired a single spell into the Mother's back. She cried out, dropped her sword, and fell face down in the blood.

The Darklings scurried past, paying their master no heed as they chased away the last of the assassins. The wizard flicked his wand and turned the Mother over, onto her back. She writhed around the floor, but her back was certainly broken, leaving her at his mercy.

"How gracious of you," he purred. "You have already given us so much, now you offer yourself..." The Crow sat on the floor beside the Mother. "Between life and death, one can glimpse all that was, all that is... and all that *will be*." The wizard considered the dark mages behind him and placed a finger to his lips. "They think it's god," he said with some amusement.

"You will never... get out of here... alive," the mother hissed.

"Hmm." The Crow looked over her crippled body. "Perhaps there is still a little too much life in you." Using his wand, he cast a spell to slash open the Mother's wrists. Warm blood poured out, adding to the already soaking floor.

"My Lord Crow?" Morvir interrupted.

"Find the thirteen," he commanded sharply. "Bring them back as Reavers."

They were no good to him as mindless Darklings and there

certainly wasn't enough magic in Nightfall to create even a single Astari. As Reavers, the Arakesh would serve him as slaves that retained their unique talents from life.

The dark mages gathered the thirteen in a neat row after shifting many of the bodies that lay strewn across the floor. The nine mages, Morvir included, went through the motions of carving the ancient symbols into the appropriate body parts, as well as painting a few on with the blood that pooled around them.

After the correct glyphs and symbols had been applied, the mages moved on to the chanting, calling on their magic to give back what portion of their life had been robbed of them. Like all resurrection spells, it didn't offer immortality, only the remainder of what they should have lived.

Using either their wands or staffs, the mages finally cast the spell that gave life to the assassins' muscles, reanimating them. Without a word or a gasp, the thirteen Arakesh sat up where they lay.

"Rise," The Crow commanded.

The assassins performed as any Reaver would and stood up before their master. They were still whole, though they all possessed deep gashes and mortal wounds to their head or chest.

"Collect your weapons," he ordered. "Your single task is to protect me at all times."

The Reavers remained standing after collecting their twin blades. They couldn't reply with anything other than unintelligible groans and so he ordered them to be silent at all times.

"We shall have to find them some new clothes," The Crow commented. "They're too ghoulish as they are."

"As you wish, Lord Crow," Morvir replied. "Where would the great Kaliban have us go next?"

The wizard shifted his attention back to the Mother, who had turned a shade paler than her already ash-coloured skin.

As always, The Crow disguised his use of dark magic. "I will perform the rites given to me by Kaliban himself. I will listen for us all…"

His response, combined with his station, afforded his lie the utmost credibility. Morvir bowed his head and backed away, giving his master the room required to make such a divine connection.

The Crow flourished his wand and tore open the Mother's clothes, revealing her bare stomach. He dipped the end of the wand into the blood, pooling around her wrists, and drew the ancient glyphs on her pale skin.

Six intricate circles of glyphs surrounded her navel by the time he was finished.

He didn't have long, he never did. With every second her life ebbed away and death laid its claim. He needed her to be between worlds...

Pointing his wand directly over her navel, The Crow began the spell he had learned Ages past. He drew the blood up through the painted glyphs until the pit of her stomach was overflowing. The incantations leaving his mouth came out at unintelligible speed, each word evoking the magic of the spell.

The Mother's fingers began to twitch as she took her final breath. While her blood still possessed some of her life, The Crow scooped up the warm liquid in both hands and washed it over his face.

Time slowed down.

The vision brought with it a degree of pain that required focus to see the details.

The Crow saw Velia, the crowning jewel of The Shining Coast and capital of Alborn. Dragons were swarming overhead and orcs were scurrying about below. Blood rained down on them all as Malliath and Ilargo fought overhead.

The future was laid out for him like a tapestry and The Crow knew exactly where he was supposed to be to see it all come true. It brought a wicked smile to his face. None could match the power of such ancient magic.

When he opened his eyes again, dripping with blood from his face, the Arakesh Reavers had taken up positions around the chamber. The mages gathered around, waiting to hear the word of their Lord. Morvir was on the floor beside him, furiously scribing away everything The Crow had said during his vision. The first servant reached over to one of the dead bodies, of which there were many, and bathed his palm in their blood, ready to sign the new prophecy.

The Crow casually removed his wand and pressed the tip to the parchment. A moment later, the scroll burst into flames, destroying the prophecy.

"We do not require such record keeping anymore," he explained. "The time of scribing is at an end, Morvir. The war is about to begin, and with it our forge is prepared." The Crow wiped some of the blood from his eyes. "Who do we have in the Tregaran force?"

Morvir looked away, consulting his memory. "Anabeth is in charge, Lord Crow."

"Contact her. I have a special errand for her to perform."

"At once, Lord Crow." Morvir bowed and commanded one of the others to fetch a diviner.

The Crow stood up, dripping with blood. "And send word. We are coming home…"

BROKEN PEOPLE

Vighon was awed by the blanket of stars that arched over The Arid Lands. With the ruins of Karath and Syla's Gate many miles behind them now, there wasn't much else to look at.

Except for Inara…

Vighon did his best to keep his eyes on the magnificence above them, but his gaze couldn't help but fall on the beautiful Dragorn. Of course, every time he looked at her, Athis looked at him. The dragon's piercing blue eyes spoke volumes, averting Vighon's interest.

"They look like they have a lot to talk about," Galanör commented as he sat down beside Vighon.

Vighon glanced at the elf before looking across the fire, to the twins. Inara and Alijah were a little way into the desert, on the edge of the firelight, and deep in discussion.

"They haven't seen each other in four years," Vighon replied. "It's just a matter of time before one of them tries to kill the other…"

Galanör unclipped his dual scimitars and ceremoniously removed the fine blades from their scabbards. "Why can we all feel the tension between them? Hadavad's never mentioned any bad blood between them."

Vighon checked the mage, sleeping soundly beside Ned. "Blood's the only thing they share anymore. Alijah walked away from the family four years ago, no word, no note. He just left in the middle of the night."

The elven ranger began wiping down the steel of his blades with a delicate cloth. "Why would he walk away? Just having his last name will open every door in Illian."

Vighon shrugged. "That's all he's ever told me, and that was three years ago. Alijah doesn't really like talking about it, or his family in general. I think he finds it easier to believe he hasn't got one."

Galanör paused with what appeared to be a deeper understanding of Vighon's explanation. "Family can be painful."

Vighon tugged on his sleeve to hide one of the many scars that marred his body. "Isn't that the truth." He looked back at Alijah, meeting his eyes briefly in the distance. "Alijah's my family now."

Galanör lifted his scimitar to eye level and examined the flat of the blade. "Does that make Inara your sister, then?"

Vighon could feel a small lump forming in his throat as he once again found Athis's eyes on him. "That doesn't make us anything," he replied, dismissing the topic with his tone.

The elf smiled. "As you say."

"I do bloody say," Vighon snapped.

Galanör turned his attention to the other scimitar. "You've certainly got that temper you northerners are known for," he said absently.

"What would you know of it," Vighon bit back, tempted to go and sit on the other side of the fire.

"By your accent I'd say you've spent a lot of time in Namdhor." The ranger wiped his cloth down the steel with incredible care. "A hardy folk from recollection."

"You can learn a lot in Namdhor," Vighon said, eyeing the elven scimitars. "We can swing a real sword for starters. Namdhorian children play with toys like those."

"Not like these they don't." Galanör showed no sign of offence. "This one is Stormweaver." The ranger presented Vighon with the scimitar in two hands.

It was impossibly light, well balanced by the hilt, and etched with elven glyphs. Vighon wanted one.

"Feels flimsy," he lied.

Galanör smiled again and took the blade back, presenting Vighon with its twin. "This is Guardian."

Again, Vighon hefted the scimitar and got a feel for the weapon. It wasn't identical to Stormweaver, which had a blue and golden hilt rather than Guardian's green and silver hilt. Vighon didn't have the best command over his own language, let alone elvish, but he was sure the glyphs on the steel were different too.

"They're so light," he commented. "Can they even cut through leather?"

Galanör chuckled to himself. "They can cut through more than just leather. They were forged by the best elven smiths in Elandril, using techniques passed down from the First Age."

Vighon looked upon the scimitar with new interest. "These were made in Elandril? In Ayda?"

Galanör nodded. "An ocean away. They were gifts from Queen Adilandra herself for my part in the war."

"The War for the Realm?" Vighon checked.

The elven ranger took Guardian back. "It's the only war I've lived through, so I just call it the war. At the time we didn't even think of it as war, it was just survival. The fancy names and tales always come afterwards, I suppose."

Vighon would never divulge his desire for the blades, but knowing where they had come from only made him want them all the more.

"What of your blade?" the elf asked, eyeing the sword laid out in front of Vighon.

Vighon wanted to embellish the sword's history and forging but, looking at it now, the blade only brought back harsh memories. "It's nothing special. I just like the balance..."

"The same cannot be said of your shield," Galanör observed.

Vighon rapped his knuckles against the shield's smooth wood. "It was a gift from Hadavad. He gave it to me three years ago after I joined this merry band of... whatever we are."

"The magic he etched into it is powerful," the ranger replied. "You took more than one spell that should have killed you."

Vighon sighed. "The old man didn't give me that shield to keep me alive. He told me exactly what I was to do with it when he put it in my hands." He looked across the fire at the closest thing he had to a brother. "He told me to keep Alijah alive."

The elf didn't reply straight away, choosing, instead, to chew his lip and glance from Hadavad to Alijah. "In the years you have been together, Vighon, has Hadavad ever referred to Alijah as his apprentice?"

Vighon's face screwed up at the question. "Why would..." It took a second longer, but he understood the meaning behind Galanör's question. "No, he hasn't. At least not with me around. As far as I'm concerned, preventing the old man's spirit from crawling inside Alijah comes under the same edict as keeping him alive."

Galanör simply nodded quietly, apparently satisfied with Vighon's answer.

"What's your part in all this?" Vighon asked, suddenly curious as to the ranger's motivations.

Galanör offered a coy smile. "You have your orders, and I have mine."

"Oh, we're back to that are we? You should know, the whole mysterious ranger thing doesn't work for you. It's just bloody annoying."

～

Where the light met the dark, Inara turned her back on Vighon Draqaro, who stole every opportunity to glance at her, and, instead, confronted her brother.

"So this is it then?" she began, struggling after only five words to contain her frustration. "Four years go by without a word and I get a pat on the back."

"Inara…" Alijah could only maintain eye contact for a second.

"You just left, Alijah. You packed a bag, *stole* Asher's blade and bow, and slinked away in the night!"

Alijah threw his hands up. "I didn't *steal* anything. They belonged to the family and they'd sat above the hearth for decades collecting dust. I've put them to much better use." He turned his back on her before quickly coming back around. "And I didn't *slink* away in the night! I just walked away!"

Inara glanced over her shoulder to see Galanör and Vighon looking at them. It seemed nothing could wake Hadavad, who slept like the dead.

"Try and keep your outbursts to a more mature volume," she said as patronisingly as she could.

Alijah gritted his teeth. "Don't start on me."

Inara… Athis's tone projected soothing emotions.

Ignoring the dragon's calming aura, Inara pressed on. "If memory serves, you always started it and I always finished it…"

"I'm faster than you," Alijah said with a dangerous glint in his eye.

"And yet you were always slower to learn," Inara fired back, clenching her fist. "I'm stronger, remember?"

Alijah flashed a cocky smile. "I've learnt a few things here and there…"

"It's a shame you haven't learnt how to shave," Inara quipped.

Alijah's face dropped before scrunching into a grimace. That was it. Brother and sister kicked up the sand and dashed for each other with murder in their eyes.

Athis brought his tail down between them like a hammer, preventing any escalation.

Somewhere beyond the fire, Inara heard Vighon say, "I told you so…"

Inara! If you cannot control yourself then you are not the Dragorn Master Thorn trained you to be. You will also find yourself grounded until some measure of control and humility can be found.

Inara wanted to reply to her companion, but she could feel the dragon close himself off just enough to give her the hint.

The Dragorn sighed and looked at her brother. "You have to help me, Alijah. You just walked out and took the only things our parents had left of Asher. Do you know what you've put them through?"

Alijah wiped his face, just as he had done as a child when he was exasperated. "Are they well?"

Inara could feel her fury rising to the surface once more. "You would know if you hadn't cut us all off! If you wanted to be a ranger you could have just said. Instead, you left our parents to split their duty to the realm and waste time searching for you."

Alijah whirled on her shaking his head. "I don't want to be a ranger. I just... I just wanted..." He swallowed all his anger and became eerily still. "You couldn't understand. None of you could."

"Help me to, Alijah," Inara pleaded, desperate to have her brother back.

"How could you understand?" he spat. "You, the *Dragorn*. Your shadow drowns us all. I could just about compete for our parents' attention growing up, but when we turned sixteen... everything changed."

"Alijah..." Inara didn't know what to say. They had both travelled to The Lifeless Isles to meet the dragons, but only one of them had remained.

"You left me," Alijah said, fighting back the tears. "For *him*." Alijah levelled his gaze at Athis, his eyes blazing with hatred. "After that, it didn't matter what I did. Inara Galfrey, the Dragorn! I became an afterthought. The one they didn't know what to do with. The one who always got it wrong."

"That's just your perception!" Inara argued. "They never saw you as—"

"How would you know?" Alijah blinked a single tear away. "You weren't there, Inara. You had an eternity of adventures ahead of you."

"That's it?" Inara bit her lip in an effort to stay calm. "You walked out without a word because you were jealous? Your talents are limitless. I grew up in *your* shadow! You could do anything you wanted, everything came naturally to you. You were just too much of a spoilt brat to see it!"

"I didn't walk out because I was..." Alijah ran out of energy and turned his attention to the ground. "You couldn't understand."

"I think you've laid it all out pretty well." Inara shook her head having heard about as much as she could handle.

"Inara..." Alijah called, turning her back. "I left *for* you, for all of you."

There was something in his tone that gripped her. For all the lies he told to himself, this was the truth.

"How could exiling yourself be for the good of the family?"

Alijah walked over, removing the tie from his messy ponytail as he did. His hair cascaded over his chest in a mixture of knots and braids. With one hand, he scraped back the hair on the right side of his head and turned his face so that Inara could see him clearly.

It took Inara's elven eyes a moment in what little light they had, but there was no mistaking the few strands of grey hair hiding among the black ones. It took another moment for her to realise what that actually meant. The Dragorn gasped and stood back with a hand covering her mouth.

"No... no you can't be..." Inara could feel eyes on her again but she ignored them. "They're just... they don't mean..."

Athis looked back at her as she called out to him for help.

Alijah let his hair fall back over his chest again. "Father started to get a few grey hairs in his early twenties as well. The magic that Asher poured into him halted any more from coming through. It's quite typical... for *mortal men.*"

Inara couldn't accept it. She looked at his pointed ears, elven cheekbones, and recalled his enviable speed growing up. If anything, he was more elf than she was.

"We're half-elf," he continued. "There was always the chance that one of us would inherit a mortal's lifespan. Unfortunately," Alijah looked down at himself, "it was the one who couldn't be a Dragorn."

Inara could feel tears welling up in her eyes. "No," she said again. "Father is immortal. Mother is immortal. We should both be—"

"Father's immortality isn't natural," Alijah corrected. "It cannot be passed on."

Inara clamped down on her emotions enough to ask, "That's why you left? Because you'll..." She couldn't say the word.

"Because one day, I'll die," he said bluntly. "I didn't want Mother and Father... I didn't want *you* to see that. To watch me die while you all live on. It's not fair. I thought, the sooner I leave the better."

There was a quiet rage building inside of Inara and she wanted to hit something. For the first time ever, the Dragorn found herself wishing she was standing in front of a hundred orcs. Instead, she darted forward and wrapped her arms around her brother. Alijah hesitated in her embrace, but he eventually lifted his arms and held her tightly.

Inara finally stood back, glancing at the side of her brother's head. ***Is it true?*** she asked Athis.

The red dragon curled his neck around to bring his head over the two of them. Athis inhaled deeply, pulling at the twins' hair.

I am so sorry, Inara. He is mortal.

Hearing it from Athis made it all the more real in Inara's mind. Her head dropped and tears fell from her eyes, thankfully concealed by her hair.

"It's better this way," Alijah said with a dispassionate practicality to his tone. "We're twenty-six years old. None of you have seen me since we were twenty-two. Twenty-two years is easier to get over than a whole lifetime."

Inara whipped her head up. "That's not for you to decide! You should have told us. We should have discussed this as a family!"

"What family?" he snapped back. "You were never around, they were always off somewhere on official business. We hadn't been a family for some time when I left."

"That's not fair," Inara insisted. "We all had responsibilities, Alijah. Places we had to be, duties to perform for the good of the realm."

"That's what I've been doing," Alijah declared with a finger in his chest. "I just had to get out from under your shadow and our parents' fame to discover it."

"You have responsibilities to the realm now, do you?" Inara asked incredulously.

"I do," Alijah stated firmly. "When your years are numbered and old age beckons, you begin to see the world differently. You don't have an eternity to figure things out, to find yourself. You have to dive right in and paddle for as long as you can." Alijah was pacing now. "I wanted my life to mean something. All I've ever wanted is to serve the realm, keep it safe as our parents did, as you do."

"You mean, you wanted to be *important*." Inara regretted her words and tone immediately. Alijah had a way of bringing this side out in her.

"You couldn't understand," Alijah said again, shaking his head. "While you've been flying around hunting down monsters in the desert, I've been making a difference. The Black Hand are the biggest threat to the realm. You didn't even know about them! They've been manipulating events from the shadows for centuries. Now Asher is back and bonded with Malliath, both of whom are slaves to The Crow's will. Whatever they're planning, it's on a scale to match the war and I've been in the middle of it for the last four years."

"You don't know what you're in the middle of," Inara maintained. "If the orcs really are returning to the world in the numbers I fear they are, a few dark mages are the least of our problems. You're in way over your head, Alijah. Hadavad has been battling The Black Hand for five centuries, Galanör is a seasoned warrior who out-classes us both. You're running around playing *hero* with Vighon when you should be—"

"Should be what?" Alijah interrupted. "Now that you know I'm mortal you think I should stay at home and read books by the fire? I've uncovered temples and relics of The First Kingdom. I've battled The Black Hand and their leagues of undead. I even found a..."

Inara could see the subtle twitches flicker across her brother's face. He had plenty of bluster left in him - he just didn't want to divulge something.

"You found what?" she pressed.

Alijah stood up a little straighter. "You have Dragorn business and we have ours."

Inara couldn't believe what she was hearing. "I think we're on the same side," she argued.

"Until today, you didn't even know there were sides. The great Gideon Thorn has been blind to the single most devastating threat to all of Illian. You keep hunting your orcs, they're on the other side of The Undying Mountains. *We* will take care of The Black Hand."

"Oh right." Inara nodded along. "So you're going to... what? Beat Asher in a drinking game? Ask Malliath to kindly fly away? You're trying so hard to prove yourself that you can't see what's going on around you. Those that you hunt and those that I hunt have allied. The Dragorn might not have known about The Black Hand's involvement, but we do now."

Alijah shook his head with a mirthless laugh. "So, you're just going to take over? This is Dragorn business now?"

"I'll tell you what I'm going to do." Inara took two steps closer to her brother and looked him in the eyes. "I'm going to escort you all to Tregaran, so I know you're safe. Then, I'm going to report back to *Master* Thorn so we can get on top of this before it gets any worse."

"Any worse?" Alijah echoed. "A cult of necromancers hell bent on religious reform have resurrected *the* Asher and enslaved the biggest dragon in the world. A horde of monsters from the past rises up to join them, but it's alright, the *mighty Dragorn* are going to get on top of it before it can get any worse."

"You think we should leave it up to you?" Inara retorted. "You might have Asher's sword and bow on your back, but neither of them will be enough to stop this evil from spreading. Maybe the mage can help you. He's only been failing to defeat The Black Hand for five hundred years... I suppose there's Galanör. A wayward elf with no sense of belonging and a penchant for killing monsters. Or

Vighon, perhaps?" Inara paused her sarcastic tirade to consider their old friend. "Why *is* Vighon with you, exactly?"

Alijah looked to be on the edge of hysteria when he gritted his teeth and sighed, calming his entire demeanour. "You do whatever you have to do and we'll keep doing what we have to do. Nothing's changed, Inara. I'm not *coming back*. You should find a way to accept that you have no brother. Try and help our parents to do the same."

He began to walk away, infuriating Inara. "You're so damn selfish!" she spat, hoping he would turn back and continue their argument. He didn't. Alijah became a cloaked silhouette as he walked back to the fire instead.

Inara's mind was a storm that swirled with a mix of emotions and thoughts.

I always knew something was wrong, she said to Athis. *Or that we had wronged him in some way and that's why he left. I just thought we would have eternity to work it out...*

I am sorry, wingless one. Athis flexed his wing slightly, concealing Inara from those around the fire. *His years may be limited, but they will be all the more vibrant. He can still have a full life of great deeds and happiness.*

I don't care about all that, Inara replied, wiping tears from her cheeks. *I just wanted my brother. I wanted my parents to have their son. I just wanted to be a family.*

Are we not family? Athis asked softly.

Inara sniffed and looked up to meet her companion's gaze. *Of course we are. You are all I will ever need, it's just...*

I know, Athis said deep in her mind. *Family is complicated for you two-legs. Being mortal as he is, Alijah will see the world and the passage of time differently. He may wish to bridge the gap much sooner than you think.*

Inara shut her eyes tight to keep the tears in. *He will still die though. Nothing will change that.*

Athis curled his tail around and Inara sat down in the centre of the coil. Being close to the dragon was the only thing that ever really comforted her.

You and I will live to see the rise and fall of many things. We are the constant. Our bond will surpass all else. This is the way of things...

Inara could sense that Athis cared for Alijah in his own way, something he couldn't avoid being bonded with her, but his words didn't come as a comfort. She felt the dragon was telling her to forget Alijah, just as her brother wanted.

I do not say these things to upset you, wingless one. I say them because you are Dragorn. Perhaps you should embrace that other half of yourself, the dragon half.

I want to, Athis. It's just... Alijah and my parents tie me to the world. I feel as if you and I, all the Dragorn, are something else, something more. My family reminds me that there is a world beneath us. A world of other families that need our help. Without my family, I'm not sure who I am or what I'm supposed to do.

Without them, you would have us go off into the unknown? Athis asked. *Despite our duty and place among the Dragorn?*

Hearing it said like that made Inara wince. **I'm just pointing out that you and I are free. We're about as free as anyone could ever be. We're Dragorn because we choose to be, not because we have to be. I'm just saying that my bond with my family is what reminds me that we're part of the world. If Alijah was to die, a part of my bond to the world would die with him.**

I understand, Athis said, coiling his tail a little tighter. *We will find our way through this, together.*

Inara rubbed the scales on his tail, enjoying the warmth that emanated from them. **We've got a lot to wade through. I feel as if the world has turned upside down in a matter of hours.**

You need rest, Athis insisted. *Tomorrow we will reach Tregaran and from there we will return to The Lifeless Isles. Master Thorn and Ilargo will offer us council.*

Inara lay back and placed her head against his tail, a restless night of broken dreams awaiting her...

25

RECLAMATION

For thirty years, Gideon Thorn had been soaring through the clouds with Ilargo. In that time, they had developed their own way of traversing the world together.

The green dragon took to great heights when journeying long distances, as they did now from The Lifeless Isles to Syla's Gate, in a bid to avoid dehydration in the warmer air below. For the Master Dragorn, however, this required magic to keep him warm and breathing.

Ilargo flapped his powerful wings before falling into a silent glide, allowing the clouds to rise above them and reveal the ground. Illian lay sprawled out beneath them in all its beauty. The snow-covered fields of the north were beginning to die away as they ventured farther south. The deserts of The Arid Lands denied winter its chilling bite.

Such views would normally be enough to distract Gideon, and the thrill of flying with Ilargo never became old, but his mind was as clouded as the skies above.

"Blood will be spilled this night…"

The Crow's words echoed in his thoughts. Gideon was aware of every Dragorn's assignment and location. Inara and Edrik were the only ones far from home and searching for creatures who had made a name for themselves hunting down dragons.

There is no connection between The Black Hand and the return of the orcs, Ilargo reminded him, sensing the storm swirling inside of him.

Think about everything we know, Ilargo. Something is happening in The Undying Mountains. Gideon squeezed the dragon's spikes all the harder, his frustration getting the better of him. **I shouldn't have left Inara and Athis down there...**

You are overprotective of her.

She's like family, Ilargo.

All Dragorn are your family. Your unique relationship with Inara has been raised before. She cannot come before others.

Gideon rolled his eyes, reliving the entire conversation he had been forced to have with the Dragorn council.

I know you're rolling your eyes...

Of course you do. Gideon closed his eyes and tried to focus his concerns, hoping to gain some kind of control over them.

They are not alone, Ilargo continued. *You sent Edrik and Aldreon.*

We both know I sent Edrik as a teaching exercise.

Ilargo flapped his wings and took them a little higher. *And I'm sure one is learning humility and the other wisdom. Either that or they're both killing each other.*

Gideon could feel the soothing emotions Ilargo was trying to share with him, but he couldn't take them on as his own. **There was something about The Crow. A confidence I can't shake. You don't tell your enemy that you're about to start a war with them unless you know you're going to win. There is more happening than we know, Ilargo.**

You can't be everywhere at once, Ilargo said.

We need to be, Gideon replied seriously. **Sixty-eight Dragorn are not enough to patrol the entire realm.**

Ilargo turned his head, looking upon Gideon with one of his large reptilian eyes. *There has been peace for thirty years.*

Yes, but then Tauren Salimson showed me a dead orc and the leader of The Black Hand was inside my mirror. I still want to find out how he—

Ilargo's head snapped to the west and Gideon followed his companion's sudden shift in attention.

"Malliath…" he whispered into the wind.

The black dragon was flying over the edges of the desert and travelling north, just below the cloud bank. Gideon knew every detail of the dragons that had remained in The Lifeless Isles rather than return to the south of Ayda with Rainael the emerald star, Ilargo's mother. The dragon flying in the opposite direction now could only be Malliath the voiceless.

We haven't seen him for twenty-five years, Ilargo said.

Gideon could feel the trepidation inside of Ilargo. In the first years after The War for the Realm, they had flown together into The Undying Mountains and even farther south searching for Malliath. As the largest and oldest of dragon-kind, Malliath was the rightful patriarch and ruler of his kin, but he had chosen exile.

Coming across him twenty-five years ago, the black dragon had told them in his own way that he intended to remain in exile…

Gideon could still feel the sting of his claws and the bite of his teeth from that fight. So too could Ilargo, no doubt.

Why would he be travelling north? Gideon asked. He hoped that the enormous dragon had decided to return to the world and was seeking them out. Something told the Master Dragorn that that wasn't going to be the case.

Gideon! There is a man on his back!

Gideon squinted into the distance but they were too far away. Now he had a really bad feeling.

Can you catch up with him? Gideon asked.

I can try! Ilargo replied, gritting his fangs.

Ilargo banked suddenly to the west and altered his flight path to bring them in line behind Malliath.

Gideon glanced over his shoulder to see The Undying Mountains fade away. The question hanging over Inara's fate, and that of Edrik's and Aldreon's, would have to wait.

Ilargo was cutting across the land and heading north now. Malliath was at least a mile ahead, if not more.

The winter sun crested low over the horizon, never daring to reach for its summer heights. Ilargo beat his wings from dawn till dusk and they both witnessed the emergence of the stars and the arrival of thick clouds from the east. More snow was being dumped over Illian, covering The Moonlit Plains and the pines of The Evermoore.

Malliath remained ever ahead.

The black dragon had perhaps been flying even longer than Ilargo, but he showed no sign of fatigue. The mysterious dark rider astride his back had disappeared into the black of Malliath's scales as the last of the light left the world. It wasn't long after that when Gideon's human eyes lost sight of the dragon too.

Looking down, the world was black, its landscapes and vistas reduced to a smooth surface of shadows. Ilargo rose higher to stay in line with Malliath and the two maintained their lofty heights for most of the night.

Can you see him? Gideon asked.

He is still ahead of us, Ilargo replied. *He's... wait. Malliath is dropping beneath the clouds.*

Where are we?

Ilargo's answer opened a pit inside Gideon's gut. *Lirian is beneath us!*

The clouds in front of them lit up as a great fire spread out underneath the white blanket.

He's attacking! Gideon held on and adjusted his position, anticipating Ilargo's dive.

The green dragon pierced the cloud bank and spread his wings to carry them over the city. As the capital of Felgarn, Lirian was the most densely populated city in the region. It was also constructed from a lot of wood.

Malliath and his rider flew low over the city and unleashed jets of fire. The torrents were so powerful as to cause some of the buildings to explode, launching the roofs high into the air. The streets were entirely consumed by the dragon's breath, cutting off escapes and trapping people in their homes.

Ilargo dropped down with little care for grace. Gideon could hear the city's bells ringing over the roaring fires. Against Malliath, however, there was nothing they, or any city, could do to defend themselves. The black dragon was a force of nature.

So are we, Ilargo answered his thoughts with righteous determination.

Gideon held on. ***Take him down!***

Ilargo banked to the west and aligned them with the perfect angle of interception. They had the height over Malliath. The green dragon hurtled towards him, having chosen an area on the edge of the city to grapple. Even if they took Malliath's attention off Lirian, two warring dragons could demolish a city between them.

Ilargo's claws came out, ready to find a purchase on Malliath's back, but the black dragon spread his wings, slowing his flight dramatically. Ilargo overshot and was forced spread his own wings to have them glide over the rooftops. The roar he released lit a fire in Gideon's soul, filling him with the need to fight.

Focus, he warned his companion. ***Our priority is the people. Now that we have his attention, let's see if we can't lure him away from Lirian.***

Ilargo banked to the north and they caught sight of Malliath stomping through the streets. His barbed tail swung freely, smashing houses and shops. A single jet of fire blasted through three buildings in a row, hurling their occupants from the windows.

Gideon, the rider is dismounting!

The Master Dragorn dug his heels into Ilargo's scales and stood up to see for himself. The rider was too far away to discern any recognisable details.

Put me down. I'll go after the rider, you keep Malliath from destroying the whole city.

Can we trade? the dragon asked as he landed in a crossroads.

Gideon dropped into a crouch and roll, coming up into a sprint. Mournblade was quick to find its place in his hand.

The streets had erupted into the kind of chaos and death that were rarely seen outside of war. People set alight from head to toe were running in every direction, their pain so agonising that they couldn't think straight and simply drop into the snow - not that it would help to extinguish dragon's fire.

Gideon navigated every obstacle, people included, to reach the spot where the rider had dismounted. The city watch clumped together with nocked bows and aimed blindly into the sky, the sky where Ilargo was flying.

"Stop!" The Master Dragorn held out his hand and expelled a wave of rippling energy into the air, knocking every loosed arrow from their path. "Concentrate on evacuating the city! Help anyone you can!"

Gideon wasted no more time and continued into the streets, leaving the city watch to murmur about the presence of a Dragorn.

Turning the corner, a team of horses came galloping across his path, threatening to trample him. Gideon dived to the side, missing the first of the horses by a foot. He rolled through the snow and came up running once again.

Three hideously sharp claws raked down his back, eliciting a sharp cry from the man. Gideon fell to his knees, hearing Ilargo's pain-filled roar reach across the night sky. The two dragons had finally collided in battle and Malliath had struck the first blow.

Calling on the magic that flowed through him, Gideon cast every healing spell he knew to at least stop the blood from running down his back. Ilargo would naturally heal quickly, but it wouldn't be quick enough if Gideon found himself in a fight soon.

He used Mournblade to push himself up, but it wasn't long before he had to move again. Anyone whose house wasn't on fire had abandoned their homes, fleeing for their lives. He could see that most were heading north, towards King Weymund's fort. The fort had passages that led deep into the small mountain, offering shelter from the hot breath of a dragon.

"Quickly!" he ushered them, grabbing the strays and pushing them in the right direction.

Gideon ran down the next street, heading west off the main road. This was where Malliath had left his rider...

"Where are you?" he asked himself, his dark eyes scanning the buildings between the fires.

Cautiously, the Master Dragorn walked through the street with a strong grip around Mournblade's red and gold hilt. The golden claw, hooked over the end, shone in the firelight.

More pain spread up his left ribs and a dull ache made itself known in his right shoulder. Looking up, the two dragons were grappling for supremacy, their sizes almost equal. Malliath, with the longer neck, had the greater reach, but Ilargo had the strength of his royal bloodline running through his muscles. The green dragon clawed at Malliath's wing joints and snapped his jaws at anything he could get his teeth into.

A window smashed in front of Gideon, drawing his attention back to the street. A man of solid build landed roughly in the snow and tumbled over himself. He had been hurled with some force to send him so far into the street, but what was more impressive was when the man got back up.

The man straightened his back, which was pocked with shards of glass, and hefted his pick-axe.

"Russell..." Gideon whispered. "Russell!" His yell was drowned out by the tavern's exploding door. The wood was ripped clean from its hinges and pushed out almost as far as Russell.

Through the flames and distorted air, Gideon laid eyes on Malliath's rider as he strode out of The Pick-Axe.

The Master Dragorn was frozen to the spot and not by the cold air.

With confident strides, the rider walked down the short steps of The Pick-Axe and came to face both Gideon and Russell Maybury.

"It cannot be..." Gideon said.

Standing in the middle of the street was an Outlander, an assassin, a ranger of the wilds, and the praised hero of The War for the Realm. To his friends, and Gideon himself for a short time, the man had been known by a single name.

"Asher!" Russell shouted over the fires. "No... you're not Asher! Whatever you are, beastie, my pick-axe will still drive through your head."

Gideon ran to join them, seeing that Russell was about to charge at Asher, but it was too late. Being a werewolf gave Russell supernatural speed and saw the two collide before Gideon even made it half way down the street.

With a two-handed broadsword, Asher raised his blade horizontally and blocked the descending pick-axe from caving his head in. Asher's broadsword, recognisable for its spiked pommel, arced through the air and twisted the pick-axe out of Russell's grip. The weapon spun through the air and landed farther down the street.

Asher swung his sword down and to the side, cutting a neat line across Russell's thigh. The owner of The Axe staggered backwards but Asher wasn't letting him get far. One step had Russell within easy reach of his arm again and the old ranger backhanded him with the spiked pommel. The werewolf fell back into the snow and spat blood from his shredded mouth.

That two-handed broadsword was coming down a moment later, its arc in line to chop Russell in half from head to groin.

Gideon turned the momentum of his sprint into a flying kick as he launched himself at Asher. Using reflexes that should have been reserved for elves, Asher spun on the spot and rotated his body out of harm's way by mere inches. Gideon continued across the gap and hit nothing but air before his feet landed on the snowy ground again.

Asher finished his spin by coming back around and plunging his sword through Russell's belly.

"NO!" Gideon cried.

Russell's yellow eyes bulged under the pressure in his gut. Asher twisted the blade once and yanked it free to face the Master Dragorn. There was no expression on his face, no glee or rage. He had stabbed and discarded Russell as if he was nothing.

Gideon raised Mournblade and tried to track both Asher and Russell. The werewolf had one hand over his gut wound while the other did its best to drag him through the snow, away from his attacker. There was a lot of blood pooling under him and melting the snow.

Asher began to walk towards Gideon and the Dragorn found

himself taking steps backwards. He was facing Asher, or at least something that looked like Asher. Fought like him too.

Was this really the ranger he had met thirty years ago? It couldn't be. In the caves of Kaliban, Valanis's fortress, Gideon had witnessed the death of Asher himself.

"You can't be him!" Gideon yelled. "I saw Asher's final moments! You *can't* be him!"

The man wearing Asher's face continued his stride, his sword held casually by his side. Gideon didn't want to fight him, but not because he was afraid, but because he knew he would kill him. Be it the real Asher or not, with Mournblade in hand Malliath's rider stood no chance of surviving.

He needed answers, not blood.

Asher burst into action. His broadsword appeared to swing wildly at Gideon but, at the last second, the old ranger turned his attack into one of finesse. The edge of his blade went left then right before coming at Gideon from above and then below.

Mournblade's magic reacted and assumed control of Gideon and his actions.

The two passed each other in a flash of sparks and quickly turned back to face the other. Their blades whistled through the cold air and connected again and again in that ancient song of battle. Asher was a fighter of many styles, coming at Gideon with the brutality of a savage and then the deadly grace of an assassin of Nightfall. It only convinced Gideon all the more that this really was *the* Asher.

As this dawned on the Master Dragorn, his intentions towards Asher changed, and, in so doing, affected the will of Mournblade. With the desire that he survived the fight, Mournblade changed its style and saw Gideon revert to form one of the Mag'dereth, a non-lethal form of combat.

Asher did his best to seek out every vulnerability and opening, lashing out with limb and blade alike. Still, Mournblade batted his attacks away and Gideon fell upon his training to defend against the blunt assaults.

A sharp pain exploded inside Gideon's thigh and he dropped to one knee, bringing his head under Asher's blade by an inch. Colossal shadows fell over the fighters as the titans of the world collided overhead. Malliath and Ilargo were entangled in a melee of jaws and claws, all the while their wings flapping furiously to keep them aloft. Hot blood rained down between the snow fall wherever they fought.

Another stab of agony ran through his gut as the dragons slammed into the ground. Ilargo's bulk flattened an entire burning house and Malliath's tail swung around to demolish a row of flaming shops.

Asher planted a boot in Gideon's chest and kicked him down the street. His broadsword came down in both hands but Mournblade shot out and intercepted the blade before it could decapitate the Master Dragorn. Gideon pushed back against Asher's might until he was able to find his feet and meet his foe face to face.

"It can't be you..." Gideon said through gritted teeth.

Asher had no reply, at least no verbal reply. With their swords mashed together, Asher reached out and gripped the back of Gideon's head, holding him firm for a headbutt. The blow opened a cut over the Master Dragorn's eyebrow, creating a trickle of blood to flow over his face.

Unfortunately, Ilargo suffered the identical blow.

The dragon roared several streets over and Malliath took advantage. The black dragon swiped one claw across his jaw, a blow felt equally by Gideon, and barrelled into the green dragon, launching both of them farther north, across Lirian's central gardens.

Staggering backwards, Gideon tried to shake off the wounds inflicted by Ilargo's fight as well as the wounds he received from Asher. He clenched his fist and called upon his magic to surge through his body and rejuvenate him.

Asher, however, was already swinging his next deadly blow.

Gideon forewent his spell of healing and opted for something with a little more kick to it. Asher's steel blade was slicing through every snowflake on its way to Gideon's neck when the Master

Dragorn flicked his fingers. The wave of energy fractured the light into a variety of colours before hammering into Asher.

His black cloak wrapped around him as he skidded and rolled through the snowy street. Somewhere to the north, Malliath roared and Ilargo pressed his attack with a solid tail to the face. Gideon was pleased to see this mirrored on Asher's face as he tried to stand. The blow knocked his head to the side and left a purple bruise that ran up to the black-fang tattoo under his left eye.

If it hurt him, there was no sign of it.

Gideon took deep breaths to try and centre himself before the fight began again. If Asher could feel Malliath's wounds, then it stood to reason that it would work the other way around and give Ilargo a better chance.

"I don't want to kill you," he told Asher as the man strode towards him, "but I *do* want to hurt you."

Asher came at him with a thrust, an attack Gideon knew he was feigning since thrusting should always be reserved for a killing blow against a crippled enemy. Knowing this, the Master Dragorn made no attempt to bat the blade away but, instead, dashed to the side in time with the twisting of Asher's sword. The opening across his ribs was too much for Mournblade to ignore. In keeping with its master's wishes, the blade lashed out in Gideon's hand and split Asher's dark leathers until it tasted blood and took a slice of rib for good measure.

Malliath roared and Asher fell to the side.

Now Ilargo!

The green dragon pounced, splintering an ancient tree on his way to Malliath. Ilargo sank his claws in and took the black dragon into a violent roll across the eastern side of Lirian. His powerful jaws clamped down again and again, drawing blood from multiple wounds.

Gideon watched as Asher thrashed about, each bite making itself known. From the look on his face, Gideon decided his enemy did feel pain after all. That he could work with.

The Master Dragorn advanced with Mournblade held high. Asher growled and rose up to meet the challenge, despite his continued pain. Gideon danced around him, whipping his scimitar high and low to both parry and attack. Blood splattered across the white snow and Asher collapsed to one knee.

Resting his scimitar against Asher's neck, Gideon asked through ragged breath, "You will tell me the truth! You cannot be him!" Asher looked up at him, his blue eyes reflecting the surrounding fires. "Who are you?" Gideon demanded.

He answered in the same gruff tone the old ranger had always spoken with, "I am a Dragon Knight."

That statement cut right through Gideon's thoughts, distracting him.

Elsewhere, Malliath succeeded in wrapping his tail around Ilargo's, flattening it to the ground. The black dragon constricted his coiled muscle and held Ilargo in place, preventing the green dragon from taking another bite. With his longer neck, Malliath sprung forward and fastened his maw around Ilargo's throat.

Gideon's moment of distraction turned into a moment of asphyxiation. The Master Dragorn stepped back and gripped his own throat as if someone had their hands around his windpipe.

Asher groaned but managed to stand, his broadsword glistening in the flames.

Without a word, he swung his blade.

26

A RED RAVEN

The world came back to Alijah in broken fragments. Sounds first. He heard familiar voices. His orientation then informed him that he was flat on his back. Blinking brought with it the pain of bright sunlight and confusion.

"What's happening?" he asked, feeling Vighon's hands gripping his arm and sitting him up.

Alijah blinked hard and forced the world to take shape again. Four faces and a dragon looked down on him with concern.

Then he remembered.

Just before the dawn, Alijah's body had erupted in pain. Claws raked at his skin and teeth sank through to his muscles. The sudden attack had thrown him from Vighon's horse, where he immediately curled up into a ball of agony.

A quick inspection proved he had come to no actual harm; he hadn't lost so much as a drop of blood.

"You fell off Ned," Vighon said.

"No he didn't," Inara replied flatly. "He was in pain *before* he fell."

Alijah looked from his sister's scrutinising gaze to the passive expressions on his companions' faces. If their knowledge of the truth was obvious to Alijah, it was blatantly obvious to Inara.

"What are you not telling me?" the Dragorn demanded.

Vighon helped Alijah to find his feet again. His friend gave the subtlest of shrugs and Hadavad and Galanör remained silent. It was clear to see that his companions would not say anything without his permission, but it was also clear that they felt Inara should know.

"I'm fine," he said, squeezing Vighon's arm as thanks.

"What's going on, Alijah?" Inara persisted.

Looking to the north, Tregaran was the size of his hand in the distance. There would be no chance of distraction in the time it would take them to travel the remainder of the journey.

"The Crow cast some kind of spell," he blurted, hoping to get it over with. "When he bonded Asher to Malliath... he connected me in some way. I feel everything they feel."

Inara's mouth dropped open and her features froze. In fairness, she had learned an awful lot about her brother in a very short amount of time; none of it good.

"Why didn't you tell me this?"

Alijah hated being questioned by his sister. "Because it's none of your business." Hearing his reason said out loud made him feel a little petty.

Inara looked away, shaking her head. "Forcing a bond between a person and a dragon should be impossible enough, but binding *another*... This Crow knows magic that simply shouldn't exist." The Dragorn stopped and held a silent conversation with Athis. "If you were in pain," she continued, "that means Malliath or Asher were as well."

Galanör nodded along with the assessment. "So who has been fighting with them?"

"And injuring them," Hadavad added.

"It could only be another dragon," Alijah suggested. "Maybe a few..." He rubbed his aching ribs.

Inara raised her eyes to the sky. A dragon as dark and large as Malliath would be easy enough to spot in the desert sky. Alijah could see the depths of her concern, beyond their current safety. She was already thinking about what she would do if Malliath attacked them again, knowing that her brother felt every swipe of Athis's claws.

"Why would the leader of The Black Hand go to so much trouble?" the Dragorn mused. "It couldn't have been easy binding a third person into the spell. Why you, Alijah?"

That was a question Alijah had been asking himself, though a part of him felt he knew the answer... he just couldn't get the words out.

"The Crow knew who you were," Hadavad answered for him. "How he knew your identity is a mystery, but I would say he wishes to use your name against you."

"My name?" Alijah had a love and hate relationship with his family name.

"Whether you like it or not, Alijah, you are a Galfrey. You are connected to the Dragorn by blood." The mage looked from brother to sister. "Even Gideon Thorn would hesitate to strike at Malliath or Asher if he knew it would bring harm to you."

"I don't like it," Vighon commented, pulling on the strap of his shield. "This Crow fella knows a lot. It's starting to feel like he's a step ahead."

Hadavad looked to argue that comment, but Athis distracted them all as he looked up sharply and turned to the north.

"Riders from Tregaran," Inara explained.

The faintest wisps of a sand cloud rose on the horizon, trailing the riders. At their speed, it didn't take long for them to reach the companions, revealing the riders to be Knights of the High Council, cloaked in yellow astride pale horses.

In the sight of Athis, however, the well-trained horses became nervous and forced their riders to take better control. Inara looked at the red dragon and he sniffed loudly before taking off into the sky, his wings battering them all with a great gust.

The lead knight jumped down from his horse and bowed his head. "I am Kel Nast-Aram, Master of the Knights of the High Council. The people of Tregaran welcome the Dragorn..." the knight looked over the others. "And their companions."

Inara bowed her head in return. "Thank you, Kel Nast-Aram.

Has High Councillor Tauren Salimson returned yet from his journey north?"

The question went over Alijah's head. What journey had Uncle Tauren been on?

The knight hesitated, possibly wondering how Inara knew of Tauren's movements. "High Councillor Salimson returned two days ago."

"We would see him immediately," Inara replied firmly.

~

With their new escort, the companions trotted through the streets of Tregaran, the new capital in The Arid Lands.

Tregaran was walled off, like every city in southern lands. The buildings were a lighter tone than the sand on which they sat and mostly topped with flat roofs.

Like every big city, it was loud and bustling with people. The bazaars and market stalls filled the streets. All offered shade by the colourful fabrics that stretched from one side of the road to the other.

If it wasn't for Kel Nast-Aram and his knights clearing the way, it would have taken them most of the day to break through the crowds and reach The Council Tower in the north of the city. Their horses were taken care of and the escort of knights halved once they were inside the tower, where every hallway was guarded by Tregaran soldiers.

"Uncle Tauren!" Inara stopped herself from running at him when she noticed the other councillors behind him. The Dragorn bowed her head and the others did the same.

"Please, please," Tauren waved the formalities away. "You are my guests here..." The High Councillor's eyes drifted past Inara and landed on her brother. "Alijah?"

"Hello, Uncle," he replied with a muted tone. Alijah hadn't considered Tauren when he exiled himself from the family. He immediately regretted calling him by the affectionate name they had given the southerner as children, but it was the only name that came forth when he greeted the family friend.

Hadavad stepped forward. "Hello, old friend."

Tauren paused, dragging his eyes from Alijah to look the mage up and down with a scrutinising gaze. "Hadavad? Is that you?"

The mage smiled and reached out to embrace the councillor. The two men laughed at some untold joke and embraced again as comrades from the war.

"I apologise, Uncle Tauren," Inara interrupted, glancing over the other councillors. "We come with grave news."

Tauren ran a hand through his curly grey hair and met Inara's eyes with some intensity. "Is this about what we discussed at Dragons' Reach?"

"I'm afraid so."

Alijah looked from one to the other, curious as to what had been discussed at Dragons' Reach. The half-elf also tried to bury the jealousy that rose up to cloud his thoughts. Growing up not far from the white tower on the coast, Alijah had dreamed of becoming a Dragorn and being privy to the prestigious meetings inside Dragons' Reach. A privilege reserved for his sister apparently.

Tauren beckoned them to follow him and the other councillors. "Come, tell us everything."

The sun was reaching for its rest by the time the companions found themselves in the home of Tauren Salimson. The impromptu meeting had gone from the discovery of orcs in the ruins of Karath to the arrival at Tregaran's southern gate.

Inara told of her dangerous encounter alongside Gideon Thorn and Alijah himself had told of events inside Paldora's Fall.

They had been vague regarding the prophecy, however, and how they came to be travelling south in the first place.

The High Council of Tregaran had listened intently to it all and finished the meeting with orders for Kel Nast-Aram. The city guard was to double overnight and the watch towers were to keep a weather eye on the sky. Malliath had never been seen by the people of Illian, but every dragon was capable of devastating a city.

Avoiding Tauren's embrace was an impossibility for Alijah. The southerner's smile couldn't be denied, neither could his hospitality. The councillor's home was large, yet its interior and decoration were humble, befitting of a man who had grown up on the streets.

Meeting his wife and son was awkward for Alijah, who only wanted to distance himself from what felt like an extension of his own family.

Isabella, Tauren's wife, hugged Alijah, filling his nose with her familiar perfume. The scent brought back memories of his childhood and the family's visits to Tregaran, a time when they were all happy.

"It is so good to see you," Isabella greeted him with a smile as broad as her husband's. "I don't think you've met Salim." Isabella moved to the side and introduced their son.

"Named for his grandfather," Tauren cut in, placing a hand on the boy's tiny shoulder.

"Hello," Alijah said. "And how old are you?" It felt like the appropriate question to ask, if not the only one he could think of.

The little boy didn't have an ounce of timidity. "I'm four and three quarters!" he announced happily.

Tauren displayed a proud smile. "Come, we shall eat together."

Alijah did his best to take part while balancing his reservations about sharing a dinner table with his sister again. He caught her looking at him more than once, though he also caught Vighon looking at Inara twice as much. Throughout it all, however, Alijah didn't miss Tauren's apprehension simmering under the surface. The news of orcs and their great numbers, coupled with the return of Asher and his bond with Malliath, had put the councillor ill at ease.

When the meal, or *meals*, came to an end, Vighon busied himself playing with Salim and his toys while Galanör found some quiet place to meditate or whatever the elven ranger preferred to do. Inara was deep in discussion with Isabella and Hadavad was chewing off Tauren's ear. It was the perfect time to slip away.

Alijah found himself searching for the source of the breeze he could feel on his face. He wasn't as attached to the cold as Vighon, but the heat of The Arid Lands wasn't for everyone.

The open balcony called to him, yet the half-elf couldn't help noticing the decoration on the wall. Centred between two short-swords was an armoured white mask, tarnished and scored with lacerations and dents. As a child, Alijah had climbed the furniture just to touch the mask of The White Owl.

It reminded him that he was not only in the house of a hero, but also that of a great warrior. Tauren Salimson, or Tauren son-of-none as he had been called, had spent his youth as The White Owl. Under this guise, he had dedicated his life to abolishing slavery by the tip of his blades.

Another overbearing shadow in his life...

How was he to accomplish any great deeds of his own if he simply ran from those who sought him harm? Tauren had faced his enemy on behalf of an entire civilisation!

Alijah walked away from the mask and swords and wandered onto the balcony, his thoughts adrift. Tregaran was spread out before him, alive with firelight and some kind of festival in the main street. The city was predominantly flat inside, with only The Council Tower and a small collection of buildings around it offering any variation.

The night air didn't provide much in the way of a reprieve from the stifling heat. Alijah leaned against the railing and wondered how in the world he had ended up where he was, not to mention the company he was in. One moment he was uncovering relics and outposts of The First Kingdom, the next moment he was running from orcs and magically bound to the biggest dragon in the realm.

Hadavad's deep voice broke his scattered thoughts. "You should have known getting in the middle of things would bring you home." The mage joined him on the balcony, his staff in hand. "Perhaps I should have warned you of that four years ago."

"I think there's a lot of things you've not said," Alijah fired back.

Unfazed, Hadavad replied, "Galanör told me about the crystal in The Evermoore. I'm sure you have questions about who else is working with us, but—"

"With us?" Alijah repeated. "It sounds like we've been taking *their* orders and you've been palming them off as your own."

The mage sighed. "I'm sorry it feels that way. I promise that any command I have given you came from me, no other."

"Who *is* the other?" Alijah asked pointedly.

Hadavad looked out at the city. "The Black Hand have finally made their move, making them more dangerous than ever—"

"Don't give me that speech," Alijah interjected. "Galanör already told us about compartmentalising and I don't buy it. Who else is interested in The First Kingdom?"

Hadavad's dark eyes rested on the half-elf. "Gideon Thorn."

The name slapped Alijah around the face. "*Master* Gideon Thorn? We've been working for the Dragorn all along?"

"He approached me not long after your parents' wedding," the mage explained calmly. "We were both intrigued and concerned by the origins of the original prophecy, The Echoes of Fate. Who wrote it? Where did it come from? Who are The Echoes? I was concerned by their connection to The Black Hand, though, of course, we now know they are one and the same. Gideon didn't like that The Echoes of Fate proved so accurate. It even steered those who had knowledge of it. Such things can start wars…"

"All this time, you've been reporting back to Gideon?" Alijah felt more like a pawn on a chessboard. "We're just a tool for the Dragorn?"

"I knew you would have mixed feelings about working with them."

"Mixed feelings?" Alijah wiped his face and ran his hand through his hair. "I wanted to get away from all that, to make something of…" He couldn't get the words out. "Does Inara know?" The idea that she had been giving Hadavad orders or even that she knew of his whereabouts over the last four years infuriated him.

"No," Inara's voice came from behind. "I didn't know."

Alijah was relieved by her answer and irritated by her presence. He wasn't finished with the mage yet.

Inara continued, "What Master Thorn does or does not tell me is up to him. I trust his discretion and I'm under no illusion that he has many projects I am not aware of."

Alijah could feel the dig that came at him between her words. "We're not soldiers in some order," he retorted quickly. "We were just the mere mortals who felt obliged to do the right thing." He could see how his choice of words cut right through his sister. He regretted it.

"We're all on the same side here," Hadavad said before the tension could mount any further. "You have both been told things exactly when you needed to be told them."

Alijah faced the mage. "If I hadn't asked you would this have been the moment you told me about Gideon?"

Hadavad raised an eyebrow. "Possibly."

It wasn't a satisfying answer, but it was the only one he would get so Alijah let it go there.

"I will leave you two to talk," the mage said. "I have some work that requires my attention…" Hadavad turned so that only Alijah could see him indicate the scroll tucked inside his burgundy cloak.

Inara joined her brother by the railing. He could feel her eyes on him.

"Stop looking at me like that," he cautioned.

"Like what?" she asked.

"Like I'm made of glass. I'm mortal, Inara; I don't have the Red Pox."

"I'm sorry." Her apology sounded genuine, but Alijah could hear that it came from a place of sympathy.

He sighed, desperate to talk about anything other than his limited lifespan. "You know, for a few years now, I've managed to find something I'm good at. I found those First Kingdom sites following my own leads. I fought The Black Hand and knew that every one I laid low would save lives. I've been doing good and I didn't need a dragon or a fancy blade or even my damn name to do it." Alijah squeezed the railing and slapped it with his palm. "Now, it turns out, I'm just a tool. No good for anything except being wielded by others…"

"We all have our part to play," Inara said, attempting to soothe him. "You didn't know about the orcs, I didn't know about The Black Hand. Still, we've both been where we needed to be and we've both done the best we can."

"You sound like mother," Alijah observed. "The best we can… That's easy to say when you're a Dragorn. You're one of the most powerful, influential people in all of Verda."

"Why does it always come back to that?" Inara asked, frustrated. "We both went to The Lifeless Isles, Alijah. The bond between me and Athis was beyond either of our control. It's not *my* fault you didn't form a bond with any of the others."

"I don't *blame* you for that," he snapped.

"Of course you do," Inara replied exasperated. "I'm sorry that your destiny hasn't been what you—"

"Now you sound like Galanör," he said, waving his hand to dismiss the topic. "Destiny is the horse shit they feed you in bedtime stories. The harsh truth is: we forge our own future. That's what I've been trying to do and now I'm right back where I started," he added, gesturing to Inara.

Appearing stung, she replied, "I'm sorry that being around me brings you so much anguish, brother." Inara made to leave.

Alijah couldn't bear hurting her, yet he had to push her away. He gritted his teeth and clenched his fist as she walked away, desperately trying to hold onto his resolve. He wouldn't have them mourn him for eternity. Just a few more steps and she would be gone and he wouldn't be able to call to her…

"Inara!" Her name almost exploded from his mouth.

His sister turned back around as Tauren came rushing onto the balcony with a small missive in his hand. Alijah held his tongue seeing the distress on the southerner's face.

"What's wrong?" Inara asked him.

Tauren held up the missive. "This just arrived by raven. Its wings were painted red…"

Alijah and Inara shared a look, their expression of concern mirrored across the other.

"What does it say?" Inara asked.

"Who sent it?" Alijah knew the message would be important since it arrived by painted raven, but he wanted to know what city would send something only used in war-time.

Tauren glanced at the parchment. "It came from Lirian. Malliath has set the entire city alight. There's more…" The High Councillor turned to Inara. "It's Gideon…"

Inara snatched the missive and read it three or four times before bursting into action. "I have to go to him!"

"Inara!" Alijah reached for her arm. "You can't go alone. What if Malliath is still in the area?"

"I'm still going, Alijah," Inara insisted. The Dragorn ran for the edge of the balcony, pausing only for a second to add, "Stay here, I'll be back!" Then she was gone. Inara dropped, perfectly in time with Athis, who glided by so close to the top of the buildings that his tail almost cut through the brick.

Alijah turned to Tauren. "Is Gideon alive?"

Tauren placed a heavy hand on Alijah's shoulder. "The message wasn't entirely clear on that. The council is convening as we speak. I must go to the tower."

The half-elf nodded absently, his thoughts still with his sister. "We'll come with you."

Tauren quickly disappeared into his home and was replaced by a frantic Vighon Draqaro. "Can you believe it? Lirian, Alijah! Do you think Russell survived?"

Of course! Alijah refrained from smacking his head. He couldn't believe he hadn't thought of The Pick-Axe and Russell.

"If anyone was going to survive a dragon attack in Lirian, it would be the werewolf, Vighon."

"And Nelly?" he asked hopefully.

"Nelly too," Alijah said with as much conviction as he could muster.

Vighon looked about. "Where's Inara?"

Alijah turned his gaze skyward. "She left. The message from Lirian mentioned Gideon; he's injured."

"You let her go?" Vighon asked, striding to the railing with his own eyes on the dark sky.

"So should you," Alijah declared. "It won't go anywhere, Vighon. Inara's a Dragorn. That's all there is to her." It was clear to see that Vighon was about to contest whatever Alijah was insinuating, but he walked away, never giving him the chance.

THE BALANCE OF POWER

Draped in dark furs, Doran's Warhog had just about reached the end of its tether. After years of short journeys and frequenting every tavern there is, the pig had forgotten what it was like to heft the dwarf's weight for so long.

The cold didn't help.

The snows had picked up after nightfall and the air had taken on an even icier edge. Still, the three companions trudged through the snow, alternating between riding their mounts and pulling them by the reins.

Namdhor was on the horizon at last. At least, it had been before the thick clouds dumped more snow.

"Bah! Ye stubborn ass!" Doran hopped off the Warhog, attired in his own furs and hood.

"We're almost there!" Nathaniel shouted over the wind.

"Ye hear that, ye stupid pig!" The son of Dorain pulled and pulled to no avail. The hog wouldn't budge an inch.

"Come on, Doran!" Reyna called back. "We need to get through this!"

The dwarf only caught every other word between the flapping of his hood and the icicles forming inside his ears. "Come on! Ye embarrassin' me in front o' me friends, pig!" The Warhog snorted, remaining perfectly still. "Fine…" Doran sighed and reached for the bottle of ale stashed inside one of the satchels hanging over the hog.

That got the Warhog's attention.

Doran had but a single swig before the hog stepped forward and nudged him with one of its tusks. He obliged and stuck the bottle into the pig's mouth, giving it only a few sips before removing it.

"Come on!" he beckoned.

The Warhog followed him through the snow and sleet until he paused to give it another swig.

"There's more when we get there!" he promised, hoping himself that the statement was true.

The three riders continued slowly through the last leg of their journey north. The wind eventually died down and the snow relented as The King's Lake came into view. The frozen lake was dominated by Namdhor in the foreground, situated on the edge of the water.

It didn't have the grandeur of a dwarven city or the beauty of an elven city, but it was an impressive sight none-the-less. Situated on a rising slope that lifted to its end at fifteen hundred feet above The King's Lake, the top half of the city was supported by a single jagged column of rock that thrust from the water.

In the dark of night, the city was alight with torches, from the sprawling lower town right the way up the slope, highlighting the ancient churches and watch towers that had been built under King Tion's reign, a thousand years past. At the top of the enormous slope, the city slowly formed into more of a fortress, with high walls and turrets. Inside the fortification sat The Dragon Keep and the throne that ruled over the north.

And the war-witch, Queen Yelifer.

Doran couldn't say he was looking forward to what came next. He was adamant, however, that he would go no farther than The Dragon Keep.

"You know," Nathaniel began, "in all my years I've never had cause to visit The Dragon Keep. Even from the base of the city, it still looks to be quite far away."

Considering the whole city was on a slope, there wouldn't be any lifts to get them to the top this time. For just a moment, Doran wondered how he was going to convince the pig to make the trip.

"It's the only city north of The Arid Lands that's entirely man-made," Reyna commented. "The first city, really. After mankind emerged from The Wild Moores, Gal Tion made himself the first king of—"

"Save ye history lesson, me Lady." Doran ushered the Warhog onwards. "I need to find meself a decent mason. It's gonna take a chisel to free me beard o' this ice!"

Despite Namdhor's vast population, the son of Dorain had the feeling that anyone not born or living in the city stood out to the natives. Every pair of eyes that fell upon them bore the recognition that foreigners had entered their country. Doran suddenly felt as if he should be looking over his shoulder.

The lower town was flat, stretching round the base of the slope and back to the lake. Its warm taverns and lively inns called to the dwarf and reminded him that his belly was rumbling. With Nathaniel in the lead, however, the companions began their ascent up the snowy slope.

The buildings grew in size the higher they travelled and eventually the square, castle-like churches started to take up precious space on the cliff. Considering the hour, Doran noticed a lack of Namdhorian guards patrolling the streets. What he did notice was the nefarious huddles in the alleyways and the eyes behind twitching curtains.

"I get the feelin' this city don' trust outsiders very much…" he commented.

Reyna looked down from her horse. "I get the feeling they don't trust *each other* very much."

Namdhor certainly had a different atmosphere to it than the last time the son of Dorain had come this way. After such a long journey, the horses and Warhog couldn't take the never-ending climb to The Dragon Keep. The companions were forced to pull all three by the reins and finish the trip on foot.

It felt like most of the night had passed them by when the

portcullis to the main keep stood before them. There was also a complement of soldiers on the other side.

Nathaniel addressed them. "We are here to—"

"Did I ask?" came the snotty interruption.

It worked to rile Doran up and the dwarf moved his head to better see the men between the steel grate. A closer inspection showed that these men weren't Namdhorian soldiers at all. Their cloaks were grey rather than the gold the northern soldiers were known for, and their armour was leather instead of the typical white. What was more interesting to Doran, was the tattoos crawling up the man's neck, a feature they all shared.

The dwarf stepped back and examined the tops of the walls that protected The Dragon Keep. The turrets were indeed filled with the Gold Cloaks, all of whom looked down on them without a word to offer in the exchange.

The skinny bald man who had interrupted Nathaniel hung his hands through the grate and ran an eye over them all.

Doran squared up when the man looked at him. "It's easy to be cocky on that side o' the gate, isn't it, laddy?"

Reyna stepped forward and threw her hood back. "Who are you to bar my way? I am Reyna Galfrey, Princess of Ayda and Ambassador to all kingdoms of men."

The skinny man found a lump in his throat and he looked over them again. His expression betrayed too much. It was easy to see that The Ironsworn thug hadn't expected to see these particular travellers.

"We've been waiting for you," he said finally, stepping back from the portcullis.

"I bet ye 'ave…" Doran replied quietly.

"Open the gate!" the thug bellowed to the real soldiers.

Nathaniel lowered his voice. "What is happening here? Why do the soldiers of Namdhor take orders from The Ironsworn?"

"Perhaps the answer lies in there." Reyna gestured to The Dragon Keep at the top of the slope.

The keep itself was a collection of towers and squat halls with tall windows. The corners of every wall were lined with dragons' teeth and claws, all taken from the corpses after The Dragon War, a genocidal act of King Tion, the first of his line.

The first line of *morons*, Doran thought. Nothing good had ever come from that bloodline, especially Merkaris Tion, the last king of the north and ally to the evil Valanis. Doran still remembered watching the treacherous whelp get trampled under the boots of his own men during The Battle for Velia. It brought the hint of a smile to the dwarf's frozen features.

The gang of thugs escorted them up the cliff and into the tall halls of The Dragon Keep. The interior decoration was one of fur rugs and massive chandeliers dotted between giant paintings of Queen Yelifer in her youth. Most portraits depicted her victory and conquest over the north.

More curious than the decoration were the Namdhorian soldiers, all of whom moved aside without protest when faced by The Ironsworn. The balance of power in this city was all wrong...

The companions were finally stopped at a set of double doors that appeared to have been custom-built for mountain trolls by the size of them.

"Weapons," the skinny thug demanded. "No one has an audience with Queen Yelifer so armed..."

Nathaniel couldn't keep the surprise from his face. "We are here at the behest of your queen to assist in diplomatic matters. We pose no threat."

The skinny man glanced at Doran before repeating, "Weapons."

Reyna was the first to remove her bow and scimitar, handing them over to the Gold Cloak standing beside the door. Nathaniel took one last look at his sword before begrudgingly unbuckling it from his belt.

Doran removed the fat sword from his back and unclipped the axe from his belt, offering it to the skinny man by the haft. Once the thug had gripped it firmly, the dwarf pulled on the axe and brought the man's face to his own.

"Unless ye want to become a notch on this here axe, I suggest ye make certain it finds its way back to me..."

The Ironsworn thug did his best to look tough, but Doran could see the fear behind his eyes. It pleased him.

In custom with the other kingdoms, the master of servants greeted them next, noting their titles ready for his introduction.

"Not this again…" Doran huffed.

The opposing double doors slowly swung open to reveal a grand hall more in keeping with a church than a throne room. Its tall windows were stained glass, its looming pillars carved into deities, and its walls adorned with religious texts.

At the head of the hall sat Queen Yelifer Skalaf, the war-witch of the north.

Her throne was the only thing in the hall that reminded Doran that he was in the home of conquerers. Yelifer sat inside the open jaws of a long-dead dragon, its upper maw hanging ominously over her head. Teeth the size of a man's hand lined the sides and the inside had been worked into an oversized chair. At least it looked oversized with Yelifer's bony frame seated in the middle.

The queen and her throne were situated between two men, one of whom was probably better described as a giant. His shoulders were easily as wide as Doran was tall and his head was entirely hidden within the confines of his helmet. Unlike the soldiers in their white armour and golden cloaks, this man-mountain wore dull silver armour and a bright yellow gambeson. The sigil on his chest was not the lion of the north, as it had been for a thousand years, but an image of a tree with a snake climbing up the trunk.

As intimidating as his frame was, the man stood with his hands wrapped around the hilt of a massive unsheathed sword, its point pressed into the ground. Doran looked at it and wondered if he could even lift the blade.

On the other side of the queen, and sat in what looked to be a throne of his own, was a normal sized man in a long black coat. His face was well shaven and his short dark hair had been shaved at the sides. For all of his expensive rings and fine tailoring, the dwarf didn't miss the garish tattoos on his knuckles and the side of his neck.

The master of servants stopped in front of the throne and

announced, "Queen Yelifer of house Skalaf, the first queen of Namdhor, ruler of Orith, conqueror of all the north, and the bringer of peace!"

Doran sniffed. "Is that all?" he uttered into his beard.

"Your Grace, may I present Ambassadors Nathaniel and Reyna Galfrey and their companion, Doran, son of Dorain of clan Heavybelly."

Reyna stepped forward and bowed. "Your Grace. We have—"

The elf stopped when the tattooed man, seated in the chair beside the queen, stood up with sudden purpose and walked down the steps from the throne.

"An elf, a man, and a dwarf walk into The Dragon Keep..." He cut between the companions and the queen and proceeded to circle them. "That sounds like the beginning of a good joke to me." His observation was met with a low rumble of laughter from the thugs that crowded around the pillars and lurked in the shadows.

"Forgive me..." Reyna started again, "Who are—"

"You made good time," he interrupted again, asserting his dominance. "The journey from Dragons' Reach must feel even farther in winter."

Pleasantries forgotten, Reyna demanded, "Who are you?"

The man shrugged. "I am but a humble lord in these lands, a servant really. Though... you might know my name."

"I assure you we don't," Nathaniel said with an ounce of irritation creeping into his tone.

"Then please allow me, *Arlon Draqaro*, to welcome you to Namdhor." The man bowed with an overly dramatic flair.

That last name nagged at Doran's memory, but it certainly rang a bell for the Galfreys, who could only look at each other in response.

Reyna struggled to compose her diplomatic tone and expression. "You're Vighon's father..."

Arlon's smile didn't reach his eyes. "On occasion. I suppose I should thank you for taking care of him and his mother for so long..."

There was an awkward pause but no such thanks ever left Arlon's mouth.

Queen Yelifer cleared her throat, a clear message to any and all, except Arlon Draqaro, who maintained his intense gaze for a moment longer before returning to his make-shift throne.

Vighon's father sat back down and crossed his legs with a bemused smile on his arrogant face. Doran imagined, with perhaps too much detail, what it would be like to plant his fist in Arlon's face.

There was a moment of silence while the queen looked down at them. "You brought a dwarf," Yelifer stated.

Doran suddenly felt like the centre of attention, but it was Reyna who appeared to take on the offence of addressing him so.

"This is Doran, son of—"

"I have ears, Ambassador," the queen interjected. "If you think adding another dwarf to this matter will bring any *peace* then you should not have come."

Reyna couldn't get much more frustrated. "Your Grace, we—"

"You must be tired after such a journey," Yelifer said without meeting any of their eyes. "Rooms have been prepared. We shall discuss the state of things tomorrow." With that, the queen of Namdhor stood up and made to leave, closely followed by the man-mountain. Everyone but Arlon stood for the queen's exit.

"If you would follow me." The master of servants held out his arm to usher them from the hall.

Nathaniel turned to Reyna and Doran and quietly mouthed. "Rooms? I thought they didn't know there would be three of us?"

"Aye," Doran agreed. "An' judgin' by that skinny fella's dumb face, I'd say they weren' expectin' any o' us to even make it this far."

Reyna nodded along, her face a picture of concern. "There is more going on here than just the events within Vengora. Maybe tomorrow I will be able to finish a single sentence and we can get to the bottom of it..."

LIRIAN'S BURNING

A this the ironheart broke through the clouds with the first rays of daybreak. The majestic colours of sunrise were muted this morning by the column of black smoke that rose up from the heart of The Evermoore.

Lirian was burning.

There didn't look to be a single building untouched by Malliath's fire, though it appeared that King Weymund's palace, situated on the side of the small mountain, had only taken minor damage.

This isn't just fire damage, Athis observed. *Dragons fought here…*

Inara looked down at the wreckage, inclined to agree. To the experienced eye, it was clear to see where the tail of a dragon had cut the top off a building. Deep grooves, matching dragon claws, marred the streets and the sides of people's homes.

This wasn't just Malliath on a rampage; Ilargo had been in the middle of this.

The sound of ringing bells alarmed across the ruins of the city. Inara checked the skies around her before realising the alarm was for them.

They think you're Malliath.

From this height I could be any dragon, Athis replied. *I fear the survivors of Lirian will live with a dread of my kin for the rest of their lives.*

Inara hated to accept that. ***How's your ice breath feeling?***

Athis turned his head to lay a single blue eye on his companion. *I haven't had need of it for some time.*

Inara glanced down at the raging flames. ***The fires burning their homes are dragon's breath. They won't be extinguished by just water or snow.***

Athis prepared to dive down. *Then let us restore their faith in dragon-kind!*

Inara braced herself and took a breath. Athis eventually spread his wings and slowed his descent before the softest landing Inara had ever known.

On street level, the city appeared even worse. The smoke and fire made everything chaotic, but it was the bodies that tugged at Inara's heart. Down here, she could see their faces, still and lifeless, their bodies tinged with licking flames. Others had been trampled and crushed by Malliath's bulk, a sight Inara could barely stand.

Athis inhaled a deep breath and the scales between Inara's legs became icy cold. The red dragon sprung his head forward and sputtered a few icicles and a cold gust of air. Athis shook his head and took another breath. This time, a torrent of ice, sleet, and freezing air blasted the nearest building, extinguishing the flames in a battle of steam.

Another two fires required extinguishing before people stopped screaming and calling for soldiers. Athis moved periodically around Lirian, his icy breath freeing up entire streets so that others might begin the search for survivors.

"Help! Please!"

Inara whipped her head in the direction of the desperate call. A woman in ragged clothes and covered in ash was banging against a door, crying for her child.

Go! Athis instructed.

Inara wasted no time finding her feet. The Dragorn ran down the length of Athis's back, navigating the spikes and flexing muscles. The dragon flourished his tail, giving the half-elf some height as she added her own elven strength to the jump. She crossed half the street and came up running.

"Please!" the woman shouted. "My daughter is in there!"

Inara looked up at the building, its windows bursting with flames and smoke. On the ground beside the hysterical woman lay a man too burnt to be alive.

"Stand back!" Inara ushered the mother away from the smoking door.

"Please! Save my baby!"

Inara dashed towards the door and threw all of her strength into the kick. Her boot slammed into the wood and decimated the hinges, breaking through the debris barring the other side. A wall of smoke assaulted her immediately, clawing at her lungs.

The Dragorn called on the magic of her bond with Athis, casting a spell that would come close to replicating the power of a dragon's breath. The spell exploded from her palm and swept through the house, banishing the smoke out of every jagged hole and crack. Only the stubborn flames of Malliath remained, promising the return of more smoke.

She had to act fast.

Inara ran into the house where her sensitive ears soon located the sound of a small girl, coughing and screaming for her parents. Debris littered the floor and thick wooden beams threatened to collapse on top of them at any moment. The Dragorn weaved through the house, tracking the sound of the girl.

The coughing was coming from upstairs…

Looking at the beams supporting the first floor, Inara wondered if the boards would take her added weight.

Inara! That house is about to collapse on itself! Get the child and get out, now!

Sprung on by her companion's warning, Inara used her innate sense of balance and agility to skip and jump up the stairs. The little girl was on the landing, curled up into a ball and cowering under a low table.

The Dragorn flipped the table away with one hand and scooped up the girl with the other. Holding her tight, Inara ran back to the stairs only to watch them cave in, creating a pit of sharp splinters. The house was creaking from every corner when the half-elf glimpsed the daylight. Ahead of them was an open room and a burning window.

It was their only chance.

Inara held the girl tight to her chest and sprinted for the window, narrowly avoiding the beams and roof panels that fell behind her. As the house collapsed in on itself, Inara cleared the window, leaping into the street beyond.

The flames ran over her, unable to grab a hold, as she flew through the air. Her landing was harder without the ability to roll, but the girl was unharmed.

The mother's frenzied screams were unintelligible. Tears streaked down her ashen face as she took her daughter in her arms. Upon seeing her father on the ground, the little girl buried her head in her mother's chest and sobbed.

Inara panted for breath, covered in ash herself now. Seeing this broken family brought tears to her eyes and weighed her down with great sorrow. She barely noticed Athis's icy breath wash over them and quash what remained of the fire.

Well done, wingless one.

Inara tore her eyes from the mother and daughter to look upon the other survivors, standing around in shock and despair.

It's not enough... she lamented.

A familiar presence pushed against the bond between Inara and Athis. To the Dragorn, the presence felt as real as a hand on her shoulder.

Ilargo?

A giant shadow was silhouetted against the rising steam, preceding the green dragon's arrival. Ilargo's wings buffeted the steam and blew Inara's dark hair out behind her. Suddenly, the dragon yelped and he fell the remaining feet, hitting the ground hard and scaring those around them.

He was badly hurt.

Majestic was always the word that came to mind when looking upon Ilargo, his green scales speckled with golden stars and his stance always that of a regal prince. Now, however, the redeemer of men stood before them with a diminished presence.

His exquisite scales were stained red with blood and the flesh between torn open by razor-sharp claws. A patch above his right eye was absent of scales and the eye itself was webbed with red veins. Some of his claws looked to be blunt and chipped, worn down by Malliath's armoured exterior.

Ilargo flexed his wings, though he was clearly in pain when adjusting the left one. The bony frame around the membranes wobbled and came into his body a lot slower than the right wing. The membranes themselves were a patchwork of cuts and holes.

If this was how Ilargo looked, Inara didn't want to think about Gideon.

Where is he, Ilargo?

The green dragon turned his mighty head towards the palace in the north. *We are healing together,* Ilargo explained. *His wounds will take a little longer, but he will recover.*

Inara tilted her head to better see his injured wings. **Can you fly?**

That was my first attempt… I think I shall walk back. Ilargo turned to Athis. *Thank you for your assistance here. I do not yet have the strength to breathe even a flame.*

Athis bowed his head in deference. Despite Ilargo's younger age, respect was something earned in a dragon's eyes, not gained by years of simply living. As Gideon's companion, the green dragon would forever have the respect of all his kin.

With Inara on Athis's back, the two dragons walked through the streets and up the small slope to the foot of King Weymund's palace. Like something out of a fairy tale, what was left of the palace stood tall with its pointed roofs and with walls of white stone. Most of those fortifying walls had now been melted under the hot breath of Malliath.

It was King Weymund Harg and his entourage that met them first, inside the courtyard that, thanks to the broken walls, could now fit both dragons.

Inara jumped down and faced the king of Lirian, though she felt he would be better described as a broken man. His left arm was in a sling and his skin and beard were dirty with ash and soot. Even his clothes were torn and unbefitting of royalty. His visage was a testament to the hell that Lirian had been put through.

"Thank you," he said exhausted. "You have stopped the spread of fire." The king glanced at his subjects. "The people of Lirian are indebted to you Inara Galfrey, Athis the ironheart."

The Dragorn wanted to ask a lot of questions, mostly about the details of what had transpired here and how many had survived the attack. But only one question found its voice.

"Where is Gideon?"

Leaving Athis in the company of Ilargo, Inara followed the king and his knights through the palace. It appeared, in the melee, that Malliath's tail had cut through the outer wall of the palace and caused one of the upper floors to collapse. The halls that were clear had been filled with the survivors, most of whom were injured and being treated by Weymund's court mages.

"I had him placed in a room of his own," Weymund commented as they came upon a lone door in the eastern tower. "I will leave you to be with him."

Inara thanked the king and gently pushed the creaky door open. The room was luxurious, decorated for guests of the king, with a massive four poster bed and more furniture than one would ever need use of.

Lying to one side of the bed was Gideon Thorn, battered, bruised, and unconscious. Inara hurried over and scanned every inch of his bare torso, arms, and face. Bandages and soothing balms had been applied to various places, but his injuries were all too clear to see.

A dark bruise spread around his ribs, beyond the confines of the bandage. His left shoulder was equally bruised and looked to have been dislocated and put back by either the court mages or Ilargo's healing. Cuts deep and shallow criss-crossed his skin, some in the shape of a sword, others mirroring the claws of Malliath. Her master's face hadn't escaped injury, with one black eye and a gash across the bridge of his nose.

Seeing him this way put a lump in her throat. He was *the* Gideon Thorn, Master of the Dragorn, and hero of The War for Realm. He was said to be the greatest warrior in the world and coupled with Ilargo, the most powerful too.

Beside the bed stood Mournblade, propped up inside its scabbard. Inara couldn't help but pick it up and slide the steel from its sheath. The metal was perfectly clean, as all Vi'tari blades were, regardless of whether Gideon had struck his foe. She slid the blade down when thoughts of Asher flooded her mind.

Gideon's wounds were proof that the Master Dragorn had fought Malliath's resurrected rider. His return would create a jumbled mess of emotions for everyone…

Gideon's hand snapped up and gripped her wrist, startling Inara.

"Master!" The half-elf crouched down beside the bed and gripped his hand.

"Inara…" His voice was croaky. "You look more hurt than I feel," he said with a crooked smile.

"Don't move," she warned as the Master Dragorn tried to sit up.

Gideon waved her concern away and struggled on his hands to sit with his back to the headboard. Inara couldn't help but wince with his every movement.

"Is it as bad out there as it sounds?" he asked.

Inara nodded solemnly. "There isn't much of Lirian left. Athis has put out the fires but…"

"What are you doing here?" Gideon asked.

"I was in Tregaran when the raven arrived from King Weymund."

Gideon nodded with a hand supporting his ribs. "He sent one to every kingdom. They need to be warned about Malliath and…" The Master Dragorn looked up at her, searching for recognition on her face.

"I've seen him too, Master. Asher has returned, bonded to Malliath no less."

"You've seen him?" Gideon said with some alarm.

"I faced him in The Undying Mountains." The memory refreshed the fight in her mind. "He killed Edrik and Aldreon."

Gideon closed his eyes and let his head rest back. Inara gave him a moment to absorb that, aware that he would take on the death as his responsibility.

"They fought bravely," Inara continued. "Malliath and Asher were just too powerful. We've never had to fight another dragon before."

Gideon finally opened his eyes, glazed with tears. "He called himself a Dragon Knight."

"You spoke to him?" Inara took another look at her master and instead of just being thankful he survived, she was curious as to *how* he survived. "What happened?"

Gideon glanced at her before inspecting his injuries. "I was flying to meet you in The Arid Lands when Ilargo and I came across Malliath, heading north…"

∼

Gideon's recollection took him back to the battle…

The dragons had ceased their thrashing and Malliath had his jaws wrapped around Ilargo's throat. Outside The Pick-Axe, the Master Dragorn stepped back from Asher and gripped his own throat as if someone had their hands around his windpipe.

Asher recovered from Gideon's attacks and managed to stand, his broadsword glistening in the flames. Gideon was gasping for air, brought to his knees with the feeling of teeth sinking into his skin.

Without a word, Asher swung his blade.

It was the perfect horizontal swipe, clean and precise. The steel, however, never touched Gideon's neck. With less than a second before the blade cleaved the Dragorn's head from his body, Russell Maybury barrelled into Asher.

The fact that his gut wound hadn't killed or incapacitated him was a testament to the strength of the supernatural creature that lived within him. Gideon only hoped it would be enough; he didn't have long before Malliath choked the life from Ilargo and himself.

The two men tumbled down the street, rolling through the snow as they grappled for superiority. To Gideon's eyes, the entire event had taken place through bleary eyes.

Russell cried out in pain under the barrage of punches that Asher buried into his gut wound. Eventually, the werewolf relented and Asher rolled over, adding an extra back-hand to Russell's face.

The backhand angered Russell, pushing him to a place that was more animal than man. With a growl that no man could replicate, Russell caught Asher's next punch with one hand and reached for his throat with the other.

Asher's response was that of a desperate gargle, a response mirrored by Malliath. The relief to Gideon was instantaneous, as both he and Ilargo took a deep breath. He could feel Ilargo shake his head to orientate himself before lashing out at Malliath again.

Gideon rubbed his throat and dug his hand into the snow to retrieve Mournblade. Looking at Asher and Russell locked in a battle of wills, surrounded by a burning Lirian, and overshadowed by Malliath's vengeful return, Gideon couldn't believe his eyes.

How was any of this really happening? Was he really about to plunge Mournblade through Asher's heart?

The Dragon Knight, as he called himself, fell into a roll, bringing Russell with him. The two contested each other's strength, but Asher possessed a larger repertoire of martial arts. The old assassin manipulated and twisted Russell's hold until he had an arm locked around the werewolf's throat.

Gideon made to help but stumbled under the weight of his own injuries. His ribs felt broken and his arms barely had the strength to lift his Vi'tari blade. The sound of clashing dragons roared over the fires, explaining his new assortment of wounds.

Malliath had gained the advantage again and laid into Ilargo, throwing the green dragon around like a rag doll. Ilargo was thrown and dragged across the city, mauled and bitten into submission. A killing bite for the redeemer of men would have been inevitable, were it not for a meaty fist slamming into Asher's face, knocking the black dragon away.

Gideon groaned through the pain and looked up from the

snowy ground. Russell wasn't giving in. The werewolf had broken the deadly hold with sheer strength and now had the Dragon Knight in a hold of his own.

"You're not Asher…" Russell was applying so much pressure that his muscles trembled. "My friend died! I won't let you wear his face, monster!"

Had Gideon blinked, he would have missed Russell's mouth change shape. An elongated snout and jaw of razored teeth replaced his human features before he clamped down on Asher's neck.

Whatever Asher was, be it man or something more sinister, he still felt pain.

His cry filled the night, quickly drowned out by Malliath's. Both Ilargo and Gideon were flat on the ground, helpless to do anything but watch.

The glint of a dagger caught Gideon's eye, but his cry of warning came too late. Asher plunged the dagger over his shoulder and into the gap between Russell's shoulder and neck. The werewolf roared and immediately backed off with the dagger still protruding from his neck.

Asher stumbled away and Russell fell to his knees, his features entirely human again. Mirroring Asher's staggering retreat, Malliath came crashing through the buildings. The black dragon wasn't without injury. The gash on his throat was obvious by the amount of blood flowing over his scales.

The Dragon Knight managed to pick up and sheath his double-handed sword before Malliath flapped his wings. The dragon struggled to gain any height for a moment and rained blood down on them all.

Before Gideon collapsed into oblivion, he watched Malliath scoop Asher up between his claws and ascend above the inferno.

"Then I woke up here," Gideon finished.

It was quite the tale to hear, and all the harder to think that her master had been beaten. Inara realised just how lucky she had been to have survived her encounter with Asher and Malliath.

"What happened to Russell?" she asked, almost afraid to hear the answer. "Does he live?"

"Oh, Russell is just as stubborn as every other ranger I've met, retired or not. It'll take more than a sword to the gut or a knife to the throat to put him down. He's the one who brought me up here."

Inara found some relief in her master's answer. "I didn't see him on my way here."

Gideon attempted to shrug and ended up wincing in pain. "He's probably out there, helping the survivors as best he can. He's a little stronger than most."

"I'm just glad you both survived," Inara added.

Gideon hesitated. "It *was* him, Inara. It was *Asher*. There are monsters out there that can look like people, damn convincing ones. That was no monster we faced. He's back…"

Inara knew the truth of Asher's return, but to say it out loud was to admit that the world she knew was upside down.

"The Black Hand brought him back."

It was a simple statement and, judging by Gideon's expression, it was a revelation more than a surprise.

"That's why they were excavating Vengora…" he replied absently. "They wanted his bones."

"I've met Hadavad," Inara continued. "I know about you helping him and Galanör." The Dragorn tried to keep the disappointment out of her voice.

After another moment of consideration, Gideon looked at Inara. "I didn't withhold this from you because I don't believe you are capable, Inara. Some things are for the council only. I would be accused of favouritism if I were—"

"I understand." Inara cut in firmly. "Did you know Alijah was working with them?"

Gideon sighed. "It sounds like you've had quite the journey since I left you."

"Did you know?" she asked again.

Gideon clamped down on his pain and struggled to the edge of the bed, where he finally managed to stand and face her on shaky legs. "I knew they were travelling through Syla's Pass," he admitted. "I gave them the crystal to open the portal from here actually. They were investigating Paldora's Fall—"

"Have you always known?" Inara pressed, seeing through his evasion.

"Yes."

Inara took a step backward and turned to the window for something other than her master to look at. "We've worried about him for four years..."

"I know," Gideon replied softly.

"You haven't just lied to me," Inara spat. "You lied to my parents. They trusted you, I trusted you..."

"Alijah's mind is a far more complicated place than yours or mine," Gideon explained. "He doesn't know who he is yet. He needed the space. I asked Hadavad to take him under his wing and give him some purpose."

"Don't talk like you know him," Inara retorted. "If you knew where he was you should have brought him back to us. He didn't leave because he couldn't find purpose. He left because he's..." The half-elf stopped herself and turned away again, wiping the tear from her cheek.

"Whatever his reason for leaving," Gideon continued, "he has been doing good. Alijah has helped Hadavad to uncover more about The First Kingdom in the last four years than he did in five hundred. He has a gift for finding lost things, Inara."

"He's lost himself," Inara corrected. "He needs his family."

Gideon appeared to have reached his limit for standing and sat back down on the bed. "I have to treat you as a Dragorn before I treat you as Galfrey," he said with an edge of authority in his tone. "I haven't always done that; a failing of mine, not yours. In this matter, you have to accept my judgments."

Inara could feel Athis agreeing with the Master Dragorn's words. In truth, she could see herself agreeing too, but she didn't want to. Her master, her friend, and mentor had kept more than one secret from her. To stop the thought of it from crushing her,

Inara allowed some of Athis's feelings to bleed with her own, offering a greater resolve.

The Dragorn bowed her head. "My first duty is to that of the order and my master."

"Your first duty is to that of the realm, Inara. I realise that having your brother in the middle of all this complicates things, but a time may come when you have to choose between him and the people of Illian."

That was a hard truth she couldn't swallow right now, but thankfully Athis was there to pour his will into her own. "We will serve the realm above all else, Master."

Gideon appeared somewhat satisfied with her answers. "Now, having only heard part of your tale, I am beginning to have this horrible feeling that everything is connected. Tell me everything you have learned since our parting."

Inara considered the events of Paldora's Fall, the orcs fighting alongside The Black Hand, and the bond forged between Alijah and Malliath.

She took a breath. "It's worse than we feared…"

PART III

10,000 YEARS AGO

Standing outside his master's bedchamber, Sarkas began to wonder if it would have been better to have lost his hearing all those years ago.

Master Vyran was entertaining a female guest in his private chamber. It always sounded like they were having fun until the screaming started, and there was always screaming.

Sarkas couldn't bear to look upon the women when they left his chamber, all bloody and bruised. After years of becoming accustomed to the sound of pain, both others' and his own, Sarkas had found coping mechanisms. One such mechanism was pouring himself into his secret studies.

Escaping the girl's torment, Sarkas decided that tonight would be a good opportunity to study the spell books in Master Vyran's quarters.

Sarkas opened the desk drawer and saw the slender black wand just lying there, under-utilised and itching to be unleashed. Just holding it made his skin tingle. In the beginning it had seemed fantastical and other-worldly to use the wand. He had never felt more powerful or in control of his life than the day he levitated a quill off the desk. That was in the beginning.

Now he hungered for more. In only a few years, Sarkas had exhausted the books in Master Vyran's personal possession, many of *which had referred to the various ways one could retain the hair on their head.*

He needed more. Sneaking off in the dead of night to experiment with new spells left him exhausted and drained. This had a negative impact on his duties and often resulted in punishment. The last time Sarkas had experimented with a fire spell, he had attempted to conjure the flames without the wand, hoping to rid his need of it. That hadn't ended well. Beside the burn in his palm, he nearly caused damage to the wand itself. That would have resulted in an investigation and his ultimate death.

After further study, Sarkas now knew it was because of the Demetrium in the wand's core. Without that special element, any human with a natural talent for magic would struggle to wield such a force with any precision.

That had only spurred him on, however, making him see that the magic already existed inside of him; he just needed the right tool.

Since the screams had yet to even begin, Sarkas decided he had plenty of time until his master would call upon him. The hesitation he had once displayed had been replaced by the courage magic offered him.

With the wand in hand, Sarkas sneaked out of his master's quarters. The door closed with barely a creak, an act that had required several months to perfect. Turning to his left, Sarkas was immediately stopped in his tracks by Edun, the first servant to the Lord Crow himself.

His expression was of both disappointment and apprehension. It was a face Sarkas had become accustomed to since his intrigue into magic had taken a hold of him.

Using the sign language they had developed as children, Edun signed, "You're going to the forbidden section, aren't you?"

Signing back, Sarkas replied, "I have nothing left to learn from the books up here. The spells in the forbidden section might have what I'm looking for."

Edun shook his head in dismay. "You shouldn't even be going down to the library in the first place. The holy texts are for priests only, Sarkas!"

Sarkas sighed. "There's nothing holy about them. I've told you what they really talk about in their meetings. There is no Kaliban; only a profit margin."

Edun's eyes dropped to the floor. Of all the brothers, Edun had had the most trouble coming to terms with the truth of Kaliban and The Echoes. In the beginning, Edun had tried to justify the horrors they were exposed to as his service to Kaliban. The truth stung them all.

"What are you looking for?" *he signed, his eyes betraying a curiosity there.*

"A way out, Edun! That's the only thing I've ever searched for. I'm trying to find a way to get us all out of this hell."

Edun sighed, his defeat beaten into him over twenty years of servitude. "There's no refuge in magic, Sarkas. Only pain and suffering. What are you going to do? Levitate every object in The Citadel until they release us? They're more powerful than you. They always will be…"

Sarkas refused to believe that. "For now," *he signed back.* "The books in the forbidden section were brought to The Citadel from Erador. From Erador! I heard Master Vyran talking about them; they were brought to Illian from the temple at the base of Mount Kaliban. Even the council don't consult them; they treat them like dangerous relics."

Edun was quick to sign back, "There's a reason for that, Sarkas! Those books contain spells that come with a price."

Now that Sarkas did agree with. He fully intended the council, if not the entire Echoes' order, to pay that price.

Having wasted too much time already, Sarkas pushed past Edun, knocking him in the shoulder as he tried to slip through the tight passage. Edun tensed, reaching for his shoulder.

Sarkas paused, looking back at his brother. "What is it?" *he signed, looking at Edun's painful shoulder. A dark patch began to show through his robes and Sarkas reached out for him in alarm.*

"Leave it!" *Edun signed.*

"What did he do to you?" *Sarkas regretted knocking his brother in frustration, always forgetting that the Lord Crow was the most violent of all their masters.*

Edun hesitated. "I smiled at his... companion. I had seen her before in the lower chambers."

Sarkas gritted his teeth and placed the tip of Vyran's wand to his brother's wound.

"Don't!" *Edun warned.* "He would notice and do far worse to both of us."

The thought of leaving his brother in pain brought tears to Sarkas's eyes. "I will find us a way out of here, I promise."

Edun shrugged hopelessly. "A way out to what, Sarkas? We either live in The Citadel or we live out there, in King Atilan's empire. The rulers of both are mad, only the empire is falling into chaos and riots now. There's even talk of King Atilan starting a war with the Dragon Riders. Have you ever thought that maybe we're better off in here?"

Sarkas considered his body of scars and the lifetime of humiliation and torment. "You only see two options, Edun. But with magic, there's always another way..."

RISE OF THE ORC

K arakulak marched down the tunnels, inspecting his warriors as they stood shoulder to shoulder in their obsidian armour.

The orcs were ready.

With sword, axe, and spear they would reclaim the world. It all started here, under the foundations of The Arid Lands' capital, Tregaran.

Glancing down the other tunnels, the king could see his forces amassing in the positions they had been assigned. Using architectural plans of the city, compliments of The Crow, Karakulak knew exactly where to strike.

Off to the side, stood a lone figure in black robes. A mage of The Black Hand, she was there to coordinate the invasion across the entire desert. Under Ameeraska, Vuruk, his war chief, was preparing just as they were. When the king ordered the invasion, The Black Hand would use their magic to communicate with each other.

Karakulak found himself clenching his fist as he looked upon the mage. He would never give up his throne, but the king couldn't deny what The Crow and his magic had granted him in the first place. Every time they used their unnatural power, he could feel the eyes of other orcs on him, judging him for allowing it into their world.

The world... The orc mulled over that word. For so long it had only meant half of the world. If The Black Hand's magic gave them the advantage they needed to claim Neverdark then he would take it. When everything was his, he would snap The Crow's neck and flay him personally.

The tremor under his feet informed Karakulak that the Big Bastards were approaching. Indeed, rounding the curve in the tunnel, a pair of giant orcs cautiously approached the king with a huge metal barrel between them. They didn't look too happy about carrying it. Behind them, a dozen more of their tribe arrived, each pair carrying a reinforced barrel between them.

"Careful! Careful with those!" came Grundi's voice. The crippled orc sucked in his belly and squeezed between the Big Bastards as he approached his king. "Put them down gently," he commanded the larger orcs. "The powder reacts to impact alone. Do you idiots know how many orcs we lose mining it?"

The Big Bastards were visibly sweating now.

"Grundi..." Karakulak regarded the limping orc. "Is the wrath powder ready?"

Grundi gestured to the nearest barrel. "Providing these fools don't drop it and kill us all..."

Karakulak removed the lid from the barrel and peered inside; the massive orcs either side held their breath. The barrel itself was filled to the brim with red powder, no different in texture to that of a grain of sand. The king knew which of those grains he would rather sit on...

Grundi ordered the Big Bastards to their positions, spreading them out under the city.

"You have done well, Grundi," Karakulak praised. "When Neverdark is ours, you will have your choice of rewards."

The crippled orc bowed his head. "I only live to serve you, Sire."

Karakulak looked over Grundi's head to the approaching chieftain. Much like the rest of his tribe, the chieftain of the

Berserkers had very little of his pale flesh left to see. In preparation for battle, the Berserkers always painted their bodies black and yellow in the war patterns of their ancestors. They wore no armour, only a loincloth and a belt of chains. They didn't believe in sneaking up on their enemy…

The chieftain dropped to one knee with a fist held to his chest. Of all the tribes, the Berserkers had required very little *persuasion* to accept him as their king. Knowing that Karakulak intended to invade Neverdark, starting the biggest war any orc had ever seen, was all the Berserkers needed to know.

"My King." Chieftain Warhg bowed his head.

"The wrath powder is in place," Karakulak said, wasting no more time. Having all the tribes mixed up and formed into new ranks was a recipe worthy of the wrath power itself.

"The Berserkers will draw the first blood in this war," Chieftain Warhg replied. Behind him, the two rows of painted orcs roared and beat their chests. "My son," the chieftain gestured to the orc behind him, "Calagah, has the honour of breaking the humans first!"

Karakulak knew he would forget that name before the day was over. "Your name shall be known by every orc yet to live, Calagah."

The king turned away and faced his warriors. "Is it to be war then?" His question was met with resounding cheers and roars. "There isn't a creature above The Under Realm who knows of our numbers, of our strength! We have been forgotten! Before the sky fire rises, I would have Neverdark tremble under the orc! Let them never forget the power of Gordomo!" The orcs chanted their god's name. "TO WAR!"

The Berserkers moved off down the various tunnels in search of their glory. Calagah butted heads with his father before walking over to the barrel of wrath powder in the cross-roads. The rest of the orcs backed off, pushed away by Grundi until they were all at least a hundred yards from the Berserkers, who all had a platform waiting for them, allowing the painted orcs to touch the tunnel ceiling.

Their prayers to Gordomo could be heard echoing down the long tunnels.

Over the prayers, Karakulak recognised the familiar voice of his mother behind him. "Gordomo will reward them with a place in his honour guard."

The king turned to look down on his mother, the high priestess of Gordomo. Her black hair was scraped back and braided between her sloping horns that curved around and almost pricked her neck. Her dress and jewellery were made from the smaller bones of a variety of Under Realm creatures... and a few orcs. A tall staff, carried ceremoniously by her, was topped with the skull of Karakulak's father, horns and all.

She had been the most grateful for the usurpation, complaining afterwards that the chieftain of The Born Horde had been too weak to lead. As a show of her dedication to Karakulak, the high priestess had slit the throat of his brother, her youngest son, and prevented any future rivalry for the throne.

"You shouldn't be here, Mother," Karakulak said, noting the small entourage of priestesses behind her.

"I do not fear a little *bang*," she replied coolly. "I come because Gordomo wills it. He would have you stand out on the battlefield. A beacon of strength and glory for the others!"

Karakulak kept one eye on Calagah, who was currently being covered in the wrath powder by the Big Bastards. The moment he jumped up, the impact against the ceiling would set the invasion in motion.

The high priestess moved in front of her son and dipped her hand into a bowl of white liquid, held out by one of her servants. "The symbol of Gordomo Himself will rest upon you this day." With one hand coated in the white paint, his mother dragged her fingers one way then the next, creating a V of eight digits on his armoured chest.

"Gordomo goes into battle with me!" He roared over the orcs around them. Their rallying cry resounded through every tunnel, infecting every orc.

Karakulak nodded at the female mage, who held up a black orb, a diviner they called it. A hundred miles away to the west, Vuruk would begin his slaughter of Ameeraska, and a few hundred miles to the east, the chieftain of the Mountain Fist would lead the attack on Calmardra.

It was time for Neverdark to fall… and the orc to rise.

Hadavad stood off to one side, his arms folded as he leaned against one of the pillars in the Tregaran council chamber. Tauren and the others were deep in discussion about what they could do to help the people of Lirian, as well as what they should do if Malliath arrived at their front door.

The old mage only took half of it in. His mind was elsewhere: in fact, it was in several elsewheres. The red raven had been vague regarding Gideon's fate, leaving Hadavad to wonder if his most powerful ally and friend was soon to leave this world.

Then there was the prophecy.

Something about it nagged at Hadavad's mind. Its age perhaps? No, the damage to the scroll over the millennia was undeniable.

What really got under the mage's skin, was Alijah finding it in the first place. He had sent Alijah and Vighon to find any dwellings that could be linked to The Echoes, but he had never expected them to find an actual prophecy. Especially one that appeared to be coming true at this very moment in time…

That was it.

Hadavad unfolded his arms and looked across the chamber at Alijah. What were the chances that he would not only find a real prophecy, but one that spoke of events happening right now? The mage felt they were being manipulated.

Still, he needed more time with the prophecy, and preferably access to the Dragorn library on The Lifeless Isles.

Hadavad's train of thought dissipated as he felt the quake under his feet. Those in the council chamber looked at each other, silently asking the question that everyone was worried about.

Hadavad looked down at his feet, feeling the vibration run up his legs. "That's not Malliath," he assured.

"Another earthquake perhaps?" Tauren Salimson suggested.

Hadavad locked eyes with Alijah, who said, "That's not an earthquake…"

An ear-splitting boom cracked the air outside The Council Tower, shaking loose a downpour of dust. Hadavad quickly followed behind Alijah, Vighon, and Galanör as they all dashed for the main doors that led out onto a balcony. More explosions resounded from around the city, soon followed by screams of pain and cries for help.

The watch towers rang bells across Tregaran, rousing every yellow-cloaked soldier from their slumber. Hadavad made space for Tauren, who joined them in looking out onto a smoking city.

Columns of black smoke and sand rose high into the night air above the buildings. Another deafening boom exploded to the north, taking a sizeable chunk out of the defensible wall.

"What is happening?" Tauren asked desperately.

His question was answered by a cacophony of roars, familiar to Hadavad and the others. A cold feeling of dread dropped into the old mage's stomach.

"Orcs…" he said without meaning to.

Tauren whipped his head around. "Orcs?" A mix of concern and horror possessed the southerner's face. "We have to evacuate the city, *now!*" The councillor turned to the guards. "Get the gates open!"

"Evacuate?" one of the plump councillors repeated incredulously. "Where to?"

Another councillor added, "We must defend our home!"

The roars of the invading orcs grew louder as the first spilled onto the streets below. Charging Yellow Cloaks met the beasts as they climbed out of their holes, adding the clash of steel to the chaos.

"Get the gates open!" Tauren bellowed again, ignoring his peers. "Direct everybody north!"

"North?" a councillor asked, clearly struggling to come to grips with what was happening.

"These creatures have come from the south, so we go north!" Tauren threw his cloak and sash onto the floor. "I must reach my family," he said to Hadavad.

The mage looked at his companions and nodded. "Then we shall help you, old friend." He tapped his staff once into the ground and they set off, leaving the rest of the councillors to be escorted by their guards.

With Tauren in the lead, Hadavad followed with Alijah and Vighon by his side. Galanör took a different route, scaling the nearest building with enviable ease.

The ground shook as more explosions rocked the earth, forcing the companions to lean against a wall more than once.

"This way!" Tauren called, taking them farther into the heart of the city.

It wasn't long before they found themselves in the thick of it. People were running away from the orcs, crying and screaming for help. No one had any idea where to run as the monsters appeared from every direction, cutting off every escape route. The Yellow Cloaks did their best to block off the roads and stand their ground with shields and spears, but it was clear to see that the orcs outnumbered them.

"Get everybody to the northern gate!" Tauren yelled over the melee.

One dead orc after another dropped from some height in front of Hadavad, their pale bodies drenched in blood. Looking up, Galanör was already clearing the gap between buildings and moving onto the next. It appeared these creatures were just as adept at climbing as elves.

Tauren took a sharp left, but the line of Yellow Cloaks to the right couldn't hold the orcs at bay. One Tregaran soldier succumbed to the jagged blades that angled over and under his shield, pushing his dead body to the ground. Once a single orc made it through the line, so did another, then the entire line was broken...

The Yellow Cloaks weren't nearly in the numbers required to beat such a horde. Blood splattered up the walls as the orcs threw themselves with abandon at the soldiers. Both sides suffered losses, but there was no end to the orcs pouring out of the ground.

Hadavad held back, his staff itching to be unleashed. The mage flicked his dreadlocks out of his face and strode back to the corner of the street.

"Hadavad!" Alijah called back.

The old mage spun his staff around and let loose a destructive spell so bright it illuminated the whole cross-roads before slamming into the chosen orc. The creature was flung across the street until his body was crushed against the wall.

Another spell exploded from his staff and tore through the mid-section of another orc, separating its top half from its bottom half.

One of the Yellow Cloaks beside Hadavad was savagely cut down. The murderous orc roared with its bloody sword raised and lashed out at the mage.

If the expression on the orc's face was anything to go by, the sound of its steel coming down on the enchanted staff was unlike anything it had heard before. Hadavad offered a cocky smile and spun his staff, sending the orc's blade flying away before he finally drove the end of the haft into its face. Another spin put the dangerous end of the staff in front of the orc again.

Blood went everywhere.

The mage was careful, however, to make sure that the force of the spell was heading away from him, blinding the orcs behind it. Hadavad wasted no time wading in with his staff. The night came alive with one brilliant flash after another, every spell sealing the orcs' fate.

Beyond the pile of dead orcs and Yellow Cloaks, the black smoke from the holes gave way to yet more of the wretched creatures. They snarled and roared as they charged, their obsidian armour gleaming under the moonlight.

"Hadavad!" Alijah called again.

The mage followed Alijah's wild gaze to the adjacent street, where even more orcs were charging. There were still people trapped and so few Yellow Cloaks in this part of the city. Hadavad instinctively backed away, heading towards Alijah and the others, but the screams of women and children rooted him to the spot.

"Go! he yelled back at his companions. "Go with Tauren! I will meet you at the northern gate!"

He could see that Alijah was hesitant, but Vighon grabbed him by the arm and dragged him after Tauren.

Hadavad turned back to the oncoming wave of monsters. He hadn't faced numbers such as these since the war... and he had missed it. The old mage had at least eleven new destructive spells he had been eager to try.

With orcs running at him from two of the four roads, Hadavad planted himself in the middle and lifted his staff, waiting for the perfect moment. When the foul beasts were within arm's reach, the mage drove his staff into the ground and shouted his spell.

The magic rippled outwards, cracking the ground, as it washed over the orcs with enough power to take them all off their feet. The walls of the surround buildings were shaken and the air filled with loose dust and sand. The first two lines of orcs lay very still, never to stir again. Those behind, however, were quick to rise and gather their weapons.

More soldiers were coming but they wouldn't reach the mage before the battle was renewed. Hadavad braced himself and readied the list of destructive spells in his mind.

In that moment of calm, Hadavad heard The Crow's voice echoing in his memory from atop Vengora.

"I have seen your end, Hadavad, and it is not a good one."

The mage stubbornly refused to believe that The Crow had such foresight, choosing, instead, to level his staff. If he was to die here, in the streets of Tregaran, giving its people more time to escape, then it *would* be a good death.

The next cluster of orcs, clad in dark armour and shaking their horned heads, leaped at the mage. The entire cluster was intercepted by the sudden appearance of an elven ranger. Twin scimitars danced in intricate patterns, batting aside jagged blades and opening arteries.

Galanör was a force of nature; something the orcs would attest to in the afterlife. Were he to possess a Vi'tari blade, he would be the greatest swordsman in all the world.

The elf dashed left and right, taking on the orcs from the northern street, leaving Hadavad to deal with the rest. The mage flicked his staff up and sent a wave of sand into the rushing orcs, blinding them all. The spells fired from his staff created silhouettes inside the cloud, as well as a growing pile of bodies.

The Yellow Cloaks arrived not long after with their spears driving the orc line back. More people took the opportunity to run from their homes and find a clear route through to the northern gate.

Galanör emerged from the sea of Yellow Cloaks and pale orcs with blood staining his leathers and blue cloak. His scimitars were red from hilt to tip.

"Come on!" The elf grabbed Hadavad by the arm and the two set off for Tauren's house. "What's happening here, Hadavad?" Galanör asked. "This isn't just a horde of orcs hiding in a cave. This is an invasion!"

Hadavad didn't have an answer and nor would he ever give one. The ground under their feet exploded without warning, separating the pair as it threw them across the street.

That single moment of chaos and pain was instantly replaced by a variety of different feelings. The mage blinked as he tried to make sense of what had happened to him. There was no chaos or pain, no sound of orcs or any fighting at all. The cold night air of the desert was amplified to a freezing wind and the dry ground was now a field of snow.

Hadavad pushed himself up, his robes and burgundy cloak covered in snow. His dreadlocks blew out behind him, revealing the peaks of mountains towering over him. He knew the shape of those mountains...

The old mage stood up and looked upon The Vrost Mountains, notable for their decline from the highest mountain in the east to the lowest in the west.

The question of whether he had just died was at the forefront of his mind, but the mage remembered the last time he had come close to death and woken up somewhere else. It took a moment longer to realise that, despite the blistering cold, he didn't feel uncomfortable standing at the base of The Vrost Mountains in the middle of winter.

Hadavad couldn't help his terrified shriek when the mountains lurched forward and the land contracted. In a blur of nauseating motion, he was now standing somewhere in the heart of The Vrost Mountains. There before him, hewn from the mountain itself, was a fortress he had never seen. It rose high into the mountain with towers protruding from the rock. Its design was that of The First Kingdom.

A bright light appeared where the fortress was, making it impossible to see anymore. Hadavad shielded his eyes and backed away, but the light intensified and advanced until he was on his knees. Between his fingers, he could see the glowing legs of a woman walking towards him. He tried to glimpse more of her, but the light concealed her features.

Find The Bastion, Hadavad...

The harshness of reality bombarded the mage, banishing the mountains and the blinding woman. There was, however, another woman standing over him with a wand in hand.

A dark mage of The Black Hand.

Hadavad reached out for his staff, curious as to why he was still alive. The dark mage whipped up her wand into a battle stance, informing the old mage that she had simply been savouring the kill. Her mistake.

An elven scimitar cut through the air and speared the dark mage, impaling her head and pinning her to the wall. Hadavad took a breath, not entirely sure if he would have reached his staff in time. For just a moment, he had thought of using the Viridian ruby and escaping his body.

Galanör rushed towards the building, skipping over the debris to retrieve his scimitar. The dark mage was slumped to the floor, dead. The elven ranger crouched beside Hadavad with a fresh cut bleeding down his face.

"Hadavad?"

Hadavad coughed and allowed Galanör to help him up. They were inside what had once been someone's shop, though now it was blown in and strewn with debris and dirt. Outside, beyond a fallen beam, orcs crawled out of the new hole that had exploded in front of them.

"We need to go!" Galanör hissed, gesturing to the back door.

Hadavad collected his staff and did his best to retain the words that echoed like a distant memory in his mind.

Find The Bastion, Hadavad…

Alijah was the last to enter Tauren's home behind Vighon. The pair of guards who had accompanied them spread out, checking every room for invaders.

"Isabella! Salim!" Tauren ran for his bedchamber on the top floor.

"Is this really happening?" Vighon asked, his sword in one hand and shield in the other. There was no hint of fear on his face, as there rarely was, but he couldn't mask the genuine shock that they were all feeling.

The half-elf nocked an arrow and let it rest in the bow. "It's not *not* happening…" He shrugged.

Vighon blinked slowly and shook his head. "You really will be the end of me."

Alijah offered a cocky smirk. "You'll die before me if that's what you mean."

Gallows humour was often at the heart of their banter before a desperate fight. Alijah found it calmed his nerves, allowing him to better aim his bow.

A scream from upstairs pierced the house before the clash of steel. Alijah was the quickest and found his way to the top floor, only to hear the main doors burst open below. The guards stayed back to tackle the invaders, leaving Vighon to join Alijah.

Tauren was quite the sight. Alijah had only ever heard of his uncle in battle, but seeing him now, with two short-swords spinning in his hands, he could easily imagine him at The Battle of Syla's Gate. The orcs climbing over the balcony fell one after the other to his fury.

Vighon instinctively ran to the side of Isabella and Salim, ready to protect them with his life. Alijah fell into the rhythm that came so naturally to him and raised his bow. The twang of the string as it propelled his arrow into an orc's face was deeply satisfying.

Tauren retreated step by step, his blades never ceasing to parry and attack. Alijah was forced to rely on his elven heritage to track the man's rapid movements, searching for the gaps to fit his arrows. One whistled only an inch from Tauren's neck before finding its mark in the eye of an orc.

Every shot gave his uncle one less foe to manage and made his retreat all the smoother. A window smashed from one of the rooms and the feral growls of more orcs echoed through the halls. Downstairs, the guards sounded to be fighting for their lives in a bid to keep the orcs off the stairs.

Vighon turned around to face the new barrage, flipping his sword before resting it over the top of his raised shield. Alijah felt sorry for the orcs who sought to flank them.

Tauren ducked what would have been a mortal injury and Alijah loosed another arrow, putting the orc down for good.

"We need to get out of here!" Tauren yelled, gesturing fervently for his family to join him.

Vighon dashed down the hall and met the first attack with his rounded shield, surprising the orc with a low slash across his belly, under the rim of its armour. The man came straight back up with a back-handed swing of his blade, slicing another orc across the face and splitting one of its horns before splattering blood up the wall.

A kick here, a strike there, and a shield to protect him, Vighon Draqaro didn't let a single orc past him. Alijah saw an opening and let fly an arrow, silencing the roar of an orc before it could reach his friend.

"Alijah!" Tauren called his name urgently. "We need to go! I need to get my family out of the city!"

The half-elf agreed. Tregaran didn't have long judging by the number of orcs scrambling out of the ground. There wasn't a city in all of Illian prepared for this.

"Vighon!" he yelled down the hall.

The dying cry of the last Yellow Cloak resounded up the stairwell. They were about to be overrun.

"Vighon!" he yelled again, adding a sense of emergency to his tone.

The northerner hacked at the remaining orc until it relented and fell to the floor dead. He wiped the blood and sweat from his face and spat on the body.

"How do we get out of here?" he asked, eyeing the shadows growing larger on the stairwell.

Alijah turned to Tauren for the answer. "The north-west corner," he replied. "This house was built with a servants' stairwell."

The word he was really looking for was slave, but Alijah felt now wasn't the time to argue the details. With Isabella and Salim between them, they ran through the house. Vighon remained at the back, ready to deal with any pursuers.

The howls and roars of the orcs chased them every step of the way and eventually preceded them as they reached the north-west stairwell. They were boxed in.

Isabella pulled Salim into her embrace with tears streaming down her face. It was gut-wrenching to see a mother cling to her son, believing that these were to be their final moments.

The rage that had steadily been building in Alijah since Paldora's Fall rose to the surface again. He offered a feral growl of his own and nocked another arrow. The first orc to round the corner or ascend the stairs was going to get an arrow through the ear.

"To the roof!" Tauren declared.

Trusting his judgment, and with nowhere else to go, they followed the councillor to the roof before the first wave of orcs fell upon them.

Under the stars once again, Tregaran's inevitable demise was clear to see. The horizon was choked with rising columns of black smoke and the air thick with death. Fires had erupted in every corner of the city and the sound of battle was matched by the sound of roaring orcs.

"Over here!" Tauren directed them to the far side of the roof, where a long plank of wood sat under the lip of the edge. "We keep these in case of fires…" he said absently, lifting the plank into place between his house and the adjacent building.

Alijah ushered Vighon across first, ensuring Isabella and Salim had someone to protect them on the other side. Salim required some encouragement from his parents having made the mistake of looking down. The drop would easily kill any of them, but the warring orcs and Yellow Cloaks below offered an even messier death.

The door they had come through burst open and the first orc caught Alijah's arrow in its neck. Tauren kissed his wife and forced her onto the plank, telling her to hurry.

Alijah nocked another arrow and killed the second orc to emerge from the house. The doorway funnelled them, making his targets all the easier to hit.

"Come on!" Vighon called from the other roof.

Alijah looked across the roof of Tauren's house to see meaty hands and metal hooks appearing on the edge. More orcs were coming.

"Go!" Tauren ordered him across the plank.

"You go!" Alijah punctuated his response with another arrow, picking off the first orc to climb onto the roof.

Tauren stopped him from drawing another arrow and shoved him towards the plank. "Go, boy!"

Alijah could see that they didn't have time to argue anymore; the roof was crowding with orcs. He turned and made a mad dash, hoping to cross the plank and cover Tauren's escape.

He saw Vighon's wide eyes before he made it across the plank and his stomach sank. Alijah whipped his head around to see the cluster of orcs moving aside, making way for one in particular. It was slightly taller than the rest with two thick horns curving over its head and flicking to the sky. Black obsidian armour protected his vital areas, though Alijah's eyes were drawn to the white V painted on its chestplate.

"Run!" Tauren yelled.

Alijah could see what he was about to do, but even elven reflexes weren't fast enough to stop Tauren from kicking the plank down to the street.

"No!" they all shouted at once.

"Uncle Tauren!" Alijah could only watch as the taller orc approached Tauren.

Isabella pulled Salim into her again and covered the boy's eyes.

The orc retrieved a wide rectangular sword from its back, the tip unusually flat. It looked to be heavier than any blade Alijah had seen before.

With his short-swords, Tauren made the orc work for his victory. The southerner was living proof that speed and agility could best height and strength. He fought fiercely, lashing out and drawing blood from the creature with every swing of his blades.

The larger orc brought his wide blade down like a hammer and Alijah fired an arrow, aiming for the gap between the chestplate and the pauldron. The arrow sank into the orc's shoulder, but it didn't stop him from taking another swing. Tauren rolled under the attack and brought his blades around to slash at the orc's legs.

Alijah fired another arrow, this time aiming for the creature's head. For the first time, the orc moved with a swiftness he had yet to display. The creature dipped its head and the arrow bounced harmlessly off its bony ridge.

"Get them out of here!" Tauren shouted across the buildings.

The large orc batted one of Tauren's short-swords away, sending it over the edge, and grasped the wrist of his other hand. Within the vice, the tendons in Tauren's hand spasmed and relented their hold on his remaining short-sword.

"No!" Alijah cried, unable to get a clear shot past Tauren

The orc flicked his hand and snapped Tauren's wrist, forcing a scream from his lips. He punched at the creature with his free hand but he might as well have been punching a wall. The orc released his broken wrist and slammed his meaty hand down on Tauren's shoulder, driving him to his knees.

"Uncle Tauren!"

Isabella's sobbing drowned out the fighting below as she cried for her husband.

The orc smiled, raised his sword, and brought it down on Tauren.

"NO!" Alijah was red in the face with tears streaking across his cheeks.

The wide blade cut through Tauren's shoulder and became stuck in his lower gut. The orc yanked his sword free and kicked Tauren at the same time, throwing him off the edge of the roof.

All sound and sensation disappeared from the world. Alijah saw only the orc, the focus of his hate and rage. Without thinking his hands went through the motions of nocking another arrow. Two rough hands gripped his arms and pulled hard, preventing him from going through with it.

The sound of Vighon's voice was distant, his words beyond comprehension. All that existed was Alijah's rage and the smiling orc.

It was the sound of Salim crying, added to his mother's that finally broke his haze. They had just watched their husband and father die under the shadow of a monster…

"Alijah!" Vighon yelled in his ear as he continued to drag him away. "We need to get them out of the city, *now!*"

Alijah blinked hard to rid his eyes of the residual tears. With clarity of vision, he could see that Vighon was directing them inside the new building and back onto the streets.

Vighon probably wouldn't count it, but Alijah knew that his friend had just saved his life again. Had he given into that rage and challenged the orcs… well, he knew the truth of that outcome: seeing Tauren's ruined body tumble off the edge of his own house would haunt him forever.

Keeping Isabella and Salim between them, the two companions found their way back onto the streets of Tregaran. Alijah had cause to fire three arrows before they even rounded the first corner.

Rounding that corner was soon added to their list of regrets. A young man, robed in black, pointed his staff at them and offered a wicked smile. Vighon held up his shield to protect them, but the spell never came… at least not from *his* staff. The dark mage was struck by a destructive spell and hurtled into the adjacent wall, killing him instantly.

Hadavad and Galanör appeared haggard and bloody before them, the mage's staff still smoking from the end.

"Where's Tauren?" Hadavad asked immediately.

Isabella and Salim fell in on each other again, relying on the comfort of the other to get them through it. Their reaction was all the mage needed to understand the fate of his friend. Before sorrow could overwhelm them all, Vighon rallied the group with a reminder that they needed to find the horses and escape the city.

Looking back one last time, hoping to sight Tauren's killer, Alijah ran from Tregaran with a promise in his heart. If it was the last thing he ever did, he would kill that wretched orc...

A LESSON IN DWARVES

Doran Heavybelly put his name to the test as he devoured every scrap of food placed before him. Bacon, sausages, and eggs, in quantities many would struggle to count, all disappeared down his gullet.

Seated in the larger room given to Reyna and Nathaniel, the three ate alone, though Reyna spent most of their intimate breakfast tapping her fingers against the wood.

The dwarf wiped the tomato juice from his blond beard. "I thought we'd be eating with the queen," he said.

"I don't think Yelifer does anything the way we expect," Nathaniel replied.

Reyna's gaze continued to pierce the stone wall.

"What's got ye in knots, me Lady?"

The elf ceased her tapping and her eyes focused for the first time all morning. "Arlon Draqaro…" she said with displeasure.

"He's got under your skin," Nathaniel commented.

Doran wiggled a sausage in the air. "I've met Vighon a handful o' times at The Axe. Nice fella! Can't see how they're related meself."

"Vighon wasn't raised by Arlon," Nathaniel explained. "When

he was only a boy, his mother, Elena, ran away from Arlon. She fled Namdhor and eventually found herself in our path. We employed her as a handmaiden for Reyna, but she also looked after the children when we were busy."

"Besides the obvious, why did the mother flee?" Doran asked.

"Arlon Draqaro was, or more likely *still is*, the head of a crime syndicate…"

Doran twigged. "The Ironsworn."

Nathaniel nodded. "Elena didn't want Vighon growing up in that, so she took him and ran south. Both of them became part of the family really…" The knight's last words were heavy with sorrow.

Reyna put down her fork. "He's found loftier heights than the head of The Ironsworn. He called himself a lord yesterday."

"A title only Yelifer could grant him," Nathaniel pointed out.

The elf shook her head. "We need more information."

"I don't think we're going to find it in The Dragon Keep," Nathaniel added. "This place is crawling with Ironsworn. The Gold Cloaks give them free reign up here."

"What ye need is some loose lips," Doran said through his mouthfuls of bacon. "For those, ye need a source o' ale!"

Nathaniel pointed his fork in Doran's face. "If you think we brought you all the way to Namdhor to sample every tavern in the city…"

Doran displayed an expression of mock offence. "I only wish to be o' service, Ambassador Galfrey."

The two shared a short laugh, but Reyna was still a hundred miles away. "I spent my entire youth learning about the display of power," she recalled. "My father would use every assembly to teach me how one could own the room, show others that you are the one in control. I never cared for it. I always thought it was a form of intimidation that kings and queens should be above."

Nathaniel arched an eyebrow. "I'd say Arlon Draqaro could teach your father a thing or two about displays of power."

Reyna nodded. "Everything he did in that hall was a display. Speaking first. Walking around us. The incessant interruptions. He also knew we had journeyed from Dragons' Reach, making him aware of the council meeting. Not to mention the way he interacted with Queen Yelifer…"

"He's been doing this a long time," Nathaniel replied. "Elena said he took over The Ironsworn in his late teens."

A knock on the door ended their conversation as a pair of Gold Cloaks arrived. The three companions were escorted through The Dragon Keep and up a level, to a new room with diminished grandeur. Circular in shape and smaller than the throne room, the chamber housed a round table with a map of Illian on it. The chamber was made to feel all the smaller by the man-mountain standing on the other side of the table, donned in his usual yellow gambeson and bucket-like helmet.

"Welcome to the war room," Arlon said with open arms.

The head of The Ironsworn was standing on the other side of the table to Queen Yelifer, who was supported by a slender cane. Behind the queen was a high-ranking soldier of the Namdhorian army with a beard as fiery as the sun. Mirroring him, behind Arlon, was the soldier's equivalent in The Ironsworn ranks, ugly as sin and painted in tattoos.

Reyna approached the table as if she belonged there. "Let's not be hasty, Lord Draqaro. War can still be avoided."

Yelifer gestured to the soldier behind her. "Ambassadors, this is General Morkas, the commander of the Namdhorian forces. General Morkas, regale our guests, if you would."

"Certainly, Your Grace." General Morkas stepped forward with his white helmet under one arm. "The mine in dispute is here," he pointed at an outcropping of Vengora, just north of Namdhor.

Doran got so close to the edge of the table that his moustache tickled the surface.

"It should be noted," Morkas continued, "that the mine was in our possession first."

Nathaniel twisted his mouth. "I think the dwarves of Dhenaheim, formerly of *Vengora*, will contest who came first."

General Morkas shot the old knight a stern look. "When the dwarves arrived in the mine, the banner of house Skalaf was already planted. It was *they* who incited violence first."

"Casualties?" Nathaniel asked.

"A small contingent of soldiers accompanied the smiths," Morkas explained. "They prevented any deaths, but three of my men suffered wounds that ail them even now."

"Smiths?" Reyna repeated. "You sent blacksmiths into the mine?"

The look Yelifer sent the general's way didn't go unnoticed.

Morkas swallowed hard, preparing his answer, but it was Arlon who spoke first. "The mine appears to have belonged to dwarven blacksmiths, long ago. Who better to inform us of the value of such a find than smiths of our own?"

Doran could tell a lot from the taste of any rock or stone, but his nose could sniff out a lie any day of the week.

Nathaniel asked, "What happened after the first retreat?"

General Morkas assumed his posture once more. "A foothold was established on both sides of the entrance hall. We occupy the southern tunnel and the antechamber. The dwarves are situated in the northern tunnel."

"And neither has attempted to reclaim the mine?" Reyna asked.

General Morkas hesitated. "There have been… skirmishes. Negotiations broke down quickly. No one can speak the dwarven tongue and when they attempt to speak our language…" The man looked down at Doran, hesitating yet again. "Well, it's hard to understand."

"Like I said," Queen Yelifer croaked, "no deaths, *yet*."

Reyna didn't look convinced. "At Dragons' Reach you told us your bannermen were already rallying."

General Morkas announced, "The Lords of Skystead, Dunwich, Longdale, and Darkwell have all answered their queen's call to arms."

"They march on The Iron Valley?" Nathaniel pointed to the arching gap in the Vengoran mountains.

"Of course," the general replied. "The valley is the only way to get an army through to the northern side of Vengora."

"Ye mean to cut 'em off from the northern entrance," Doran mused aloud.

Morkas looked down on Doran with contempt. "It is a simple strategy, Master Dwarf. In the confines of the mine, our numbers count for nothing. We must find their entrance to the mountain and seal it."

"A simple strategy…" Doran stroked his beard. "Aye, it is that."

Nathaniel nudged his foot. "Doran…"

The dwarf didn't have the patience for this kind of chatting. "I'm jus' sayin' what's not bein' said! They've clearly found the workshop o' a dwarven smithy, somethin' I can see why ye'd get so excited abou'. Callin' it a mine ain't gonna make it what it's not, mind ye. Now they're talkin' abou' usin' *simple strategies* to best me kin!"

"Doran." Reyna added her own tone of diplomacy.

The dwarf waved her away. "Ye brought me here for me knowledge, din' ye? Well, they're gonna hear it!" Doran looked at the general. "Ye're talkin' about goin' to war with a civilisation that's been perfectin' the art o' killin' since before yer bloodline even started, laddy!"

General Morkas lifted his chin. "You underestimate the men of the north, Master Dwarf."

Doran sighed. "The arrogance o' man won't stand up to the mettle o' the dwarves."

"Doran!" Reyna's voice went up an octave.

If Morkas hadn't taken offence yet, he certainly did now. "How dare—"

Doran shook his head and waved the man's reply away. "I'd say ye're brave for diggin' that far into the mountain, but ye're *stupid* for stayin'. I'll tell ye what I told these two; take yer men, pull back yer army an' leave Vengora alone. Ye're sparkin' a war with an enemy ye can' hope to beat. Piss 'em off enough, an' they'll not stop at reclaimin' the mine. They'll take Namdhor, then the entire north. Keep pissin' 'em off, an' the entire realm will be forced to take up arms!"

Queen Yelifer spoke, silencing any further response from her general. "Were you not in the company of the ambassadors, Master Dwarf, I would question your allegiance. My banner stands in that mine; I will not relinquish it to anyone, dwarf or otherwise."

Doran could see no part for him in all of this. "Well, I wish ye all luck!" He turned to leave and found the man-mountain standing in his way. The son of Dorain had to pull his head right back to see the man's head.

"He can leave if he wishes to, Sir Borin," the queen added.

Without a word, the yellow guard stood aside, revealing the door his wide frame had completely hidden. Doran marched out with a lasting look at Reyna and Nathaniel. This wasn't the way he wanted to leave it, but he had said all he could on the matter.

The hours of the day flitted by and day turned to night as the grey clouds relented to an ocean of stars. Doran, of course, missed it all, hidden from the outside world in the comfort of a tavern. The name of the establishment, however, had rolled out of his head some time ago.

A variety of different crowds had come and gone as the day waned. The heavy drinkers arrived earlier than Doran did, but even they had failed to compete with the dwarf's stamina. The tavern had an eerie silence in the afternoon, but it was soon filled again by the evening crowds.

Doran's day had been filled with stories of his own, for those who wished to hear them, as well as few from other patrons. The ale had flowed freely and the son of Dorain had built up a tab he wasn't entirely sure how to pay. Still, he was having fun!

It seemed the Namdhorians only required time and drink to warm to newcomers. Unlike Russell Maybury, the owner didn't mind the Warhog who, when left alone, only wished to fall asleep at Doran's feet.

When Reyna and Nathaniel walked in, later that night, the dwarf couldn't say he noticed until they were both sat comfortably in his booth.

"Bah! How did ye two find me?" he asked, sloshing his tankard of Strider Cider.

"It wasn't that hard," Nathaniel answered. "We just entered the first tavern we came across."

Thinking about it, Doran didn't recall travelling very far after leaving The Dragon Keep. "Well, here we are…" The son of Dorain burped and did his best to focus his vision.

"It would appear you've had a more interesting day than we have," Reyna said.

"Well, I thought to be leavin'," Doran began, "but then I thought, hang abou', why don't I see if there's any beasties that need dealin' with before I go. Get some coin out o' Namdhor before there *is* no Namdhor…"

Reyna looked around at the patrons. "I hope you haven't been telling a tale too many, Doran."

The son of Dorain pretended to turn a key into his tight lips. "Sealed, me Lady."

Nathaniel leaned over the table. "You're not really leaving, are you?"

Doran huffed and put his tankard down for the first time in many hours. "I rightly should, lad. I've said all that needs to be heard. If the old war-witch doesn' want to hear it…" The dwarf shrugged. "I know I'd rather be on the other side o' The Evermoore when me kin sees an army o' Gold Cloaks."

Reyna met Doran's eyes across the table. "We're going into the mountain tomorrow, at dawn. We would very much appreciate your dwarvish tongue."

"*I bet ye would*," Doran replied in his native language. Seeing their quizzical faces, he elaborated, "O' course ye'll be needin' me! I only said all o' that so I could get out from under their watchers." Something about that statement didn't ring entirely true, but the dwarf couldn't concentrate enough to decide what was what. "I've been in here gatherin' information!" he declared. "If ye tell a tale or… six, then ye'll always find some folk willin' to tell ye some o' their own."

Nathaniel narrowed his gaze. "You said all that and stormed off so that you could gather information? Not so you could drink in a tavern all day?"

"Wait," Reyna put a hand on her husband's arm. "Doran, are you saying you will come with us tomorrow? Into the mountain?"

Doran blinked once, but not in sync. "O' course I will, me Lady! *I am at your service*," he added in dwarvish. Again, something didn't sound right to the son of Dorain, but Reyna's big green eyes robbed him of further thought.

"So," Nathaniel said, picking up the dwarf's tankard and giving it a sniff, "what *have* you discovered, Heavybelly?"

Doran could feel a story rising to the surface, as it always did when given the chance. "The north," he began. "It's a different world up here. They've got so much land the rest o' Illian might as well not exist. They're proud, though, I'll give 'em that. They think the cold makes 'em hard." The dwarf laughed to himself. "I said it just makes 'em cold!"

Nathaniel raised an eyebrow. "Where exactly did you get your source of information?"

"Hey now!" Doran scowled at him. "Don't ye doubt. I've... learnt stuff." The dwarf took another swig of his sweet cider. "Now, where was I? Oh, the north, right. From what I can gather, it's like The War for the Realm never happened up here. They've already forgotten King Tion and all the shit he put 'em through. Most have never even heard the name Valanis!"

Reyna replied, "I suppose his alliance to Valanis put all the north at odds with the rest of Illian. I can see why they would be quick to forget Merkaris Tion."

"Up here," Doran continued, "the war for the *throne* is what matters. We all went abou' our lives, rebuildin' Velia and The Arid Lands but, up here, the war was only just gettin' goin'. The lords o' the north fought tooth and nail for The Dragon Keep. Some said the whole o' The White Vale was red with blood for an entire summer!"

"We tried to mediate several times," Nathaniel emphasised. "We weren't welcome unless we were pledging the force of other kingdoms."

"I recall the lord of Skystead requesting a battalion of elves," Reyna added with a bemused smile.

"Well," Doran continued, "their little civil war was beginnin' to break up the country. Things only got worse when the lord of Namdhor didn't wake up one day."

"You mean Lord Gaillart Skalaf?" Nathaniel clarified. "I remember hearing about that. Died in his sleep, didn't he?"

"Poison, the folk here say. Either way, it left Namdhor open for the other lords. That is, until Lady Yelifer Skalaf stood up to them. 'Pendin' on who ye ask, she's either a hero or a tyrant, though ye won't hear much o' the latter this close to the Keep."

"I heard the war-witch earned her title," Nathaniel chipped in. "Used magic to best the other lords."

Doran gave a sharp laugh. "Sometimes, when folk see the impossible, they call it magic. In this case, the Lady Skalaf was just more willin' to compromise than the others that fought for the throne."

"What do you mean, Doran?" the elf asked.

"The civil war was apparently very good for the gangs. The Ironsworn used the chaos to set themselves up in every town an' city north o' The Evermoore. Now, the exact details are hazy, a bit like all o' ye right now... *But*, a couple o' shady fellas I got to speakin' with had their own take on events."

Reyna looked skeptical. "Doran, were these men even alive during the civil war?"

"O' course they were! A couple o' retired Gold Cloaks, in fact. They weren't proud o' it, but they served under King Tion himself. Anyway, after I bought 'em a few rounds, they said their bit. Turns out, Lady Skalaf struck a bargain with The Ironsworn. Overnight, her forces swelled and she suddenly found herself with allies in every town."

Reyna sat back, her face a picture of revelation. "Yelifer gives them a free pass."

Nathaniel didn't look convinced. "There must have been boundaries set in place. They might have helped her claim the throne, but Yelifer wouldn't give them keys to the entire north."

"Perhaps once she did keep some form of order, but the years have not been kind to her. As she has declined, heirless, Arlon has assumed more control."

"Exactly!" Doran agreed, or at least he thought he did. "They said Arlon runs everythin'. Well, everythin' but that walkin' slab o' a beast."

"Sir Borin?" Nathaniel asked.

"Aye, that one. Sir Borin the Dread they call 'im. He's Yelifer's through and through. Probably why Arlon hasn't got rid o' her…"

Nathaniel was inclined to agree. "He certainly inspires a degree of dread, I'll give him that."

"I have to say, Doran, I am impressed with your ability to gather information while so… hindered" Reyna looked at his near-empty tankard.

"It's no problem, me Lady." Doran burped. "So, what did ye learn after I left? Did they say what's in that workshop that's got 'em all…" The dwarf could feel the world slipping away. "Hold that thought. There's rope in one o' the pig's satchels."

"What's that for?" Nathaniel asked.

"For me," Doran replied. "Ye're gonna have to tie me to the pig. He'll drag me back to the Keep."

Reyna tilted her head, or was it heads? "What will we need to do that for, Doran?"

The son of Dorain could see his peripheral vision blacking out. "Because o' this…" The dwarf fell sideways and slammed face first into the tavern floor.

ABOVE AND BELOW

Between the thick columns of rising smoke, Karakulak watched the inevitable return of the sky fire. The eyes of Gordomo began to fade away as the first rays of light threatened to scorch them all.

Turning away from the east, the king of the orcs looked out on his first victory. In a single night, the city of Tregaran had transitioned from a dwelling of humans, to a trophy room of bones.

Karakulak walked through the streets, enjoying the sights, sounds, and smells. The remnants of the city's survivors were screaming their last words, some dying on their feet, others crawling until a spear ran them through. Bodies of all ages littered the ground and the smell of fear had been replaced by death.

Everywhere he looked, orcs were roughly grabbing at their human victims and going to work on removing their skin; eager to get at the bones. Every warrior was entitled to the bones of their first kill. They each believed it would make them rich, a notion Karakulak found amusing. By the time they had conquered Neverdark, they would be swimming in human bones, a fact that would see the value of their bones diminish.

Still, they were blood drunk. Many of the orcs currently

scavenging among the dead had never seen so many bones, at least not from a creature on two legs.

An orc of the Steel Caste roared at the changing sky and made a run for the nearest tunnel, pausing only to pick up the sack of bones he had filled. His retreat was soon followed by others who had no desire to see the sky fire.

Karakulak was inclined to join them when he came across the body of the man he had been instructed to kill. Why The Crow had demanded the death of this particular man was beyond the king. He couldn't see how ending his life would lead to victory across the entire realm, but seeing the future wasn't his gift; forging it was.

On his way back to the comfort of The Under Realm, another body caught his sharp eyes. Cloaked in black, the dark mage lay dead in an awkward position. It didn't take an expert in bones to see that the mage's spine had been snapped. The king bent down and picked up the small orb hanging off his belt. Karakulak gave it a smell and shook it in his hand. Nothing. He had no idea how it worked.

"I advise caution, my king!" came the shrieking voice of his mother.

Karakulak rolled his eyes before turning to face her. Were she not the High Priestess of Gordomo, he would have put a blade in her hand and forced her to lead the invasion. As it was, her position was seen as second only to Gordomo... and the king, of course.

"The sky fire rises, Mother. You should be below ground."

"And you should not be touching magic," his mother shot back. The priestess dismissed her entourage before continuing, "You walk a thin line with magic, my son. There are murmurs that you have come to rely on it."

"I do not fear murmurs, Mother."

His mother moved about in the manner of a banshee, her dress of bones rattling every which way. "I stamp them out where I can, but dissent has a way of spreading, like an infected wound."

Karakulak's curious nature couldn't be denied and he pocketed the diviner when his mother's back was turned. "What would you have me do?" The king spat on the ground. "Magic is foul, but it is a weapon in the hands of our enemy, a weapon they would turn on us. Our ancestors were forced a thousand miles from Vengora to The Undying Mountains because they couldn't challenge the magic of the elves."

The rising sky fire continued to chase away the eyes of Gordomo and shed its nightmarish light over Neverdark. Karakulak could feel it burning his eyes, stealing his vision. The remaining orcs grabbed whole bodies and dragged them into The Under Realm for flaying.

"Your victory here, and across The Arid Lands, will see every orc chanting your name. Now is the time to break away. You have used The Black Hand to your end. We have the ancient tunnels. All nine tribes are united under a king! You don't need their filthy magic anymore..."

The light began to irritate Karakulak. "What would you have me do?" he demanded.

"Turn your back on this... *Crow*. He has his dragon. We don't need them to take Neverdark. The wrath powder is of our creation, the spores too. Let *me* help you, my son."

"Is this Gordomo's will you speak of?" he asked skeptically.

"I speak of no other!" his mother shrieked. "This Kaliban The Crow speaks of - he is beneath Gordomo!"

"The Crow's foresight has proven true at every turn," Karakulak countered. "That is a tool we cannot afford to lose."

"You don't need his seeing eyes!" The High Priestess danced in front of her son, stamping her staff into the ground. "The Arid Lands fell in a single night. The might of Gordomo flows through you, my son. You do not need the power of Kaliban."

Karakulak bared his teeth, frustrated. There wasn't an orc alive who shared his vision nor his intelligence. His kin spoke of strength and might, the very things that had been beaten into the ground by the elves and the dwarves five millennia ago. They would need more than their strength if they were to win this war.

"The Arid Lands have fallen," he agreed, "and the northern kingdoms will suffer a similar fate. The world of man is weak, *but...*" the king turned on his mother, "when Neverdark is ours, the *elves* will come. That's if we don't fight the dwarves first—"

His mother jumped in, eager to interrupt him. "With you as our king we can—"

Karakulak roared, silencing the High Priestess. "Should we find victory against the humans *and* survive the elves from the east *and* the dwarves from the north, we are still opposed by the Dragorn. I will use any weapon I must to see the orc risen above all, to see Gordomo rule above *and* below. If magic is needed, then magic I will use."

His mother spat on the ground. "Gordomo spits on magic! Look at what he did with the strength of the orc!" She gestured to the smoking city.

Karakulak could barely see anymore and the pain was shooting through his head. The king growled and snatched his mother by the arms. "Gordomo didn't do this! Gordomo wasn't here! Look, even now his vision is taken away by the sky fire! *I* did this, King Karakulak!"

His mother hissed. "You wouldn't say that if He could see us!"

Karakulak huffed and released his mother, turning for the nearest tunnel. "Until Gordomo *Himself* tells me to find another way, I will use The Black Hand to my end."

The High Priestess hurried ahead of him with her usual sporadic movements. Once inside the shadow of the tunnel, she faced her son again. "I will make the appropriate sacrifices on your behalf, my son, as penance for your words..."

Karakulak clenched his sharp teeth, aware that the eyes of many orcs were on him now. Striking the High Priestess of Gordomo would be considered blasphemous. Standing by the edge of the encroaching light, the king turned his back on his mother. The sky fire had created a stark contrast now between the darkness of the tunnel and the surface beyond.

Seeing the approaching light, The Crow's words came back to him from when first they met.

"If the orc goes to war with Neverdark, the earth will go to war with the sky fire."

Yet here it was. The sky fire rose and the orcs retreated. The king could feel himself being pulled in two directions, splitting the fury that coursed through his veins. Should The Crow and his words prove false, even once, he would flay the entire Black Hand himself. On the other side of that, he could see that everything had happened just as the wizard had said it would. With every victory, however, Karakulak knew his mother's protests would grow louder.

The truth was... the king had never seen any proof that Gordomo existed. And if He did, He had shown no care for the orc. Karakulak was thankful that for all the eyes on him, none could read his thoughts. His mind, superior to that of his kin, could also see that there had been no proof of The Crow's god, only that the wizard could grasp magic better than most.

Let the gods watch, he thought. Let them all watch as he conquered Neverdark. When the whole world was his, it would be Karakulak who was worshipped as a god. A god that the orcs could see and hear, a god that cared for his realm.

Karakulak looked up at the pale blue sky, squinting to focus his eyes in the light. It pained him, but the king continued to stare defiantly at the light. Gordomo hated the light, and so the orcs were chained to the dark with Him. That thought saw the king raise a hand, pushing it into the light as he had done in the ruins of Karath. Again, the light did nothing to his skin. It didn't burn or poison him. Karakulak pulled his arm back and inspected it, realising that the sky fire affected only his eyes.

Once, he had been too weak to lift his father's sword, but that hadn't stop him from picking it up every day. Eventually, he was strong enough to lift that sword over his head.

Eventually...

ILYTHYRA

After two days of following The Selk Road into the unwelcoming north, Vighon finally stopped looking over his shoulder for any sign of the orcs. The heat of The Arid Lands had finally fallen away as they entered The Moonlit Plains and the desert ground gave way to snow-covered grass.

It felt like walking home to Vighon, but he could see the distress on the faces of those who had lost their homes.

Looking to Isabella and Salim, both astride Ned, it was clear to see that they too were struggling to cope with the drop in temperature.

"Here," he said, removing the black fur cloak from one of Ned's satchel bags.

Isabella thanked him and selflessly wrapped Salim in it. It seemed Tauren's wife was made of stronger stuff as she gritted her teeth and pulled her son closer.

Vighon went to remove the dark cloak hanging over his own shoulders when a Tregaran soldier offered her his yellow cloak. He was one of very few soldiers to have fled the city, with most falling to the orcs. Vighon was glad that a few had survived and now helped to keep their little caravan safe. The line of refugees didn't quite cover half a mile, but Galanör told of other survivors who had chosen a different direction.

The truth remained, however, that there were more dead than living now.

Vighon ploughed through the snow-covered fields, his mind cast back to the fighting. He considered the orcs he had laid low. They were stronger than the average man, but their skin was just as vulnerable to steel.

Then there was the other orc, the one with the rectangular blade. Vighon glanced back at Alijah, his face still a picture of sorrow. Uncle Tauren might not have been related by blood, but he was still family to the half-elf. Looking beyond his friend, Vighon could see Alijah's expression on the faces of every man, woman, and child. They had all lost family.

Up ahead, something moved in the lightly falling snow, catching Vighon's eye. He reached for his hilt, wondering if he was to see his first Centaur. There hadn't been a reported incident between their two kinds for years, not since the elves returned, but Vighon wasn't taking any chances; they were notoriously territorial.

The sound of galloping hooves was enough to have Vighon pull his blade an inch out of its scabbard. The white haze finally gave way to a familiar pale horse and elven rider. The northerner let his blade rest as Galanör brought his horse to a stop in front of him.

The ranger, protected from the snow within his blue cloak and white furs, hopped off his horse and pulled his hood down. "The weather only gets worse," he reported. "The road becomes impossible to see and the snow is heavier. We could end up walking in circles."

Vighon had seen enough chattering teeth to agree. "There are a few forests dotted around The Plains, but even they won't offer much in the way of warmth."

Galanör looked briefly to the north-west. "There is one forest that can provide shelter - protection too."

Vighon cast his eyes over the empty plains, wondering if the elf had been out in the cold for too long. Then he remembered exactly where they were.

"The elves?" he questioned. "You want to go to Ily..." Damned if he could say the name.

"Ilythyra," Galanör finished. "It's not too far from here. They can shelter us until this blows over."

Vighon considered the trail of people, *human* people, behind them and wondered how happy the elves of Ilythyra would be to see so many. "I don't know..."

"We have nothing to fear from my kin," Galanör assured.

The idea of walking into an entirely elven domain was comparable to getting in a boat and sailing to Ayda in Vighon's opinion. It wasn't a place humans visited. Then again, humans weren't supposed to be exposed to elements such as the freezing cold either.

"I don't fear elves," Vighon clarified. "I've just... only met two."

Hadavad came up beside them astride one of the horses he had charmed outside the city gates. "Well, what are we waiting for?" It was the first time the mage had spoken since they left Tregaran, he himself struck hard by Tauren's death. "Show us the way, Galanör."

With Alijah stuck in his own head, Vighon decided to keep his reservations to himself as they set off in search of Ilythyra.

The day stretched on and the snows came upon them with a vengeance when finally they stood on the edge of the forest. The trees were tall and somehow more foreboding than those of The Evermoore or even The Wild Moores.

Something more than nature breathed life into this forest...

Galanör led the way, breaking through the tree line first. Alijah came to stand beside Vighon, his eyes set high into the canopy. It seemed the sense of wonder evoked by the forest was enough to re-awaken the inate explorer that the half-elf could never deny.

"I came here as a child," he said, "before you and your mother joined us."

"What's it like?" Vighon asked, refraining from using the elven name.

Alijah stared wistfully into the forest. "It's like a different world." He turned to his friend with the first smile he had seen in days. "You'll hate it."

"I won't hate it," Vighon argued. "If it's warm and they have food I might never leave."

Alijah chuckled softly to himself. "Of all the people I've ever met, Vighon Draqaro, no one likes what they know and knows what they like more than you."

Happy to keep his friend's spirits up, Vighon went along with the banter. "I'm a very cultured man, don't you know. An artist, in fact."

"Don't start that again," Alijah pleaded.

The caravan followed them in and the refugees wove between the trees in silence. When their discussion ran dry, Vighon tried to comfort his friend.

"I'm sorry about Tauren," he said seriously. "He seemed like a good man."

"He was," Alijah replied into his chest.

Vighon nodded along, unsure what to say. "He also seemed like a fighter, a warrior born even."

"I know what you're thinking," Alijah said, gripping the strap of his quiver. "He died a good death, fighting on his feet as all warriors should. But you saw what that orc did to him. The price of honour is a cost his family must pay."

"You're blaming yourself," Vighon observed.

Alijah glowered. "I blame *all* of us. Hadavad's magic, Galanör's skills, my arrows, your… *everything*. We should have done more. We live in a world under the protection of the Dragorn. After Tregaran, that means *nothing*. We can't keep people safe."

"We can't keep *everyone* safe," Vighon corrected.

"Well, maybe we should…" Upon spotting Isabella and Salim, Alijah retreated into himself again and slowed his pace to fall behind.

Vighon gave him his space, aware himself that time was the best of healers.

The forest was quiet. Only the sound of their feet crunching through the snow pierced the trees. Vighon hated it. The feeling of being watched burned in the back of his head. Still, they walked in the wake of Galanör, who passed the trees with little trepidation.

"Interesting," Hadavad muttered beside him. The mage was guiding his horse on foot, but his eyes were fixed on the ground.

"What's that?" Vighon asked, wincing at the volume of his voice in such a quiet place.

Hadavad stamped his staff once into the ground and looked up. "Where's the snow?"

Vighon frowned and looked to his feet, where there was indeed a lack of snow. Where it should have remained piled around their ankles, there were now only patches here and there. The dark ground and green moss were steadily taking over the farther they journeyed.

"It's warmer too," Alijah commented, sneaking up on them.

Vighon hadn't noticed, but Alijah was right. The cool air had grown musty and thicker than any winter chill.

"Look at the trees," one of the Tregarans said.

Vighon walked a little farther and found himself standing before the thickest tree he had ever seen. Looking around, the ordinary trees of the forest were becoming as sporadic as the patches of snow. These, larger, much thicker trees dominated the heart of the wood. The northerner was careful not to trip over the web of roots that looped in and out of the ground.

It was as if they had walked through an invisible wall. On the one side, the forest was cold and silent and, on the other, it was warm and filled with bird song and woodland creatures.

Vighon ventured farther in, his eyes running over everything. The leaves of the great trees possessed colours that shouldn't be seen for months to come. He stopped when he came across a stag, drinking from a shallow stream. Without fear, the stag looked up at him and assumed its regal pose before strolling off. Butterflies flitted about and animals ran between the trees; even the air was sweeter.

"It's beautiful…" he whispered.

Alijah walked past him. "We're not there yet."

They walked through the stream and navigated the enormous trees until winter became a bitter memory. It was Galanör who soon led them to the entrance of Ilythyra, an arch of vines between two trees. The arch was decorated with flowers and small orbs of soft light.

Vighon longed to enter and see the little piece of Illian the elves had claimed back, but they were met under the arch by a group of elves.

Galanör bowed his head and said something in elvish, quickly followed by Hadavad and Alijah. Vighon copied the bow and didn't even bother trying to say the greeting that threatened to knot his tongue.

The elves that filled the arch were a myriad of beauty, both male and female. Their long hair flowed like honey over robes of blue and green. Intricate patterns of gold and silver decorated their clothes, all of which appeared too clean for life in a forest.

The most beautiful of them all stood ahead of the group, her eyes a brighter shade of green than the most exquisite emeralds. A deep forest green hood crested the golden circlet that crowned a head of rippling blonde hair. Under her cloak was a vision, an iridescent dress that sparkled as if the stars of the heavens had been plucked from the sky and trapped therein.

Vighon was captivated by her.

"Welcome to Ilythyra," the elf said, her eyes meeting every one of theirs as she took in the growing crowd. "I am Ellöria of house Sevari."

Vighon almost rocked back on his heels. Alijah spoke very little of his family these days but, having spent most of his youth with the Galfreys, Vighon knew that his mother, Reyna Galfrey, had once been a Sevari. He shot his friend a questioning look only to have the half-elf shake his head in response.

"I am Galanör," the ranger replied, leaving out his own house name. "These people hail from Tregaran. They are in dire need of your hospitality, Lady Ellöria."

The elf of the woods looked over Vighon and his dreary companions. "I would say you are all in need..." Her melodic voice worked its way into his bones, reminding him immediately how far they had travelled.

"Come," she bade. "There is room in Ilythyra for all." Ellöria turned to her kin and spoke in elvish. The elves proceeded to glide across the ground and intercept the weary Tregarans, helping them with their belongings and injuries. "You four will follow me," she added, talking to the companions.

Alijah hesitated, looking back to Isabella and Salim. They were both being tended to by a pair of elves, as well as Ned.

"They are safe here," Ellöria assured, noting his lingering gaze.

Isabella nodded at Alijah from across the clearing and he relaxed a little, happy to accompany them. Tauren's wife saw Vighon and offered him his fur cloak back, having been offered replacements by the elves. He took back the cloak, hoping, as Alijah did, that they would find some reprieve from their loss. Thinking of those he had lost himself, Vighon knew it would take more than the comfort of elves...

Seeing the others follow Ellöria through the arch, Vighon held the hilt of his sheathed blade and jogged to catch up. He couldn't help but slow down, however, when the entrance gave way to Ilythyra. In fact, he stopped, lost control of his jaw, and craned his neck to look at everything.

Beyond the arch, a mossy plateau descended into a set of wide curving stairs. At their base, Ilythyra was spread out before them as an oasis, a place where the line between magic and nature blurred.

The trees were just as tall and thick, but now their branches wrapped around giant orbs of light. Some of the orbs were on the ground, tied within the mighty roots. Vighon noticed one to the side of the stairs and he reached out, curious as to its feel. The orb was warm and its surface as soft as a baby's skin.

The sky between the canopy was blue, though Vighon couldn't recall seeing any blue since they were in The Arid Lands. Looking back down, the world had taken on a softer look, as if the orbs had removed the harshness of reality.

Stone plateaus and spiralling staircases decorated the picture of Ilythyra. The dwellings in which the elves resided were hollowed out of the trees themselves, reaching high into the canopy above.

Vighon hurried again to catch up with the others on the stairs, careful to keep one eye on the steps as he continued to marvel at Ilythyra.

Galanör leaned in. "Wonderful, isn't it?"

Vighon nodded, his eyes still fixed on the environment. "I can't believe this is in The Moonlit Plains."

"It sort of isn't," Galanör replied cryptically. "Ilythyra works much in the same way Hadavad's satchel does."

Vighon looked at the old tattered bag hanging off the mage's shoulder. He had seen the old man pull a horse's saddle out of it once.

"It's a pocket dimension," Galanör elaborated.

Vighon understood what the elf meant, but that didn't mean he could wrap his head around it either. He was happy, however, to simply follow Lady Ellöria through the elven village. It was like walking through a dream.

It was something of a climb before the companions found themselves on a higher plateau, standing in front of a knot of vines and branches. Ellöria waved her hand over the knot and the branches recoiled and the vines snaked apart, revealing an entire chamber carved out of the tree. The interior walls were decorated with murals, interspersed with smaller orbs of light and flowering vines.

The chamber itself was that of a small amphitheatre, with neat rows of seats curving around the room until it flattened out at the bottom. In the centre sat what looked to be a throne to Vighon's eyes. Its high back rose almost to the top of the room, where it was styled in the shape of a pair of antlers. Ellöria chose the chair beside the throne, one of simple design and carved from wood, like everything else, with elvish glyphs highlighted in golden paint.

"Only the queen sits in the throne," Galanör whispered in Vighon's ear.

"You are right, Galanör," Ellöria announced. "Only my sister is permitted to sit there. In thirty years I believe she has had that pleasure only once." The elf let her eyes fall over Alijah. "When Queen Adilandra visits Illian, she chooses to stay with her daughter…" Under her gaze, Alijah could do nothing but look away. "I do not believe you came here to discuss chair arrangements," she continued. "The elves of Ilythyra would never turn a soul away, but I would know what has happened in The Arid Lands to bring so many and in such strife?"

Hadavad took a seat on one of the rows, looking to Galanör to answer the Lady's question. Vighon shuffled a little closer to Alijah, entirely unsure how to behave around the female elf. Everything about her commanded respect and attention, but he had no idea where she fitted into the hierarchy of this new world.

Galanör stepped in front of the throne. "Our tale is long, my Lady. And somewhat hard to believe…"

"I still recall sailing away from Illian's shores at the end of The Dragon War, nearly a millennia ago. Now, here I am, hundreds of miles inland again, living in the heart of The Moonlit Plains, and sitting in a room with a five hundred-year-old man and an elf with a human father." Ellöria leaned over. "*Hard to believe* is my speciality, Galanör of house Reveeri…"

Vighon shared a glance with Alijah; it was obvious that Lady Ellöria was well informed, despite their remote location.

Galanör bowed his head apologetically. "A great many events have transpired to see us stood before you, my Lady. We are here and the people of Tregaran have been run from their homes for a single reason."

"And that is?"

Galanör straightened his back and answered with but a word. "Orcs…"

Galanör's tale got as far as their arrival in The Arid Lands before Vighon's legs couldn't take it any longer. He had taken a seat on the row behind Hadavad and done his best to stay awake for the elf's retelling. Lady Ellöria had been very clear about hearing every detail and she had done so without moving a muscle.

"No city could prepare for an attack such as that," Galanör said, drawing near to the end of his tale. "Tregaran was almost destroyed before they even emerged from the ground. There was nothing we could do but try and get as many people to safety as we could…"

Ellöria looked away for the first time since the elf had begun to speak, and Vighon would have happily believed it was her first breath as well.

"The orcs have returned…" she whispered, as if saying it herself would make it more real.

"My Lady," Hadavad said, standing up for the first time. "Has there been any word from the other cities in The Arid Lands? Calmardra? Ameeraska?"

"I'm afraid Ilythyra rarely receives missives from any of the six kingdoms. I don't believe the people of Illian have warmed to our presence here yet."

"In my experience," Hadavad replied, "humans always require time."

Ellöria didn't appear convinced. "If the orcs have returned, I fear time is something none of us have." The Lady of the wood adjusted her posture. "You are all welcome to stay in Ilythyra for as long as you wish. The people of Tregaran are extended the same invitation. I will have messages sent to all the kingdoms warning them of the orcs." The elf considered her next words. "I will send scouts to Calmardra and Ameeraska to confirm their fate."

"We thank you for your hospitality, Lady Ellöria." Galanör bowed his head and the companions made to leave.

"Alijah," Ellöria called softly. "It is good to see you…"

The half-elf had nothing to say but to nod his head in agreement. They left the Lady of Ilythyra and descended the winding staircase in silence, feeling between them that they were in a sacred place.

Back on the ground, the elves had welcomed the refugees who had accompanied them north. Small campsites were already being established in the clearing with healers seeking out the injured. Vighon stopped and stared when a pair of elves stepped away from the cluster and began to sing. Their arms waved about and their hands twisted in hypnotic patterns. He was a second away from inquiring when new roots wormed out of the ground as if they were alive.

"Look at that!" he exclaimed to an uninterested Alijah.

The roots twisted and wove in and out of each other until they formed a dome with a small hole in the side. More and more began to sprout from the ground, wherever the elves directed their voices. More elves arrived, this time carrying baskets full of the fleshy orbs, each glowing softly in their piles. The elves fitted the orbs into the makeshift nests, illuminating the interior for the refugees.

Galanör was one of very few who could still offer a smile. "How do you think the trees became so big?"

"It's incredible…" Vighon said with wide eyes.

The soft approach of bare feet preceded the appearance of a female elf. She greeted the companions with a genuine smile and bowed her head. "I am Aenwyn," she said in the common tongue.

Vighon was captured by her beauty and that of her ethereal dress, its fabric that of the breeze itself. Vighon wondered if mankind was destined to be spellbound by the exquisite beauty of all elves. Seeing Aenwyn and her long dark hair, the northerner couldn't help but think of Inara. Then again, a lot of things made him think of Inara…

"Rooms have been prepared for you all inside the Evertree," Aenwyn continued, gesturing to the giant tree behind her.

Alijah glanced back at the Tregaran refugees, his eyes briefly resting on Isabella and Salim. "Thank you, but we'll stay down here."

"Lady Ellöria has—"

Alijah cut Aenwyn off. "We'll stay down here if it's all the same." His tone was as definitive as his words.

Aenwyn bowed her head again. "As you wish, Prince Alijah." The elf walked away before the half-elf could protest.

"Prince?" Vighon immediately repeated.

Alijah held up his hand. "Don't," he warned,

The two singing elves arrived, preventing the conversation from getting started. Distracted by their magic, Vighon missed Alijah disappear into the crowd of refugees. He was easily found, however, beside Tauren's wife and son. The half-elf dropped to one knee and embraced Salim, though his words were lost from such a distance.

Hadavad was the first to enter his private bower. The mage found a comfortable spot and retrieved the prophecy from within his satchel. With his eyes fixed on the ancient scroll, Hadavad waved his hand over the entrance and the branches and roots snaked and coiled until the hole was sealed.

Galanör unclipped his sword belt and placed the scimitars inside his bower. "A great evil stirs in the realm again," he began. "If I were you, Vighon Draqaro, I would take rest wherever I can find it."

After fighting the orcs and two days of trekking north, Vighon could feel his every muscle aching for sleep. "You saw the orcs," he replied. "Do you really think we're safe here?"

"Safe enough to rest for the night," Galanör countered. "Let us face the world tomorrow, when we can better understand it." With that, the ranger ducked into his bower and waved the entrance shut.

Vighon turned his attention to Alijah again, troubled by the idea of sleeping while his friend suffered through the loss of what felt like an uncle. He removed the round shield from his back and decided to sit against the wall of his bower. He watched Alijah for some time, talking to Tauren's family and other refugees. The soft glow and heavenly surroundings did nothing to keep him awake, and the northerner soon found his eyelids refusing to open again.

The sound of familiar voices woke Vighon from his slumber. Disorientated, he looked about and found the daytime sky had been replaced by the stars. Still, winter's bite couldn't find him, despite having fallen asleep outside his bower.

The familiar voices came from the left and he turned to find the source. The campsites were quiet now, the refugees asleep, and the native elves with them. Ilythyra was entirely peaceful but for these two voices.

Vighon left his shield and scrambled to his feet. His muscles stung and he regretted not stretching after his fight with the orcs.

One of the voices belonged to a woman, though her words were elvish. Vighon followed the melodic sound, navigating a series of hedges and smaller trees.

Ellöria and Alijah were beyond the patch of trees, occupying a small garden which was home to a miniature waterfall and a stream. Vighon clung to the nearest tree and remained hidden. He knew to eavesdrop was rude, but his years living in Namdhor had replaced his older instincts with newer and far more inappropriate ones.

"Have you forgotten your mother's tongue?" Ellöria asked.

"I am a child of two worlds," Alijah replied. "That gives me the privilege of choice." He shrugged. "I prefer the common tongue, it suits me better."

Except for when you're chatting up the young wives of old lords, Vighon thought.

"How does life without a family suit you?" Ellöria asked knowingly.

Vighon could see Alijah trying to hide his surprise. "For a group of people who never leave their homes, you surely know a lot."

Ellöria smiled. "The free folk of Illian see what they wish to see. The elves of Ilythyra secretly walk the streets of every kingdom, though I know of a couple who like to frequent a tavern in Lirian…"

Vighon slunk back behind the tree, racking his memory to think of anyone he might have seen in The Pick-Axe resembling an elf.

"You've been spying on me?" Alijah's accusation sounded more curious than offended.

"You are second in line to the throne of Elandril," Ellöria answered. "Of course you are being watched."

Alijah shook his head and slumped down onto a large rock. "What does that matter? My grandmother rules: an elf of what… fifteen hundred years? Being the third in line to an elven kingdom is just as far from the throne as a beggar is to a king."

"You are part of a royal family that has reigned over two continents and survived five wars over eight thousand years." Ellöria walked over and came to stop in front of him. "Whether you like it or not, you are a *Sevari*."

"I'm barely a Galfrey," Alijah replied with some venom. "And I won't be either of them for long."

Vighon scrunched his face in confusion and moved around the trees to see them better. Ellöria crouched down in front of her great nephew and tilted her head until Alijah was forced to make eye contact with her. The Lady of Ilythyra took his hand in hers and examined it, stroking her thumb over his knuckles and along his palm.

"Stand up," she commanded. The elf turned away from Alijah and walked a little farther into the garden.

Leaving Asher's green cloak behind, along with his bow and short-sword, Alijah acquiesced and joined her in the clearing.

"Since you arrived here," Ellöria said, "I have sensed something in you. A recklessness…" The elf turned around to face her great nephew. "A trait born to mortals in my experience."

Vighon crouched down and crawled to a small boulder on the edge of the garden. He had no idea what they were talking about.

Alijah held up his hands, eager from the looks of it to be done with this conversation. "I appreciate everything you—"

Ellöria whipped out the hand concealed within her cloak and expelled a sharp breath. A cloud of blue powder washed over Alijah, cutting off his words.

Then there were two of him!

Vighon, mouth ajar, watched as an ethereal twin of his friend was blown out of the back of him, mirroring his very stance. It took the northerner another moment to realise that Alijah's movements had slowed down to a crawl, yet his face remained tormented by the powder.

"Oi!" Vighon yelled as he ran into the garden.

Ellöria held up a single hand and the northerner ceased his charge. It wasn't magic that stopped him, but the expression on the elf's face. She wasn't harming Alijah.

As the half-elf slowly fell backwards, Ellöria casually walked around him until she was beside the blue, ethereal Alijah. The elf reached out and cupped the ghost's head before running her other hand down his face, to his chest. She stopped over his heart, hesitating with a glance at the real Alijah. Then she dipped her fingers into the smoky image.

Ellöria's eyes lit up with revelation and she looked at her great nephew again. Vighon had seen enough sorrow to recognise it now.

"What's wrong?" he asked.

Ignoring him completely, the Lady of Ilythyra reached out and gripped both Alijahs by the shoulder. The elf simultaneously corrected his falling posture and forced the ethereal version back inside.

With a gasp and a look of surprise, Alijah turned from Vighon to Ellöria with blue powder smeared across his face. "What happened?" he asked frantically. "What did you do?"

Ellöria sighed. "Something your mother should have done long ago."

Alijah glanced at Vighon, but kept his attention on the elf as he wiped a finger full of powder from his cheek. "What is this?"

"Something you cannot find in Illian," Ellöria replied cryptically. "Centuries ago, it was thought that we could see into the very soul of our kin. We are a little more enlightened now. It allows one to see what they look like on the magical plane. It is this plane of existence that ties elves to their immortality: an abundant source of magic that resides inside of us, bridging the gap between the two realms."

Alijah made sense of her explanation before Vighon did. "I already know what you're going to say."

Ellöria cupped his face. "I am sorry…"

Vighon looked from one to the other, his confusion growing into frustration. "What in all the hells are you talking about?"

Alijah moved away from Ellöria's tender touch and wiped more powder from his face. Vighon didn't miss the stray tear he also caught with his thumb.

"I'm mortal, Vighon," he stated flatly.

"I don't understand," the northerner replied, looking from Ellöria to his friend. "You're a…" he gestured to Alijah's pointed ears. "You have…"

"This should have been discovered when you were born," Ellöria interrupted. "There hasn't been a child of our two people since the earliest years after humans emerged from The Wild Moores. You and your sister are the first of your kind in nearly a thousand years."

"You're not immortal?" Vighon just had to say it out loud to really take it in. "I always thought..." He couldn't finish the sentence. The northerner had always assumed is friend would live forever, like his family...

Vighon experienced a revelation of his own but was sure to clamp down on his mouth. He could see it all laid out now. He could see why Alijah had done everything possible to distance himself from his family, his *immortal* family.

"Have you told anyone?" Ellöria asked.

"Inara knows." Alijah's response was almost a whisper.

"Is she mortal as well?" Vighon asked without thinking.

Alijah moved to retrieve his cloak and weapons. "If she was we'll never know. Once Inara bonded with Athis, his life force became her own." The half-elf turned to Ellöria. "My grandmother had you keeping an eye on me to make sure I'm safe, yes. After what I saw in Tregaran, I don't think it matters whether I'm mortal or not; no one is safe anymore. I take it I can trust you to keep this between us?"

Ellöria considered his request. "You are third in line to the throne and therefore in higher standing than myself. Unless Queen Adilandra asks me specifically about your mortality, I will guard it as you have asked." The Lady of Ilythyra bowed her head and Alijah reciprocated.

"You have both survived quite the ordeal," Ellöria continued. "There are only a handful of elves still living who can say they have fought against the orcs. I suggest you find some rest."

Vighon waited until the elf had disappeared from the gardens before asking, "Are you alright?"

Alijah finished strapping his quiver up. "I've known about this for a while now. I've come to terms with the years I have."

"That's why you left, isn't it?" Vighon's question halted Alijah in his tracks.

Without turning back, he said, "There's no need for them to suffer."

Vighon hated to see his friend in such turmoil. "Alijah—"

The half-elf turned on him before he could say anymore. "It doesn't matter, Vighon. Think of everything that's happened since we found that prophecy. Asher, Malliath, Tauren... Tregaran is *gone*. The world is being plunged back into chaos and war. My mortality grows more trivial by the hour."

Vighon took a breath. "I was just going to say; nothing has changed for me. We will still fight together or die together. Brothers..." That took the edge off Alijah, softening him somewhat.

The half-elf held out his hand and the two clasped forearms before pulling each other in for an embrace.

"You're blue," Vighon observed.

It took Alijah an extra second to understand. "You're talking about my face, aren't you?"

The northerner chuckled to himself. "You look ridiculous..."

The two shared a quiet laugh before Alijah went in search of water to clean his skin. It took Vighon some time to find rest that night, his mind wondering about a life in which the two friends grew old together. Would they still be fighting, laughing, and up to no good in their old age?

Images of the orcs and the smell of Tregaran burning plagued Vighon, reminding him that dreaming of old age was a fool's game.

They would be lucky to see another winter...

A PRECIOUS GIFT

I nara stood to the side as King Weymund's court mage, Theatred Atherlarde, directed the servants about Gideon's room, rearranging the furniture according to the Master Dragorn's specifications. An oval table was moved from the corner into the space at the bottom of the bed and seven chairs were situated around it.

Theatred removed a diviner orb from within his colourful robes and placed it in the very centre of the table.

Having rested for a couple of days, Gideon was finally able to walk from his bed to the chair at the head of the table unaided. Inara didn't miss his wince, however, when he put his shirt back on. The bruises and cuts had all but gone, but some of his bones were still mending.

With a great sigh, the Master Dragorn took his seat and looked to the mage. "If you would be so kind, Theatred."

The court mage bowed his head and stamped his staff into the floor, evoking the magic within the diviner. Four of the available six chairs were suddenly occupied by the ethereal form of the Dragorn council.

Inara took an extra step aside to make certain she didn't create an ethereal projection of herself.

A chorus of greetings went around the table, followed by questions of concern for Gideon's wellbeing. The Master Dragorn reassured them that he was healing and asked about the empty chairs.

Ayana Glanduil, the only elf on the council, glanced curiously at the other councillors before turning back to Gideon. "Garin and Jorla have flown to Tregaran. Have you not heard? The city has fallen."

Inara felt the room wobble as reality tried to tilt on its axis and swallow her whole. She reached out for the nearest solid object that would keep her upright. Athis flooded her with his bolstering aura and the room corrected itself almost immediately, but nothing would be able to shift the pit opening inside her gut.

He's a survivor, the dragon declared with some force.

"Fallen?" Gideon echoed.

"They've all fallen," Rolan Baird clarified. "Tregaran, Ameeraska, Calmardra... The orcs have claimed them all."

Inara took a deep breath, wishing more than anything that Athis could be inside the room with her. Alijah, Vighon, Hadavad, Galanör... They were all in Tregaran. Uncle Tauren! Visions of the city being overrun by orcs consumed the Dragorn's mind.

He's a survivor, Athis reminded her again. *They all are, Tauren included.*

Alise Trubek leant forward in her chair. "When the orcs attacked you in the ruins of Karath, you said they numbered in the hundreds. In a single night they torched three whole cities, Gideon. There must be thousands of them."

Gideon sat back, rocked by the news. "Garin and Jorla have gone to Tregaran?" he confirmed.

"Along with Flint and Morkas," Ayana replied. "We sent Roddick and Alessandra to Calmardra and Galwyn and Aled to Ameeraska."

"We received the red raven from Lirian," Rolan said, "but I

thought you would have received word from at least one of the southern cities."

Gideon shook his head. "It's chaos here. King Weymund is in the process of sending what remains of his people south, to Vangarth."

"They might be better going north," Alastir Knox, the youngest among the council, suggested. "These orcs were first discovered in the south and now The Arid Lands have been invaded…"

"I'm inclined to agree," Gideon said. "Get word to Garin and the others; have them escort any survivors north. Those in Ameeraska and Tregaran will find shelter in Grey Stone. The people of Calmardra should follow the coast to Velia."

Gideon had drawn up plans before Inara was even a Dragorn, detailing the evacuation process for every city should it be attacked.

Focusing on such rational thoughts was quite a strain. Inara couldn't stop looking at the door, tempted to simply run out, find Athis, and fly as fast as they could to Tregaran.

"We should take this fight to the orcs," Rolan added determinedly. "Every Dragorn, every dragon. We could wipe them from the face of Verda for good."

"We have no idea where they are, Rolan," Ayana countered.

"We could attack the cities they've invaded," Alise said.

"You're assuming they intend to hold them," the elven councillor replied. "From what we know about orcs already, they despise the surface world. I don't believe they attack our cities just to make them their own."

Alastir looked down the table at Gideon. "If they do intend on keeping the cities they sack, they will do it from an underground position."

Gideon winced as he lifted his hand to end the topic. "Since last we spoke there have been… developments." The Master Dragorn half turned his head to regard Inara. "I told you all of The Crow who appeared to me in the library…"

"The Black Hand?" Alise's ethereal face scrunched into confusion. "Are they involved in this?"

Gideon nodded. "He has played his hand, just as he said he

would. Before Malliath came to Lirian, he faced Inara and Edrik in The Undying Mountains." He took a breath, chewing over his words. "Edrik and Aldreon are dead."

Alise put her hand over her mouth and Rolan ran a hand through his thick hair. They were the first fatalities the order had suffered since The Dragon War, a thousand years past. Inara could still see Edrik's neck snapping in time with Aldreon's...

"There's more," Gideon continued. "Inside Paldora's Fall, he used the darkest of magic to resurrect..." The Master Dragorn still struggled to believe it himself. "He brought Asher back."

There was visible shock around the table. "*The* Asher?" Rolan asked.

"Of course," Ayana said. "The excavation above Grey Stone, in the mountains."

"I'm afraid so." Gideon took a breath. "It seems they were searching for Asher's bones all along, but it gets worse. Somehow, The Crow has enslaved Asher to his will and bonded him with Malliath the voiceless."

Alastir's ethereal eyes went wide. "Asher was with Malliath when he attacked Lirian?"

"Impossible," Ayana argued. "Such a bond cannot be forced, that kind of magic simply doesn't exist."

"Not only that," Gideon continued, "but this Crow has found a way of binding Alijah Galfrey into the spell. He feels everything they do."

"Inara's brother?" Alastir questioned.

"Why would The Crow do this?" Ayana asked the question that had been plaguing Inara.

Gideon sighed. "The Crow's motivations are something of a mystery for the time. His knowledge of ancient magic is all we know right now."

"That and his ability to see the future," Rolan replied seriously. "He said one of us would die that very night."

Gideon challenged his perspective. "Edrik and Aldreon's death doesn't prove that The Crow can see the future, only that he knew Malliath would outmatch them."

Alise added, "As Gideon pointed out, I think it is more likely that The Black Hand have access to ancient magic and spells heralding from The First Kingdom."

Rolan shook his head. "And I think it's time we stopped underestimating our enemy."

"Enough." Gideon ended it there.

Ayana continued the meeting with a more harmonious tone. "How exactly are The Black Hand intertwined with the orcs?"

The Master Dragorn's response was simple. "The Black Hand are in *allegiance* with the orcs. I wouldn't be surprised if they were the reason for the orcs sudden return."

Silence filled the room as the councillors stared at each other across the table.

"How did we not see this coming?" Rolan asked incredulously. "There was no word from Hadavad?"

"The last I heard was from Galanör," Gideon explained. "Though, since then, Inara has met with him." The injured master hesitated. "There appears to be a prophecy…"

That piece of information had them all shuffling in their seats and asking questions at once.

"The information I have is very limited," Gideon said. "It currently resides with Hadavad and Galanör."

"We need to examine it as soon as possible," Ayana pointed out.

"Where was it found?" Alise asked.

"In The Wild Moores," Gideon replied. "They believe it to have come from the same place as The Echoes of Fate prophecy." That set the councillors off again. "Its words have little weight until we can compare it to the original prophecy," he said a little louder.

"Where is the mage now?" Rolan asked. "We can send someone to retrieve it."

Gideon glanced at Inara. "The last time they were all seen was in Tregaran, in the company of High Councillor Tauren Salimson."

Alastir replied, "We shall have word sent to Garin and Jorla."

Rolan sighed. "If there is a new prophecy, then it came from The Echoes, another First Kingdom thorn in our side. I'm starting to think we should have prioritised The Black Hand ourselves instead of using the old mage."

Inara stood a little straighter. That was another remark against Gideon's leadership. It was no surprise hearing it from Rolan, who had always favoured a slightly different approach when it came to the role of the Dragorn. Peacekeepers was to be their way, however, not tyrants who used fear to force peace upon the realm.

Gideon pinched his nose. "The First Kingdom and all of its secrets can do nothing but wait to be uncovered. In the meantime, we have their descendants to worry about and their new allegiance with the orcs."

"Agreed," Ayana offered her support, moving the conversation on.

"Going forward," Alise added, "we should assume the orcs have an army comparable to that of the six kingdoms."

"Combined?" Alastir clarified.

"That remains to be seen," Gideon answered. "For now, let's escort all the survivors north. The orcs have dealt the first blow; The Arid Lands belong to them for now."

"We're just fleeing north?" Rolan challenged again.

Having had years of dealing with Rolan Baird, it was clear to see that Gideon's patience was wearing thin. "Ameeraska, Tregaran, Calmardra, *and* Lirian have been reduced to ash in a matter of days. That's a lot of broken families and no homes. We will ensure any and all survivors reach a place of safety. Then, we will convene a meeting with the rulers of Velia, Grey Stone, and Namdhor."

"Convene a meeting?" Rolan repeated. "We need their armies marching south as we speak. What remains of the Lirian army?"

"If a counterattack is to be organised, Rolan, we will need the kings and queens of those three kingdoms to be in open discussion—"

"They will have already received the red ravens," Rolan interrupted.

Gideon shook his head. "They won't grasp the need for an allied front right now. *We* need to be the ones who—"

Rolan interjected again. "*We* need to be the ones who remind the orcs where they belong. They should have stayed lost in their mountains and—"

"This is not a discussion, Rolan." Gideon's tone was absolute. "Our first priority is always the people."

"We still need more information about our invaders," Alastir commented. "The orcs' motives for attacking The Arid Lands are not certain."

Alise agreed. "For all we know, they won't go any farther than the desert."

Inara didn't agree, but she could see her own feelings reflected on Gideon's face. The Dragorn decided to stay out of the meeting, lest Gideon be accused of favouritism again...

Gideon replied, "The Black Hand are working with the orcs. They didn't resurrect Asher and take control of Malliath for nothing. They were *sent* to Lirian. I fear The Arid Lands are only the beginning."

"We will see the survivors to safety," Ayana said.

"And begin a patrol pattern," Alise added. "We'll make sure there are Dragorn guarding the border between The Moonlit Plains and the desert."

"What about this prophecy?" Rolan asked, speaking up for the first time since Gideon had silenced him.

"I will find Hadavad and bring it back to The Lifeless Isles," Gideon answered.

Alastir flexed his ethereal fingers on the table top. "What should we do if we come across Asher and Malliath?"

Inara knew the answer she would give, but the young Dragorn had never known Asher as others did and she had no love for Malliath. Killing them over saving them felt the most logical choice.

"If lives are in danger," Gideon commanded, "then all Dragorn are to intervene. If he is spotted away from the population, you are to track him and wait for reinforcements."

The councillors nodded in agreement and wished the Master Dragon a speedy recovery before Gideon gave Theatred the nod to end the conversation. Their ethereal forms lost their cohesion like smoke dissipating into the air.

Gideon sighed heavily. "Thank you, Theatred. I would appreciate it if you could ask King Weymund to come by my chamber. He should be made aware of the dire situation in The Arid Lands."

Theatred bowed his head, collected the diviner orb, and left the chamber in a rustle of robes.

Gideon sat back and turned to regard Inara. "The Arid Lands are gone... On my watch, three whole cities, four including Lirian, have crumbled under foreign invasion." He sounded broken to Inara.

The young Dragorn felt selfish for asking, but there were only a handful of people she needed to know about. "Do you think Hadavad and the others made it out?"

Gideon met her eyes with an apologetic expression pulling at his features. "I'm so sorry, Inara, I didn't think. I'm sure Alijah is fine. In fact, of everyone south of The Moonlit Plains, Alijah and the others are the only ones I would bet on surviving. As we speak, Tauren will be leading them and any survivors to safety. He's done it before..."

Inara nodded, but her features betrayed her real concern. "If something had happened to Alijah, I would know it."

"I'm sure you would," Gideon agreed. "We will fly south tomorrow," he said with confidence. "We will find them."

Tomorrow felt like an awfully long time away, but Inara could see that the Master Dragorn needed another night of rest and recovery, even if Ilargo was fit to fly.

"So," Gideon changed the subject, "how did you find your first council meeting?"

Inara could see the distraction for what it was and she welcomed it all the same. "With all due respect, Master, why did you appoint Rolan Baird to the council?"

Gideon smiled wistfully. "When I was first assembling the council, when the order was younger, I didn't just want people who saw everything as I did. Rolan had a way of seeing things from a different perspective; something I valued... at the time. He has become rather impatient of late." Gideon reigned his comments in.

"Forgive me, I shouldn't speak ill of the council. They all offer something the order needs. With the threat of mass invasion on our doorstep, I am sure Rolan's perspective will be much appreciated."

Inara could only hope that the orcs intended to stop at The Arid Lands, even if she knew in her heart that it was only just beginning. "I should go, Master. Russell Maybury has asked if Athis and I could help him recover some of his belongings from The Pick-Axe before the people move on."

"Go," Gideon gestured to the door. "I will inform King Weymund of the orcs and advise him to reach out to King Jormund of Grey Stone."

Inara bowed her head and promptly left her master's chamber.

You would slay them both? Athis asked from nowhere.

Through their bond, Inara could feel Athis's concerns for Asher and Malliath. **Do we have a choice?** she asked. **Look around; they destroyed a capital city in one night and nearly killed Gideon and Ilargo.**

But they are slaves to The Crow, Athis argued. *They know not what they do.*

You could say the same about most of the soldiers in an army. How many armies have been torched by dragon's fire over the millennia?

Soldiers can choose to live by the orders of one side or the other, Athis countered. *Asher and Malliath have been robbed of that privilege.*

Inara knew he was right, she just couldn't reconcile their safety with the potential destruction they were capable of.

We are Dragorn, Athis reminded her. *We do not need to choose between such stark decisions. We have the power to find our own path.*

You're talking about freeing them, Inara stated.

Malliath is the oldest living dragon, Athis explained. *He has seen and lived through more than any other being. His captivity under the mages of Korkanath lasted a thousand years and he has never been given the time to heal from that. Asher's life, though shorter, was marred with just as much torment. He sacrificed himself to rid the world of Valanis and end the war. I think they both deserve a second chance...*

Inara stopped in one of the palace's halls and leaned against the wall. Her head was swimming. Alijah might be dead, Lirian was still smoking, and thousands of people had been killed in the south. She wanted action and justice and she wanted it now.

Yet, she could not argue with Athis's wisdom. He always offered her an insight and a greater font of knowledge that most people could only dream of. The truth was; he made her a better person.

And you make me a better dragon, wingless one.

Inara smiled to herself, comforted by her eternal companion. Comfort was something she needed, but felt she didn't deserve right now. There were many people in greater need than her.

If we do not look after ourselves, we cannot look after others. Come, I shall take you down to Russell.

The thought of being close to Athis put her legs in motion again. **Can we really do it, Athis? The spell that binds Asher and Malliath is likely ancient and very powerful.**

As Dragorn, we carry the most precious gift and the most powerful weapon. With it, there is nothing we cannot accomplish.

Inara raised an eyebrow. **What are you talking about?**

Can you not feel it, wingless one? It has passed down the generations of our order for thousands of years. We carry hope…

AN EMPTY KINGDOM

D oran cursed the light of the new day. It did nothing but worsen his headache. Still, to look away from the rising sun was to look upon Vengora; it wasn't much better…

The dwarf stood at the very base of the mountain range, an indomitable wall of rock that had once been home to all of his kin.

"Are you ready, Doran?" Reyna asked, gesturing to the small entrance up ahead.

The cave, tunnelled by the Namdhorians, was guarded either side by a group of soldiers with the lion sigil emblazoned across their golden cloaks.

"Bah!" The dwarf waved the question away. "I shouldn' even be here! I said I wasn' goin' in there an' I meaned it!"

"That's not what you said in the tavern," Nathaniel pointed out, pulling the collar of his coat over his neck.

"You said we would need you in there," Reyna reminded him.

"I had more cider an' ale in me than all o' the other taverns in Namdhor combined!" In a quieter tone, he added, "I got ye into the know abou' what's goin' on here, didn' I?"

Reyna held onto her hood to prevent it from blowing off. "I

would not lightly enter such a place without a dwarf so brave as yourself, Doran son of Dorain."

"Ye canna' change me mind with such sweet words, Me Lady." Doran looked up at the mountain again. "That way leads to a place I didn' wanna go back to. I don' belong there anymore than ye do…"

"Is there a problem?" The call came from ahead, where their Ironsworn guide stood waiting in the freezing cold.

"An' there's another reason not to go inside that bloody mountain," Doran insisted. "We still have no idea why Arlon had his boys spyin' on us in Grey Stone or why they attacked us on the road to Namdhor. Do ye really wanna go into the dark tunnels o' their makin' when they could slip a knife in ye back?"

"It will be their end if they try," Nathaniel declared.

"Doran," Reyna began. "We are going into that mine and we are going to face your kin. I would much rather do that with you by our side."

Doran dropped his head.

"Are you coming or what?" the thug shouted back.

"Bah! Keep a hold o' yerself, laddy!" The dwarf looked at Reyna. "We're coming…"

The three companions followed the Ironsworn up the rise and through the small camp of soldiers. Again, Arlon's man passed through the group without a word of protest from the Gold Cloaks. Doran walked through them with a wary eye and one hand resting on the haft of his axe, under his cloak.

Leaving the Warhog in their company wasn't easy, but he instructed the pig to kill anyone that messed with it. He also instructed it not to steal too much ale…

The wind howled as they entered the tunnel, threatening to blow out the torches that lined the interior walls. The gloom came alive in Doran's eyes, his dwarven senses easily attuning to the dark atmosphere that all his kin were born to.

They walked in silence for some time before the Ironsworn stopped abruptly at the end of the tunnel. Here, the jagged rock ended and the tunnel opened up into a taller corridor of hewn stone. It was the first piece of dwarven architecture Doran had seen in sixty years.

The son of Dorain pushed past the thug and put a hand to the cold slab, running his fingers along the grooves carved in straight lines. The stonework in these tunnels was far older than any found in Dhenaheim, constructed well over five thousand years ago. Vengora had never been his home, but the dwarf couldn't deny the feelings a simple wall evoked in him.

The Ironsworn pointed down the western corridor. "Follow this until you reach the stairs. If you get lost, look for the torches, they'll show you to the mine."

"You're not coming?" Nathaniel questioned.

"It's a long way, even from here," the thug answered. "Just don't get lost," he added with a wicked smile.

"Unlike ye," Doran replied, thumbing to the tunnel over his shoulder.

The Ironsworn disappeared back the way they had come, leaving the three companions in the eerie silence of an empty kingdom.

"Does anyone else think this is strange?" Nathaniel asked.

"Strange ain't the word I'd use," Doran said gruffly.

"Not this," Nathaniel gestured to the dwarven walls. "That tunnel must have taken years to dig through. This isn't a recent project Yelifer has undertaken."

"Yes," Reyna agreed. "And why here? The mountains of Vengora are beyond massive, yet the queen successfully chose the one place where they could dig straight through to dwarven halls."

"What are the chances?" Nathaniel asked with a suspicious tone.

Reyna looked down at Doran. "Perhaps we should have left you in the tavern after all. It seems we are still without all the answers."

"We should probably get going." Nathaniel looked down the long corridor.

"I don' like it," Doran maintained. "Dwarven halls can be akin to mazes. Lots o' dark corners an' doorways. It would be easy for The Ironsworn to ambush us."

"And yet there is no step to take but forwards," Reyna replied, pulling down her hood.

Doran sighed. "The logic of elves..."

With bow, sword, and axe in hand, the three followed the torches and entered the dwarven kingdom of Vengora.

They soon came across the stairs the thug had spoken of. Again, they were such a simple thing, but Doran found himself fascinated by them. Everything they saw from here on in was of dwarven design, made by dwarven hands.

After an arduous climb, they found rest at the top, where a pair of rectangular pillars framed the entrance to the city proper. Leaving Reyna and Nathaniel behind, Doran wandered ahead until he could see past the pillars and gaze at history.

With mouth ajar, the dwarf looked upon the home of his ancestors. Arching ceilings, taller and far grander than any church or palace in Illian, decorated the dizzying heights above. Every pillar and wall was traced in the perfectly straight lines preferred by his kin. Stairs could be seen between the pillars, leading to places unknown and beyond the reach of the torches planted by the Namdhorians.

Nathaniel joined him on the platform. "What happened here?"

His question removed the dreamy veil which Doran had been gazing through. Looking again, he saw the ruin of his ancient home. There wasn't a single pillar that hadn't been damaged and a handful of them weren't even whole anymore, rising into jagged ends.

Construction sites had been set up throughout the great hall, with scaffolding climbing the walls and pillars. Small makeshift hovels had been set up, sprawled across the floor, where the dwarves had slept between their shifts.

Scattered amongst it all were skeletons, discarded weapons, and damaged armour. Dark stains were splattered up the stone here and there.

It was a mass graveyard.

"War," Doran finally replied. "War is what happened here."

The three companions descended the next set of stairs and

walked among the ruins. Up close, it was so much worse. Bulky pieces of armour encased long dead skeletons, their bony hands still clasped to their axes and swords. Cobwebs connected them all in the gloom, stretching cross the hall.

Nathaniel crouched down and picked up a horned skull. "War with the orcs…"

Doran spun about and stared hard at the skull in his friend's hands. Its fangs were still sharp and its horns still thick and tough. Just seeing the beast's empty head drove Doran to snatch the skull from Nathaniel's hands and launch it into the nearest pillar.

The dwarf spat on the ground. "Shits o' the earth, the lot o' 'em!" Doran paused and frowned. "How are ye knowin' that were an orc's head?"

Nathaniel stood up and looked to Reyna with a question in his eyes. The elf didn't say a word, but the old knight had his answer.

"We saw one not ten days past," he said.

Doran stepped back, almost knocking over one of the torches planted on the path. He couldn't believe the words that had just left his friend's mouth.

"Ye seen one?" he questioned pointedly. "A dead one, aye?"

"Dead, yes, but only recently."

"Bah!" Doran threw his hands into the air. "Ye lie, Galfrey!"

"Doran!" Reyna rebuked.

The dwarf shrugged apologetically. "Ye must be mistaken, I mean. Ye saw somethin' that resembled these beasts."

"I'm afraid not, Doran," Nathaniel continued. "We were summoned to the tower of Dragons' Reach by Tauren Salimson. A small band of orcs killed the soldiers guarding Syla's Gate."

Doran couldn't find the words to respond. He hadn't heard anything so hard to believe in nearly three hundred years of life.

"They're back?" he managed but a whisper. "It cannot be… Ye talking abou' the foulest creatures to ever walk the earth. They ran us from our home, they damn near wiped out the elves! Thousands, tens of thousands o' me kin died driving them into The Undying Mountains! There's not a dwarf who don' know the tales! They're supposed to be dead! Long dead at that!"

"Gideon Thorn is looking into it personally," Reyna assured.

"I don' care if the whole damn Dragorn are lookin' into it! Wha' are we even doin' here? We should be goin' south! That's where the real fight is!"

"The council have ordained it Dragorn business," Reyna explained. "We all have our roles to play, Doran. What could we three do against any orcs that the Dragorn could not?"

The dwarf was pacing now with an iron grip around his axe. "Ye don' understand. It's in me blood!" Doran beat a hand against his chest. "There ain't a dwarf still livin' who's actually seen an orc, but we can still feel The Great War in our veins! No dwarf could rest knowin' that these foul creatures have returned to the world."

Nathaniel held up a hand to calm his friend. "I wouldn't say they've returned, Doran. A handful found their way up through the ruins of Karath. They killed the watch at Syla's Gate and Tauren's men made them pay for it. Any few who remain will have to deal with Gideon. How many do you think will survive after that?"

Doran stopped his pacing, eyes fixed on the corpse of another orc. Every dwarf had dreamt of burying their axe in the head of a smelly orc for what they had done during The Great War. That opportunity had been robbed from him and, to make things worse, he was soon to be back in the company of his kin. Muttering and cursing to himself, the son of Dorain kicked the leg of the dead orc and continued down the torch-lit path.

"When this is all done," he called back, "we're goin' south to hunt some orc!" That thought alone cheered him up and he laughed to himself. "I'd be the first dwarf to slay an orc in five thousand years! Aye... Doran the orc-slayer! Doran the orc-cleaver!" He laughed again. "It's abou' time I got meself a legend o' me own."

With dreams of where they could be and lamentations of where they were, Doran led the companions through the towering halls. Everywhere they went, there was only more evidence of war and death.

The next hall they entered had once been a temple devoted to the dwarven gods. Doran gasped and broke into a jog, weaving between the skeletons and debris to better see the chamber. Two rows of pillars supported the temple, but Doran was more concerned with the enormous statues reaching for the ceiling.

"Would ye look at that…" The dwarf's eyes lit up and he lifted his chin right up to see to the very top.

"What is this place, Doran?" Nathaniel asked.

"Considerin' the age o' all this," he replied, "it could very well be the first temple o' the gods." Doran pointed to the broad dwarven statue on their left. "That's Grarfath, the father. He spat on the world and the oceans roared to life, revealing the peaks of the first mountains. He pulled them up with his bare hands and set them on the land as monuments to his strength. Grarfath offered the mountains as a gift to Yamnomora," Doran pointed at the statue on the right, "the mother…"

The son of Dorain laughed as he recalled the liturgy. "Yamnomora cracked the mountain with her fist and reached deep inside for the purest block of stone she could find. Together, they moulded dwarves from that very stone."

Nathaniel admired the enormous statues. "I never took you as a religious one, Doran."

The dwarf frowned. "Ye don' have to be *religious* to appreciate the works o' ye mother an' father!"

"Do you not worry," the old knight continued, "that, like Atilan and all the human gods, they're just legends made into something more?"

"Bah! Only humans an' elves could turn some old evil bastard like Atilan into a god an' worship him for ten thousand years! Don' ye worry, laddy. Grarfath an' Yamnomora are the real thing!"

Doran could see that neither Nathaniel nor Reyna were convinced about his deities. He couldn't blame them after the discovery of Atilan's true place in history, as the last king of The First Kingdom. His evil scheming, from beyond The Veil, had seen him risen to the heights of a god, a false god, but worshipped all the same to this very day.

Doran could only dream of the day when every race realised

Grarfath and Yamnomora were the creators. They just didn't like humans, or elves, or anything but dwarves really...

Leaving the temple behind, the three companions climbed several sets of stairs carved from the mountain. By the taste of the stone, Doran could tell they were heading north, deeper into Vengora.

Nathaniel and Reyna wondered aloud many times about how many hours had slipped past on their journey under the mountain. Doran would always answer. As a dwarf, he had the uncanny ability to keep track of the time without the need for the sun. In these wintery months, he knew the light would already be fading outside.

The sound of Namdhorian soldiers found the companions before the sight of them did. Echoing through the bare halls, Doran could hear plates of armour scraping together and feet shuffling on the cold floor. The crackling of a fire and the scent of smoke didn't escape Doran's senses either.

"Sounds like this is the place," the dwarf said to his friends.

Reyna shook off any signs of fatigue and straightened her back before rounding the corner and facing the camp. Doran happily kept to the back, unsure if he was about to come across any other dwarves.

The Namdhorian soldiers were startled by their sudden appearance. The closest of them shot up and reached for the swords on their hips, while the others dropped their drinks and food and stood to attention.

"Stand down, fellas!" The order came from the other side of the makeshift camp. "They've come from our side," he added.

The soldiers visibly relaxed and parted for their commander. He strode through with the confidence of a man in charge, attired in a gold cloak and white armour emblazoned with the lion sigil. With short grey hair and a trimmed beard to match, he was older than those around him, though, in Doran's eyes, they were all babes.

"You must be the ones we've been waiting for," the commander said, facing Reyna. "My name is Captain Adan."

Reyna bowed her head. "I am Ambassador Reyna Galfrey, this is my husband, Ambassador Nathaniel Galfrey—"

"We've been expecting you. Who's the dwarf?" the captain asked bluntly, one hand resting on the hilt of his fine sword.

Reyna half turned to regard Doran and he had no choice but to walk out from behind Nathaniel. He felt the eyes of every soldier fall on him and burn with hate. It was possible that these soldiers were the very same who had held the dwarves back and suffered for it, or at least their friends had.

"This is Doran son of—"

The dwarf held up his hand to stop Reyna. "Doran is just fine, me Lady."

The ambassador nodded once in understanding. "You see him as the enemy, but I assure you, he is an ally."

Captain Adan folded his arms. "Whether its words or steel he offers, the stubbornness of his kin knows no bounds. They will not be budged."

"That, we actually agree on," Doran said with a shrug.

Nathaniel stepped in. "Perhaps we could see this mine everyone is willing to die for?"

The captain didn't move an inch as he considered Nathaniel's request. "You can see the entrance," he replied. "No one's seen the *mine*."

That statement raised the eyebrows of all three companions. "No one has entered the mine?" Reyna clarified.

"Not yet," Captain Adan confirmed. "Before the dwarves showed up, we tried everything to force our way in, but those doors are as stubborn as those who made them. Queen Yelifer sent smiths, ready to explore the contents of the mine, but when we failed to get inside, she sent for those who could translate the dwarvish surrounding the doors."

"Let me guess," Doran interrupted. "They've had no luck."

Captain Adan looked down at the dwarf. "Apparently the language is older than any dwarvish known to man."

"Aye, it will be," Doran said. "This deep into Vengora…" The dwarf looked about at the hewn walls. "It's likely to be the earliest form o' dwarvish. Very old!"

"Can you read it, Doran?" Reyna asked.

"To be honest, I'm better at speakin' it. Me great grandfather used to blabber on in it when I was a young'un'."

"Either way," Nathaniel said, "it would be of use to see more than just your camp, Captain Adan."

The captain squared his jaw before relenting. "Follow me."

The soldiers moved aside for them, revealing a small antechamber in the middle of a T-junction. The southern corridor was home to the Namdhorians and to the north was a darkened tunnel that appeared to have no end. The antechamber was lit by a single shaft of diagonal light that was brightest in the late afternoon's waning sun. The light hit the door and illuminated the runes that lined it.

Doran looked up to see the hole in the mountain side. It was a natural formation that none but a small animal could clamber through, but its presence was most likely the reason for this particular chamber being built where it was.

Stepping into the diagonal shaft of light, Doran's shadow fell over the double doors that barred the way. Arched at the top, it was an unusual design to be found inside a dwarven kingdom. Until now, every door the son of Dorain had come across was rectangular. It was a small detail, but it damn near shouted at the dwarf that something was wrong.

Nathaniel, in his typically human way, had to push against the black doors and feel their resistance for himself. They didn't so much as rattle under the pressure.

"Aye, this is a *mine*..." Doran said with no lack of sarcasm. "Ye see those markin's there?" The dwarf pointed to the runes shaped like a hammer coming down on a flat line. "Even now, that's the symbol for a dwarven weaponsmith. Yelifer wants herself some dwarven weapons it seems."

Captain Adan puffed out his chest. "What *Queen* Yelifer wants and doesn't want inside that chamber is not our concern. Getting inside and keeping the dwarves of Dhenaheim *out* is all that matters to me and my men."

"Then our priorities do not align, Captain." Reyna turned from the runes carved into the stone. "We are here to prevent a war and any further bloodshed. Guard the way if you must, but *we* must speak to the lords of Dhenaheim."

Captain Adan glanced at the darkened tunnel to the north. "The dwarves are down there," he said. "I've got six men on patrol in those tunnels."

"And the rest..." one of the soldiers muttered behind the captain.

Adan sighed. "Ah, yes. The *historian*..."

"What's that?" Nathaniel asked.

"Corbyn here will escort you to the dwarven line," Captain Adan replied. "Be warned, you aren't the only ones trying to open a dialogue. Queen Yelifer believes these runes may hold the answer to opening the doors." Adan took an exasperated breath. "A specialist in everything dwarf was sent for... Master Devron has been here almost since the beginning."

"Who is Master Devron?" Nathaniel asked.

"He's a... I don't know what his proper title is. He's from The All-Tower in Palios. Claims to have been studying dwarven culture all his life. All twenty-eight years of it..."

"What exactly is he doing?" Reyna asked with a look at the dark tunnel.

"He's asking them to translate some of the runes. Or at least that's what he was doing the last time I clapped eyes on him. He's a little... well, you'll see."

Corbyn led the three companions a little farther into the northern tunnel, where they passed three of the six guards Captain Adan had spoken of. They eyed Doran with heavy suspicion.

The tunnel broke off into a maze of corridors and ancient halls, but Corbyn continued along the straight line, taking but a single corner to reach the dwarven line. There really wasn't much distance between the two camps.

A shrill-like scream preceded the lanky man who came skidding around the corner. He slipped under his own momentum, an error that saved his life from the flying axe. His hands slapped against the stone floor and he scrambled on his knees until he was able to dive behind the corner and land at Nathaniel's feet.

Doran's eye tracked the axe as it dug into the wall at the end of the hall. It was a fine axe and definitely dwarven in make and style.

Nathaniel bent down and helped the man to his feet. "Master Devron, I presume?"

Brushing down his robes, the young man replied with a beaming smile on his face. "Master Petur Devron, at your service!"

Doran scrutinised the man, wondering if he had knocked his head running from that axe, an axe he seemed to have immediately forgotten about.

"Well met, Master Devron. I am Ambassador Nathaniel Galfrey and this—"

"Reyna Galfrey! *The* Galfreys! It's such an honour to meet you both!" Petur grabbed their hands one after the other and shook them profusely. "I've never met an elf before. I studied The War for the Realm in my earliest years at The All-Tower. Fascinating stuff!"

Doran looked from the eccentric master to the dwarven axe. "Is no one else bothered by the axe in the wall?"

Petur quickly turned on the dwarf and his mouth fell open. "A dwarf?" he exclaimed in a pitch few men could manage. "A dwarf on this side of the line!" The master looked Doran up and down. "I know you! You're Doran Heavybelly! That's great! You're—"

"Master Devron," Reyna interjected with her melodic tone. "Should we be concerned by the manner of your arrival?"

Petur's eyes went wide and he tried to run a hand through the knots in his manic hair. "Oh, that? No! That's just... That's just their way of saying 'Not today, thank you'." He laughed to himself and wiped the sheen of sweat from his pale brow.

"He's not wrong," Doran said.

Reyna continued, "Captain Adan tells us you are inquiring about the runes around the door."

"Yes!" Petur launched a finger in the air. "The runes! Fascinating stuff, it really is. A much older dialect than any I have researched before. This is quite the opportunity, let me tell you."

"This is how wars begin, Master Devron," Nathaniel added in a serious tone.

Petur attempted to bring his excitement down a peg. "You're

quite right, Ambassador Galfrey. I thought that working with the dwarves to translate the runes might offer a better recourse. Of course…" The lanky man turned to the axe in the wall. "You have to catch them in the right mood."

"Ye still alive, ain't ye? I'd say that's as good a mood as ye're gonna get."

"A dwarven tongue might delay the next axe," Reyna suggested.

Doran sighed. He had finally arrived at the moment he had hoped to avoid and the moment he had always known he couldn't outrun forever. Home has a way of dragging people back, whether they like it or not.

Pushing past the young master, Doran positioned himself on the very edge of the corner. He stole a glance with one eye and discovered the silhouettes of his kin against a roaring fire in the middle of the tunnel. A dozen at least, all armed to the teeth and plated in silvyr by the smell of it.

He exhaled a deep breath, blowing out his bearded cheeks. "*Did one of you lose an axe?*" he asked in dwarvish.

Their chatter and general hubbub came to a sudden stop. All eyes fell on Doran's head, poking around the corner.

"*Name yourself, stranger!*" came the gruff response. "*No mud-dweller can speak like that!*"

Doran rolled his eyes, having forgotten the dwarven slang for humans. "*That's because I'm a son of Grarfath, like yourself!*"

There was a pause. "*How do we know this ain't a trick? Mud dwellers love them some magic!*"

"*I'll put myself at your mercy, friend.*" Doran stepped out into the hall, aware that to his kin, he was just as hard to make out as they were.

"*Aye, you look like a dwarf from here!*" The lead dwarf briefly turned to the others. "*You're going to have to come into the light… friend!*"

Doran motioned for Reyna and Nathaniel to accompany him.

"*Hold!*" The lead dwarf warned as he brought up his axe. "*What are you about then? Who are they?*"

"*You've got a lot of warriors behind you,*" Doran answered. "*These two are with me. They're ambassadors, not soldiers.*"

Nathaniel whispered. "I hope you know what you're doing Heavybelly…"

"*You mean they're talkers,*" the lead dwarf replied. "*Like the other one,*" he added with the same exasperated tone as Captain Adan.

"*He does seem like an irritating bugger,*" Doran agreed. "*I don't suppose you could use the common tongue for my friends here, could you?*"

"*He's lucky to still have two legs to run on! You tell him, if he comes back here one more time with those drawings, we're gonna take his feet…*"

Doran stepped into the light of their fire and the lead dwarf froze. Not a word escaped the lips of any of his kin. Doran swallowed hard when he looked upon the sigil raised against their breastplates. An upright axe with double-sided blades on one end and a hammer at the base…

The sigil of clan Heavybelly.

The lead dwarf dropped to one knee, quickly followed by the others. They kept their heads bowed and weapons pressed to the ground.

"Prince Doran!" the lead dwarf said in the common tongue.

Both Reyna and Nathaniel turned on the son of Dorain. "*Prince?*"

A COLD FAREWELL

A lijah couldn't help but feel at home inside the warm embrace of Ilythyra. He tried to convince himself that it was because of the magic that kept winter at bay or the soft lighting that made everything feel as if he were in a pleasant dream.

Living in Illian, it wasn't very often that he came across a place that brought the elf out in him. If he stayed in Ilythyra for much longer, he was likely to shave his beard off and start singing to the trees.

Alijah looked down from the branch he was lazing on. The camp of survivors from Tregaran were still in shock and prone to gathering in huddles for support. They had warmed to the elves, welcoming their help and advice.

Alijah hoped that wherever the rest of the survivors had fled to, they had all found refuge.

He searched the huddles until he spotted Isabella and Salim. He had spoken with them both shortly after dawn, offering yet more sympathies. Isabella was as strong as they came; the southern lands had a way of forging such tough skin. Alijah knew she would honour Tauren and stand up for her people in his stead.

Salim, on the other hand, had lost his father, one of the pillars in his life. It was hard to say how his loss would affect the small boy, but Alijah had offered himself, pledging to be there whenever Salim needed him, just as Uncle Tauren had always been there for him and Inara growing up. For now, he was satisfied that they were safe among the elves of The Moonlit Plains.

Beyond the camp, nestled between the tall arching roots of a massive tree, Alijah caught sight of Hadavad and Galanör talking to Ellöria. The half-elf noted the ancient scroll in the mage's hands.

Alijah wasted no time falling backward off the branch and turning it into a flip. He caught the next branch down by his hands and let his momentum carry his swing forward until he hopped and skipped between the lower branches. Only seconds after spotting the huddle, he was striding across Ilythyra's gardens.

It felt awkward to demand entry into their conversation, so he tried the casual approach. "Has there been any word from Lirian?"

The three, whose combined lifespan was over two thousand years, halted their discussion and regarded Alijah for a moment. He began to wonder, with slightly laboured breath, if he hadn't been casual enough in his approach.

Ellöria replied in her soft tone, "No word, I'm afraid."

Alijah had asked the question as a way of entering their conversation. He hadn't realised that the answer would have an effect on him. No word from Lirian meant no word from Inara…

Alijah could feel his concern growing out of control. With some focus, he remembered that Inara had no doubt been in peril during his four year absence and he had rarely worried about her safety then.

That was before Malliath and Asher started killing Dragorn…

He forced that worry away. If Malliath had been fighting Athis, Alijah would know about it. The black dragon might win, but Athis would certainly cause him enough pain that Alijah would feel it.

He had to believe that she was alright.

"If Gideon is injured," Hadavad said, "Inara is most likely aiding him. She will be fine."

Alijah hated it when his thoughts and concerns could be so easily read. The half-elf straightened up and took a breath, pushing aside all his fears. He had no family. Alijah repeated those words again and again until he was sure that his expression was unreadable, comparable to his Galant-playing face.

"You're looking at the prophecy…" he said.

Hadavad nodded. "I thought the experienced eyes of Lady Ellöria would offer better insight."

Ellöria turned from Alijah and looked down on the ruined scroll. "As you say, Hadavad," the elf resumed, "it will require comparison to The Echoes of Fate prophecy for better authenticity. It is undoubtedly ancient…"

"That's the part that doesn't make any sense," Galanör insisted. "If it's as old as we suspect, it should have perished in that cave long ago."

"Vighon raised a good question," Alijah added. "He wondered if we were meant to find it."

Ellöria was hard to read, but it appeared his comment had sparked an idea. The elf carefully took the scroll from Hadavad and held it up. They could all see the painted black hand at the bottom of the parchment and the few lines of prophecy that remained. Its edges were frayed and tattered, the skin itself stained with dark patches.

Ellöria ran her nose up a short length of the edge. Her head snapped back and she rolled the parchment up before throwing it away. Hadavad's arms shot up with a great deal of alarm on his face, but Galanör put a hand on his chest, preventing the mage from reaching the prophecy.

Alijah shielded his eyes as Ellöria opened her palm, bringing to life a ball of blue flames. A flick of the wrist hurled the fiery spell at the scroll and it instantly succumbed to the burning element. Another flick of the wrist extinguished the fire, leaving the scroll to smoke in the grass.

"What have you done?" Hadavad asked urgently.

Ellöria eyed the scroll with great suspicion. "Nothing, it seems."

Alijah tentatively picked up the scroll and unravelled it. There wasn't a trace of the flames. No scorch marks, no holes, not even a burning odour. The tattered edges were just as they had been, the verses too, and the black hand was still intact.

"Impossible," Hadavad whispered. "It should be ash."

"The spell I used wouldn't even have left ash. A powerful protection spell has been placed over this scroll," Ellöria concluded.

Galanör examined the scroll in Alijah's hands. "The question is; why would The Black Hand protect a half-destroyed prophecy? Why not just write a new one?"

Alijah shrugged. "Perhaps they couldn't remember everything it said."

Surprisingly, it was Vighon who offered wiser words. "Have you considered it may have been ruined on purpose?" The northerner was behind them, leaning against the tall roots with his arms folded. "Maybe they didn't want us to have the whole picture. The *real* question is," he added, looking at Galanör, "did they know *who* would find it?"

Ellöria slowly walked around the group. "If your question has a sinister answer, Mr. Draqaro, then whoever wrote this prophecy intended for a particular person to find specific information." The elf turned to Alijah.

Hadavad caught on. "Information that would see them act upon it." The mage laid his own eyes on Alijah.

The half-elf was putting the pieces together in his mind. "You're saying, someone, ten thousand years ago, wrote this prophecy, damaged it so that only specific parts could be read, left it in a cave in The Wild Moores, and made certain it would stay there until, what? I came along eons later?" He scoffed. "That's more than a little far-fetched, even for us."

The ranger folded his arms. "Not unless they've been telling the truth all this time." Galanör met Hadavad's dark eyes. "If The Echoes' priests, *The Black Hand*, can really see the future, they would know, well, everything. Some ancient priest could have foreseen Alijah retrieving the scroll and known exactly what to do to make sure that happened."

"No," Hadavad replied adamantly. "They know their way around dark magic, but *no-one* can see into the future. Not elves, not dragons, not the most powerful mages in the world. It's just a trick The Crows use to pull in followers, nothing more."

Galanör argued, "We have to accept it as a possibility, Hadavad. There's a reason The Echoes have survived the Ages, survived the wars and genocide. It all makes sense if you—"

"If you what? Accept that The Crow *can* see the future?" The mage dropped his head. "We might as well give up now if that's the case. They've already won if they know what we're going to do next."

Seeing them lock horns over the subject was oddly uncomfortable, reminding Alijah of the times he caught his parents arguing.

"To what end?" Ellöria asked, breaking the mounting tension. "What would The Echoes of ages past have to gain by ensuring the prophecy was found by Alijah?"

"We went south," Vighon offered. "That led from one nightmare to the next. We were lucky to have survived any of it."

"From your recollection," Ellöria continued, "none of you were required in the spell to resurrect Asher or bind him to Malliath. So I ask again; to what end? What do The Black Hand of today have to gain from your presence in Paldora's Fall?"

The answer hit Alijah in the form of an image. He was momentarily back in Paldora's Fall, staring into the blazing purple eyes of Malliath. When he returned to the present, Ellöria was watching him closely.

The elf said, "As impossible as the spell would seem, the only advantage to having you present would be your binding to Asher and Malliath."

Alijah broke their eye contact. He hadn't enjoyed Galanör's retelling upon their arrival and he hated hearing it from Ellöria even more. He couldn't shake the feeling that they were talking about something incredibly private to him.

"That would complicate any encounter with Malliath," Galanör agreed. "But only to a few."

"It is often only a few who can make a difference," Ellöria wisely replied.

Alijah could see that Hadavad disagreed with it all. The old mage was beyond certain that The Crow and his predecessors were lying about their prophetic skills. In truth, Alijah was equally convinced. He believed, as Hadavad did, that they had put themselves in the middle of The Black Hand's schemes, nothing more.

"I would say it's more likely that the prophecy was damaged thousands of years ago," he said. "They must have put the protection spell on it to make sure they didn't lose the whole scroll. Maybe they considered it sacred…"

"I agree," Hadavad said. "Like The Echoes of Fate, the words are open to multiple interpretations. They can be used to explain any narrative depending on the reader's perspectives."

Galanör placed his hands on his hips. "It says *a warrior will be resurrected in the heart of a fallen star*, Hadavad. How open to interpretation is that?"

"Paldora's Star is not the first to fall from the heavens," Hadavad countered. "Where do you think the silvyr mines in Dhenaheim come from? You could easily have interpreted it a different way and travelled north instead of south."

"Wait?" Alijah held up a hand. "You know it says warrior?"

The ranger gestured to their host. "Lady Ellöria can read the ancient glyphs better than all of us."

"Do we know what else it says?" the half-elf asked.

Sitting on one of the smaller roots, Ellöria maintained her regal posture. "There is only a collection of lines that can be read. It should be noted that out of context, they have even less meaning."

"What does it say?" Alijah asked again, annoyed by his own eagerness in light of his recent opinion. He chalked it up to being the one who had found the ancient relic in the first place.

From memory alone, Ellöria said, "From the first verse, it says: *As the Age turns to ruin, so too will the light turn to darkness.* There is mention of a pact, also. Between who or what I cannot say and I believe it folly to speculate as the rest is damaged."

Ignoring Ellöria's advice completely, Vighon speculated, "It's most likely talking about The Black Hand and the orcs."

Hadavad shook his head. "That's the narrative…"

Ellöria waited for silence before continuing, "The second verse reads: *A warrior shall be resurrected in the heart of a fallen star*. There is a broken line regarding a dragon, but the rest is too damaged to make sense of. The next part of that verse, however, is very interesting. *Only magic wrought of unity can break the chains*. I find the choice of words unusual, though I cannot speak of their meaning. The last line has only two words that remain intact: *immortal ash*."

To Alijah's understanding, the second verse made as little sense as the first, lending more to the opinion that it meant nothing at all.

"What about the last verse?" Vighon asked.

"*Through the forge of war, the world will have…*" Ellöria trailed off. "The rest is too damaged."

Alijah sighed and rolled up the prophecy. "Our initial translation may have seen us travel south, but I think it's fair to say that the rest of it is useless, regardless of your perspective or belief."

"What matters is what we do next," Vighon added.

Alijah gave his friend a hard look. He had never heard anything so determined from the northerner.

"You are welcome to stay in Ilythyra," Ellöria offered. "When we have heard back from Ameeraska and Calmardra, we will ensure the survivors of Tregaran find their way south again; under the safety of our escort, of course."

"North is our course," Hadavad announced. "Gideon Thorn is in Lirian, or what remains of it. The schemes of The Black Hand remain to be seen and the orcs are even more unpredictable." The mage turned to Alijah. "I would say the only problem we can face is your bond with Malliath and Asher."

It wouldn't have been Alijah's first plan. "And you believe that Gideon can help me with that?" he asked incredulously.

"If there's anything that can help us to undo this spell it will be found in the library on The Lifeless Isles. Besides, I fear it won't be long before we hear from Malliath and Asher again. When that happens, it would be best for everyone if your life wasn't tied to theirs."

"A sound course of action," Ellöria agreed. "We shall provide you all with enough supplies for the journey."

Thoughts of his sister crept back into his mind. Alijah tried to ignore the relief he felt at knowing he would see her again. He hid his smile well.

～

On the northern edge of the forest, where the trees met the snow-covered plains, the four companions said their farewells to the elves of Ilythyra. A small escort had accompanied Ellöria, each providing them with various supplies.

Alijah subconsciously straightened his posture when his great aunt approached. In both hands, the Lady of Ilythyra presented him with a quiver.

"Thirty years ago, I gave one of these to your mother before she first sailed to The Shining Coast. Like hers, the quiver is enchanted."

Alijah's eyes lit up. As an archer, he had marvelled no end at his mother's quiver, enchanted to never run out of arrows.

"I cannot accept this gift," he replied without thinking. "You have already given us so much."

"I did not ask if you would accept it," Ellöria said, lifting the quiver a little higher.

Alijah bowed his head and took the quiver in his hands. The surface was laced with beautiful patterns of gold and the wood itself was engraved with ancient glyphs. He wasted no time removing his arrows and placing them inside the new quiver. He pulled one out and smiled as it was immediately replaced by a new one.

"Thank you, Lady Ellöria." Alijah bowed again, dropping his head even lower this time.

The elf offered a warm smile and embraced him. "You do not bow to me…" she whispered.

That was a concept Alijah would always struggle with. Had he been born and raised in Ayda, among his mother's people, Ellöria was right; he wouldn't bow to her. The elven hierarchy was absolute, making his place among them indisputable.

But he didn't belong in a land of immortals.

Alijah stepped back and bowed again. "That is not the world I know," he said. "Thank you for the quiver."

With that, the four turned to begin their journey north. They each had their own horse now, a fact that made Vighon very happy.

Ellöria's voice cut through the cold air. "There is one more gift I would see you take."

The companions stopped as one and turned back to see an elf break free of Ellöria's escort. He presented the Lady of Ilythyra with an ornate wooden box and opened the lid for her. Alijah's interest was piqued when he saw the contents glow.

"The journey to Lirian is long," Ellöria continued. "If Gideon Thorn has the means to break the bond between you and Malliath, I would see you with him as soon as possible." The elf removed the crystal from within the ornate box and walked beyond the tree line, into the plains.

"Lady Ellöria," Galanör began with some concern. "Such a thing is precious, but to open a portal from here to Lirian would cost you greatly."

"It would cost *you* greatly, Galanör of house Reveeri." Ellöria came to a stop with her green dress blowing gently in the breeze. "Besides, I am not opening a portal to Lirian. I can get you as far as Vangarth, just south of Lirian. There simply isn't enough magic in this crystal to go any farther."

"Thank you," Alijah said earnestly.

With Vighon on one side and Galanör on the other, they prepared to enter the portal. Only then did Alijah realise that Hadavad was astride his horse, apart from them all.

"What's wrong?" Alijah asked.

The old mage looked briefly to the east. "This is where we part ways."

"Part ways?" Alijah echoed, looking to the east himself. "What are you talking about?"

Vighon nodded his head to the north. "You said we were to find Gideon Thorn."

"And you will," the mage said boldly. "You don't need me for that."

"Where are you going?" Alijah demanded.

Hadavad sighed and he struggled to find the words. "I can't explain it. I just know I have to go another way."

The mage looked at Ellöria but the half-elf couldn't decipher their expressions. It was apparent, however, that this was no surprise to the Lady of Ilythyra. It had most likely been Hadavad who suggested the crystal to see them parted beyond reunion.

"I don't understand…" Alijah glanced at the open plains. "Why are you going another way?"

Hadavad's mouth opened but he appeared displeased with whatever his answer was to be. "I'm going to get answers, Alijah. At least, I think I am."

"You're making less sense than normal," Alijah argued. He turned to the silent ranger. "Don't you have anything to say?"

"Answers are in short supply," Galanör said from within his hood. "I would welcome any that Hadavad might find."

Alijah shook his head in despair. "Where is this coming from? You're suddenly just leaving?"

"Why don't we discuss this in Vangarth?" Vighon suggested.

Hadavad shook his dreadlocks. "My path lies to the east," he persisted. "Whatever The Black Hand are doing, they've been planning it for a long time. We need answers if we're going to get in front of them."

Alijah still wasn't satisfied. "How do you know the answers lie to the east? I thought the library in The Lifeless Isles had all the answers."

Hadavad could only offer a stoic expression. "I'm still going, Alijah. We will meet again, I am sure of it." Before any further protest, the mage turned his horse to the east.

"Wait!" Alijah ushered his horse to cut in front of Hadavad. "We need to compare the prophecies. You need to be there; nobody knows The Black Hand or The Echoes like you do."

Hadavad eyed one of the satchels on the back of Alijah's horse. "You have the prophecy now, boy."

Alijah looked over his shoulder to see the cylindrical tube given to them by the elves.

"Don't doubt yourself," the mage continued. "You're a quick learner and you've got a hunger for it now. You *need* answers. You get yours and I'll get mine. Only then can we put it all together and make a real difference." Hadavad slapped Alijah's arm affectionately before digging his heels into the horse. "Keep each other safe!" he called back.

The three sat on their horses and watched the mage ride off towards the white horizon. Alijah had gone off into the world plenty of times without Hadavad, not always sure when they were going to meet up again. For some reason, this felt different.

Ellöria's melodic voice offered comfort. "Those who live in the currents of magic will always be called to a different path. Hadavad must go his way now, and you must go yours."

The Lady of Ilythyra threw the crystal into the open air and flexed her fingers, awaking the magic stored inside. The crystal exploded into a portal of pitch black, distorting the snow around it.

"Let him go…" Galanör said as he guided his horse forward.

Alijah watched the mage ride away without turning back. Thankfully, Vighon ushered Ned forwards and cut off his view of Hadavad. It reminded him that he wasn't as alone as he felt.

"Shall we?" The northerner had to battle with Ned to walk through the portal.

Alijah followed behind his friend and offered Ellöria one last bow of the head. Unlike Galanör, the elf showed no sign of fatigue or discomfort at holding open a portal. She was strong, like all that shared the Sevari bloodline. It took Alijah a moment longer than it should have to realise that he was included in that bloodline.

Watching Hadavad, his mentor, ride away as they entered a portal and travelled hundreds of miles in but a few steps, Alijah reminded himself that he *was* strong enough to do this. He held onto that thought and rode into the abyss.

PARTING WAYS

J ust beneath the cloud cover, Inara and Athis flew side by side with Gideon and Ilargo. The young Dragorn was sure to keep a close eye on her master. Both dragon and rider appeared in good health now, but having seen their injuries up close, Inara struggled to shed her concern.

Through their bond, she could feel Athis's alertness. His senses were far more acute than normal, even when compared to hunting.

What troubles you? she asked.

The red dragon kept his eyes on the sky. *They could be anywhere…*

Inara knew Athis was talking about Asher and Malliath. She lifted her head a little and joined him in searching the skies. Between the snow-covered world and the grey clouds, there was nothing but air.

It's unsettling, the Dragorn commented. **I'm not used to feeling vulnerable in the sky.**

Nor am I, wingless one. I am hoping that after their fight with Master Thorn and Ilargo, Malliath and Asher are in need of rest.

Don't you think it's unusual, Inara said, **that Asher would come all the way to Lirian just to reclaim one of his swords?**

Perhaps they were instructed to destroy Lirian, Athis countered. *Though, I see your point. If Asher's will is truly enslaved to The Crow, why would he seek out a weapon that belonged to him personally?*

Maybe there is something left of him in there.

Athis's voice was soft in her mind. *We can hope…*

The dragons continued their flight south, following The Selk Road below, until they came across Vangarth, nestled in the bottom of The Evermoore.

For most of their journey, the road below had been filled with people. Gideon's warning to King Weymund hadn't fallen on deaf ears. Now, everyone under his rule was on their way to Grey Stone, seeking shelter from not only Malliath, but also the invading orcs.

Inara couldn't help but think of Alijah and the others again. The orcs had set The Arid Lands on fire and she had left them.

The two dragons circled the town for a while, making sure that the majority of its inhabitants evacuated safely. It was as troubling as it was frustrating to think that the orcs could attack from underground without any notice.

Through the bond that they all shared, Inara became aware that Ilargo had spotted something only a moment before Athis did. The red dragon shared their discovery, guiding Inara's curiosity to the western edge of Vangarth. From their high vantage, all four could see the spark of a portal open and a trio of riders emerge as if from nowhere.

To her eyes, the riders were only distinguishable by their horses. Besides Gideon, there were only a few individuals in all of Illian who could open portals and most of them resided in Ilythyra.

Have the elves come to help?

Athis adjusted his angle of approach to better see the riders as they emerged from the tree line. *It's Alijah!* he exclaimed.

Inara felt a wave of relief wash over her mind. **Who is he with?**

Athis began to descend alongside Ilargo. *He is with Vighon and Galan*ör.

There was a name missing. **No Hadavad?**

The portal has closed, Athis replied.

Inara didn't know what to make of the mage's absence, but she decided the portal was a good sign; it meant they had been assisted by her great aunt, Lady Ellöria.

With most of the town already packed up and travelling north, the southern end of the town was largely abandoned; perfect for two large dragons. All but Galanör's horse became rattled by the sudden appearance of the great wyrms of the sky.

When the cloud of unsettled snow found its rest once more, Inara joined Gideon in the street. Those at the end of Vangarth's human trail stopped what they were doing and stared at the dragons. For most, it was the first time they had ever laid eyes on one close to.

"Well met," Galanör greeted as he climbed down from his horse.

Gideon offered his old friend a warm smile. "It's been too long since we met in person." The two clasped forearms and fell into a tight embrace.

Their journey together, thirty years previously, had been the subject of countless bedtime stories for Inara and Alijah. Since becoming a Dragorn and having the opportunity to learn from Gideon himself, Inara had come to hear his version of such tales. They were far more gruesome and life-threatening than the version her mother had told them. It was almost enough to put her off ever crossing The Adean and visiting Ayda.

Inara was faced with Vighon before she could greet her brother. As before, there was an awkwardness between them that should have been left in the past. Indeed, to Inara, the feelings they had once shared for each other were long buried, but it seemed Vighon still held a more intimate place for her in his heart.

The northerner moved to embrace her until a sharp gust of air bombarded the man from above. Athis loomed overhead and made one distinct sniff of the air, conveying his feelings.

"They're not going to eat the horses, are they?" he asked, his eyes darting from one dragon to the next.

They do look tasty... Athis's tongue licked his front teeth as he eyed Vighon's horse.

Inara answered his question in the hopes that it would prevent her from laughing. "The horses are safe," she assured.

Vighon swallowed hard and settled with offering her a friendly nod. "It's good to see you again."

"And you," Inara replied. "I'm glad to see you made it out of Tregaran. We heard what has happened."

Alijah pulled his green cloak about him and purposefully came to a stop beyond Inara's reach. Like Vighon, he bore a few new cuts and bruises, but all three of them looked to have escaped the southern city largely unharmed.

Inara wanted to tell her brother how good it was to see him safe. What she really wanted to do was hug him and pretend for a moment that everything was as it had been, before he left. Back when they thought they would both live forever…

Alijah met her eyes briefly. Inara was sure she could see some trace of relief there. He could claim to have no family, but his feelings would forever betray him.

"Where is Hadavad?" Gideon asked.

Galanör glanced at Alijah before replying, "He has chosen a different path."

"A different path to what?" Gideon asked.

"Hadavad's reasons remain his own," Galanör explained. "He claims to be in search of answers."

"Somewhere to the east," Vighon added.

Gideon paused as he regarded the northerner. "You must be Vighon Draqaro."

Vighon stood a little straighter. "I am," he declared.

"Gideon Thorn." The Master Dragorn held out his arm and the two clasped forearms. "Well met."

Gideon casually scanned Alijah from head to toe. "Hadavad has been a mysterious person since before any of us were born. If there's one thing he's proved good at; it's finding answers."

Galanör replied, "It was his suggestion that we travel north to find you."

"What chance," Gideon remarked. "We were travelling south to find you."

"Perhaps we should find some shelter before going any further," Inara suggested.

"I'd say we've got our pick of the town." Vighon gestured to the empty buildings.

The Stags Inn was the closest and offered a number of chairs and tables. Vighon moved to kick the door in.

"What are you doing?" Inara interjected. "This is someone's property."

With his boot in the air, the northerner paused. "I was just..."

Inara ushered him out of the way. "Let's assume everyone's coming back." The Dragorn waved her palm over the lock and used a simple spell to open the door.

Somewhat flustered, Vighon stepped aside and waited for everyone else to enter the tavern before he followed. Inara rolled her eyes when the northerner proceeded to help himself to a jar of dried food behind the bar. Beating her to it this time, Galanör deftly unhooked the small pouch of coins on Vighon's belt and left it on the bar top. Vighon followed the elf with an exasperated look, but he offered no protest.

Inara was pleased to be in a gathering at last that didn't consist of kings, queens, and council members to her own order. The Dragorn took a seat beside Gideon and did her best not to watch Alijah the entire time. Seeing him twice in as many days after losing contact for four years made him food for the eyes. It would take some time to get used to his beard, but more than anything, it was his demeanour that Inara struggled with the most. Sat opposite her, the fun, outgoing, and carefree brother she had known appeared trapped inside his own mind, haunted almost.

Gideon didn't wait for Vighon to finish rummaging behind the bar. "Since you'd already used the crystal I gave you, I'm assuming you come by Ilythyra."

Galanör pulled back his blue hood and ran a hand through his short hair. "Lady Ellöria was most gracious considering the strain we put on her home."

"There were survivors then?" Inara pressed. "From Tregaran?"

A sombre moment passed between the three of them, even giving Vighon pause.

"Inara…" Alijah's voice croaked. "Tauren didn't survive."

Those three words knocked Inara back in her chair and brought tears to her eyes. Gideon cupped his beard and looked to Galanör, who could only nod solemnly.

"He was slain by an orc," Alijah continued.

"What of Isabella and Salim?" Inara asked desperately, unsure if she was ready for the answer.

"They're safe," Alijah replied quickly. "We left them with the others in Ilythyra."

Gideon released a long sigh and stood up from his chair. The Master Dragorn rubbed his eyes and paced the bar. Inara blinked hard and wiped away the only tear to have broken through.

Galanör said, "I'm sorry for your loss, Inara. I know Tauren was like family to you."

"He was a good man," she managed, clearing her throat to stop it from cracking.

"He was a hero," Gideon proclaimed, his back to them all. "An entire generation were born free from slavery because of him." The Master Dragorn dropped his head. "Now it's all gone…"

"All gone?" Vighon echoed.

Inara caught the confusion pass between the three companions. "Did word not reach Ilythyra? The orcs have taken Ameeraska and Calmardra as well."

"*What?*" Alijah and Galanör asked at the same time.

"The Arid Lands have fallen," Inara clarified. "There are refugees fleeing north up both coasts. Velia and Grey Stone are taking them in."

Alijah and Galanör could do nothing but stare at the table. Vighon walked around the bar and slumped into one of the chairs, his manner one of defeat.

The elven ranger looked over to Gideon. "I thought… I *hoped* Tregaran was a random event." Galanör sat with a disquieted agitation not usually seen in his kin. "Are we being invaded?"

"It would seem so," Gideon whispered, bracing himself against the bar and letting his head fall between his arms.

"How did no one see this coming?" Alijah jibed. "I thought the all-seeing Dragorn were to protect us from everything."

"Alijah…" Inara imparted her feelings by tone alone. "Until very recently, no one knew orcs still existed."

Gideon's stare looked to penetrate the tavern walls. "Someone knew…" he insisted.

The Master Dragorn was a thousand miles away, his arm folded over his chest and a hand cupping his jaw. Inara had never seen him this way before.

"Master?"

Gideon snapped out of it immediately. "Why did Hadavad send you to find me?"

"To help me," Alijah said without meeting the master's eyes.

"Your bond with Malliath and Asher," Gideon reasoned.

Inara could see Alijah closing himself off even more. There was once a time when she could have looked upon his face and known everything he was thinking. Looking at him now, he was a blank slate.

In the absence of any response, Galanör offered, "It's only a matter of time before another city suffers the same fate as Lirian. It was felt that our best course of action would be to break the bond between Alijah and this… *Dragon Knight*."

"Agreed," Gideon said. "Evil though it may be, this spell has brought Asher back into the world. Our enemy may see him as a weapon, but I see it as a second chance. If we can free him, we will."

Inara was about to ask how they go about breaking an impossible spell when the ground shook. The tankards and glasses rattled and smashed, dust rained down from the beams above, and somewhere in the street a window shattered.

"Those are getting worse," Vighon observed.

"Wait," Inara had a thought. "The orcs are using tunnels underground to reach the cities. What if that's what the tremors are?"

Galanör looked down. "They're tunnelling…"

That would mean they are beneath us, Athis warned in her mind.

Gideon met her eyes across the tavern, having heard something similar from Ilargo, no doubt.

"New plan." The Master Dragorn strode across the tavern with his hand bracing Mournblade. "Inara, you and Athis are to escort the people of Vangarth and any survivors of Lirian. Get them safely to Grey Stone."

Inara had a few points she wanted to raise immediately, but her master turned on the others.

"Galanör, Vighon, the two of you will accompany them by ground. Be wary of these quakes."

"Hang about!" Vighon raised his hand. "I don't take orders from you." The northerner looked at his two companions for support and found nothing. "*Do I?*" he asked Alijah.

"Hadavad received his orders from Gideon," Alijah explained. "So, aye, it would seem we do take orders from him." Vighon looked to have some follow up questions, but Alijah waved them away. "What am I doing?" he demanded of Gideon.

The Master Dragorn glanced at Ilargo through the dusty window. "You're coming with me."

"Wait." It seemed Vighon blurted the command involuntary. "Where he goes, I go."

Gideon offered an apologetic smile. "Not this time, Vighon. We're going to The Lifeless Isles. Alijah will be safe there, you have my word."

Alijah's face broke into confusion. "I don't need protection, Vighon's not my keeper," he protested.

"Bodyguard is probably closer…" Vighon added.

Alijah's mouth opened and Inara expected a stream of expletives and one of his brattish rants about the people who cared for him.

In a surprisingly calm tone, he replied, "Vighon, go with Galanör and Inara to Grey Stone. Your sword will be of great value should the orcs attack. Gideon is right; no harm can come to me on The Lifeless Isles."

Vighon resembled an abandoned pup, unsure of what he was to do next. "Then you'll come and meet us in Grey Stone?" he asked, looking from Alijah to Gideon.

"If we find a way to break the bond," Gideon answered diplomatically. "I would say your farewells. We may be some time."

Shortly after, they gathered outside again. Galanör and Gideon held a private discussion that Inara was too far away to hear, even with *her* ears. Vighon and Alijah embraced, squeezing each other tightly before pulling away and patting each other on the arm.

For just a moment, it was like stepping into a memory for Inara. As children, the three of them had been inseparable, always off on some adventure around the farm or making trouble on one of their parents' trips. Alijah and Vighon had always shared a stronger bond of friendship, at least until they stopped being children. Then, other feelings rose to the surface and her bond with Vighon became the stronger.

You made promises to each other, Athis said, sharing in her memories.

It was the youngest of love. We thought we would be together forever. I told him I would become the queen of Ayda and he would be my king, the first human king of the elves. Inara internally scoffed at the idea now, seeing how naive they had been.

Recalling her farewell to Vighon, the day she left for The Lifeless Isles, was painful. She had been sixteen, Vighon nineteen. He hadn't taken it well. It had been easier for Inara, as the bond between her and Athis had already taken hold and started the process of pushing Vighon out.

"We will see each other soon," Alijah promised him. "Leave some orcs for me, eh."

Vighon nodded along. "Try not to fall off," he jested, looking to the sky.

The approaching crunch of snow turned Inara's attention to Gideon, who had left Galanör to tend the horses.

"Are you ready?" he asked.

"I would rather help in your errand," she replied. "You'll need more than your eyes to find a way of breaking this bond. Not to mention the prophecy; it will need comparing."

"I will have more than my own eyes." Gideon gestured to Alijah. "He is quite efficient when it comes to digging through the past."

There was but a single spark of jealousy at the thought of Alijah spending time alone with Gideon. Already annoyed that Athis would be aware of it, the Dragorn quashed it with the weight of her duty.

"I will ensure everyone makes it to Grey Stone safely, Master."

"I know you will." Gideon's smile was full of pride and confidence. "I will send others to oversee the protection of Grey Stone and offer you relief. Remember what I said to the council: don't engage Malliath and Asher on your own. Wait for the others."

It was a sound course of action, but the reality of Malliath attacking the caravan was very different. There would be no scenario in which Inara didn't put herself between the black dragon and the people. Of course, she couldn't kill Malliath or Asher without killing her own brother.

"I will, Master. Find a way to break the bond before he returns," she added quietly. Gideon's eyes rolled over Alijah and he nodded.

With Vighon and Galanör astride their horses, towing Alijah's horse, there was nothing left for Inara but to say farewell to her brother. The internal battle that waged war among his feelings was manifesting in his body language. Alijah still loved her, she could see that. Whether he exiled himself for selfless or selfish reasons, that fact would never change.

He made to walk past her and offer a simple farewell, but Inara reached out and gripped his hand. One tight squeeze spoke volumes of her love for him, and she hoped he knew then and there that she would never give up on him. In his defiant stride, he continued to walk past and their hands began to part.

He squeezed her fingers. It felt like hope to Inara.

She watched Gideon instruct him on the correct way to mount Ilargo. Together, both dragons rose into the air, one to fly east, the other west. Across the widening gulf, Alijah and Inara watched each other disappear beyond sight.

I feel it too, wingless one. Fear not; we will see him again…

Inara clung to the dragon's words as tightly as she clung to his horns.

37

BROTHERLY LOVE

The day had passed into night and back into day, yet Doran Heavybelly still grumbled and muttered under his breath.

"O' all the clans…" he kept repeating.

Shortly after discovering that their prince was standing before them, Rorin, son of Galahag, had sent two of the fastest from his camp to bring back a dwarf of equal standing, since Rorin was not counted among royalty.

"So let me get this straight." Master Devron crouched in front of the sitting dwarf with a parchment and a scribe in hand. "Rorin cannot speak to you because your hierarchy only allows dwarves of similar stations to commune."

Doran shook his head and clenched his fist. The wild-looking Master from The All-Tower had badgered him for information since they left the tunnel. He was sure the young man had yet to sleep.

"What are ye abou'?" Doran looked up at him. "He's sent for me brother, otherwise he'll end up stuck between my commands… an' me father's."

"Your brother?" Reyna inquired lightly.

"Aye, he's the only one o' equal standin' that can enforce me father's decree an' stop me from sendin' them home. It's safer for Rorin to cut off all negotiation with us now an' wait for further orders."

Petur Devron edged closer. "So what exactly is—"

"One more question out o' ye an' I swear I'll fit ye through that there hole!" Doran pointed to the shaft of light that illuminated the workshop doors.

Master Devron looked to reshape his mouth and ask a different question when Nathaniel put a firm hand on his shoulder. "Get some rest. You'll want to be ready for the talks, won't you?"

Petur hesitated before finally relenting to the advice. He left them in front of the workshop doors and retired to his cot on the outskirts of the Namdhorian camp.

Nathaniel shifted his long coat and sat down opposite the dwarf. "So, should we call you Doran or *Prince* Doran?" he asked with a cheeky smile.

The son of Dorain spoke through the pipe he put in his mouth. "Don' think any fancy sword skills will stop me from fittin' ye through that hole as well…"

Nathaniel silently laughed to himself and held up his hands. "There was a serious question in there somewhere."

"Aye, I bet there was," Doran replied in a puff of smoke.

The dwarf sighed. This was exactly the thing he had been avoiding for sixty years. Seeing the inquisitive faces of the Galfreys, however, he knew the truth would have to come out.

Damn Galfreys…

"A'right," he began begrudgingly. "Aye, I'm a prince o' sorts. In Dhenaheim, I was Prince Doran, son of King Dorain of clan Heavybelly. It changes nothin'!"

Nathaniel shrugged apologetically. "I have to ask. What is a dwarven prince doing living as a ranger in Illian?"

For six decades the answer to any such questions had been, *mind yer own business.* Sitting in an ancient dwarven hall, his friends having witnessed his kin bend the knee… There was no running away from it now.

"Like I've been tellin' ye," Doran said, "there's no one better for killin' dwarves than dwarves. It's one o' our best talents an' we excel at it." The son of Dorain couldn't look the Galfreys in the eyes as he recalled the bodies and blood that littered the valleys beyond Vengora.

"I grew tired o' it," he continued gruffly. "All that killin'… After a while, war didn' beget honour or courage. It was just pettiness an' greed. I've killed more o' me kin than ye can rightly count. An' for what? Clan Heavybelly? Me father? No. I killed because I liked it." Doran closed his eyes in shame.

"What happened?" Reyna asked softly. "Why did you stray from that path?"

Doran remembered the moment with perfect clarity. "Sixty years ago, I found meself standin' in the middle o' a valley. When we arrived, it was a single sheet o' white that rose up into The Whisperin' Mountains. The snow was undisturbed, perfect. Before the sun had set that day, I stood in the same valley, only there wasn' a single speck o' white to be seen. I was surrounded by the bodies o' me kin. Not just o' the Heavybelly clan, but the Hammerkegs. We slaughtered them all…"

"You were at war with these… Hammerkegs?" Reyna pressed.

"The Hammerkegs were at war with us," Doran mumbled. "We were at war with the Stormshields. Ye go to war with the clan above ye, an' defend against the clans below ye. That's the way o' it."

"What changed that day?" Reyna continued. "What turned you to Illian?"

Doran removed the pipe from his mouth. "As the eldest son of King Dorain, it was me duty to lead the army o' clan Heavybelly into battle. I'd not long returned from an assault against one o' the Stormshield's keeps. That battle went for them much the way ours did against the Hammerkegs. We were beaten back an' at the cost o' many Heavybellys.

"When I returned home, there was no parade, only the shame o' returnin' as survivors instead o' victors. Then the Hammerkegs took their chance, thinkin' we would be vulnerable after such a defeat. I was furious. The Stormshields had made certain I was fixed in a foul mood an' not ready to put me axe down.

"Later that day, I stood in a valley o' blood. We'd killed every one o' them Hammerkegs an' with fewer numbers too. I couldn' tell ye how many o' me kin were never to rise from that field because o' me axe. Because o' me fury an' me needless sense o' honour."

Doran could still remember the warm blood that quickly froze to his armour and skin. It covered every inch of him in red. The smell had followed him for days, weeks after he walked out of the valley. Crusted blood had remained stuck in his fingernails for even longer, reminding him of the lives he took every time he used his hands.

"So you left," Reyna stated.

"Aye. I dropped me axe an' walked off that battlefield. I didn' stop until The Iron Valley was behind me an' Illian was under me feet. It took a decade or more, but I met a couple o' rangers," the dwarf added with a wink, "an' discovered the meanin' o' real honour."

"Asher and Jonus Glaide," Nathaniel said with real warmth.

"They showed me the way," Doran declared. "That's why I didn' wan' to come back here. It's gonna end in blood; it always does."

"Were the clans always like this?" Nathaniel asked.

"Depends who ye ask. Me great grandfather would talk o' better times, back when me kin used to call this place home. He always said it were them orcs that drove us mad for blood. It were the first real taste o' war we had an' we liked it. An' I cannot deny that I didn', for a time that is. Turns out I had me limit."

Nathaniel placed a comforting hand on Doran's armoured pauldron. "Well, on behalf of all the people you've saved over the last sixty years, we're glad you did."

"Thank ye, lad," Doran replied.

It had taken sixty years, but the dwarf could say he was finally accustomed to the familiarity shared between the other free folk of Verda. The friendships he had forged were more real than anything he had experienced in over two hundred years in Dhenaheim.

"How many clans are there?" Reyna asked out of interest.

Doran regarded the Namdhorians camped by the edge of the

antechamber, opposite the workshop. He couldn't tell if any of them were listening, but the dwarf turned his back to them all the same.

"At last count there were six o' 'em." Doran shrugged. "There might well be fewer now, I suppose."

Nathaniel checked the boiling water that bubbled over the small fire they shared. "It's an interesting hierarchy they all share," he commented, preparing a cup of Velian tea for his wife.

Doran chuckled. "As they say in Namdhor, shit rolls downhill. The clan considered to be the rulin' lords o' Dhenaheim are the Battleborns. King Uthrad, son o' Koddun, sat on the throne when I left. They rule from Silvyr Hall. They're forbidden from goin' to war, being at the top an' all, but that don't mean they can't incite war between the other clans, for amusement an' the like…"

"So the Heavybelly clan doesn't sit at the top?" Nathaniel mused.

"Never have," Doran replied. "We're slap ban' in the middle. Above us, the Stormshields o' Hyndaern have forever lorded their superiority. Ruled by a shit o' a king: Gandalir, son o' Bairn. He never won no battle. Just inherited his kingdom from his father. Now there was a king!"

"The Hammerkegs go to war with the Heavybellys, then?" Reyna said, trying to get her head around the dwarvish system.

"Oh, aye. They were hammerin' at our doors before I were born. King Torgan has always had his eyes on Grimwhal's halls."

"Grimwhal?" Nathaniel frowned.

"Home o' the Heavybellys," Doran replied. There was still a part of him that swelled with pride at the thought of his home. "Thankfully, the Goldhorns always kept the Hammerkegs busy. Now, the Goldhorns have got a real bee in their bonnets abou' the Hammerkegs. King Thedomir, son o'…" Doran scratched his head. "Son o' who cares! Old King Thedomir tried to arrange a temporary alliance with me father, hopin' to wipe out the Hammerkegs an' all o' Nimdhun."

"I take it that didn't work out," Nathaniel assumed.

"Me father said no. He preferred havin' King Torgan knockin' at his door than Thedomir. The devil ye know an' all that…"

Reyna looked astonished at the dwarvish hierarchy. "So which poor clan is at the bottom of this violent ladder?"

That brought a smile to Doran's face. "The Brightbeards. Ye can't miss 'em." The dwarf gripped his own beard. "They live in a little city called Bhan Doral. Bein' at the bottom, they enjoy more peacetime than the rest o' us ever did. The Goldhorns would occasionally raid some o' their mines, but there was very little bloodshed. They spend most o' their time gobblin' 'em colourful mushrooms an' dyin' their beards. Funny lot! Probably the most un-dwarvish o' 'em all."

"It's the strangest hierarchy I've ever come across," Reyna admitted.

Doran stared hard at the workshop door. Strange wasn't the word he attached to his people. War-mongering would probably suit them better, he thought.

The dwarf sighed. "I really don' want to be here..."

Reyna put a surprisingly warm hand over his. "I'm sorry to have brought you back to all of this."

"Don' fret, me Lady. Helpin' ye to avoid that lot from descendin' on Illian is me duty, whether I like it or not. That's what rangers do..."

Seeing that he had been the source of the sour mood now firmly set between them, Doran looked about for a change of subject. The shaft of light angling at the doors to the workshop tugged at the dwarf's curiosity.

"That's a natural formation," he observed with a scrutinising eye. "That hole wasn' made by no dwarf."

Nathaniel looked up at the source of light. "What of it?"

Doran followed the shaft of light from the hole to the doors. "It just happens that a natural formation in the rock provides light over this particular door... I don' buy it!"

Reyna's curiosity was piqued now. "Are you saying this workshop was built here for a reason?"

Doran eyed the ancient dwarvish that surround the doorframe. "Aye, I think I am. Me ancestors built this here, in this cavern, for a reason. Must 'ave!"

Nathaniel stood up to stretch his legs. "Why would dwarves build this one room because the sun shines on it? I thought your kin didn't care for the sun."

"We don'," the son of Dorain agreed. "We're much happier with a mountain over our heads than the sky."

"Can you read any of these glyphs?" Reyna asked, running her hand over the engravings.

Doran's face screwed up as he looked upon them. "One or two, but it's like pickin' words out o' a sentence. They don' make any sense on their own."

"What are the words?" the elf pressed.

Doran shrugged. "I think that one might actually say *elf*."

"Elf?" Nathaniel repeated in disbelief. "Why would a dwarven door have the word elf written above it?"

"Beats me," Doran admitted. "Me ancestors got on with elves abou' as well as they do now."

Reyna put her hand into the light and followed it back to the jagged hole in the mountain side.

"What is it?" Nathaniel asked.

"I was—"

Before the elf could finish her thoughts, Captain Adan and the Namdhorian soldiers created quite the commotion as they all stood up at once. Two of the patrol guards came rushing down the tunnel from the dwarven end, their armour clattering and echoing off the walls.

"Captain! More dwarves!"

Captain Adan glanced at the three companions in front of the workshop before looking back to his patrolmen. "How many?" he asked, dropping a heavy hand onto the hilt of his sword.

"Half a dozen maybe," the soldier answered.

"Shields, boys!" Adan called back to his men.

Doran stood in their way. "They ain't fixin' for a fight yet, Captain. Best not provoke 'em while they're still in a mood for talkin'."

Captain Adan raised his chin. "Dwarves do not give orders in these halls anymore."

Reyna and Nathaniel added themselves to Doran's barrier.

The elf stated plainly, "Until it comes to violence, Captain, we will oversee all negotiations."

Captain Adan had the face of a man slapped. "They've sent for reinforcements, Ambassador!"

"I don't think six dwarves counts as reinforcements," Nathaniel rebuked. "You still outnumber them three to one."

"Like that matters," Doran muttered under his breath.

"Remain stationed here, Captain," Reyna added with some finality. "We will return shortly with more information."

A dishevelled Petur Devron hopped between the soldiers with his arm raised. "Can I come? Can I come?"

"No!" all three replied as one.

With a satisfied smirk on his face, Doran led the Galfreys back into the dwarven tunnels. Only when he rounded the next corner did he remember what he was walking into.

His brother...

"*WHAT AM I WAITING FOR?*" came the booming voice.

"What was that?" Nathaniel asked, the dwarven language lost on him.

Doran sighed. "That was Dakmund, son o' Dorain... Me brother."

The dwarven camp had increased in size and been illuminated by more torches to add to the firelight. One figure stood out among the rest.

A helm of brilliant silvyr, coated in gold, rested on Dakmund's head, covering his balding scalp. His breastplate shone in the firelight, accentuating the Heavybelly sigil in the middle of his chest. A jewel-encrusted axe adorned each side of his hips and a mighty sword of pure silvyr was sheathed over his back.

"*I've been waiting,*" Dakmund said bluntly.

"*Still impatient as ever, baby brother.*"

Reyna cleared her throat.

Dakmund squared his shoulders. "*I've told you not to call me that...*"

Doran took the measure of his brother's stature. "*You've grown fat.*"

Reyna cleared her throat again.

Dakmund visibly sucked in his gut. "*Well, you've shrunk,*" he spat back.

Doran stuck a thumb into his armoured chest. "*This shrunken dwarf can still knock you into Yamnomora's waiting arms.*"

Reyna cleared her throat for a third time.

"*What's wrong with your elf?*" Dakmund asked, tucking his thumbs into his belt.

"*There's nothing wrong—*" Doran snapped his head around to Reyna and back to his brother. "Use their tongue or they can' understand."

"*That's not my problem.*" Dakmund eyed the Galfreys with suspicion.

"Dak…" Doran growled.

"A'right, a'right!" he relented. "What are ye abou'?" he asked, struggling as Doran did to pronounce his words in the common tongue.

Reyna and Nathaniel appeared unusually flustered. "I am Ambassador Reyna Galfrey," the elf finally managed, "and this is my husband, Ambassador Nathaniel Galfrey. We have come on behalf of Queen Yelifer Skalaf and, indeed, all of Illian."

Dakmund groaned. "I'm gettin' sick o' hearin' that woman's name!" The stout dwarf turned on Doran. "What are ye doin' with the likes o' an elf an' workin' with the Namdhorians, eh?"

Doran presented his brother with a solid fist. "Watch ye mouth, Dak! These 'ere are friends an' ye'll treat 'em as such, ye hear!"

"Friends?" Dak echoed, looking at his fellow dwarves with an amused smile pulling at his ginger beard. "Doran the conqueror is friends with an elf?" The group erupted in hearty laughter.

Doran ground his teeth. It had been a long time since that title had been attached to him and he hated Reyna and Nathaniel hearing it.

The words that rumbled out of Doran's mouth were closer to a snarl. "Call me that again…" he warned.

Dakmund leaned in to Doran's face. "Take a care, brother. Ye stand before Prince Dakmund, son o' Dorain o' clan Heavybelly! Not some human streak o' piss that can' even lift a sword."

Before he knew it, Doran was holding his axe.

Dakmund straightened up and turned to his camp. "Right, ye lot! Bugger off! Ye not to be seein' the sight o' royal blood." The other dwarves hesitated, clearly enthused at the idea of such a spectacle. "I said get lost!" Dakmund roared.

Doran squeezed the haft of his axe until his knuckles paled. The other dwarves collected their weapons and shuffled out of the hall and into an adjacent tunnel.

Only when the doors closed did Dakmund throw out his arms and embrace his brother with fervour.

Doran's arms were pinned to his side and his eyes bulged in surprise. "What are ye—"

"It's damn good to see ye again, brother!" Dakmund released his older brother and clapped both of his hands around Doran's face. "Look at ye, eh! Ye've aged well on Illian's air!" Seeing Doran's confusion, Dakmund continued, "Oh, sorry abou' all that. Things have changed since ye left." The dwarf held up a clenched fist. "Got to keep up appearances or they get mighty unruly…"

Doran blinked hard a couple of times in an effort to orientate himself. "What are ye talkin' abou', Dak?"

Dakmund casually picked up a half-burning log and aimed it at the door between them and the dwarfs. "Morale really took a dive after ye walked away." He threw the log at the door and shouted, "Take that ye stupid oaf!"

"What are ye doin'?"

Dakmund shrugged his heavy armour. "Got to make it sound real."

Doran shook his head, happy to see that the Galfreys appeared just as confused at the situation. Of all the reunions he had expected, this wasn't even a consideration.

Dakmund gave him a friendly dwarven punch to the arm. "It's so good to see ye, brother!"

Doran put his hands up. "A'right! What is goin' on?"

"After ye left, father's entire rule was brought into question,"

Dakmund said with a sigh. "Ye were the commander o' Grimwhal's armies, the first born son, an' future king. The clan took ye leave as a sign o' no confidence in father's rule. I had to step up, give the clan a future to think abou' after father dines in Grarfath's halls."

"Step up?" Doran took note of his brother's assortment of weapons.

"I started leadin' the campaigns against the Stormshields an' organisin' our defence o' the city to keep them Hammerkegs out. It's been a bloody sixty years, Doran…"

A sudden weight fell upon Doran's heart and he chastised himself for being so selfish. How could he have never considered the consequences? He had always assumed, dwarves being dwarves, that they would call him every name under the mountain and move on to the next war. He never stopped to think about his brother.

"I'm sorry, Dak," he said, unable to meet his brother's eyes.

Dakmund took a step back. "Did ye jus' say *sorry*?" The helmed dwarf looked to Reyna and Nathaniel as if they had put a spell on Doran. "In nearly two hunnered years I never heard ye say that word." Dakmund's quizzical expression expanded into a broad smile again and he clapped his hands around Doran's shoulders. "If I'd known Illian would be so good for ye, I'd have paid the traders me weight in silvyr to take ye through The Iron Valley a century ago!"

Between any other dwarves, Dakmund's response would have been one of ridicule, but Doran knew his brother better than anyone, even their mother. He had always been a gentle soul, for a dwarf, and Doran had done all that he could growing up to protect that nature.

Then he left.

Now, his baby brother had been forced to take on the title of conqueror and crack open the skulls of his kin. Doran had slaughtered dwarves of the other clans for a hundred and sixty years before the nightmares began, in which, every night, he would drown in the blood he had spilled. Dakmund had taken his place for sixty years but he had been of a different nature. How long could he really keep fighting for?

"Do ye still paint?" Doran asked, hopeful that something remained of the brother he knew.

Dakmund flashed the Galfreys a pair of paranoid eyes. "No," he said gruffly. "The overseein' o' clan Heavybellys' art was given to Tolim." He said the name with no lack of venom. "He replaced all the murals an' artwork with axes an' swords. He made an exception for any art that depicted a battle… providin' it had enough blood in it…"

The hint of a smile returned to Doran's face. There was still something of his brother in there. The smile faded when he considered Dakmund's inevitable future. Without Doran, he would assume the mantle of king after their father died. Then, if he was still young enough, he would be expected not only to decree the wars, but also to keep fighting in them. It would break him.

"I'm sorry," he said again.

"Oh, that reminds me." Dakmund's helmed head shot across the gap between them and slammed into Doran's forehead, knocking him clear off his feet. "That's for ye very worst crime!"

With one hand covering his face, Doran held out his other to keep the Galfreys calm, as Nathaniel had pulled his sword an inch from its scabbard. It had been a long time since he had been struck by silvyr… he had forgotten how much it hurt.

"I thought ye were jus' pretendin'!" he said, staggering to his feet again.

"Oh, that wasn't for them lot," Dakmund clarified. "I meant that. Do ye know what happened after ye left?" The red-bearded dwarf reached into his armoured collar and displayed a fine chain of silvyr.

"Oh no…" Doran managed.

"Oh yes!" Dakmund replied with a hint of fury. "Ye didn' think the weddin' would be called off, did ye? Oh no! Father jus' put me in ye place! For sixty *very* long years I've been married to her!"

That was a fate perhaps worse than all the fighting…

"Married who?" Reyna asked.

"Ilgith, daughter of Lord Dorryn… me father's cousin."

With a face like thunder, Dakmund said, "I would rather face all the barbarians o' The Iron Valley in nothin' but me socks than have to go home to her every night." Doran opened his mouth to apologise again. "Don' ye be sayin' yer sorry! It's not gonna cut it!"

"It's not a fate I would o' wished upon anyone," Doran said honestly. "Even the Stormshields... Well, maybe the Stormshields. Have ye never thought o' puttin' a weapon in her hand an' lettin' her loose?"

"Oh, aye! O' course I did." Dakmund looked away in disbelief. "She's gettin' a better reputation than ye had. I even posted her in the western gold mine. It's rumoured she turned away an entire raidin' party o' Hammerkegs with nothin' but a look!"

Doran believed it.

Reyna cleared her throat. "Perhaps we should discuss our current situation before Captain Adan comes charging around the corner?"

"There's no situation *yet*, elf. This only becomes a problem if ye don' pack up yer men and leave."

It was strange to hear his brother talk in such a way. Still, at least he was talking. In another sixty years he would most likely be swinging his axes before a word left his mouth.

"What's inside that workshop that has everyone ready to go to war?" Nathaniel asked.

"Don' know an' don' care," Dakmund replied flatly. "It's ours by right. It was built by dwarves, it's got our writin' on it an' in all likelihood, it's got our weapons inside. It's ours."

Reyna shook her head, but not at Dakmund. "I can't believe Queen Yelifer would be so willing to go to war over a room that *might* have some very old weapons in it."

"They can't even translate the glyphs," Nathaniel pointed out. "How did they know it belonged to a weaponsmith in the first place?"

Dakmund looked at Doran with a furrowed brow. "Are these two listenin' to me?" He eyed the Galfreys. "It's — ours!"

"Our concern, Master Dwarf, lies with the knowledge possessed by the Namdhorians."

"What's that then?" he asked before throwing another log at the door and shouting a new profanity.

Reyna waited until the dwarves' cheering calmed down. "Judging by the point of entry and the extensive journey to reach the workshop, it would appear Queen Yelifer knew exactly where to find it."

Doran agreed. "There can' be a dwarf *alive* who could tell ye how to find this particular workshop."

"So how did she know where it was?" Nathaniel posed.

Dakmund puffed out his chest and nodded his head. "Sounds like ye've got a real mystery on yer hands. Should probably pack up yer men an' be on yer way to find the truth o' it."

"I'm afraid that is only part of our errand, Master Dwarf," Reyna apologised. "We are also here to find a peaceful solution to this claim."

Dakmund twisted his mouth and glanced at the door holding back the dwarves. "Ye want me opinion?" he said quietly. "Ye need to find a way o' openin' them doors an' fast. I can guarantee ye there ain't nothin' o' interest in that dusty ol' workshop. Ye queen might be willin' to fight us for some treasure that don' exist, but me kin *will* go to war with all o' Namdhor over the simple right that an empty room belongs to us. I don't think either o' us want our people dyin' over an empty room now, do we?"

Doran thanked Grarfath that Dakmund still had a level head on his neck. If it had been Doran standing in his place, it would have come to blows by now.

"The sooner ye discover that it has nothin' to offer, the sooner ye'll all be leavin'," Dakmund continued.

"Have you any idea how we open them?" Reyna asked hopefully.

Dakmund shrugged. "I did suggest to father that we consult the library in Silvyr Hall, but he thought it were a stupid idea."

"Ye mean he didn' want to ask King Uthrad for permission," Doran corrected.

"That's abou' right."

"Are you allowed to enter other dwarven kingdoms?" Nathaniel asked. "Would that not be an act of war?"

Doran shook his head. "Silvyr Hall is the rulin' clan, remember. Any clan but the Stormshields would be treated as guests, providin' ye ask permission first."

Dakmund held up his rough hands. "Look, ye've got two more days before father's patience evaporates. After that, these boys have been ordered to march on that workshop and take it back, consequences be damned."

"There is also the problem of Namdhor's army," Reyna added. "They are amassing in The Iron Valley as we speak."

"Oh, we know abou' them. The Goldhorns have already volunteered to stand in their way. Any conflict there is out o' our hands."

Reyna sighed, an unusual demeanour for the elf. "Then we had better find a way to open those doors…"

Doran rubbed his sore head. "I told ye this weren' goin' to end well!"

38

THE EYE OF THE STORM

A stride Ilargo, high above the world with nothing but the clouds for company, Alijah could almost forget his troubles. The green dragon soared over the land with a grace no other creature in all of Verda could claim.

As they broke from The Shining Coast and headed east, over The Adean, the clouds faded to memory and blue skies reigned supreme. The rays of sun that shone down on Ilargo highlighted the golden specks that decorated his scales.

Alijah had taken to flying straight away, settling in behind Gideon. Ilargo was careful with the speed at which he ascended and descended, preventing his stomach from jumping into his throat.

Banking south, they passed by the island nation of Dragorn. The city lay sprawled across the entire island, packed tightly inside its high walls. It possessed one of the largest populations in Verda, though most of its inhabitants took little notice of the rest of the world.

Flying over the hundreds of trading ships, Ilargo journeyed ever southward. The massive archipelago of The Lifeless Isles began with a single island, like the point of a spear, and quickly spread out across The Adean where it finally curved to the west, at the bottom of the isles.

Those in the middle rose high above the ocean, providing towering canyons and lazy rivers of sea water. Alijah sat back and craned his neck to see over Ilargo's horns. The skies above The Lifeless Isles were teaming with dragons, some with riders, some without.

It was an incredible sight, one that he hadn't seen since he was sixteen upon his first visit. A congregation of dragons would never fail to awaken a sense of awe in any being.

The green dragon glided lower and lower until they could fly between the canyons of white rock. Dragons of every colour dropped from the sky and perched on the edges of the cliffs, lining the high valleys. To Alijah's eyes, it looked to be the dragons' idea of a royal welcome.

Alijah had forgotten that to the dragons, Ilargo was seen much in the way Gideon was viewed by the people of Illian. The green dragon was the offspring of Rainael the emerald star, the queen of the dragons.

Ilargo flew effortlessly through the canyons. Alijah looked everywhere he could to see the dwellings of the Dragorn. They inhabited the ancient ruins of their predecessors, inside the small towers that protruded from the rockface and atop the plateaus. Ilargo glided past so fast that the Dragorn looking up at them were gone in a blur.

With a subtle twitch of his wings, Ilargo cut his speed and altered his angle. A large rectangle had been carved out of the canyon on their left, leaving a hollow large enough for a dragon to land inside. Alijah instinctively ducked his head as Ilargo came in to land, missing the rocky ceiling by a few feet.

Following Gideon's lead, Alijah made his way down and onto the hollow's smooth floor. Ilargo grunted once and slipped off the edge, disappearing below the lip, before flying straight up with enough force to blow Alijah's braids about.

"Come with me," Gideon bade.

Doing his best to appear casual after his first flight with a dragon, Alijah turned from the hollow's wide entrance and faced the intimate dwelling therein.

He was standing in the heart of the Dragorn...

The cave walls came to an abrupt stop halfway through and gave way to hewn stone and four circular pillars. Torches lined the walls beyond, illuminating a smaller chamber with a long table and chairs inside.

"Is this..?"

"Yes," Gideon said. "This is the council chamber. It's also my private quarters, but we are here to see neither." The Master Dragorn walked around the table and made for a door on the left.

Alijah's intrigue for all things ancient slowed his own progress and he found himself taking in the detail of everything. His hands reached out and touched the table and chairs, aware that Dragorn had sat in this very room for thousands of years.

Three murals, carved from the walls, depicted long forgotten battles between good and evil.

"I found murals such as these a few years ago," Alijah said, running his fingers over the carvings.

"In that half-buried keep off the west coast," Gideon concluded.

Alijah was on the verge of demanding how he knew that when he remembered who he was talking to. "Of course you know... Was it you who told Hadavad to send me there?"

"You had to cross a mile of The Hox to reach that island. If I had known you were going I would have sent a Dragorn and saved anyone from sailing on those waters."

Alijah recalled the trip well, if only for the monsters he had seen briefly cresting The Hox's surface.

"You found that place following your own leads and instincts," Gideon continued. "You have a talent for such things. That's why I encouraged Hadavad to take you under his wing; we need you."

Alijah stepped away from the mural. "So, you know everything I've found over the last four years?"

Gideon nodded. "I looked into a few of them myself after you left. That site you found in The Spear, the royal graves, was most enlightening."

"I'm sure it was," Alijah replied sardonically.

"I won't apologise for the deception, Alijah." Gideon leaned against the wall with his arms crossed. "You needed this and you would never have taken to it if you knew you were doing it on behalf of the Dragorn."

Alijah scoffed. "Oh, so I should be thanking you for steering my life from behind the scenes? Typical Dragorn…"

Gideon corrected his posture and uncrossed his arms. "Speak ill of me, but I won't hear you speak of the order in such a manner. Your personal feelings towards us will not change the fact that the Dragorn have done nothing but good."

Alijah could feel his calm attitude beginning to fray. "I think the Graycoats would argue that point."

"The Graycoats were an antiquated order of knights. Even your father would attest to that. They couldn't maintain peace."

Alijah smirked. "You mean they weren't deterrent enough?"

Gideon appeared almost hurt by the response. "We don't *force* peace upon the kingdoms, Alijah."

"You misunderstand," the half-elf said, shaking his head. "Half the world is on fire right now. I think you *should* be a little firmer…"

There was a hint of shame on Gideon's face. "The orcs were unforeseen. I can assure you we will be quite *firm* with them."

That calm demeanour was burning away by the second. Alijah could feel rage bubbling under the surface again, its origin unclear, but its intent as strong as ever. He needed to lash out, to hurt. His heart pounded in his chest.

"And after they've been dealt with?" Alijah snapped, unable to contain his mounting frustration. "What then? How long until war breaks out again? I've been trawling through history for a while now and if there's one thing I've found, it's that history repeats itself. War, peace, back to war, peace, war *again*. Eventually, one kingdom will fall out with another or some foreign invader will arrive at our shores."

Gideon took a deep breath, irritatingly calm. "And what would *you* have the Dragorn do?"

Alijah took a step forward. "I would have any enemy of Illian look upon us and tremble. The Dragorn have the power to enforce an everlasting peace that would see every generation thrive better than the last!"

"Alijah..." Gideon was staring at the his hand, which was gripping the hilt of his dagger so tightly that the blood had drained from his knuckles.

The half-elf had to take a breath and collect himself before his hand relinquished the dagger. He flexed his fingers and clenched his fist, examining it as if he didn't recognise the appendage.

Gideon's concern, coupled with the half-elf's flushing cheeks, saw Alijah turn away. As the pounding in his chest began to slow, the pounding in his head only increased. The half-elf rubbed two fingers into his temple, hoping to massage the pain away.

"Forgive me, Master Thorn," he stammered. "I speak out of turn."

Gideon paused for a moment, his expression impossible to read. "Come with me."

Alijah's guilt was soothed by the distraction the library offered. Three tiers of ancient knowledge interspersed with relics and weapons of old, the Dragorn library was a paradise for the half-elf. He wanted to pick up every book and handle every weapon at once.

Gideon led him down to the lowest tier, where several tables were hidden beneath piles of books and rolls of parchment. Alijah took the leather tube, containing the prophecy, off his back and laid it on the table. His eyes couldn't help but take in the titles of the various books.

"You've been reading about The Great War," he observed.

"What do you know of it?" Gideon asked casually, his attention fixed on a cabinet between two bookshelves.

"Not very much, only what Inara told us. The dwarves and orcs fought over territory in Vengora. Then it spilled out into the rest of Illian and the elves became involved."

Gideon opened one of the drawers inside the cabinet. "It took the combined forces of the surface world to win that war."

Alijah flicked lazily through one of the tomes. "With The Arid Lands gone, we're already down one army."

Gideon closed the cabinet and turned back to Alijah. Whatever he had removed from the drawer remained hidden in his closed fist.

"Tell me about Paldora's Fall," the Master Dragorn commanded.

Alijah swallowed and closed the book he had been perusing. "The Crow laid out Asher's bones—"

"Not that part," Gideon interrupted. "Tell me about the first time you saw him."

"Asher?"

Gideon shook his head. "Malliath," he said.

Alijah thought back to the moment he saw those reptilian purple eyes looking back at him. Describing the feeling felt too personal to him, as if he were being asked to bare his soul.

His silence was apparently more telling than anything he could have said, prompting Gideon to continue. "I have spent more time with Malliath the voiceless than any man or elf in a thousand years, since he was first enthralled to the mages of Korkanath. Yet, something tells me you know him better than I do…"

Hearing about Malliath's captivity to the mages only worked to awaken a fire within Alijah. He felt his knuckles crack and the blood return to his face as his teeth clamped together. The thought of the dragon being a slave to anyone clawed at the Alijah's insides.

"Did The Crow do anything to you before the binding spell?" Gideon asked, distracting Alijah from his mounting rage.

The half-elf looked down at the table in an effort regain his composure again. "No. He hit me with a spell that froze me to the spot. He made me watch."

"But you did see him mark Asher?"

Alijah took another breath. "Yes. Malliath looked to have already been marked, around his eye."

Gideon nodded and began to slowly walk around the long table. "I have very few books on The Echoes of The First Kingdom, but those I do have mention nothing of such magic. They can raise the dead, they boast of seeing the future, but there is nothing, not even a scrawl that connects them to dragons. How The Crow bonded

Asher to Malliath is beyond me, but how he bonded *you* to *them*... I do not believe it to be possible."

Alijah could feel Gideon's eyes boring into him. The Master Dragorn's words had an edge to them, as if he were accusing him of something.

"What are you saying?" he asked impatiently.

Gideon flicked his wrist and threw a small object at Alijah. The half-elf snatched it from the air and opened his palm to look upon a pebble. Etched in white across the grey surface was the elvish rune for Dragorn.

Alijah frowned and threw the pebble once into the air before catching it again. "What's the meaning of this?"

"Look again," Gideon said.

Alijah looked down at the engraved pebble and saw nothing but the elvish symbol.

"Turn over your hand,' Gideon instructed.

Alijah sighed, not understanding the point of this exercise. Still, he closed his fingers around the pebble and turned his hand over. He had to look twice when he realised the elvish symbol was glowing under the skin, just below his knuckles.

"I don't..." Alijah couldn't finish his words. Instead, he turned his hand back over and examined the pebble again. It appeared entirely ordinary. Looking at the back of his hand again, the symbol continued to glow through.

"It's called a dragon stone. We don't use them anymore," Gideon explained. "They were created during the time of Elandril, the first Dragorn. The bond between elf and dragon wasn't as understood as it is now. Back then, they believed that you were *born* a Dragorn. They eventually came to realise that a bond needed to be formed *first* before the stone could detect it."

Alijah had devoted his life to putting cryptic puzzles together and connecting dots that spanned thousands of years. It didn't take more than a second to put the Master Dragorn's words together and understand his meaning... He just couldn't comprehend their consequences.

"You're saying…" Alijah held out the pebble, inspecting the back of his hand. "You're saying I'm…"

"Bonded to Malliath the voiceless," Gideon finished. "Naturally, that is…" he added softly.

Alijah couldn't focus on anything and he dropped the pebble on to the table. The elvish symbol faded immediately, leaving his head to spin.

He was a Dragorn? No. Alijah shook his head; he didn't want to be a Dragorn. He had given up on that dream years ago. He didn't want anything to do with their order. He didn't need a dragon to make him special. He wasn't even… immortal?

There was no denying the sense in Gideon's words, that much he could rationalise. That meant his entire being would be shared with Malliath, granting him eternal life. *Is* that what it meant? Alijah put a hand to his forehead, struggling to contain the thoughts and questions that wanted to come out at once.

The Master Dragorn walked back around the table to face him. "In the time I spent with Malliath, his most defining trait was his rage. He had always harboured a temper, but a thousand years under the mages of Korkanath ignited a fire in him that has yet to be extinguished. I see that same rage burning inside of you now."

"You don't know me!" Alijah spat.

"I know this anger that bubbles under the surface is new to you. You don't know how to control it yet. That's because it's not your anger. It comes from Malliath…"

Alijah ran his hand over the table and launched a pile of books across the floor. "You don't know what you're talking about! You know Malliath as well as you know me!"

"It doesn't change the fact that you're bonded to him, and naturally. When you saw him, did the whole world come to a stop, as if the two of you were the only ones in it? Did you see yourself through his eyes?"

Alijah didn't answer any of his questions, but it was clear to see from Gideon's face that his expression alone had told the truth.

"That's a relatively common occurrence," he continued. "More than half report a similar experience."

Alijah stepped back, seeing Gideon's attempt at comforting him. He didn't need it and he didn't want it.

"It's alright," Gideon said quietly. "Your feelings towards me and the order are reflective of the way Malliath feels about us. He too doesn't want to be a part of this."

"My feelings are my own," Alijah insisted.

"To an extent," Gideon agreed. "The bond has yet to be fully formed. You need more time with him, though I suspect the spell between Asher and Malliath will be something of an obstacle."

Alijah whipped up a finger. "Stop. Talking." He needed a moment to collect himself. Just looking at Gideon made him angry, let alone listening to his voice talk about him as if he knew everything.

The significance of the single, most important thing to ever happen to him was clouded by a mist of rage. The rational side to his mind could see that his rising temper had increased dramatically since being around Gideon and other Dragorn.

Quite out of character, Gideon turned away and frowned at nothing. "What?" he exclaimed suddenly.

Alijah searched the otherwise empty library, wondering what Gideon was reacting too.

"Sorry," he apologised, looking back to Alijah. "I was talking to Ilargo. The Dragorn I sent to The Arid Lands have just reported their findings."

The drastic change in subject worked to pull Alijah from his angry haze. "What is it?" he asked.

"They've checked all three cities. Tregaran, Ameeraska, Calmardra... There isn't a single body to be found."

The half-elf looked away, recalling the streets of Tregaran, littered with bodies. "That's impossible. I was there, I saw them. There were hundreds of dead in the streets."

Gideon cupped his beard. "Not anymore."

"The orcs took them?" Alijah mused.

Gideon looked to the books sprawled across the table. "There was mention of bones in one of Elandril's biographies. They hold some significance for the orcs."

Alijah thought of Tauren's body being taken underground by those foul beasts and torn apart for his bones.

"There are more answers here," Gideon stated, taking in the library. "We just need to find them."

"We?" Alijah echoed.

"You have skills I would utilise. Also... You're a Dragorn now; you belong here."

Alijah shook his head. "I'm not a Dragorn, Gideon." He waited for the anger to resurface but it stayed buried this time, offering him a measure of control.

"Not yet," Gideon quipped.

Alijah concerned himself with the orcs and their sudden attack, hoping that the gravity of that situation would keep his anger in check and distract him from thoughts about his potential immortality.

"Sorry about these," Alijah said, picking up the books he had launched from the table.

"You can make up for it by reading them," the Master Dragorn replied. "The books on this table are everything I can find that relates to the time of The Great War."

"What are you going to do?" Alijah asked, getting the feeling that he would be the one doing all the research.

"I'm going to give this new prophecy a look."

"Not without me you're not," Alijah protested, careful to keep his tone light. "I found it. I want to be present for any examination."

The Master Dragorn tilted his head, weighing Alijah's demands. "Fair enough."

Gideon walked up to a tall set of shelves lined with red books. Thin chains ran across the shelves, though they appeared more decorative than anything else. Showing no interest in the books, Gideon pushed his hand into one of the stone slabs beside the shelves. The whole slab disappeared into the wall and set off a series of grinding noises and cogs.

Alijah had seen something similar in The Pick-Axe.

The bookshelf spun around to reveal a cabinet with glass doors on it. Inside were only two objects: a rolled up scroll the length of a man's arm and a very thick, ancient-looking book.

"When do *I* get my own secret wall?" Alijah asked.

"When I'm confident you won't gamble away the contents..." Gideon replied, his attention on the scroll he was delicately removing.

"Is that what I think it is?" Alijah asked, his eyes on the book rather than the scroll.

Gideon closed the cabinet doors and returned to the table, scroll in hand. "That depends on what you think it is."

"I *think* it's Atilan's grimoire and I *think* I'd love to read it." Alijah barely noticed the scroll Gideon was rolling out on the adjacent table. "That book was found by my grandmother," he said, his feet taking him towards the cabinet.

"Yes," Gideon agreed. "At the end of The War for the Realm. She was with Galanör at the time."

"And in Ayda," Alijah added, excited by the mere presence of such an ancient relic.

"I was hoping, some day, that you and Hadavad might get a chance to explore some of south Ayda. There may well be other locations Atilan put down his flag."

Alijah's hands rested against the glass of the cabinet. "The fact that Atilan's kingdom even stretched to Ayda is incredible. He commanded the largest empire the world has ever seen."

"Yes." Gideon's voice was right behind him now and a firm hand rested on his shoulder. "And that book is very dangerous," he warned. "It's written in the ancient language, making it a pain to translate, but what I did learn put dread in my bones. Atilan was a mad wizard with a lust for power and a penchant for hurting people. Much like our Crow problem..."

Alijah wanted desperately to get his hands on that book. It was the kind of find he could spend his entire life searching for and never come across it.

"Come," Gideon steered him away from the cabinet. "I need your eye for detail. We need to learn all that we can."

The Master Dragorn laid out his prophecy and Alijah removed

his from the leather tube and put it down beside the other one. Side by side, there was an immediate similarity.

"They're both human skin," Gideon observed.

Alijah tried his best to contain his excitement at looking upon The Echoes of Fate, the prophecy that foretold of The War for the Realm. It was in exquisite condition compared to the one he had found in The Wild Moores, with every word legible and barely a stain on it.

"They look roughly the same age," Alijah added. He tentatively reached out and thumbed both scrolls at the same time, feeling for the texture.

"There is some significant damage to this one," Gideon said, pointing out the water stains and patches.

Alijah retrieved his notebook with the words written down that Ellöria had translated. "Did Galanör tell you about the protection spell?" he asked, flicking through the pages of his notebook.

"Yes, he said it cannot be destroyed. That means all this damage was done thousands of years ago."

"Exactly," Alijah agreed. "So, did The Echoes deliberately ruin it so that we could only read a few words, or did it get accidentally damaged and they put a protection spell on it to prevent further decay?"

Alijah watched Gideon study both scrolls, his inspection intense. "Do you believe it then?" he asked the Master Dragorn. "Do you believe The Echoes could see the future? Or that The Crow can see it now? He boasts of such."

"I'm more than aware of his boasting," Gideon replied with a strange glance at the long mirror in the corner. "Whether The Crow can see the future or not, the ancient priests of The Echoes certainly could. Every line of The Echoes of Fate came true."

Alijah looked down at the immaculate prophecy, aware that the first verse actually had a reference to Gideon, if it was believed to be true. "Hadavad believes it can be applied—"

"To any narrative," Gideon finished. "I know what Hadavad thinks. His judgement of The Echoes, and especially their current iteration, has always been clouded by his hate and fears. I would ask that you suspend disbelief and accept anything and everything as possible. Only an open mind will get to the truth, Alijah."

"But how can anyone see what hasn't happened yet? That magic doesn't exist."

Gideon folded his arms. "You've been mentored by a man who has survived the centuries by transferring his essence from one host to the next. I would start believing in everything until proven otherwise…"

Alijah couldn't argue with that. He had seen a lot of strange things over the last four years. Most folk would call him a liar if he told them of his exploits.

"Here's Lady Ellöria's translation." Alijah handed over his notebook.

Gideon read aloud, "*As the Age turns to ruin, so too will the light turn to darkness.* Some mention of a pact… *A warrior shall be resurrected in the heart of a fallen star.*" He looked down at the damaged prophecy. "Something about a dragon… *Only magic wrought of unity can break the chains…*" Gideon stopped reading for a moment and looked up, his musings private. "*Immortal ash?* It's a shame that part's damaged. *Through the forge of war, the world will have…*" The Master Dragorn sighed. "Well, that's suitably irritating."

"Lady Ellöria believed we were meant to find it," Alijah explained. "She believed the only thing The Black Hand had to gain from it was our travelling south, to Paldora's Fall."

Gideon nodded along. "Therefore placing you in front of Malliath and binding you into the spell with Asher. It certainly complicates things."

Alijah considered the master's conclusion. "It would mean The Crow knew I would naturally bond with Malliath…"

Gideon reluctantly agreed. "More evidence that The Crow can see the future."

Alijah shook his head. "Or it was foretold in an ancient prophecy The Black Hand have access to."

Gideon kept his eyes on the scrolls. "Were you given directions to the cave in The Wild Moores?" he asked.

Alijah thought for a moment. "No. Vighon and I were searching those woods for two weeks before we came across it. It was Hadavad who suggested we search the heart of The Wild Moores. He said that when the survivors of The First Kingdom fled the dragons, they would have travelled deep into the forest."

Gideon leaned over the table with both hands supporting him. "As ruined as it is, I would say it's useless to us now. If its intent *was* to see you travel south, the damage has already been done. Hadavad was right, our priority should be finding a way to break the spell. We need to strengthen your bond with Malliath and separate him from Asher."

Alijah could see the ranger thrashing around on the hewn table when he closed his eyes. "Regardless of the bonding spell between them, Asher is still enslaved to The Crow. I saw him burn the spell into his chest."

"We'll deal with that when we can," Gideon replied. "If Malliath attacks again, we'll have no choice but to engage him. That could be life-threatening for you."

The idea of the Dragorn hurting Malliath caused Alijah's fist to clench again.

"We won't kill him," Gideon assured in a soothing tone.

Alijah took a breath, believing the Master Dragorn. "What do we do next then?"

Gideon stood up straight and blew out a long breath. "We have our work cut out for us. We need to find a way of breaking the forced bond between Asher and Malliath, or at least weakening the bond between *you* and Malliath; that way you won't feel everything he does. We also need to research the orcs and The Great War." Gideon looked down at the two prophecies. "*And* we need to examine these in more detail."

Alijah took in the size of the library. "The orcs will have taken over all of Verda before we get through all this."

"Agreed," Gideon said. "I've got most of the Dragorn patrolling Illian right now, but some of our younger members remain in the isles. I will recruit some help."

It was a strange thought, but Alijah didn't like the idea of researching without Vighon looking out for him. His northern friend might not have a love for learning anything other than swordplay, but his company was always welcomed. He found explaining things to Vighon helped him to grasp a better understanding himself.

He could really do with talking to him now. The knowledge that he was, in fact, bonding to Malliath continued to push out from the back of his mind, attempting to distract him from the tasks at hand.

Excitement, anxiety, and fear raged in his mind like a storm. For the first time in his life, there was a sense that he was meant for something more, though Malliath's essence, now a part of him, coloured his emotions and beliefs.

In the eye of that emotional storm, Alijah had a moment of peace and clarity. It was an inescapable thought, but he knew right then, bonded with Malliath, that he was capable of something truly great... or something truly terrible.

CLOUDLESS THUNDER

Vighon could see that Galanör was becoming frustrated and it did nothing but encourage the northman. He continued through the motions of his stretching regime, determined to finish them.

The ranger pulled one face after another, waiting with his scimitars in hand, as the night moved steadily closer to day.

"How long does this go on for?" the elf asked.

Vighon put his fingers into his left shoulder joint and rotated his arm. "Stretching's important."

Galanör sighed. "The entire caravan will be on the move again soon."

"Are all elves as dramatic as you?" Vighon bent down and touched his toes.

Galanör's eyes narrowed and a wicked grin pulled at his mouth. "Not every foe will allow you time to stretch."

The elf flicked up his scimitars and lunged at Vighon, crossing the snowy clearing in two quick steps. Vighon had anticipated this response, however, and easily reached for his shield. Galanör's blades came down as one, failing to even dent the enchanted shield.

Crouched under the assault, Vighon took the force of it as he clenched his other fist. Surprising the ranger from under the concealment of his shield, Vighon punched him in the gut, lifting the elf from his feet for just a second. The northerner jumped up and roughly grabbed Galanör's belt, over his doubled form, and pushed him into the snow face down.

Galanör's face lifted from the ground, spitting snow, with red fury in his eyes. "You said you wanted to spar!"

Vighon retrieved his sword from the ground and spun it around once. "I said, *let's see what you're made of.* Sparring is for lords and children." The northerner hammered his blade against his shield. "Come on then."

Galanör sneered and picked himself up, shrugging the excess snow from his shoulders. "You should have said spar…"

The elf dashed forward and combined running with some kind of dance, confusing Vighon as to which blade was going to come down first. The northerner turned his body at the last second and raised his shield to catch the edge of one of the scimitars. As he brought himself back around, behind the elf now, he swung his sword backhand only to find that Galanör was no longer standing there.

The ranger had dropped into a roll and come up a few feet away, his blades spinning about him hypnotically.

"Your defence and movements were good," Galanör observed. "Your counterattack was predictable."

Vighon cracked his neck and advanced on the elf. A short jump into the air allowed him to come down on Galanör tip first with a skewering thrust. The ranger reacted just as Vighon knew he would and imitated the same defensive spin that he had just used. When the northerner's feet touched the ground, he had but to push out with his shield and knock Galanör off his balance.

The ranger was pushed back, but he turned his momentum into an unorthodox flip, bringing him back comfortably onto his feet.

"Predictable enough for you?" Vighon grinned.

Galanör stalked back into the centre of the small clearing. "You use your shield as a weapon too, that's good. But its size also blocks your sight any time you use it. I'll demonstrate." The elf matched his grin.

Vighon didn't wait for the ranger to attack him. The northerner started forward and dropped one knee, swiping his blade low at Galanör's legs. A simple lift of the leg saw the elf avoid the sword and the slightest shift in his shoulders saw him avoid the next swipe as Vighon reversed his swing.

With reflexes and strength Vighon could only dream of, Galanör gripped his wrist, squeezing the hilt from his hand, and slammed one boot into the northerner's gut. Vighon rolled back through the snow, gripping his stomach.

Galanör examined one of his scimitars and threw it perfectly into the nearest tree, where it didn't so much as wobble.

Vighon used his shield to help himself to his knees. His sword shone in the moonlight, half buried in the snow. The northerner feigned his reach for the blade and turned his movement into a forward roll, bringing him directly in front of Galanör. The elf side-stepped the first swing of his steel-rimmed shield and came at Vighon with three strikes of his own, all of which were met by the enchanted wood.

Of course, every time he lifted the shield to parry, Galanör was lost from sight. The elf appeared in a different place every time, coming at Vighon from a different angle of attack. Eventually, he lifted the shield to block an attack that never came. Instead, Galanör had dropped to one knee and tucked his scimitar under the shield, where it now rested against Vighon's chest.

"Your shield is good," the elf commented. "But your sword is better. Don't substitute it for the shield."

Vighon had a witty response on the end of his tongue when the sound of clapping broke across the clearing. Both elf and man turned in surprise to see Inara Galfrey leaning against one of the trees with a bemused smile on her face.

"The king of Lirian offers you both a place at his table, yet you would prefer to fight in the woods…"

"You mean that big fancy tent of his?" Vighon strapped his shield over his back again and retrieved his fallen sword.

Galanör was inclined to agree. "It is a little... big, considering the circumstances of everybody else."

"That's why I convinced King Weymund to turn it over to the cooks," Inara said with the hint of a smile on her face. "The queues are so long you'll be lucky if there's anything left for the two of you."

"Thank you for your concern, Inara." Galanör bowed his head. "We are part of a small camp on the southern edge of the caravan for tonight. I'm sure we will find something."

Vighon heard every word that passed between them, but he barely took any of it in. The northerner was desperately trying to think of something to say to Inara, anything. He wanted to make her laugh and smile.

"Have you eaten?" Galanör asked the Dragorn.

Vighon hid his dismay, deciding that he should have asked that question instead of standing there like an idiot.

"Not yet," Inara replied in a melodic tone that reminded Vighon of Lady Ellöria. "Athis is patrolling the skies, so we have yet to find anywhere to rest."

"You can rest with us," Vighon blurted, drawing an amused look from Galanör. "If you want," he added. "I'm sure King Weymund has another big tent..."

Inara waited patiently for him to finish his babbling. "I find kings to be a little stuffy," she said.

The lightest of chuckles came from the ranger as he patted Vighon on the arm. "Let's make for camp. I can't feel my feet anymore..."

Vighon waited for Inara to start following the elf before he fell in behind them. He just needed to take a breath and have a quiet word with himself. They weren't fifteen anymore.

Breaking through the tree line, The Selk Road was entirely hidden from east to west. Small fires had been lit in the middle of the makeshift camps and tents had been erected in every available space. The survivors of Lirian had been taken in by the larger caravan from Vangarth: the people of The Evermoore looked after each other.

This is how it should be, Vighon thought.

Galanör led the way, weaving between the different camps and heading south-west. King Weymund's tent, easily spotted, had smoke pouring out of it and long queues of people holding empty bowls.

The barking of a dog told Vighon that they had arrived at their camp. "Nelly!" The northerner crouched down and intercepted the running dog. She paced in circles as he scratched and stroked her shaggy fur.

Finding both her and Russell Maybury alive had brought the first smile to Vighon's face after Alijah left with Gideon. Camping with them had seemed the obvious fit, considering their history... and Russell's supplies.

"You've missed most of the food," the werewolf announced, "but I saved you both some sausages."

Vighon felt his stomach lurch at the mere sound of sausages. He rubbed his hand into Nelly's head and made for the fire.

"I'm a vegetarian," Galanör said apologetically.

Russell thought for a moment. "Oh, there's some veggies in the cart! Help yourself, Master Galanör."

Vighon sat down on one of the logs and tried to subtly glance at the moon above. It wasn't quite full.

"Fear not, Mr. Draqaro," Russell said quietly. "If it was a full moon I wouldn't be here."

"I meant no offence," the northerner replied.

"None taken," Russell said happily, handing over a plate of food to both him and Inara.

The Dragorn sat beside him on the log, ushering in an awkward silence between the two. Russell soon left to help Galanör search for food and the silence stretched on until it became an almost physical presence.

Thankfully, Nelly turned up, though whether she was after more attention or one of his sausages was debatable. Vighon busied himself with the dog until the rangers returned to the fire.

A few others came and went, but the four unusual companions shared food and swapped a few tales. There was certainly no end of stories between a werewolf, a Dragorn, and an elven ranger with four hundred years on his life. Vighon kept on the quiet side, keeping his own life experiences to himself.

As the moon began to disappear over the top of the trees, Galanör and Russell made for their tents. It was only after they left that Vighon realised there was no one but him and Inara around the fire. Even Nelly had fallen asleep.

"Don't you need rest?" he asked.

Inara shrugged. "Rest is good, but we don't need it as often as others. We are sustained, in part, by the strength of the dragons."

"That's… handy." Vighon berated himself immediately. Did he really say that?

Another awkward silence fell upon them.

"You were quiet this evening," Inara commented. "I don't ever remember you being quiet when we were younger."

Recalling those earlier days brought a smile to Vighon's face, easing the tension he felt. Those days contained some of his best memories.

"I enjoyed listening to all of your tales," he said, unsure what else to say.

"You're worried about him, aren't you?"

"Alijah?" Vighon thought about his friend. "Worrying about him is what keeps him alive, usually."

Inara offered him a warm smile, melting more of his tension away. "You look out for him. You always did. In fact, I remember the first time he tried to use my mother's bow. She had warned us plenty of times that it wasn't a toy." The half-elf let out a little laugh. "He could barely pull back the string, but with that bow it didn't matter."

Vighon remembered. "The arrow went straight through the barn doors," he laughed.

"It *destroyed* the barn doors," Inara corrected. "You grabbed the bow off him and said it was you."

Vighon sniggered. "Your mother was furious."

"She knew it wasn't you," Inara added.

"So did *my* mother, but I still got punished for lying…"

The pair went quiet again after that. The camps had followed suit, with only the sound of fires crackling and the occasional patrol of knights.

Vighon turned to see Inara watching him intently, her eyes passing over the scar that cut into his right eyebrow and the continuation down his cheek. The scar on his forehead caught her eye too and her features softened.

"What happened to you, Vighon?" she whispered. "I left for The Lifeless Isles and the next time I heard from home you had gone."

Vighon looked away, deciding the fire was a better place to focus his gaze. There were two things he and Alijah never talked about: the half-elf's family issues and Vighon's time in Namdhor. Still, Inara's voice was like honey, compelling him to do anything to hear more of it.

"Shortly after you left," he began, "my grandfather died. He had a fishing business in Skystead. There was no one left but my mother to take over." Vighon paused, aware of the story's final destination. "We said our farewells to your family and left for the north again. A year, maybe two, after we took over the business, the Red Pox hit Skystead. My mother died soon after."

Inara looked hurt. "I'm so sorry, Vighon. Your mother was a wonderful person."

Vighon tried to smile, but his memories were resurfacing now. "I had no idea how to keep the business going after that," he continued. "It all fell apart. By the time I was twenty, I was living on the streets of Skystead. That was a cold and… hungry time." He tried to say it jovially, lightening the dark tone he had placed over their conversation.

"That sounds awful," Inara replied, her body turned towards him now.

"I was only on the streets for a year or so. Word reached my father in Namdhor."

"Your father?" Inara looked confused. "I didn't know your father was still alive."

"He's the reason my mother fled south and ended up in your

family's employ. She didn't want me growing up around him." If Vighon could thank his mother for the years she gave him out of his father's reach, he surely would.

"What happened?" Inara asked before he could fall into his memories.

"I welcomed the warmth and the food without question," he replied. "Arlon had quite the estate in Namdhor, servants too. He lived like a king and for a very short time, I wondered why my mother had fled from him."

"Why? Was he that bad?"

"Bad? Bad is too small a word to describe Arlon Draqaro. He's got wickedness in his bones." Vighon turned to look at Inara. "My father is the head of The Ironsworn gang."

Inara looked away for a moment. "I've heard of them. Master Rolan has had dealings with them. Vicious by all accounts."

"They basically rule the north — that is to say, my father does. He used the civil war for the throne to gain leverage and power. Now they have control over every town and city in the region."

The Dragorn's beautiful eyes bored into him. "What did he do to you, Vighon?"

The northerner took a long breath and pulled back the sleeve covering his left arm. The underside of his forearm bore a long tattoo of straight lines and sharp angles. The two lines were entwined and ended at his wrist in a spear-like point.

"I joined The Ironsworn willingly at first. I'd been on the streets living like a beggar and before that we had struggled to survive with the business. Arlon gave me power, resources, men at my back. Of course, he gave me the easier jobs in the beginning. Collecting *taxes* as he called it." Vighon closed his eyes and did his best to recall everything without the images and sounds.

"Don't pity me," he said softly. "I actually enjoyed it for the first few years. I became a regular in the fighting rings. *Arlon's* fighting pits. Two enter and only one comes out. I was easily the best fighter he had, but I wasn't brutal enough for his liking. He started giving me different jobs in the hopes of making me more like him. I did… things. Things that will stay with me for the rest of my life."

Inara put a gentle hand on his shoulder, though he didn't feel he deserved it.

"When I refused or failed him…" Vighon licked his lips and gestured to the scars on his face. "He hated that I had enjoyed years with your family."

"I'm so sorry." Inara had the beginnings of tears in her eyes.

"I was trapped in that world for ten years," he said. "Until one day, when Arlon sent me to one of his rackets. He told me there was a young man who had been caught cheating at one of the tables."

Inara met his eyes with a knowing look. "Alijah…"

Vighon finally smiled and meant it. "They had him in the back, hanging by his wrists from the ceiling. They had already beaten him pretty bad, but Arlon had commanded me to take his fingers and thumbs. *Never kill them*, he would say. *You need them to spread the word.*" Vighon shook his head, deeply ashamed that there had been times when he had obeyed that command.

"But you didn't," Inara said. "You helped him instead."

"I just reacted. I couldn't explain it then and I can't now. I drew my sword and… well, we walked out of there. He told me what he was doing with Hadavad and I joined them. It was either that or return to Namdhor and face Arlon. Son or not, he would have killed me slowly for what I did."

"It would seem my family owe you a great debt, then. If it were not for you, my brother would be dead."

"He'd be dead eight times over," Vighon added with a mirthless chuckle. He waved her questioning look away. "No one is in debt to me," he said. "There are families out there that are still broken because of me."

Inara's tone took on a firmer edge. "You are a good man, Vighon Draqaro. I know—"

The Dragorn's words were cut off as panic beset the entire caravan. The ground shook violently beneath their feet, disturbing the horses and collapsing tents in a single quake. Russell's cart toppled over and the supplies fell across the fire, extinguishing the flames. The people screamed from one end of the camp to the other.

"What is this?" Vighon cried. It was stronger than any of the recent quakes.

The trees swayed with some of the weaker ones snapping and falling into the road. More screams followed and the snow was shaken from the branches of the pines as if hit by a wave.

Inara looked down and Vighon followed her gaze. The ground had cracked here and there but, thankfully, remained intact.

Galanör and Russell scrambled out of their tents and Nelly barked, adding to the chaotic din.

"What's going on?" Russell asked, bracing his legs against the rumble.

"The orcs?" Galanör suggested.

Vighon recalled the attack on Tregaran. "The ground didn't shake like this! This is something else!"

Scared horses galloped through their camp, forcing people to dive out of the way.

Then it stopped.

Vighon joined the others in searching the ground. "Is it over?"

Cries for help spread across the caravan. Vighon knew the sound of people in pain when he heard it. Between their combined strength, Galanör and Russell were able to shift one of the fallen trees, allowing Inara and Vighon to drag two men to safety. Others were bloodied and injured, walking around aimlessly in search of help or loved ones.

Boom!

A collective gasp filled the night air as the sky cracked. Above them, the stars shone over the icy night, not a cloud in sight.

Boom!

Vighon winced every time the sky thundered. "What is that?"

"I've never heard anything like that," Inara said.

"I have," Russell panted. "Thirty years ago, when Paldora's Star hit The Undying Mountains. That's what it sounded like."

Boom!

Everyone gasped again and flinched. The mighty crack was sharp, startling the senses.

"I'm going to find King Weymund!" Inara declared, making for the largest tent.

"We need to get everyone moving again!" Galanör called after her.

Inara paused, looking back. "I'll advise him to give the command!"

Vighon watched her disappear into the chaos.

"Come on!" Galanör patted him on the arm. "Let's help as many as we can!"

Vighon inhaled a deep breath and took in the sight of a few thousand people, all panicked and several injured. It was going to be a longer night than he thought...

40

THE ENEMY OF MY ENEMY...

The sound of small pumice raining over his armour roused Doran Heavybelly with a start. The dwarf snapped his eyes open and reached instinctively for the axe on his hip.

Then the very rock under his feet shook, rattling the loose stones and pebbles. The Namdhorian soldiers jumped to their feet, snatching at their swords.

"They're attacking!" one of them cried.

Nathaniel and Reyna huddled closer together, wary of the ceiling above. Doran picked himself up and pressed his palm to the nearest wall.

"Whatever that is," he said, "it's comin' from the deep, not in these tunnels."

"You can feel it?" Nathaniel asked incredulously.

"Aye." Doran listened to the mountain through his hand. "It's mighty strong whatever it is..."

The quake stopped as abruptly as it began, leaving them all clueless to its source. Doran had felt quakes for months now, but nothing strong enough to shake Vengora.

Captain Adan sent six more of his men into the tunnels, just to be sure that the dwarves weren't in the midst of planning an attack. Doran left them to it.

"Are ye a'right?" he asked the Galfreys.

They stood to their full height, still cautious of the ceiling and the tons of rock that concealed the night's sky.

"Those quakes are getting worse, it seems," Reyna said.

"It's over now," Doran assured. Now that he was awake, he was confident he would feel any more before they affected the structure of the tunnels.

Nathaniel looked at the dwarf. "I can't believe you can sleep at a time like this. Your brother just told us—"

"I know what he told us," Doran snapped, irritated by the whole situation. "Sorry, lad. This is just... Well, it's not what I wanted. Threats from me father don' help either. I don' suppose ye've figured out how to open those doors then?"

Reyna glanced at her husband. "Actually we were about to try something a little more drastic."

Doran followed her eyes to the bow in her hand. "Ye mean to hit 'em with that?" The dwarf had seen the power of that enchanted bow many times and knew better than to get in front of it.

"I've yet to see anything it can't penetrate," Reyna replied, admiring the weapon.

Doran shrugged. "I'd be more concerned with the damage it does on the other side..."

Taking up their positions in the middle of the T-junction, the elf nocked an arrow and aimed at the doors.

"You must be joking," Captain Adan remarked. "You think an arrow can open those doors?"

Nathaniel turned to the captain. "This is the bow of Adellum, general to Valanis for over a thousand years." Captain Adan looked at the bow again, his eyes betraying the awe he felt. "They called Adellum Valanis's battering ram during The Dark War," Nathaniel continued. "There was a reason for that..."

Reyna pulled back the bowstring until her hand rested comfortably by the corner of her mouth. The arrow was launched from the bow as any other only, from this bow, the arrow was gifted the strength of magic.

The arrow bounced off the doors.

Doran had been bracing himself for the almighty explosion. "Are ye sure ye brought the right bow, me Lady?"

Reyna's elven composure had been cracked, exposing a confusion seen more often on humans. The ambassador retrieved the arrow from the floor and inspected the head.

"It's blunted..." she said to herself.

Nathaniel came to stand before the doors of the workshop and ran his hand over the area where the arrowhead struck. "It didn't even dent the doors."

"I told you," Captain Adan said. "We've tried all manner of magic. That's why Master Devron was sent for."

"Yes!" Petur Devron burst forth from the Namdhorian soldiers with two arms full of scrolls and parchments.

Doran sighed. "Here we go," he said quietly. "His voice is like a hammer to me head..."

"Queen Skalaf, erm, well, that is Lord Draqaro, believes the dwarven symbols tell us how to gain entry," Petur continued happily.

"The more Arlon Draqaro wants to get inside," Nathaniel commented, "the more inclined I am to hand it over to the dwarves."

"Those are treasonous words, Ambassador Galfrey." Captain Adan's voice had the edge of a threat.

Never one to back down, Nathaniel pressed, "Is that because Arlon Draqaro is the one ruling Namdhor?"

Adan raised his chin. "He might not be on the throne, but Arlon Draqaro is still a lord of Namdhor. That means we serve him."

Nathaniel nodded along. "Remind me, Captain, what was *Lord* Draqaro before he became a lord?"

Adan glanced back at his men nervously. Doran looked to the soldiers as well and wondered which of them were in Arlon's pocket, more than ready to stab Captain Adan in the back.

"He was a businessman," the captain replied confidently, as if he had been given the line previously. "When the north was fighting for the throne, he maintained the supply of food and drink for the city. He was granted the title of lord by way of a gift, from Queen Skalaf herself."

Reyna discarded her blunted arrow. "Perhaps we should focus our efforts on the door," she said, her melodic voice extinguishing the tension. "First Commander Dakmund warned us of our timeframe."

"Bah!" Doran was becoming frustrated as the eve of battle approached. "We've been tryin' to open this door for two days. They've been tryin' for even longer. This door is sealed by magic an' it ain't dwarven magic, I'll tell ye that for nothin'."

"How do you know it's not dwarven magic?" Petur asked before anyone else, his eyes reflecting his hunger for knowledge.

"Dwarves have a natural resilience to the affects of magic, praise Grarfath, but there are a few who possess the talents to use it. Trust me, dwarves don't know how to do anythin' with magic that ain't destroyin' stuff."

Petur Devron didn't look so convinced. "But this is a dwarven kingdom. It stands to reason that dwarves placed the spell over the doors. The writing is—"

"I know what the writin' is an' I know where we are," Doran cut him off. "An' I'm still tellin' ye, that ain't dwarven magic, lad!"

"This chamber is thousands of years old," Master Devron argued, still wearing his idiot's smile. "Who else could it be?"

"Elves…" Reyna's answer came from behind them.

Doran turned around to see Reyna with her hand pressed to one of the doors. The elf closed her eyes as if listening for something. Then her attention turned to the hole in the rock, opposite the doors.

"What is it?" Nathaniel asked.

"I do not know," Reyna admitted. "But I believe it was *my* kin who sealed these doors, not dwarves."

Petur scratched his head through his wild mane. "I don't mean to cast doubt on you, Ambassador Reyna, but from all that we know about dwarves, both ancient and present, they never got on with elves. Present company excluded, of course!" he added, looking down on Doran.

"They were allies during The Great War," Reyna replied, her attention still on the doors.

Petur's mouth twisted into an apologetic grin. "Sorry, which war was that?"

Reyna's attention had flitted up to the engraved symbols now. "Five thousand years ago, our two people allied to fight the orcs," she said absently.

This did nothing to clear things up for Master Devron. "Fight what? I don't... I..." the master looked at his many scrolls in confusion.

"Orcs, lad! Ye must o' seen those ugly skeletons on yer way in!"

"Yes, yes, yes..." Petur's face screwed up. "There's no mention of any Great War in the archives."

Doran laughed. "Maybe ye should think o' changin' the name from All-Tower to Some-Tower!"

Nathaniel joined his wife. "Reyna, what are you thinking?"

The elf couldn't rightly say. "This magic reminds me of the spell Lady Syla placed upon the gates in The Arid Lands. It will budge for nothing."

"What were elves doin' this far into Vengora?" Doran asked. "Even durin' the war, they fought on the surface, never in the mountains."

Reyna looked to reply, only the words were drowned out by the loud echo of chanting dwarfs. It had been a long time since Doran had heard one of the Heavybelly's rhythmic war cries. It certainly sounded different on the receiving end of their march.

"Doran?" Nathaniel gripped the hilt of his sword.

"Times up," the dwarf replied solemnly.

"Shields!" Captain Adan barked. "Corbyn, find the patrols and bring them back, *now!*"

The son of Dorain watched the Namdhorians form up and draw their swords behind their pointed shields. They looked fierce packed together, well trained too judging by their reactions. It would make no difference, he knew. Those shields wouldn't stand up to silvyr weapons, nor would their fine white armour.

Petur Devron didn't seem to grasp the gravity of their situation. "Perhaps we could get a message to the elves in Ayda? There might be someone who—"

"Get behind us, ye fool!" Doran pushed the wiry man back and drew his sword and his axe.

The chanting resounded off the stone, growing louder with its promise of violence and death. Between their words, the dwarves of the Heavybelly clan beat their weapons against their armour.

Reyna nocked an arrow and strode out in front of the Namdhorian line. Her defiant stance reminded Doran that this elf wasn't just an ambassador, she was an elven princess and a veteran of war. A man without fear, Nathaniel drew his blade and joined his wife in front of the soldiers. All the silvyr in Dhenaheim wouldn't keep these two from laying low any dwarf who attacked them.

"Get out of the way, ambassadors!" Adan ordered from behind his shield.

Doran walked out to meet them. "Yer gonna want them right where they are." The dwarf examined the state of his weapons, all too aware that they wouldn't be enough to keep him alive.

First Commander Dakmund, son of King Dorain of clan Heavybelly marched around the corner at the end of the tunnel. Behind him, nearly twenty dwarves beat their armour and cried out to Grarfath and Yamnomora. They were quite the sight.

His brother had surprised him when first they met, but there was nothing of that dwarf marching towards them now. Dakmund's face was one of bloodlust, his war cry louder than the others behind him.

"You cannot kill your brother," Reyna commented.

"He doesn' look to be givin' me much choice," Doran replied through gritted teeth.

"Brace!" Captain Adan shouted behind them. "No mercy, boys! We kill 'em all!"

Doran shook his head. His kin didn't even have a word for mercy.

The marching and chanting came to a sudden stop. The dwarves were breathing heavily, every one of them pent up and eager to spill the blood of their enemies. It was a frenzy Doran had often whipped up among his ranks when he was in command.

"This is ye last chance, Doran!" Dakmund bellowed down the tunnel. "Fight with us… or die today."

Captain Adan seethed as he threatened, "If you turn on us dwarf, I will gut you first."

That alone made Doran want to turn around and bury his axe in the man's head. Reyna and Nathaniel met the dwarf's gaze, their eyes full of sorrow. They knew their friend would never turn on them; they were just sorry it had come to this.

Doran called back, "I'll see ye in Grarfath's hall, brother!" The son of Dorain hefted his axe and sword.

Dakmund's face dropped and he lost some of his rage. "So be it…"

In the silence that followed, dread filled every beating heart as distant howls and screeches echoed through the tunnels. Doran knew that sound, though he had never heard quite so many at the same time.

"What was that?" Captain Adan asked, his mounting horror mirrored in his soldiers.

Nathaniel sneered and gripped his sword with both hands. "Gobbers!"

"A whole damned pack by the sound o' it!" Doran added.

The howls and screeches were complemented by feral roars and beastly growls. Their monstrous cries were soon followed by their deadly claws scraping against the tunnel floors. They were getting louder.

"*Where are they coming from?*" Dakmund demanded in dwarvish.

The Heavybelly dwarves turned every which way as they tried to locate the source. Doran copied his brother and placed a hand to the stone under his feet. The mountain told them everything they needed to know.

"They're comin' from everywhere!" Doran warned.

Both dwarven and human ranks turned around to search the

darkened tunnels behind them. Being in the middle of both, Doran couldn't see a thing past their tight formations. It wasn't long, however, before the hungry roars and foul stench of the Gobbers found their tunnel.

"Move," Reyna commanded the knights of Namdhor.

The soldiers parted as she aimed along her arrow, down the tunnel. The faintest of whispers left her lips in time with the departing arrow, a spell to ignite the missile. The flaming arrow cut through the tunnel and briefly illuminated the Gobbers, who numbered so many they were crawling over each other, their lizard-like heads snapping at the air.

War cries from the dwarven end indicated that they were similarly challenged.

"We've been cornered…" Doran grumbled.

Captain Adan pushed his way to what had become the new front line, facing the Gobbers. He had no encouraging words to bolster his men this time.

Without provocation, the Gobbers charged, sprinting down the tunnel on all four of their scaly limbs.

The thunderous clash of claws and steel filled the halls of Vengora. Their gnashing teeth snapped at the soldiers of Namdhor and blood shot across their formation. Beastly limbs and heads were chopped from their bodies, creating a bloody and chaotic mess.

Reyna loosed an arrow with perfect precision, sending the bolt between the clamouring soldiers and into the eye of a Gobber. The arrow passed straight through and continued down the tunnel, slaying another six before it met the wall.

Nathaniel and Doran braced themselves, waiting for the inevitable break in the soldiers' ranks. Once the Gobbers poured through, the tunnel would become a dangerously tight field of battle.

Petur Devron caught Doran's eye as he scrambled into the workshop's antechamber. Now he seemed to be grasping the gravity of the situation.

Farther down the tunnel, Dakmund and his dwarves laid into

the Gobbers with axe, sword, and hammer. It would be a while before the Gobbers broke through their ranks.

The back line of the Namdhorians fell into disarray when three Gobbers leaped over the top and came crashing down on them. Claws raked at their armour and dug into their skin as the soldiers viciously stabbed at the monsters' green hides.

"Come 'ere!" Doran brought his axe down with enviable strength and buried the entire blade in the Gobber's back before it could bite off the soldier's face.

Dragging it off the man, Doran proceeded to thrust his sword into the beastie's head. When it went limp, the dwarf launched it at the others breaking through.

With the sound of his kin singing behind him, Doran was taken back to his days on the dwarven battlefields. He spat the Gobber's blood from his mouth and roared.

Nathaniel's warning fell on deaf ears, the son of Dorain lost in the fray. The soldiers around him dropped under the barrage of claws and teeth, leaving the dwarf to face the monsters. Captain Adan had been forced back into the antechamber, his life saved more than once by Reyna's aim.

Doran barrelled into the Gobbers. His axe and sword swung freely, easily cutting through their unprotected flesh. One particularly brave, or perhaps stupid, Gobber charged directly at Doran. The dwarf slammed his axe into the beast's chest and pushed forward, using the creature as a shield while he stormed through their ranks.

"Is that all ye got?" he bawled, finally throwing the Gobber off his axe and swinging with his sword.

The tunnel floor was beginning to feel slippery under his boots, slick with blood. Still, they came, a relentless force of starving monsters. Doran's black and gold armour kept the clamping teeth at bay, but the numerous claws eventually found his body between the joints. The son of Dorain ignored them all, focusing on the strength in his arms and the angle of his blades.

The sound of Dakmund gleefully swinging his mighty sword

proved a distraction. He had never heard his brother so happy in the middle of a slaughter.

Taking advantage of his divided attention, the Gobbers swarmed him. Their combined weight was enough to topple the dwarf, piling him on top of Namdhorian bodies. Doran shifted his head this way and that to avoid the biting jaws filled with rows of teeth. The weight was crushing, preventing him from swinging his weapons with any efficiency.

A slightly larger Gobber than the rest hunched over him, his scarred maw opening to fit Doran's entire head. There was nothing he could do to stop the beastie from clamping his teeth around his face and ripping him to shreds.

A flash of steel passed over Doran's face and through the Gobber's head, splitting it nicely into two halves. Nathaniel Galfrey didn't stop there. The old knight hacked and chopped at the Gobbers, pushing them back and giving them something to think about beside Doran. A product of Graycoat training, Nathaniel danced with his sword, swinging it into arcs and patterns that gave the monsters pause. Any who crawled within reach of his sword arm found themselves missing a limb.

"Get up Heavybelly!" he cried.

Doran only got to his knees before the next Gobber needed the taste of his axe. The dwarf joined the old knight and the two slowly retreated towards the antechamber, where Adan and Reyna were making short work of the Gobbers who slipped past.

Down the tunnel, not a single dwarf had fallen to the beasts. They sung from deep in their barrelled chests and ploughed through the Gobbers with glee.

"We need to fall back!" Nathaniel advised mid-swing. The Gobber's head flew through the air and hit Petur Devron in the arm, ushering him back.

Reyna fired arrow after arrow, never slaying less than two Gobbers with each bolt. As the antechamber began to fill with the scaly beasts, the elf swapped her bow for the scimitar resting on her hip. The blade sliced through Gobber flesh as easily as it sliced through the air.

"Retreat!" Nathaniel shouted over the gore. "There's too many!"

Guarding the defenceless Petur between them, the three companions and Captain Adan made their way towards the dwarven battle. Reyna kicked out and sent one monster into the other, opening them up for Doran's axe. The dwarf chopped them down, but one of the prone Gobbers lashed out and bit down on Adan's thigh, dragging him to the floor.

"Captain!" Reyna flicked her scimitar upwards and left the Gobber with nothing but a few tendons between its head and neck.

"Pull him back!" Nathaniel jumped out of their retreat and cut down two more who threatened to attack Adan.

Doran and Reyna did their best to get the captain to safety, but they were soon at the back of the dwarven battle, where the Gobbers from their side were beginning to break through. Petur pressed himself to the wall, abandoning his scrolls.

"Hello, brother!" Dakmund hailed, his sword gutting two Gobbers at once. "Are ye havin' fun yet?"

Doran growled and backhanded the nearest creature with his axe. Battlefields weren't for talking.

Captain Adan tried to stand up, but his torn leg gave way, dropping him to his knee. Reyna and Nathaniel did what they could to keep the monsters at bay, but in the chaos of flaying limbs and raking claws, they missed the Gobber bursting from the swarm. Its jaws wrapped around Adan's leg with a vice-like grip and the captain screamed in agony.

"Nathaniel!" Reyna called, but the old knight had been separated, placing him too far to be of any help. The elf dashed to the captain's side but it was too late.

"Help me!" he screamed in terror. There was nothing any of them could do to prevent the Gobbers from dragging him into their clutches. Teeth and claws pulled him in every direction, quickly tearing through his leathers and flesh until he was scattered across the tunnel.

Doran cared little for the captain of Namdhor, but he hated that the Gobbers had claimed another life; the ranger in him couldn't live with the injustice.

A war cry to Grarfath exploded from his blood-soaked lips and he charged into the monsters. His bulk alone saw him push through their attacking line, hammering them under his boots. Reyna's and Nathaniel's warning calls were impossible to make out between the dwarves' singing and the Gobbers' screeches. Doran ignored it all and swung his axe and sword.

Through the entanglement of their nightmarish bodies, the son of Dorain caught flashes of an elven scimitar and silvyr blades hacking, chopping, and slicing. Doran charged the Gobber in front of him and flattened it against the tunnel wall, adding a headbutt for good measure. Carnivorous claws hooked around the back of his armour, however, and dragged him back into the thick of it.

"Brother!" Dakmund called over the din.

Doran swung his sword back and twisted his body to throw the Gobber off his back. The sword continued its arc, cutting through three more of the beasts and spilling their insides.

"Brother!" Dakmund's silvyr sword chopped down enough Gobbers to open a path back to the rest of them.

"We need to get out of here!" Nathaniel shouted, pushing Petur Devron away from the Gobbers crawling along the walls.

Doran stepped behind the fighting line of Heavybelly dwarves and panted for breath, safe within their perimeter for a moment. The Gobbers numbered a hundred at least and there seemed to be an endless supply of the monsters.

The way back to the workshop was cut off.

"There's only one way we're to be goin'!" Dakmund bashed in a Gobber's head with the hilt of his sword before decapitating it with a single swipe.

Doran dashed out between two dwarves and added his axe and sword to their efforts. The Gobber bodies were piling so high now that the rest of the beasts were struggling to crawl over their own dead.

The dwarf beside Doran turned to Dakmund. "*The northern tunnel is clear, First Commander!*" he said in their native tongue.

Dakmund glanced at Doran with a question on his face; *stay and die fighting or retreat north, to Dhenaheim?*

Doran buried his axe in the next Gobber and looked to his friends. The Galfreys were still on their feet, which was something, but even they couldn't keep this up. Petur Devron would most likely die in the next minute if they didn't leave now.

"Go!" Doran barked. "Get out o' the tunnels!" He put himself between the Galfreys and the oncoming Gobbers, ushering them north. "Be on with ye!" A swing of his sword and a chop of his axe cut down two more monsters. "Go!" he ordered, retreating with them.

Reyna exchanged her scimitar for the enchanted bow and sent a single arrow through four Gobbers unfortunate enough to be in line behind the other. It gave Doran some breathing room to turn around and sprint after them as they were led out of the tunnel by the dwarves.

The howling Gobbers chased them relentlessly, scaling the walls and ceilings to attack from all sides. Reyna released two orbs of white light to follow the fleeing band overhead. Dakmund assumed the lead, taking them back through the passage used as a camp by the dwarves. Together, they sprinted, stumbled, and scrambled through the ancient halls of Vengora, desperate to stay out of the Gobbers' shadows.

Reyna was the only one with a ranged weapon. Her arrows flew past Doran at the back and never failed to hit their target.

A wide set of stairs slowed them down, or at least the dwarves, allowing the Gobbers to catch up. Doran kept his eyes front and concentrated on ascending the stone steps as Reyna fired her arrows from the top. Every twang of her bow prevented a Gobber from harming a dwarf.

They ran through great halls and several intimate chambers that Doran would have loved to explore, but the cracks in the walls and shadows were coming alive with more Gobbers.

"How much farther?" Petur asked with a hoarse voice. The man clearly wasn't built for running for his life.

"In here!" Dakmund made a sharp right and barrelled his way through two very tall doors.

The dwarves followed him in and the Galfreys made sure Petur joined them. Doran blinked through the sweat dripping into his eyes and jumped sideways through the closing doors, barely making it before his kin slammed them shut. The Gobbers crashed into the doors, pushing the dwarves back a step.

"*Bar the way!*" one of them commanded, gesturing to the alcove beside the doors.

The nearest dwarf reached up and yanked on the thick column of wood stood upright inside the alcove. The wood fell into place across the doors and took the brunt of the next barrage. Every hit the doors took elicited a creak from the old wood.

"That ain't goin' to hold..." Doran commented between laboured breaths.

The screeches and howls stopped and the doors stood still for the first time since being closed. Doran knew better than to hope they had become bored, especially since they had all stopped their assault at the same time.

An ear-splitting roar carried through the stone walls and settled in their bones like death's icy grip.

Doran sighed and looked at Nathaniel, recalling his words from their reunion in The Pick-Axe. "Are ye ready for another adventure, old friend?" he repeated sarcastically, shaking his head.

That same monstrous roar came again, just beyond the doors.

Doran hefted his axe and sword. "We're all about to die..."

PART IV

10,000 YEARS AGO

Sarkas rushed to his master's window. From the highest towers of The Citadel, he was offered a view of Ak-tor that very few ever got to see. Judging by the dragon's fire that consumed the city now, it seemed likely that even fewer would have the opportunity to see it from this vantage ever again.

To the east, King Atilan's magnificent palace had already become a smouldering ruin. The Dragon Riders, or what remained of their hunted order, had targeted the king first, ensuring his legendary talent for magic didn't put a stop to their invasion.

This war had dragged on for years, though Sarkas only heard of it through The Echoes' council meetings. The servants of Kaliban had been spread thin during the war, their prayers required on every battlefield.

Thanks to the hearing he wasn't supposed to have, Sarkas had heard his masters complaining no end about the Sermon strategies they had been forced to devise in order to keep the masses and soldiers under control. Sarkas had grown to pity his own people; taken in by a greedy religion and their faith used to enslave them. Kaliban was no more real than the love his parents had pretended to have when he was born.

A black dragon with glistening scales soared past the window and

Sarka's master jumped back and gasped with fright. For all the magic possessed by The Echoes, they had never used it for anything other than amassing wealth and tricking the empire into following their beliefs. Fighting a dragon was entirely beyond them.

"What has that fool of a king done?" his master muttered to himself.

Unlike his master, Sarkas didn't cower in the shadow of a dragon. This wasn't how he died.

"Atilan has doomed us all..." the master continued, sweat building upon his brow.

"Not all," Sarkas replied boldly, speaking aloud for the first time in thirty-four years.

His master whipped his head around and stared dumbfounded at his slave. His mouth fell open but not so much as a syllable came out.

Sarkas always thought he would be beaming when this day came, but now that it had finally arrived he could only look back at his tormentor with a focused gaze.

"You are right to some extent," Sarkas continued casually, wandering away from the window. "Atilan has doomed most of you. After today, The Echoes, this entire kingdom, will cease to exist. Our kind will return to our savage ways and what grows from the ashes won't recall any of this. Today, the empire dies... and you with it."

His master's contorted expression began to smooth out as he composed himself. "Impossible! You shouldn't even be able to talk!"

Sarkas sighed. "I just told you the end of days has arrived, yet you are still too narrow-sighted to understand that which lies beyond your very nose."

The master's face screwed up into rage and his eyes watered. "Silence, whelp! You will be punished beyond comprehension for this!" The old man was frantically patting his robes down.

"Looking for this?" Sarkas presented his master's wand from across the chamber.

"How dare you even touch that! You will suffer before you die, wretch! It will be slow, I promise you that!"

Sarkas slowly shook his head. "Look outside, Master. Do you think there's time to do anything slowly? As we speak; Garganafan and

Malliath, the most ferocious of their kin, lay waste to Ak-tor with a dozen dragons behind them. I have seen how this ends and I promise you, your end will be that of suffering. But fear not, your death will serve a purpose."

The master sneered. "You wouldn't know what to do with that wand if you read every book in The Citadel."

"Oh, but I have," Sarkas replied, relishing in the sound of his own voice. "At least, the books that matter anyway. There is enough knowledge in this tower to have usurped King Atilan years ago! If only you and those other leches hadn't been clouded with greed and lust."

Sarkas considered the wand in his hand and decided to give the master a taste of his studies. A quick flick of the wrist ripped the master's tunic from his body, shredding the fabric before it fell to the floor. The old man jumped back, his bony body quivering. Sarkas thrust the wand out and cast a spell to push the priest over his own desk. The blast of energy knocked everything from the surface and the master tumbled off the edge, bleeding and bruised.

Another strong flick of the wrist and the desk was cast aside and broken to splinters, revealing the cowering master. He crawled across the floor, confused and terrified. It had been a state of living that Sarkas had come to understand all too well over the decades.

The Citadel shook under his feet, but Sarkas knew he had until sunset before the tower was brought down. In his vision, he had seen Garganafan's fiery breath and Malliath's incredible bulk snap the tower in half, its tall walls orange in the dying sun. Until then, he had all the time in the world to exact his revenge.

An intricate flourish of the wand and a little spell was all that was needed to pick the master up and pin him to the wall. He yelled as his head slammed against the cold stone. Sarkas closed the gap between them and cast a new spell to create a scorching furnace at the tip of the wand. Maintaining eye contact, he slowly dragged the wand tip up the inside of the master's thigh, enjoying every squeal and shriek. He stopped before he could do any damage that would see the old man pass out or die. He still needed him, after all.

"While you slept, I studied," Sarkas boasted. "I read the forbidden books from cover to cover, many times in fact. You've spent all these years fearing their content, when really you should have seen them as tools. Written in the temple at Mount Kaliban, the very birth place of magic! How could you not see them for what they are?"

Sarkas stepped back and looked out of the window, where giant clouds of ash dominated the horizon. "I was always careful," he continued. "I only killed the lowest of priests, those who could disappear and no-one would really care. But every life I claimed showed me a little bit more of what is to come." Sarkas stepped in, bringing his lips close to his master's ear. "I have seen a future where all can prosper. A future without greedy kings and make-believe gods. A realm where children aren't abandoned for coin and used by men like you."

Recalling the images of that future kingdom almost brought tears to Sarkas's eyes. In the beginning, he had been fighting for his freedom and that of his brothers, but now... now he had a world to build.

"There's only one piece of the puzzle missing," he said, meeting his master's eyes with a hunger that could only be satiated by magic. "I need to see who will lead this new kingdom."

Sarkas stepped back and lowered his wand. The spell he muttered was among the earliest he had learned, but never had he had the opportunity to use it. Four glowing tendrils grew from the end of the wand and wormed down to the floor, where they ended in hooks. The magic whip cracked and sounded like thunder when he tested it out on the floor.

"In order to see this new world, Master, I will need some of your blood." Sarkas smiled for the first time. "I'll try not to take too much..."

Only when the sun began to kiss the western horizon did Sarkas allow his master to fall to the floor. His body was a canvas of horrors, making the old priest almost unrecognisable as a man. With laboured breaths, the wretch clung to life. Good, Sarkas thought. He needed him somewhere between life and death; too far either way made the old man useless to him.

With little time left, Sarkas drew the runes onto his master's stomach, using the blood from one of his many wounds. When six interlocking circles of runes were painted around his navel, Sarkas began the incantation, drawing up more blood until it overflowed the priest's stomach and spilled across the floor. The ancient magic took a hold of him, as it had done many times over the years.

The future was laid out before his very eyes, as real as the world he lived in right now. He felt as if he could reach out and touch those he saw.

When the vision ended, his master having finally succumbed to his wounds, Sarkas opened his eyes to see his six brothers. They were all standing in the chamber with bloodied knives in their hands. Sarkas looked upon them all, proud. Just as they had planned, the other high priests of The Echoes had been slain by their slaves. He hoped the wretches had seen his brothers before they died.

"Well done," he signed, picking himself up from the floor.

"We don't have long, Sarkas," Edun signed quickly as The Citadel began to rumble. "The dragons will bring the tower down soon!"

Sarkas held his hands up to calm them. He had seen exactly how they each died but, more importantly, he had seen how they all survived.

"Did you bring it?" he signed, asking Edun specifically. He could have stated it rather than ask the question, but Sarkas had learned years ago, when he first began his ventures into the future, that his brothers didn't like the way he spoke to them when he already knew what they were going to do or say.

Edun removed a small wooden box from inside his robe. Sarkas glanced out of the window, where the sun was slowly but surely fading. They didn't have long.

Sarkas took the box and wasted no time in removing the glowing crystal that resided inside. It was beautiful, hypnotic even. Its potential was so much more.

"We must hurry," Edun signed. "Word has spread that everyone is taking refuge in—"

"The Wild Moores," Sarkas finished. "Yes, I know. That too is our destination." He met the eyes of his brothers. "From there we shall plant a seed that will grow into a new tree of life. The Echoes are gone. Atilan's empire is gone. We, brothers, we will build something better."

Sarkas launched the crystal across the room and conjured a portal *of pure darkness. His brothers jumped back but he soothed them and quickly ushered them through the gateway. They all gasped when a single step took them from The Citadel to the mossy ground of The Wild Moores. Before them sat a cave, quiet and unassuming. There were no dragons laying waste and no screams to fill the background. It was peaceful.*

He turned back to his brothers as the portal disappeared. "This is where we shall change the world…"

41

DRAGORN UNBOUND

Alijah's head shot up from the library desk with a sheet of parchment stuck to his face. The disorientation quickly faded when a pair of young Dragorn offered him bemused smiles. The half-elf peeled the parchment from his face and smiled with them, wondering all the while how long he had been asleep.

The Dragorn library was a windowless pocket dimension that prevented any of its readers from even guessing the time of day outside.

On the adjacent table, the two Dragorn Gideon had brought in for extra eyes were studiously scouring through book after book, showing no sign of fatigue. Alijah looked at the pile of books on his table, ashamed that he hadn't read nearly as many as they had. He decided that his search for anything about the orcs had been in more detail…

"Good evening," Gideon greeted from behind, making him jump out of his skin.

"Evening?" Alijah replied quietly. "Is that what it is?"

"Come and look at this," the Master Dragorn said, gesturing to the table behind them. "Get some rest you two." He dismissed the younger Dragorn.

"How long was I asleep?' Alijah asked, dragging his chair back.

"You've been combing through these books for two days, Alijah; don't worry about how much sleep you've had."

"What have you been doing?" Alijah asked curiously.

"Gathering ingredients…" he replied cryptically.

The table used by Gideon had the two ancient prophecies laid out side by side. They were surrounded by mixing bowls, some filled with pastes while others housed fine powder. Other herbs and plant life had been discarded here and there and two sticks of incense gave off a trail of smoke into the air. If Alijah had to guess, he would say Gideon had been attempting multiple spells.

The Master Dragorn gestured to the scroll on the left. "The prophecy you found." He gestured to the prophecy on the right. "The Echoes of Fate."

Alijah's head was still a little fuzzy and he silently thanked Gideon for explaining everything as simply as possible. He also noticed that the cuts and bruises had disappeared from the Master Dragorn's face and hands now; a miraculous recovery.

Side by side, the prophecies were easily distinguished by their conditions. Found a thousand years ago by Alijah's grandfather, the disgraced and exiled king of elves, The Echoes of Fate had been kept in perfect condition over the millennia, its every verse legible. By comparison, the scroll found recently by Alijah was ruined from top to bottom, its every verse damaged in some way.

"I had been staring at them for hours when I started to see the similarities," Gideon explained. "I finally had cause to use an old spell I was taught in Korkanath," he added happily.

"What have you found?" Alijah asked, glad to be looking at anything that wasn't a book or connected to The Great War.

"A few things," Gideon replied with a wry smile. "The first thing I noticed was the calligraphy. They were both written by the same person." The Master Dragorn stopped there, adding a dramatic pause to the revelation.

"You're sure?" Alijah questioned, looking closely at the two scrolls.

"I wasn't until I used a spell to confirm it. They're a perfect match. As are the hand prints."

"They were written at the same time then," Alijah said, failing to see how this would help them with anything.

"Yes," Gideon confirmed. "I used another spell to date the parchment, or skin rather. Both were scribed around ten thousand years ago."

Alijah tapped the edge of the ruined prophecy. "But this one was placed under a protection spell after it was damaged."

Gideon smiled knowingly. The Master Dragorn flicked his fingers and cast a small destructive spell. The flames hit The Echoes of Fate and rolled over the parchment until they extinguished, leaving the prophecy entirely unharmed.

Alijah's heart skipped a beat, horrified for a moment that such a relic was about to be destroyed. "They're both protected..."

"Indeed," Gideon answered. "I suppose no one ever thought to test The Echoes of Fate prophecy, too concerned with keeping something so ancient intact."

Alijah was amazed. "So you hit it with a fire spell!" he said incredulously.

Gideon chewed his lip. "Not exactly. I may have accidentally knocked a candle over. But, all the best things are discovered by accident!"

Alijah was beginning to wonder if he should have been the one to examine the scrolls. "So, they were both written by the same person and they're both under a protection spell," he concluded.

Gideon turned to the half-elf. "Would you like to see who wrote them?"

Alijah couldn't stop his face crumpling into confusion. "You can't be talking about what I think you're talking about."

Gideon gestured to the mixing bowl beside the ruined scroll. Alijah noted the fine blue powder inside.

"You have Krayt dust."

Gideon took the bowl in hand. "It's not impossible to come by. The spell, on the other hand, takes some practice."

"It doesn't matter," Alijah protested, familiar with the spell's parameters. "The scrolls weren't written here. You would have to use the dust wherever they were originally scribed to see into the past. Even then, no one has ever looked back ten thousand years!"

Gideon nodded along. "That's all true enough. The scrolls, however, are imbued with magic, magic placed upon them by the one who scribed them. That works as a tether, forever connecting them. Also, that isn't your usual Krayt powder," Gideon added with a hint of mischievousness about him.

For just a moment, Alijah glimpsed a much younger Gideon Thorn, a young man who gave his teachers at Korkanath hell.

"Why is it different?" he inquired.

"Because *I* made it," Gideon replied confidently. "This library is full of wonders. There's a whole section on the top floor devoted to spells rather than history. I've been itching to use this spell since I discovered it a few years ago," he insisted. "Though it took me some time to gather the extra ingredients."

Alijah was keen to see the spell in action. He had only ever witnessed Hadavad use it, almost four years ago. They had been investigating a recently abandoned dwelling of The Black Hand and the old mage had wanted to see if The Crow had been present. Once the blue powder took flight, it rained down inside the room and gave shape to the dark mages who had been inside. It was a spectacle to watch, glimpsing into the past.

Gideon poured a small handful of the Krayt powder into his palm and uttered the spell. Alijah paid special attention to the words and enunciations, committing them to memory.

The spell completed, Gideon waved his hand through the air and released the blue powder. As it had done with Hadavad, the powder rained down over the scrolls, glistening in the firelight. As the powder descended, it clung to an invisible body, giving shape to a man who crouched over both scrolls, as he had done ten thousand years ago. The more powder that clung to the forms the more detail became apparent.

"Incredible..." Alijah whispered, moving around the table to better see the duplicated man.

The two forms were certainly the same person; a bald man,

skinny by his build. A delicate hand scribed over both scrolls, their movements almost in time.

"He looks young," Gideon commented.

"But who is he?" Alijah asked, his curiosity burning like a flame inside of him.

"A priest of The Echoes, perhaps?" Gideon suggested, his eyes fixed on the scriber's hand as he wrote words that couldn't be seen on the ruined prophecy.

"It's hard to say," Alijah replied. "Both prophecies were found in The Wild Moores, which suggests The First Kingdom had already been destroyed by the dragons of the time. Then there's the black hand printed on both, which suggests The Echoes might have been replaced by The Black Hand we know today when these were scribed."

Alijah had wondered for years how The Echoes, the dominant religion in The First Kingdom, had evolved into The Black Hand. Both worshipped Kaliban, yet one showed all the hallmarks of an ordinary, if powerful religion, while the other practised necromancy and other dark magic.

It was a time in history when the humans of Illian had taken refuge in The Wild Moores, hiding from the dragons. As they grew to be as wild as the forest they inhabited, their historical notes faded away, leaving only questions.

"Look!" Gideon pointed to the scribing of the ruined prophecy.

The bald man sat back after finishing, perhaps marvelling at his foretelling. Then he lifted a wand from within his powdery robes. He placed it to the scroll and the blue powder imitated the damage seen on the real scroll on the table.

"He ruined it deliberately," Alijah said, his eyes as fixed as Gideon's.

The bald man proceeded to wave his wand around, over the scroll, and the blue powder glistened here and there.

"He's placing the protection spell over it," Gideon observed. "The other one's doing the same."

Alijah froze. Outlined in blue powder, the invisible man working on the ruined prophecy slowly looked up and tilted his head. He was looking directly at the half-elf.

"Gideon..." he whispered.

The Master Dragorn followed the figure's gaze to Alijah. "He must have been looking at some—"

The blue figure whipped his head around and looked directly at Gideon. The Master Dragorn took a step back. The bald man regarded Alijah briefly again before turning back to Gideon, his gaze intense.

"Is he... He can't really *see* us, can he?"

Gideon shook his head. "The spell doesn't work both ways. He's dead, long dead in fact. We're just seeing an echo." As the Master Dragorn moved around the table, the blue powdered man followed him with eerie precision.

The truth of what was happening hit Alijah, filling him with dread. "Unless he could see into the future." His words garnered the bald man's attention again. "If he was looking into the future ten thousand years ago, he could see us doing this now, looking at him in the past."

Gideon moved to end the spell but the bald man flourished his wand and the blue powder fell from his form and that of his twin. The spell had been broken from his end...

"What just happened, Gideon?" Alijah knew the answer to his own question; he just couldn't accept that someone could really see into the future.

"I think your doubts about seeing the future have just been answered," Gideon replied, cupping his trimmed beard. He sounded collected and calm, but his body language betrayed his grave concern.

"Why would he destroy only part of the prophecy?" Alijah asked, inspecting the damaged scroll.

The library door opened above them, ending any further discussion. A Dragorn somewhere between Alijah's and Gideon's age walked in, alarm etched across his dark features.

"Master Thorn." He bowed his head.

"Corrigan," Gideon greeted. "Do we know anything about those massive quakes?"

"Yes, Master. We've just received word from Roddick and Alessandra in Calmardra. It would seem a volcanic eruption has taken place in The Undying Mountains, a *massive* one."

"Volcanic?" Gideon repeated, his focus growing distant.

"Yes, Master. They can see it all the way from Calmardra. They say the skies are turning black with ash and smoke."

"Have them set up relays across the realm," Gideon ordered. "I want Dragorn situated with just enough distance to stay in mental communication with each other. Have them pull back from The Arid Lands and start patrolling cities and towns that have yet to be targeted by the orcs."

"Yes, Master." Corrigan bowed again and hurried from the library with his commands.

Gideon folded his arms and ran a thumb over his lips, lost to his thoughts.

"You are concerned by this volcano," Alijah stated.

Gideon paused, dragging himself from the depths of his mind. "I'm concerned about a northerly wind…"

Alijah followed the Master Dragorn's thinking and found himself faced with the same concern. "The orcs," he said. "They couldn't have known the volcano was going to erupt."

"No," Gideon agreed. "But an ally who can see the future could."

Alijah was shaking his head. "All of this…" The half-elf gestured to the prophecy, though he was referring to everything that had happened since The Black Hand found Asher's bones. "It would take a level of orchestration that couldn't be achieved if it was conceived ten thousand years ago. It's too long. Too many variables stand in the way."

Gideon sighed. "Yet here we are."

Alijah opened his mouth to further his protests when a burning jolt of pain shot through his gut and threw him over the table. Parchments and herbs followed him over, creating a loud clatter and a mess.

"Alijah!" Gideon skipped over the table with the grace of a cat and landed by the his side.

Alijah tried to get up as another searing bolt gripped his left elbow, causing his hand to go into spasm. He cried out, rolling his head against the cold floor.

"It's Malliath…" he groaned. "He's in pain…"

Gideon turned away as if someone was speaking to him. "It's Korkanath! Malliath's attacking the school!"

Alijah gritted his teeth and found the strength to stand. "We need to go to him."

Gideon didn't look convinced.

"You said it yourself," Alijah continued. "I need to strengthen my bond with him. Maybe my presence will weaken his bond with Asher."

Again, Gideon looked away, listening to Ilargo no doubt. There was a sense of urgency about him as the dragon relayed the devastation Malliath was causing.

The Master Dragorn picked up Mournblade in its sheath. "Grab your bow."

Under the stars, Ilargo led the way, trailed by six other dragons, five of whom possessed riders. Gideon could feel all of them in his mind as they relayed their thoughts through the minds of their dragons.

He could feel their trepidation as they flew over The Adean, crossing the short distance to the island of Korkanath. None of them had ever fought another dragon before, but fighting Malliath was perhaps the worst dragon to fight.

We are still here, Ilargo reminded him, bolstering his resolve.

I don't think our fight with Malliath and Asher has filled anyone with courage, Ilargo. We nearly died in Lirian…

Careful, the green dragon warned. *Our thoughts are not entirely guarded.*

Gideon turned to his right, where three Dragorn were hugging closely to their companions' scales. He could sense their anticipation through the bond, worried for the first time that they might not survive the next hour.

You need to say something, Ilargo insisted. *Before they see him…*

Gideon considered his words before reaching out to acquire permission to enter everyone's mind at once. It was a jarring experience to speak to so many in such an intimate way, each Dragorn and dragon attempting to guard their most personal thoughts.

When we reach Korkanath, split into two teams. One to help any survivors and put out fires, the other to help me drive Malliath away. Figorax, it's probably best you help me with Malliath and leave Korkanath to dragons with riders.

Figorax, the only dragon without a Dragorn, roared into the sky in agreement.

Ilargo's voice sounded deep in Gideon's mind, where the others couldn't hear him. *Perhaps something a little more rousing?*

Gideon sighed. He'd never had cause to give any speeches before a battle, yet he couldn't deny the fear he felt through the bond.

We outnumber Malliath six to one, he began. **Ilargo and I will serve as his main distraction, flying low. That will give the rest of you a chance to come at him from above; height is the key. Go for his wings and neck.**

Gideon… Ilargo's warning tone was accompanied by an image of Alijah, who was currently behind the Master Dragorn and holding onto the dragon's spine horns.

We can't kill Malliath, he said, addressing the others again. **Or Asher for that matter. Both have been forced to act against their will. Our task is to drive them away from Korkanath. If possible, separate Malliath from Asher.**

A mumble of agreements came back at him through the bond, most still unsure how to engage in aerial combat, let alone figure out how to separate dragon from rider.

Ilargo cut off the bond, speaking directly to Gideon. *We'll work on your motivational speeches…*

Gideon sighed. ***Just get Alijah down on the island as fast as possible.***

They soared through the night's sky, over the island nation of Dragorn and across the small stretch of ocean. Korkanath was a beacon on the dark horizon. Malliath's distant roars told of anguish and retribution to those who understood dragon-kind.

"Is that Korkanath?" Alijah shouted over the wind.

Gideon didn't want to say yes, but the flaming inferno was none other. The school for mages burnt, a towering tornado of flames and smoke. The massive shadow of Malliath swooped down here and there, adding more fire to the wreckage.

Gideon, Ilargo called softly, *no one could survive that, not even mages…*

Gideon thought of the hundreds of children inside. Malliath's capacity to murder hundreds, if not thousands, in a matter of minutes was unthinkable. The Master Dragorn was instantly torn between his anger and the safety of Alijah. Everything they did to the black dragon would be shared with the half-elf.

He's leaving! Ilargo declared, sharing his sight with the others.

Where's he heading? Gideon asked, struggling to spot the dragon outside of the inferno's light.

He's heading west. Ilargo paused and Gideon could feel the tension in the dragon's muscles. *He's heading towards Velia…*

Gideon looked from the empty blackness in the west to the blazing island in front of him. Korkanath was lost. Velia had twenty times its population.

Go after him, Ilargo.

The green dragon banked to the left and headed west. The other dragons followed his lead and banked with him, perfectly in time.

"What's going on?" Alijah shouted from behind. "Where are we going?"

Gideon half turned to regard him. "Malliath's going to Velia!"

Alijah looked at Korkanath and the same realisation Gideon had experienced a moment ago flashed over the half-elf's face. There was nothing anyone could do for the mages now.

The lights of Velia provided a luminous backdrop, allowing Gideon's human eyes to make out Malliath's flying form. Backing up to the very edge of The Shining Coast, Velia was a port city with a fleet of ships sitting in her harbour.

They were the first to go.

Gideon and the others were too far behind to prevent Malliath from attacking Direport. A thick jet of fire exploded from his mouth and brought the light of the sun into the night. The flames clung to the ships, determined to burn their way through every plank of timber and sail. The fires were so big that the ships that missed Malliath's attack still caught the flames from adjacent vessels. In a matter of minutes, the entire harbour was a burning wreck.

Get some height! Gideon ordered the others.

Ilargo roared, hoping to get Malliath's attention and draw him away from the city itself. Velia's high walls meant nothing to a dragon and its densely populated streets were easily destroyed by a single jet of fire. There were three times as many people in Velia as there were in Lirian. Gideon didn't even want to think about the potential death toll.

Malliath paid no heed to Ilargo's roar and continued to fly around Velia, weaving between the four giant statues that stood tall on the city's curved western wall. One of the old kings was only built up to the chest, having been destroyed in The Battle for Velia at the end of the war, thirty years ago. Gideon had a feeling the city would suffer far worse than a broken statue today.

The black dragon halted his flight and dug his claws into the most northern of the stone kings. Malliath looked down on Velia and unleashed an ear-splitting roar.

Ilargo swooped down as quickly as he could, aiming for the southern curve of the main wall. The Velian soldiers scrambled to get out of the way, their red cloaks billowing behind them.

"I need you on the ground!" Gideon said to Alijah, pouring as much urgency into his voice as possible.

Alijah didn't argue. "What can I do?" he asked as he made his way down Ilargo's scales.

"Stay alive," Gideon replied simply.

The ground shook, sending a shockwave up the wall. Gideon looked around, expecting to see Malliath somewhere, but the black dragon was still residing over the city from atop the ancient king.

The ground shook again, followed by a distant explosion on the other side of the city. A column of black smoke was pushed high into the night's sky and the air was filled with screams. Another explosion, only a few streets away from them, threw slabs of rock into the air, destroying houses and shops in the process.

"It's them!" Alijah cried from atop the wall. "Orcs!"

Gideon looked back over the city as three more explosions ripped jagged holes in the earth. One was just outside the main gates, in the centre of the western wall. The screams of the city were soon accompanied by the feral roars and growls of the pale beasts.

Dragorn, separate from your dragons and take to the city! Defend Velia! Figorax, go back to The Lifeless Isles and alert the others. Bring reinforcements!

The bronze riderless dragon roared in protest but he turned mid-flight and headed back to the isles. The other dragons landed at various points around the city to drop off their riders.

Ilargo...

I know what to do. The green dragon lifted his head to Malliath high above.

Gideon considered the Galfreys' son. **Don't kill him,** he reminded the dragon.

You deal with the orcs. We will take care of Malliath.

Try and separate him from Asher if you can. And... be careful, old friend.

Ilargo roared, matching Malliath's tone with a regal call to arms. It set off the other dragons, all of which spread their wings and added their own roar to the cacophony.

Gideon joined Alijah on the wall as all the dragons took flight.

Malliath remained fixed to the old king, showing no sign of concern for the teeth and claws that were coming for him.

The Master Dragorn wanted to watch their clash, but the sound of orcs filled the air with their hungry growls. Gideon ran to the edge of the battlements, above the main gate, and looked out on the small village that lay sprawled across the field. It was beyond the protection of Velia's walls, though the inhabitants were fleeing out into the night, desperate to get away from the orcs piling out of the hole in the central road.

Gideon gestured to Asher, astride Malliath. "I hope you're as good with that bow as he was."

Alijah snapped the bow to life and nocked an arrow. "What's the plan?"

"Stay up here out of the way." Gideon continued before Alijah could argue the command, "Malliath and Asher are about to feel pain; that means you will too. Stay out of the battle."

The Master Dragorn approached the other side of the battlements and looked down at the interior of the city. It was a hundred foot drop at least. The orcs were charging in from outside, cutting off any escape for those running away from the orcs ascending into the streets.

"What are you going to do?" Alijah asked.

Gideon removed a small vial from his interior pocket and pulled the cork out of the end with his teeth. The pink liquid was far too sweet for anyone's liking, but it wasn't intended to be pleasant; he kept the Tempest elixir for emergencies since it only worked for a matter of seconds.

"What was that? Wait, what are you doing?"

"I'm going down there," he replied, throwing the empty vial away.

It had been too long since he had cause to unleash his power.

Without another word, Gideon took Mournblade in his hand, dragging it from its scabbard, and ran for the edge. Alijah swore at the top of his voice, sure that the Master Dragorn had just leaped to his death. Gideon focused on the ground, which was quickly rushing up to meet him, and uttered a destructive spell under his breath.

The charging orcs didn't see him coming from above, nor would they live to ever discover the cause of their death. Gideon landed in a crouch in front of the main gate with Mournblade pointed to the ground.

The effect was devastating.

The elixir coursing through his veins prevented his bones from shattering on impact, but the spell that exploded forth from Mournblade broke bones, tore through muscles, and bruised flesh in every direction. The stone of the main gates cracked and the ground shuddered under the Master Dragorn.

In the aftermath, there was an eerie quiet as a cloud of dust and debris settled over the courtyard. Gideon slowly stood up and inspected the tip of Mournblade, happy to see the scimitar still in one piece. He could hear his pulse beating in his ears and his skin itched. Along with the bitter aftertaste, they were the worst of the elixir's side-effects.

Inspecting his environment, orc bodies were piled around him in a neat circle, their limbs twisted and pulled into unnatural positions.

The eastern street, directly opposite the courtyard, quickly filled with the rushing soldiers of Velia. They looked upon the ruin that Gideon had caused and stared at him in awe.

There wasn't time for that. He could already hear the next wave charging towards them through the small village outside.

"On me!" he cried, rallying the soldiers. "Don't let them through the gates!"

A quick assessment told Gideon that the soldiers wouldn't make it to the gates before the orcs rushed through, but bottle-necking them in the entrance was the only way to get on top of their superior numbers. The Master Dragorn clenched the red and golden hilt of his ancient sword.

He charged.

The orcs made it half way through the short tunnel before Mournblade came down on them. The scimitar cut through the air from right to left, slicing through obsidian armour and pale bodies as if they weren't even in the way. Gideon lashed out with magic next, hurling a fireball down the length of the wall. Those that caught fire created chaos inside the tunnel, filling it with smoke and an acrid smell to accompany their screams.

Gideon moved like a dancer, weaving between their swords and spears, as he flipped and twisted to confuse his opponents. Every time, he countered with Mournblade, never failing to kill the orcs. Every swipe of the Vi'tari blade cut down two orcs or more, and magic defended Gideon where the sword was too occupied.

Then the Velian soldiers entered the fray.

Gideon jumped back and rolled to the side before the two sides collided in the small space.

"Don't give them an inch!" he barked over the melee.

The Master Dragorn felt his free hand cramp up before teeth marks appeared over his skin. Looking up, Ilargo was tumbling through the air, locked in battle with Malliath. More pain erupted up and down his arms and at the base of his neck. Gideon gritted his teeth and turned away from the fighting.

The other dragons came to his aid and crashed into the black dragon with claws and teeth. Ilargo fell a couple of hundred feet before spreading his wings and correcting his flight-path.

Gideon shook his injured hand and clenched a fist. ***Try and get them away from the city.***

Gideon! Asher isn't up here!

The Master Dragorn looked out on the courtyard, scanning the building tops for any sign of the Dragon Knight. If he could subdue Asher, Ilargo and the others could beat Malliath…

I'll find him!

Gideon ran off into the city, eager for a re-match.

FIRE AND ICE

Vighon pulled his fur cloak about him as the bitter winds of The Ice Vales bombarded the sheer face of Grey Stone's mountainous walls. The northerner was stood at the base, beside the main entrance to the narrow ravine that served as the city's central road in and out.

He surveyed the fields of white snow sprawled before him, looking upon the many refugees from Lirian and Vangarth. There were even a few from Ameeraska, having travelled up the western coast seeking shelter.

Tents had been set up for those who couldn't fit inside the already cramped city and its narrow web of streets. The city watch had done their best to place as many of the southerners inside the city, since most of them hadn't even seen snow, let alone known temperatures this low.

The howling wind did its best to put out their fires and blow their tents away. Still, they were safe from Malliath's fire and under the protection of King Jormund's soldiers. Snowfell and Kelp Town had sent many of their soldiers to bolster Jormund's ranks.

Vighon tried to keep his mind on the here and now. Thoughts

of Alijah tried to distract him, worried as he was for his friend. The width of Illian separated them now and he hated it.

"You don't look happy." Inara surprised the northman as she joined him in the cold. The Dragorn was sporting a flowing cloak of red over her leathers now, offering some extra protection against the elements.

"I can't decide what's worse," Vighon replied. "Dying from the heat in there or dying from the cold out here."

Inara glanced back at the warm glow emanating from the tall ravine. "It is hot in there," she agreed. "It would seem the perfect temperature is at the top, inside The Black Fort."

Vighon turned to regard the Dragorn. "Been dining with kings have you?"

"King Jormund has welcomed King Weymund with open arms, but there is a degree of… measuring going on."

Vighon laughed, the noise lost in the wind. "Is Galanör up there too?" he asked.

"No. He went with Russell to investigate the old tunnels that lead into Vengora. I think they both like to have a way out."

Vighon nodded, unsure what to say. He had told Inara some things about his life that he had worked hard to bury. Telling her had made it all very real again. There was also a part of him that worried Inara would see him differently now. Perhaps he deserved that judgement, he thought. Alijah had accepted him for who he was, making them brothers, but it had been easier than he deserved.

The northerner considered lighting his pipe as something to do, but the winds would never allow it. Instead, he looked to the night's sky, where a thick blanket of dark clouds greeted him.

"Where's Athis?" he asked, curious.

Inara looked at the sky with him. "He's…" The Dragorn pointed to a patch in the sky. "There."

Vighon followed her finger but saw nothing but more clouds. "As you say."

"He doesn't like it here, either," she said. "There's nowhere for a dragon to fit. Even the upper city is too cramped for his size."

Vighon agreed. There was barely enough space to fit the

inhabitants of Grey Stone, never mind all the refugees and a dragon.

Another awkward silence befell them.

"I'm sorry if I—"

"Thank you for sharing—"

Having both cut each other off, yet another awkward silence filled the air between them. Vighon didn't remember it ever being like this when they were younger. The relationship between them had been so natural and easy. He couldn't deny, however, that they were two very different people now.

"Thank you for sharing your... *story*, with me, on the road. I know that couldn't have been easy to talk about."

Vighon shrugged. "I'm sorry if I made you uncomfortable."

"No," Inara replied quickly, shaking her head. "I just wish... things had gone a different way for you."

The northerner had shared that wish many times over the years, but never more than when he was in the company of Inara. His dreams of 'what may have been' had returned of late, leaving the young man to wonder what life with her would have been like. He'd certainly have a lot less scars. He might even manage a whole night's sleep without waking up in a cold sweat.

Vighon turned to Inara, intending to ask her if she ever dreamt of different times, but the words never had a chance. The ground to the left of the sprawling camp exploded, followed by another, then another.

Vighon and Inara braced themselves under the Dragorn's protective shield as chunks of rock and debris hammered down. Black smoke poured out of the large holes, preceding the monsters of mans' nightmares.

The refugees scrambled from their tents and huddles and dashed for the light of Grey Stone's only entrance. The screams were loud, being as close to the tall ravine as they were, but Vighon and Inara still heard the roars that came from the explosion sites.

"Orcs!" Vighon spat, drawing his sword and lifting his shield from his back.

Inara unclenched her hand and released the magic that had

protected them. The Dragorn strode away from the main entrance, towards the oncoming orcs, with her Vi'tari blade in hand. Vighon often looked upon her and saw great beauty, but now he saw that beauty harden into a resolve of heroic stature. Deciding she was a distraction, the northerner hefted his sword, getting a feel for the weight of it.

He would need to focus if he was going to survive the next few minutes.

The black smoke stretched its ethereal hands through the camp, hiding the emergence of the first orcs to crawl out of their hell. Their growls reached his ears before the first of them charged through the haze. The pale beasts were clad in their obsidian armour, their helmets crafted individually to curve around their unique horns. Vighon clocked jagged swords, razor-sharp axes, and obsidian-pointed spears in the hands of his foes. It was nothing his shield couldn't handle.

"Come on then!" he yelled at the rushing orcs.

As one, Inara and Vighon leaped into the fray with their swords raised. The northerner switched his attack mid-fall and presented the nearest orc with his shield instead. The force of his impact launched the beast backwards, knocking over two more behind it. With a roar and a mighty swing, Vighon brought his sword to bear, cleaving off the head of one of the orcs unlucky enough to have remained on its feet.

Now he was in the thick of it.

The orcs came at him through the smoke, navigating the piles of supplies and tents to reach him. Vighon stood his ground and beat his sword against his shield, drawing them to him. He ducked one swipe, letting the orc rush past, and came up swinging his own sword to open up the neck of another. Shield, sword, shield, sword; the rhythm of battle took over his body.

A particularly crazed orc painted in black and yellow burst out of the smoke and ran at Vighon with abandon. Its feral roar was the only weapon it had, devoid of armour or a sword. The northerner twisted his sword and lifted it to his head in the manner of a spear. His aim true, he launched the sword at the orc, impaling it in the chest and dropping it to the ground immediately.

With only his shield now, Vighon could hear Galanör's warning voice in his head about relying on it too much. The blade was now more than a few paces away and more orcs were coming for him. Vighon growled and dashed forward, rolling under the first swing of his enemy, and jumping up to reach out for his sword. An orc's axe came down between him and the blade, forcing the northerner to pull back his hand and leave the sword. Vighon didn't hesitate to grab one of the orc's horns and yank it down, exposing its throat to the edge of his shield.

The orc went down under the impact, spluttering at the air for a desperate breath. Vighon ignored its dying moments and put his whole body behind his shield as he bashed into another orc. He blocked the swing of another and twisted his body on the spot, gripping the hilt of his blade on the way round. When he came back at the orc, he was swinging both his sword and shield until the beast had steel thrusting though its gut. He kicked the impaled orc back and freed his blade again.

Vighon stumbled back trying to catch his breath for a second. The refugees were still fleeing towards Grey Stone, but the narrow ravine was slowing everyone down. Jormund's hardy soldiers were doing their best to get through the stampede and present a defensive wall, but the orcs slipping past Vighon and Inara were almost upon the refugees.

The sound of magic being discharged was made all the more satisfying by the yelping orcs and the bodies flying through the air. Inara leaped out of the smoke like a banshee, one hand extended to expel magic and the other lashing out with her Vi'tari blade. Her scimitar flashed in every direction, cutting the orcs down in droves.

By comparison, Vighon felt he was moving through mud with all the grace of a hammer on an anvil. Where Inara glided over the snow, whipping her scimitar around in intricate patterns, he was hacking and chopping as he ran into every charging orc that got in his way.

Blood pounded in his ears and his heart threatened to beat its way out of his chest. With ragged breaths, Vighon matched the roar of the orcs and ran for those that had set upon the refugees.

The orcs were like animals as they attacked the back of the crowds. They had no problem slaughtering unarmed people as they stained the snow with blood. The assault created more chaos and the refugees began to flee in every direction, scattering across the face of the cliff. The soldiers tried to push through but the orcs killed someone with every strike of their weapons.

Then Vighon arrived.

The northerner had been known for giving into his anger in the past, during his time in The Ironsworn, and this usually led to a display of violence and no small amount of blood. Tonight, he decided, was going to be one of those moments.

Vighon ran blade first and thrust the tip through the back of an orc, shoving him so hard that he fell forwards and the blade ran through another orc. He yanked his sword free and turned on the next beast, slashing at its throat with enough force that its head almost rolled off its neck. The shield came up next, but not to defend. He repeatedly punched the next orc with the rim of the shield until it dropped and didn't get back up.

A few more savage displays and Grey Stone's entrance was littered with dead orcs. The soldiers picked up the people that had fallen and ushered them into the city as quickly as possible.

Vighon turned on the charging orcs again, ready to tackle any who tried to get into the city. Only a handful of the beasts were running for him, an unusually small number considering three holes had been blown out of the ground. Then he caught sight of Inara and realised why there were so few. The Dragorn was cutting down the orcs with such swiftness and efficiency that only a few escaped her scimitar. Her deadly display seemed to be attracting the beasts, distracting them as they emerged from their dark realm.

Vighon turned his head to the soldiers. "Hold this line!" he barked.

The northman braced himself for the handful of orcs that were about to descend on him. A dash to the left, then right, then left again; each dash a swing of the sword followed by a backhand.

When he finally stopped moving, the first three orcs lay on the ground with mortal wounds spilling out large volumes of blood. The remaining three tried to surround Vighon, slowing their charge.

The sound of a sharp object whistling through the air rushed past Vighon's ear. A flash of steel later and Stormweaver was sticking out of an orc's chest. Galanör held onto Guardian and sprinted across the snow to join Vighon, but his long-range attack spurred the remaining two orcs to attack the northman. His shield blocked an axe while his sword reached high to parry a sword. The elven ranger skidded on his knees through the middle of them and swiped his scimitar across the belly of one before thrusting his blade up into the head of the other.

"I could have handled it..." Vighon panted.

Galanör retrieved Stormweaver. "You're welcome."

"Get back!" Inara shouted over the feral orcs. The Dragorn was running towards the main entrance, away from the emerging beasts. "Get back!" she shouted again.

Vighon feared whatever Inara had seen to make her flee the battle in which she had clearly been dominating. Both he and the ranger stepped back, keeping their eyes on the orcs as they charged out of their holes.

The night came alive and the icy cold was banished in a brilliant jet of orange fire. Athis swooped low over the makeshift camp, setting it alight from east to west. There was no escape for the orcs. Dragon's fire had a way of sticking to everything it touched and didn't stop burning until everything was melted away.

The beasts' roars and growls turned into nightmarish screams and howls, yet the pale creatures continued to crawl out of their holes, searching for a path around the line of fire. Athis came down again and the red dragon unleashed his horrifying breath. The jagged holes were filled with flames and the burning bodies of dead orcs. Those few who survived the initial attack dived into the snow, desperate to be free of the flames.

One last flyby scorched the earth and halted any further attack.

More smoke and a foul stench covered the white plains. Athis remained in the air, awaiting any reprisals.

"Is it over?" one of the soldiers asked.

Murmurs broke out among the soldiers and the refugees, speculating about these new monsters from the deep. With the exception of the survivors from Ameeraska and Tregaran, this was the first time anyone else had laid eyes on the orcs.

Inara took charge. "Get everyone inside the city," she ordered. "I don't care about how cramped it is; find the space. Fill the halls of the upper city if you must, but everyone will be inside Grey Stone before they come again."

"Come again?" a soldier echoed with trepidation.

"They mean to take the city," Inara replied. "They won't stop until it's theirs." The Dragorn squared herself in front of the captain and spoke slowly. "Get everyone inside the city, now. If King Jormund or any of the lords has a problem with using the upper city, send them to me." She punctuated her last word by forcefully sliding her blade back into its sheath.

The soldiers wasted no more time and set about finding the refugees who had fled along the mountain wall. They ushered those at the main entrance back and the captain barked orders to fortify the ravine.

Still panting, Vighon examined the rocky walls. "They don't have any gates," he said incredulously.

"Why would they?" Galanör asked. "You would have to be mad to invade a city with such narrow streets. Numbers count for nothing in there."

Inara added, "And getting an army up those steps would be near impossible even if they were only defended by a handful of men."

Vighon looked out at the burning bodies. "Well, you might want to tell them that. I don't think numbers is something they're worried about."

The giant holes might be on fire, but they all knew that more orcs were waiting in the dark. They had the numbers to attack and conquer all three cities in The Arid Lands in a single night...

They would return.

GODS DO NOT BLEED

C utting across the land, Hadavad led his horse by the reins, giving the animal a rest. They had journeyed with barely a stop since setting off from Ilythyra. The old mage fell upon his steely resolve to uncover the mysteries that plagued his mind.

Find The Bastion, Hadavad...

Those words haunted him. Where had they come from? Who was the woman made of light?

The mage had more questions than answers, a pattern that had followed him through his long life. He was more than hesitant to believe in gods or any such divine entities; he had seen too much to have that kind of faith. But he couldn't deny what he had seen and heard. Her voice had been soothing, her light comforting.

Whoever she was, The Bastion had been revealed to him. He could see it clearly in his mind, nestled in The Vrost Mountains, north-east of The Evermoore. The keep itself was a mystery right now, but Hadavad knew there were answers inside. It had all the architectural designs of The First Kingdom, though it appeared more intact than anything they had come across before.

By moonlight alone, Hadavad navigated the rough ground until he found The Selk Road. Thinking of his horse, the mage decided that he would stop in Velia and resupply before continuing his journey north.

Only when the howling winds died down and the snow finally stopped pelting his face did the mage actually see Velia. Fires roared inside the curving walls, illuminating the dragons flying above. Columns of black smoke rose high into the air, just as they had in Tregaran.

Without delay, Hadavad leaped onto his horse and spurred it into a gallop.

Alijah Galfrey could probably count on one hand the number of times in his life he had done as commanded. Tonight would not be adding to that list. After watching Gideon perform a daring leap and descend upon the orcs with unmatchable fury, the half-elf had made for the stone steps.

With an arrow nocked in his bow, Alijah followed a group of red-cloaked soldiers down into the city. He made it to the last five steps before excruciating pain raked at his back. The half-elf yelled and fell into the main wall before sliding down and rolling off the side. The short drop went unnoticed due to the pain that lashed at his body.

Never once was a drop of blood drawn, but he was certain his insides were being shredded by dragon claws. Through the strain, his face turned red as he looked up into the night's sky. A maelstrom of dragons surrounded Malliath, raining hot blood down on Velia.

Only when the black dragon escaped their ambush did the pain subside. It was instant relief to his body, but he wouldn't likely forget the pain any time soon.

Looking up again, Alijah saw Malliath and felt his storm of emotions settle as he finally understood what bond really connected them. It was surreal to see the black dragon flying above and know that they were to be something so much more.

The scope of that revelation was almost too much to think about. The thought that he was indeed a Dragorn, bonded to the oldest dragon alive, and on the verge of immortality… It was more than he could comprehend in the middle of an invasion.

Springing to his feet, Alijah decided to add his bow to the Velians'. Pain or no pain, he wasn't going to let the city fight without him.

The Velian soldiers he had followed down the wall had already put themselves between a group of families and the oncoming orcs. Their swords clashed and both sides suffered immediate fatalities. The families were pressed against the buildings, the fathers creating a line to shield their wives and children.

"This way!" Alijah called, drawing them towards him.

They scrambled, staying close to the buildings. The Velian soldiers were outnumbered, however, and the last of them soon fell to the might of the orcs. Alijah pulled back the string of his bow and fired an arrow between the cluster of families, narrowly missing four of them by an inch. It didn't miss the pursuing orc. Catching the missile in the face, the beast was flung backwards and dropped to the ground.

"That way!" Alijah gestured to the next street where there was no sign of any orcs yet.

Stepping aside to better see his foes, Alijah aimed down the next arrow and dropped another orc. Then another, and another. His aim was true every time, always finding the gaps in their obsidian armour. Seeing their pale flesh stain red with blood was almost as satisfying as the enchanted quiver on his back. It felt freeing to know that he would never run out.

That wasn't how the orcs felt.

The last of the charging beasts made it as close as ten feet before an arrow ran through its eye. A little farther north, Alijah saw bodies flying into the air so high they could be seen over the row of buildings. It was the main gate. Woe betide any orc foolish enough to rush Gideon Thorn.

More screams pulled at Alijah's attention, drawing him deeper into the city. The ground shook under his feet and two streets over the buildings were rocked by another explosion. Tregaran was happening all over again…

The streets became harder to navigate as Velians ran from every corner seeking shelter when their homes were overrun. Windows smashed, shattering glass across the streets, and doors were kicked in by orcs hunting for prey.

Alijah could feel Malliath's rage boiling his blood. It was an anger, a fury that surfaced from somewhere primordial inside his mind. Firing arrows wouldn't be enough to satiate his bloodlust.

He flicked the locking switch on the bow and snapped it in the air to close the limbs. He needed the feel of silvyr in his hand. The short-sword was drawn from over his shoulder, its hourglass shape glittering under the light of the moon. The silvyr sparkled in its diamond-like way, a beautiful weapon of death.

Alijah rammed it into the nearest orc, preventing the beast from kicking in someone's door. He thrust again and again and again. The orc's cry became a gargle then it became nothing at all. The half-elf stood over the body with blood dripping off the blade. The silvyr had pierced the obsidian armour with such ease that Alijah hadn't even felt the resistance.

More orcs were coming for him now, angered by the death of their comrade. Alijah sneered and stepped over the dead body to face them. Using his greatest advantage, he weaved between their attacks and dodged every swing of their jagged blades, turning the orcs in circles. It wasn't long before one of the orcs drove his blade into the neck of another, missing Alijah entirely. The half-elf rolled across the ground and came up behind that orc with his silvyr blade angled to run through his ribs.

That only left one. The beast growled but it didn't rush him as expected. The two combatants circled each other amid the chaos that surrounded them. Alijah could only hold back so long before his rage urged him to attack. It was all-consuming, demanding that he slay orc after orc.

An enormous shadow was silhouetted against a distant fire, the only warning they received before one of the dragons plunged into the ground, dead. Its massive bulk slammed into the street and continued to skid between the houses and shops. Somewhere else in the city, a Dragorn had just fallen dead.

Alijah darted up the wall beside him, using the stone blocks to grab a firm hold. The orc made the mistake of running down the street, where the dragon's corpse soon barrelled over it. When its momentum at last ran out, the blue dragon had left a trail of devastation and bodies behind it.

The half-elf dropped back to the street, his rage quashed by the sight of a dead dragon. He had never seen one die before. It was a sobering image...

Malliath soared overhead with such speed that Alijah's green cloak was blown out behind him. He turned and watched the black dragon fly over the eastern edge of the city, chased closely by Ilargo and three other dragons. Malliath dipped low here and there and used his claws to rip roofs off houses and swing his tail through towers.

The dragon was a force of destruction. Alijah struggled to imagine a world in which they could ever be bonded.

A man running for his life knocked against his shoulder, dragging him from his reverie and reminding him that he was in the middle of a battle. Alijah sheathed his silvyr blade and nocked an arrow, letting it fly with barely an aim; the orcs were so clustered that he couldn't help but hit one of them.

"Run!" he shouted at the Velians, directing them away from the horde charging down the street.

The orcs bared their fangs and ran at Alijah with abandon, their weapons raised high. He slew four of the beasts with arrows before the Red Cloaks intercepted them as they passed a corner in the street. Velian spears pierced the side of the charging orc horde, creating bloody chaos in front of Alijah.

Only a few continued their charge, determined to kill the half-elf, and only one of the five remained on its feet before it was too close for Alijah to launch an arrow. The half-elf drew the arrow from his quiver and ducked under the obvious swing that looked to cleave off his head. He came back up on the other side of the swing, shoulder to shoulder with the orc, and thrust the arrow into its neck. It was a redundant habit thanks to his enchanted quiver, but Alijah still withdrew the arrow from the corpse and nocked it before firing again into the melee.

The Red Cloaks spread out across the street and formed a line to prevent the orcs from gaining any more ground. Swords clashed and warriors fell on both sides, adding to the mounting bodies.

Alijah decided he would hold back and pick them off with his bow, but the sound of galloping horses stopped him from pulling the bow string. On the other side of the street, where the orcs had come from, a team of horses galloped with Velian riders astride. They were led by the king.

The Red Cloaks retreated immediately, withdrawing from battle before they complicated things for the riders. King Rayden bellowed as he swung his sword, opening up the first orc too stupid to get out of his way. The horses charged through the horde with ease, trampling any who didn't fall to a flash of steel.

King Rayden pointed his sword. "Drive them back!" They turned the corner and rode up another street, leaving a pile of dead orcs behind.

The Velians had been faster at responding to the invasion than the Tregarans, but over the din of battle, the dominant sound was that of the orcs. There were just too many of them...

Alijah followed in the wake of the horses, assuming he would make it farther into the city without being challenged. He wasn't sure where he was going yet, but he knew who he was searching for. If the orc that killed Tauren was in Velia, he would find it and kill it.

King Karakulak looked upon the densely populated tunnel that stood as Velia's main gate. The humans had fortified this particular entrance with an abundance of soldiers. It was a good opportunity for the king of orcs to show his mettle, but there would be time for that later.

Now was the time to demonstrate intelligence and tactics...

Standing outside the main gate, Karakulak turned to the hole they had blasted out of the ground. "Big Bastards!" he roared.

The ground thundered as six of the overly-large orcs emerged from The Under Realm in full armour and spiked knuckle-dusters. They were a sight to behold, even from Karakulak's perspective. He imagined the humans would relieve themselves under the shadow of such monsters.

The king pointed at the main gates with his rectangular blade. "Don't stop until you reach the other side of the city!" he commanded.

The Big Bastards grunted and beat their chests, roaring into the night. They were dumb and slow, but the same could be said of any battering ram.

The six lumbering beasts charged at the main gate and Karakulak followed closely behind, eager for his blade to taste man-flesh. The orcs already inside the short tunnel pressed themselves against the walls, making way for the two rows of Big Bastards. The humans grounded the ends of their spears, hoping to impale the massive orcs, but their momentum could not be repelled.

Karakulak jogged behind, smiling at the sound of human bones being crushed under the Big Bastards. His living battering ram threw humans around as if they were no more than sacks of fluid, spraying blood across the courtyard. As commanded, they didn't stop after pushing their way through. They would create a bloody mess from west to east.

Standing inside the city, the king breathed in the air of victory. There were already orcs swarming into Velia from four other locations; it was only a matter of time now.

Looking around, it was clear to see the damage created by the Dragorn. Karakulak ran a finger through one of the many cracks in the stone, noting the circular spread of dead orcs around the entrance. It had been that particular show of power that held Karakulak back after emerging from The Under Realm.

The dragons fought overhead, adding an extra layer of chaos to the battle. It was the first time Karakulak didn't feel like cursing The Crow. Malliath and his rider were keeping the Dragorn from decimating the orcs, just as he had promised.

The king hefted his blade as his baser instincts rose to the surface. There was an animal in him that very much wanted to challenge a dragon, slaying it with his own might. Karakulak took a breath and focused on the city again. He was king because he was smart, not because he was strong. It was a flaw in his kin that they failed to see the former would always triumph over the latter.

"Let dragons deal with dragons!" he yelled over the horde piling into the city. "Take your bones! Burn the city! Bring Neverdark to its knees!" Every command elicited a cheer from the orcs as they spread out.

Karakulak looked to the sky. "I hope you're watching Gordomo," he said softly. "I'm coming for you…"

The king of orcs strode through the city streets. Just the sight of the white V painted over his obsidian armour was enough to send the orcs into a frenzy. It pleased Karakulak. Soon, they would associate him with a god.

The sound of horns drew Karakulak to the south. The pretty beasts the humans rode across their world might serve as a ferocious sight in Neverdark but, to the orcs, they looked like a good meal. The king watched as the tight cluster of horses charged through the street, cutting orcs down with ease. The lead rider wore a golden crown, fixing Karakulak to the spot. The Crow had told him the meaning behind such jewellery.

His grip tightened around the hilt of his sword and he braced himself in the middle of their path. The king of Velia rode on, sure that he was only seconds away from killing another orc. Karakulak roared with all his might, defiant to the last moment. Then he moved. His strength offered him a burst of speed no human could match and he dashed to the right, clearing the galloping riders. At the same time, however, he raised his blade under the jaw of the king's horse, slitting its throat.

The horse's dying cry was a garbled moan, but its body tumbled over itself, launching the king of Velia from his saddle. The riders in his wake were brought down with their horses as they tripped over the king's dead mount. In a matter of moments, the street was littered with fallen horses and crushed riders, all of whom were speared by surrounding orcs.

Karakulak tilted his head, looking down the street at the crowned man. The king of Velia crawled slowly through the blood and dirt, his sword a few feet in front of him. With a wicked grin, Karakulak stalked alongside him and waited for him to grip his sword. A strong boot came down on his hand, breaking the bones therein, and forcing a cry of pain from the man.

With one hand, the orc reached down and picked him up by the back of the neck. Karakulak deliberately laughed, knowing that it would draw the attention of every orc in the street.

"My first king of Neverdark!"

Now was the time to display his brutality and strength. Without magic or steel, Karakulak would kill this king and remind his kin why he was the Bone Lord of The Under Realm.

The pathetic man squirmed in his grip and pushed at Karakulak's arm with his one good hand. The orc king lifted the man and drove his bony brow into his skull. Again and again he head-butted the king of Velia, only stopping when his face was caved in, no longer recognisable as human, let alone a man. Karakulak made certain the golden crown stayed with the body, a message to all the people of Velia.

The orcs began to chant his name, drowning out the battling dragons above. Karakulak soaked up the praise, deserving as he was.

Proving he was yet to reach the heights of a god, an arrow sank into the muscle at the base of his neck, dropping the king to one knee. The orcs ceased their chanting and Karakulak growled, searching for the origin of the arrow. Then another whistled through the night and buried itself in the king's thigh. He roared and looked up to the roof tops, where a familiar archer was crouched.

A low growl rumbled out of Karakulak's throat. It was the archer from Tregaran. This made it three times that the man had drawn blood from the king. He would die slowly for that...

A FIEND IN THE DEEP

Doran ran the edge of his axe along the length of his blade. The doors weren't going to hold much longer; the barrier splitting a little more with every thunderous knock. The Gobbers had retreated by the sound of it, having been replaced by something much larger and far stronger.

"What is that?" Nathaniel asked, his sword already dripping with Gobber blood.

Doran shared a look with Dakmund, the two dwarves well aware of what monster hammered at the doors. It had been a long time since either had come across one, but there was no mistaking its distinctive roar.

"It's a fiend from the depths o' Vengora," Doran replied. "A monster so foul, Grarfath dropped the mountains on top o' the lot o' 'em."

The doors began to cave in and the barrier almost cracked in half. Five of the dwarves barrelled into the entrance before the hinges came loose. Every blow to the doors knocked them back a step.

"Does this fiend have a name?" the old knight pressed.

Doran smirked. "Ye looking' to add a beastie to yer list,

Graycoat?"

Even in the face of death, the immortal knight could still find a cocky smile. "I just like to know what I'm killing."

Dakmund lifted his large sword with both hands, his eyes fixed on the doors. "We call 'em Dwellers, lad. Imagine a Gobber mated with a rock. That's what's comin' through them there doors."

Doran couldn't argue with his brother's description. Its head was as long as a man and its body stood at twenty-feet. Dark red scales blended between the patches of black rock that decorated its hideous form from head to toe. A pair of thick arms ending in four razor-sharp claws were always quick to snatch dwarves out of the dark tunnels and drag them back to its lair. Unlike Gobbers, the Dwellers had reptilian tails as long as a horse.

Just thinking about the nightmarish creature made Doran itch to bury his axe and sword in its hide. "Ha! Wait 'till Rus hears abou' this!"

Reyna didn't share his enthusiasm. "That's if we ever get back to The Pick-Axe..."

"Fear not, elf!" Dakmund placed himself square in the entrance. "This only ends with me sword in that monster's skull!"

The doors caved in and the hinges broke free from the stone, throwing the five dwarves backwards onto the floor. A giant lizard-like head poked through the entrance and hissed, its forked tongue tasting the air.

"Basher!" Dakmund bellowed, dropping to one knee in front of the monstrous head.

The dwarf beside Nathaniel charged forward with his mighty two-handed hammer. It was a nostalgic sight for Doran, who had invented this particular move to break through the front line of an opposing army.

The hammer-wielding dwarf jumped onto Dakmund's back and leaped towards the Dweller's flat snout. His golden hammer came down between the monster's eyes with all the dwarf's weight behind it. The Dweller bowed under the strike and its reptilian eyes rolled into the back of its head. It wasn't a killing blow, but it allowed the fallen dwarves to scramble to their feet and collect their weapons.

"Bring it down boys!" Dakmund bawled in dwarvish.

The dwarves charged with a war cry as the Dweller shook off the disorientating blow. A single roar preceded its own charge. The Dweller barged its way through, tearing down stone and digging its claws into the walls.

The hammer-wielding dwarf was the first to suffer the creature's wrath. The Dweller picked him up in one claw and bashed the stout dwarf into the wall, then the ground, before bending down and tearing him in half with its jaws.

Enraged, the other dwarves threw themselves at the beast. Two succeeded in climbing up its head before it finished chomping on their dead comrade, but the Dweller flicked its head back and launched them out of the chamber.

Axes cut through the air, though only a couple found their way into the monster's scales, between the patches of hardened rock. Dakmund swung his silvyr blade and swiped a chunk out of the Dweller's inverted ankle bone. It roared in agony and backhanded the dwarf into a pillar.

"Dak!" Doran didn't have time to wait and see if his brother stirred; the beast was upon him.

The son of Dorain dropped and rolled out of the way, missing the descending jaws by a foot. The floor shook under the pressing weight of those jaws and its hot breath waved over his face. Doran came up swinging, landing a satisfying strike from his axe into the Dweller's eye.

Anger and pain caused the monster to snap its head back, only Doran's axe was still embedded in its eye… along with Doran's firm grip. The dwarf was taken from the floor and launched into the air so high he flew over the top of the beast. His flight was brought to an abrupt stop when he pummelled into the ceiling. He did, however, fall onto the Dweller's back, where his sword scraped along its tough hide until finally impaling its scales.

Doran clung onto the hilt of his blade with both hands and dug his feet into the patches of rock, steadying himself. The unique sound of Reyna's bow contested with the Dweller's roars for the dominant sound inside the chamber. Every arrow pierced its rocky hide, devastating its insides before bursting out of the other side. More than one of the missiles exploded through the monster's back and chipped Doran's armour.

Nathaniel leaped and rolled to avoid the claws that raked at him. Those same claws tore chunks out of the stone pillars, promising instant death to the old knight.

Doran put his weight forward and buried his sword a little deeper into the fiend's back. The more the Dweller thrashed about, the harder it became for the son of Dorain to focus his eyes. The dwarves below became a blur of armour and flashing silvyr. Judging by the beast's irritated hisses, they were slowly but surely hacking it down.

Another arrow from Reyna exploded out of its back having torn through the creature's chest. The dweller moaned in pain and stumbled, crushing one of dwarves under a clawed foot. The elf dashed out of the way and avoided a snapping bite. Nathaniel took advantage of the lowered head and chopped down with his sword, causing the beast to flinch and fall away. Doran braced himself as the Dweller shoulder-barged a pillar, raining dust and debris down on all of them.

The son of Dorain took his opportunity and rushed over the creature's back, pulling his sword free with him. As the Dweller straightened again, the dwarf had steadied himself over the monster's head. He lost count of how many times he drove his blade down, but the clawed hand that reached up to snatch him changed his priorities.

It was a long drop for a dwarf, so Doran took some of his speed out of the fall by throwing himself into one of the pillars. He bounced off and landed awkwardly over his brother, who finally woke up under the sudden pressure.

"Are ye finished nappin' yet, brother?"

Dakmund ignored the jab and reached for his silvyr sword, his rage renewed. Together, both brothers charged the Dweller, just as they had under the watchful eye of their father, a hundred and fifty years ago.

Their swords hacked and chopped at its legs. Distressed, the

Dweller lashed out at anything and decapitated another dwarf with one of its claws. Doran and Dakmund weaved in and out of its legs, careful to avoid getting in the way of its thick tail. The remaining dwarves ran around the Dweller, coming at it from various angles. It worked to confuse the beast, offering too many victims to keep track of. All the while, Nathaniel dived in and out with his precision strikes, never failing to cut through the scales and miss the patches of rock.

The Dweller hissed, stopped moving around, and reached down to grab Dakmund. One of the other dwarves shoved him out of the way and found himself in the monster's deadly grip instead. The dwarf cried out for only a second before the Dweller squeezed its four fingers and crushed his insides.

With fury as his guide, Dakmund swung his silvyr sword up and impaled the monster in the thigh. The exquisite blade had no trouble splitting the rock and piercing the scaly hide. The Dweller's hiss morphed into a roar and it released the dwarf's misshapen corpse. Dodging the falling body, Dakmund yanked his sword free again, removing the only thing that had prevented the stream of arterial blood from pumping out. The Dweller stumbled and fell into another pillar as the floor quickly began to run red with its blood.

Taking advantage of the creature's distress, Reyna dashed into the gap between its clawed feet and aimed her bow straight up. The arrow impacted the Dweller in the soft pallet under its jaw, but the magic of the bow launched the arrow with enough explosive speed that the monster's head burst open, decorating the ceiling with its brain matter.

"Watch out!" Doran warned, seeing the big beast sway on its feet.

The Galfreys dived out of the way and the Dweller toppled over, slamming into the wall on the far side of the chamber. The ancient wall was pushed through and reduced to a pile of broken stones under the creature's weight.

The Dweller dead, everyone took a breath, slumping against whatever was closest. A handful of dwarves lay dead in different parts of the chamber, their bodies horribly mutilated. No one spoke for a minute, happy, instead, to simply catch their breath and thank the gods that they had survived where others hadn't.

Doran straightened up, cracking his back, and made to retrieve his axe. It was lodged deep in the Dweller's eye and required a boot to its face and two hands to pull it free. The son of Dorain eyed the arrow in the ceiling, surrounded by a web of cracks and gore.

"That's some bow…" he said absently. "Hang abou'! Where's the lad?"

Reyna's confusion quickly turned to realisation and then guilt. "Petur?" she called.

They all heard the excited squeal in the far corner. Petur Devron was crouched by a series of runes carved into the wall.

"This is fascinating!" he said, though no one was sure who he was talking to. "I've never seen runes such as these before!"

Doran gave the man his most indignant look. "How is it he's jus' been sat there this whole time?" The dwarf looked from the eccentric fool to the dead Dweller.

Completely oblivious to the question, or indeed the large corpse in the middle of the chamber, Petur replied, "I'm going to have to get a sketch of these runes. Someone needs to catalogue this language!"

Doran blinked hard. There wasn't a scratch on him. "Lucky fool…" he growled, turning back to the mess.

The four dwarves who had been killed by the Dweller were lined in a row. Dakmund himself went from each one, offering prayers to Grarfath and Yamnomora on their behalf. The dwarf in Doran was looking at their discarded weapons and wondering which would feel better in his hands. They were his old ways, however, and the son of Dorain shook his head, ridding his mind of such thoughts.

His feet detected the subtlest vibration in the stone. It was too subtle for any but a dwarf to notice and looking around, his kin had felt the same thing.

"What's wrong?" Reyna asked, perceptive as always.

Her question was answered by a cacophony of howls and hissing roars. The Gobbers were returning!

"Ready yerselves!" Doran squared himself in front of the entrance.

Reyna declined to nock an arrow. "We cannot win against those numbers," she protested.

One of the other dwarves grunted. "Speak for yerself, she-elf!"

That poked at Doran's temper, but he couldn't deny the reasoning behind Reyna's protest. They had already lost dwarves fighting the Dweller, after all...

"Reyna's right, Dak," Doran agreed, glancing at his brother. "I love killin' Gobbers more than anyone, but a pack this size... It'd spell death for us all."

Dakmund was fixed on the ruined entrance, waiting for the howling Gobbers to descend upon them. "What choice do we 'ave, brother? It's fight in 'ere or fight out there. At least in 'ere they're funnelled on the way in."

"Or," Nathaniel announced from the back of the chamber, "we could go this way?" The old knight was standing on the Dweller's head, on the other side of the wall it had brought down. "There's another passageway here that runs parallel to the chamber."

Doran shared a look with Dakmund and pleaded with his eyes to make his brother see sense.

"A'right!" Dakmund relented, pretending he had been up for a good fight. "We go that way!"

The Gobbers were almost at the entrance now, their howls and roars echoing off the chamber walls. Reyna collected Petur Devron, ushering him towards the broken wall.

"Where did that thing come from?" he asked, stepping over the Dweller's head.

Doran grumbled and pushed him through, eager to get them all as far away from the Gobbers as possible.

The son of Dorain jogged alongside Reyna and Nathaniel, his mood sour. "Did I mention how much I love travellin' with ye two?"

DRAGON FALL

Velia was falling into ruin. Fires were spreading out of control, bodies were piling up in the streets, and the sun was far from rising.

Gideon Thorn had cut a bloody swathe through the city, slaying any orcs that got in his way. Only twice had he been forced to seek immediate shelter due to the pain Ilargo shared with him.

Above the city, the dragons continued their aerial battle, adding their snarls and roars to the din of the chaotic city. Malliath had already killed Falmir and his dragon Jorlaxa. Gideon had felt them separate from the bond, their death so swift that Jorlaxa hadn't been able to pass on her memories to one of the other dragons.

Their loss would have to be grieved later. If he thought about it too much, Gideon feared he would miss the swing of a sword and find himself and Ilargo joining the fatalities.

What he couldn't miss, however, were the six massive orcs charging up the street. They were much larger than the orcs currently filling the streets, with impossibly thick arms and legs. They carried no weapons and nor did they need any. The orcs rammed their way through every cluster of Red Cloaks, throwing the soldiers around like rag dolls.

Gideon shot out his hand at the three orcs who stepped in his way, hurling them all through a shop window with a single spell. He stepped into the middle of the street, putting himself between the six massive orcs and the Velians attempting to fortify the crossroads.

Twice the size of the largest man and crowned with thick horns, the orcs caught sight of Gideon and bared their fangs. The lead orc backhanded a much smaller orc to clear its path to the Master Dragorn.

With two hands wrapped around Mournblade's hilt, Gideon braced himself in the street. His intentions towards them were clear to the Vi'tari blade and he knew the scimitar would work tirelessly until they were all dead.

Only a few feet remained between him and the charging behemoths when Ilargo swooped down and snatched four of them from the ground. His tail dragged through the street behind him and clobbered the two remaining orcs, throwing them in opposite directions.

Leaving Gideon behind, the green dragon gained tremendous height in a single beat of his wings. Then he released the orcs from his claws. All four of the massive beasts fell to their deaths, impacting the city walls at great speed.

I could have handled them, he said into his bond with Ilargo.

You haven't got time, Ilargo replied, his voice relaying a sense of urgency. *Asher is on the northern wall!*

Gideon turned to his right and focused his sight down the length of the street until it met the northern wall. Looking up, he couldn't see the old ranger, but he knew better than to doubt Ilargo's eyes.

I'll find him!

Hurry, Gideon…

He didn't like Ilargo's hopeless tone, betraying his sense of defeat. Malliath wasn't even fighting his companion at that moment, but he was ferociously clawing and biting at Sabitha and Galda, pinning the yellow dragon onto one of the towering statues. It was only a matter of time before the raging dragon killed another Dragorn…

Gideon sprinted towards the northern wall, pausing only to cut down an orc and save the life of another Velian. He easily threw two orcs aside who challenged him on the steps. On the wall itself, there were very few orcs, with most of their horde in the streets. A handful of Red Cloaks showed a cluster of orcs that they wouldn't abandon their home without a fight.

Their victory over the orcs was but a small one in the grand scheme, though Gideon still found himself elated to see the knights of Velia slay their enemies.

That elation was instantly replaced by dread.

Beyond the Red Cloaks, a figure in dark armour and a flowing black cloak strode towards them. Asher's two-handed broadsword was already in hand, his greying hair hanging over his face in knots. His expression was that of a grimace, marred with cuts that mirrored Malliath's own.

"Get out of the way!" Gideon warned.

The Red Cloaks had no idea who Asher was, but he certainly wasn't an orc and therefore he was seen as an ally. They turned to Gideon, confused as to why he was running towards them and shouting.

They missed Asher raising his sword. The Dragon Knight brought his blade down, splitting the first Velian down the back, killing him instantly.

"No!" Gideon ran as fast as he could.

Asher had their full attention now, but there wasn't a knight among them who possessed the skills to beat the old ranger. His broadsword sprang left and right, parrying and slashing. One by one they dropped at his feet, dead. The last of them received a boot to the chest and was launched from the ramparts and down into the city.

Without thinking, Gideon leaped over the bodies and came down on Asher with Mournblade. The Master Dragorn allowed some of Ilargo's feral nature to bleed with his own emotions, giving him the thoughts and feelings of a superior predator.

Asher stepped back with every blow from Gideon, his broadsword rising to meet Mournblade. The two warriors collided again and again in a clash of steel, the Master Dragorn careful to keep the old ranger on the defensive.

An unorthodox twist of Mournblade cast Asher's sword aside, opening him up for a backhanded swipe. The scimitar cut across the Dragon Knight's face, tracing a red line over his right cheek and the bridge of his nose. Gideon jumped and turned in the air, his form that of the Mag'dereth, and kicked Asher in the chest.

Baring his teeth in the manner of an orc, Gideon looked down on Asher as he rolled back across the ramparts, bleeding from the cheek. In the distance, Malliath roared twice; once for the new gash over his face and a second time when Ilargo took advantage. Teeth marks dug into Asher's arm and the fabric of his shirt became wet with blood.

The old ranger scowled at his opponent and glanced at his fallen sword, resting beside Gideon's foot. The Master Dragorn saw Asher as Ilargo would see a bison; a vulnerable prey that could do nothing to stop him.

He took a step towards the Dragon Knight and stopped, thoughts of Alijah rising to the surface. He couldn't kill Asher, nor did he want to. For all the damage he could cause, Malliath too, neither of them deserved what was happening to them. His reservations set in, affecting his will over Mournblade, just as it had done in Lirian.

He couldn't allow a repeat of Lirian.

How many had the pair killed since then, all because he couldn't find the will to cut Asher down? His moral dilemma gave him pause for too long and the Dragon Knight leaped at him. Mournblade came up and intercepted the dagger that flashed in Asher's hand, but Gideon's mixed feelings prevented any counterattack from the Vi'tari blade.

Asher, enslaved to The Crow, didn't harbour any mixed feelings. An uppercut with his free hand caught Gideon under the jaw and a second jab connected with his windpipe. Two steps he stumbled before the Dragon Knight planted a foot in his chest and kicked him down the ramparts.

Gideon felt his grip release Mournblade and the scimitar

clattered across the stone until it disappeared over the lip of the rampart. His hands instinctively reached for his throat and he opened his mouth wide as he tried to suck in any air. He coughed and spluttered, scrambling backwards on the floor to put some distance between him and Asher. The Dragon Knight moved towards him, bruised and bloodied with his dagger in hand.

With some air finally reaching his lungs, Gideon succeeded in standing, only now Asher stood between him and Mournblade. Through ragged breaths, the Master Dragorn clenched his fists and cracked his knuckles. His knowledge of the Mag'dereth offered him multiple fighting styles with or without a sword.

Hurry Gideon! Ilargo cried out.

Gideon and Asher clashed in a flurry of fists and kicks. The Master Dragorn slipped between the openings and hammered the Dragon Knight. Asher took the blows and never failed to demonstrate the skills he had learned as an assassin of Nightfall. Gideon felt the nerve clusters in his shoulders taking the brunt of Asher's counterattacks, steadily wearing his reflexes down.

Before either could claim victory, both men crumpled to the floor in agony. High above them, Ilargo had violently crashed into Malliath. Their claws raked and their jaws snapped, as all the while their wings fought to keep them airborne.

The Master Dragorn writhed around with veins bulging under his skin. Claw marks raked across his chest and teeth clamped down on his limbs, drawing blood and tearing at his muscles. Asher silently endured the same torture, doubling over and grabbing at his wounded limbs.

Malliath used all four of his claws to push away from Ilargo, who dropped a hundred feet before spreading his wings into a glide. The bond between the remaining Dragorn was becoming harder to focus on, but Gideon knew the other three dragons were hurtling towards Malliath. It was perhaps the only reprieve he and Ilargo would get. He had to make it count.

Gritting his teeth through the pain, Gideon stood up and faced Asher. The Dragon Knight appeared to be in just as much pain and

Gideon shared a thought for Alijah, who, somewhere, was feeling everything they did.

"If you're in there, Asher…" Gideon wiped the blood from his eyebrow. "If you're in there, I need you to fight this. Illian is nearly gone! We need to fight the orcs, not you!"

Without a word, Asher lunged at him with his dagger. The small blade swiped left then right, each move angled to open Gideon's throat. The Master Dragorn evaded every strike and opened his arms, offering his chest as the perfect target. The inevitable thrust came at his heart and Gideon twisted his body, bringing him alongside Asher's outstretched arm. With two hands gripping the Dragon Knight's arm and wrist, Gideon powered his chest into his foe's elbow, bending the arm against the joint.

The dagger dropped to the floor and Gideon whipped his arm under and round, throwing Asher's arm out wide and exposing his chest and face. Two swift punches to the jaw and nose knocked the Dragon Knight's head back and a third, open-palmed attack to the chest threw Asher to the floor.

Gideon blinked the blood out of his eyes. "There must be something of you in there!" He circled Asher, pausing to kick his dagger off the edge of the rampart. "Don't you recall any of this? You've been up here before. You've fought on these very walls for the good of the realm!"

Asher groaned and slowly rose to his feet again, his eyes dead. Whatever it was looking back at Gideon, it wasn't the Asher he had known.

Gideon shook his head, despair creeping into his voice. "I'm so sorry, Asher… You didn't deserve this. You should have been allowed to rest."

Asher responded with his fists. The Dragon Knight came at Gideon with renewed fury, demonstrating the deadly hand-to-hand techniques perfected by the Arakesh of Nightfall. Gideon was forced to use every limb to keep Asher's attacks at bay, only succeeding twice to land his own counterattacks. The old ranger took the hits without care and always came back at Gideon with successful punches of his own.

Look out!

Ilargo's warning came without explanation, but the dragon imparted a great sense of danger combined with the overwhelming need to leap out of the way. Gideon kicked Asher backwards and used his resistance to launch himself back down the rampart. The two separated as Malliath hammered the wall, pinning Yorva to the stone.

The rampart was violently shaken before Gideon could jump into the air, throwing him sideways towards the inner edge of the wall. Before he fell over the side, he glimpsed Malliath's jaws wrap around Yorva's purple neck and heard the dragon's neck snap. Malliath pushed off the wall, beating his wings over the ramparts, and left Yorva's long neck and head to follow her body off the wall and plummet to the ground.

Gideon held on to the edge of the inner wall by his fingers. Looking down, the drop was a hundred feet, only this time he didn't have any elixirs to save him from the impact. The Master Dragorn groaned through the pain and lifted his body weight by his arms alone.

Asher was standing over him.

Gideon let his shoulders drop back down and hung by his fingers once again. He was at the mercy of the Dragon Knight.

"Asher…" Gideon could feel his fingers going numb. "Asher, you have to fight this. Don't let him control you!"

Without a hint of emotion, the old ranger lifted his broadsword, holding it directly above Gideon's face.

"Asher!" Gideon pleaded.

In the seconds he had before Asher plunged his blade, Gideon imagined Ilargo falling from the sky, dead. Ilargo's life would always be the thing he fought for, no matter what trials he had to endure. He would survive.

Gideon let go of the wall.

~

Alijah skipped over the roof tops of Velia, narrowly avoiding the obsidian arrows and spears that scraped and rebounded off the slate. More than one of the black arrows cut holes through his green cloak as he leaped over the chimneys.

His elevated vantage gave Alijah a view of the city in all its fiery horror. Trapped inside Velia's high walls, the people had nowhere to run and the Red Cloaks fell in every street defending them.

Above it all, the dragons were too occupied with Malliath and their riders were nowhere to be seen. Their inability to protect the people of Velia set Alijah's blood on fire. It should be Gideon trying to kill that orc, not him. He felt like roaring into the sky to let out some of that anger, a feeling that reminded him he was being influenced by Malliath.

Stealing a glance below, the king-slaying orc was in pursuit amidst those who fired upon him. Yet again, the pale beast had taken Alijah's arrows and continued as if they were nothing more than splinters. The orc barked a harsh and guttural language at the others, directing the archers.

The half-elf skidded down the angled roof and nocked an arrow, relying heavily on his elven heritage to keep his balance. Alijah released the arrow before propelling himself along the edge of the building, killing one of the creatures and evading another salvo from the orcs.

Looking ahead, his sprint was about to come to an abrupt end. One of the main streets cut through the row of houses, presenting the half-elf with an impossible leap. Nocking and firing another arrow faster than most could even observe, Alijah impaled the orc climbing over the lip of the roof, the same roof he was moments from running out of.

A spear whistled through the air in front of him, helping Alijah to decide on his change of direction. He lost speed dashing up the angled roof, but his immediate change in direction caused all of the orcish archers to overshoot. Alijah rolled over the apex of the roof as obsidian bolts bounced off the slate. Tucking his legs up, the half-elf slid down the other side of the roof and sprang across the narrow alley, leaping from one wall then back to the adjacent until he landed on the street.

The alley was dark and deserted, offering Alijah a moment to catch his breath. He had hoped to kill that orc with an arrow, saving him from the hordes that followed the commanding creature around.

A whimper pulled his attention to the stack of barrels behind him.

Alijah's senses were on high alert and he found himself aiming an arrow at a man guarding his family. The blood was pounding in his ears and sweat ran down his temple and over the nocked arrow, resting against his cheek. He took another breath and lowered his bow.

The roar of an orc invaded the alley and Alijah didn't hesitate to raise his bow again and let fly. The arrow sank into the creature's face and threw him back into the main street, where a cluster of the horned beasts took note.

Alijah tensed his jaw and nocked another arrow. "You need to get out of here, *now*!" he instructed the family.

Looking down to the other end of the alley, more orcs were coming, blocking any escape. The half-elf growled and turned to the nearest door. He had no idea where it would lead but he kicked it in anyway.

"In here!" he barked. "Find somewhere to hide; I'll hold them off!"

The mother thanked him as the father scooped up their daughter and disappeared through the door. Alijah had promised he would hold off the orcs and so he would. He just had no idea how yet...

"Come on, then!" he yelled, channelling some of Vighon's pre-fight fervour.

He loosed three arrows in quick succession before folding the bow and hooking it back onto his quiver. The silvyr short-sword was in his hand before the three dead orcs hit the floor.

Alijah slammed the door shut behind the family and stood his ground in the alley. With enemies coming at him from both sides, he wished more than ever that Vighon had his back.

An orcish word filled the alleyway, so loud and so harsh that it could be heard over the charging beasts. Then they stopped. Their ragged hot breaths could be seen in the icy air, their reflective eyes fixed on the half-elf. Not a single orc moved.

Alijah's head snapped from one end of the alley to the other, checking that both hordes had ceased their charge. The group in front of him began to part, giving way to the orc who had killed Tauren and King Rayden. A white V marked his black chestplate, though its meaning was lost on him. Perhaps it was a symbol he could decipher when the orc was naught but a corpse.

The orc tilted his head and his eyes looked to settle on Alijah's pointed ears. The beast's lip curled into a growl and it hefted the rectangular blade in its meaty hand. Stepping clear of the others, the arrow impaling its thigh was clear to see, though it made no difference to the orc's stride.

Determined to maintain his resolve and hide any fear that might creep into his bones, Alijah dropped into an aggressive stance before pouncing at his foe. The silvyr blade flashed left and right but the orc moved with every swipe, evading the bite of the blade. The watching horde of orcs backed up, giving the combatants space.

Alijah used the left-hand wall to gain height and come down on the orc with a strong thrust. The orc, however, showed incredible reflexes and spun on the spot, providing Alijah's blade with nothing but air to pierce. The sound of the beast's mighty sword cutting through the air behind him gave him cause to drop and roll across the alley. When he jumped back to his feet, the orc examined the rectangular blade in its own hand, glancing briefly at Alijah.

Then he tossed it away and sneered. Alijah was sure it was a smirk.

The crowding orcs cheered and beat their armoured chests. Alijah didn't care; let the stupid orc think it could kill him without a weapon. One way or another, Tauren's killer was about to become acquainted with a blade of silvyr.

It was tempting to lunge at the orc, weaponless as it was, but Alijah moved cautiously, taking the measure of the beast. Its pale skin was pulled tightly around its muscles. Its face was all angles and its bony brow formed up into a pair of thick curving horns that flicked into the air at the end. Everything about their breed was the stuff of man's nightmares.

Still, the orc didn't possess anything that would prevent silvyr from opening up its insides.

The orc roared with the bravado of a lion and lashed out at him. Its meaty hands ended in sharpened nails designed to tear through flesh, or in this case, the leather of Alijah's light armour. The half-elf dashed back before those nails could pierce his leathers and open his chest, but the orc was relentless, coming at him again and again in the narrow alley.

Alijah dodged and weaved between the clawing hands, using the blade as a threat to keep the orc from pinning him. Twice he batted one of the pale hands away with the silvyr, drawing red lines across the orc's arms and hands. One particular cut pushed the beast back a step, luring Alijah in for a killing thrust.

The half-elf unleashed a roar of his own and advanced on the orc, so sure was he that his blade was a moment away from ending the fight. The tip of the silvyr pierced the obsidian armour over the orc's heart and tasted but a single drop of its monstrous blood. Alijah grunted under the exertion of his thrust, his blade only an inch from slaying his foe, but the orc's vice-like grip around his wrist saw his efforts go to waste.

The orcish hand had snapped around Alijah's wrist with such speed that the half-elf couldn't say he saw the beast even move. The more he pushed the harder it squeezed. The orc's free hand shot up into the his throat and five thick digits coiled around his windpipe. Taken from the ground, Alijah was slammed against the alley wall and pinned. One hard shove from the orc forced his hand into the brick, causing him to drop the silvyr blade.

Alijah struggled in the monster's grip and kicked out, desperate to be free if only to breathe again. The orc held him firm and drew closer until his hot breath stung his sense of smell. It looked to be struggling with something in its mouth before a single word found Alijah's ears.

"Elf..." it growled.

It was a strange thing to see such a beast conjure a word from the common tongue, but Alijah's lack of air prevented him from dwelling on it. He kicked out, pushing his boot down on the arrow protruding from the orc's thigh. The bolt didn't snap straight away, forcing the beast's leg to buckle in the direction of Alijah's foot. It was just enough pain to see the orc release his grip.

Alijah's fists were swinging before his feet hit the ground. He didn't have the strength of his elven heritage, but he did have its speed. The half-elf planted four fists into the orc's face before it had chance to recover from the pain in its leg. Unfortunately, Alijah's last punch went wild and struck the beast across its bony brow.

Cursing, Alijah snapped his hand back to discover bloodied knuckles and numb fingertips. The orc gnashed his fangs and retaliated with a backhand to Alijah's face, a strike so hard it knocked the half-elf back into the wall and down to the ground. With a beard stained red with his own blood, Alijah crawled across the ground hoping his disorientated sight would correct itself as soon as possible.

Through the slush and snow, his hand nudged the hilt of his short-sword. His grip was strong and his swing true, but the orc snatched his wrist mid-strike and pulled him back to his feet before hammering a solid fist into his chest. Alijah felt the air rush from his lungs as he was launched down the alley. He rolled and tumbled over himself, between the parting orcs who didn't dare interfere.

Forced to crawl again, Alijah gasped for breath as he entered the main street. The Red Cloaks were dying in the streets, outnumbered by the swarming orcs. Innocent people lay strewn over each other, caught in the middle of the battle. Alijah was desperate to help them; he wanted nothing more than to solidify his bond with Malliath if for no other reason than to decimate the orc legions.

A strong hand gripped the back of his neck and easily lifted him from the ground. The half-elf swung his arm out, breaking the hold, and threw all of his weight behind his fist. The orc took the punch, its nose bloodied, and brought his forehead down on Alijah's face. The bony brow cut his cheek open and sent an impact through his skull that caused him to temporarily black out. When his eyes snapped open again he was back on the ground and blood was trickling across his cheek and over his nose.

The orc was relentless. It picked Alijah up again and thrust its fist into his gut. The assault lifted Alijah from the ground and he vomited. The orc's triumphant roar sounded distant despite his close proximity. The feel of his bow and quiver on his back reminded Alijah that he needed to put some distance between him and his foe; only then could he put an arrow in his eye.

Staggering to his feet, Alijah looked about, hoping to see a way through the melee so that he might turn back and fire his bow. But the orc was upon him. One back-hand followed by another threw the half-elf around. His hair was gripped in one orcish hand while the other pounded him in the face. Alijah fell backwards and crashed into one of the orcs fighting a Velian soldier. The Red Cloak took the advantage and stabbed his enemy in the ribs before turning to defend Alijah against the pursuing orc. Alijah wanted to warn the Velian but the soldier lunged at the pale beast.

The orc side-stepped the soldier's thrust and trapped his head in a vice-like grip. One quick tug snapped the man's neck.

Alijah watched hopelessly as the Red Cloak fell to the ground, dead. Looking around, more Velians were falling by the second. There was no sign of any Dragorn and even the sky was clear of warring dragons. No one was coming to help him. No one was going to save Velia.

The orc with a V painted on his armour stood over Alijah and looked down on him. Another of his kin arrived by his side and handed the fiend his rectangular blade. Alijah lay on his back, his body exhausted and beaten. In his last moments, he wondered what would happen to Malliath if he died. Would the dragon suffer the same fate or was their bond not strong enough?

He hated the thought of never knowing.

The orc roared and lifted his blade, ready to plunge it down into Alijah's chest. Had he not been so wounded, Alijah might have spared an amusing thought for the moment. To think of all the time he had wasted being miserable about his mortality when it didn't really matter. He was still going to die in his twenties.

The orc stabbed down with his black blade but the deadly edge never touched Alijah's skin. A blinding light erased the night and the orcs were hurled from where they stood in a cacophony of roars and clattering armour. Behind the great clamour, Alijah could hear a familiar voice casting spells at the top of his lungs.

Hadavad leaped into view with his staff swinging and spells firing. All manner of destructive magic erupted from his staff, blasting orcs into walls and severing limbs with ease. The mage launched an orb of brilliant light into the air, creating a miniature sun over the street. It highlighted the death that surrounded them in stark contrasts, but it also kept the sun-fearing orcs at bay.

"Come on!" Hadavad crouched and helped him to find his feet.

Alijah could barely stand, let alone walk. The ground failed to register under his feet and he was forced to lean on Hadavad for support. The mage wielded his staff in one hand and continued to unleash a magical torrent of death upon the orcs. Any Red Cloaks that still survived had taken to the side streets, desperate to escape the nightmare.

"Quickly now!" Hadavad turned Alijah around and guided him down the street. "We need to get out of here. The city is lost."

They were half way through the city before Alijah's mind caught up with the fact that he was being supported by Hadavad. Were he able to string a sentence together, he would have asked the mage what he was doing in Velia.

Everywhere they turned, every street and alley they traversed, the orcs were winning. The Velians were being slaughtered and between them all there were dragon corpses littering the city. Velia was dying.

Hadavad hurled orcs every which way when they chose foolishly to get in their way. The end of the mage's staff was smoking from all the discharged spells, but every one cast ended in a dead orc.

Alijah did his best to stay alert for their escape, but when the eastern gates came into view, the half-elf found his vision finally fading at the edges as his head pounded with every beat of his heart. He felt Hadavad's grip on him falling away and the ground rushing up to meet him. The sound of another orc being cut down by magic was the last thing he registered before oblivion swallowed him whole.

~

Gideon Thorn groaned deep in his chest, the pain in his leg too sharp to even utter a word. Lying awkwardly across a broken collection of boxes and barrels, the Master Dragorn looked up the outer wall of Velia's defences, unbelieving of his survival.

He had let go, avoiding Asher's killing blow, and slid down the stone wall until his hands gripped a protruding block. The snow on the wall and the blood on his hands had prevented him from maintaining his grip, but the brief pause had taken some of the momentum out of his fall. It had been just enough to stop the fall from killing him. But it hadn't been enough to stop his right leg from breaking.

Hidden within the debris of his own making, many orcs had passed him by without notice.

Ilargo... Gideon called out across their bond.

I am here, Ilargo replied, his voice equally strained by pain.

I'm sorry, Gideon apologised. **I couldn't beat him.**

That thought haunted the Master Dragorn. How many more would die because Asher and Malliath were still enslaved to The Crow? He was the head of the Dragorn; he should be able to defeat any foe!

Nor could I beat Malliath, Ilargo added.

Where are you? Gideon asked.

When you let go of the wall, I abandoned my attack on Malliath and turned for the coast. I'm on the beach now, just north of the city.

How's your leg? Gideon glanced at his own and knew Ilargo's would be similarly broken.

I can't use it, but I'm not the one trapped inside the city.

Gideon peered over the splintered boxes and inspected the street. It was clear since most of the fighting was taking place in the centre of the city.

Where's Malliath now? he asked.

I saw him and Asher take to the sky, but Malliath appeared to be in some distress.

Gideon remembered Alijah then. He had left the young man on the wall. Where was he now? Was he still alive?

Calm your mind, Ilargo bade. *Alijah Galfrey has a knack for surviving and he is bonded with Malliath. If he were dead, we would know about it.*

I need to find him, Ilargo. I brought him into this mess.

No, what you need to do is survive. We must find our way back to each other and recover.

Gideon disagreed, but the jolt of pain that shot through his leg was overpowering. He wouldn't be helping anyone in his condition. Looking around, the Master Dragorn discovered an arching storm drain at the base of the wall, not too far from his position. If he could make it through there, he could crawl all the way through to the fields of Alborn.

Gideon struggled to contain his agonised groan. **I'm coming, Ilargo...**

∾

Karakulak blinked hard several times before his vision returned. The king was flat on his back and under the weight of a dead orc. The sound of fighting continued around him, but it was distant now. Rolling the dead orc away, Karakulak found his feet and shook off the after effects of the spell.

Magic...

The king sneered, searching the street for any sign of the elf or the mage who had dared to interrupt his kill. He discovered only more of his dead kin and his rectangular sword, now broken in two.

A deep growl rumbled from within his throat, but the effort sent searing pains through his chest where the spell had struck him. Still, he was alive. Even magic had failed to bring him down.

Sighting their king, more orcs appeared from the side streets, their pale flesh coated in blood. The dying screams of the Velians seemed distant now.

"The city is ours, my King!" one of the orcs declared, oblivious to the fight Karakulak had just lost.

The king shoved the orc aside and strode through the street, checking the bodies again. The elven archer had escaped death and not for the first time. It took Karakulak another moment to realise the sky was empty of any dragons, the only creatures that posed a serious threat.

Surprising them all, the ground thundered under their feet and the corpses that littered the ground shook. Karakulak turned around to see his kin backing away from a black dragon whose bulk filled the entire street. Its mighty wings spread over the buildings on either side and its horned head dipped low to reveal a man on its back.

The Crow's puppet…

Asher climbed down from Malliath and paused by the dragon's neck. The man had taken a beating by the looks of him, the wyrm too. Karakulak was convinced the Dragon Knight was going to fall over as he weaved through the bodies between them.

Finally, Asher stopped in the middle of the street, taking no care of the orcs that watched his every move. Karakulak could see their caution and he shared it to some degree. This man had been brought back from the dead, his bones reforged and his body made whole again. It was unnatural, as all magic was.

With Malliath behind him, the Dragon Knight wasn't a foe to challenge, though The Crow had assured the king that he was an ally, or at least an ally of The Black Hand. The distinction between their order and the orcs was something Karakulak was growing to see more clearly every day. He didn't like the fact that they had a dragon on their side.

Without a word or so much as a glance at any of them, Asher crouched down and retrieved a short-sword that had been poking out from under one of the bodies. It was the elf's blade, and an exquisite one at that. Though too small for Karakulak to wield, he wanted it as a trophy.

"That is mine," he demanded in his guttural language.

Karakulak presented Asher with a wall of muscle and

determination, not that the Dragon Knight took any notice. Malliath, on the other hand, raised his head and exhaled a sharp hot breath, warning the king not to take another step.

Asher, ignorant of the exchange, held the hour-glass blade in both hands, transfixed. The Dragon Knight deftly spun the sword in his hand before returning to Malliath. The man's dark cloak billowed out behind him and the short-sword flashed a brilliant silver as he ascended the dragon's scales.

They were all buffeted by those mighty wings. Malliath lifted off, revealing more wounds on his thick legs and tail. Karakulak watched the dragon disappear, wondering when and where the two would show up next.

"My king!" one of the orcs called. "The dawn is coming!"

To any creature of the Neverdark, the approaching sky-fire would not become apparent for a short while, but to eyes of The Under Realm, the subtle changes in the night sky were obvious.

"We still need to secure the northern wall," another orc pointed out.

Karakulak considered the state of his victory over Velia and found himself displeased with retreating before every human was dead. How many bones would escape the city while the orcs waited in darkness?

The smell of magic and man-flesh carried on the breeze. The orcs parted to allow one of the mages of The Black Hand to stand before their king. There was blood on the mage's robes but none of it belonged to the man. At least they were adding their spells to the cause of the orcs…

"My master made you a promise, king of orcs; one that has yet to be fulfilled." The mage's command of the orcish language was commendable, considering the rigidity of his tongue.

"What promise is that?" Karakulak asked.

The mage eyed the top of the southern wall, behind the king. "See for yourself."

It wasn't an answer, and so Karakulak decided that if he was displeased with what he discovered atop the southern wall, he would remove the man's spine with his bare hands. He couldn't, however, deny his curiosity.

Meaningful strides placed the king of orcs on the southern wall only minutes later. Those that accompanied him were clearly becoming agitated with the idea of ascending rather than returning to the shadows of The Under Realm, but no one would disobey him.

The sight that greeted Karakulak was perhaps the most expansive vista he had ever seen. Having lived underground since birth, the orc had never looked upon so much of Verda. Laid out before him were the snowy fields of Alborn and choppy waves of The Adean to his left. That horizon went on and on for more miles than his eyes could fathom.

For all of Neverdark's majesty, it was that which approached across the sky that rooted the king to the stone. The orc laughed from a place deep in his belly as The Crow's words echoed in his memory.

If the orc goes to war with Neverdark, the earth will go to war with the sky fire...

Karakulak looked from the black smoke choking the sky to the rising sky fire in the east. How The Crow had achieved such a feat was beyond the king, but what he did know was undeniable.

"A new Age has laid siege to Neverdark!" he bellowed over the ramparts. "THE AGE OF THE ORC!"

46

THE LONG NIGHT

Vighon Draqaro kept one hand on the hilt of his sword and one on the strap of his shield, keeping it slung over his back. He did his best to push through the dense crowds of Grey Stone without knocking anyone over.

From every ravine-like street, the city's population was steadily evacuating through the ancient cave network that connected Grey Stone to the southern curve of Vengora.

Vighon paused and looked up the high walls of the mountain that encased the city. The zig-zagging stairs were occupied by the lords and ladies who had no choice but to join the commoners. They marched down the stairs with their servants in tow, carrying the many useless sundries they couldn't bear to be without.

The northerner had briefly inspected these tunnels and knew it would be hours before they were all safely inside. Whether they had that time remained to be seen. The presence of a particularly ferocious red dragon had kept the orcs at bay for the rest of the night and Inara had assured them the sun would halt any further attack.

Eager to get out of the crowds, Vighon scanned over the hundreds of heads in search of Galanör. The elven ranger was always above it all, never failing to find a high perch that separated him from the population. True to his nature, Vighon spotted the elf sitting atop one of the few stairways that wasn't packed with people. With his legs hanging over the edge of the first platform, between the stairs, Galanör surveyed the humans with intense scrutiny.

Vighon bounded up the steps carved out of the mountain and came up behind the elf. The view was narrow thanks to the high walls, but the central courtyard could still be seen at the head of the street. Soldiers were stationed at every corner, guiding the populace into the depths of the city.

"Where do the tunnels lead?" he asked the elf.

Without turning to face the northman, Galanör replied, "They go north as far as I could tell."

Russell Maybury's heavy steps sounded from above as he descended towards them. "They're as old as Grey Stone itself," the werewolf explained. "Built as a last resort in case of a siege."

"A last resort, eh?" Vighon considered that phrase from King Jormund's point of view. "The orcs only attack us once and we're turning to the last resort. I bet the king is thrilled."

"I believe Inara was quite persuasive," Galanör added. "King Jormund agreed to evacuate his people into the caves, but no farther. If… *when* we are next attacked, there will be time to evaluate the need for complete abandonment of the city."

Vighon turned his head to the sky. They were running out of time. When the sun finally found its rest, the orcs would rise.

"Where's Inara?" the northerner asked. When violence ruled the day, he wanted to know exactly where the Dragorn was going to be. He tried to convince himself it wasn't because he liked keeping her close.

Russell lifted his chin. "Still in the upper city. She's helping the kings to coordinate both of their forces."

Vighon hated the waiting. He was restless, but it would be foolish to ask Galanör to spar with him when they needed to conserve their energy. The northman wondered what Alijah was doing. Had they already found a way to break the spell that bound him to Malliath? How long would it be before they saw each other again?

Russell hefted his pick-axe and hammered it once into the stone plateau, where it remained perfectly still. "I don't think it'll come to a complete evacuation. Grey Stone is going to get bloody for sure, but the people will return. This city is just too hard to invade."

Vighon was happy for the distraction. "One way in, one way out. Narrow streets. You'd think the smell would be enough to send the orcs packing."

The elf, man, and werewolf remained above the din for some time, watching the people slowly gather their belongings and idle down the streets. Only when the last rays of light faded away did they turn back to the main entrance and the fields of white snow beyond. Stood square in the middle was Athis the ironheart. The dragon was perfectly still, his red scales dulled without the light.

The sound of marching boots and armour filled the narrow streets. The soldiers of Grey Stone filed down the main street in neat rows of lancers, shield men, and archers. The Black Cloaks were a tough group of fighters. Raised in the tundras of The Ice Vale, their skin was more akin to hide and their resolve as hard as steel. Tonight, they would be tested.

Vighon descended the last flight of steps with Galanör and Russell in tow. Donned in his black fur cloak, the northman blended right in with the soldiers of Grey Stone. He looked around, ascending one of the steps to better see if Inara was among them. Her red cloak would allow the Dragorn to stand out among the sea of black.

Captains barked orders over the marching boots, directing their men to take up their positions. The lancers stood aside and three rows of archers walked through the human tunnel. They were commanded to take position beyond the main entrance and line up along the cliff wall. Athis moved for the first time and walked towards the jagged holes blasted out of the ground.

"Only fire when the dragon is clear!" one of the captains yelled.

The lancers and shield men formed rows in the street, bridging the gap between the two walls. There weren't many soldiers, but in the narrow passage the orcs' numbers would count for naught.

It wasn't long before everyone was in place and an eerie silence fell upon Grey Stone. The light of the sun had well and truly gone, leaving them at the mercy of the long night. Vighon had always preferred the cold, and indeed winter, but right now he could wish for nothing more than the short nights of summer.

The northman struggled to see over the helms and spear tips of the Black Cloaks. "Can you see anything?" he asked the others.

Galanör nimbly climbed up the scaffold of a nearby stall and focused his elven eyes. "Athis is investigating the breaches. I see no sign of any orcs."

Russell sniffed the air. "There's not so much as a scent on the breeze."

Vighon didn't like it. He had seen what the beasts had done to Tregaran and heard of the ruin they left Calmardra and Ameeraska in; there wasn't a hope that they would simply give up now.

"Maybe it isn't dark enough yet?" Russell suggested.

Galanör let go of the scaffold and dropped back down without a sound. "Something isn't right…"

Vighon was used to the overly dramatic expressions on the elf's fair face, but this time he was inclined to agree with the assessment. The orcs had to know that there was a dragon barring the way.

A feeling of dread crept into the northerner's bones. What if they were waiting for Malliath to arrive? He would take care of Athis and Inara, leaving the city exposed.

He was wrong.

Somewhere deep in the heart of the city, the ground shook and a thundering *boom* blew grit from the walls, filling the narrow streets with thick clouds. Another explosion resounded through the maze-like city, then another and another.

Vighon reached out to balance himself against the wall. "They're in the city…" he rasped, struggling to breathe through the debris.

The Black Cloaks turned around and ran back into Grey Stone. Galanör dashed up the first flight of steps and leaped out into the main street, using the market stalls and discarded wares as platforms to avoid the rushing soldiers. Vighon didn't even have time to call the elf before he had disappeared into the distance.

Behind them, Athis clawed at the walls of the main entrance and roared. The dragon was simply too large to fit through the ravine and his fire was useless when the streets were filled with soldiers.

"Come on!" With his pick-axe in hand, Russell charged after the soldiers before the archers blocked their way.

Angry that the orcs had no doubt spilled innocent blood already, Vighon drew his sword and gripped his shield.

By the time they reached the central courtyard, bloody battle had broken out in every ravine. The howl and roars of the orcs came from every direction, accompanied by the sound of steel clashing with obsidian. Being attacked from all sides, the people yet to escape into the caves ran for their lives, creating chaos.

Vighon left Russell's side and jumped between a young couple and a trio of orcs. His shield bashed the closest, knocking it into the beast beside it. Before they hit the floor, the northman was bringing his sword down on the third, preventing it from lashing out at the couple. A clean downwards strike scraped over its dark armour and into its pale arm. The beast yelled in pained outrage, but Vighon shoved his boot into its chest and kicked it back into the wall. Without losing any momentum, the northman advanced and thrust his blade into the orc's gut, pinning it to the wall.

"Run!" he shouted at the couple.

Leaving his sword to keep the orc pinned, Vighon turned on the recovering beasts behind him. The first to rise was struck in the throat by the steel edge of his enchanted shield. It gargled for breath as it was launched backwards, soon to die from such a blow. The last survivor of the trio swung at Vighon's legs as it found its feet, forcing the northman to retreat.

A feral snarl preceded the orc's attack with a slash to the left then the right, each strike forcing Vighon to step back. When the opening presented itself, no matter how small, he took it. Dropping to one knee, the northman hammered the edge of his shield onto the orc's foot, eliciting a howl of pain from the creature. Lifting the shield with all his strength, Vighon drove it up into the beast's jaw, a strike that put the orc on its back.

He fell upon the creature with a lust for violence that had been born in him years earlier. Using both hands, Vighon brought the shield down on the orc's face again and again until it stopped moving.

Another orc dropped dead in front of him to reveal Galanör and his bloody scimitars.

Vighon pushed himself up, keeping his eyes on the elf. "Looks like I do just fine without a sword, eh?"

Galanör rolled his eyes before a flash of imminent danger crossed his face. Vighon whirled around to see a pair of soldiers be cut down by a pack of orcs that had their sights set on the northerner. Vighon regretted his quip to the elf and dashed for the sword he had left pinned to the wall. The orcs were upon him, however, and he was forced to throw his shield at them to slow the pack down.

Sensing the proximity of the nearest orc behind him, Vighon yanked his blade free and continued to swing it around, ducking low as he did. The beast was stopped in its tracks by a length of steel slicing across its gut. The northman came up with a rage-filled cry and a swinging sword. One orc after the other missed him, but every one of the pale creatures tasted his blade. After the last of the pack fell to the ground, absent half of its head, Vighon dropped into a roll and scooped up his shield.

Ready to fight, the northman unhooked his fur cloak, leaving him free to move around in his padded gambeson. Galanör didn't appear hindered at all by his flowing blue cloak - in fact, the elf often used it to his advantage, misdirecting his foes and hiding his form.

Stuck in the central courtyard, Vighon turned on his heel this way and that, parrying and attacking any who strayed within reach of his sword arm. As more orcs poured out of their holes, the narrow streets became all the harder to fight in. More than once,

Vighon was forced to alter his swing at the last second to avoid killing one of the soldiers.

"This is chaos!" Vighon shouted over the din.

Galanör, close by, yelled back, "We need to plug their entry points! Stem the flow!"

Vighon pushed one orc away with his shield and slashed another across the throat before turning back to the sound of Athis's roar. "What we need is a dragon!"

A shadow fell over the pair as Russell Maybury launched himself across the courtyard. Using his supernatural strength, the werewolf easily leaped over the heads of many soldiers, bringing him, and his pick-axe, down on the orcs in front of Vighon and Galanör. His years as ranger shone through. The pick-axe was buried in the skull of the central orc being torn free and swung around with mighty power. The next three orcs all found their chest cavities caved in and their jaws shattered by the wooden haft.

Together, the three fell in, back to back, and faced the next horde. Vighon sighted a pair of orcs advancing from the northern ravine, their combined width almost filling the entire street. They stood at least three heads above the rest, though they wore less armour. Vighon cricked his neck and squeezed the hilt of his blade. He fancied plunging his sword through one of their heads.

The monstrous orcs added their roars to the pitch of battle, easily drowning out the growls of their smaller kin. Spotting the trio slaying orcs in the courtyard, the pair set into a jog, barrelling through orcs and humans alike to reach them.

"Come on then you big bastard!" Vighon yelled, resting his blade over the top of his shield.

Russell stepped ahead and threw his pick-axe with both hands. The weapon, as it was in his hands, spun end over end until it found rest in one of the orc's face. The sudden impact and instant death launched the orc backwards and its legs high into the air. Vighon quickly forgot about that orc and focused on the remaining behemoth. The northman braced his legs and prepared himself to meet the rushing wall of muscle.

Galanör moved like a cat, using the nearby orcs as stepping

stones to attain height until he was able to leap off the curved walls and across the behemoth's path. Either Stormweaver or Guardian, Vighon didn't know which, cut a neat red line from one side of the beast's neck to the other. As it fell to its knees, the elf landed back on his feet, where he had the audacity to slay another orc before the larger one finally hit the ground face first.

Vighon's expression froze into that of a disrespected man. "One of those was mine!"

Galanör flashed Vighon a cocky smile. "It's not your fault you were cursed with the speed of a mere man!" The elf fell back into the rhythm of battle, his scimitars dancing hypnotically around him.

"Less talk and more killin'!" Russell warned as he yanked his pick-axe free from the dead beast. He dashed down the next street, claiming orcish lives with every swing.

"Right," Vighon hissed under his breath. He hefted his sword and charged down the street after the elf and the werewolf.

The upper city of Grey Stone had fallen into disarray. The lords and ladies in the process of descending the stone steps or waiting for their turn on the lift were trying to return to their large homes where they could hide. The soldiers turned them back around wherever they could, forcing the noblemen into the battle below.

"Get them down!" Inara shouted over the howling winds. "We need everyone in those tunnels!"

Looking around at the collection of grand houses and even The Black Fort, there was nowhere for them to escape to and their homes wouldn't keep out the orcs once they took the city. The ancient cave network was their only hope of surviving now.

King Jormund stormed out of The Black Fort in the finest armour. His hammer, as tall as any man, was carried easily in one hand by the mountainous king. His knights followed after him, having formed a natural shield around the king's family. Behind them came King Weymund of Lirian, his arm still in a sling. He didn't have nearly as many knights to protect him or his family, but a complement of soldiers had been assigned to them by Jormund.

"We will not run, you hear!" The hardy king bellowed at Inara. "My people will find shelter in the mountain, but we will not hand Grey Stone over to these monsters!"

The Dragorn didn't have time to listen to the belligerent king. As long as he encouraged his men to fight while others took refuge in the caves, Inara didn't care what words spouted from Jormund's mouth.

Turning to the east, beyond the edge of the cliff, Inara searched the black skies. ***Can you sense the others yet?*** she asked Athis, hoping the Dragorn Gideon had promised were close.

The red dragon sounded frustrated and furious. *No,* he replied curtly. *Nor could they help. This city was not designed with dragons in mind.*

Inara could feel Athis clawing at the walls of the main entrance, desperate to get inside the maze-like city and slaughter some orcs.

Then pain exploded across Inara's left leg and hip. The Dragorn screamed and dropped to one knee under the strain. If it weren't for the relentless wind, she would have heard Athis roar like thunder.

What's happening? she managed.

Orcs! Athis growled deep in her mind. *They're flanking me from the holes outside the city. I have a spear in my leg…*

Inara felt blood soaking through her trouser leg. ***I'm not going to disagree***.

The Dragorn grunted through the pain as she put weight on her injured leg. Opening the right side of her jacket, Inara examined the vials that normally lined her ribs. She quickly pulled free an orange tonic from its tight pouch and popped the cork with her thumb. It was spicy running over her throat, but the horrid taste was worth the immediate pain relief. The wound would heal before long, but for now, her thigh was numb, allowing Inara to break into a sprint.

I'm coming! she promised, running for the edge of the cliff.

No! Athis warned, halting her in the snow. *I can handle them out here. Get as many people into the caves as you can.*

Inara wanted to be by her companion's side in a fight, but she couldn't argue with the dragon's wisdom. She never could. As always, her duty would come first and, right now, that meant saving as many lives as possible.

Kill them all, she said determinedly.

Athis unleashed his primal fury upon the orcish horde, a fury that ignited a fire inside Inara. The half-elf drew her Vi'tari scimitar and made for the steps. The wooden lift was already halfway down the ravine and a queue had formed at the top.

"Behind me!" Inara commanded, grabbing the attention of the two kings and their lords. "We make for the caves!"

There were only a handful of people still journeying down to the lower city via the steps, with most preferring to wait for the lift. They didn't have that kind of time. Trusting them to follow her, the Dragorn jumped down the steps two or three at a time.

Just over halfway down, those same steps were now thronged with orcs. Inara glanced back, looking up to ensure that the king and his people were following. She would clear the way for them.

The orcs howled when they saw her, thinking foolishly that they were challenged by a weak woman, and alone at that. Inara, however, was neither weak nor alone, not when she had her Vi'tari blade in hand.

The Dragorn dropped into an unorthodox position and kicked the first orc to attack her. With the power of her mother's kin behind her, Inara booted the beast into those behind it, creating a cascade effect. Many of the foul creatures were pushed from the edge of the steps and thrown to their deaths. Not realising how many of its kin had just died from a single boot to the chest, the next orc continued to charge up at Inara.

Down came the Vi'tari steel.

The fine blade cut through armour and flesh and another boot sent the corpse over the edge. Two more flashes of the scimitar claimed the lives of two more orcs. As the bodies piled up, the following orcs struggled to reach the Dragorn. The Dragorn didn't struggle to reach them. Again and again her blade came down and across, cutting them down in droves. A flick of the boot pushed the bodies over the edge, allowing her to gain more ground.

With the trail of people catching her up, Inara decided to clear the steps with a little more efficiency. Calling upon the magic she shared with Athis and that of her natural heritage, Inara pushed out her hand and cast a wave of condensed air over the orcs. Their pale skin rippled across their muscles and their obsidian armour crumpled into their bodies as they were all thrown from the steps.

The wave pulled a cloud of debris from the ravine wall and cracked the flat plateau between the zig-zagging stairs. That crack snaked into the rocky wall and became a larger crack that ran along the wall. A moment later, sheets of rock were falling into the western street below, blocking the advancement of the orcs.

Inara experienced a moment of clarity. "We need to collapse the streets…"

The Dragorn ignored the steps in front of her and dropped down from one flight to the next, pausing only to slaughter orcs. With only two more flights between her and the circular courtyard in the heart of the city, Inara spotted Vighon and Galanör fighting at the head of the northern street. They had been separated from Russell, who was farther into the ravine and swinging his pick-axe with abandon. The courtyard was quickly being overrun by orcs flooding through the side streets and alleys that cut through the rock.

They were being swarmed.

Inara leaped without thinking. The very centre of the courtyard was rushing up to meet her, but the Dragorn had a special landing in mind. With her arm pulled back, Inara's free hand summoned a destructive spell that gathered more energy as she fell. As her feet touched down, the half-elf dropped into a crouch and thrust her palm into the stone. The telekinetic magic that burst forth expanded over the ground in every direction, collecting orcs in its wake. The pale beasts were slammed into the walls, their bodies broken beyond repair.

Standing up, Vighon and Galanör took refuge behind a wall of soldiers to marvel at her work. The courtyard was free of orcs, for a moment.

Inara nodded at the pair and flicked her scimitar into form four of the Mag'dereth. The Dragorn twisted her body into every unorthodox position she knew, flipping around the oncoming orcs and weaving between their attacks. In such numbers, they were clumsy creatures compared to what she could do with a Vi'tari blade. Once fully surrounded, just where she intended to be, Inara spun one way then the next, her blade whipping out and claiming limbs and opening arteries. Finishing with a kick that knocked an orc off its feet, the half-elf plunged her sword into its chest and looked back at Vighon and Galanör. They were staring at her like half-wits.

"If you two feel like helping, I have an idea..."

47

HOME

Doran never thought he would be so happy to see the light of the world. Not once had he been in the warm embrace of a mountain and even thought about the sky.

Being hunted by an enormous pack of Gobbers had a way of changing one's mind, even a stubborn dwarf's.

Reyna let loose another arrow, as she had continued to do since they fled from the dead Dweller. The Gobbers had picked up their trail almost immediately and resumed their chase. The elf's arrows kept the fastest of their wretched kind at bay.

At the end of the ancient hall was a rectangular wall of morning's first light. It wasn't the brightest dawn the son of Dorain had ever seen, but compared to the shadows of Vengora, it might as well have been a blazing fire.

Winter's icy touch kissed his cheeks as they ran towards the light. A light fall of snow blanketed the northern ridge of the mountains, though the contrast prevented the dwarf from seeing any detail.

"Fast as ye like, brother!" Dakmund shouted back at Doran.

Lagging behind the party, Doran had come to see what areas of his life required improvement. Long-distance running was at the very top of his list.

"Where's that damned pig when ye need it?" he muttered under his breath.

Another arrow whistled past his head and caught a Gobber in the head. So close was it that Doran felt its dying squeal on the back of his neck.

One by one, the dwarves disappeared into the light, followed by Reyna and Nathaniel. Doran bellowed at the top of his lungs digging deep for that last bit of energy. The dwarf burst into the light at such speed that he failed to see the edge of the path and, like the others, tumbled straight over the edge.

Curses in more than one language escaped his mouth on the way down the slope. His armour saved him from the rocky outcroppings, but his bulk and speed hurled him down the mountainside without reprieve.

When finally he came to a stop, his face was buried up to his ears in the freezing powder. He came up spitting the snow from his mouth and groaning from a plethora of new sores that ached in his muscles.

At the top of the ridge, the Gobbers gathered in a line and shrieked at the sky. It wasn't long, however, before their exposed hides began to shiver. The definition of cold was very different north of Vengora. The pack soon decided against hunting their prey in the elements. When the last of them disappeared from sight, Doran lowered his axe and took a breath.

"Foul beasts!" he growled.

Doran's spine cracked as he straightened his back. They had been running from the Gobbers for most of the night, but they wouldn't find any rest sitting around in the snow, especially when the thick clouds promised to dump more on them.

"We need to find shelter and fast," he observed, wondering how long it would take for an elf to freeze to death.

The son of Dorain strapped his axe back to his hip and turned to face his companions and the grubby faces of his kin. The dwarf's eyes went wide and his heart doubled its beats in his ears. Held on their knees in the snow, Petur, Reyna, and Nathaniel each had a silvyr blade held to their throats.

"What are ye abou'?" Doran demanded, taking his axe in hand again.

Dakmund's reluctance faded away, replaced by dwarven resolve. "Look at where ye are, Doran," he said, gesturing to the mountain peaks behind him. "Ye're on the other side o' Vengora now. This is Dhenaheim…"

Doran examined the barren landscape of white tundra and mountains peeking through the mist. It could have been anywhere in the north, but his brother was right; north of Vengora belonged to his kin.

"Ye weren' invited to these lands," Dakmund continued. "If ye're not invited, ye're trespassin'. And if ye're trespassin'… ye're to be prisoners o' clan Heavybelly."

Doran glanced at his friends before eyeing his brother. "Don' do this, brother."

Dakmund apologised with his eyes, but his thumbs hooked into his belt and he puffed out his chest. "*I* am the prince o' Grimwhal. I'll do whatever I like, an' I'd like to take me prisoners before the king for judgement!"

"The king?" Doran echoed, a pit growing in his stomach. "Ye wanna take me before father?"

Dakmund licked his lips. "Ye have no other choice." Doran knew his brother well enough to understand that it was, in fact, he who had no other choice.

His options laid out before him, Doran had to decide between slaying his kin to free his friends or go willingly back to Grimwhal. Back to his father.

The dwarf gripped his axe and he moved to retrieve the sword from his back. But he stopped. If he pulled that blade free, he would have no choice but to cut down his kin, maybe even his brother. He had walked away from that, determined never again to spill dwarven blood.

He looked to his friends, who silently pleaded for him to lower his axe.

With a great sigh, the son of Dorain dropped his axe into the snow. He seethed, unable to speak or utter so much as a curse. Two of Dakmund's dwarves approached cautiously before removing his sword from its sheath. His axe was scooped up and the dagger taken from his belt. Manacles were fixed around his wrists and another chain tethered him to one of the dwarves, who was more than happy to drag Doran along.

"Let's go!" Dakmund ordered, leading the party into the north west.

"I'm so sorry," Reyna said as Doran was dragged past. The Galfreys were similarly stripped of their weapons and chained, each assigned to a different dwarf and separated on the march. Petur Devron offered no challenge but clung to his satchel, which the dwarves allowed him to keep.

Doran was glad to have been separated; he was fuming with them. Not only had he entered Vengora, but he had interacted with his kin, his very brother in fact. Now, he was on the other side of the mountains and exactly where he didn't want to be. To say things had gone from bad to worse was an understatement.

Day had turned to night and back to day by the time the first kingdom of Dhenaheim came into view. In the setting sun, Doran looked upon Grimwhal, the city of his birth.

He was home.

For two days, Doran had kept his mouth shut, not speaking a word to either of his friends or Petur. Dakmund had stayed away while they briefly camped overnight, clearly too ashamed to face his brother.

Now, standing before the central pillar of his father's kingdom, Doran conjured but a single word.

"Damn..."

Grimwhal's entrance was an enormous hollow carved out of the mountain and supported by a substantial pillar. The top of the pillar was that of an inverted pyramid without the apex, creating a larger surface area for the pillar to hold up the mountain roof. Though vast within its hollow, Doran knew that the city was even larger underground, where the majority of his clan resided.

His teeth gritted and jaw set, Doran allowed his captors to drag him past the ancient pillar and into the very halls of Grimwhal. Dwarves appeared from everywhere, muttering and gossiping about Doran's reappearance in chains. The word elf was thrown about too, and not in a kind way.

The heavy doors of the throne room were pulled back by unseen dwarves, revealing a chamber of great opulence. The pillars were encrusted with diamonds, the marble floor polished until its reflection was that of a mirror, and the roaring fire pits illuminated the golden statues of his forebears. Two silvyr thrones sat at the head of the chamber, atop a platform lined with fierce dwarven warriors.

It was those who occupied the thrones that held Doran's attention.

The heavy doors were swung shut behind them with a mighty bang and the sound of the fires filled the chamber. Doran could feel eyes boring into him from all around, but none more so than those who sat upon the thrones.

A moment of regret rested on the son of Dorain. He hadn't said a word to his friends since the chains had touched his skin, but they were most likely only minutes away from execution. He felt it to be a failing on their behalf that he had found himself back in his ancestral home, but he now considered it a failing on his behalf that husband and wife were about to have their lives cut short at the hands of his kin.

Still, there was nothing left to do now but face their fate. If he had to, he decided, he would fight to see them released. Two days past he couldn't bring himself to kill a dwarf to see them freed, but standing here now, Doran knew what truly mattered to him. He knew *who* truly mattered to him.

Doran stood before the thrones and lifted his chin with squared shoulders. He would face his fate.

"Hello, Father…"

48

JOURNEY'S END

Alijah's eyes opened sporadically, but always he was looking up at the sky. Sometimes it was day, sometimes it was night. Thick clouds were replaced by blue skies and when next he awoke, the stars greeted him from the heavens.

All the while, his head pulsed with great pain. In those brief moments of clarity, he feared his skull had been broken. Whenever he tried to move, his limbs felt heavy, and his energy ebbed away before he could come to.

Every now and then, Hadavad's face would loom over him and the mage would apply ointments or utter incoherent spells over him. It always hurt and he always passed out before he could ask the old man any questions.

As Alijah's health improved, he became aware of the motion that carried his body. He was lying on something hard, and at an angle too. Judging by the constant rocking, Alijah guessed himself to be on some kind of sled behind a horse. Of course, such thoughts were momentary before blissful oblivion took hold of him again.

It was sound that woke the half-elf this time. He heard the crackling of a fire. It took some effort and a short bout of nausea, but Alijah managed to open his eyes and focus on his surroundings.

He was layered in a missmatch of blankets that felt so heavy they weighed him down. Beside him was a modest fire and on the other side sat the mage, cross-legged with his staff resting across his legs.

"Hadavad…" he croaked.

"Easy, boy." The mage came to his aid with caution in his eyes. "You took more than one knock to the head, not to mention the rest."

"What happened?" Alijah struggled to sit up, but when he did a jet of vomit shot from his mouth and onto the snow. Next came the dizziness and a coughing fit that he thought would never end.

"Easy now," Hadavad said. "Drink this, you need to stay hydrated."

Alijah blindly took the water skin from the mage and sipped at the cold liquid. The feel of it going down his throat brought broken images of Hadavad pouring small amounts of water into his mouth while he was semi-conscious.

"You need to rest," Hadavad continued with a steadying hand on Alijah's shoulder.

"How long have I been asleep?" Alijah straightened his back and groaned through the stiffness and pain. "Where are we?" he added, seeing nothing but darkness beyond the fire.

"Three days," the mage replied bluntly.

Alijah stopped sipping the water and stared wildly at the mage. "Three days?" he echoed incredulously.

"As to the where," Hadavad continued. "We're in The Vrost Mountains."

Alijah was hit with another fact that he found hard to swallow. They weren't even in Alborn anymore, let alone Velia. The mage had carried him north, into Orith and the deep snows.

"It doesn't seem cold enough to be The Vrost Mountains," Alijah commented absently.

Hadavad raised his hand and touched an invisible field with his finger. The air rippled in the light, revealing a small dome that encompassed their camp and the horse.

"A trick I learned from your sister actually."

Mention of Inara brought recent events to the forefront of

Alijah's mind, each revelation hitting him like a hammer. Velia was gone, overrun by the orcs. Gideon had disappeared and was potentially dead beside Ilargo somewhere. Korkanath had been razed to the ground and all of its students gone with it. Then there was the matter of the prophecies, apparently written by the same person who had seen him and Gideon through time. The Black Hand actually being able to see into the future was a nightmare scenario, but it paled in comparison to the last revelation that sat in Alijah's gut like a stone.

He was bonded to Malliath...

"Alijah?" Hadavad said his name as if it was the second or third time he had tried to get through to him. "You need more rest."

"No," Alijah protested, holding up a hand. "I've rested long enough." The half-elf was about to lay it all out for the mage when a single question blurted from his mouth. "What are we doing in The Vrost Mountains? In fact, why were you in Velia?"

Seeing that Alijah wouldn't return to sleep, Hadavad sat back by the fire and sighed. "This was always my destination. I was on The Selk Road outside Velia when I saw the invasion. It was just luck that I found you when I did. That orc looked to be ending your life."

Flashes of the orc painted with the white V struck Alijah like lightning. "Where's my blade?" he asked suddenly.

Hadavad hesitated. "Lost, I'm afraid. You have your bow and quiver," he said, gesturing to the pack on the side of the horse.

Alijah was disheartened to have lost Asher's short-sword. For the first time since he left home, the half-elf felt a twinge of guilt for taking the weapon.

Hadavad's words cut through his train of thought. "I would say by midday tomorrow we'll reach our destination."

That comment placed Alijah back in the present. "And where is that exactly? You never did say."

The mage stared into the flames, considering his reply. "There's something out here, Alijah. Something very old and full of answers. I'm sure of it."

The half-elf glanced at their barren surroundings. "Hadavad, there's nothing out here but more snow."

The mage shook his head. "I've seen it. The Bastion…"

The name meant nothing to Alijah. "I've never heard of it."

"I don't think there are any still living who have," Hadavad replied cryptically. "It looks to be from The First Kingdom by the design of it."

"Looks to be? You've seen this place before then?"

Hadavad dropped his gaze. "Twice I have been close to death and twice I have been… somewhere else."

Alijah scratched his head and felt nothing but pain for his effort. "Are you sure you're not the one who hit his head?"

Hadavad offered a wry smile. "I know how it sounds. I'm no more convinced of the gods than you are." The mage's expression grew serious again. "But I have seen it. It was as real as you are now. There was a woman, or at least something resembling a woman. Made entirely of light too!"

"Hadavad…" Alijah was becoming increasingly concerned for his old mentor.

The mage held up a hand. "I'm not saying it was a *god*. But perhaps it was something in between. Something above all of this. We already know that such places exist. When Atilan and his wretched lot disappeared beyond The Veil, they were transported to another realm, a place where they could observe us for millennia without ageing."

"And you think that, what? This higher being is guiding you to answers?" Alijah hoped his tone conveyed his serious doubts.

Hadavad sighed. "I don't know. What I do know terrifies me. The Arid Lands are gone, all three cities wiped out. Lirian has been decimated. Velia… There was no victory to be had there - it's probably ash by now. Illian is falling into ruin, just as that damn prophecy said it would. The orcs are rising and The Black Hand have yet to reveal their true motivations. We desperately *need* answers, Alijah."

He couldn't think of a time the mage had steered him wrong,

and so he decided to go along with it. "This Bastion, it's not far from here then?"

Hadavad perked up a bit. "Yes," he replied eagerly. "Hidden in the heart of the mountains, but I can find it."

Alijah swallowed his disbelief and nodded along. "Then tomorrow, we shall find it."

Hadavad offered an appreciative smile. "Thank you, Alijah."

He wanted to tell the mage everything he had learned during his time in the Dragorn library, but the brief time he had been awake was beginning to take its toll on him. If they really did find any answers in these mountains, perhaps then he would share all that he knew. But, for now, he would keep the truth of The Black Hand's power to himself. More importantly, he would keep his bond to Malliath to himself...

By mid-morning the following day, The Vrost Mountains did everything they could to turn the trespassers away. The blizzard that fell upon the land blew sideways, buffeting the horse Hadavad had taken from outside Velia's gates. Alijah found the strength to leave the sled and so they abandoned it in the snow, freeing the horse of the extra burden.

By late afternoon, however, the burden of its two riders, combined with the increasing cold, saw the horse drop with exhaustion. With no way of helping the horse in such elements, Hadavad placed his staff to the mount's head and put it out of its misery.

Alijah swaddled his cloak about him and used a torn piece of cloth from one of the blankets to wrap around his face. It would have been easy to give up, but watching Hadavad plough through the snow ahead of him was inspiring. The mage simply didn't have it in him to give up.

The Vrost Mountains were unique in their shape, rising highest in the east and gradually descending to the west. It often made for easy navigation when journeying through it, but today, those notable peaks were concealed from view.

"Hadavad!" Alijah shouted ahead. "How much farther?"

The mage half turned in the tracks. "It's in the heart of the mountains!" he replied unhelpfully.

"Is that close?" Alijah yelled back, unable to discern east from west.

Despite dire weather and the exhaustion they both shared, Hadavad managed to offer a smile. The mage turned away and lifted his staff into the air, his bellowing voice a distant call in the whipping wind. When his spell was complete, Hadavad stamped his staff into the ground and expelled a wave of magic strong enough to temporarily push the snow, wind, and cloud from their view.

Alijah craned his neck to take in the mountainous wall that sat a few hundred yards in front of them, completely unseen before Hadavad's spell. Before the magic ran out of momentum, the half-elf caught sight of an unnatural shape against the black rock. There was a broken arch set into the slope at the base of the mountain wall.

The storm that swirled around them could not be denied and it soon closed in on them again. Any thoughts of abandoning their search were quickly forgotten, replaced instead by a sense of urgency that always stoked the flames of Alijah's need for knowledge. The explorer that lived inside of him found the much-needed energy to press on and battle the icy veil that raged between them and the arch.

Following Hadavad, Alijah began to feel the ground under his feet change from that of thick snow to a coarse and rocky incline. With his green cloak billowing out behind him now, the half-elf ignored the burning in his calves and pushed on until the outcropping from the mountain shielded them from the blizzard.

His breath was ragged and every part of his body complained of ailment, but seeing anything from The First Kingdom made Alijah almost giddy. He pulled down the cloth wrapped around his face and marvelled at the broken arch. The runes carved into the stone

were definitely that of The First Kingdom and Alijah couldn't help
but reach out and run his fingers over them.

"You were right!" he called to Hadavad over the howling wind.

"This is only the beginning," the mage replied. "What we seek is
up there!"

Alijah followed Hadavad's gaze to the curving slope that
disappeared behind the mountain wall. It was quite the illusion, as
the path could never be seen from the valley unless standing under
the arch, which did its best to blend in with the surrounding rock.

For all his excitement, Alijah couldn't deny the state of his body.
Ascending the mountain began almost immediately to take its toll
on him. Hadavad appeared to be suffering equally by the time they
passed through the low cloud cover. Their brief pauses to recover
their breath became more frequent and the call of sleep grew all the
stronger.

It was finally under the glow of the moon that they saw it. The
Bastion. Alijah had discovered several dwellings and ancient keeps
of The First Kingdom, but none could boast of holding against the
decay of time as The Bastion did.

Set into the mountain, it was a collection of towers and rounded
buildings with steps hewn from the stone here and there. It had all
the hallmarks of a First Kingdom design, but its condition was too
exquisite to be ten thousand years old. Yet here it was, intact and
hidden away from the world.

"What is this place, Hadavad?" Alijah asked through laboured
breath.

Leaning on his staff, the mage answered, "I don't know. It's built
high into the mountain, though. We know King Atilan preferred to
build high. Perhaps it's one of his fortresses. Either way; it has
answers."

Defying his age, Hadavad straightened his back and made for
The Bastion. Alijah summoned what dregs remained of his energy
and followed the mage. Even if there were answers inside, he hoped
they could rest within its shelter for a while before they scoured
those ancient halls.

They passed under another arch, five times the height and

thickness of the broken one at the beginning of the path. Beyond, a shallow set of stairs took them to the looming double doors that marked the top. It was tiring to say the least, but Alijah held onto the resolve that Hadavad exuded, believing himself that the answers therein would be worth their efforts.

It required both of them to shoulder through the doors. A loud creak resounded off the interior walls as they pushed through. Alijah and Hadavad stood side by side, mouths ajar, and exhausted from head to toe. With what little energy they had left, the pair took in the darkened entrance hall that greeted them.

The doors slammed shut behind them.

The pair jumped and a series of fire pits began to come to life around the outside walls of the hall, giving shape to two rows of pillars and an arched ceiling. One by one, the fire pits breathed light into the room, revealing its true length. The final pit was much larger and sat at the opposite end of the hall.

There was a single figure silhouetted against the fire.

Alijah felt his stomach drop but his exhaustion kept his reflexes from responding with any speed. The figure stepped forward and the light from the smaller pits betrayed its identity.

"Welcome!" The Crow shouted, his arms outstretched.

Hadavad gasped gruffly and pointed his staff. A mage of The Black Hand stepped out from behind a pillar and flicked his wand, snatching the staff from his hands in one smooth motion. The tug yanked Hadavad forward and left him on his hands and knees. Only then did Alijah's hands respond to the threat, retrieving his bow and nocking an arrow.

A concussive spell slammed into his chest before he could even aim the weapon, launching him back into the closed doors. From the floor, Alijah watched The Crow stalk towards them.

"Welcome to The Bastion, friends." The Crow came to a stop in front of them, his wand in hand. "Welcome to my home…"

49

LAST STAND

Vighon fell against the ravine wall, desperate for rest as the siege of Grey Stone went into its third day. For three days they had fought the orcs in the narrow streets, keeping the hordes at bay for as long as possible. Most of the city's inhabitants had fled into the cave network of Vengora now, the kings included, but Vighon and a portion of Jormund's army had been cut off from the caves.

The northman watched now as Inara and Galanör used their magic to collapse yet another street. The idea had been the Dragorn's and so far it had been the only thing that kept the orcs' numbers from overwhelming them. Together, they cast destructive spells against the high walls, bringing down massive sheets of rock to close up the holes blasted out of the ground.

It also blocked the only street that led to the caves...

At the time, there had been little choice but to barricade the street with rock, since a new wave of orcs had been tasked with hunting down the people.

Only midday offered reprieve, for the light of dawn failed to penetrate the dark maze-like city and its high walls. As the orcs were forced back into the shadows, the remaining survivors went to work removing the heavy slabs of rock that lay between them and the cave network.

One or two terrified soldiers had attempted to climb over the mountainous debris of jagged slabs, but they inevitably fell prey to the loose rocks and slid back down, marred with fresh cuts.

To prevent any attack from outside, Athis had raked at the entrance to the city until one of the walls caved in, blocking any from entering or leaving Grey Stone. Now, however, it meant they were trapped inside the city with an army of orcs under their feet.

Vighon had decided that making strategic decisions while exhausted and under duress was to be avoided. Of course, hindsight was a wonderful thing. Every choice they had made saved lives and snatched victory away from the orcs, but if they couldn't get back to the cave network, they would be the ones to pay the price for that heroism.

Vighon had decided that being a hero wasn't everything the stories made them out to be.

"They won't be coming through there," Inara said, stepping back from the cloud of debris that rushed out of the collapsed street. "We should get back to removing the rock."

"Russell is already there," Vighon said. "He's got them forming a line to pass the rocks along."

"We don't have long," Galanör observed, looking up at the midday light. "As soon as there is enough shadow, they will return."

Vighon's head dropped as the will to fight on ebbed away. They had been battling for hours without pause and there had been no aid from the Dragorn Inara promised. Galanör and Inara had the strength of elves, Russell that of his condition, but Vighon was just a man. He gripped his sword, sheathed on his hip, and knew he couldn't squeeze the hilt as well as he could a few hours previously.

Trying not to overthink it, the northerner followed his companions through the maze of streets until they came across the long line of soldiers. Rocks large and small went from man to man until they could be dumped elsewhere. At the head of the line, Russell Maybury lifted slabs of rock with ease, his forearms pulsing with thick veins.

Galanör hurried to the werewolf's side and began to shift rocks as well. They had to be careful which ones they moved or face another avalanche of rock, burying them all forever.

Vighon could see Inara looking away from it all, her expression full of concern. "What is it?" he asked.

"Athis," Inara said bluntly. "He's a little… *furious*, to say the least."

"He doesn't like being separated from you," Vighon replied, nodding his head absently. "I can understand that." He regretted saying it as soon as the words registered with his ears. He chalked it up to fatigue.

Ignoring the comment, Inara continued, "He's angry that the other Dragorn have yet to arrive."

Vighon sighed and had to work at keeping his eyes open. "I wouldn't say no to a *little* help."

Inara straightened her posture and turned back to the efforts of Grey Stone's soldiers. "Come, we should offer our strength."

Vighon shook his head, thinking of the inevitable fight to come. "I can barely lift my sword. A few of us should conserve our energy for the next battle."

Inara looked upon the northman with a critical eye. Vighon didn't like to think what she saw, aware that he was as haggard and weary as he had ever been. He didn't want to appear weak in her eyes, but he couldn't deny his limitations and that of his kin.

"Here, drink this." Inara opened one side of her short jacket and removed a vile of red liquid.

Vighon held it up to the light, noting the sparkle inside the dense liquid. "What is it?"

"Essence of…" Inara shrugged. "I can't remember. I just know the red ones will keep you on your feet."

Vighon was hesitant to drink a potion that its owner couldn't describe very well, but he trusted Inara. "Don't you need it?" he asked.

"Athis lends me his strength," the Dragorn explained. "He will keep me going a while longer."

The northman pocketed the potion, deciding to take it when he really needed it. Looking up at the faint light, he knew that would be all too soon.

The monotonous work of receiving and passing along heavy rocks prevented Vighon from keeping track of time. His hands ached and, like many others, he had to take breaks to work out the spasms that tormented his grip.

Every now and then, word would come down the line reporting on their progress. The last word to reach Vighon was that Galanör and Russell could see the other side of the collapse now. How long it would take to make a hole large enough for a man to fit through was another question.

Small rations of food and water made their way around the soldiers, helping to keep their energy up, as well as morale. They had what precious light the winter sun had to offer them and they all used every minute of it.

Only when the torches were relit and the braziers brought back to life did Vighon realise the day had slipped away. Then came the call they had all been waiting for. Russell's booming voice filled the narrow ravine, informing them all that a hole large enough for a man to crawl through had been made.

Their cheers were immediately drowned out by the roars of orcs.

The slabs of rock were dropped by whoever was holding them and replaced by swords and shields. Vighon dashed across the street and retrieved his own weapons, glad to see that the thought of battle had given him the boost he needed.

Russell's voice resounded off the walls again, ordering the men to begin their crawl through to the other side. Judging by the sound of their foes, the men of Grey Stone didn't have time to make their escape.

Galanör appeared by the northman's side, his scimitars in hand. "We need to hold them back," the elf said. "Give them all as long as possible."

"Agreed," Inara replied with no lack of determination. Her Vi'tari blade slipped from its scabbard, the enchanted steel perfectly clean.

Vighon hefted his sword and shield, catching the eyes of the soldiers around him. They were scared. He could see the hopelessness in their faces. The soldiers did their best to form defensive rows, blocking the street from the central courtyard, but most barely had the strength raise their weapons. Those at the front knew their fates were sealed.

The northman walked out into the courtyard and faced the men. Over the last few days, Vighon had gained their respect, leading charges, stepping between them and certain death. Without a king and many of their captains already dead, they needed someone to bolster them if they were to stay on their feet and face the orcs.

Vighon paced the courtyard, careful to keep one eye on the men and one on the other streets. "Take heart brothers of the north! The darkest day has come for us all! But no man of the vales was born in the light! You were born with steel in your hands and iron in your beating chests!" He met the eyes of every one of them, being sure to let them see his courage.

"Monsters have come for your home!" he continued, noting the growing sound of his enemies. "But they will find only the bite of our steel waiting for them! This night is ours, brothers! Will they take it while you still draw breath?"

A solid cheer came back at him, a roar that came from somewhere deep in their souls. One of the soldiers began to beat his sword against his shield, a drumming that carried back down the street until every man was hammering his shield in time.

Vighon pointed his sword down the adjacent street, on the other side of the larger courtyard. "Whatever manner of beast comes at us, we *will* push them back! Protect the man to your side and you will all make it through to the other side! FOR GREY STONE!"

The soldiers repeated the cry again and again, beating their shields all the while. Inara and Galanör were off to the side, watching Vighon with great interest. Were he not so worked up after his speech, the northman might have blushed.

With his companions joining him in the centre of the courtyard, ready to slow the approaching horde down before they slammed against the soldiers' defensive wall, Vighon rested his sword over his shield and dropped low into a fighting stance. His muscles ached and his head throbbed from lack of sleep, but all he had to do was draw blood - then everything but the fight would be forgotten.

"Here they come," Galanör commented under his breath, dual scimitars rotating by his sides.

The orcs poured out of the adjacent street and spread out to fill the courtyard. Those who charged ahead found three stubborn warriors in their way. Galanör whipped his blades up and down, cutting through four of the beasts in the first couple of seconds. Inara flicked her Vi'tari scimitar, slicing through the necks of two orcs, before exploding into action. Every limb became a weapon as she danced around her foes, dispatching them with grace.

Vighon matched his enemy's roar and dug in. His shield blocked the obvious attack and his sword shot out, thrusting through one orc then another before he had the room to raise his blade and come down swinging. Orc blood went everywhere.

It was only a moment later when he heard the pale beasts crash into the soldiers behind them. The three companions had taken out the point of the orcs' spear-like attack, but those who spilled around wasted no time, leaping into the men of Grey Stone. They could only hope that the men at the other end were busy crawling through the hole Russell and Galanör had made.

Vighon dashed left and right, raising his shield and swinging his sword in time with the battle. It was a rhythm he was becoming accustomed to.

An orc shoved its way through and surprised the northman. His shield deflected the jagged blade, but a backhand caught him across the face and knocked him back, where he tripped over a dead body. Vighon was able to turn his fall into a backwards roll and return to his feet, but it came at the price of his shield. Leaving it at his feet, he rushed back at the orc with a two-handed grip. Vighon hammered the orc's defence with heavy downwards strikes until he overwhelmed the beast and buried his blade in its skull.

Without a shield, Vighon adapted his style of attack. Gone were his firm stances and heavy attacks, replaced now with quick movements on the balls of his feet. His sword had to work twice as fast to parry and strike. Only once did he note that Galanör's blades extended to slay an orc that would have killed Vighon. The northman didn't doubt it wasn't the only time the elven ranger had saved his life; he could feel himself getting slower.

The three companions retreated towards the soldiers, adding their unique talents to the melee. When the orc bodies began to pile up, the beasts showed their first signs of caution. Vighon liked to think that he was the cause for their slowed approach, but with Inara Galfrey and Galanör Reveeri either side, he knew the real reason.

A distant chanting sounded from the back of the orcs. "Algamesh! Algamesh! Algamesh!" The beasts cheered and howled and the chanting became louder. "ALGAMESH! ALGAMESH!"

Vighon was almost doubled over with exhaustion. "I don't suppose... that's their word... for 'I surrender'."

Panting beside him, Inara winced from some unseen pain. "I don't think so..."

Vighon stood up straight to see the surrounding orcs thrusting their spears and swords, but remaining several feet away. It might only be a brief pause, but it would give a few more the time needed to escape this hell.

The ground shuddered under their feet and the chanting came to a stop as the largest orc Vighon had ever seen strode out of the narrow ravine. A double-sided axe rested in both of its meaty hands and a pair of thick horns curved around its face to point at its square jaw of yellow fangs.

"I think that's Algamesh," Galanör said tiredly.

"Right..." Vighon popped the cork on his gifted vial and downed the red liquid with little thought to its sour taste. He threw the bottle away and twisted his sword, wondering if he was in the final moments of his life. If any of these foul monsters was going to claim his life, it would be the mountain of muscle that stood before him now.

The northerner inhaled one deep breath and prepared to throw himself back into battle, when the magic of the ingested potion came alive in his veins. The shadowed streets became a hue lighter, his reflexes sharpened with better vision and his fingers wrapped around the hilt of his sword until his knuckles matched the white of the orcs themselves. All aches and pains abated and Vighon felt light on his feet again. Every breath he inhaled felt like the world was filling him up with energy.

"Whatever this is," he said to Inara, "I need more!"

Inara, sword held into form two of the Mag'dereth, offered Vighon a coy smile. "Too much will kill you. Use it well."

Vighon eyed the giant orc. He fully intended to.

Algamesh unleashed a roar that shook the occupants of the courtyard to their bones. It also kept the other orcs rooted to the spot.

"Come on then!" Vighon yelled, charging forward.

Galanör and Inara were a couple of steps behind him, leaving the northman to break through their front line. And break it he did. His strength renewed, Vighon came down hard on those first orcs. He kicked one back and cut through the neck of another before parrying and killing a third. A fourth came at him, but his initial attack had enraged Algamesh, who swept the fourth orc aside with the flat of his axe.

Now there was nothing but air between the northman and the behemoth.

That double-sided axe went high and then came down with the full force of the orc's mighty strength. It wasn't an attack Vighon could defend. Rolling to the side saved his life and the quick swipe of his sword ended that of another orc running past him.

Vighon sprang back onto his feet and Algamesh turned to face him, shoving its kin aside wherever they got in its way. That devastating axe came down again and again, scarring the bear sigil carved into the courtyard stone. Vighon weaved between the smaller orcs and rolled out of the axe's way wherever he needed to.

A quick kill here and a dive there were the only things keeping him alive.

Algamesh roared, becoming frustrated with its prey's continued survival. The behemoth began swiping its axe across the field of battle to reach him, taking orcish lives with every swing. After a particularly hard downwards strike, Vighon dashed in and swung his sword at the beast's face, cleaving a chunk of its horn off and drawing a red line down its face.

The axe came out of the ground immediately and Algamesh assumed its towering stance again. The lion-like roar was painful to hear up close, but the curved blade cutting through the air promised a lot more than just pain. Vighon ran towards the incoming axe and skidded on his knees to slide under it. The northman leaped forwards from his skid, deliberately rolling over his fallen shield before jumping back to his feet.

Spinning about with his shield and sword ready, Algamesh was already upon him. That heavy axe looked to come down on him again and Vighon decided that even with the shield the crushing weight of such a blow would break his arm. With nowhere else to go, the northerner dashed forwards, inside the behemoth's reach. The axe overshot him and Vighon was presented with an exposed gut of muscle.

Using both hands, he thrust his sword up into the beast's gut, twisting as he did. He didn't stop until the hilt guard pressed against the pale flesh. The behemoth's yelp turned into a pained growl when Vighon yanked the blade out, spilling blood all over the ground.

Algamesh didn't go down, however. The beast hefted its axe and bashed Vighon's head with the blunt end. The northman blacked out for a few seconds, recalling nothing of his fall or hard landing. With Inara's potion still coursing through him his senses returned faster than normal, gifting him the extra second to see the axe coming down over his head.

A strong hand gripped his gambeson and dragged him sideways as the curved blade dug deep into the ground. Vighon felt that same hand pull him up before he finally turned his head to see Inara. The

Dragorn had saved his life while simultaneously parrying a group of swarming orcs. She said nothing, but simply released him from her grip and dived straight back into the fight.

With Algamesh turning on him once more, Vighon had no choice but to do the same.

The giant orc killed three more of its kin trying to remove the northman's head, leading Vighon to wonder if it would be better to keep the behemoth alive at the rate it was killing orcs.

Wiping the fresh blood trickling over his left eye, Vighon went to work. Steel flashed left and right, hacking through the orcs between him and Algamesh. If today was the day he met his end, he would make certain that monster left the world first.

Algamesh's erratic movements had turned their fight around, placing Vighon in the middle of the courtyard now. The orcs flooding in behind the northerner would have been a concern, were they themselves not too concerned with interfering in Algamesh's fight.

The giant orc raised its axe high into the air over Vighon's head. The beast's attack never came, however, when three spears were launched from the soldiers of Grey Stone, all of which impaled Algamesh's back. The giant orc swung about in an attempt to rid itself of the spears, its recklessness bringing an end to so many orcs. Vighon ducked and dropped to the ground more than once to avoid its wild axe.

Galanör skidded past the behemoth, whipping both of his scimitars across its legs. Algamesh roared and one of its thick legs buckled, forcing the orc to support itself on its axe. The soldiers foolishly thought they saw an advantage and charged out from their defensive line with a war cry on their lips.

Algamesh grunted, finding its reserves, and rose up to meet the men with its axe gripped horizontally. The first four were shoved back by the haft and taken from their feet. It was enough to give the soldiers behind pause, but those on the ground found themselves at the beast's mercy.

Vighon bashed the nearest orc around the head with the hilt of his sword, clearing his path to the back of Algamesh. The northman had no plan - he simply reacted.

A flip of his sword saw him grip the blade like a spear and he threw it without delay.

The steel ran through Algamesh's back as the orc was lifting his axe, preparing to hammer the fallen soldiers.

Vighon burst into action before the hilt guard had even sunk to the skin.

He knocked one orc aside with his shield before dropping it, reaching now for the dagger on his hip.

With determined strides, he bounded up the wide back of Algamesh and used the protruding hilt of his sword to steady himself above the monster's head.

The dagger came down in the side of the orc's neck and was twisted. Vighon held on to the unbroken horn and plunged his dagger again and again until Algamesh's gargled cries died away.

First it dropped the heavy axe. Then both of its legs buckled. Finally, it fell face first into the ground and Vighon jumped forward, staggering to his feet. His breath ragged and face splashed with orc blood, the northman looked upon the blank faces of Grey Stone's soldiers.

They let loose an almighty cheer and charged into the fray.

Vighon was happy to take a moment to catch his breath and retrieve his sword from Algamesh's back. He wanted to sit on the monster's tremendous bulk and marvel at his works, but the sound of Inara and Galanör dominating the courtyard drew him back into the melee.

There were still a few more orcs to kill.

50

THE BASTION

There was only darkness. Rough hands grabbed at Alijah's arms, dragging him down cold halls, and over wet floors. His feet could do nothing but follow in his wake, his every muscle still aching and desperate for a reprieve.

A foot went into the back of his leg, forcing him to his knees. His hands were already shackled behind his back but, now, someone out of sight lifted his arms back and connected his shackles to another chain bolted into the wall.

The sack cloth was torn from his head and the world returned to the half-elf in the blinding light of a roaring fire. Alijah blinked in the contrasting light, trying to orientate himself in a chamber of flickering shadows.

This new chamber appeared to have a single purpose - housing a large fire pit built into a circular chimney. Above the flames rested a wooden plank, chained at the corners to the curved walls. Alijah craned his neck to see the circle of white light at the top of the chimney.

Was it daytime?

Had he been unconscious?

He remembered being dragged down several corridors and

through various opening and closing doors, but there were fuzzy parts of their journey inside The Bastion that he couldn't hold on to.

Since he was still alive, Alijah decided it wasn't important. He, instead, examined his surroundings and discovered Hadavad beside him, similarly chained. The mage was wounded with a plethora of cuts and gashes on his face and blood dripped down his long dreadlocks.

"Hadavad?" he hissed, noting the absence of the dark mages now.

"I'm here, boy…" he rasped.

Alijah tensed his muscles and strained against his chains. He sighed, bereft of strength, and gave up.

"What happened?" he asked, tasting blood on his lips.

Hadavad couldn't bring himself to lift his face. "I… I was…" The mage choked on his words, unable to answer.

"Hadavad?" Alijah prompted.

"He's broken." The harsh voice came from the shadows.

The Crow emerged, walking out in front of the crackling fire that rose over his head. Draped in his usual dark cloak and crow feathers, the leader of The Black Hand came to stand before them. His expression wasn't smug, however, but apologetic. The harsh lines and creases of his pale face furrowed around his brow as he looked down on them.

"For five hundred years," The Crow continued, "Hadavad has stood up to The Black Hand. Every victory brought with it the confidence that he would inevitably win." The Crow flexed a delicate finger and lifted Hadavad's chin. "I am sorry, mage. You fought for what you believed to be right. And you fought hard. But you could never see what *we* were fighting for…" Cold eyes settled on Alijah.

"How did you know we were coming here?" he asked. In truth, he cared little for the answer; he just needed to buy some time to figure out how they were going to survive this.

"I knew because I told him to come here," The Crow replied boldly.

Alijah stopped inspecting the chamber and turned to Hadavad, confused. "The visions…"

"Yes," The Crow whispered. "Dreams are easy to manipulate when the person has been forced into sleep. A knock to the head is usually adequate."

Hadavad finally lifted his face and fixed The Crow with a glowering stare. Tears filled his bloodshot eyes but the mage still couldn't find any words.

"The future is a fickle thing," The Crow explained, unfazed by the mage's scowl. "The smallest of things can knock everything out of alignment. Here and there, I must occasionally apply pressure to keep everything on course."

"You're mad!" Alijah spat. "You and all of your fanatics!"

The Crow tilted his head. "Fanatics? What is it we're fanatical about exactly?"

Alijah felt as if he had been asked a trick question. "You worship Kaliban," he answered, ignoring the pain creeping into his knees on the stone floor.

The Crow crouched in front of him, his gaze intense. "There-is-no-Kaliban."

Those four words turned Alijah's world upside down. It was the foundation of the entire order. If nothing else, it was the only thing they knew about The Black Hand for sure. Even Hadavad's scowl softened into surprise.

The Crow stood up and turned to the fire. "Ten thousand years ago, The Echoes, an order of mages, created Kaliban to maintain order over a growing population of magic users. During the time of The First Kingdom, magic was an everyday tool for humans, or at least those educated enough to use it. Control was needed. And so religion was born."

"You're lying," Hadavad finally blurted. "I've seen The Black Hand worshipping at secret shrines to Kaliban."

The Crow turned to them again, his expression one of regret. "I hate what I am, what I have become. I am fooling them just as the priests of The Echoes did so long ago. It wasn't what I intended for The Black Hand. I gave them a new vision, a new order with which to live by. In my absence, however, the old ways returned, *over time*. Now they are slaves to their beliefs. Still, I have seen firsthand how the faithful can be herded. Though blind to the truth, I can still use them to better the world."

Alijah was sure he was hearing The Crow's words correctly, but it didn't make any sense. "Who *are* you?" he asked.

The Crow ran his hand slowly over his scarred scalp. "My name… is *Sarkas*." He paused as if tasting the name in his mouth. "It has been a very long time since that name has reached my ears." The Crow briefly closed his eyes and tilted his head with a pained expression. "Who I am is not important. It never was. Acknowledging that you're no more than a pawn in destiny's hand is a hard truth to come to terms with." The Crow looked down at Alijah. "But when I saw you… When I saw everything you're going to accomplish…" The old man crouched down again and cupped Alijah's face in his hand. "I will do anything I have to, *be* anything I have to, to see that future realised."

"You're mad!" Alijah spat again, shaking The Crow's hand free.

The lanky man straightened and stepped back. "No. I have seen madness. I saw the madness that corrupted the most powerful man in the world. King Atilan plunged his empire into chaos and death because of his insanity and insatiable hunger for immortality."

Alijah shook his head. "Have you heard yourself? You're the insane one! You're talking about events from ten millennia ago!"

The Crow's gaze grew distant and he looked through them. "Ten millennia… It only feels like a handful of years to me."

The Crow pulled on the knots of his cloak and shook the material free of his shoulders, leaving him bare chested with only a long skirt to hang from his waist. Alijah scanned his pale body, taking in the patchwork of scars that marred his flesh. It was easy to understand why The Crow was insane when he had obviously been subjected to a staggering amount of torture. The most obvious of his scars was the thick line that ran diagonally over his heart.

"I left strict instructions," The Crow continued. "When The Black Hand was born in the ashes of The Echoes, I left them with a map of sorts. When Paldora's Star fell from the heavens, thirty years ago, they were to come here, to The Bastion. This place used to be one of Atilan's laboratories. Can you not feel it? The magic of the place rolling over your skin."

Alijah had been too exhausted to register it, but now that he thought about, he could feel something pressing against his skin. There was certainly magic permeating The Bastion.

"I had to be vague, of course. It was paramount that they found it at exactly the right time. Along with my body, buried in The Wild Moores, they were to come here and grant me new life. Astari!" The Crow declared with his fingers resting over the scar on his chest. "Don't you see, Alijah? I *died* for you, long ago, before your ancestors were even born. I plunged a blade into my heart and rested in the ground for ten thousand years! All so that I might guide you. I couldn't leave such a task to any other."

"Shut your mouth!" Hadavad growled. "You lie with every breath!"

Alijah could feel his heart pounding in his ears. He looked upon The Crow's chest again. The truth of that mortal wound couldn't be denied.

"It's hard to hear, I know," The Crow purred. "For ten years I have walked this earth again, hardly believing myself that events have truly unfolded as I foresaw. But you should see it! The world that is to come… It's beautiful!"

"What does this have to do with me?" Alijah asked, tears gathering in the corners of his eyes.

"Don't Alijah," Hadavad warned. "Don't get pulled into his lies! This is what Crows do!"

Ignoring the mage, The Crow focused on Alijah. "Verda has endured many rulers, empires, kingdoms. All were corrupted by individuals, fractured by meaningless wars, and left to spiral out of control. Because of these individuals, the many have been made to suffer for the lavish lives of the few. What Verda needs is something new! Kings and queens don't work, emperors are weak, lines on a map create only division. Under one banner, the banner of one *strong enough* to maintain peace, the people of Verda could live in harmony."

Alijah couldn't believe what he was hearing. "And you think that's me?" he asked incredulously.

"Not alone," The Crow replied cryptically. "But with the wisdom and power of a dragon... there would be nothing you cannot accomplish."

"Malliath..." he uttered.

"I have already seen it, Alijah. Together, you will bring peace to this world."

The half-elf looked away, shaking his head. "No, no you... You brought Asher back. You bonded them and turned them on the world! You're allied with the orcs! You talk about peace and harmony for the many, but you've started a war that will set the world on fire!"

With a soft tone, The Crow replied, "It will not be an easy road for you, Alijah Galfrey. You're not nearly strong enough yet. No one is simply born with the power to do all that I have seen. That type of strength is *forged*! There is no better forge than war. There will be pain and suffering before the end, but you will emerge as something new, something the world sorely needs. When I am finished with you..." The Crow smiled. "You will be reborn!"

Hadavad lunged forward with gritted teeth, but his chains held him firm.

"Ah yes, the mentor..." The Crow turned away and looked to the plank of wood above the blazing fire.

With a closer look, Alijah thought he could see something lying on the plank, but the details were impossible to make out from such an angle.

"There can be no attachments," The Crow said. "No bonds to your old life that bring you down and stop you from realising your potential."

"What are you talking about?" Alijah asked, fearing for Hadavad's life.

The Crow paused, considering his words, before looking at the mage. "Five hundred years ago, before old age could truly claim you, you used the Viridian ruby to transfer your soul into that of another. But whatever became of your original body? You had but one friend, one friend you trusted with the most precious thing."

Hadavad looked from The Crow to the plank of wood above the fire, his expression growing terribly concerned.

The Crow waved his fingers in the air and his wand appeared in his hand, plucked from an unseen pocket dimension. "Rupert Flint, I believe his name was."

Hadavad's eyes glazed over, his eyes locked on The Crow. Alijah could see everything the mage clung to unravelling with revelation after revelation.

"You tasked Rupert Flint with taking your body and burying it where none would ever find it." The Crow had a dangerous glint in his eyes. "You should have had him burn it…"

"Impossible!" Hadavad hissed, tugging at his chains.

"That's always been your problem, Hadavad. *Impossible* is simply a thing that the narrow-minded cannot fathom. I found Rupert Flint's grave in Longdale. I dredged him from his eternal rest and put sharp things into his body until he told me where you were hidden. A glacier in The Lonely Wastes, if you were wondering."

Hadavad appeared to have lost some of his bluster. The mage stared at the plank, shaking his head in disbelief.

"I've had to go to some lengths to see this happen," The Crow explained. "That ruby around your neck is troublesome. I could kill you with a spell but the magic of the stone would spit your essence out and you would assume another host. But," The Crow said, holding up his wand, "if your original body was to become whole again, if it was to have life breathed into it… It would drag your soul back kicking and screaming."

Hadavad growled and struggled in his chains. "It won't work! I *will* end you! *All* of you!"

"I'm afraid it *will* work," The Crow replied. "I did tell you, mage; I have seen your end." The ancient man looked back at the fire. "And it is not a good one."

Just as he had in Paldora's Fall, The Crow began to chant in the ancient language, his arms outstretched and his wand glowing at the tip. Alijah and Hadavad fought with what little strength they had left and twisted their bodies into every position, hoping to free themselves of their bonds. The chains held.

The Crow continued his spell and a light was sparked on the surface of the plank. The bones rattled on the wood as the magic coalesced, bringing the broken form back together.

Hadavad's every muscle tensed. The mage was in pain and it wasn't from the chains digging into his skin.

"Alijah," he said, ceasing his struggle. "Don't..." Hadavad clamped his jaw shut for a moment, mustering whatever he had left. "Don't give in to him. Don't become what he..." The mage's final words grew into a pained scream.

"NO!" Alijah raged, pulling on his chains.

Hadavad's body went limp, suspended in the air by his chains. His eyes remained open, staring into the abyss.

Alijah's breath was ragged as he slowly looked from the dead body beside him to the plank of wood above the fire. An old man sat up with white scraggy hair around the side of his head and a beard that fell below his chest.

"Hadavad?" Alijah whispered.

Returned to his original body, Hadavad looked down at his wrinkled and bony hands. Horror and shock contorted his face.

"No," Alijah urged, seeing what was to come. "No, no, no! Don't do this! Don't do this! Please! You don't have to do this!"

The Crow looked back over his shoulder at him. "Your journey begins here, Alijah."

A single flourish of his wand lifted the flames of the fire, engulfing Hadavad's ancient body. The mage's dying screams were drowned out by the roaring of the flames, its light concealing his final moments.

"NO!" Alijah cried through tears.

The fire dropped back to its natural height, revealing a single arm hanging over the plank. It was charred black.

Alijah gasped for breath with tears streaming down his cheeks and into his beard. His despair turned into raw anger when he looked from Hadavad to The Crow.

"I will kill you!" he snapped. "I will kill you!"

The Crow knelt down in front of him. "I have seen my end, but it is not you who stands over me. Fear not; this rage you feel will have its day. There are those who will stand in your way, who don't understand the importance of what you're going to do. That anger you share with Malliath, soon it will become yours alone. You will learn to control it, to wield it even. Inside these walls, we will work together."

Alijah spat in his face. "If you let me live, I *will* kill you."

The Crow stood over him again. "*Let* you live?" he echoed. "You don't know what it is to be alive. Not yet…"

Alijah stared down the length of the wand pointed at his face. First there was pain. Then there was nothing at all.

THE FALL OF ILLIAN

Inara thrust her hand out and cast a destructive spell into the attacking horde of orcs. Tired as she was now, the spell did nothing more than push them back, offering the Dragorn a few extra seconds before they renewed their assault.

Vighon was beside her, his shield held low and the grip on his sword becoming tentative. The northman had proven his courage and great skill in battle over the last three days, but never more so than the last few hours. How much longer he could stay on his feet was uncertain, however. The elixir she had given him wore off soon after his victory over Algamesh.

Galanör's angular face glistened with sweat and streaks of orcish blood. Even the hardened ranger was showing signs of fatigue, his shoulders hunched and all form forgotten. Still, the elf wielded his scimitars with deadly accuracy, always finding his foe's weak points.

Together, the three companions had been pushed away from the street that led to the caves. The soldiers of Grey Stone had steadily disappeared down the narrow ravine, escaping through the hole in the barricade one by one. Inara hoped they had all found safety on the other side, Russell included, but the likelihood was that the street now possessed a lot more human bodies.

There were just too many orcs...

Inara couldn't believe their never-ending numbers. They were a plague that had no cure, a swarm that couldn't be satiated. She could see it in their eyes, that hunger for blood and war. The orcs wouldn't stop until the surface of Illian was wiped clean of life.

Not while we breathe! Athis exclaimed deep in her mind, bolstering her.

Inara levelled her Vi'tari blade in front of her face and presented the orcs with a face of fury. Grey Stone was lost, but the Dragorn would only relinquish the city when it was buried under a mountain of orcs.

The enchanted scimitar embraced her intentions towards the pale beasts and had Inara strengthen her grip. The blade slashed across the oncoming wave and cut down three before jabbing and swiping to claim the lives of two others. Their jagged swords and axes came at her from awkward angles, but the Vi'tari blade parried them all before opening them up. Blood spilled across the ground and the three companions continued to retreat down the street.

"Where are we going?" Vighon asked through laboured breath, his sword flashing in front of them to slay any orc that jumped out of their line.

Galanör held the right side of the street, making sure their enemies didn't get around and flank them. The elf's dual scimitars couldn't be denied their taste of blood.

"This street just leads us deeper into the city," Vighon continued. "We'll hit a dead end soon."

Inara dashed forward and chopped down on a spear aimed for Vighon's chest. The Vi'tari blade went down, through the spear, and out to the side, whipping across the orc's throat. The northman yanked her back immediately as a cluster of the beasts looked to stab her in the back. Together they paved the street with more orc corpses.

Where are we going? Inara asked inside her bond with Athis.

The red dragon was above them, at the top of the ravine. His bulk was too large to crawl down and so he was left with following them from the upper city. Inara knew Athis had considered exhaling a breath of fire down the narrow ravine, but in such a cramped environment, there was a chance the fire would spread and engulf them all.

I'm looking, Athis assured.

Inara craned her neck and stole a glance. Athis had disappeared from the pale sky above.

Pale sky!

"The sun is rising!" Inara exclaimed.

"Not nearly quick enough!" Galanör replied, thrusting his scimitar through two orcs at once. "Only the light of midday can reach these streets!"

Inara's hope faded fast. Midday was hours away. They would reach the end of this maze before then and be worn down by the hordes.

One particular roar drowned out the others and an almost naked orc burst through the line. Painted in black and yellow, the orc was a solid build of pure muscle and rage. Its head was a crown of small horns, four of which pointed out from its forehead. In its frenzy, the beast took no heed of the four blades between them and lunged at the three companions.

Vighon's steel tore a mortal gash across its ribs and Inara's Vi'tari blade opened up an artery in its arm, but the orc's momentum couldn't be stopped. A brutish backhand knocked Vighon back and Galanör was forced to step in front of the fallen man and protect him from the others. Inara, on the other hand, was thrown back when the painted orc barrelled into her.

Trapped under its body and her scimitar out of reach, Inara was at the creature's mercy. With blood pooling out of two severe injuries, the painted orc attempted to headbutt the Dragorn with those devastating horns. Inara shifted her head to the right and the horns slammed into the ground instead. Abandoning the search for her blade, the half-elf thrust her forearm up into the orc's neck, preventing it from getting any closer.

Looking down at her feet, Galanör was stemming the flow by himself, allowing Vighon a moment to get back up and add his blade to the fight.

Had she not been so exhausted, Inara knew she would have possessed the strength to simply throw the painted orc off her. That strength had left her a whole day ago. The orc looked her in the eyes and growled, baring its fangs. Then its breath became ragged, its limbs dead weights, and its gaze distant. Due to blood loss, the beast finally died... on top of her.

Inara dug deep and grunted as she pushed the orc up and to the side, rolling its corpse off her. Galanör and Vighon were about to step on her in their continued retreat. The Dragorn rolled aside and retrieved her Vi'tari blade on the way up. Her addition to the trio saw the end of three more orcs who had Galanör in their sights.

The lift! Athis declared without warning.

It took Inara a moment longer than normal to understand her companion's words, but when they finally registered the Dragorn felt her hope rising once more.

"We need to reach the lift!" she told the others.

"The lift?" Vighon questioned, raising his sword to keep an axe at bay.

Galanör kicked his foe away and faced Inara with revelation. "The upper city," he said. "Where is it?"

There is an alley that leads off the street you are on, Athis explained to Inara, hearing the elf's question through her mind. *It's on your left, Inara. Follow it to the end and turn right. Keep going until you see the lift on your left.*

Is it down? Inara asked desperately.

Yes!

"Follow me!" she barked, turning and sprinting away.

The trio ran as fast as they could, or at least as fast as Vighon could. Galanör deliberately slowed down and stayed at the back while Inara took the lead. Putting some distance between them and the orcs gave Athis the opportunity to unleash his awesome breath.

Inara didn't need to be bonded to the dragon to know a jet of fire had been spat down the ravine. They turned the corner into the alley as the flames scorched the ground behind them. The orcs screamed in agony and the fire gave the trio more time to escape, rushing down the adjacent ravine.

The lift was ahead of them, on the left as Athis had said. Beyond the lift, at the end of the street, a wall of orcs were running past. It took only one of the pale beasts to notice the three companions before they charged towards them, howling with glee that there were still people to slaughter.

"Run!" Inara shouted, despite the fact that they were already running. If they didn't make it to the lift before the orcs met them in the street, they would never get out of this hell.

Galanör, the fastest among them, ran ahead and began investigating the mechanisms that controlled the lift. "It's too slow!" he called back.

Inara chastised herself for only thinking of it now, for she knew the lift was on a counter-weight that had to be cranked by someone at the top or bottom. The orcs would swarm them before the lift was raised even a foot into the air.

The elven ranger hopped over the railing and confronted the orcs with Stormweaver and Guardian. Every slash and swipe of his magnificent scimitars ended the life of an orc. It wasn't long before a handful slipped past him and continued their charge towards Inara and Vighon. The Dragorn dropped to her knees and skidded down the street with her blade out to the side. She cut down two orcs before jumping back to her feet and planting her boot in the chest of another.

Vighon used an abandoned crate to leap into the fray and come down with his sword. The northerner followed his swing with a punch from his shield, lodging the steel rim in an orc's throat. He yelled out in pain when one of the beasts caught his arm with its blade. Having none of it, Vighon kicked out and snapped the orc's knee, bringing it to its knees - the perfect height to thrust the tip of his sword through the monster's face.

Inara! You need to get out of there! Athis urged from above. *More are coming!*

More? Inara repeated, her tone somewhere between despair and exhaustion.

Thanks to Galanör's blades, Inara was only left to deal with the few lucky enough to make it past the elf. While her Vi'tari scimitar kept her body fighting, the Dragorn inspected the lift in as much detail as she could.

That is not a good idea, Athis protested.

I ran out of good ideas hours ago, Inara replied, decapitating an orc. **You've got ten seconds to come up with a better one!**

Inara! Athis objected.

"Get in the lift!" the Dragorn commanded.

"It won't work!" Galanör shouted over his shoulder. "It's too slow!"

With even more urgency and a touch of authority, Inara yelled back, "Galanör, get in the lift!"

Vighon ran into an orc, shield first, and slammed it into the wall before hammering it with the steel rim. "Just do what she says!" he bawled, hopping over the railing and turning to face any who followed him.

Galanör's retreat was like the breaking of a dam. The swell of orcs that chased him back to the lift numbered so many that death was an inevitable certainty. Vighon put his sword through two more orcs, preventing them from hindering the elf's arrival. Inara, inside the railings herself, couldn't wait a second longer, for fear that the weight of the horde would ruin her plan.

"Galanör, jump!" She ordered, hoping the ranger could see her swinging her blade and knew what was about to happen.

Almost as sharp as silvyr, the Vi'tari steel sliced through the thick cord of rope that connected the lift to the counter-weight mechanism. Galanör, having already sheathed his fine blades, leaped high, reaching for the floor of the lift as it shot up the ravine. Only elven hands could have maintained such a grip, as the lift was launched at great speed.

The counter-weight dropped past them, bashing violently against the side of the rising platform, and plummeted into the orcs left in the street below.

Inara and Vighon lost their balance and fell to the floor. "Hold on!" the Dragorn shouted.

Galanör's fingers were the only part of the ranger that could be seen for those agonising seconds it took the lift to reach the top of the ravine. The supporting struts at the top were damaged when the lift stopped with more momentum behind it than the entire mechanism was designed for. Inara and Vighon were thrown into the air before slamming back down on the platform. Galanör's hanging form was similarly thrown into the air. Only the grace of his kin allowed the elf to land on his feet.

The sound of wood snapping filled the cold air.

"Run!" Vighon hissed, scrambling to his feet.

Inara felt Galanör's hand scoop under her arm and she was dragged off the tilting lift. Vighon jumped as the whole lift, supports and all, collapsed, promising more death to the orcs below.

The northman came up with a face full of snow. "Are we dead?" he muttered.

Inara took a breath and nodded her thanks to Galanör.

The ranger held up his hand. "That was quick thinking on your behalf. We owe you our lives, Inara."

The Dragorn waved the thanks away and searched for Athis. The red dragon was easily found, bounding over the gap between the ravines to be by her side again. Just seeing him lifted a crushing weight from her shoulders.

"I can't believe we made it out of there," Vighon said, rising to his feet.

They all peeked over the lip of the ravine and watched the orcs scrambling about below.

Most of the city made it to the caves, Athis said. *The soldiers too. I watched Russell escape with many of them.*

Inara managed a smile. "They made it," she said for the benefit of those who couldn't hear a dragon speaking in their minds. "Russell and the others; they made it."

Vighon mirrored her tired smile. "At least this wasn't for nothing. I could sleep for a week."

"We shouldn't linger," Galanör warned, serious as ever. "We only have until nightfall before we become the hunted again."

Inara... Athis's tone opened a pit in her stomach. The dragon moved aside, turning their attention to the east. *We no longer have the light...*

Inara moved away from the lip of the ravine with tears gathering in the corners of her eyes. From the south, a cloud of black swallowed the world, its ethereal edges reaching out to block the rising sun. The pale sky slowly disappeared and the first rays of light with it.

Vighon came up beside her, his eyes fixed on the foreboding horizon. "What... what is that?"

As evil spread across the sky and they witnessed the dying of the light, the Dragorn could think of only one answer for Vighon.

A lone tear broke free and streaked down Inara's cheek. "The end of the world...

EPILOGUE

Alijah's head came forward as the sack cloth was torn from his head again. He had been moved through The Bastion in darkness, leaving him clueless as to its layout.

The only constant now was the oppressive cold. This new chamber was vast and filled with shadows. There was no roof and the walls ended in jagged stone; the only part of The Bastion he had yet seen that was in some state of ruin.

Alijah's body shivered, his cloak, boots, and coat taken from him along with his bow and quiver. His hands were chained above him now, but he could still stand on the icy wet floor.

When the dark mages closed the door behind them, Alijah poured all of his grief and rage into a feral roar.

Hadavad was gone...

He could still see the mage's final moments when he closed his eyes. Smell his burning skin. Hear his dying screams.

His frustrated roar turned into tears and he let his head droop as he sobbed in the freezing cold. He had lost his mentor, the only one who had seen something in him, trusted him.

What was happening? How could this be his life? Everything had turned upside down. The Crow's explanation for all of this made no sense to him and he didn't want anything to do with it. He didn't want to rule the world, especially at the cost The Crow spoke of.

Alijah tried to work it all through in his mind, struggling to believe what that wretch had told him. Having witnessed Asher's resurrection, he knew Astari were possible, but the motivations of this Sarkas... The thought that The Crow had witnessed The First War and lived in Atilan's empire was hard to fathom when his mind was clouded by grief and searing hate.

"I won't..." he stuttered. "I won't give in." He started shaking his head, searching for any kind of resolution. "I won't be broken. I WON'T BE BROKEN!" he screamed at the door.

Alijah didn't care what The Crow thought he had seen, be it the future or in him. He would die before he let The Black Hand do anything to him.

Something in the shadows moved.

Alijah's head whipped up, but he failed to pierce the darkness with nothing but the stars for light. Something shuffled and loose gravel was dragged across the stone. The half-elf pressed himself against the wall, his eyes darting from side to side.

Two purple eyes opened in the abyss.

Malliath's long breath exhaled over the chamber and hit Alijah's cold face. The black dragon shifted in the shadows and his form became apparent with a long tail coiled around one side of the chamber. His wings were closed in around him, but his face was pointed directly at Alijah, his gaze intense.

Looking around, there was no sign of Asher, but from what he knew about the old assassin, he could be hiding anywhere in the dark.

"Why are we here?" he asked, suddenly aware of the volume of his voice.

The dragon continued to stare at him with those hypnotic purple eyes.

Alijah's initial fear faded away and his frustration and anger returned. "Why are we here?" he shouted. "Why is any of this happening?" he asked, his voice breaking. "Oh, I forgot; you're Malliath the voiceless. Maybe it should be Malliath the useless."

The dragon huffed a mighty breath and his horned head slid out of the darkness and rested in front of Alijah. He immediately regretted his words, but not because of the threatening dragon in front of him, but because they were hurtful words. He was, in fact, addressing the oldest living dragon, a dragon who had been subjected to torment and suffering at the hands of others.

The more Alijah stared back at those purple eyes the more he lost himself. Their fates were entwined. Everything The Crow was going to put him through, Malliath would share. There would be no end to their misery, and the longer he resisted The Crow the longer they would suffer. The ancient wizard would never stop; he had already braved the threshold of death to reach this far.

Malliath's hot breath was the only thing keeping the cold at bay.

"Is it real?" Alijah whispered into the night. "Is our bond real?"

Malliath continued to stare at him, his thoughts his own. The dragon breathed on him again and he basked in the warmth. There was more to it than warmth, though. Alijah could feel his muscles tensing and his skin tingling. He pulled against his manacles, only this time the pain of them digging into his skin didn't hurt as much.

"What are you doing?" he asked, not expecting an answer.

Malliath let out a long breath of steam into the icy air. His reptilian eyes bored into Alijah, drawing the half-elf into another world where there was no pain or suffering.

Tears streaked down Alijah's face. He could feel Malliath's feelings bleeding with his own. The black dragon didn't want to endure any more torture at the hands of others. He was frustrated and angry with the way the world had treated him, forcing him into exile for fear of his own wrath. Most of all, he was tired. Malliath wanted it all to be over, a sentiment that Alijah shared.

The thought of sitting on top of the world, a world built upon the graves of so many, made Alijah feel sick. Yet, there was a fury that seemed to exist in both of them that would witness The Crow's vision come true. They could do the hard thing if it meant creating a better realm. A place where dragons weren't enslaved and the downtrodden were championed.

But how many would die before that was achieved? How much suffering and pain would the two of them have to experience before The Crow released them?

No. He wouldn't let that happen, not while he still had sense enough to choose. He would end it.

A crack of thunder exploded overhead, preceding the downpour of rain. Malliath's hot scales steamed in the shadows and Alijah's body shivered. The dragon's hot breath, however, continued to breathe life into Alijah's limbs. If he was going to do anything, he would have to do it now, before he lost the will and the energy gifted to him.

"I will end it," he promised. "I will end it before it can go any further. You will find peace."

Malliath stood up in the roofless chamber, his thick claws digging into the stone beneath him. The dragon arched his neck and looked down on Alijah, though he was content to do nothing but look at hime.

Alijah could feel it.

Their bond was a cord of three strands: Alijah, Malliath, and magic. The longer they were together the tighter those three strands entwined.

The half-elf darted forward and pulled down as hard as he could on the chain that connected him to the wall. The rusted square bolted to the stone began to shift forward. Alijah gritted his teeth and grunted with the exertion, telling himself that it was the last thing he would ever need to do. He put all his energy into it, all his strength, and determination. The bolts popped out of the wall one by one. Alijah pressed his feet into the wall and pushed with a deep cry on his lips.

The last bolts sprang out of the wall and his body fell forward, onto the wet floor. A single claw came down in front of him and snapped the links in the chain between his hands. Alijah looked up through the pouring rain and met Malliath's blazing eyes. There was recognition in those eyes.

"I will end it..." he said again, his own tears mixing with the rain water.

With only the bindings around his wrists, Alijah staggered to his feet and made for the door. His whole body was splayed across the surface as he forced it open. There wasn't much strength left in him anymore.

The Bastion's winding halls were a maze to Alijah, who had only seen the inside of three chambers. Remaining as quiet as he could, the half-elf stumbled down the corridors, hugging the walls before checking the corners. There could be dark mages anywhere. Cold and wet, he struggled to stop himself from shivering as he left footprints behind his every step.

An icy draft blew against his exposed skin, drawing him down the hall to his right. The Bastion was high up in The Vrost Mountains and the chamber he had just escaped from must have been near the top of the fortress since there had been no sign of any mountain above him.

The next corridor ended with an open arch that led onto a circular balcony. The stonework under his feet looked to be in some kind of pattern, but the heavy rain made it impossible to decipher. Alijah walked to the very edge, where there were no railings, and looked down. He was above the bulk of The Bastion and indeed The Vrost Mountains. It was a drop no man could survive.

Alijah clenched his fists, tears still streaming down his wet face. If he was gone, The Black Hand would have no reason to continue their fight. It could potentially unravel the entire war with the orcs. It would also save Malliath from torment...

He knew, above all else, that he would do anything for the dragon. His only regret, and it weighed heavily on his heart, was not saying goodbye to Inara or making peace with his parents. The truth of his love for them was something he had tried to bury deep in his soul.

But this was the only way.

Alijah edged forwards until his toes were hanging over the lip. It would be instant death from this height. He wouldn't feel anything. One step and it would all be over.

"Don't do it, Alijah!" The Crow called over the rain.

Looking his shoulder, Alijah kept his body facing the edge. "I won't let you turn me into something else! I won't let you hurt Malliath!" Alijah looked down again, his breathing ragged. "Not while I can still choose…"

"To build a better world, Alijah, the old one *must* be broken. You won't do this from a place of malice; you're not evil and you won't be when you're ready to leave this place." The Crow stepped into the rain. "Killing yourself won't save lives. It will only ensure the suffering of generations to come. You don't see that yet, you don't see how truly flawed this world is. But you will."

Alijah clamped his jaw and kept his eyes on the chasm below. He had to be strong now. One last time.

"Alijah…" The Crow purred, drawing closer.

"You would have me become a monster!" the half-elf snapped.

"No," The Crow reassured. "*I* will be the monster. I will kill everyone you love and hold dear if I have to. I will break the chains that hold you back and set you free! I have come too far, seen too much to let this world rot under the reign of lesser beings. You, Alijah Galfrey, will rise above them all and show the world a better way. I will do whatever I must…"

Alijah let his head drop. "No," he whispered. "I won't let you hurt any of them…"

To take a step was a simple thing, a small thing even. But right now, in the hammering rain, it would take such a simple and small thing to change his destiny.

Alijah exhaled a slow breath. There would be no more pain.

And so he stepped off the edge, and let the darkness swallow him…

THE ADVENTURE CONTINUES...

THE ECHOES SAGA

KINGDOM OF BONES

BOOK V

BY
PHILIP C. QUAINTRELL

AUTHOR NOTES

Here I am again. I just couldn't stay away from this world! The broad strokes of this particular story came to me when I was halfway through writing Empire of Dirt. As Reyna and Nathaniel grew closer in that story, I came to see that whatever came next would be about family.

As always, I've got a few other characters who have their own journey to go on. I always like to make sure that every character has their part to play and is vital to the story as a whole. Boring side characters can ruin a book.

I've read a few books over the years where extra characters were slotted in for no good reason, or they were simply boring and I switched off.

So, Asher is back! Like I said, I had this story in mind before I finished Book 2, so I always knew the old ranger would return. Though, he is an enslaved Dragon Knight with a penchant for burning things at present. I guess we'll just have to see how that goes...

It was hard seeing the reviews for Relic of the Gods, with some people stating they wouldn't read this series because Asher wouldn't be in it. I *really* wanted to say something, but I *hate* spoilers! So, thank you to those of you who held on and picked up this book.

If you make it as far as the appendices at the back of this book, you'll see that this world has a lot of history that has yet to be fully fleshed out. I can't say for sure how many years I'm going to spend in Verda, but I know there's a lot of stories therein that need to be told.

It's possible by this point that you've already got a favourite character from this book, or maybe a few. One of my favourites that I just loved writing from the POV was Doran Heavybelly. I knew he had to return from where we left him Book 3 and I received a lot of messages from fans wanting more of him too. This worked out great because I always had plans to go to Dhenaheim and introduce readers to my dwarven kingdoms; they just didn't fit into the previous 3 books.

I apologise to those of you who were really hoping I would dive head first into Dhenaheim. Doran has a very different perspective to most other characters but, more importantly, he has a unique perspective on his own people. It felt important to tell the beginning of his tale through the journey to Dhenaheim since he was returning home and what that meant to him. Needless to say, Kingdom of Bones will plant the reader in the heart of dwarven culture.

One of the biggest differences in my writing, since finishing Relic of the Gods, is the amount of time I get to spend actually writing. Thanks to the success of the first 3 books, I have been able to transition into the Author life full time, so again, thank you to all of my readers for giving me this fantastic opportunity. I promise I've got plenty more stories to come!

With writing as my job now, I plan on publishing around 2-3 books a year, so you can expect this series to be finished in 2020. No more long waits! Yay!

I used to cram writing in to whatever available spaces I could, between working and having a life, seeing my wife etc. Now I have the joy of continuity, rather than having the days or sometimes weeks between writing. It feels very freeing from a story-crafting point of view.

The new routine starts with coffee, or at least it used. My newborn son laughs in the face of routine. I was getting up at 7am (believing foolishly that I was getting a nice early start on the day) and writing 3000 words before midday. Now I write in between my parenting duties and those many hours where I find myself simply staring at him.

When I first transitioned from nursing to writing full time, I had no routine and enjoyed one too many lie-ins. It took me a while to figure out that I write better in the mornings. Every author is different, with some that I know preferring to write very late at night. I tried this once, earlier on, and I just fell asleep at my desk.

The strangest aspect has been the perspective shift. Where writing used to be a hobby, it's now my job. Thankfully, my years as a nurse has left me fairly disciplined and an early riser. For you guys, the readers, that's a good thing, because it means I write every day without fail. In fact, my wife struggles to convince me to take the weekends off. I just love it!

I may be doing this full time now, but I am still a self-publisher. No takers yet I'm afraid. With that in mind, I would ask that you take a few minutes to leave a review on Amazon. Your comments and opinions help me to get the word out and keep me in this chair. I've got a lot more stories to write and share with you all.

For updates and news, you can find my author page on Facebook and you can follow me on Instagram, *PhilipCQuaintrell*. Please feel free to email me at philipcquaintrell@gmail.com. I reply to every message and I love hearing from fans of the books.

Until the next time…

APPENDICIES

Dwarven Hierarchy:

1. **Battleborns** - Ruled by King Uthrad, son of Koddun. Domain: *Silvyr Hall.*

2. **Stormshields** - Ruled by King Gandalir, son of Bairn. Domain: *Hyndaern.*

3. **Heavybellys** - Ruled by King Dorain, son of Dorryn. Domain: *Grimwhal.*

4. **Hammerkegs** - Ruled by King Torgan, son of Dorald. Domain: *Nimduhn.*

5. **Goldhorns** - Ruled by King Thedomir, son of Thaldurum. Domain: *Khaldarim.*

6. **Brightbeards** - Ruled by King Gaerhard, son of Hermon. Domain: *Bhan Doral.*

~

Orcish Hierarchy:

1. ***The Born Horde*** - Ruled by Karakulak, Chieftain of the Born Horde, Bone Lord of The Under Realm, and king of the orcs.

2. ***The Berserkers*** - Ruled by Chieftain Warhg the terrible.

3. ***The Big Bastards*** - Ruled by Chieftain Barghak the mountain-maker.

4. ***The Grim Stalkers*** - Ruled by Chieftain Lurg the unseen.

5. ***The Fallen*** - Ruled by Chieftain Orlaz the devastator.

6. ***The Savage Daggers*** - Ruled by Chieftain Raz-ak the swift.

7. ***The Steel Caste*** - Ruled by Chieftain Nilsorg the unbearable.

8. ***The Bone Breakers*** - Ruled by Chieftain Dugza the marrow drinker.

9. ***The Mountain Fist*** - Ruled by Chieftain Golm the fiend-slayer

~

Kingdoms of Illian:

1. ***Alborn*** (eastern region) - Ruled by King Rayden of house Marek. Capital city: *Velia*. Other Towns and Cities: Palios, Galosha, and Barossh.

2. ***The Arid Lands*** (southern region) - Ruled by the elected High Council. Capital city: *Tregaran*. Other Towns and Cities: Ameeraska and Calmardra.

3. **The Ice Vales** (western region) - Ruled by King Jormund of house Orvish. Capital city: *Grey Stone*. Other Towns and Cities: Bleak, Kelp Town, and Snowfell.

4. **Orith** (northern region) - Ruled by Queen Yelifer of house Skalaf. Capital city: *Namdhor*. Other Towns and Cities: Skystead, Dunwich, Darkwell, and Longdale.

5. **Felgarn** (central region) - Ruled by King Weymund of house Harg. Capital city: *Lirian*. Other Towns and Cities: Vangarth, Wood Vale, and Whistle Town.

6. **Dragorn** (island nation off The Shining Coast to the east) - Ruled by the three crime families; the Fenrigs, the Yarls, and the Danathors.

~

Other significant locations:

Elandril (northern Ayda) - Ruled by Queen Adilandra of house Sevari. The heart of the elven nation.

The Lifeless Isles (south of Dragorn) - An archipelago and home to the dragons and the Dragorn.

Korkanath (an island east of Velia) - The most prestigious school for magic.

Stowhold (an island north of Korkanath) - The headquarters of Illian's largest bank.

Syla's Gate (south of The arid Lands) - Entrance to The Undying Mountains.

The Tower of Dragons' Reach (south of Velia) - The meeting place for all the rulers of Illian and the Dragorn.

Ilythyra (in the The moonlit Plains) - Governed by Lady Ellöria of house Sevari. Home to a small population of elves from Elandril.

Paldora's Fall (inside The Undying Mountains) - The impact site of Paldora's Star, a well of powerful magic.

~

Significant Wars: Chronologically

The First War - Fought during The Pre-Dawn (before elvish-recoded history). King Atilan started a war with the first Dragon Riders in the hopes of uncovering their source of immortality.

The Great War - Fought during the First Age, around 5,000 years ago. The only recorded time in history that elves and dwarves have united. They fought against the orcs with the help of the Dragorn, the first elvish dragon riders. This war ended the First age.

The Dark War - Fought during the Second Age, around 1,000 years ago. Considered the elvish civil war. Valanis, the dark elf, tried to take over Illian in the name of the gods. This war ended the Second Age.

The Dragon War - Fought in the beginning of the Third Age, only a few years after The Dark War. The surviving elves left Illian for Ayda's shores, fleeing any more violence. Having emerged from The Wild Moores, the humans, under King Gal Tion's rule, went to war with the dragons over their treasure. This saw the exile of the surviving dragons and the beginning of human dominance over illian.

The War for the Realm - The most recent war of the Third age, fought 30 years ago. The return of Valanis saw the world plunged back into war and the re-emergence of the Dragorn. Gideon Thorn became the first human to bond with a dragon in recorded history. Valanis was killed by the ranger, Asher, who died in their final battle.

Made in the USA
Monee, IL
26 November 2020

49618010R00370